INSIDE STAR TREK®

The *Real* Story

For orders other than by individual consumers, Pocket Books grants a discount on the purchase of **10 or more** copies of single titles for special markets or premium use. For further details, please write to the Vice-President of Special Markets, Pocket Books, 1633 Broadway, New York, NY 10019-6785, 8th Floor.

For information on how individual consumers can place orders, please write to Mail Order Department, Simon & Schuster Inc., 200 Old Tappan Road, Old Tappan, NJ 07675.

INSIDE STAR TREK®

The *Real* Story

Herbert F. Solow and
Robert H. Justman

POCKET BOOKS
New York London Toronto Sydney Tokyo Singapore

POCKET BOOKS, a division of Simon & Schuster Inc.
1230 Avenue of the Americas, New York, NY 10020

ISBN: 0-671-00974-5

Book design by Richard Oriolo

First Pocket Books trade paperback printing June 1997

10 9 8 7 6 5 4 3 2 1

POCKET and colophon are registered trademarks
of Simon & Schuster Inc.

Printed in the U.S.A.

For Yvonne

For Jackie

Contents

Who Are They?

As Vice President of Desilu Studios, Vice President of Paramount Television, and Executive in Charge of Production of the *Star Trek* series, Herb Solow was responsible for the sale, development, and production of both pilots and the series. Gene Roddenberry and the entire *Star Trek* cast, crew, and studio personnel reported to him. No decisions regarding personnel, casting, budgets, or *Star Trek*–NBC affairs were made without his approval.

As Associate Producer and later Co-Producer of *Star Trek*, Bob Justman, working hand-in-hand with Gene Roddenberry, was in charge of and responsible for all phases of preproduction, production, and postproduction of both pilots and the series. All production and postproduction personnel reported to him.

Preface

HERB: I guess, for me, this is not only a preface, it's also a confession. Having been involved in the development and production of many theatrical and television movies and in the development, sale, and production of seven prime-time television series (of which *Star Trek* was one of the least successful during its original run), writing a book about the bewitched voyage of the *Starship Enterprise* never really entered my mind.

But in the entertainment industry, as participants enter that gray-haired dinosaur segment of their lives, they suddenly are sought out for their knowledge of the past. And so it happened. Authors, seeking information on what used to be, came calling. I discussed *Star Trek* in general terms with Kathleen Brady for her biography of Lucille Ball, Coyne Steven Sanders and Tom Gilbert for their book on Desilu, and Patrick J. White for his book on *Mission: Impossible,* and I gave a few background facts to Joel Engel for his biography of Gene Roddenberry. Bill

Shatner never called me regarding his book, *Star Trek Memories*—which accounts for some of its inaccuracies. David Alexander asked Bob Justman if I would speak with him for his biography of Gene Roddenberry. I told RJ to thank him and say no. Alexander then proceeded to deal with my *Star Trek* involvement not only as insignificant, but as if I rarely showed up for work during those years. My reason for silence was simple: since I finally had something to say about *Star Trek*, I intended to say it myself.

I have never been to a science-fiction convention, much less a *Star Trek* convention. Other than those mentioned above, I have been steadfast in not giving interviews to authors, the press, or the public.

And yet, I know more about the very beginnings of *Star Trek*—its development, its sale to NBC, its two pilots, and the production of the series—than any other living being. Most of that knowledge has never before been made public.

Unfortunately, much that has been "made public" has often come from the recycling of stories, events, facts, and figures—apocrypha that, inevitably, have been embellished during the retelling. At times, little of the truth remains.

The fact that there does remain so much interest in the series, quite frankly, surprises me. But our publisher, Pocket Books, is interested; our editor, Kevin Ryan, is interested; and obviously, millions of *Star Trek* fans are interested. So to borrow a contemporary expression, I guess this book is my way of coming out of the *Star Trek* closet.

BOB: I, too, have a confession. I've wanted to write this book for many years. The all-encompassing and intense experience I had in making *Star Trek*—as well as the show's contribution to world culture, science, and the exploration of space—practically demanded that I do so.

Oddly enough, during the early eighties, I attempted, several times, to interest publishers in just such a book. Unfortunately, or rather fortunately, the timing was wrong. Although the mystique of *Star Trek* was a fact, its hold upon, and appeal to, the general public was not yet fully realized.

In the spring of 1986, with my friend, Stephen Poe (formerly known as Stephen Whitfield), I began to assemble research for a new, comprehensive book about the birth, life, and premature death of the original show. Years before, during production of the series, Steve had written a book entitled *The Making of Star Trek*. It afforded readers a close-up look at some of the events of its first two seasons. But I knew there was much more to tell—things that only Gene Roddenberry, Herb Solow, and I knew—and I felt it was time to tell the real story before it was too late.

Steve and I never finished our research. He was busy with his other writing obligations, and I was soon hard at work preparing what was to become *Star Trek: The Next Generation*. The book was put aside.

And then, Gene died. Now, there were only two of the original trio left. The book that needed to be written was still unwritten—and would remain unwritten, I feared.

And then, Herb Solow stopped by to see me one day. "RJ, I'm going to write a book about *Star Trek.*"

"But what about me?" I exclaimed.

"What about you, RJ?"

"Well, I should be writing that book. *We* should be writing that book. Do you want a partner?"

"Great idea, RJ. Why didn't I think of that?"

Of course, he had thought of it; that's why he came by in the first place. And that's why you're reading this now. So settle back, take the phone off the hook, and get ready for an exclusive and revealing look into the past—and the astonishing future it created.

Prologue

Riding the Red–Eye

HERB: February, 1966. The ritual of pilot season was finally over. I refused to let lack of sleep bother me as I impatiently encouraged the New York cabbie to step on it, to take the short cut up the East Side Drive and over the bridge by Riker's Island. The last thing I wanted was to miss this night's last flight out of New York City back to Los Angeles.

Before jumping in the cab to the airport, I telephoned my production advisor, harbinger of bad things to come, and eventual lifelong friend, Bob Justman. I had already told creator-producers Gene Roddenberry of *Star Trek* and Bruce Geller of *Mission: Impossible* the good news, but I hadn't given them the final, locked-in, not-to-be-overturned details. Better to meet with them later, at the studio, and use the momentum of the good news to extract some much-needed understandings about their parking spaces, their offices, and the little matter of not bankrupting the studio. I'd congratulate them as producers of network series and wish them well, before they told their wives and children the news that they'd be missing around the house for, I hoped, many, many years to come.

"Hug the kids and kiss the wife good-bye. Welcome to the television series production business, the new bare-bones Desilu style," I'd add.

When I called Bob Justman, I told him to be at the studio at 6:30 the following morning for a meeting.

"What about you?" asked Bob plaintively. "You didn't sell anything, did you?"

"We'll talk about it in the morning, RJ. I have to rush to catch the plane."

"You sold one, didn't you?"

"I gotta go. Hang up. . . ."

"You sold both of them."

"We'll talk tomorrow. I'm hanging up now. . . ."

"Does anyone know the mess you've probably gotten us into?"

"In the morning, RJ. If I miss the plane, it's a long walk home." I hung up, not daring to confirm that his ultimate fears had been realized. We had to make both series—at the same time. Better he doesn't know for sure, I thought, because if he did, by morning he'd have twenty typewritten pages about the impossibility of making the shows and thirty typewritten pages about how to do it. Let Bob have a good night's sleep. He'd need it.

But for now, I was on my way home. Sales season was over. It wouldn't be until next year, twelve long months, when that odd group of Hollywood-based studio heads, agents, and producers would descend on New York's network and advertising agency screening rooms, boardrooms, and trendy Midtown restaurants. We came to town to fight the good fight: to get our expensive pilots sold and an order for twenty-six first-year episodes—to sell a network television series.

And if we were lucky enough to get a series sold, then would come the struggle, the head-to-head combat to get our series scheduled at a certain time and on a certain night, to protect our newborns from the competitive networks' established "killer" shows. To the participant—the inside player—the ritual was an aggressive, lying, take-no-prisoners rat race. Success was returning to Los Angeles with a prime-time series order stuffed in your attaché case, your head held high, and a silly grin on your face.

Failure meant figuring out all the excuses why, after putting your career on the line and spending so much of your company's money, you failed miserably. There was no such thing as an average pilot season. You either won or you lost, sold something or got shut out. There wasn't any place or show money in this race. An unsold television pilot had all the value of a Good Humor bar laid out on the pavement in the hot Madison Avenue sun.

When the network fall schedules finally came out, the Hollywood crowd, bags packed and waiting in hotel lobbies, fled the New York television scene. It could be dangerous to hang around any longer. Why tempt fate by saying something stupid over lunch at the Oak Room of the Plaza or late-afternoon drinks at 21 and reveal the possible production or money problems you have back at the studio—or even breathe a mention about your leading actor already making demands for a bigger salary (contract be damned) or a better parking space or a private phone in the dressing room or using his own makeup and hair people or demanding to approve press releases and publicity photos? Bad move.

Suppliers had to be careful about sudden changes in the network hierarchy. The head of the network may not have liked the pilots chosen for development and production by the current Program Vice President. There could be a new marshal in town shortly, a new marshal who'll hate everything developed by his predecessor. You sure as hell don't want to be there when he arrives. Get out of town fast—as soon after sundown as possible.

So even though I was physically and mentally drained, uncomfortable from a week of dining and entertaining, and tired of wearing my wrinkled New York–sincere suit and tie, I boarded the crowded late-night TWA flight to Los Angeles, and nothing, absolutely nothing, would interfere with the joy of my successful trip.

Other production heads and salespeople were aboard the plane. It was obvious who had picked up orders for series. They drank and laughed and strutted up and down the aisle, displaying a sudden lifelong friendship with their competitors, whom they would have stabbed in the back hours earlier if it meant a sale.

It was also obvious who struck out, who were the losers. They looked depressed when they drank. And then they drank some more. It would be tough for them to go to work the next day. It would be tough facing the studio gate guard and his happy "Good morning," and the expectancy of his secretary and staff: "Did they like our pilot? Are we going to be a series?"—and the questioning eyes of his boss: "I put my faith in you. What happened?" It would be tough picking up the Hollywood trade paper, *Daily Variety,* and reading the box score: who sold series and who lost series. It would be a full year before you had another crack at it—that is, if you still had your job. It would be a year of watching your competitors producing their new series. It would be a year of laying people off because, with no series, there's no money to cover your overhead. It would be a year of regenerating interest in your studio, trying to attract the top pilot writers, the top horses. Because, without the top horses, it's tough to win the race. Flying back to Los Angeles without an order was the end of the line.

As I watched the unhappy Production Vice President of a major studio slugging down a drink, I imagined headlines in the next *Daily Variety*: "TWA PASSENGER LEAPS TO DEATH OVER NEBRASKA. Studio Chief Sings 'It Isn't Fair' as He Plummets into Corn Field." The major studio guy called the stewardess and ordered another drink.

But for me, this was a joyful time. It had been a long, tough, anxiety-ridden year. I was the new kid on the block at a dying studio. Competition for salable talent was as tight as it ever had been. The hypocrisy of Hollywood is competitors saying nice things about you in public, then cutting you up in private in ways that hurt. So far as I was concerned, there had been too much cutting up, both inside the studio by the old-line management with their old-line ideas and sensibilities, and outside the studio by the agents, managers, and competitive studios and production companies. It had been a tough year. But I'd won big; I'd batted 1.000. I had come to New York a week earlier with two pilots for sale. And I was flying home with both pilots sold and orders for two prime-time one-hour network series. CBS ordered twenty-six episodes of *Mission: Impossible,* an expensive and innovative television series where the real stars of the show were the stories and the surprise endings. The five actors were merely tools to unravel and solve the complicated plots. The "experts" had predicted *Mission* didn't have a chance to get on the schedule. "No one's going to watch a complicated series without any big stars," the influential and expert production head of Universal warned CBS programmers. I filed his name away for future reference. A few years later, I was offered his job. I was delighted to get the offer and glad to turn it down. *Mission: Impossible,* by the way, went on to become a seven-year television hit. So much for experts.

The biggest surprise of the sales season was that NBC ordered our highly complex science-fiction, fantasy-driven dramatic-adventure series, *Star Trek,* seemingly impossible to produce on a weekly basis. The CBS, ABC, and studio bigmouths couldn't understand it, so they knocked it. "They'll never be able to make it every week. NBC and Desilu have some kind of death wish." The street rumor was that NBC was interested in snatching *The Lucy Show* away from CBS, and the scheduling of *Star Trek* was the initial step in its master plan. It was a stupid rumor that only served to give some competitors a reason for their failure to sell their product.

This was a particularly sweet time for me. *Star Trek* and *Mission* were the first projects I'd put into development after I joined Desilu. After making the development deals with NBC and CBS, I'd worked every day with writer-producers Gene Roddenberry of *Star Trek* and Bruce Geller of *Mission,* developing the concepts and characters and taking the projects from idea to story to script and then to pilot film. I'd fought the budget battles and the casting problems, the network egos and the studio's old-fashioned policies. I knew I could take a good deal of the credit for the development and production of the two pilots, but could take only passing credit for closing the sales. Lucy was a big player at CBS, and the network would do nothing to aggravate her, unless, of course, the *Mission* pilot was an absolute failure. Happily, it deserved to sell; it was a spectacular effort. And having Lucille Ball and Mickey Rudin—Lucy's attorney and my mentor—waiting in the wings to apply the weight of their importance to the CBS Television Network was pretty good insurance.

NBC wanted to have a Desilu show on their network. They had never had a series from this studio. As a matter of fact, they had never even had a development deal with Desilu. And now they'd invested a lot of money in *Star Trek,* from the earlier "too cerebral" and "too erotic" ninety-minute (seventy-eight minutes without commercials) pilot film to the newer one-hour version that I hustled in and out of the halls of 30 Rockefeller Plaza.

In addition, they had invested extra money for two alternate pilot scripts. Networks don't like to throw money down the drain with nothing to show for it. Since NBC was very pregnant with invested money in *Star Trek,* they wanted the next step to happen. They wanted a new show to be born. The *Star Trek* pilot film was an exciting sales tool, a new, visually provocative and thought-provoking possibility for a successful prime-time series. Gene Roddenberry, Jimmy Goldstone, and Sam Peeples had produced, directed, and written a solid piece of science-fiction entertainment. It deserved to sell.

Desilu was represented by a topflight talent agency, Ashley-Famous. Alden Schwimmer in Los Angeles and Ted Ashley and Jerry Leider in New York had worked the clients and the networks well. They had done a first-class job in setting the scene for success.

What made me even happier was that the Hollywood network executives with whom I'd be working on the newly ordered series were friends, good guys who wanted to make good things happen. Unfortunately, there were the others, the "kiss of death" executives, the envious and bitter ones who wanted you beholden to them or they'd do their best to knock you out of the box. Let Ashley and Leider deal with them, I decided. They have more patience. Happily, I'll be working with Perry Lafferty, Vice President of Programs at CBS Television City in Hollywood. Lafferty was a former producer and director, later to become a successful novelist. Perry's response was always, "Let's see how we can make this work." *Mission: Impossible* was going to be a very difficult show to do well and do weekly. It surely needed a positive attitude from the network.

Years before, when I was a recently-out-of-college executive with the NBC Film Division in New York, I met and worked with a bright, personable, recently-out-of-college lawyer, Herb Schlosser. "Schloss," as he was known to his face by me and a handful of others, would eventually become the President of NBC. But in 1966, he was the newly appointed NBC Vice President of Programs, West Coast. That was great, I thought. Schloss and I had spent many hours together, early in our careers, discussing our futures. I wanted to be creatively involved in television and movies, producing and writing. Schloss wanted to head a big entertainment company. Now both of us were in the process of achieving our dreams.

When the NBC schedule had been finalized, Grant Tinker left his role as NBC West Coast Vice President and returned to NBC New York to work directly with Mort Werner, Vice President of Network Programs. My old friend Schloss would be running things in Burbank. It went without saying this was a fortunate move, as it helped maintain a very close, friendly, and mutually understanding relationship with the network, a relationship we'd certainly need. We knew that *Star Trek* would be expensive and difficult to produce, but never anticipated it would be the most difficult to write, the most difficult to produce, and one of the most expensive series in television history at that time.

NBC had a legion of New York executives, headed by Program Vice Presidents Mort Werner and Grant Tinker, two men who were strong supporters of *Star Trek.* Grant considered it to be groundbreaking television entertainment "cast like a family group . . . embraced by the *Enterprise,* which is their home." Unfortunately, there were network skeptics, major players who resented how much the series was costing NBC, disliked Desilu because of Lucy's tight relationship with prime competitor CBS, disliked science fiction in general, disliked *Star Trek* in particular, and had grave doubts about the show's chances for success. The "skeptics" could best be summed up as NBC Sales, a network department that could be a very formidable adversary.

All these dreams, all these facts and impressions colored my thoughts as the plane droned on toward Los Angeles and I leaned back in my seat and stared at a glass of cheap champagne. Tomorrow would be one helluva day.

INSIDE STAR TREK®

The *Real* Story

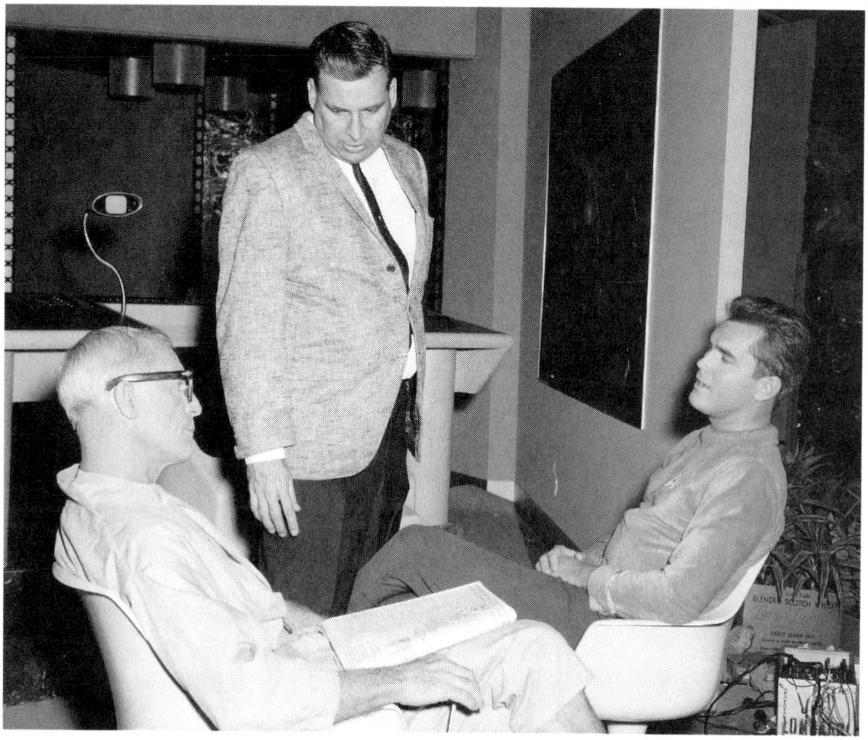

Courtesy Greg Jein

Gene Roddenberry (center) with actors John Hoyt and Jeffrey Hunter.

Courtesy NBC/Globe

The bridge of the *Enterprise* in "Where No Man Has Gone Before."

A C T O N E

Genesis: The Two Pilots

Courtesy NBC/Globe

Lucille Ball and Desi Arnaz, who, together, built a Hollywood studio.

1

The Back Story: Boy, Could He Tap-Dance

The applause did not subside; the cheering continued. Finally, America's sweetheart, the fabulous redhead, Lucille Ball, walked onto the stage and took another bow. It was another Thursday night, like so many other Thursday nights, as Lucy finished shooting a *Lucy* show before a live audience on Desilu Studios' Stage 12.

That it wasn't *I Love Lucy* was unimportant. If Lucy was in it, it was a "Lucy" show. After all, everything else was still the same. Ethel had a different character name, but she was still Ethel. The director was the same, most of the writers were the same, the sets were the same, Wilbur Hatch still struck up his band, little Desi Jr. still played the drums during the preshooting warm-up, and Lucy would still tell the after-show audience that her red hair was real because it came from a real bottle of Clairol.

But there was something missing. Something as tangible as a person, something as intangible as a presence. Missing was Desi Arnaz.

Lucy, the brassy red-haired showgirl from Jamestown, New York, and Desi Arnaz, the flamboyantly hot-blooded entertainer from Havana, Cuba, together, as husband and wife, built a Hollywood icon, Desilu Studios. They were brash enough to name it for themselves—none of this International Pictures or Zenith Studios stuff, thank you very much. They made it work; they were entitled. Lucy, the comedienne, and Desi, the sort-of actor and brilliant producer and executive, not only built the studio, but were the linchpin that held it together. They wisely surrounded themselves with old-line, experienced Hollywood professionals who dealt with the nuts and bolts of picture making. Their success grew to such proportions that they ran out of space and had to expand, buying two other studios. Their original studio, which they had rented first and later purchased, was Motion Picture Center. They bought it from the owner, Joe Justman. Coincidentally, years later, Joe's son, Bob Justman, would be part of Desilu's renaissance, a renaissance that enabled Lucy to sell the studio and close a cheerless chapter in her life.

BOB: My father and Desi liked each other a lot and saw eye to eye about almost everything. Dad always said that Desi was a "great guy and a great businessman." Although he called every man he met a "great guy," for him to call Desi a "great businessman" was the height of praise.

Years later, in an ironic twist of fate, I went to work for Lucy at Desilu's main studio on Gower Street, which she and Desi had purchased from RKO. She never seemed to get used to my presence on "her" lot. I'd pass her on the studio street and she'd stop to stare at me. She'd look me up and down. I couldn't tell whether she trusted me or suspected me, but she wasn't hostile. It seemed as if she wanted to say something but didn't quite know how to go about it, as if she saw some small vestige of my father in me and wanted to find more. He was a vital, attractive, and magnetic man with a busload of personality—outgoing and friendly to one and all, especially strangers.

I was nothing like that. Maybe she just couldn't figure me out. I guess that, to Lucy, I was one of the strangers that Herb had brought in, and just as she couldn't figure Herb out, she couldn't figure me out either. But she kept on trying.

With Desilu's expansion into the studio rental business, the production business, and the domestic and foreign film sales business, the daily problems grew. But the linchpin was still there. Lucy and Desi were a team; they were partners in life and business—they could do no wrong. Until the unimaginable, the unspeakable happened.

The linchpin broke. The weight of broken promises, broken lifestyles, and broken dreams caused the good ship Desilu to rupture and spring a leak. Lucy and Desi divorced, leaving behind successes like *I Love Lucy* and *The*

Untouchables. But that was then and this was now; important changes were in the offing.

Using borrowed money, purported to be $3,000,000, Lucy bought out Desi's interest and ownership of the studio. Desilu was now Lucy and her "old guard" professionals. However well meaning they were, the nuts-and-bolts production and financial people failed to grasp the changing times and overzealously tried to protect Lucy from the future.

With hundreds of workers toiling at three widely separated physical plants, two in Hollywood and the other miles away in Culver City, Desilu's nondirective management made wrong decisions, and the good ship began to list. Desi was a very hard act to follow, both personally and professionally.

Lucy married "second banana" comedian Gary Morton. Apparently she was happy and no longer lonely, but Morton had neither the experience nor the talent to function in any studio capacity. Those close to Lucy didn't beat around the bush about Gary trying to fill Desi's shoes. It wasn't necessary; Lucy knew. When studio problems got too much for her, she continued to call upon Desi for advice, advice warmly and freely given. She trusted him in business, if not in marriage.

HERB: The film business is a small world. In 1974, in an office building on the Universal Studios lot, I met Desi Arnaz. Desi, who had just moved into the office next door, burst in, threw his arms around me, and with an expansive grin exclaimed, "Amigo! You the one what's focking my wife, Lucy?" I shook my head "no" and smiled, hoping that this was merely Desi's friendly way of saying "hello." Luckily, it was.

Desi no longer had Lucy, but CBS surely did. She was their biggest and one of their most loyal stars. CBS countered in kind and kindness, establishing a major development fund for the studio's use, and Lucy began to develop new series. But nothing seemed to work. Lucy was brilliant in knowing what was good for her "Lucy" character, her writers, her costars, her directors, her show. But she didn't have the foggiest idea how to deal with the networks and the creative community, how to play the television production game. That wasn't her job. She was only the red-headed actress on Stage 12 and unquestionably one of the biggest television stars in the world. Running a studio, developing new pilots, and making television series was Desi's job. But Desi was gone, and the pilots and the series dwindled down to a precious few; and then there was only one, *The Lucy Show*.

Enter Ted Ashley, the powerful head of Ashley-Famous. Until then, agents had always represented individual artists, actors, writers, producers, directors, composers, and others in the entertainment world. Agents didn't represent studios. Studios represented studios, themselves. But that was about to change.

CBS saw the need to protect their investment in Desilu; Ted Ashley saw a very good business deal. After the smoke of the divorce had cleared, Ashley-

Famous became the agents for Desilu. They would receive a percentage of gross sales of television series to the networks—in perpetuity.

There was still a void. CBS and Ashley-Famous needed someone to run the studio, take charge of the development fund, make good pilots and series, and get the studio up and running once again. New Yorker Ted Ashley, New Yorker Bill Paley (owner of CBS), and several influential New York CBS executives agreed New Yorker Oscar Katz would be the man for the job. Katz was a highly regarded CBS television network executive who had been Vice President of Network Programs and, and prior to that, Vice President of Daytime Programs. In due time, Katz resigned from CBS and moved to that foreign region of America called Hollywood.

HERB: The problem was, as in the best-laid plans of mice and men, Oscar didn't speak the local language. But there wasn't a nicer or brighter man than Oscar Katz. He was expert in many fields: network programming, the New York stock market, New York advertising agency media buys, network ratings and research, and, after his move west, the house odds at the craps table in Las Vegas, the betting line at Hollywood Park, and on what street in Hollywood, on which day and at what time, you could find the seltzer truck that sold Fox's U-Bet chocolate syrup in a bottle.

A look-alike for famed comic Myron Cohen, Oscar Katz could hold his own with stories and anecdotes. But there was something lacking of a practical nature. Katz was almost totally devoid of experience with Hollywood-style television development, knowledge of the operation and the workings of a film studio, of the Hollywood creative community—the system. As it turned out, he knew less about the Hollywood studio side of the television business than Desilu President Lucille Ball, the valued CBS property he came in to rescue.

HERB: In early 1964, I was working at NBC Burbank. This was my second tour there. I'd returned for two reasons. First and foremost, an executive shuffle at CBS-TV City in Hollywood, where I was also responsible for Daytime Programs, forced me into network oblivion. Secondly, I wanted to work for Grant Tinker, then Vice President of Programs, West Coast. I'd met Grant several years before, during my first NBC tour, when I was Program Director of the NBC Film Division and Grant was Vice President of Benton & Bowles, an important New York advertising agency. But a year later, boredom had set in. And for a nervous, high-energy, high-strung, left-handed person, boredom is a difficult bedfellow.

The big event on that particular day was a "Standards and Practices" (censors) problem dealing with a Pillsbury chocolate cake. The live commercial during a game show featured a spokesman slicing the cake and announcing, "It's three days old and still fresh and delicious." One of the censors had kept the cake in a vault to make sure the cake was really three days old. However, he'd been drink-

ing heavily and had forgotten exactly when he'd taken possession of the chocolate cake. So how old was the cake, really?

I decided to end my stay at this particular nuthouse and returned to my office to make some phone calls to find out what other kinds of jobs were around. A message was waiting on my desk; Oscar Katz had called. I had known Oscar when I was at CBS. I returned the call.

"Hi, Oscar. What are you doing in Los Angeles?"

"I moved here," he replied, dourly. "I'm the new head of Desilu." He didn't sound happy, but then he never did.

"That's great." I was really pleased for him because I remembered the CBS executive shuffle a year ago, the same one I was caught in when Oscar was moved down a notch. "What can I do for you?"

Oscar's voice got more serious. "Do you know about film studios and labs and development deals and pilots?"

"Sure," I said, not knowing how excited I should get, if at all.

Courtesy Grant Tinker

NBC V.P. Grant Tinker, who would later become the Chairman of the Board and CEO of NBC.

"Do you want to come over and take care of those things for me? I'm a kind of fish out of water here."

"When?"

"As soon as possible!"

The next morning I met with my boss, Grant Tinker. I couldn't have been happier if I'd found the Dead Sea scrolls in a box of Crackerjacks. Grant wished me luck and told me to keep in touch.

"Keep in touch? Of course I'll keep in touch. You're one of the three buyers in the television business!"

Within the week, I arrived at Desilu (next door to Paramount Studios) on Melrose Avenue and was escorted to my new office by an aging studio guard. The studio looked and smelled old. There was even a sense of despair in the peeling paint. "We're going to where the senator has . . . or had his office. They gave it to you," he said sadly.

"The senator. What senator?"

"What do you mean, what senator? Why, George Murphy, of course. He was one of our executives. Boy, could he tap-dance!"

But then, what senator couldn't, I mused. (Former hoofer/actor George Murphy was a one-term U.S. senator from California during the years 1964–1970.)

I hadn't been on the lot for five minutes, and based on what I'd already seen and heard, I then understood the seriousness in Oscar's voice.

One of the many unwritten dictums in the film production business is to sell the minimum as the maximum and sell it hard. Or, to put a different spin on it,

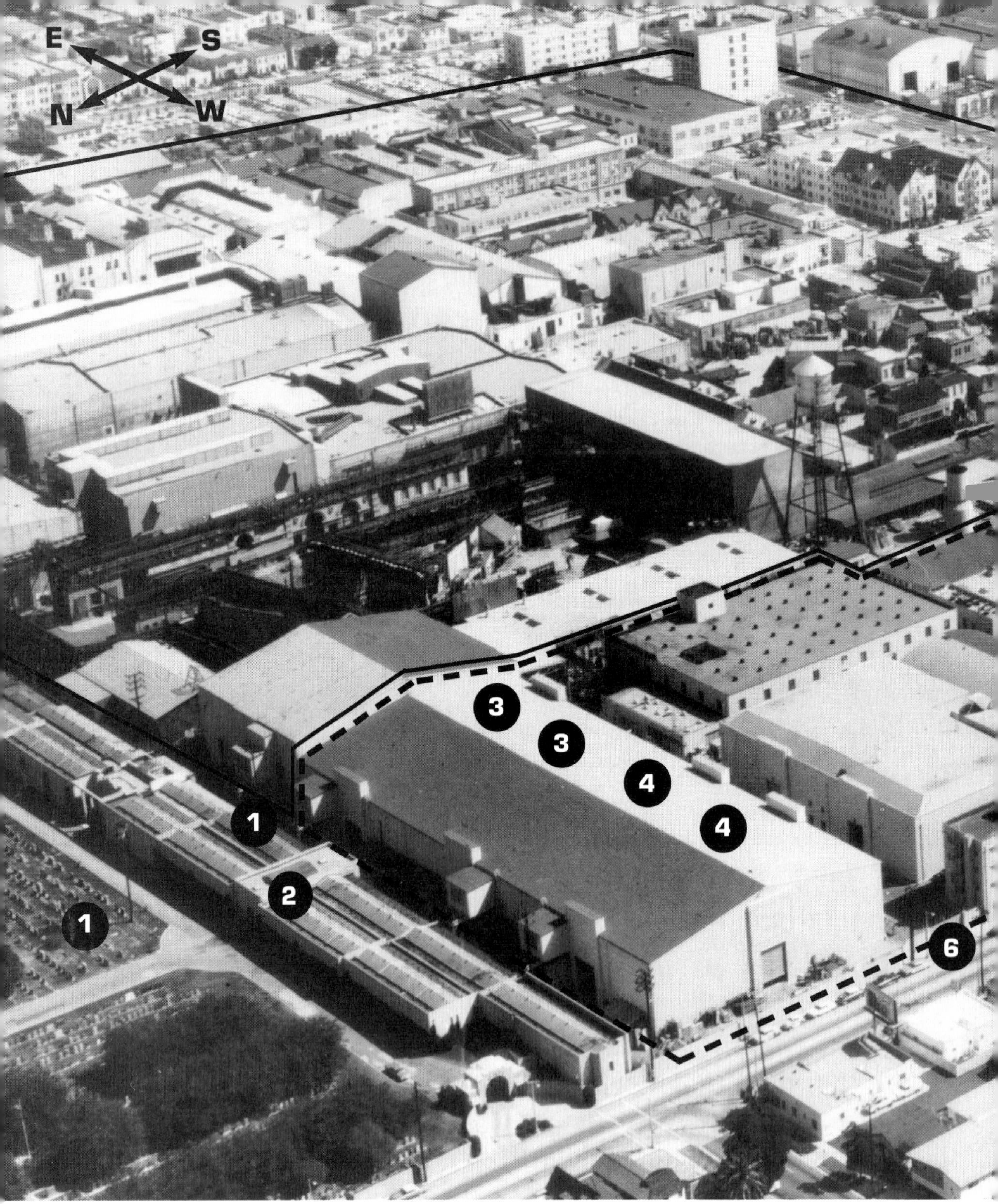

An aerial view of the Paramount lot (bordered by solid line) and Desilu studios (bordered by broken line).

1) Cemetery
2) Cemetery Crypts
3) *Star Trek* sound stages 9 and 10
4) *Mission: Impossible* sound stages 7 and 8

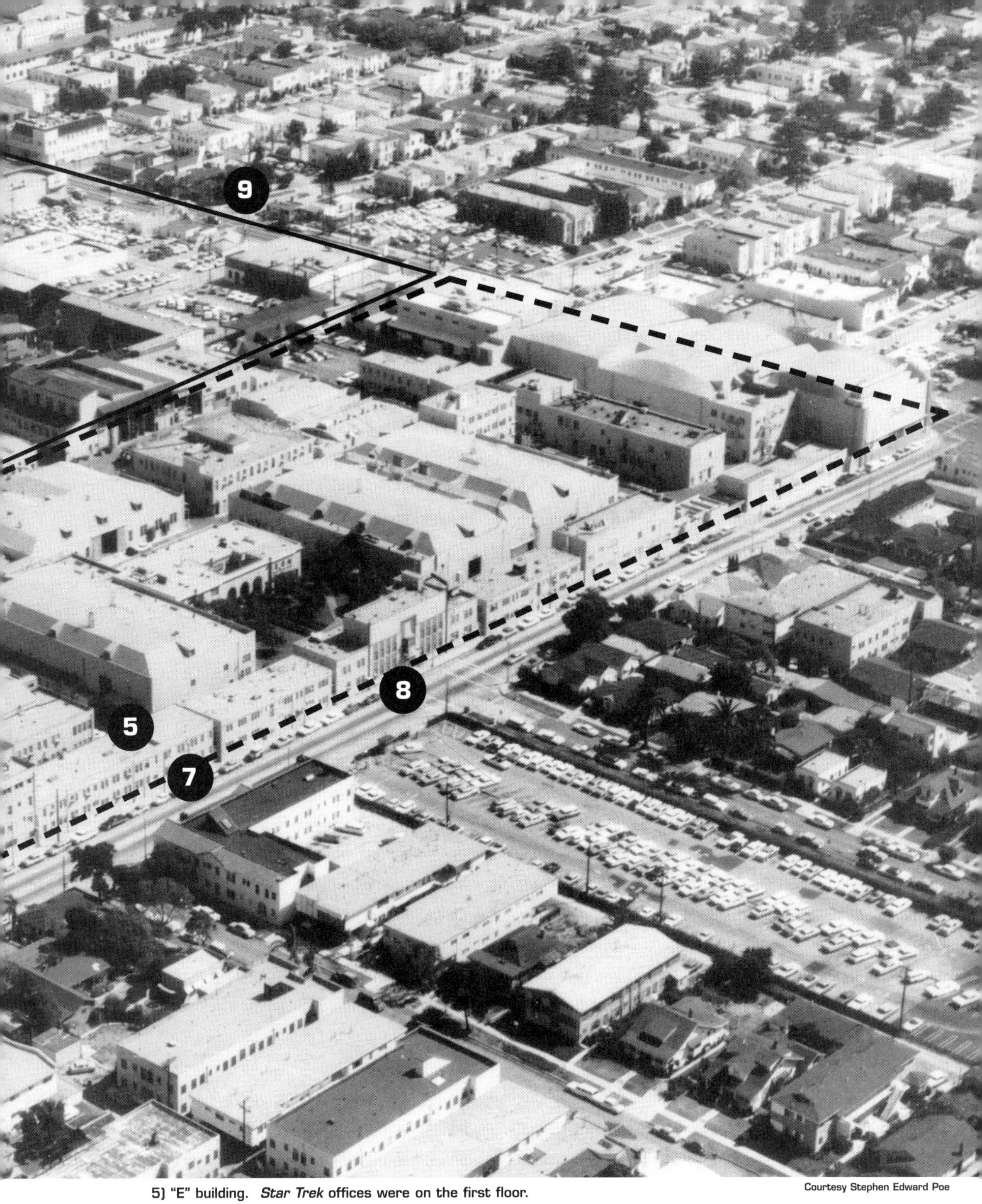

Courtesy Stephen Edward Poe

5) "E" building. *Star Trek* offices were on the first floor.
Mission: Impossible offices were on the second.
6) Desilu main auto entrance
7) Gower Avenue
8) Desilu main entrance (pedestrian). Herb Solow's office was in this building.
9) Melrose Avenue

"If you don't ask for it, you ain't gonna get it!" The assistant studio manager, waiting for me in Senator Mur . . . ah, my new office, knew the routine well.

"They sure don't make furniture nowadays the way they used to make it," he pronounced as he walked me through and around the oddest collection of prewar RKO Studios office leftovers. But this was my first day on the job, and I was determined to be good and diplomatic. As I looked over the sorry assortment of furniture, I said, "Don't tell me. Let me guess. This stuff is from a Jimmy Cagney movie!"

The guy shook his head.

"Okay, a Humphrey Bogart movie!"

The guy continued shaking his head.

But then I wised up. "Of course, it's from a George Murphy movie!" The guy's smile exploded into a full-blown grin. He even named the movie the furniture was from, *For Me And My Gal*—1942.

"Good," I continued, having been somewhat accepted into the fold, "let's talk about a little modern furniture."

"Modern? But modern means money," he countered. He sounded frightened. "I'll have to speak to Argie Nelson, the studio manager. Christ, we'd have to buy the stuff."

I nodded, and *my* smile exploded into a full-blown grin. He was the first person at the studio to meet the advance man for the new group that would repair the good ship Desilu and set it back on course. And we'd have a real good time doing it.

Probably the last studio vestige of Desi Arnaz, other than part of his name on the sign above the entrance, was his office. It was wood-paneled, carpeted, and decorated in exceptionally good taste. I was told Lucy rarely used it after Desi left, preferring to handle her business from within the yellow-painted walls of her dressing room–bungalow that bordered the small park just across from the studio office building. But now, Desi's office had become Oscar's office. I sat with Oscar and discussed what was expected of me. In the meantime, workmen removed the last vestiges of George Murphy from my office and replaced him with more modern furnishings.

Oscar would deal with important Desilu policy matters, the Board of Directors (of which he was a member), Lucy, financial and legal matters, and that sort. I would take care of the series development, pilots, networks, and that sort. Responsibilities divided, Oscar and I walked down the studio street to Stage 12 where I would meet Lucy.

Lucy was not happy with her rehearsal. She was having problems with the script, the director, the guest star (famous movie star and Lucy's friend, Ann Sothern), and the paint smell in the air, a pet peeve of hers. Lucy did not like to rehearse if the paint on the sets was still wet and the odor permeated the stage. It was a condition to which she was entitled. Since everyone knew paint odor was a no-no, few were surprised when she flew off the handle a little. So perhaps it wasn't the best of times to meet Lucy; or perhaps it *was* the best of times to meet Lucy. We shook hands and smiled. "Get some shows for the studio," she ordered. I nodded that I'd try.

Lucy continued, "I'm just the girl from Stage 12. That's what I do."

I nodded again, said, "Get back to your rehearsal," and added firmly, "It needs you." She nodded and returned to her rehearsal, and I walked away. The tone and demeanor of our relationship had been established. She does what she does; I do what I do. The twain should not meet. Except for a handful of occasions, that's the way it was for the next four years—until I resigned a few months after Lucy sold the studio.

Gene Roddenberry and a dancer on the set of "The Cage."

Courtesy Greg Jein

2

A Dreamer of Dreams

HERB: The day after meeting Lucy, I began series development with a search for the writers who would create pilots for us. It was my agent and good friend, Leonard Hanzer, who referred to them as horses. He always reminded me, "Herb, remember, you can't get into the race if you don't have the horses, and you can't win the race if you don't have the really great horses." As in so many other things, Leonard was right. Although all phases of the entertainment business usually start with the writer, in television the process can *only* start with the writer.

We had a plus with our agents, Ashley-Famous. They represented many quality and network-salable writers. Desilu would have a crack at many of those who weren't committed elsewhere, and thank goodness, we had the CBS development fund that enabled us to afford them.

The head of the Ashley-Famous office in Los Angeles was Alden Schwimmer. A warm, intelligent, fair-minded former New Yorker with a very urbane sense of humor, Alden, aka "Schwim," personally represented a basketful of superwriters: Rod Serling, Reginald Rose, Tony Webster, Howard Rodman, and similarly important talents. The superwriters were super–in demand, superbusy, superexpensive, and usually superunavailable to new clients like Desilu Productions. But that was to be expected. An agent, even a powerful agent, can push his client around just so much. If the superwriter didn't want to work at some run-down, headless studio with a terrible track record for getting shows on the air and keeping them there, a studio somewhere on Melrose Avenue sandwiched among Paramount Studios, Nickodell Restaurant, Channel 9, and the Hollywood Memorial and Beth Olam Cemeteries, then we'd be out of luck.

But Alden and the agency had many other writer clients: some good, some bad; some successful, some not. Remember, in television you can be bad and successful or good and a failure. Let's not confuse futures with definitions. Two of the writers, guys with pilot-series ideas attached, sent over to the studio at various times, were of the star-crossed variety.

They were as opposite as night and last Thursday morning. Bruce Geller: Yale graduate, Jewish, liberal exotic, son of the famous "Hanging Judge" Justice Abe Geller of the New York State Superior Court. Gene Roddenberry: Columbia Adult College night course, Southern Baptist, mumbling exotic, and son of a bigoted Texan (as Gene later described his father), a small-town peace officer. Yet, both men seemed to have been born for this moment. Both seemed to have a streak of madness that would protect them and stand them in good stead at the reawakening Desilu. It was as if I'd posted a sign reading "Normal People Need Not Apply," and they were both jockeying to be first in line.

Gene Roddenberry

Courtesy Richard Arnold

Much has been written about the personal history of Gene Roddenberry. Some is factual; some is not. Gene himself, over the years, tended to intermix fact and fantasy. But then, that happens with many who are in the public eye. Yes, as Gene told me during those early years, he was a pilot for Pan-Am who "deadheaded" on a Middle-Eastern flight from Karachi that crashed in the Saudi Arabian desert. But no, Gene did not pull all the passengers from the burning wreckage by himself, fight off a raiding band of Arab tribesmen, and walk across the desert to the nearest phone and summon help.

Yes, Gene was a contributing writer for *Have Gun, Will Travel,* but not "head writer" of that series—nor did he create it. That was done by Sam Rolfe and Herb Meadows. But yes, Gene did write more scripts than any other of the show's freelance writers.

Yes, Gene was a police officer for the LAPD. Yes, Gene wrote speeches for Chief William A. Parker. No, as a sergeant, Gene was not in line to replace Parker as Los Angeles police chief.

Yes, Gene created and produced a television series, *The Lieutenant.* Yes, the series was unsuccessful, lasting less than one year. Yes, Gene Roddenberry was out of work. That's when he showed up on my doorstep.

It was April, 1964. Lydia Schiller, my secretary, buzzed me on the intercom to advise that Mr. Roddenberry had arrived for his appointment. Never having met or spoken to Roddenberry, but having seen several episodes of his series *The Lieutenant* and knowing he was once a cop and an airline pilot, I very much expected a straight-backed, bright-eyed, dynamic, quick-paced individual who'd snap his way into my office. "Thanks, Lydia. Send him in."

The door opened, and there was Gene Roddenberry. My first impression was that this tall, unkempt person recently learned how to dress himself but hadn't yet quite gotten the knack. His gait reminded me of tepid water flowing from a slow faucet, and his hair unidirectionally flopped over his eyes like a very shaggy dog's. He smiled boyishly and mumbled, "Hi, I'm . . . ahh . . . Gene Roddenberry. Ahh . . . Alden sent me." He handed me a piece of paper wrinkled in the corner by his nervous fingers. "This is a series idea I have. It's . . . ahh . . . like *Wagon Train* to the . . . ahh . . . stars. It's called . . . ahh . . . *Star Trek.*"

A month earlier, in March, while Gene was still at MGM, finishing up the final episodes of *The Lieutenant,* he approached his Executive Producer and boss, television legend Norman Felton, with a sixteen-page presentation of the same idea for a new series. It was about a spaceship that flew around the universe getting in and out of trouble. Felton, just having had a year working with Gene, passed.

Dorothy Fontana

Courtesy Stephen Edward Poe

Gene Roddenberry's secretary at the time was Dorothy Fontana. She liked the concept and, after typing the presentation, questioned him as to who would play Spock. Gene told her he had already decided on Leonard Nimoy, a little-known actor who had just finished appearing in an episode of *The Lieutenant* along with a then little-known actress named Majel Barrett.

As further evidence of the small world of *Star Trek,* while working as a studio secretary years before *The Lieutenant,* Fontana sold her first story to a television series called *Frontier Circus.* One actor who appeared in the episode based on her story was Leonard Nimoy. *Frontier Circus*'s creator-producer was Sam Peeples, who later wrote the second of two *Star Trek* pilots, "Where No Man Has Gone Before."

Gene sat anxiously in the chair near my desk and stared at me as I read his words on the wrinkled paper.

I could understand why Felton had passed on Gene's original presentation. Although inventive, it wasn't a totally new kind of television series. Years before, in the infancy of television, Channel 5, the old Dumont Network station in New York, telecast a live series called *Captain Video.* Soon after *Captain Video* came *Space Rangers.* And the movies had covered the subject fairly well, especially with the popular serials *Buck Rogers* and *Flash Gordon.* However, while Gene Roddenberry's subject was familiar, the concept and characters he'd created, and later defined and refined, were compelling. And he'd solved one of the problems of audience familiarity by using contemporary navy terms, ranks, names, and jargon. It was captain and yeoman and medical officer; it was "starboard" and "port," and it was the *U.S.S. Yorktown* (later changed to the *Enterprise*), rather than "Rocket Ship X-9." However, the *"Wagon Train* to the stars" concept, while an ear-catching phrase, didn't work as conceived. It needed something else. I looked up at Gene, but before I could say anything, Gene volunteered he'd written a complete presentation for "A one-hour dramatic action–adventure–science-fiction" television series that included character breakdowns and story springboards.

"I'd like to read it later," I told him, "but first, let's see if we can make a deal to develop your idea."

Roddenberry stared at me quizzically. "You're kidding. You haven't read any of my writing."

"I've seen the way you dress," I countered, "and I figure you must be able to write. You sure as hell aren't going to make a living impressing employers with your wardrobe!"

I made a script development deal with Gene, and the process began. The development deal was with Desilu only; we still needed a network involvement. But it was too early to pitch the networks. A lot of the pedestrian elements (what every other action-adventure series offered) had to be removed from Roddenberry's concept. And that *"Wagon Train* to the stars" business had to be rethought and improved upon.

But it was not to be. Apparently eager to show CBS that Desilu was really getting cracking with a development deal, Oscar arranged for Gene to pitch the series to CBS. On hearing the news, I had three concerns.

First, the concept needed a lot of work and wasn't ready to be taken to market, because once a network turned down an idea, there was no going back. Second, Gene Roddenberry was probably the most ineffective pitchman for a series, especially one this different, that I had ever met in the television business. Third, pitching shows was my responsibility; yet I wasn't told anything about the meeting until after it was over. The problem was further magnified: CBS represented our best shot, because of Lucy and, more significantly, because it was their development money we were playing with. My fear was that impatience with the development process might blow our chance of getting a network development deal for *Star Trek.*

From the collection of Herbert F. Solow

Gene Roddenberry (l.) and Herb Solow (r.) on the set of "The Cage" with three "dancing girls." They are "looking" for Desilu head Oscar Katz.

Gene filled me in on the pitch meeting. The main CBS guy present was its President, James T. Aubrey, Jr. Both Oscar and I had worked for Jim Aubrey and knew his business acumen and his personality fairly well. Jim was exceptionally bright. He knew television, and he knew what he wanted on CBS. He had a rapier-sharp mind that, in less than a split second, could turn into a rapier-sharp mouth. The famous "smiling cobra," at first gentle as a lamb, became as ferocious as a bull before you had time to dive for cover. (I became all too familiar with this side of him in 1970 when I was Production Vice President at MGM and Jim was its President. Working with him was never dull.)

Oscar introduced Roddenberry, and Gene nervously mumbled his way through the presentation, pushing the *"Wagon Train* to the stars" business. The CBS party line was that they had a Fox series in development called *Lost in Space,* and *Star Trek* was the same kind of show. So they passed on *Star Trek.* I told Gene I didn't buy their excuse for not making a development deal. In recent years, Desilu had been known as a producer of small, half-hour, three-camera situation comedies, and suddenly, we're talking a one-hour, outer-space, dramatic-adventure series with complicated optical and special effects. The only special effect taking place at Desilu at that time was Lucy getting her hair dyed each week.

Gene, Oscar, and I made a pact: no more running off to the networks half-cocked. We would develop the concept properly, to where it was so damn good networks would take the gamble on letting us make such a complicated series. The development process was restarted, knowing Big Daddy CBS was already out of the batter's box. The ill-fated CBS meeting managed to do one thing, however. Concerned over the CBS setback, Oscar rarely involved himself in any future network and/or studio meetings or discussions about *Star Trek.*

Gene and I met every day, just sitting around and talking about *Star Trek.* Gene was relatively inexperienced in the art of writing series presentations and very much needed someone to use as a sounding board. We'd discuss concepts regardless of how ridiculous they seemed. At times he was the pitcher, and I was the receiver; at times the roles were reversed.

The continuing problem with *Star Trek* was the need to place it in a viewer-understandable time frame. Gene's pet metaphor for *Star Trek,* "*Wagon Train* to the stars," came from a very successful television series about a wagon train moving from St. Joseph, Missouri, to Oregon during the nineteenth-century migration to the American West. But that was a time and event most viewers knew from school, or from the movies, and accepted because it had already taken place. *Star Trek,* according to Gene's concept, was out there in the future and was going to happen.

There was the possibility that the 1964 television audience wasn't going to accept that premise on a continuing series basis. Having studied Jonathan Swift and *Gulliver's Travels* at college, I accepted what Swift wrote because he treated it as something that had already happened. Swift was merely telling me what had gone on, setting up and highlighting the adventure for me. My recommendation to Roddenberry: "The voyages of the Enterprise have already taken place; all *Star Trek* adventures are already history. The captain is setting up and recounting the particular adventure. He clues in the viewer very quickly as to what is going on and where, so we don't have page after page of boring exposition." It was an unusually quick way to deliver needed information, using a flashback to move the action from the past to the present. We kicked the idea around for a while, and Gene accepted the concept. The "captain's log–stardate" introduction to each episode was born, and each adventure became a flashback. To commemorate the event, we went further and changed the series title from *Star Trek* to *Gulliver's Travels* and the name of the ship's captain to Captain Gulliver.

Several days later, we met again. Gene looked at me in despair; I looked at him in despair. We had both come to the same conclusion. We had just gotten caught up in the moment and gone too far. Narration: "Yes!" *Gulliver's Travels* and Captain Gulliver: "No!"

Who knows? Bill Shatner could have been Captain Gulliver, and the sequels to the original series would have been *Gulliver's Travels: The Next Generation* and *Gulliver's Travels: Deep Space Nine.* Rather than "Trekkies," we would have had "Gullies." Changing the name back was a wise move.

With the captain's log–stardate concept in place, with the main characters more defined, the time had arrived to confront another network. NBC was the choice. Desilu had never had a series development deal with NBC. Whether it was CBS's desire or NBC's refusal or Desilu's lack of quality series, the reason wasn't known. But having recently left NBC, the wanna-be "full-color network," I decided, with a series like *Star Trek* just begging for color, you can go home again. I called Grant Tinker and set up a meeting. Jerry Stanley, NBC Program Development Vice President, would join Grant. Gene would join me.

We discussed the pending meeting. I told Gene the more he was considered exotic, strange, and mysterious, the more the network would believe he knew about other planets, alien creatures, and benevolent monsters. So Roddenberry was coming to the meeting, having agreed to the following provisos: He would look unkempt—not a problem; he would mumble some—not a problem; and he wouldn't volunteer anything—hopefully not a problem.

Several days later, in early May, 1964, Gene and I drove over to NBC Burbank for our meeting. It was like most network meetings: fifty percent small talk, twenty-five percent network gossip, and twenty-five percent business. I made the pitch, explaining the series idea, the characters, and the stories. Gene was great. He sat there in some odd, grinning stupor, as if he were jet-lagged from the long voyage back from Alpha Centauri. Jerry Stanley wanted to know more about the pilot story. I asked Gene to explain. He did, very succinctly describing the premise of the "The Menagerie."

But neither Grant Tinker nor Jerry was convinced it would make a commercial television series, that there was enough of an audience out there to support this mixture of science fiction and fantasy. It was "well, I really don't know" time. Experience told me if we didn't get a deal before we left the room, we'd never get a deal at all. Grant and Jerry were friends of mine. You can take advantage of friends at network meetings.

Jerry stood up to end the meeting. "Listen, Herb, let Grant and me talk it over, and we'll call you."

Gene stood up to leave. I told him to sit down and turned to Jerry. "Jerome, there comes a time when you guys have to gamble on something that's worth the gamble. Sure, *Star Trek* is a gamble, but it's worth taking. It's also a gamble for Desilu, a big gamble. If it doesn't work, we've all lost, but we've lost trying to do something worthwhile. And if you give us a commitment for a ninety-minute script instead of one hour, and we make the pilot, you can always run it as a TV special and recoup your investment if it doesn't sell as a series. Besides, I'm not leaving this room until you give us a script order." I sat down as authoritatively as I could.

Grant smiled. "What do you want for dinner?"

"Whatever you're having." I smiled back.

So there we all sat, stubbornly waiting for a shoe to drop. Jerry broke the silence with a smile. "Solow, you're a real pain in the ass."

"I know," I replied. "Does that mean we have a deal, Jerome?"

He looked at Grant. Grant smiled. Jerry nodded. "Have your guy call Business Affairs."

"Thanks, Jerry; we'll do a good job for you."

Something popped into Jerry's mind. "Oh, by the way, Herb, do you know that goddamn bump of yours ruined my car?"

(During my last boring days at NBC, I won a Personnel Department safety contest, suggesting that a speed bump be installed at the entrance to the executive parking lot and received a $25 U.S. savings bond for my effort.)

"My driveshaft is bent," Jerry continued. "Who's going to pay for that?"

"Jerome, Tommy Sarnoff liked my suggestion and gave me the prize. Let him repair your car," I retorted. I turned to Roddenberry. "Let's get outta here, Gene, before they take back the script order. Because they sure as hell aren't getting back my $25 U.S. savings bond!"

As Gene and I drove back to the studio, we marked the day as the beginning of *Star Trek.* We didn't know it would take almost three years of anxiety and frustration before the *Star Trek* series would debut on NBC.

NBC always had doubts as to whether or not the supposedly reborn Desilu could pull off something like *Star Trek.* They wanted to hear more stories before one of them was chosen as the basis for the pilot script.

We had more meetings, and Gene gave them more stories. Realizing his inability to dramatically pitch his material, Gene fell into a new and highly successful mode of delivery at network meetings. Rather than attempt to speed up his remarks, raise his voice, and wow them with fancy footwork, Gene slowed his delivery even more and all but whispered his words. Soon, network executives were sitting on the edges of their chairs, leaning over and straining to hear his words. He became the absolute center of the room. It worked so well, Gene Roddenberry used the technique for as long as I knew him.

The pilot story NBC chose was named "The Cage," and after we spent many hours straightening out the twists, turns, and bends in the plot, Gene began to write the script. In some way, he found the process easier than writing other pilot scripts. That little person who sits on a writer's shoulder demanding reality and real life was conspicuous by its absence. Gene had no reality to write, only fantasy with a dose of "non-science" science fiction, to boot.

The reality would come when the script was finished, the reality of money. Easy for Gene to hinge a scene on a "laser cannon," tough to go down to the local hardware store or gun shop and buy one. But like the old joke about selling sardines but never eating them, the network draft wasn't for shooting, the network draft was for selling. When we got the order for the pilot film, then we'd face the budget problem head-on. Sure we would!

As Gene completed the first-draft pilot script, he unfortunately became overly protective of his new baby. He began to establish scapegoats, failing to recognize that others had not only emotional interests in the project, but monied interests as well. NBC Programming, NBC Standards and Practices (the censors), and the Desilu Production Department were destined to become his three leading scapegoats. I cautioned Gene that having good reason at times was no excuse to continually cast blame, especially when dealing with people who had a lot to do with the future of the series and his ultimate survival. He didn't listen. He didn't want to. And as series development progressed, his behavior foreshadowed a continuing rocky future for Gene Roddenberry and *Star Trek.* Though I ran interference for him with Desilu management and its Production Department, NBC was a different story. It helped no one to get involved in a very personal war, but Gene couldn't resist tilting at windmills.

Gene and I met with NBC to get their script comments. He took offense at most of them, at times unnecessarily so. Some ideas were really good. And a new side of Gene slowly appeared: ownership of ideas. If a good story or series point came from anyone, be it NBC, Ashley-Famous, or Desilu, Gene Roddenberry appropriated it. This subtle "these are all my ideas" syndrome would eventually affect Gene's relationships with many who worked on *Star Trek:* writers, composers, actors, agents, story editors, art directors, producers, and me. A few years later, Bob Justman coined a name for him, "the Great Bird of the Galaxy." As Gene continued to absorb ideas and concepts from others, I would jokingly tell Gene that he was really "the Great Blotter of the Galaxy." It seemed more appropriate.

BOB: Probably because she never interfered with his show, Gene always had kind words to say about Lucille Ball. Nonetheless, there was, and has been, a lot of speculation as to Lucy's involvement in the development of *Star Trek.*

HERB: Several incidents should set the record straight:

First, although I wasn't a member of the Desilu Board of Directors, I was called upon to make appearances at board meetings to report on and update our series development status, network deals, important casting choices we'd made, and the like. Lucy rarely asked questions during the meeting, content to listen to her executives discuss the state of her company. Surprisingly, at one particular meeting as I was about to begin my presentation, Lucy interrupted me.

"Herb?"

"Lucy?"

"Herb, what's happening with that South Seas series?"

"The what?"

"You know, Herb, that South Seas series you mentioned last time."

"South Seas series? Gee, Lucy, I wish I could remember, but I don't recall any South Seas series. Are you su—?"

"Herb," Lucy interrupted, a slight anger sounding in her tone, "of course you talked about a South Seas series. With the USO entertainers who went there during the war to visit the troops!"

I looked around the room. The faces of the board members weren't happy. Mickey Rudin, Lucy's attorney and my support system at Desilu, silently indicated for me to answer her question. I tried to be calm as Lucy was getting more and more upset.

"Lucy, perhaps it's something I've forgotten, but for the life of me, I do not recall ever mentioning a series we have in development about a group of USO entertainers visiting our troops in the South Seas during World War II!"

"Oh, yes, you did," said a now defiant Lucy. "Oh, yes, you did!"

I stood speechless, trying to remember what I'd obviously forgotten, when Lucy, having remembered more information on the subject, suddenly blurted out, "Oh, yes, you did, Herb. You called it *Star Trek*!"

Later, out of hearing of the others, I explained *Star Trek* to Lucy. And I realized what an honest and human mistake she'd made. After all, in Lucille Ball's world, a star trek could mean only movie stars travelling somewhere in the world for the USO to visit our troops. The South Seas was as good a place as any.

In addition, to avoid potential confrontations, I'd made a decision never to involve Lucy in the casting of our television pilots. In fact, the only actor Lucy would ever ask to meet before we hired her was Barbara Bain of *Mission: Impossible.* Possibly because Barbara was to be the female lead—probably because Barbara was married to Martin Landau, star of *Mission*—Lucy suspected a little favoritism. Favoritism in casting would eventually cause a "Lucy problem" for me because of Gene and his "Number One," actress Majel Barrett.

And finally, all the top executives received copies of our pilot scripts to read, review with others, and comment on. I personally walked the *Star Trek* pilot script into Lucy's dressing room and handed it to her. "Lucy, this is the *Star Trek* pilot script. There'll be lots of changes, so if you have any comments, let me have them, because there'll be ample time to implement them." Lucy never mentioned the script, and the day the completed pilot was screened for NBC on the West Coast, I walked into Lucy's dressing room to tell her NBC's reaction. The pilot script was still there, apparently untouched.

I know Oscar read his copy of the pilot script, but he never offered any comments. He allowed me to do my work without interference. When you think about it, could anyone have had better bosses than Lucy and Oscar?

The two-hour pilot script was finally finished. Gene's original concept had been greatly altered by suggestions from both NBC and Desilu. In the early sixties, there was but one pilot season. To be in contention for pilot film orders, scripts had to be in the network's hands by a particular date, usually late summer. The networks distributed copies of all their pilot scripts to their many executives, and by Halloween, decisions had been made. It was "trick or treat" time. Weekends and the Thanksgiving and Christmas holidays became secondary in our minds. We had primary concerns: Would they like our script, and, more importantly, would they commit to making the pilot film? The wait began.

Then the unthinkable happened. Desilu was going to make a pilot for NBC. Really. NBC, the archrival of Lucy's CBS, had put its faith in the new Desilu and *Star Trek.* NBC's financial contribution to the pilot would be considerable. After Oscar made the announcement at the Desilu board meeting, I fielded the questions.

"Will the pilot cost more than they give us?"

"Yes, the pilot will cost more than they give us."

"How much more?"

"We won't know until the revised script is budgeted. But more."

"Can we make this kind of show?"

"Of course we can!"

"Are you sure?"

"Of course, I'm sure."

The board was nervous. Production of a ninety-minute science-fiction pilot was an expensive business move, a risky business move. We were in the arena where the big boys played: Universal, Warner Brothers, Fox, MGM, United Artists, Paramount, Screen Gems (Columbia Pictures). As I answered more questions about the soon-to-be-produced pilot, keeping up a positive demeanor as best I could, I desperately wanted everyone in the room to form a circle, hold hands and repeat after me, "Our Father, which art in Heaven . . ."

(l. to r.) Actress Susan Oliver, Gene Roddenberry, director Robert Butler, and Bob Justman on the set of "The Cage."

Courtesy Greg Jein

3

Get on Board, Li'l Chillun

BOB: There was a foot of snow on our balcony. My wife, Jackie, and I were at the El Tovar Hotel on the south rim of the Grand Canyon where we'd come for a long-planned vacation. Although it was early in May, 1964, there had been a storm the night before and all the buttes and mesas were carpeted white. It was a stunning sight.

Jack Berne, production manager for famed movie director Robert Aldrich, was on the phone. This was the third time Jack had called, pleading with me to go to work preparing the next Aldrich film. There was a note of desperation in Jack's voice. "You can't turn Bob Aldrich down."

"I have to, Jack. I made a commitment to go back to *The Outer Limits.* I gave my word."

"But he said, 'Get Bobby J.' What will I tell him?"

"Just tell him the truth, Jack. He'll understand."

"No, he won't!" Jack sounded angry and bitter. "You're gonna regret this, Bob."

"I hope not, Jack. But it just can't be helped."

Jack hung up. He didn't call back.

Aldrich and I had been close friends for years. We'd worked together when he was still just an ambitious assistant director. He helped get me into the Directors Guild and was the first person to shake my hand and welcome me as a fellow member. I'd been his second assistant director on *The Doctor,* the first TV series he ever directed, and later worked with him on his movies *Apache, Kiss Me Deadly, Attack,* and *The Big Knife.* He was a great guy, and I had learned more with him and from him than anyone else. Bobby Aldrich was my hero and friend. I hated to turn him down, but in our business your word is your bond. Things happen so quickly that there's seldom time to draw up a contract. If you can't be trusted to keep your word, you can't be trusted for anything. I hoped that he would understand and forgive me, but I had no control over what Jack would tell him. I hoped I'd made the right decision.

I hadn't. The first intimation of trouble came when I returned to *The Outer Limits.* As the B. B. King song lyric goes, "The thrill is gone." And so was Joe Stefano, screenwriter of *Psycho,* who was the producer-writer responsible for the high quality of *The Outer Limits* series. The dialogue he wrote was so poetic and filled with metaphor that his scripts read like blank verse. But Joe had made the mistake of saying "no" to sensationalizing the show at the request of the network buyer, ABC.

With Stefano's departure and ABC's installation of a new management team, the magic of the series begin to dissipate. Many of the new scripts were unintriguing but "the bear" was always present. "The bear" was the nickname we gave to the monster ABC wanted in each episode. There had been monsters during the first season, but they weren't just for exploitation value. Often, the real monsters turned out to be the humans who came into contact with these unworldly creatures—another case where art imitates life.

HERB: Gene and I, by now good friends united in a common cause, celebrated the pilot order at lunch with our daily Cobb salad at the Hollywood Brown Derby on Vine Street. Dave Kaufman, the venerable television reporter and columnist for *Daily Variety,* sat at his usual table eating his usual lunch: scrambled eggs and french fried potatoes. David ate the same lunch at the same table each and every day for the thirty years that I knew him. As you can probably guess, he wasn't too thrilled with change. So when he dropped by to say "hello" on his walk back to the nearby *Variety* offices, I excitedly told him of our success.

"I knew it before you did," he said, leaning over to shake Gene's hand, then continuing wryly, "The question is who's going to make the pilot? Desilu does comedy, and quite frankly, Herb, I've never known you to be that funny." I invited Dave to join us and have some dessert. I knew he didn't eat dessert, so the expense account was protected. As expected, David declined the invitation.

"I was just joking, Herb," he allowed, "but seriously, where are you going to find the kind of people you need to make the thing?" David knew Desi quite well, knew Desilu's history, and knew the production personnel deficiencies at the studio. As we acknowledged his insight, Dave was on his way. "Good luck with the pilot. Whatever the paper can do to help you, call me." For many years, I often took him up on his offer, and David Kaufman was a man of his word.

David had laid out the problem for us, and it was a serious one. Pilot season came once a year. Production companies that were actively making long-form films or series had experienced crews on their payroll. With advance planning, they'd split off members of those crews and put them together as one or more production units that worked on pilots. Desilu had *The Lucy Show* crew—period. As professional as the crew was, most of them would be of little help when confronted with the overwhelming demands and technical requirements of the planned *Star Trek* pilot. Basically, Gene and I were faced with the job of building a production unit from scratch at a time when the availability lists from the unions were scant or empty. And if people were still on the list during pilot season, they were usually drunks, undependable, or semiretired. But first things first. We needed a director.

Robert Butler was chosen by Roddenberry and Solow after numerous conversations with NBC Programming and Alden Schwimmer at Ashley-Famous. Networks had their "approved" lists of pilot directors, based on prior experience with particular individuals. NBC liked Bob Butler's work very much. His track record and credits were excellent. And he was perfectly suited for the task. Roddenberry and Solow knew Butler was St. Francis of Assisi. If faced with the end of the world—cool, calm, and collected—he'd just keep on going about the business of directing. And happily, as Butler prepared the film, nothing about the challenges fazed him, nothing beat him down, nothing sent him scurrying back to his agent, crying, "What have you gotten me into?" Step one was completed.

Since no one, previously, had ever attempted to film a complicated television script like "The Cage," finding the key creative personnel was easier said than done. The production designer–art director was the next key to the puzzle. Roddenberry had written about the *Starship Enterprise*, but he was never able to visualize what the ship actually looked like. He had already spent many hours with writer friend Sam Peeples, looking through hundreds of old science-fiction and fantasy magazines in an effort to visualize what the *Enterprise* should look like, and he finally took photos of the cover illustrations of some issues of *Thrilling Wonder Stories* and other science-fiction magazines dating as far back as 1931. A visual translator was needed, a designer-draftsman-artist, well versed in flight and aerodynamics, who, starting with the magazine covers, could combine, reduce to paper, and eventually make a reality of what was flying around inside Roddenberry's head.

While Pato Guzman, the underchallenged Art Director on *The Lucy Show*,

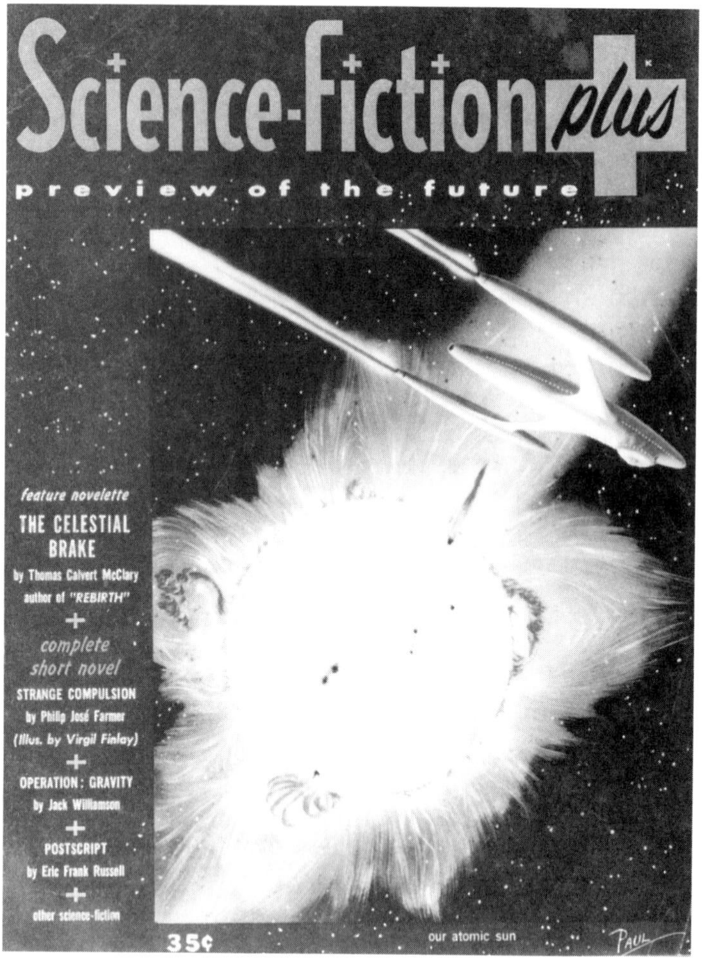

One of the pulp magazine cover illustrations that intrigued Roddenberry. Note certain design elements used for the *Enterprise.*

would design the sets, Set Designer Walter "Matt" Jefferies—artist, designer, illustrator, and aviator—was given the assignment of designing the spaceship. All that Roddenberry knew was what the *Enterprise* shouldn't look like. It shouldn't be a dinky *Flash Gordon* spaceship, and it shouldn't be rocket-powered. Rather, its power should be something as yet unimagined by present-day science. Given the tall order, Matt Jefferies made trip after to trip to Roddenberry's office with what he felt was the answer, and time after time returned to his drawing board until, at long last, they both agreed. Matt Jefferies had successfully pulled something out of thin air and the science-fiction magazine covers that had such an influence upon Roddenberry.

Luckily, Costume Designer William Ware Theiss was between assignments and available. An intense dabbler with fabric swatches, Theiss was given the assignment of designing costumes that had to be different from anything ever seen on commercial television. "And by the way, Bill, do it without much money. Budget problems, you know." Theiss utilized the pictures of scantily clad women in pulp science-fiction magazines like *Amazing Stories* and *Astounding Stories* as his point of departure. His costume designs permitted the actresses to show as much leg, breast, and skin as possible, while attempting to adhere to the dictates of NBC's Broadcast Standards Department, the network censors.

If there's one thing a producer learns early in life, it's that his greatest needs are good Associate Producers to do the dirty work and ride herd on both the production and the postproduction phases of the show.

James Goldstone had direct and indirect influences on *Star Trek.* He was Herb Solow's classmate at college; he directed an episode of Roddenberry's MGM series, *The Lieutenant;* and he would later direct the second *Star Trek* pilot. But on that day in early October, 1964, Goldstone was directing "The Inheritors," a two-part episode of *The Outer Limits,* when Gene Roddenberry called and asked

(left) Inspiration for Bill Theiss's futuristic costumes came from science-fiction pulp magazines like this one from 1952. (right) Actress France Nuyen wearing one of Bill Theiss's *Star Trek* costume designs.

him for an Associate Producer recommendation. Goldstone told Roddenberry he was again working with an assistant director named Bob Justman, who he thought was more than ready to move up to Associate Producer. "Talk to Bob Justman. He's the one you want," Goldstone advised.

BOB: Jim Goldstone told me I would be getting a call from a guy named Gene Roddenberry. "He's making a science-fiction pilot and he's looking for a good Associate Producer. I lost my head and lied and told him you're the best."

"You've got great taste, Jimmy. Who's this Roddenberry? I've never heard of him."

"You'll like him," he said. "I directed *The Lieutenant* for him over at MGM. He's bright. And he's unusual. It could be a big step up for you."

Gene phoned, and I agreed to meet with him during my lunch break. As I drove over to Desilu, I was excited by the possibility of moving up from what was, for me, a dead-end career.

As an assistant director, other than an early film I made with my father, I'd been on my own for almost fifteen years. I'd done it all: at least thirty-five movies

and more than a dozen television series, pilots and episodes, from kid shows like *Superman* and *The Mickey Mouse Club* to whodunits like *Phillip Marlowe* and *The Thin Man,* and science-fiction shows like *One Step Beyond* and *The Outer Limits.* I was very good at my job, but I wasn't getting anywhere and was still working as an assistant director. I wanted creative input into the product I helped make.

So I was hopeful as I parked my car and crossed Gower Street to the Desilu studio entrance. Maybe today was the day. Maybe this meeting with Roddenberry would result in another chance. I was soon in Gene's small, temporary office. He was alone; his secretary, Dorothy Fontana, had already gone to lunch.

He rose to greet me and shook my hand. "Hi, Bob. I'm Gene Roddenberry." He was quite tall, and when he smiled, he was immediately likable. Goldstone was right; as Gene and I talked, I realized he had great intelligence. He spoke softly, philosophically. He asked me about myself, my career, what I wanted to do in the future, and what was important in my life. No one in the film business had ever asked me about what was important in my life. I told him I wanted to use my creativity and contribute ideas rather than merely contributing my time and energy.

Gene smoked throughout our meeting, his long, slim fingers holding the cigarette in a most unusual fashion, midway between the two middle fingers. When he brought the cigarette up to his lips, the other fingers on his hand remained extended and covered his face from his nose to his chin. When framing a new thought, he would drag deeply on the cigarette while he gazed upwards toward something else, somewhere else, not in that room, perhaps not in any room.

I enjoyed speaking with him. After no more than thirty minutes of exchanging views on a wide variety of subjects, he asked if I'd be interested in the job of Associate Producer on his pilot.

Interested? Try desperate! I had recently given myself one more year to make a move up or forsake the film business. But I knew I lacked the sort of extensive postproduction knowledge a show like this would demand; it would be the wrong thing to do. I explained that to Gene and turned down his offer.

Before leaving, I recommended my friend, director and postproduction photographic effects whiz Byron Haskin. ("Bun" Haskin was famous for his work on the movies *Conquest of Space, Robinson Crusoe on Mars, His Majesty O'Keefe,* and the classic science-fiction opus, *War of the Worlds.*)

In an odd coincidence, on my way out of the studio, I met Byron on his way in.

"Hi, Bun. What are you up to?"

He was his usual crusty self. "Hi, Bobby. I'm gonna see some guy with a really weird name, Rodenberg or Rosenberry . . . or whatever. I don't know. Probably another rank amateur who doesn't know diddley and wants me to save his ass. He's looking for an associate producer type for some kind of science-fiction show."

"Well, good luck, Bun." I smiled. I didn't mention where I'd just been. I went back to work on *The Outer Limits,* and Byron got the Associate Producer job with Gene.

On Friday, October 30, 1964, we wrapped "The Brain Of Captain Barham," my last episode of *The Outer Limits.* By the middle of the following week, I was back with Leslie Stevens, with whom I had worked on *The Outer Limits* pilot and a series entitled *Stoney Burke.* Leslie was both boss and friend. He had brought the talented Joe Stefano in to produce *The Outer Limits* series, but now Stefano was gone and it seemed likely that the show wouldn't be renewed.

Leslie had just written a feature motion-picture script, entitled *Incubus,* that he wanted me to prepare for filming. Upon reading it, I was horrified to discover it was to be filmed with the actors all speaking Esperanto, an artificial worldwide language that was invented back in 1917 by Polish oculist L. L. Zamenhof.

Remonstrations did no good; Esperanto was one of Leslie Stevens's unusual and eclectic hobbies, and at the time it was his favorite. He was fixated upon it. "There are millions of people in the world who speak Esperanto, Bob. They'll all go see it."

What a dilemma. My chances to move on up the ladder of success had been drastically diminished: I'd turned down Roddenberry's offer; *The Outer Limits* was kaput; I was persona non grata with Bob Aldrich—and now I had to do a film in Esperanto.

HERB: A lot of Hollywood jargon is totally nondescriptive. Take, for example, assistant director. He really doesn't help the director direct. Although he does stage the background action in shots requiring "extra" players, an assistant director is primarily a traffic cop, making sure everything and everyone is scheduled, ready, in place, and prepared before turning the set over to the director. A great assistant director is a blessing; a lousy one is a curse. The first *Star Trek* pilot needed a great one.

I didn't want to use any first assistant who'd worked with Bob Butler in the past, feeling that too much familiarity might be a disadvantage on this mind-boggling science-fiction pilot. I checked with producer and director friends around town. "This pilot we're doing is a bitch. We need a very talented, very independent assistant director who'll push the crew and keep his director wound up." There were several "maybes" and two firm recommendations. One "maybe" and both "firms" were Bob Justman.

I checked with Gene Roddenberry. "Wasn't he the guy you wanted for Associate Producer?" He told me Justman had gone back to work for Leslie Stevens. "He's on staff there as assistant director," Gene added. "I don't think you'll get him."

Gene scoffed at my guarantee. "If I can't get Justman, I'll buy you dinner. If I get Justman, you buy lunch next time." At that time, Gene wasn't much for spending money, so I knew this was the only bet he'd make. He gagged a bit but finally agreed to the wager.

Actually, I'd hoodwinked him. What he didn't know was I had a development deal with Justman's boss, Leslie Stevens. We'd optioned Burt Standish's series of 1920s dime novels about the adventures of Frank Merriwell and were talking with Leslie about writing the script. I called Leslie, we discussed his ideas on the Merriwell material, and then I got down to the business at hand.

"Leslie, I need a favor. You have a guy working for you named Justman, an assistant director. We're preparing the *Star Trek* pilot, and I need him."

"Well, I don't know. For how long?"

"With prep time, the shooting, and some wrap-up, figure I'd be borrowing him for no more than a month at the most. Remember, Leslie, it's only a loan, a temporary loan, and he's yours again. Guaranteed."

Leslie okayed the temporary transfer, and I called Justman. I'd never spoken to him, so I introduced myself and told him he was moving.

BOB: Herb Solow phoned me out of the blue. I'd never even heard of him before, and here he was, speaking to me as if he'd known me for years: "Hi, Bob. How've you been? Who? Herb Solow. Call me Herb. I hear from my sources you're pretty good—at least that's what Jimmy Goldstone says. Of course, you and I both know that he's a terrible liar. Anyhow, how would you like to be assistant director on this little *Star Trek* pilot you turned down?"

I told Herb that I was busy preparing a feature and unavailable. His response? "No problem, Bob. I've already spoken to Leslie. It's all arranged. Come by my office at Desilu tomorrow morning. Say, nine o'clock? We can talk some more then. And I'll take you over to see Gene Roddenberry and your new office. 'Bye!"

So I went to work for Desilu on what I thought would take no more than six weeks. It would get me out of the Esperanto business, and besides, I was amused by this man whom I had never met. His breezy, informal manner made him likable, even over the telephone. And I was also highly intrigued by the challenge of *Star Trek* and the chance to work with Roddenberry. That "no more than a month" would lengthen into more than three years on *Star Trek* and a further stint on *Star Trek: The Next Generation* more than twenty years later.

The next morning, I met Herb Solow for the first time. He was as breezy and informal in person as he had been on the phone. "Welcome aboard, RJ. I'm glad you're here. Now I can relax while you guys make the show. Remember, it's how you play the game—*and* how you win."

Herb introduced me to his boss, Oscar Katz, and then took me down to Roddenberry's office. Gene was in a small office bungalow, working on the pilot script. He stopped long enough to greet me, warmly, and went back to work. It had been my intention to begin my preparation, but there was no final shooting script for me, yet. It was undergoing yet another one of its many rewrites, so after moving into one of the rooms in the bungalow, I decided it was time to "press the flesh." Herb had told me I would have to make the required visit to the Desilu Production office to meet Desilu VP and overall studio manager Argyle Nelson.

I had a good reputation as an assistant director. Curiously, I had been available a number of times when Desilu was hiring, and I'd never even had a phone call, much less a job offer from the studio. And yet, I was certain Argyle Nelson was aware of my existence. After all, Nelson and my father had business dealings when the growing Desilu Productions was renting studio space from him. "Argie's a great guy," my father used to say. "You ought to work for him." But Argie never called.

The visit to Nelson's bailiwick was fully as uncomfortable as I had anticipated. The other men in the office nodded, coolly, when I was introduced to them. The hair rose on the back of my neck. I could feel Argyle's eyes on me. His unspoken question was, "Can he cut it?" His unspoken opinion, "Not a chance."

Where does an alien go to register? It was Argie's prerogative to hire all assistant directors—and he certainly hadn't hired me. I was an outsider, one of Solow's and Roddenberry's boys and not one of his. Nevertheless, as production manager, Argyle had to approve my hiring by officially putting me on salary. Someone handed me a "start slip" and a withholding form. I signed both and got the hell out of there as fast as I could.

After Justman read the latest script rewrite, he began the schedule and budget "breakdown" process. Not only was the film equivalent in length to any movie, it was replete with enormously difficult production challenges, special effects and optical effects that had never even been attempted on a television schedule and budget. Some of the optical effects would require time-consuming tie-in elements that would slow the filming process.

The Howard Anderson Company, an optical effects house, was a tenant on the Desilu lot. It created special optical effects for many Hollywood production companies. Under its arrangement with Desilu, it was to handle all *Star Trek* special optical effects shots.

Darrell Anderson was the man with whom Butler and Justman would have to coordinate filming these special shots, and he had to be on the set to approve each camera "setup" involved in the optical process. The Anderson Company would also film, in its own off-lot stage, the miniature model of the *Starship Enterprise* that Matt Jefferies was still designing.

Justman had a theory about being a good assistant director: first, to have everything ready on the stage—actors, equipment, whatever—before his director even turned around to ask for it. And second, to plan ahead so well and so thoroughly that when things go wrong, and they will, he'll have several alternate plans ready to put into action. Justman often quoted Murphy's Law, stating that "whatever can possibly go wrong, will go wrong." He also quoted Parkinson's Law, stating that "work expands or contracts according to the amount of time available." Both these "laws" would be grievously tested and found to be still operative on "The Cage."

Already concerned about meeting an impossible production schedule man-

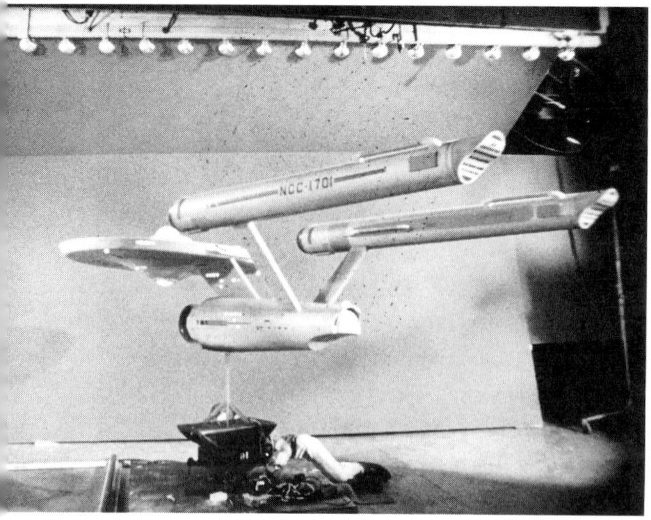

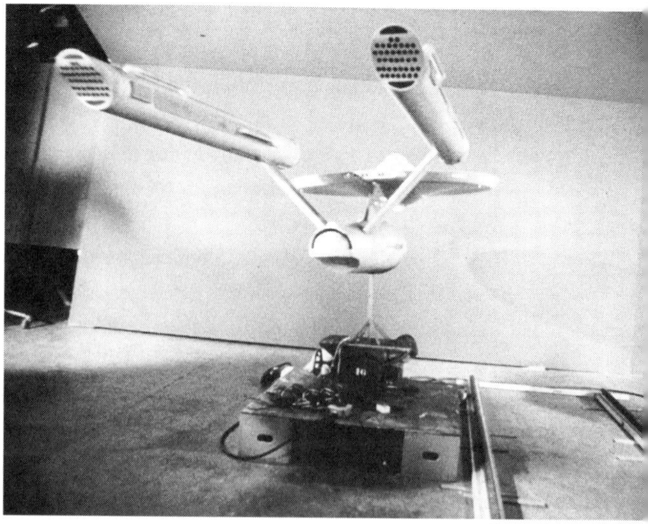

From the collection of Robert H. Justman

dated by the front office, Justman met with Roddenberry and Associate Producer Haskin to question the show's creator closely about how he wanted various elements of the pilot's production handled: which effects were necessary and which others could be eliminated or revised to make them more doable.

Even in this preproduction phase, Justman saw signs of escalating tension between Roddenberry and Haskin. Instead of accepting Roddenberry's ideas and working to make them feasible, Haskin sometimes refused to compromise. He was brilliant and knew everything there was to know about optical effects, but to paraphrase the old popular song, "Bun knows a little bit about a lot of things, but he doesn't know enough about Gene." Roddenberry had immense patience with people whose ideas differed from his, but little, if any, patience with people who were dogmatic about what could or couldn't be done.

BOB: "You can't do it that way," Byron would say to Gene.

"Why not?"

Byron folded his arms across his chest. "Because it can't be done that way. I've been in this business forty years. You can't reinvent the wheel."

Gene would look at him and then me, exasperated.

So later, when Byron and I were alone, I'd step in, gently. "You know, we're all after the same thing, the effect that Gene wants to see. It's not how we end up doing it; it's the final result that counts. Maybe you can find another way to do it, Bun. Or maybe you can dream up an even better effect—and one not so expensive."

Byron would harumph a bit and allow as how he could try; and sometimes, he'd come up with an answer to the problem. And sometimes not. But it was like pulling teeth. Gene greatly disliked going through the same motions constantly.

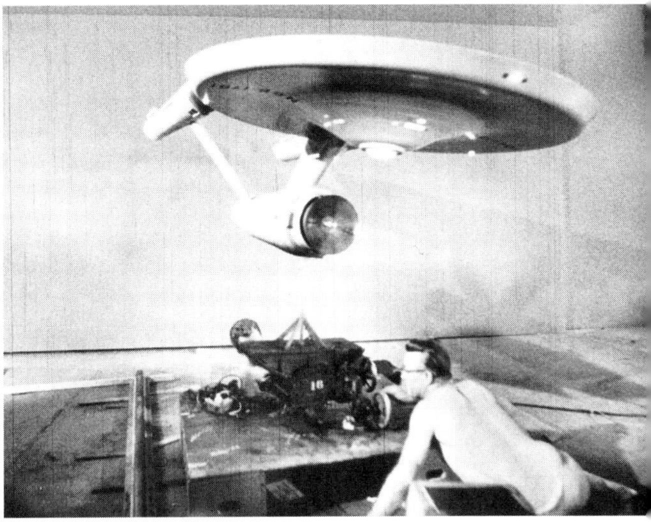

The large *U.S.S. Enterprise* model on the Anderson Company's "miniature" stage.

There was a temporary setback in the Art Department as Art Director Pato Guzman left the project. Homesick, Pato returned to his native Chile. His replacement was a veteran Art Director, German-born Franz Bachelin. But the design process continued. Matt Jefferies worked closely with Bachelin and not only designed the main *Enterprise* set, the Bridge, but also designed the various consoles and readout screens in the *Enterprise* sets.

Adhering to Roddenberry's original concept of contemporary navy, everything about the vessel had a "nautical" feel. There were no floors; there were decks. There were no walls; there were bulkheads. There was no front and rear or left and right; there was forward or aft and port or starboard. The *Enterprise* itself was a vessel, a space cruiser attached to Starfleet. And she, not it, was commanded by a captain.

Jefferies continued to bring revised designs of the vessel to Roddenberry for approval. The show's creator-producer was difficult to please, but slowly, painstakingly, an unusual craft took shape: a torpedo-like cylindrical lower body, its rear somewhat akin to that of a World War II flying boat, connected on top by a large forward-raking pylon to the bottom rear of an immense saucer-shaped superstructure. Two elevated smaller cylinders were connected by struts or pylons to either side of the rear lower body. This was no aerodynamic vessel and was, all in all, a strange-looking contraption that, in the real world, couldn't even get off the ground. Certainly, it was entirely different from anything usually seen on the pages of science-fiction pulp magazines like *Amazing Stories.*

After a well-pleased Roddenberry approved a three-foot *Enterprise* model built by talented model-maker Dick Datin, Jefferies gave the Anderson Company plans for another miniature. Some miniature! At almost fourteen feet in length, its size would create problems in filming, but not because the model was difficult to move through a shot. The model wasn't supposed to move; it was the camera that moved, and therein lay the problem. The model was so large, and took up so much of the Anderson Company's "miniature" stage, that camera movement was severely limited. Another one of those "best-laid plans" stories!

Fortune smiled as Director of Photography Bill Snyder, a superior cameraman, became available and, as was the custom in the industry, brought his own camera crew and lighting "gaffer" with him. (Although Jerry Finnerman, the first Director of Photography on the series, has been erroneously credited in other books as the camera operator on this first pilot, Bob Justman says that the actual camera operator was Dick Kelley, who later became a "first cameraman" in his own right. Justman still has the original crew sheet from the first pilot.)

BOB: It was apparent that we needed the best makeup man we could find. There were numerous "appliances" (latex or rubber prosthetics) that would have to be designed, built, and affixed, on a daily basis, to the actors who would portray non-human aliens. In those early days of special makeups, most makeup artists didn't have the prosthetic expertise we needed. Certainly, the studio had no one; the studio didn't even have a makeup department. Lucy's makeup was done in her private dressing room. Other makeups were done on stage.

There was only one person I could trust to handle this difficult job. I'd worked with Fred Phillips on several television series, the latest of which had been *The Outer Limits,* a series that required scads of special makeups and prosthetics. Although Fred was busy, I managed to spring him long enough to do our pilot. He would design and build, or have built in a makeup lab run by special makeup creator John Chambers, the ears for Mister Spock, ears that would become famous and, eventually, come to plague all of us: Freddy, Gene and me, Herb Solow, the studio, NBC, Leonard Nimoy—and eventually, Bill Shatner. Especially Bill Shatner.

Surprisingly, the casting process was not a difficult one. All the roles were specific and well defined. While Roddenberry and Bob Butler prepared their lists of actors, Solow decided against using only *The Lucy Show*'s casting director and sought help from two people who had worked with Roddenberry in the past. Joe D'Agosta, later made Casting Director for Desilu by Herb Solow, was working at Twentieth Century Fox. Moonlighting from Fox, D'Agosta made suggestions and set up weekend interviews for the major roles. Morris Chapnick, who had worked with Gene at MGM, came on board to help with the casting and also functioned as a jack-of-all-trades assistant to Roddenberry. Taciturn, possessed of a dry wit, and utterly dependable, Chapnick was later put on the Desilu payroll as an assistant to Herb Solow.

NBC, Solow, Roddenberry, and Butler were thrilled that they were able to get Jeffrey Hunter to star as Captain Christopher Pike (in Roddenberry's original pitch to Solow, the captain's name was Robert April). Bob Butler worked exceptionally well with actors. Hunter had appeared in over twenty movies, including *The Longest Day*, *The Last Hurrah*, and John Ford's *The Searchers*, and had starred as Jesus Christ in *King of Kings*. He had also starred in the television series *Temple Houston*. He was aware of the often unrewarding daily grind. Solow felt he had the nucleus of a winning team.

Courtesy Greg Jein

Jeffrey Hunter as Captain Christopher Pike.

Making long-term contracts with potential television series stars that called for prenegotiated pay increases for future years was like walking into a buzz saw. For the opportunity to be in a pilot that could become a series, actors and their agents, business managers, and attorneys would agree to almost any future episodic salary. They operated on the basis that, when the actor became an important series star, he could just refuse to show up for work, threaten to walk out of the series, and his employer would have to come up with more money to get him back. But when studios negotiated future episodic salaries, series budgets were prepared on the previously "agreed upon" basis. There would be some big surprises in store for Desilu.

Leonard Nimoy, a struggling actor who had worked on *The Lieutenant* for Roddenberry, was the one Roddenberry wanted to play the alien Mister Spock. His saturnine face and introspective appearance were perfectly suited to that mysterious character. But early on, Nimoy had misgivings about the ears he would have to wear. He didn't want to be perceived as a television freak and didn't want to end up in a career dead end, typecast as an actor who could play only weird roles.

HERB: Like the other actors on the series, Leonard signed one of those standard series contracts with prenegotiated pay increases. But the chickens came home to roost during the high drama of Nimoy's holdout after *Star Trek* was renewed for its second season.

DeForest Kelley had made a reputation playing "bad guys" during the golden years of Hollywood Westerns. And as so often happens in the Hollywood typecasting mind-set, it was assumed that was about all he could do. Kelley was at the top of Roddenberry's list for the role of the ship's doctor. But Bob Butler had recently seen the much-traveled and better-known actor John Hoyt perform

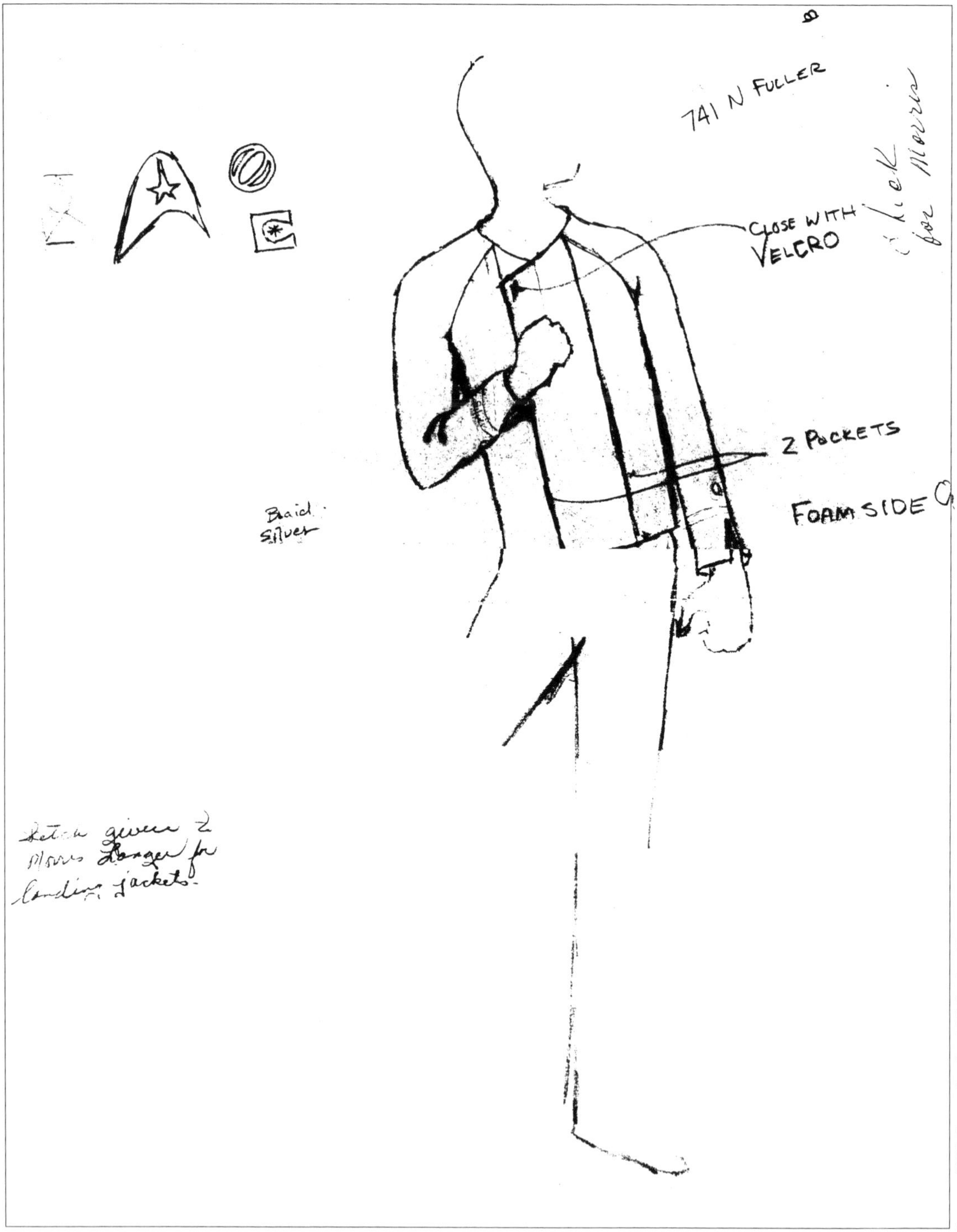

Courtesy UCLA Theater Arts-Special Collections Library

Bill Theiss' design for a "crew landing jacket."

at a Shakespeare festival. Butler was very impressed. John Hoyt got the role. Roddenberry raised no objections.

Susan Oliver, one of Hollywood's really nice and talented people, was set as the guest star and love interest for Jeffrey Hunter. Her role included several manifestations, one of which was Vina, the green-skinned alien dancing girl. While the "dancing girl" part worked out fine, Justman would soon discover that the green skin would be something else again.

Roddenberry gave final approval on Bill Theiss's velour uniforms for the *Enterprise* crew.

But approval of some other costumes took quite a bit longer. Roddenberry's penchant for unusual female costume design was fulfilled as he personally checked out the skimpy, diaphanous costumes worn by Susan Oliver and the dancing girls. His verdict: "Good job, Bill. But not revealing enough." Then, rhetorically to Butler, Solow, and Justman, "I think we can show more, don't you?"

Solow began, "Well . . ."

Roddenberry didn't wait for him to finish. "Yes, definitely. Let's show more."

HERB: Gene wanted to costar Majel Barrett, an actress who had worked for him at MGM, as Number One, second in command of the *Enterprise.*

"You'll like her, Herb." Gene insisted. "She's solid."

"It'll be a hard sell, Gene. I don't know her work. In some lesser role, okay, no problem, but NBC will want a better-known actress for the female lead. It could hurt us if she's not up to the part."

Whenever Gene wanted to make a point, he always took a long drag on his cigarette, spoke even more softly, and dropped his speech into slow-motion mode. (I would translate for him during network meetings when the various Vice Presidents strained to hear, and understand, what he was saying.) He did it now, "It's important . . . ahhh . . . to me, Herb. Call it . . . aaah . . . professional devotion. You'll . . . aaah . . . like her."

Since he couldn't be moved, I went along with his request, devised some obtuse sales pitch, and met with NBC to try to sell the notion.

"Guys, listen. Roddenberry has this strong feeling he's found a marvelous woman for the role of Number One. The fact that she's still unknown to the public is to our advantage. It'll add humanity and believability to the concept. After all, this is science fiction. Right?"

NBC Program Executive Jerry Stanley stared quizzically at NBC Vice President Grant Tinker. Then Jerry grumbled, "Christ, Herb, this is madness. She's his girlfriend. I remember her hanging around Gene's office at MGM when he was doing *The Lieutenant* for us."

The simple truth is that NBC resented being put into such an awkward position, but in the end Grant and Jerry didn't want to rock the boat with Gene. Majel

was cast as Number One, the *U.S.S. Enterprise* executive officer, playing opposite Jeffrey Hunter's Captain Christopher Pike.

BOB: When I came to work at Desilu, Majel Barrett was already set for the role of the ship's second-in-command, Number One. Gene said, "She's a good friend, Bob, and as a favor to me, she'll do the green dancing girl makeup tests for free." Majel had worked for him before, and in fact, they had rather more than a professional relationship, a fact of which I was blissfully unaware until much later.

Majel seemed nice and allowed herself to be smeared with various shades of bilious green makeup and then photographed in front of a neutral backdrop. Surprise, surprise! Next day, when we viewed the makeup tests, Majel came out looking somewhat green, but not green enough. Perhaps Fred Phillips should have used more green because the Eastman film negative we were using couldn't replicate that color.

Fred Phillips was surprised. "Sure, it was green enough. I don't understand it."

"Use more green, Fred," said Gene. We did the test again. Next day, same results.

We called the film lab. "How come this film stock can't handle green?"

The reply: "You saw it, too? It's the strangest thing. We had to work like hell to correct the color prints but we still couldn't get all that green out."

Ever on the lookout to save money, Unit Manager James Paisley from the Desilu Production Department suggested we use a green wig that Lucy had worn in one of her comedy sketches, but Gene Roddenberry nixed it. He wanted Vina to have "strawberry roan" hair, which he thought would contrast nicely with the dancing girl's green skin. I was impressed that, for the first time, someone from the old regime at the studio had tried to help us out. I decided I liked Paisley and, soon, so did Herb and Gene. By the time we finished the pilot, Jim had become a staunch friend and supporter.

The pilot was scheduled to be filmed at Desilu's antiquated Culver City studio, Desilu Culver, because of its large stages and proximity to the famous "forty acres" back lot where Atlanta burned in *Gone with the Wind.* Since that time, local government had taken over part of the acreage to build a flood control channel, so the historic and romantic "forty acres" had become thirty-one acres. Was nothing sacred?

After Justman "broke down" the script and scheduled it for filming, the usual battle began. The schedule was too long, and the budget was too high. The old guard had a fit: "It's gonna cost *what?* Cut it down!"

Herb Solow, already uncomfortable about the difference between what NBC would pay and what the pilot would cost, had to agree with the studio. So by getting Roddenberry to effect some important changes that didn't compromise the story, Justman was able to trim the budget and shorten the shooting schedule from sixteen days to fourteen. That didn't do the trick. The budget was still too high.

It was necessary to "chop" again, but now there was little Roddenberry could change in the script. Justman knew that unless everything went perfectly (and no show ever goes perfectly), the pilot would take a lot longer to film and cost much more than the studio wanted. Solow knew it too, but conveniently looked the other way.

In setting a shooting date, Justman had convinced everyone it was safer to begin production on a Friday, rather than a Monday, so that the cast and crew, unused to that great unknown, science fiction, could get their feet wet for a day and then collapse over the weekend. Principal photography would begin on Friday, November 27, 1964, and was scheduled to finish eleven working days later, on Friday, December 11, 1964.

"Eleven days? Okay," agreed the assistant director, "and for an encore, we'll shoot *Gone with the Wind*."

Justman had suggested to Roddenberry and Solow that three days of rehearsals with Butler and the cast would pay off in a better product. Cast rehearsals began on Monday, November 23, 1964. Then came Thursday, Thanksgiving day. And next would come Friday, "magic time," the first shooting day.

BOB: A few days prior to the Thanksgiving day holiday, cameraman Bill Snyder; his gaffer, Bob Campbell; and the electrical crew began to "prelight" the Planet set on Stage 16, the largest stage at Desilu Culver. The set was encircled by a huge backing painted green to simulate an alien planet sky. On Wednesday night, after two days spent pouring light onto the green sky backing, Snyder and Campbell complained, "No matter how much light we throw on it, it's never enough. The damn backing just soaks it all up. Bob, if this is the way it's going to be when we're actually in production, you can kiss your f.....g shooting schedule good-bye."

This was definitely not what I wanted to hear. Campbell patted me on the back. "We're already on overtime, so we're going home now. See you Friday morning—and have a nice Thanksgiving."

The painted-sky problem later sparked me to an innovative idea, should the series ever sell. But for now, I worried about what else Murphy's Law would bring to this bedeviled production. My Thanksgiving day holiday was already ruined; I didn't want the same thing to occur on Christmas.

Magic time had finally arrived. Without a foot of film exposed, the pilot was already over budget. *Star Trek* was just hours away from birth.

Courtesy Greg Jein

(l. to r.) Majel Barrett, Gene Roddenberry, and Leonard Nimoy on the *Enterprise* Bridge set of "The Cage."

4

Magic Time: The First Pilot

BOB: I never sleep the night before starting a new show. I just lie in bed, with my eyeballs burning, tossing and turning and conjuring up all the things that can possibly go wrong. But nothing I could conjure would match the madness of what actually occurred.

Everything was ready. We'd had a final dress rehearsal for camera. Filming would begin with a dialogue scene on the Captain's Quarters set. The actors, Jeff Hunter and John Hoyt, were in position. The camera was loaded with film. We had placed "wig-wag" red lights outside the stage to warn visitors not to come in when we were shooting and to warn passing truck drivers on the studio street to kill their engines so the noise wouldn't ruin our sound tracks.

"Quiet, please. This will be a take," I announced. Everything became very still on the stage when I ordered camera and sound to "roll" for our first shot. But we hadn't counted on . . .

"Coo, coo . . . ."

"Slim" Haughton, our sound mixer, ripped off his headphones and looked around. Everyone looked around.

"What's that, Bob?" asked director Bob Butler.

"Sounds like pigeons."

"Pigeons?"

"In the rafters. I think they live here."

Butler was a gentle soul. "Ask them to be quiet."

I deployed some pigeon herders up high, but the pesky critters just moved to another rafter every time someone got close. Then they'd coo even louder and flap their wings, noisily. The pigeon wranglers tried yelling and waving their arms. This frightened the birds, which began to fly around in the darkness, bumping into the rafters and scaffolding and then thrashing their wings in pain. I finally ordered the electricians to turn off all the lights, figuring that the birds might settle down. They did, but as soon as we turned on the lights, they began cooing again.

"Turn off the lights and open the stage doors!" I ordered. "It's dark in here and light outside. The birds will fly to the light, so stand by to close the doors when they leave."

The big doors were opened. A few pigeons flew out. But some other pigeons, waiting outside, flew in to join their friends. That called for an agonizing reappraisal. Someone suggested shooting them down, but I decided to live and let live. The pigeons were here first. For years this had been their home. We'd just have to learn to be good neighbors. Besides, who wants a bunch of wounded pigeons flapping around? Not us. And definitely not the Humane Society. I imagined the Channel 2 TV news promo: "Tonight! Pigeon slaughter in Culver City! Innocent bystanders wounded as shotguns miss their mark! Film at eleven."

We rehearsed quietly. The pigeons continued to coo, but more softly now. Evidently, the more frightened they were, the more noise they made. Luckily, there wasn't much dialogue in the scenes, so we finished the day's work despite some "pigeon breaks" from time to time because the birds' cooing overlapped the actors' speeches. Slim Haughton was not amused. Neither was Bob Butler. Neither was I.

The following morning, I was prepared for pigeons. We left the big stage doors open and scattered a mess of stale bread, birdseed, Cracker Jacks, whatever, on the studio street outside. By the time we'd finished lighting for the first shot, most of the pigeons were outside, chowing down. We closed the doors and went to work with the hope of no further interruptions. Other than an occasional "coo" from a late riser who had slept in, things were quiet.

I looked at Bob Butler. He nodded, ready. I yelled, "This'll be a take! Quiet, please!" and then, "Roll it!"

"Speed," said Slim Haughton

"Marker," said Dick Kelley.

"Action," said Bob Butler.

BANG! BANG! BANG! BANG! BANG!

Someone was hammering inside the next-door stage. I didn't wait for Butler's question. "Everybody stay ready!" I yelled as I raced out the door and into the studio street, scattering a flock of feeding pigeons. I flung open the door to the adjoining stage and burst in. A group of carpenters were busy building a set for us. They hadn't noticed the red light that was wig-wagging away to let them know there was a take in progress on the next stage. I employed some refined language to impress upon them that the red light was to be obeyed or else.

As I ran out, I yelled, "Red light on, no hammer! Red light off, hammer!" I was sure they understood, now. Scattering the pigeons again, I raced back onto the shooting stage. "Quiet!" I yelled, screeching to a stop. "Roll it!"

"Speed."

"Marker."

"Action."

WHOOSH! CLANG-RATTLE! Someone, somewhere, flushed a toilet and the pipes rattled.

"Bob . . . !"

"I know, I know . . . ." I raced outside, again. The pigeons moved aside for me, but grudgingly this time.

I found the problem—and the culprit. The woman in the ladies' room was not amused. When the stage was erected, money was saved by not building double walls between the outside toilets and the stage interior. Not only that, the toilets' water and sewage pipes ran inside along the stage wall before heading out to the main lines in the street. Every time a toilet was flushed, we heard it loud and clear. This stage was truly a "sound stage."

So red lights were placed in both the men's and ladies' facilities to warn people when we were "on a take." Problem solved. I returned to the stage singing a parody of a famous parody: "Passersby will please refrain from flushing toilets down the drain while visiting the rest-rooms, I love you."

Bob Butler raised an eyebrow. I gave him the thumbs-up.

"Roll it!"

"Speed."

"Markers."

"Act . . ."

WHOOSH! CLANG-RATTLE!

The red lights in the rest-rooms didn't solve our problem. When you gotta go, you gotta go.

"Bob?" My director was getting just a smidgen agitated.

"I know, I know."

So toilet monitors were deployed outside the stage lavatories. No one was allowed in until each new shot was over. Sometimes the shots took a long time. What one doesn't do for art's sake.

Things went along pretty well after that—until we moved to the stage next door and prepared to film our next shot. This stage had no bathrooms attached. Things were looking up. Everyone was in place.

I looked at Butler. "Okay, Bob?" He nodded.

I looked at Dick Kelley. "Camera ready?" He nodded.

I looked at Slim Haughton. "Sound ready?" He nodded.

"Quiet, please. This is a take!" The stage became quiet.

"Roll it!"

"Speed!"

"Marker."

Bzzz-bzzzz-bzzzz.

Courtesy Greg Jein

Gene Roddenberry and actor Peter Duryea on the set of "The Cage."

"Cut," yelled Slim Haughton as he tore off his headphones and looked around. "What's that?" he asked.

"What *is* that, Bob?" Director Butler had begun to sound a touch testy.

"Sounds like bees."

"Bees?"

"Yeah. I guess they live here, too—and have for a long time. Remember, this is an old studio. It's where they burned the city of Atlanta for *Gone with the Wind.*"

"They should have burned this stage as well. Are there going to be any more little surprises?"

"No."

"Good."

"At least I hope not."

That night, a beekeeper was brought in and the problem was solved. Or so we thought. We hadn't seen the last of the "killer bees."

As I've already mentioned, we were on a very tight budget. Little money means big problems. Before we started filming, we discovered we couldn't afford to build the main Talosian set the way we'd like to. It demanded lots of scope and we didn't have the space or the money for it. I thought about it overnight and then held a meeting.

"I've got the answer, guys. Midgets!"

"Okay, Bob, the answer is midgets," replied Herb Solow. "So, tell me, what's the question?"

"We use 'forced perspective.' Matt builds the set smaller and smaller as it goes away from camera. And then we use midgets at the back of the set. Get it?"

"Yeah . . . but Bob, aren't midgets more expensive than real . . . ahhh . . . I mean, bigger people?" asked Gene. His face reddened a bit from the faux pas. He'd tried to show Herb what a thrifty producer he could be, and in so doing, he'd stuck his foot right in it.

"Not that much more. And we'll need only two or three of them. We'll save money on wardrobe, too. Smaller strokes for smaller folks." Herb began to laugh, which only encouraged me. "And we'll serve them cheap little open-face tea sandwiches for lunch."

By this time, we were all hysterical with laughter. After we wiped the tears from our eyes, Art Director Matt Jefferies seized the concept and ran with it. He built a full-scale set in the foreground that diminished in size until it was quite small at the back.

To make the idea work, we used the Talosian actors in the foreground and Talosian midgets in the rear, one of whom was famous for having had a "small" role in *The Wizard of Oz.* Now he could be famous for being in *Star Trek,* too—in an even smaller role.

The set looked enormous in dailies, due in large part to the midgets in the background of the forced-perspective set. Later Bill Theiss, our Costume Designer, complained about how time-consuming and difficult it was to make garments on such a small scale.

My response was, "Just think of the money we saved on fabrics, Bill."

He didn't understand why I began to laugh. But the laugh was on me; while the shot looked great, it was never used in the final version of the film.

Fred Phillips applying green makeup to actress Susan Oliver.

Courtesy Greg Jein

As a result of the preproduction makeup tests on Majel Barrett, Fred Phillips had mixed a batch of makeup that was the right shade of green for Susan Oliver's portrayal of a wanton and enticing dancing girl temptress. But while the green makeup was applied as evenly as possible, it didn't stay that way for long. Evidently certain areas of her skin were oilier than others. In just a few minutes, the guest star began to look blotchy. A "body-makeup girl" was assigned to her and kept "touching her up" all day long. The exertion of dancing caused the actress to perspire, which only exacerbated the problem. Susan Oliver was patient and remained good-natured throughout the whole process. The constant repair jobs slowed filming down, and everyone breathed a sigh of relief when that sequence was completed.

Another time-consuming makeup job was the difficult transformation of Susan Oliver from a supposedly young and exotically beautiful Vina, kept captive by the Talosians for many years and used by them to entice Jeff Hunter, captain of the *Enterprise*, into the incredibly old and wrinkled creature she had actually become during her years of captivity. Bob Justman called the transformation "the old Wolfman–Jekyll and Hyde caper."

A separate "tie-down" camera was angled for a closeup of Vina as she "aged." Once it was in place, no one could walk or work near the camera, as any slight movement during the lengthy process would ruin the shot, which wouldn't be realized until dailies were run the following day. A special head brace was built to hold Susan Oliver's head immovable and positioned. The device was hidden from view when the actress was in it.

Then Oliver was photographed in her "beauty" makeup. After fifteen seconds' worth of film was exposed, she was carefully removed from the head brace and went to get the first of her "ugly" makeups. An hour or two later, back again, into the head brace with great care, and then another fifteen seconds' worth of film before she left to get the next, older stage of "ugly." All the while she was being photographed, Susan Oliver had to emote without moving her head at all until near the end of each shot, lest the illusion be spoiled. But near the end of each of the "getting really ugly" phases, she moved her head down and to one side, as planned, as she scrunched up to simulate extreme old age. When she returned for the next phase, she resumed her last position, which was double-checked by means of two 8 x 10 tie-down still cameras, positioned on either side and chained to the floor to prevent movement. Her various head positions were grease-penciled onto the ground glass of each still camera, so that her previous posture could be duplicated at the head end of each succeeding piece of film. When all the individual shots were edited together, the makeup changes were to occur gradually by means of "dissolves," the optical process in which the end of one shot would gradually disappear as it was replaced by the beginning of the next shot. As a result, Susan's character, Vina, would look as if she was shriveling from age. The process began first thing in the morning and wasn't completed until late in the day. While the green makeup had been uncomfortable for her, it was nothing compared to what she went through to complete this one short piece of film. Luckily for her, the complicated shot went off without a hitch and her transformation looked great in the finished film.

Although Susan Oliver fell ill with the flu and needed the ministrations of a physician on set, she never complained. Thanks to her professionalism, the whole process was enjoyable for everyone.

BOB: The Spock ears were another makeup problem. Fred Phillips had taken a cast of Leonard's ears from which he had molds made that incorporated the kind of pointed tips that Roddenberry wanted. The theory was that, once the molds were made, duplicate ears could be cranked out when needed and glued onto

Courtesy Greg Jein

Bob Justman (far right) demonstrating his vein-control technique to Roddenberry. Also shown are actors Meg Wyllie (left), who played "The Keeper," and in background, Peter Duryea.

Leonard's ears. Easier said than done. Once a pair of them had been painstakingly attached and colored to match the rest of Spock's yellowish complexion, that was it for that pair. And when they were removed (a painful and time-consuming process for Leonard, since they were attached with spirit glue and could be removed only with the use of strong solvent), they couldn't be saved for use the next time. New day, new ears. And the rubber being used wasn't dependable. The makeup lab had to cast pair after pair of ears until a good set was made.

Later, when the series was filmed, Charles Schramm of the MGM makeup department would use an improved latex formula and crank out ears on an assembly-line basis. But when Fred Phillips first applied them to Leonard, a new problem arose. The pointed ears were beautifully modeled, but Leonard looked like a bus coming down the street with its doors open; his ears stuck way out. Freddie had to pull them back to the sides of Leonard's head with double-faced "wig tape." That finally did the trick. And for the entire run of the series, that's how it had to be done.

Gene had cast small-boned women to play the Talosians, captors of our brave captain and his damsel in distress. The Talosians were weak-looking humanoids with enormous craniums. Actress Meg Wyllie portrayed the chief Talosian, known as "the Keeper." We, meaning Captain Pike and the audience, could hear her even though her lips didn't move; her dialogue was to be dubbed in later using a male-sounding voice. Large "veins" traversed the Keeper's skull, and they pulsated as she spoke.

The huge rubber heads of the Keeper and her cohorts were created by Wah Chang, a designer-sculptor with whom I had worked on *The Outer Limits.* He also created some unusual creatures that were kept captive, along with Captain Pike, in the Talosians' "menagerie." Wah would later become a source of other creatures and devices for *Star Trek*—and a source of considerable friction to both Desilu's labor-relations department and the Hollywood propmakers' union.

In reality, the Keeper's veins were airtight and connected to a tube behind and below her neck that, concealed by the costume she wore, led down her back to the bottom of her gown and then up to a rubber squeeze bulb. When the bulb was compressed and released, air pressure inside the system caused the veins to expand and contract. I hid below camera while Meg was being photographed, manipulating the pulsating veins of the Keeper's oversized head in time with the Keeper's dialogue, which was spoken on stage by script clerk George Rutter.

While Roddenberry wanted *Star Trek* to cover new ground, he sensed the importance of convincing the audience that what they were seeing was actually happening in this strange new world of the future. One of the many creative and thought-provoking ideas he employed was to have a male voice emanating from a female character. He did this with the Keeper by "revoicing" her previously recorded dialogue to make it sound masculine.

BOB: I had reservations as to how we could afford certain aspects of "real" space travel on a television budget and schedule. So before reading the script, I talked to Gene. Since there's no gravity in outer space, reality dictated that for the actors to give the appearance of floating in space, they would have to be "flown" on wires. Gene's solution: artificial gravity. It solved the believability problem for me and also made it possible to film the show in something less than a year's time. Years later, in a flight of fancy, I created my own one-sentence parody of the show, one that might well rival the justly famous *Star Trek* parody seen on *Saturday Night Live:*

"The Enterprise is reeling from phaser blast after phaser blast, but somehow the artificial gravity never fails and continues to anchor everyone's boots to the deck, but not so firmly that Kirk can't move forward to take center stage, and as the bridge crew is being thrown from one side to another, Scotty calls to complain, 'Captain, we've lost war-r-r-p power-r-r-r, sir-r-r,' and Spock calmly informs Kirk, 'Life-support systems are failing rapidly; we have exactly 32.95 seconds left,' and Sulu reports, 'Main phasers disabled, sir,' and Chekov announces, 'Keptain, werry deefeecult to mentain power to sheelds,' and Kirk orders, 'Open a hailing frequency!' and Uhura, her incredibly cantilevered superstructure preceding the rest of her, struggles back to her station, jams a gizmo into one ear, and announces, 'Hailing frequencies open,' and Doctor 'Bones' McCoy growls, 'Damn it, Jim. Do something!' and Kirk, gut sucked in and chin thrust out, moves into an extreme closeup, each of his eyes never quite aligned properly with the other, and holds position, heroically, for the fadeout."

Thank God for artificial gravity!

My other major worry was the enormous cost of optical effects to land the *Enterprise* on a new planet every week. Gene's clever solution: the transporter effect, "beaming" people to other locations with no apparent loss of molecules, other than when required for story purposes.

Courtesy Greg Jein

The transporter, cost-effective solution to landing the ship every week.

When I first viewed the transporter effect, I was as curious as anyone else might be and asked the inventive Darrell Anderson how he achieved it. Darrell said, "I just turned a slow-motion camera upside down and photographed some backlit shiny grains of aluminum powder that we dropped between the camera and a black background."

And using a piece of Sandy Courage "shimmer" music, we gave the visual effect its distinctive sound.

Gene's creative solution to my "landing" dilemma resulted in a new catchphrase and a wealth of bumper stickers, "Beam me up, Scotty."

Incidentally, did you ever ask yourself "How were those *Enterprise* guys able to communicate with different alien creatures each and every week?" Well, I did. The answer was simple. Enter the "Universal Translator." You couldn't see it, you couldn't hear it, but you could depend upon it. And you could also forget about it, which is what we did soon after the device was introduced.

HERB: Despite everyone's best efforts, the pilot took sixteen days (including some retakes), just as Bob feared when he first scheduled the show for shooting. At the conclusion of the pilot, I said thanks and goodbye to RJ. "Have you learned to speak Esperanto yet?"

"I won't have to." He grinned. "Leslie got someone else to do the picture."

"He didn't tell me he couldn't wait. I'm sorry, RJ."

"I'm not. Let somebody else suffer. This pilot was rough. I'll take some time off first and then either go back to Daystar Productions [Leslie Stevens's company] or find something else."

"Keep in touch, RJ. We've got some new pilots in the works for this spring."

I called Leslie Stevens. "I want to thank you, Leslie, for Bob Justman. He did a great job for us, and as advertised, I'm sending him back to you."

"Fine, Herb, as long as we have the understanding that I'm going to need him here at Daystar. So if you sell your series, you'll have to get someone else."

"Leslie, he's yours, and I'll never lean on you again to 'borrow' him."

I hung up the phone. And then I uncrossed my fingers.

Months later, Leslie Stevens "just had to" screen a film for me. "Did it relate to our Frank Merriwell project?" I asked.

"No," replied Leslie, "it's something else, something different, and you won't be wasting your time."

Meeting with Leslie was never a waste of time. His enormous creativity always seemed to wrap him up in fascinating, if not always totally practical, projects. But in this instance, I had no idea what I was in for.

Leslie arrived at the Desilu screening room with a partially completed feature film, entitled *Incubus.* Leslie had used his own money to get the production this far and was seeking additional funds to complete the film. Perhaps Desilu would be interested? The film starred William Shatner, our new skipper of the *Enterprise.* The lights dimmed, and the film began.

The actors began to speak. And I began to realize Leslie had done the unimaginable. He'd shot a film in Esperanto, and I couldn't understand a word the actors were saying.

The incomplete film was over; the lights came up. I didn't know what to say. Everyone liked Leslie. Everyone highly respected his talents. And he was the recent "owner" of Bob Justman.

Happily, Leslie spoke first. "As you've gathered, Herb, the film is in Esperanto. Before you say anything, you should know that there are millions and millions of people in the world who speak the language."

I don't know what made me say it. It was a terrible thing to say—but I said it. "Leslie, I understand that millions of people in the world do speak Esperanto. There are three hundred in Chicago, a hundred in Spokane, four hundred in London, seventeen in Bakersfield—but not enough in any one city to even partially fill any one theatre more than any one night." Left unsaid was, "Why would anyone make a feature film in Esperanto?"

I'm sure Leslie had heard it all before, as he was good-natured about the remarks. It was one of the most memorable screenings of my life.

NBC Programming V.P. Mort Werner, the man who gave the show its second chance, indulging in his favorite pastime.

Courtesy Carole Werner Teig

5

The Good Witch of the East

And suddenly it was still. No actors, no technicians, no hair problems, no makeup. No pigeons. No bees. Nothing. The *Star Trek* cast and crew had done what the studio asked them to do. They took their well-earned salaries and went on to their next assignments.

Butler, Roddenberry, and Solow remained as the custodians and protectors of tens of thousands of feet of 35 mm picture negatives, positive work prints, and sound tracks. All the wisdom of the concept, the thoughtfulness of the script, the ingenuity of the production, the creativity of the director, and the performances of the actors were reduced to little rolls of film on yellow plastic cores, just waiting their turn to be cut, trimmed, reversed, blown up, and literally glued together. Then and only then would *Star Trek* become a pilot.

A team of picture editors, shortly to be joined by sound and effects editors, worked on the process under the guidance of Bob Butler. Out of the rough assemblage of all the pieces came the "first cut," the director's cut, his version. Butler then moved on to his next assignment, returning to the lot occasionally to touch base with Roddenberry, who guided the next step, finishing the second cut or refinement of the film. Solow sat in on the screenings, approving the various cuts on behalf of the studio. Time was important. To be in contention for the few time periods NBC intended to fill for the next fall season, the pilot had to be completed by the end of February. Quickly arriving at the final cut, the studio next had to score the film while waiting for the completion of the much-needed optical film effects.

HERB: Wilbur Hatch was Lucy's musical director. Lucy, through her secretarial grapevine, asked if I'd consider using Wilbur as our musical contractor, handling the scheduling and hiring of musicians when we scored the pilot. Why not? Wilbur was very experienced in the Hollywood music world, and we needed a contractor regardless. But we wouldn't depend on him to hire our composer, the person to score our precious pilot. After all, Wilbur was best known for his years as the conductor of the Lucy Band. What did he know about music for our science-fiction–fantasy dramatic adventure?

You know, when you're wrong, you're wrong. And in this instance both Gene and I were wrong. Stubbornly wrong. We approached agents and managers, only to discover their top film and pilot composers were working elsewhere or not interested. Desilu? Who? *Star Trek*? What? Big-time composers wanted to score pilots that had a chance of becoming a series. Why waste a good score on an unsold pilot? Would you throw your creative baby away with someone else's uncreative bathwater?

Rejection became dejection when Wilbur came to us with a suggestion, volunteering the name of an arranger working at Twentieth Century Fox. "He's a really good composer," Wilbur said. "Sure, he arranges for all those legendary movie composers, but he makes a lot of them more legendary than they deserve." The arranger-composer's name was Alexander Courage.

"Sandy" Courage and his contribution to *Star Trek* have never received the plaudits they truly deserved. Hired after a meeting with Gene and me, Sandy, though not at all a fan of science fiction, wrote a truly exciting score that magnified both the adventure of outer space and the mysteries that lay somewhere in that beyond. But Sandy's brilliance lay in arranging and orchestrating his main title theme music. Rather than relying upon a man-made musical instrument, Sandy placed a soaring human voice, that of soprano Loulie Jean Norman, just above the orchestra. It created an ethereal human quality and sent it out into the galaxy as if opening a door of welcome to one and all who might be out there—listening, watching.

Roddenberry often spoke of his idea of giving planets their own "personality" by arranging for the exterior of the planet Talos, for example, to have a high-pitched wavering sound. One particular plant, growing on the planet surface, was also given its own individual "singing" sound. This plant was different in color and structure from species growing on Earth. When anyone came near it, the plant would vibrate, thanks to a self-contained battery-driven motor.

The concept of a musical sound for planet surfaces, however, actually came from composer Sandy Courage. Not a particular fan of science-fiction sounds, Courage proposed that the noises of distant planets and planet surfaces would be more unusual if they came from music rather than sound effects. He assembled five musicians on a recording stage at Glen Glenn Sound Studios and recorded both individual instruments and assorted combinations of instruments. The result of his efforts made the sounds of the galaxy not only unique, but almost human.

Courtesy Greg Jein

Captain Pike inspects a "singing" plant on Talos IV.

Another Sandy Courage contribution, and a very personal one at that, is heard in the series's main title. Roddenberry and the sound editors were having great difficulty finding an acceptable sound effect for the fast fly-bys of the *Enterprise.* Whatever they tried just didn't work. Always the ingenious one, Courage picked up a microphone and made several "whooshing" sounds into it. The recordings of his whooshing were laid into the main title and synchronized with the passage of the ship. They were perfect, even though there really is no sound out in space.

The dubbing process, the marrying of all of the many audio tracks into one master track in sync with the picture, was marred and greatly slowed by the need to invent and/or manufacture the seemingly endless number of cosmic and futuristic sounds. But as with all things in life, the filmmaking process ended. *Star Trek* had become a pilot.

The old guard's reaction to the pilot can best be described as "haltingly neutral." "The Cage" went over schedule and over budget. The reality was that a *Star Trek* series would also go over schedule and over budget. Then the studio financial folks could lay off the stage, office, and equipment rental against the series, just as they'd done against the pilot. When push came to fiscally conservative shove, the general understanding was that the outsiders would fail, gather up their strange toys, and go away.

But the real world was calling. "The Cage," the *Star Trek* pilot, was ready to be screened by the NBC executives, who would decide whether the show that sprang from Roddenberry's original wrinkled piece of paper would fly as a weekly series or disappear into failed-pilot oblivion as a midsummer Movie of the Week.

HERB: Mort Werner was head of Programming for NBC and was the best programming executive at any of the three networks. Mort spoke directly and spoke the truth. You always knew where you stood with Werner, as virtuous a virtue as there could be in the 1964 edition of television land. And when he wasn't playing the piano at any cocktail lounge that would permit him, or working his Sunday

Even though it didn't sell the show, the first pilot's scope and production values impressed NBC.

Courtesy Greg Jein

morning shift behind the counter at a Scarsdale, New York, deli, Mort was developing pilots and series for the soon-to-be full-color network. *Star Trek* was one of those pilots; and when Mort arrived in Los Angeles to view the results of NBC's many efforts, a brand-spanking-new 35 mm print of our pilot was waiting for him. We were all very nervous.

The screening took place at the projection room in the Desilu executive office building. Mort arrived with his usual joviality. Grant, Jerry, and several other NBC Burbank executives joined him. The screening was definitely a family affair for me; but then, families have been known to be dysfunctional, sometimes very dysfunctional.

(The worst screening I ever had for top network executives was also for NBC. Several years later, as the lights came up at the NBC screening room at 30 Rockefeller Plaza, after two hours of viewing a romantic and lyrical pilot about a motorcyclist who "traveled America to see what's over the next rise," the President of NBC turned to me and said angrily, "Herb, where's the pilot we paid for?" The result of that screening, after cooler heads and NBC Research prevailed, was that *Then Came Bronson* was scheduled by NBC and debuted as a new series in the fall of 1969.)

The best screening I ever had for network executives was running the first *Star Trek* pilot for Mort, Grant, Jerry, and the others. They were blown away with the production, the scope of the film, the music, the whole physicality and feeling of the film. They were less impressed with some of the actors and the acting, but that's what pilots are for—as research and development tools, to see what works and what doesn't. Actors were replaceable, but production capability wasn't. A studio either had it, or it didn't. We'd made our point and made it well.

Mort made no promises as he shook my hand. "I must tell you something, Herb. I've seen many science-fiction, outer-space films. You name it. I've never felt I was aboard a spacecraft. I never believed the crew was a real crew. But you guys gave me the feeling of total belief. I loved it. Grant and I will be in touch." But the result of that screening, after cooler heads and NBC Sales prevailed, was that *Star Trek* was not scheduled by NBC as a weekly series.

Depression? Sigmund Freud never knew depression like Gene and I knew depression. Big talk! Big splash! No cigar!

The NBC party line was that "The Cage" was too "cerebral." That description has been bandied about in all the books about *Star Trek* and was a rallying cry in the early days of the series. The unspoken reason, however, dealt more with the manners and morals of mid-1960s America. NBC was very concerned with the "eroticism" of the pilot and what it foreshadowed for the ensuing series. Their knowledge of Roddenberry's attitude toward, and relationship with, the fairer sex didn't help. NBC Sales was equally concerned with the Mister Spock character, him being seen as demonic by Bible Belt affiliate-station owners and important advertisers. Their concern, perhaps not accepted by all executives at the network, nonetheless had presented a serious stumbling block to the sale of the hoped-for series.

HERB: But Mort Werner did not forsake us. Soon after the fall schedule was set, we met again. Mort, Grant, and Jerry were still taken by what we'd accomplished. And Mort had a complaint: "Herb, you guys gave us a problem."

"Sorry, Mort, we tried our best."

"That's the problem. I didn't think Desilu was capable of making *Star Trek,* so when we looked over the pilot stories you gave us, we chose the most complicated and most difficult one of the bunch. We recognize now it wasn't necessarily a story that properly showcased *Star Trek*'s series potential. So the reason the pilot didn't sell was my fault, not yours. You guys just did your job too well. And I screwed up."

I shook my head in awe. No, no, this wasn't a network executive talking to me. This was the Good Witch of the East come to lay gold at our feet. I conjured up all my good thoughts. "So let's do another pilot."

"That's exactly why we're here. We'll agree on some mutual story and script approval, and then, if the scripts are good, we'll give you some more money for another pilot."

I was thrilled even though I knew that the first pilot, which had budgeted out at $451,503, went well over schedule and ended up costing $615,751. Most of the cost had been absorbed by Desilu. What I couldn't know was that eventually, the second pilot, which would be budgeted at $215,644, would end up costing $354,974—and Desilu would have to bite the bullet again. But *Star Trek* was still alive; that's what mattered to me.

But I wanted the pilot guaranteed. They agreed. They also agreed Desilu would select the stories and NBC would guarantee to finance the writing of three pilot scripts. Both NBC and Desilu would agree on which one of the three scripts would be filmed for the pilot.

Then came their wants and desires; after all, there's no such thing as a free lunch or a free pilot order.

"In varying degrees, we're not too happy with some of the cast. We support the concept of a woman in a strong, leading role, but we have serious doubts as to Majel Barrett's abilities to 'carry' the show as its costar. We also think you can do better with the ship's doctor, the yeoman, and other members of the crew. We applaud the attempt at a racial mix; it's exactly what we want. Hopefully, there'll be more experienced minority actors available for next year. Jeffrey Hunter was okay, and if you want to use him again, that's fine with us.

"Leonard Nimoy isn't a problem, but the role he plays is a major problem! If you want to lose Nimoy, that's also fine with us. You've already heard the Sales Department reaction to the character. We can give you research numbers that support their reaction. Herb, we have to say this to you and Roddenberry: Though the Mister Spock character is interesting and probably has potential, its inclusion in our new pilot could possibly keep *Star Trek* off the air as a series.

"And one last thing, Herb. For God's sake, no more scantily clad green dancing girls with the bumps and grinds, okay?"

So we were still alive. I filled Gene in on my meeting. He was thrilled with the rebirth, especially the guaranteed pilot film. And we made a decision. Majel had to go. Gene seemed both upset and relieved at the same time. Desilu wasn't about to endanger more pilot investment on Gene's personal relationships. Yes, we could do better with casting. I hoped to hire a full-time casting director for this and, hopefully, other pilots.

Despite NBC's position, both Gene and I were adamant about Mister Spock. The character was a huge plus; there was no way we could lose it. But that wasn't what NBC wanted to hear. We agreed to tap-dance around that one for the time being. Sometime down the line, I'd pick the time to reopen the Spock discussion with our friendly local executives at NBC Burbank.

Gene wanted to get cracking writing the three new one-hour scripts. That wasn't quite what I had in mind. Simply put, Desilu had a golden opportunity and the requirement to prepare three "different" scripts. There wasn't enough time for one person to write all of them. I also wanted the diversity that other writers would bring to the project. Gene finally agreed, as long as he discussed his story ideas with the writers and he could write one of the scripts. He didn't want to give the appearance that he'd relinquished control over his own project. That was understandable and accepted.

BOB: It was heartening when Gene Roddenberry phoned. "Great news, Bob! We're going to make another *Star Trek* pilot."

"Wonderful, Gene. I'm very happy for you."

"I want you with me again, and this time you have to be my Associate Producer. I won't take no for an answer."

"But what about Byron?"

"He won't be back, period. You're the one I want."

It was Gene's ball game and he had decided to keep Haskin out of the lineup. It stood to reason; the two of them didn't get along. Gene reassured me that I wasn't cutting my friend out of the running. He and Herb Solow also had plans for me to be the Associate Producer on a number of other pilot films at Desilu that year. I was overjoyed. Finally, I had the break I wanted, and just in time. It was just a few months short of my self-imposed deadline to move on up or else leave the film business.

Shortly after a private meeting with Justman at Roddenberry's home, Roddenberry wrote a personal letter to Justman on April 7, 1965.

Desilu Productions Inc.

780 NORTH GOWER STREET · HOLLYWOOD 38 · CALIFORNIA

HOLLYWOOD 9-5911

April 7, 1965

Mr. Robert H. Justman
236 Loring Avenue
Los Angeles 24, California

Dear Bob,

Good to see you the other day. My daughters still want a ride in your torpedo.

Here is the situation on STAR TREK -- we plan to begin photography July 5. Therefore, in order to bring you in with plenty of time for preparation, would like you to plan tentatively to report on June 7. That's a week more than planned in the budget and if we add some post-production time to it, it could create difficulties. However, these could be resolved by your working as associate producer overall plus first A.D. during actual filming. In other words, taking the budget allowance for both and applying it to your overall cost. Does this create any problems?

At any rate, we should get together again soon and discuss all this, plus get an idea of salary and other terms for me to present to the business people here. Also, as quickly as I get some basic stories into work for myself and the other two writers, would much appreciate getting your comments on dangerous production and cost areas.

On the same subject, am enclosing with this Morris Chapnick's compilation of department and crew comments and suggestions growing out of the original STAR TREK pilot. Please keep this copy confidential since I prefer not to risk giving offense to Argyle Nelson and any of his production people. I think they did an excellent job for us and I would not for a moment want them to think that this was some sort of implied criticism of them. We'll keep it for our own consideration and use.

2

Regarding ASSIGNMENT 100 (or POLICE STORY which may become the title) Oscar Katz and others here feel that trying to shoehorn production of it into our schedule before STAR TREK might create some problems with NBC and injure our chances on the hour show. Therefore, the plan now is to go into production on the police show immediately after STAR TREK. If this should change, will let you know immediately.

Have made Oscar Katz and Herb Solow aware of our conversations and my earnest desire to have you associated with these future ventures. They, along with many others here, are delighted with the idea. You have many friends.

I hope you can work all of the above out in your schedule somehow.

Sincerely yours,

Gene Roddenberry

A letter from Roddenberry asking Justman to become Associate Producer on the second *Star Trek* pilot.

HERB: We had an option on Jeff Hunter for a series, but not for another pilot film. The idea of a network financing a second pilot film after the first one failed to result in a "sold" series was unheard of, so there was no reason for such a contract provision. We therefore had to devise a plan that would enable us to keep Jeff Hunter in the fold.

In the eyes of the New York and Los Angeles television world, *Star Trek* was already a failure. But we knew differently and looked forward to running the completed pilot for our star, Jeff Hunter. We hoped it would convince him to do another pilot. Gene and I waited in the Desilu projection room for him to arrive. He never did. Arriving in his stead was actress Sandy Bartlett, Mrs. Jeff Hunter. We traded hellos, and I nodded to Gene. He flicked the projection booth intercom switch. "Let's go."

And so it went. As the end credits rolled, and the lights came up, Jeff Hunter's wife gave us our answer: "This is not the kind of show Jeff wants to do, and besides, it wouldn't be good for his career. Jeff Hunter is a movie star." Mrs. Hunter was very polite and very firm. She said her good-byes and left, having surprisingly and swiftly removed our star from our new pilot.

Well, now, boys and girls, we weren't left with much of our cast. No star, no Number One, our demonic alien—Mister Spock—in serious question, no ship's

doctor, no yeoman, and our only ethnic actor due for replacement. But first, we had to get the writers to their typewriters.

NBC's audience research was interesting. It indicated that women, early twenties to mid-thirties, while not opposed to action-adventure, were definitely not serious fans of fantasy or science fiction. And since that age group controlled the purse strings of most American families, they were the prime television viewer audience. Roddenberry continually stroked NBC's top management via letters and phone calls, but distrusted any middle-management-level advice, which he saw as an unnecessary intrusion. Contrary to NBC Research's "adventure" recommendation, Roddenberry took his own "Omega Glory" story and would write the script.

Steve Kandel, a quality writer who seemed to thrive on self-imposed delivery deadlines, met with Roddenberry. Roddenberry wanted "a sort of swashbuckling" character as the guest lead, and they thrashed around various story concepts. Several weeks later, Kandel returned with his version of Roddenberry's story idea, "Mudd's Women," and after discussions with Roddenberry, proceeded to write his script. Though he enjoyed working with Roddenberry, Kandel very much disliked his continual rewriting: "I told him I'd polish my own script, but Gene always hemmed and hawed about how he just wanted to change a few minor things." When screen credits were submitted to the Writers Guild for approval, Roddenberry took credit for Kandel's story.

Sam Peeples was the writer whom Roddenberry consulted while researching the first pilot, "The Cage." As Peeples relates, "Gene was particularly pleased with me for introducing him to the works of many science-fiction writers, not the least of whom were Robert Heinlein and Isaac Asimov. We discussed Heinlein's *Space Cadet* [which became the basis for *Star Trek*'s Starfleet], and I loaned him my copy of Olaf Stapledon's *Last and First Men*, as Gene was particularly interested in future history."

Peeples further supplied a list of those science-fiction writers whom he felt Roddenberry should contact to write for the series. The actual contacts with the writers were later made for Roddenberry by science-fiction writer Harlan Ellison.

Roddenberry, continuing to seek both Peeples's guidance and the use of his voluminous research library, contracted with him to write the third script. Arguably the most experienced science-fiction writer of the three, Peeples discussed concepts with Roddenberry. But Peeples devised his own story and went on to script. He enjoyed working with Roddenberry and welcomed Gene's continual rewriting. After viewing the completed pilot, however, Peeples preferred his original version of the script to the one that was filmed. When screen credits were submitted to the Writers Guild for approval, Roddenberry did not take credit for the story. Later, there was some discussion regarding who had originated the title, "Where No Man Has Gone Before." Peeples states unequivocally that he, not Roddenberry, wrote the phrase as the title to his own story.

Peeples's script, "Where No Man Has Gone Before," was an action-adventure story with science-fiction overtones. It was clearly the best candidate for the new pilot.

Desilu management seemed content with the new pilot order. Granted, there would be no "after-use" for the one-hour film if the series didn't sell, but at least it would cost the studio less over-budget money for a one-hour pilot than it had for the ninety-minute "The Cage." Typically, they tended to lose sight of the upside. Desilu was still in the running to have its first-ever series on NBC, a series that would make groundbreaking television history. But for the money folk, faith was not in the future, so to speak; faith was in government bonds and high-interest savings accounts.

HERB: We knew that when we had an approved second pilot script in hand and a new pilot director in tow, the non–star recasting process would not be a major problem. And the actor–agents at the Ashley-Famous Agency were already making quality recommendations as to Jeff Hunter's replacement. William Shatner was among the suggestions. Gene and I screened a marvelous episode from Rod Serling's *Twilight Zone* series and a low-budget feature film that starred Shatner. The feature was Roger Corman's *The Intruder*. Interestingly enough, the film had been written by Charles Beaumount, a brilliant science-fiction writer we would have loved to hire for *Star Trek*. Beaumont recommended that Roger Corman hire an actor-writer friend of his to play a Southern sheriff. Corman agreed. Little did Gene and I realize as we watched Shatner's performance that we were also watching the acting debut of science-fiction writer George Clayton Johnson, later a contributor to the *Star Trek* series.

The multiple problems inherent in selling the second pilot boiled down to Leonard Nimoy's Mister Spock character. The time had arrived—the time to confront NBC with our position. I left Roddenberry home. Not only was he less experienced playing the network meeting game; but more important, I could use him as the reason for not committing to anything at the meeting. It was "good cop–bad cop" with the bad cop remaining at the studio as my backup.

The Mister Spock–NBC meeting would be the first of many such encounters. Programming understood our position. Spock was needed to balance the contemporary reality we tried so hard to achieve. To have Spock aboard the ship advertised science fiction, fantasy, and endless new worlds to the viewer.

But what to do about NBC Sales? Easy. We tabled the decision. If *Star Trek* didn't make the NBC schedule, it was all academic. Should *Star Trek* make the schedule, then we'd reconvene to rediscuss what to do with Mister Spock.

"If it means not getting the series on the air, Desilu would certainly have to reconsider its position," I agreed. But the matter of Mister Spock was a non-matter for the second pilot. We would rehire Leonard Nimoy.

The three scripts were in contention. "Mudd's Women," the story of a intergalactic trader-pimp, was just what NBC didn't want for their new pilot. It was very well written, it was fun, and it featured three beautiful women-hookers sell-

The Mister Spock character became a major stumbling block with NBC, who were afraid of his "satanic" appearance.

ing their bodies throughout the galaxy. It later became a standout and much-loved episode in the series. Strike one!

Gene Roddenberry's script, "The Omega Story," wasn't very good. It was unnecessary to point it out to him; he was the first to recognize the fact. It later became a less-than-mediocre series episode. Strike two!

Sam Peeples's script, "Where No Man Has Gone Before," personified NBC's expectations for the pilot. The new captain, soon to be named Kirk, was heroic and valiantly fought to the finish against crew members who had developed demonic powers. Mister Spock was present but not too importantly; the script called for shots of the *Enterprise* bridge pulsating with futuristic bells and whistles and shots of the ever-evolving galaxy; the "transporter effect" and the hand-held "communicators" (originally called "transicators") were both still there; the action-adventure story was light-years away from being too cerebral. And not even the most conservative of conservatives could characterize the female guest-star role, later performed by Sally Kellerman, as being too erotic.

One of the prime reasons for hiring director James Goldstone early was to get his input into the three scripts. Ironically, Jimmy's closest friend, then and now, was and is Steve Kandel. Regardless, Goldstone recognized our particular need and was in agreement with our choice, "Where No Man Has Gone Before."

Gene called Steve Kandel and awkwardly explained why we weren't using his script. Steve understood. In the second year of the series, Kandel wrote an additional "Mudd" script and polished two other scripts as a favor to Gene.

I recommended Sam Peeples's script to NBC. They agreed wholeheartedly; they loved it. My June 10, 1965, memo to Gene Roddenberry (see facing page) explained the three-script situation and instructed Gene to put "Where No Man Has Gone Before" into production. With copies going to Fred Ball, Lucy's brother and board member, and Argyle Nelson of the old guard, the memo was designed to lay out our status with NBC and to keep Ball and Nelson as positive as possible toward Gene. It specifically pointed out that NBC preferred his "Omega Glory" script, which, of course, NBC did not.

In the last at bat of the ninth inning, after being down to an 0 and 2 count, we'd hit a home run.

So from a stillbirth came the first unprecedented resurrection of *Star Trek*—a new, shorter, less creatively fulfilling second pilot with major changes in both cast and crew. The process of making the pilot began—all over again.

Desilu Productions Inc.

Inter-Department Communication

cc - Oscar Katz
Fred Ball
Argyle Nelson
Bernie Weitzman
Ed Perlstein

TO GENE RODDENBERRY

FROM Herb Solow

DATE June 10, 1965

SUBJECT STAR TREK - EPISODE 2

The situation as to which of the three STAR TREK scripts we will shoot for episode two is as follows.

The scripts, WHERE NO MAN HAS GONE BEFORE, by Sam Peeples, and the OMEGA GLORY, by Gene Roddenberry, have been completed. The third script, MUDD'S WOMEN, by Stephen Kendal, has been delayed due to the illness of the writer. We have therefore taken the following steps.

We have submitted the Sam Peeples script and the dGene Roddenberry script to NBC, and requested of them their opinion as to which of these two scripts they would prefer for episode two. Coupled with the submission of these two scripts to NBC was the statement that the third script would not be available until sometime next week and to wait until that time to obtain an answer from NBC would seriously delay our production plans since we must shoot on July 14. I've had discussions with NBC today, the result of which is a decision on our part and on the part of NBC to shoot WHERE NO MAN HAS GONE BEFORE, by Sam Peeples, as episode two.

From a writing point of view, I must say NBC preferred THE OMEGA GLORY. However, from the point of view of doing a more straight-line adventure show, they felt that the Peeples script as a finished film would better complement the first pilot, and would also show the two different ranges in which the series can go. As you know, this was also our feeling.

I would appreciate, therefore, Gene, if you would put the Peeples script into production. I have made NBC aware of the fact that you will be polishing the script yourself and alter the story so as to get us down on the planet surface earlier.

NBC has, however, inquired as to what would happen should they much prefer Steve Kendal's script, MUDD'S WOMEN, to Sam Peeples' script. I have told them that after a reading of the first draft of the Steve Kendal script, it would still be our recommendation that we do Sam Peeples' as MUDD'S WOMEN is a little too light and frothy and would not be a good example of the overall series. NBC has agreed with this thinking but has reserved the outside right to make a pitch for the MUDD'S WOMEN script if they like it. I gave them that right. I do not think we are running any risk, however, and therefore should get into preparing Sam Peeples' script just as soon as you've had a chance to rewrite it.

H.F.S.

hfs:ls

Memo from Solow to Roddenberry instructing him to put "Where No Man Has Gone Before" into production as the second *Star Trek* pilot.

Courtesy Motion Picture & Television Arch

Captain Kirk and Mister Spock, as they appeared in the second *Star Trek* pilot, "Where No Man Has Gone Before."

6

Magic Time Revisited: The Second Pilot

BOB: Director Jimmy Goldstone grumbled, "Christ, Bob, no matter where I go, you keep popping up."

I smiled. "That's part of my resilient charm."

"Well, since I can't avoid you, let's go to work."

"If you insist. By the way, thanks for telling Gene about me."

"My pleasure. It's lucky for me this is only a one-hour show. It should be twice as easy as your first pilot."

"Or half as hard." I grinned.

With the friendly amenities behind us, Jim and I began our preparation. Desilu was cheap and Herb Solow was thrifty, so my deal with the studio meant doing two jobs simultaneously, Associate Producer and First Assistant Director. It was simple arithmetic: One person doing two jobs cost less than two people doing two jobs. But I didn't care. I would have paid the studio for the chance.

My past working experiences with Jim Goldstone had been personally rewarding. I had always challenged myself to come up with creative approaches to a script and presented them to the director I was assisting. "Ego trip" or not, I wanted to contribute something in hopes of making the film better. Many directors rejected my help, seemingly threatened by their ambitious AD. Jimmy was one of the few directors who not only welcomed my suggestions but actually used them. I was thrilled that he would direct the pilot. This second voyage of the *Enterprise* would be an affair to remember.

HERB: The nuclear clock couldn't have timed it better. At the predictably exact and precise time, "Old Faithful," in the guise of Bob Justman, erupted into my office waving a handful of papers.

"Do you f.....g believe this stuff, what your studio has mandated for the budget and shooting schedule? The budget is pure science fiction, and the schedule allows only seven paltry days to shoot a very complicated show that anyone in his cockamamy, cotton-picking mind knows will take a full nine days. Minimum! Unless, of course, we're talking Jupiter moon days during the vernal equinox!"

I looked up from my work. "May I have your name, please?"

"Justman. Robert H. Justman."

"And what exactly can I do for you, Robert H. Justman?"

"Let's not shoot the show. Let's film the budget instead. Talk about going where 'no man has gone before . . .' "

"Now, now, Robert H. Justman. Get yourself out of warp drive and just do the best you can. No one's asking you to do the unattainable. Just the impossible."

"Oh, okay. That we can do. No problem." Then he grinned. "But it's still going to end up nine days."

"I believe you, RJ, but I'd rather we schedule seven and work nine than schedule nine and risk ten. Let me keep this paper bag over my head for a while, okay?"

"Be my guest."

"And please don't bother Gene with this kind of trivia. Since he carries his police revolver in his attaché case, we wouldn't want him shooting Argie Nelson or Ed Holly [Desilu's Financial VP]. At least not yet. I'll arrange to have some overhead charges moved around, do a little creative bookkeeping, and the budget should make a little more sense."

"Okay, but just don't tell me. I don't want to be implicated when they come looking for you."

"But you see, they already have. The thought police are loose. Last week, Ed Holly came here with his newest concept of togetherness, the very latest in 1965 gadgets from the phone company. Beepers. I never heard of beepers, but Lucy, Oscar, Argie, Bernie, and Ed all have them. And Ed gave one to me. That way, at any time, any place, wherever we are, whatever we're doing, we can beep each other and always stay in touch to discuss escalating costs, parking spaces, phones in dressing rooms, fan mail—you know, all the important stuff."

"He still hasn't figured out you make it a practice to be out of touch?"

"Nope."

"So how do you avoid getting beeped?"

I asked Bob to follow me into my private bathroom. There, sitting in a sink full of water, was the beeper, happily rusting away.

"It drowned," I suggested to RJ. "Ed dropped in the other day to ask why I wasn't responding to his beep. I told him the truth. I never heard it. Ed figured there must be some malfunction in the transmitting equipment and was having the phone company look into it."

RJ said a few proper words over the deceased beeper and returned to his office to begin doing the impossible.

William Shatner, selected by Roddenberry, Solow, and Goldstone and approved by NBC, was the new captain of the *Enterprise.* His background was extensive. Born on March 22, 1931, he grew up in Montreal, Canada, and attended McGill University. To quote a Desilu press release, "When he was graduated in 1952 with a B.A., he was already a well-known voice on Canadian airwaves." He was soon working at the Repertory Theatre of Ottawa and the Stratford, Ontario, Shakespeare Festival, followed by his first role on Broadway in the play *Tamburlaine.* He performed in many of the top New York television shows. Shatner's movie debut was in *The Brothers Karamazov.* He returned to Broadway to star in *The World of Suzie Wong* and *A Shot in the Dark.* More films followed, including the classic *Judgment at Nuremberg.* In Hollywood, he became a sought-after TV guest star and worked on *Route 66, Dr. Kildare, Alfred Hitchcock Presents, The Twilight Zone,* and, in another quirk of fate, an episode of *The Outer Limits,* "Cold Hands, Warm Heart," on which Justman was the assistant director.

Courtesy NBC/Globe

William Shatner as Captain Kirk.

BOB: Bill co-starred with Geraldine Brooks in that episode; he played an astronaut who visited the planet Venus in a planet colonization program titled "Project Vulcan"—a name that would later become familiar to *Star Trek* fans.

That was the first time I ever worked with Bill, and it was a rewarding experience. He was already a well-respected actor within the filmmaking community. I liked him a lot and found him to be enthusiastic, good-humored, and hardworking; we never had to wait for him when he was called to the set for a shot, and he gave his all to make the episode as good as it could be. So when I heard that Bill would be the new captain of the *Enterprise,* I was pleased. I knew he would bring

a much-needed energy to the role, an energy we hadn't gotten from Jeff Hunter.

Other coincidences ensued from that *Outer Limits* episode. Actors Malachi Throne and Lawrence Montaigne had important roles; they both later had important roles in *Star Trek.* Malachi worked in the two-part episode titled "The Menagerie"; Larry Montaigne, wearing pointed ears both times, performed as Decius, a Romulan officer in "Balance of Terror," and as Stonn, Spock's Vulcan adversary in "Amok Time."

Oddly enough, as late as a month prior to filming Shatner in his role as the new captain of the *Enterprise*, the character's name was still up for grabs. Roddenberry came up with some ideas and invited suggestions from his associates. Then he sent a "short list" to researcher Kellam DeForest's office and asked for the sixteen possibilities to be checked out and cleared for use in the show. The name "Kirk" was next to last, followed by the penciled-in name, "North."

Roddenberry's memo to researcher Kellam DeForest regarding the name of the ship's captain in the second pilot.

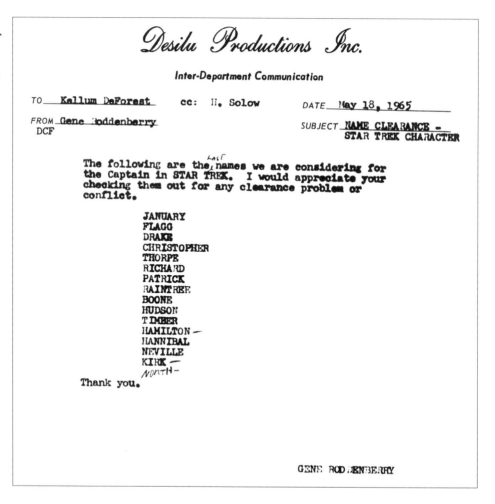

Desilu Productions Inc.

Inter-Department Communication

TO Kellum DeForest   cc: H. Solow   DATE May 18, 1965

FROM Gene Roddenberry
DCF

SUBJECT NAME CLEARANCE - STAR TREK CHARACTER

The following are the last names we are considering for the Captain in STAR TREK. I would appreciate your checking them out for any clearance problem or conflict.

JANUARY
FLAGG
DRAKE
CHRISTOPHER
THORPE
RICHARD
PATRICK
RAINTREE
BOONE
HUDSON
TIMBER
HAMILTON —
HANNIBAL
NEVILLE
KIRK —
NORTH —

Thank you.

GENE RODDENBERRY

Justman and Roddenberry worked well together and had liked each other from the start. Their friendship, born during the harried production of the first pilot, had deepened with time. In addition to spending their workdays with each other, they began to cement their friendship after hours as well.

Justman invited the Roddenberrys out to dinner. Stopping by the Roddenberry house in Beverly Glen, Justman and his wife, Jackie, were given a tour of the baronial-style mini-mansion. It was evident that the Roddenberrys were very proud of their new home. After all, Holmby Hills was a decidedly upscale section of the city.

Before they left for dinner, Roddenberry took his guests to a room behind the kitchen where he and his wife, Eileen, pursued their favorite hobby, polishing semiprecious gems and mounting them in handmade jewelry.

BOB: We had dinner at Trader Vic's, a famous Polynesian restaurant in the Beverly Hilton Hotel.

Until that night, Jackie hadn't met Gene, and I hadn't met Eileen. I ordered up a mess of appetizers and potent tropical-fruit and rum drinks, Zombies and Navy Grogs. Eileen was polite, but distant. I assumed she was either shy or very reserved because she contributed little to the conversation. Gene, however, having sluiced down a few Zombies, took center stage, telling stories about his World War II flying days as an Army Air Force bomber pilot in the South Pacific.

From that, he progressed to his job as a Pan Am pilot after the war. I listened, fascinated, as he relived his Middle East "plane crash in the desert" while deadheading on the return run from Karachi to Cairo. He described how he had dragged injured passengers from the wreckage, and then how he saved the lives of the survivors by outwitting some marauding Bedouins who raked the plane with gunfire in an attempt to kill the survivors and rob them. Somehow, he made his way across the desert on foot, to a town where he made telephone contact with someone in a phone booth in Manhattan who dispatched a rescue team.

Gene finished his "life story" by describing his career as a cop in the Los Angeles Police Department who rose to the position of speechwriter for famed L.A. Police Chief William Parker. Then he ordered another Zombie.

"What an exciting life this man has led," I thought. The stories Gene told were the kind that occur only in the movies and rolled right off his tongue as if he had been telling and retelling them for years. I didn't disbelieve Gene; the stories had some ring of truth to them, embroidered a bit perhaps, but then, who amongst us doesn't "improve" his own truths? However, I wondered why Gene would quit his job as a well-paid Pan Am pilot to become a beat cop in L.A. It also seemed odd that a man as politically and socially liberal as I already knew Gene to be would be so trusted by Chief "Bill" Parker, well-known in Los Angeles for his ultraconservative views.

The evening ended back at the Roddenberry house. There were warm goodbyes from Gene. But Eileen was less forthcoming. She seemed eager for the

evening to end; her good-byes were perfunctory. I had the distinct impression she was quite uncomfortable with her husband's new friends and new lifestyle.

"Maybe she's just ill at ease with people she doesn't know," I thought. But after a moment's reflection, I discarded that idea. "Why kid yourself? She probably had dinner with us only because Gene insisted."

Back home, I asked Jackie about her reaction to Gene. She didn't mince words. "I liked him—but I listened to all his stories and I have only one thing to say. Your friend Gene is either crazy—or he's the greatest storyteller in the world."

"Maybe he's a little of both," I theorized. But having worked closely with him, I thought I sensed a touch of genius. And I remembered having read somewhere that geniuses were often thought to be madmen or liars by their contemporaries. I liked Gene a lot, and he had already become a hero of sorts to me. Would he turn out to be a flawed hero? Only time would tell.

In the late sixties and early seventies, two of the most popular and commercially successful motion pictures were *M*A*S*H* and *2001: A Space Odyssey*. Among the stars of those films were "Hot Lips" Sally Kellerman and "Astronaut" Gary Lockwood. And in the summer of 1965, the two guest stars of the second *Star Trek* pilot were Sally Kellerman and Gary Lockwood, whose characters, during the story's development, mutated into godhood. In typical Hollywood fashion, within a period of five years, Sally went from a goddess to the pompous, sex-starved nurse in Korea, and Gary went from a god to an astronaut who is outmaneuvered by a computer named HAL. They were no longer gods, but they certainly were stars, and Roddenberry later joked that he "gave them their start."

Sally Kellerman as Dr. Elizabeth Dehner.

Courtesy NBC/Globe

Roddenberry, Solow, and NBC were thrilled to have them in the guest-star roles. Gary Lockwood had starred in Roddenberry's *The Lieutenant* series, while Sally Kellerman was one of the hotter leading ladies in the world of Hollywood television. (She had starred in an *Outer Limits* episode, "The Bellero Shield," written by Joseph Stefano. Justman was the assistant director on the episode, which also starred John Hoyt, who played the doctor in the first *Star Trek* pilot.)

Then came the hard part: recasting the series regulars. With Jeff Hunter's Captain Pike now history, the only holdover from the first pilot, ironically, was the one character NBC really didn't want, Leonard Nimoy's Mister Spock.

Roddenberry was still looking for the right actor to play the ship's doctor. During the casting for the first pilot, Gene wanted DeForest Kelley but was talked out of it by Bob Butler. Once again, with the second pilot, Roddenberry had the chance to push Kelley. When the veteran actor Paul Fix was recommended for the part by director James Goldstone, Roddenberry again pulled back and accepted the decision of his director.

Courtesy NBC/Globe

Paul Fix as the second pilot doctor, Dr. Mark Piper.

HERB: When casting was discussed with Gene, the only performers he would stand up for were the actresses with whom he'd had a previous personal relationship: Majel Barrett, Nichelle Nichols, and Grace Lee Whitney. After the casting of Fix, I told Gene, "Too bad De Kelley hadn't been born a woman!"

Gene's version of the ship's yeoman role came straight out of old Hollywood movies: cute and shapely, and cute and bubbly, and cute and not too bright—and cute. Laurel Goodwin as Yeoman Colt fit Gene's vision for the first pilot, but she was swept away by the NBC broom. Model Andrea Dromm, also fitting the mold, came aboard for the second pilot as Yeoman Smith. Actually, it was a non-part. But during the casting process, director Jimmy Goldstone overheard Gene say, "I'm hiring her because I want to score with her." It was not only a non-part, I'm sure it was a non-score as well.

Paul Carr was hired as one of the ship's officers, Lt. Lee Kelso. Carr was a good actor, but it, too, wasn't much of a part.

Andrea Dromm as Yeoman Smith.

Courtesy NBC/Globe

For the climactic fight action, Justman hired his two favorite stuntmen, Hal Needham to double Gary Lockwood and Paul Baxley to double Bill Shatner. Many years later, Needham went on to a successful motion-picture career, directing *Smokey and the Bandit* and other action movies.

As a matter of principle, NBC promoted racially integrated casting in its shows. Programs Vice President Mort Werner reiterated the network's racial policies in his August 17, 1966, letter to Gene Roddenberry.

Roddenberry and Solow were in full agree-

NBC TELEVISION NETWORK

[illegible]

THIRTY ROCKEFELLER PLAZA, NEW YORK, N.Y. [illegible] CIRCLE [illegible]

August 17, 1966

Mr. Gene Roddenberry
DESILU STUDIOS
Hollywood, Calif.

Dear Gene:

Census figures, in the mid 1960s, indicate that one American in every eight is non-white. It is reasonable to assume that this percentage also applies to the television audience.

I choose this statistic to call your attention once again to NBC's longstanding policy of non-discrimination. Our efforts in the past to assure the fact that the programs broadcast on our facilities are a natural reflection of the role of minorities in American life have met with substantial success. I would like to congratulate those producers who have extended themselves in this regard and I invite all of our creative associates to join us in an even greater effort to meet this fact of American life.

NBC's employment policy has long dictated that there can be no discrimination because of race, creed, religion or national origin and this applies in all of our operations. In addition, since we are mindful of our vast audience and the extent to which television influences taste and attitudes, we are not only anxious but determined that members of minority groups be treated in a manner consistent with their role in our society. While this applies to all racial minorities, obviously the principal reference is to the casting and depiction of Negroes. Our purpose is to assure that in our medium, and within the permissive framework of dramatic license, we present a reasonable reflection of contemporary society.

(continued)

We urge producers to cast Negroes, subject to their availability and competence as performers, as people who are an integral segment of the population, as well as in those roles where the fact of their minority status is of significance. An earnest attempt has been made to see that their presence contributes to an honest and natural reflection of places, situations and events, and we desire to intensify and extend this effort.

We believe that NBC's pursuit of this policy is pre-eminent in the broadcasting industry. It is evident in both the daytime and nighttime schedules and particularly in such popular programs as I SPY, THE ANDY WILLIAMS SHOW, THE MAN FROM U.N.C.L.E., RUN FOR YOUR LIFE, and many other presentations. While we have made noticeable progress we can do better, and I ask for your cooperation and help.

Sincerely,

Mort

MORT WERNER

MW/lh

Letter from NBC V.P. Mort Werner reaffirming his network's long-standing policy of nondiscrimination and multiethnic casting.

ment with NBC and many African-American actors were interviewed. Lloyd Haynes, later the star of *Room 222*, caught everyone's attention. Herb Solow, incidentally, had known him as a Production Assistant on *Video Village*, a day-time game show during Solow's days at CBS. Haynes was one of the first African-American actors hired to play an important role in a network television pilot.

BOB: Years later, in my other career as a reserve uniformed Los Angeles County sheriff's deputy, I was working the streets of West Hollywood in a black-and-white patrol car at night. My regular deputy sheriff partner and I made a traffic stop on a vehicle for a minor infraction. After my partner asked for some identification and we talked with our nervous stoppee, I recognized him as Lloyd Haynes, who

by then had become a TV director. I told the other deputy, "Hey, I know the dude and he's okay. Let's just give him a warning and let him slide."

Lloyd was duly cautioned. He expressed his thanks to the two officers and drove away, never realizing that one of them was Bob Justman, the television producer.

Courtesy NBC/Globe

Lloyd Haynes as the ship's communications officer, Lt. Alden.

The one-hour length of the pilot and the relative simplicity of the script exposed a major chink in the *Star Trek* armor. Roddenberry, Solow, and Sam Peeples soon realized the shortcoming. Other than Kirk, Spock, and the guest stars, the other characters—particularly the projected series regulars that Roddenberry had placed aboard the *Enterprise*—were boring and bland and had absolutely nothing to do but occupy chairs on the ship's bridge. Roddenberry reverted to his navy analogy and pulled several distinctive characters from his old-time movie memories.

One of them was the ship's irascible engineering officer. James Goldstone had directed Canadian-born actor James Doohan and recalled Doohan's marvelous facility for dialects. He recommended Doohan read for the part.

The actor faced a critical audience: Roddenberry, Goldstone, Justman, Joe D'Agosta, and Morris Chapnick. Doohan was handed a page of dialogue and asked to deliver the same speech using his various accents. He did many, and he did them well. Everyone was pleased with Doohan, his look, his vocal range, and his ability. Roddenberry, undecided as to what nationality the new character should be, asked Doohan's opinion. Doohan responded without hesitation, "Well, if he's going to be an engineer-r-r-r aboard a ship, then he ought to be a Scotsman." And so Engineer Scott was born. Jimmy Doohan not only got a job, he had "made" his own role.

James Doohan as Chief Engineer Montgomery Scott.

Courtesy NBC/Globe

Another distinctive role was the strong and always dependable ship's helmsman. But the actual casting was very unusual for its time. George Takei, a second-generation Japanese-American, was set to portray Sulu. Other than comic-book hero Green Hornet's trusty manservant, Kato, Sulu was one of the very first "good guy" Oriental characters ever to appear in a television series. Justman thought the character's name came from the Philippine Islands' Sulu archipelago, which bomber pilot Roddenberry knew about from his World War II experiences flying in the South Pacific. Actually, the name "Sulu" resulted from Roddenberry's decision to "honor" Herb Solow by using a mispronunciation of his name "without the w," a running joke between Solow and many of his friends.

Magic time was closing in on Justman again. Of his remaining preproduction duties, one of the most important was to obtain "silver eyes" for Sally Kellerman and Gary Lockwood. The script called for their characters to mutate into all-powerful godlike creatures, the outward signs of which would be their normal eyes transformed into shiny, silver-colored orbs.

Justman phoned around only to find that a few optical houses still made old-fashioned "scleral" lenses that covered the entire eyeball, but not one of them wanted to undertake the difficult and possibly lawsuit-provoking task. One firm gave him the name of the Roberts Optical Company, stating, "If John Roberts can't make them, no one can!"

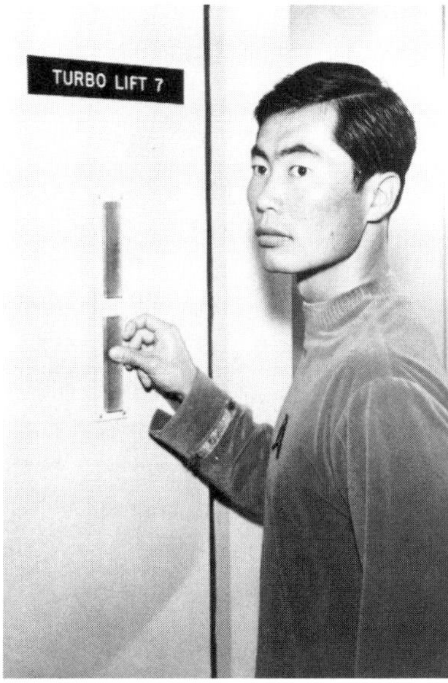

Courtesy NBC/Globe

George Takei as Lieutenant Sulu.

BOB: "Silver eyes?" John Roberts was incredulous.

Over the phone, it sounded bad, the way the optician said it. But I persisted. "Yes, Mister Roberts. My name is Bob Justman. I'm from Desilu Studios. We're making a new science-fiction television show and two of the stars have to have silver eyes."

"Silver eyes," he repeated. He sounded gruff.

"Yes. We need silver eyes. The people at Security Contact Lens recommended you. They said if anyone could make them, you could."

"They did, did they?" He sounded skeptical. Less gruff but skeptical.

"Yes, they said something about 'schollario' lenses—"

" 'Scleral,' " he interrupted. "Not like what we use today. Scleral lenses cover the whole eyeball. You sure that's what you want?"

"Yes, that's exactly what we want."

"Nobody else does. They're too damned uncomfortable. Who's going to wear them?"

"Sally Kellerman and Gary Lockwood. They're . . ."

"Never heard of them."

"Well, they're both pretty well known and . . ."

"How you get them to look like silver, that's the problem."

"Gary had his own series, *The Lieutenant,* and . . ."

"You could maybe coat the outside with silver enamel, you know, paint it on."

"You could? That's great!"

"But it wouldn't work."

"Oh . . ."

"What you'd have to do is laminate something inside the lens. That would make it double-thick, but it could work."

"Great!"

"Naw. They'd be too damned uncomfortable. Maybe even dangerous if you had 'em in too long."

"Oh . . ."

"It's a challenge. I've never done anything like that. Come on by my office on Monday at nine and take a look. I'll dream something up over the weekend."

"Gee, thanks. . . ." He'd already hung up.

When I arrived at John Roberts's Beverly Hills office at nine on Monday, he had a sample pair of silver eyes waiting. "Stayed up the whole damn weekend, working on this," he grumbled. "I had to crumple up tinfoil and laminate it between the two outer layers. See?"

"Yes, they're real silver-looking, all right. Tell me, how are the actors going to see through them?"

"See through them? You didn't say anything about seeing through them."

"Oh. Well . . ."

"It wouldn't take much, though. Just a small hole in the tinfoil. You'd never notice it unless you looked for it. Come back Wednesday."

I did. And he had silver contact lenses that could be seen through. "Great work, John." By this time, we were on a first-name basis. But now came the tough part. "You said they might be dangerous."

"Damn right. You wear things this thick for any length of time, heat builds up in the eyeballs behind the lenses and it gets damn uncomfortable—painful, in fact."

I couldn't in all good conscience ask the actors to wear the lenses if I couldn't. So I tried them on. As John had said, they were damn uncomfortable. But they could be worn. And I could see with them on, not well but well enough to navigate. And John assured me that if the actors wore them for only short periods of time, they'd be safe.

Eureka! We had our silver eyes!

(A personal note: Afterwards, John Roberts became my family's optician. Although he passed away some years ago, we still get our glasses from the John Roberts Optical Company, but now from his son, John, Jr.)

I arranged appointments for Sally Kellerman and Gary Lockwood to be fitted for the lenses by John Roberts. Sally's fittings went fine. She was in and out in no time at all. Before delivering the custom-made lenses to her, I tried them on. After a minute or two, they drove me nuts, but Sally could pop the lenses in and out at any time, without difficulty, and wear them without any pain. Even the buildup of heat between the lenses and her eyeballs didn't faze her.

But Gary Lockwood was a whole 'nother story. His fitting took a long time. Later, on stage, after much fussing, he'd finally manage to get the lenses in between his eyelids and his eyeballs. But he could hardly see while wearing them. In order to have any vision at all, Gary had to raise his chin and look down his

Courtesy Paramount Pictures

Sally Kellerman and Gary Lockwood wearing their silver contacts.

nose at the other actor in the shot. Happily, this gave him an unearthly appearance that worked well for his character and even helped his godlike progression.

HERB: Although he appeared only in the second pilot, Gary Lockwood's association with the series continues to this day. Gary loves to drive fast cars fast—very fast. And on four separate occasions, in four separate states, Gary was pulled over by either the Highway Patrol or the local Sheriff's Department for speeds in excess of 130 miles per hour. On three of those occasions, a "particular kind" of peace officer stopped him. Gary noticed that those officers were *"Star Trek* kind of guys with that old *Star Trek* look." The cop would stare at Gary, check out his eyes "to see if they were silver," and treat him as "a special person."

"They remembered me from the pilot," recalls Gary, "and forgave my speeding indiscretion. No ticket."

The fourth time he was pulled over, now traveling at 139 miles per hour, the Highway Patrol officer failed to remember him from *Star Trek.* "But he did remember me from *The Lieutenant* series." says Gary with a smile. "The guy was an ex-Marine."

"Hey, you guys ought to be proud of my record," maintains Gary. *"Star Trek,* 3; *The Lieutenant,* 1."

It was getting uncomfortably close to magic time, and Justman's last important duty was to find a topflight cameraman to photograph the show. Unfortunately, the first pilot's cameraman, Bill Snyder, was busy elsewhere.

Goldstone received cameraman Conrad Hall's blessing to hire his camera operator, Bill Fraker, and move him up to full cameraman for the pilot. Though both Hall and Fraker were Bob Justman's old friends, the pair's current employer, famed writer-director Richard Brooks, took angry exception to the proposal and threatened Goldstone, "If Fraker goes, he'll never work in this industry again!" So the search for a cameraman began again.

It was the time of year when most studios and production companies were busy making both series and network pilots, and even competent technicians were scarce. It was so bad that some studios were even hiring nonunion off-the-street "permit" workers to help build sets.

Justman called the Cameramen's Union and was told the list was empty; they had no one available. This was not welcome news to Solow.

"Christ, RJ, how can there be no cameramen? Can you see me calling Mort Werner and telling him we're such a dumb studio we can't even locate a dumb cameraman to shoot the dumb pilot?"

"Herb, the local said they'd search the bars and old-age homes and would call when they found someone." Justman had learned how to relieve Solow's tension.

Failing to get Bill Fraker, Goldstone wanted an experienced cameraman who had photographed complicated films. He recalled an old-timer he once knew, now probably retired, and suggested Justman check him out.

The next day, Justman got a message. The union had located Goldstone's old-timer.

Ernest Haller, a man with graying hair, showed up in Bob's office. Roddenberry and Solow sat in on the interview. Haller seemed nice, but Justman knew nothing about him. He was getting worried. Should he be wasting time with this guy when he could be out beating the bushes to find a cameraman? After the usual amenities, Solow broke the ice. "Could you tell us what you've done? Recently?" Haller took a long time to respond, "Not much, recently. I've been sort of semiretired."

"Sort of semiretired?" Now, Justman was very worried. Solow was persistent. "Well, have you done anything that, you know, we might have heard of?"

"Well, yes. I did do a picture you might have heard of. Back in thirty-nine."

Justman and Solow looked at each other. They both quickly calculated. "Let's see, it's now 1965. If he's talking 1939, that's . . . Christ, that's twenty-six years ago!"

Then it was Ernie Haller's turn to break the ice. "It was called *Gone with the Wind*."

"Oh, that's right. I almost forgot," said Solow. "Listen guys, if it's all right with you, I think we ought to . . ."

Roddenberry jumped in. "I couldn't agree more, Herb. . . ."

"Same here," overlapped Justman. "Can you come to work tomorrow, Ernie?"

So Ernest Haller was hired on the spot to film the second *Star Trek* pilot. And he filmed it at Desilu Culver, the same lot that had once been owned by famed producer David O. Selznick, the same lot where twenty-six years earlier, Haller had worked on *Gone with the Wind*.

Finally, magic time came, and shooting began on Monday, July 19, 1965. As usual, Justman showed up an hour early on the first day, bleary-eyed from lack of sleep and totally hyper, flying on nerves alone.

This time, past experience had the pigeons under control. They still lived in the rafters, but were kept busy in the daytime eating food an assigned pigeon wrangler scattered outside the stage. And experience also caused toilet monitors to be deployed ahead of time. With only a seven-day schedule, no flushing noises would ruin takes and slow down the filming. Nevertheless, again Murphy's Law was not to be denied.

BOB: We'd been shooting for days and falling further and further behind schedule, just as I feared. One morning, after an overnight move to our next stage, it was time for the first shot. I looked at Jimmy Goldstone. He nodded. I announced, "Quiet, please. This will be a take. Roll it."

"Speed."

"Marker."

"Action."

"Bzzz-bzzz-bzzz . . . "

It was a case of déjà vu all over again. The "killer" bees were back and on the same stage as the previous year.

Courtesy NBC/Globe

Captain Kirk in a climactic moment from the second pilot.

"What the hell is that, Bob?" demanded director James Goldstone. He was much more impatient than Bob Butler.

"Don't ask."

"Yeah, Bob. What the hell is that?" joked Bill Shatner. He stopped joking when an avenging bee swooped down and stung our new starship captain on the eyelid. Luckily, it was Friday so we had a whole weekend for the swelling to diminish. But Bill's face was still puffy and we had to shoot around him on Monday and film him from behind.

Sally Kellerman was stung, too, but not on the face, so it didn't show. Luckily, all her shots that day were done standing. Even though the sting must have hurt, to her credit, she never complained—not even when she sat down.

But Goldstone complained. He turned to me and muttered, "Bob, she's doing it again." And then to her, "Sally, what the hell are you doing with your hands?"

"Oh, nothing."

But it wasn't nothing; it was something. Sally had gone into her protective mode. For a reason that it seemed only I could fathom at first, namely embarrassment, she was very uncomfortable wearing the Starfleet uniform of velour tunic, boots, and tight black pants. The reason wasn't the tunic, and it wasn't the boots. It was the pants. They were very form-fitting and clung to her legs and torso, especially in the area of her *mons veneris*. So every time we got ready to do a take, she'd fold her hands in front of her nether region and assume what I called her "crotch cover" posture.

Jim walked over to her and said, softly, "Keep your hands at your sides, Sally. Okay?"

"Okay."

He came back. "Okay, Bob."

"Roll 'em."

"Speed."

"Markers."

"Action."

Sally folded her hands.

"Cut!" Jim looked at me. I shrugged. Jim told the propman to give her a "space clipboard" prop. She held it in front of her. It solved Goldstone's problem and covered Sally's "problem" as well. And whenever possible, Jimmy filmed her from the waist up.

HERB: Earlier, Jimmy had handled a suggestion from Sally. After trying on her costume for the first time, she approached her director. "Jim, you know that in the future, women won't wear brassieres. So I've decided not to wear one."

"Well, Sally, this really isn't that far into the future. On this film you'll wear one . . ."

"But . . ."

". . . because you need one."

Sally changed her mind about what the future would hold; the brassiere stayed.

Roddenberry, Goldstone, Solow, and Justman viewed every previous day's work in the projection room. Shatner's portrayal of the ship's captain was exactly what Roddenberry had been looking for. Kirk was heroic, undaunted by adversity, and a swashbuckling adventurer, to boot. *Star Trek* had an energetic leading man who could excite an audience.

Courtesy NBC/Globe

Mister Spock at his station. Note the "primitive" printout and microphone.

And Leonard Nimoy, now portraying both science officer and the ship's second in command, brought a heightened sense of mystery to the supposedly unemotional Mister Spock. There was something intriguing about this alien humanoid. Roddenberry liked Nimoy's cool, self-assured portrayal. Bob Justman predicted that women would be attracted to him, likening Spock to the new foreign sailor in town who was strangely attractive to all the local females.

While the new characters of Engineer Scott and Helmsman Sulu worked well, the ship's doctor role played by Paul Fix didn't ring true for Roddenberry. He felt that something was missing in the role. He told Solow that if *Star Trek* became a series, he would come up with the right person for the role. He still had DeForest Kelley in mind.

Production of the first pilot did nothing to disprove the old guard's lack of confidence in Solow and his interlopers. In fact, it only made things worse. Realistically, the first pilot, massively complex and futuristic, wasn't a fair test. On the other hand, "Where No Man Has Gone Before" was a fair test. It was, as the hoped-for series would be, a one-hour science-fiction action-adventure rather than science-fiction–fantasy. It would have a doable complement of optical effects and a talented group of actors. Besides, there was the all-important learning experience from the first pilot. So "Where No Man" was not only a pilot to sell a series to NBC, it was demonstrable proof to Desilu's old guard that the interlopers could put its money where their mouths were.

The original nine-day shooting schedule had played on the old guard's fears: "They say nine, it'll damn sure be ten, maybe even eleven." Solow had prevailed upon Justman to cut the schedule down to seven days.

Despite director Jim Goldstone's detailed preparation and efficient shooting style, despite Bob Justman's strong hand with cast and crew, despite the support and expertise provided by Desilu's Unit Manager Jim Paisley, whose main responsibility was to watch over the shooting schedule and how Desilu's money was spent, and despite the efforts of all the others concerned, the second pilot fell further and further behind schedule. Instead of wrapping up at the conclusion of the seventh day of shooting, the company was two full days behind.

The break came during the eighth day of principal photography. Goldstone, Justman, and the crew faced the challenge and really did the impossible. They managed to pack two days of work into one. The pilot finished in eight days plus one day of pickup shots and "inserts," a total of nine days, as Justman had originally scheduled.

Late in the evening of that last principal photography day, Wednesday, July 28, 1965, everyone was fighting the clock to avoid going into another payday for the cast and crew. The scene was Shatner and Lockwood confronting each other in a fight to the death. A portion of the stage had been converted into a rocky terrain covered by sand. However, with everyone fighting fatigue, each take would cause the loose sand to scatter over the camera dolly tracks, causing further delays. Justman and Solow, seeing the problem, grabbed brooms and resolutely swept the scattered sand from the dolly track after each shot. Suddenly, they noticed another broom was in the act. They looked up and into the equally resolute face of Lucille Ball, as she determinedly swept away. Brandishing her broom, Lucy approached Goldstone. "What do I have to do to get you to finish?" Then she looked back at Solow and Justman and smiled. "What I won't do to get the wrap party started!"

Courtesy NBC/Globe

7

Strange New Worlds

HERB: The last thing I wanted to do was have a wrap party for Bob Justman. *Star Trek* was in the editing stage, and RJ was moving onto our *Police Story* pilot. The problem was, when that half-hour pilot finished shooting, there was no longer a job for Bob; we had no other way to pay him. He would be absolutely necessary when we went into series production, and though Gene remained anxious, I had convinced myself *Star Trek* was going to be a television series. Neither Gene nor I wanted or could afford to lose our favorite workaholic.

Desilu's ever-growing group of youthful interlopers believed in a slight deviation from an old saying: "a team that plays together stays together." The old guard wasn't at all happy with the concept or with me. They felt I was ignoring them and their suggestions and that I was becoming more obnoxious when it came to listening to any suggestions from Lucy's husband, Gary Morton. I was guilty on both counts. Considering that no one at the studio would ever tell me not to do anything, however, I just did what made sense.

And since we were fortunate to have attracted a number of pilot orders, it just made sense that Justman should be the Associate Producer on all of them.

Desilu had an interesting group of pilot films to produce. Roddenberry put his previous career as a member of the Los Angeles Police Department to dramatic use when he wrote a half-hour pilot for the studio, titled *Police Story.* (It was originally titled *Assignment 100.* Later, a different one-hour *Police Story* anthology series was created by ex-LAPD detective Joseph Wambaugh.)

Actor Steve Ihnat starred in Roddenberry's *Police Story* pilot, the same Steve Ihnat who was starring in "The Inheritors," a two-part episode on *The Outer Limits* that not only was directed by Jim Goldstone, but was the episode Justman was working on when Roddenberry first interviewed him for *Star Trek.* It was truly a small world.

And the world got even smaller when DeForest Kelley was cast as the third lead in Roddenberry's *Police Story* pilot and eventually became Doctor McCoy on the *Star Trek* series.

BOB: It was a long, hot summer. During the worst of the heat, two events took place simultaneously. One was Gene Roddenberry's half-hour cop-show pilot for NBC, *Police Story.* The other was the 1965 Watts riot. All the cops in the city were on overtime, working double shifts. The National Guard was called out. Structure fires erupted in the riot-torn areas, and when firefighters responded, they became targets for snipers. The sound of National Guard machine-gun fire made some Los Angeles streets sound like a war zone. No one knew where trouble would erupt next.

In the midst of all the real action, some fake action was taking place. Exterior scenes from the *Police Story* pilot were being filmed on a street just around the corner from Gene Roddenberry's house in Holmby Hills, one of L.A.'s wealthiest enclaves. The script called for us to set an auto ablaze in the middle of the street after actors, portraying bad guys, riddled the vehicle with shotgun fire. Then our good-guy stars, Steve Ihnat and Gary Clarke, piled out of the burning car and fired back at their assailants. I think you can imagine what happened next. Frightened nearby residents, believing the riots had finally come to their upscale neighborhood, panicked and phoned the cops. Just like the old complaint, they called for help but nobody came.

Actually, there were two off-duty cops assigned to the production that day. They'd just come from working a straight thirty-six hours in Watts, and we let them sack out in one of the dressing room trailers. One citizen later complained to us, "Cops! They're never around when you need them."

HERB: Late one afternoon during the Watts riots, while the *Police Story* crew was out filming on location, Gene Roddenberry and I were alone at Desilu Culver going over show costs while closely monitoring a local news broadcast. Our attention quickly turned away from the *Police Story* pilot on hearing ". . . and the rioters are now headed for Culver City."

"Do you have a gun?" asked Gene. "I left mine home."

"A gun, Gene? I've never even shot a gun, much less owned one."

"If we're to protect the show's sets, let's go buy some guns."

I always figured you protected shows from overscheduled directors, bad scripts, mad actors, greedy agents, and sometimes ourselves—but from looters and rioters? Roddenberry was insistent. He knew of a gun shop on Washington Boulevard. So we went to buy guns.

The gun shop walls were bare, the display cabinets empty. The shop owner apologized to Gene. Sold out!

"Hey, man," threatened Gene while he flashed his retirement badge, "there's no time for bullshit! Me and my buddy, we're protecting Desilu Studios. We need guns!"

"Okay, but I can't discount them," responded the owner. He returned from his storage room with two guns. "They're all I have." Gene was amazed; he stared at two "Ithaca Gun Company model X-15 Lightning" .22-caliber rifles.

". . . Twenty-two rifles?" bellowed Gene. "You really expect us to take on rioters with twenty-two-caliber rifles?"

"Sorry, guys, you'll have to take 'em or leave 'em."

We "took 'em," also buying cases for each gun, and drove back to the studio. Luckily I had a key, as both the guard at the gate and the few people who had been there were long gone.

So two grown men, Gene Roddenberry and I, sat in the production office in silence, holding our "powerful" weapons, waiting for the rioters to storm the studio. Newscasters continued to recite vivid details of buildings going up in flames and gun battles on the streets in Watts. But nary another mention of Culver City.

"Gene, maybe we can find the phaser cannon from the first pilot. Remember, it melted rock?"

"Or Captain Kirk's phaser rifle from the second pilot."

"Yeah, we can throw them at the rioters."

After hours of "guarding" the studio, a bemused Gene Roddenberry turned to me. "Herb, are you hungry?"

I nodded. "Yeah. Chinese food?"

Gene agreed. The chagrined defenders stashed their weapons in the trunks of their cars and, after hot and sour soup and kung pao chicken, drove home.

The Battle of Desilu Culver was over well before it began! I still have the .22-caliber rifle.

Sam Rolfe was one of the quality television pilot writers and producers. His most successful series were *Have Gun, Will Travel* and *The Man From U.N.C.L.E.* Attempting to follow up on his success, Solow hired Rolfe to write a pilot script for Desilu, and almost instantly the project was "laid off at" (financed by) ABC. *The Long Hunt of April Savage* was a Western and was great television fodder, following a nonviolent man who seeks to avenge the brutal murder of his family at the hands of a crazed gang of outlaws. Part of the deal with Rolfe, however, was that due to a prior commitment in London, he could not produce his own pilot.

HERB: Gene Roddenberry had written many *Have Gun* episodes for Rolfe, and they enjoyed working together. Continuing the effort to keep our group busy and employed, I hired Gene to produce the *April Savage* pilot. Rolfe was pleased and went off to London with his wife, Hilda, and his kids.

His trip turned out to be a bad move. Gene, for some reason, coasted along and halfheartedly produced Sam's pilot. His interest seemed to be mostly in the paycheck he picked up. He even went so far as to officially inform ABC that he

From the collection of Herbert F. Solow

Herb Solow (l.) and Gene Roddenberry (r.) on the set of *The Long Hunt of April Savage.*

would not be available to produce or supervise the series should it sell. ABC made Rolfe aware of Gene's position. Sam phoned from London, furious with me. He had left his project in my hands. I explained that Gene had let us both down. Sam's close friendship with Gene ended in anger.

BOB: *The Long Hunt of April Savage* starred Robert Lansing, later to star in "Assignment: Earth," an episode made to be a *Star Trek* spinoff. We filmed the pilot on location above the famous mountain resort of Big Bear, California. The set, a log cabin exterior and interior, was built near the shores of a small lake at an altitude of 9,000 feet.

Actor Rip Torn, portraying the leading bad guy, had an undeserved reputation for being "difficult" with his directors. To the contrary, Rip was totally cooperative and, during this production, minded his own business. He even stayed nearby and fished for trout in the lake while waiting to work.

Bruce Dern and Charles Dierkop portrayed Rip Torn's henchmen. Bruce soon found a prop that helped him come across as being totally psychotic. He continuously carried and stroked a chicken while on camera. Once more in training for the 1,500 meters at the upcoming Olympic Games, Bruce ran the mountainous terrain when he wasn't needed on the set. He ran too far afield several times and, after the day's wrap, had to sprint furiously after the crew bus in order to get back to the hotel.

Not only was I working again as both Associate Producer and First Assistant Director, I also had to cover for my Second Assistant Director, who had a drinking problem. Since I was turning in incredible hours and working at such a high altitude, it was small wonder that, every night, crew members watched with fascination as I literally fell asleep in my plate while eating dinner. They had to do something for excitement. Big Bear in the summertime was dull.

During the filming, something happened that later returned to haunt Gene Roddenberry. I never found out what had angered Gene, but he also decided to show who was boss and ordered me to throw ex-quiz kid and ABC program executive Harve Bennett off the set. Harve not only was the network executive assigned to the pilot, he'd been my fraternity brother at UCLA. It was an awkward and unnecessary moment. Ironically, years later, after *Star Trek: The Motion Picture* went substantially over budget and fizzled at the box office, Paramount hired Harve Bennett to produce and write several *Star Trek* movies, movies on which the studio gave Gene Roddenberry only a perfunctory "consulting" credit.

The Desilu pilot parade continued with two half-hour comedies and Bruce Geller's *Mission: Impossible*, all for CBS. Geller's pilot began filming on December 8, 1965. Bernie Kowalski directed for Geller, his former partner at Four Star Productions. It was the last of that year's pilots for the overworked Bob Justman.

BOB: My education in the many phases of postproduction, which had begun with the second *Star Trek* pilot, continued with *Mission: Impossible.* I helped Bruce with the editing of the show and sat with him as he spotted the music cues with composer Lalo Schifrin. The night we recorded the score for the pilot, Bruce and his wife, Lalo and his wife, and Jackie and I all went out to dinner to celebrate. After dinner, Bruce took me aside and asked me to meet him early the following morning. Although the score was terrific, he was not happy with the main title music cue.

The following morning, I was stopped outside the sound and music cutting building by Bill Heath, head of Desilu's Postproduction Department. He had already heard that Bruce was recutting the music and knew that it would cost more time and money. Red-faced with anger, he blustered, "Stay out of F Building!" I just looked at him. "Stay out of F Building, or else," he repeated, but he couldn't back up his threat. He was on a fool's errand, I thought. Argyle probably sent him.

I waited until he stalked away and entered F Building to find Bruce hard at work in the music cutting room. Bruce, who had written a successful off-Broadway musical comedy and was well versed in music, felt Lalo's music cues were good, but some were misplaced. He was busy recutting the recorded score. The major move was dropping the theme Lalo wrote for the main title and substituting something else. There were two candidate cues. I liked one; Bruce liked the other. He was more equal than me, so he won. He chose a "throwaway" cue Lalo had written for the final chase and escape sequence. Television history knows that throwaway cue as the famous *Mission: Impossible* music theme.

While working on *The Outer Limits*, Justman used full-time accountant and part-time singer Robert Johnson for "voice-over" work. At this point, a voice was needed to give instructions to the famous *Mission: Impossible* team. Justman again tapped Johnson. When the series sold, the accountant struck pay dirt. Compensated for all seven years of original episodes, Johnson was repaid each and every time an episode was rebroadcast and he said: "Good morning, Mr. Phelps. Your mission, should you choose to accept it . . . This tape will self-destruct in five seconds."

HERB: Anyone would hate to be in the middle of a tug-of-war between Gene Roddenberry and Bruce Geller. Each had his own way of playing the game, and each had his own pigheaded conviction that losing anything just wasn't an acceptable circumstance.

Gene spoke to Bob Justman to ensure his loyalty and availability should *Star Trek* become a series. Bruce spoke to Bob Justman to ensure his loyalty and availability should *Mission: Impossible* become a series. Bob Justman spoke to me:

"I hate to put you in between them, Herb, but my dilemma will be your dilemma if both series sell."

From the collection of Herbert F. Solow

(l. to r.) Bruce Geller, Herb Solow, Leonard Nimoy, and Bob Justman at a surprise party for Solow in December 1966.

My solution was simplistic and totally unemotional; it dealt purely with mathematics. Since Justman had done two *Star Trek* pilots but only one *Mission: Impossible* pilot, Roddenberry got first "dibs." Both producers bought the rationale. Mister Spock couldn't have been more logical.

However, it really didn't end there, as Bruce had the combined memory of a herd of elephants. The following year, I developed a detective show with writers Link and Levinson, creators of a host of top-ten series, not the least of which was *Columbo*. The Desilu project was called *Mannix,* and it had no producer attached to it. A producer was needed, however, after CBS ordered production of a pilot film. I went to Bruce and asked, even though he didn't create the series or write the script, if he'd be interested in producing the pilot. Bruce's response? "It's about time you gave me something after taking Justman away."

NBC's Research Department concept-tested *Star Trek* just as they did all their pilot films. The tests were performed by a Los Angeles–based independent research company and took place at Preview House, basically a large theatre fit-

Courtesy Paul Lenburg

The "high-tech" computer equipment at Preview House.

ted with individual dials that the audience manipulated during the screening of a pilot on a "like" or "dislike" basis. The dials were connected to a computer that segmented the audience on the basis of sex and age groups. A master readout indicated the audience's fluctuating opinion of the pilot being tested, with an overall score at the conclusion of the film. There were small group discussions held after the screenings, but a bad computer score almost always resulted in a pilot not being recommended for the fall schedule.

Before a pilot was tested, there was an established routine at Preview House. Despite what was inaccurately reported in another "authoritative" book, every test showing *began* with the same *Mister Magoo* cartoon, which was a research standard test to determine whether the audience was an "average one." If the audience reaction to the cartoon did not match pre–established criteria, the test results for the particular film that followed were discarded and the film would be retested later with another audience.

Star Trek was tested in the afternoon before an audience of, as Solow later complained, "little old ladies with blue hair." The test was a disaster, and Solow was irate. His experience as a network Daytime Programs executive convinced him the daytime audience's viewing habits, likes, and dislikes were enormously different from those of the nighttime, prime-time audience.

Solow complained angrily to Program and Research executives at NBC, demanding a retest before a nighttime audience "when husbands are home from work and kids are out of school." To NBC's credit, they acquiesced. *Star Trek* was retested at night. The results were considerably better and indicated substantial audience interest in science-fiction action-adventure, especially among sixteen- to thirty-five-year-olds.

Overjoyed with the retest results, Solow packed up *Star Trek* and *Mission: Impossible*, and his suit and tie, and flew east for "PSR," the annual Pilot Season Ritual.

Every day, Roddenberry, Geller, and Justman waited anxiously for news. There were a lot of rumors, a lot of gossip as to what was on the network schedules on a particular day and what took what's place the following morning. Basically, no one would actually know until the three networks locked in and announced their fall schedules.

Roddenberry became even more anxious. He had an overwhelming fear that *Star Trek* wouldn't sell. Justman suffered from a different sort of high anxiety. He had an overwhelming fear *both* pilots would sell.

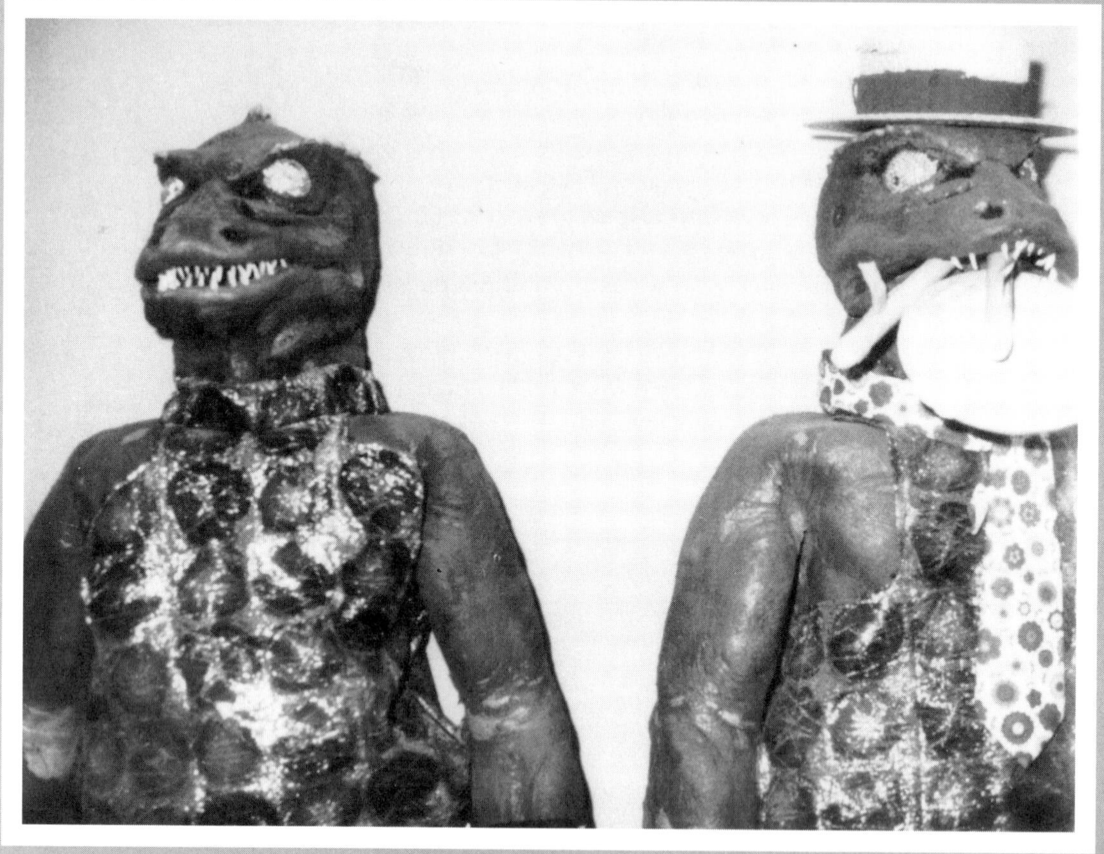

Courtesy Scott S. Smith

8

The Key to the Asylum

HERB: Yes, tomorrow would be one helluva day.

It had been a late, long, and tiring TWA flight back to Los Angeles. But I didn't care; I'd sold two big one-hour series, *Star Trek* and *Mission.* And now that I'd sold them, I had to figure out how to actually make them.

I left my Brentwood home at 6:00 the following morning. As I drove along Sunset Boulevard through Beverly Hills and into Hollywood, the problems I faced cancelled out any memories of my successful New York trip. There was one serious problem in particular that I purposely avoided mentioning to NBC—the possibility that the studio was incapable of deficit-financing the series the network had just bought. Forget whether the shows were producible—that's some other discussion. The reality was that we might not even get a turn at bat.

Some years earlier, especially when advertisers, via their agencies, purchased series and then bought broadcast time on the networks, the studios and the independent producers were paid the actual cost of the series they produced.

The studios looked for their profits from foreign sales or syndicated sales of network series after they'd been cancelled, or merchandising the series' ancillary rights, but the initial cost would be covered. The financial gamble just didn't exist unless your production ran wild and costs exceeded your sale price. The networks looked for their profits from commercial time purchases from advertisers.

But things had changed. Now networks bought new shows, locked them into time periods of their choosing, and then sold the broadcast package to advertisers. The networks had wised up as to who was making what money and when. They figured out, roughly, the overall projected profitability of the series and just paid the network-run portion of the series' costs. This policy had a massive impact on television series in general, and expensive television series in particular. If the network figured that their broadcast portion of the series cost was eighty percent, then the studio had to cover the remaining twenty percent of the series' cost. The twenty percent could come from foreign sales, and, if the show became popular on American television, from syndicated sales in this country—but only if there were enough episodes to sell to local stations. Money from merchandising toys and games and clothing would come only when, and if, the series was a success and usually not until years after the series premiered. What it all boiled down to was that the studio had to use its own money or borrow from a bank to pay for its share of the production cost of a television series.

While costs of other comparable series were around $160,000 an episode, *Mission: Impossible* and *Star Trek* were each roughly budgeted at nearly $200,000. The networks would pay Desilu roughly $160,000 an episode. Simple arithmetic indicates Desilu would have to ante up, beg, borrow, or steal about $80,000 for every week for twenty-six weeks in order to honor its contractual obligations for both series. And there were no guarantees the studio would ever recoup its investment, much less see a profit.

More frightening was what would happen if we went over budget. An $80,000 weekly deficit could grow to $160,000 or even $200,000 a week. I couldn't imagine little Desilu having to deficit to the tune of $200,000 a week. I mean, Lucy's "red" hair would turn white first.

Making things worse, the Ashley-Famous Agency received a "packaging fee," ten percent of the network sale price—five percent now and an additional deferred five percent from any future profits. Forget white hair. Lucy would go bald first.

When I arrived at the studio, Bob Justman, of course, was already there, patiently standing by the Desilu drive-in gate. His arms were full of schedules and budgets. He was ready for serious business, just waiting to get at me.

"Hi, Bob. What's new?

"You did it, didn't you? Both of them!"

"I had no choice. Good is good. I wanted you to hear the news directly from me, before the fall schedules come out in this morning's *Variety.*"

"Did you tell CBS that Steve Hill is an Orthodox Jew who won't come in on religious holidays? And he has to stop work an hour before sundown every Friday so he can get to synagogue in time to pray? And we always shoot late on Friday nights to catch up on the schedule? And he's in almost every scene in every *Mission: Impossible* show? Did you tell them that?"

I shook my head. (But Bob and I later joked that Steve Hill was more devout than either one of us had anticipated. In one of the very few cross-pollinations between *Mission: Impossible* and *Star Trek,* Bill Shatner laughingly burst into my office to tell me that Steve Hill was not as serious a guy as everyone thought, that he really had a great sense of humor, to wit: "Steve asked me how many Jews worked on *Star Trek.* He was recruiting a prayer group of ten guys [per Talmudic law] to worship together on top of the studio's highest building and only had six Jews so far from *Mission.* He asked if I would come and bring Nimoy and Justman and you." And Bill laughed. I said, "Don't laugh, Bill. He's not kidding." Shatner left the office in disbelief.)

Bob continued, "Did you tell NBC how much time it takes to put on Leonard's ears every morning and do all the weird makeups and hairdos?"

I shook my head.

"Did you tell them Desilu is the worst-equipped studio in town?"

I shook my head.

"Did you tell them anything?"

"I thanked them for the orders and said they could depend on us," I replied with a smile. "And then I gave them your name and office extension as the person to call if they have problems. And they will."

RJ smiled. "What did Lucy say?"

"I haven't spoken to her," I said, "but I'm sure Ted Ashley and Oscar Katz have filled her in on everything."

"But you know she listens to you."

"I'll speak to her, Bob. Honest."

Bob got to the heart of the matter: "Does she have the money to make the shows?"

"There's a meeting later today to discuss that minor point. I told the network people we have the money."

"Well, do we?"

I thought a bit and stared at Bob. "I certainly hope so."

Bob and I walked around the studio, discussing our production needs so that I could act a little more knowledgeable when I met with Lucy and the Board of Directors. A very mundane thought entered my mind. "RJ, where the hell are we going to put everyone? And where will they park?" Desilu was a small lot. It lacked most things, especially space to park. And having a parking space on the lot was up there with birth, taxes, and death.

"They can park at the cemetery next door and walk," Bob responded with a sardonic smile.

I knew I could always depend on Bob for the practical side of things. But later it didn't seem like such a bad idea. By the time filming began, we ran out of parking spaces at the studio. When we checked out the possibility of temporarily renting more at the cemetery, we discovered that we couldn't afford the cost; the cemetery got much more money from its permanent tenants. (See aerial photo of Desilu and surrounding area on pages 8 and 9.)

Eventually, so many people were constantly complaining to me about wanting a parking space—or a better parking space—that I sent an angry memo to every producer on the lot suggesting, "If your people still feel they are being put upon, then I would recommend that you tell them to seek employment elsewhere." It put a temporary stop to the complaints, and I got only one response. Bob Justman wrote, "Dear Mr. Solow: I have received your two-page, single-spaced memo on the subject of 'Parking Spaces.' I want you to know that, I, for one, think the memo is very well typed. Thank you."

Desilu itself had only one thirty-minute show on network television, *The Lucy Show.* It was extremely light on production requirements. It was no big deal in the overall scheme of things.

The *Lucy* staff had been in the same office building for years, and they used only one small audience stage, Stage 12. They used the same sets each week, the same actors, the same music and, in latter years, it seemed like the same scripts. They were stuck in low gear on a severe downward slope.

But two separate and totally different hour-long adventure-dramas, big productions with many starring roles, meant the studio's film output would multiply five times over, from thirty easy minutes a week to two backbreaking hours plus thirty easy minutes each and every week.

Each new series needed at least two huge sound stages. They needed dressing rooms and makeup rooms and wardrobe and prop rooms. They needed cutting rooms and dubbing rooms and projection rooms. But first, they needed office space. All of this would cost money—money to build from scratch, money to refurbish what could be saved, lots and lots of money.

Almost all the stages and office buildings on both Desilu lots were rented to tenants; the studio was full. There were twelve stages alone on the Gower "home" lot and, in addition, another twenty-two stages on the Cahuenga Boulevard and Culver City lots. So between stages, ancillary support facilities such as dubbing and music scoring stages, cutting rooms, construction facilities, lighting equipment, and offices, rental shows brought a great deal of money to Desilu and helped pay the overhead. And if you chose not to reinvest any of the rental money into studio upkeep, as bottom-line-minded Desilu chose not to do, it's a great cash business—that is, unfortunately, until the studio begins to decay and falls apart at the seams.

Walking with Bob, I recalled my attempt to have the studio install an additional power line in a building for a window air-conditioning unit. It was needed to prevent one of the *Star Trek* pilot writers from sweating to death during the hot summer months.

"Sorry, Herb, this just isn't possible," I was told by the studio electrician. "The buildings are so old that the termites have eaten all the wood studs in the walls. Christ, the only thing holding up the building is the old stucco wall. Now, if we break into that stucco wall to run in a new power line or to install an air-conditioning unit, dimes'll get you doughnuts the goddam building will just come crashing down." The decision: buy a desk fan for the writer.

We needed space for *Star Trek* and *Mission: Impossible.* The studio couldn't throw out *The Danny Thomas Show, The Dick van Dyke Show, Ben Casey, My Three Sons, Gomer Pyle, I Spy, The Andy Griffith Show,* and *Hogan's Heroes.* That's a battle I knew I'd lose. There's no way Lucy's attorney, Mickey Rudin, would support me on that. The tenants paid cash. We'd have to make do with the leftovers.

Bob and I made a quick appraisal. Each series needed at least ten offices. *Star Trek* was big on special effects and required a separate optical-effects staff. Neither show took place in Hollywood or in any one big city. *Star Trek* needed a different planet each week, strange sets, strange costumes, strange props, strange people, and things that fly. *Mission* needed the back streets of Hong Kong one week and the Bank of England the next, only to be followed by a rug bazaar in Casablanca and a Romanian prison. "Tough to find a Casablanca rug bazaar on Melrose Avenue in Hollywood," Bob and I agreed. "Maybe even tougher to find planet Alpha 7 and its eleven moons."

Both series needed special makeup, ranging from Leonard Nimoy's ears to Marty Landau's complicated makeups, from warlike outer-space humanoids to scruffy alien creatures that suck salt out of people. That means a massive and complex makeup department. Additionally, all the sets, all the props, all the wardrobe for *Star Trek* had to be designed and manufactured. Common sense dictates you can't rent anything that doesn't yet exist. *Star Trek* needed a minimum of two large sound stages, so we could build planet Alpha 7 and hang all eleven moons up high. And another smaller stage was needed for new sets that would be used only once.

Bob Justman made his point. "Easy for a writer to casually jot down 'Mr. Spock picks up the phone.' Just where do we find this phone—on Venus? And sound effects? What does it sound like when you departicalize people? We'll have to invent every single sound effect. We'll have to invent every single everything."

I had an idea. "Hey, RJ, while we're at it, let's invent some money to pay for all this stuff."

Another thought struck Bob. "Wait a second! We forgot one important thing, the most important thing. We actually have to make these shows! We weren't able to produce the pilots on schedule, and those were pilots! Meaning we had extra time to shoot and almost enough money. How are we going to make twenty-six episodes of *Star Trek* and twenty-six episodes of *Mission: Impossible* on budget with only six-day shooting schedules?"

I thought a moment. "Easy, Bob, we just do it. And besides, because we have a better deal with CBS, I think we can get seven days for *Mission.*" (For some strange reason, my reply tickled the hell out of him.)

The more Bob ticked off the out-of-the-norm ingredients of the shows, *Star Trek* in particular, the more he convinced himself there's no more excitement in the world than challenging the impossible. I'd put together a group of aggressive young professionals who loved to surmount obstacles, who didn't know how to quit or what it meant to fail. What frightened me was, even with all the deficit-financing money in the world, was this small studio creatively and physically capable of turning out two quality one-hour shows each and every week?

We tried out for the big leagues when we made the pilots. Now were playing in the big leagues with big-time series. You just don't call the network and tell them, "Listen, guys, forget the advertisers, all your publicity, the listing in *TV Guide,* and the millions of viewers—something unforeseen came up here at the studio and we're not finished with the next *Star Trek* episode. So could you do us a small favor? Please put on something else this Thursday, because we won't be ready. Thanks a lot, guys; we'll try to be ready for next week!"

To make matters worse, NBC subsequently advised us they'd placed the show on Canadian television. "One small detail," they added. "Canada will be televising the series one week before the States. We hope this doesn't give you guys any delivery problems." (In a twist of fate, in order to meet the Canadian schedule, an almost wet-from-the-lab 16 mm print of each week's episode was air-freighted to NBC in New York, hustled by messenger across town to the ABC facilities on West 66th Street, and then fed into Canada via NBC's competitor's transmission lines—an unusual practice for those, or any other, times.)

I had the series order from NBC. I had a die-hard group of professionals to make the series. I had a lot of sleepless nights. Now all I needed was the financial support of the studio elders, the very conservative Desilu loyalists. This would all start, and end, with America's favorite redhead, Lucille Ball herself.

The boardroom was a woody affair that was part of Desi Arnaz's domain, the palatial offices of the man who built Desilu. As mentioned earlier, when Oscar Katz joined Desilu, Lucy gave the offices to him. A year later, after Oscar departed, I expected to move in. Gary Morton convinced Lucy to take it herself. "Just keep Solow out of it" was the apparent slogan for Gary's campaign. Studio scuttlebutt was that Gary actually wanted it for himself. I didn't really care, having found a comfortable home down the hall that I shared with the spirit of George Murphy. Lucy used her big office only on Fridays, when she wasn't rehearsing or shooting her show. She used it to play Madame President, but seemed uneasy sitting behind the desk and even more uneasy playing the role.

Two board members—Lucy's personal attorney, famed Hollywood lawyer Milton "Mickey" Rudin, and Lucy's tax attorney, Art Manella, head of the firm of Irell and Manella—had to come from offices off the lot, so of course they were on time. The studio locals—Program VP Oscar Katz, Financial VP Edwin Holly, Production VP Argyle Nelson, Lucy's brother Fred Ball, Business Affairs VP Bernie Weitzman, and President Lucy—drifted in.

Mickey Rudin was the best of the lot when it came to an understanding of

From the collection of Robert H. Justman

Bob and Jackie Justman at the annual Desilu weekend party in spring 1967.

the television business, its character, and its practicalities. And he was never one without a position. You always knew where you stood with Mickey, and in a business that ofttimes features hypocrites and blatant liars, he was a blessing. More important, Mickey always had Lucy's best interests at heart. Some of the other board members decided issues on how such decisions would affect them; Mickey decided issues on the basis of how they would affect Lucy.

Without Mickey's support, Lucy's new husband and her loyal and ancient camp followers wouldn't let me on the lot to use the men's room. So I tried never to disappoint him.

Art Manella was a highly respected professional who purposely kept himself above the political infighting, preferring to concentrate on the issues at hand.

Oscar Katz was my boss. But his relationship with Lucy and the board soured later as they realized Oscar's lack of studio experience made him only a titular chief operating officer. (This problem came to a head many months later. Several board members advised that Oscar had presented a report, a mathematical formula based on the production of multiple series and the prediction of the ensuing profits. It seemed so impractical and blue-sky to the powers-that-be that they soon nodded him away. I'd heard rumors earlier that day, and when I went to see Oscar to find out what was happening, he was already gone. That same day,

Lucy with second husband Gary Morton.

Mickey Rudin called me over to his offices, where he confirmed the news. Mickey gave me a new contract and the Vice President of Programs title. I officially became creative head of the studio. Oscar was gone; he was a good friend, but his actual involvement with *Star Trek* was minimal. Nevertheless, in interviews since then, he greatly exaggerated his involvement with *Star Trek.* Oscar's role as titular head of Desilu is documented; any record of his direct involvement with *Star Trek* has yet to be found.)

Financial VP Edwin Holly was a very smart street fighter disguised as a mild-mannered accountant. He used numbers to forward his own agenda. But his efforts were obvious to me and, as such, self-defeating.

Argyle Nelson was an old-line Hollywood production guy. You know the type: "The director is insane, the writer should always be locked up, all actors steal wardrobe, and there's something subversive about producers who graduated from college." He referred to Bruce Geller as "that crazy college kid." He was annoyed that he couldn't accuse Gene Roddenberry of being a college graduate, so Argie put down Gene by referring to him as "that crazy ex-cop." When word got back to Gene, it caused bad blood between the two men. After that, Argie was on the receiving end of Gene's continued finger-pointing as to the production ineptness of the studio. And Argie was well aware of Gene's flaunted relationship with actress Majel Barrett. Because Gene Roddenberry was a married man with two daughters, this greatly offended the straitlaced Desilu executive.

Lucy's brother, Fred Ball, had an office on the lot, but no one really knew what he did. The studio rumor mill said Fred was in charge of real estate, as he ran Lucy's Indian Wells Hotel and Country Club near Palm Springs, where all Desilu employees gathered for their annual company weekend (see page 103).

Bernard Weitzman was the only long-time Desilu executive who had the courage to support Solow's "radical" group. A true Desi Arnaz friend and loyalist, he was thrilled with the rebirth of Desilu and helped dramatically to enable us to achieve that renaissance.

There were actually three Lucys with whom I dealt. There was Lucy Ricardo, the scatterbrained redhead who delighted audiences around the world. There was President Lucille Ball, promoted by others as the hard-driving business tycoon who turned a few bucks into a major Hollywood institution. And there was the real Lucy, the former showgirl from Jamestown, New York, the surprisingly decent, reserved, and dedicated comedienne who was happiest on her Stage 12, starring in and supervising *The Lucy Show.*

The old guard made its position quite clear. It wasn't a difficult position for them to take, considering the high costs of both pilots. And their position was, simply put, "Don't let Solow and the rest of the crazies loose. Things are good. Things could get worse. If it ain't broke, don't fix it. Don't give the inmates the key to the asylum."

Before the board meeting I'd laid it out to the owner of Desilu: "You'll always have a show, Lucy, with the same actors, the same staff, the same people to write and direct. Everyone will be happy. The studio will keep renting space to other shows. So fame isn't a problem, and money isn't a problem. But wouldn't you like to rebuild Desilu's prestige, importance, and value as a major player? Wouldn't it be great to have two exciting and successful Desilu television shows on the air?"

So it was up to the third Lucy. Forget about Lucy Ricardo's "Vita-meata-veg-emins" and those chocolates coming down the conveyor belt and Lucy crushing grapes with her feet. Forget Ricky Ricardo and his "Ba-ba-loo" band. Don't even think about Fred and Ethel Mertz. Forget all the fluff about President Lucy, the brilliant executive, the Hollywood mogul. On this day, she could be the real Lucy, the one who respected talent, hated confrontation, and held the future of a lot of people in her grasp. "Say 'yes,' Lucy, and we'll all go to work."

Lucy nodded. And we all went to work. The inmates had the key to the asylum.

Part of NBC's eight-page ad in *TV Guide*'s 1966–1967 Fall Preview issue.

ACT TWO

The First Season: A Struggle For Life

Courtesy NBC/Globe

9

Another Fine Mess

HERB: When little Virginia O'Hanlon wanted to find out whether there was a Santa Claus, she wrote to the *New York Sun* because "if it's in the *Sun,* it has to be so." And the editor told her, "Yes, Virginia, there is a Santa Claus."

We had our own *New York Sun.* It was called *Daily Variety,* and when columnist Dave Kaufman wrote that *Star Trek* and *Mission: Impossible* were on the network fall schedules, "it had to be so." There was a Santa Claus. It felt great to be publicly stamped APPROVED, to proceed directly to GO and collect $200, to watch Desilu return to the winner's circle. But the light of our success had not really showered down on everyone. Worrywart Bob Justman continued to accept the news with mixed emotions—joy and fear—joy that he'd be the Associate Producer in the strange new world of *Star Trek,* and fear that he was going where no Associate Producer had ever gone before.

"Smile, RJ, you're on *Candid Camera,*" I called out to Justman as he swept into my office.

"I am smiling," Bob replied as he frowned, nervously twirled his mustache, and sank onto my couch. "Could you really get me on *Candid Camera*?"

"Sorry, since you helped get us into this mess, you have to stay. I'm not easy like Leslie Stevens."

RJ got down to business. "Argie wants us to use only his 'key' people. Some of them haven't got the skills for our show. Gene and I don't want them."

"Just ignore him. Anything else?"

"Yes. Bill Heath, the Postproduction head? He wants us to hire no more than three teams of cutters, max. We'll need four if we're going to make our airdate schedule."

"Ignore him, too. Anything else?"

"Yes. Both Argie and Bill are going to go over your head to Lucy because you keep ignoring them."

"Actually, RJ, they'll be going to Gary Morton. He'll go to Lucy and wind her up until she goes to Mickey Rudin and complains about Solow and his crazies."

"And?

"And Mickey will once again tell her to 'leave Solow alone.' RJ, in the long run, ignoring them will be the path of least resistance."

"Oh," said Bob, and he left to go about staffing the series his way.

But while Justman was feeling less pressure from the Desilu old guard, Roddenberry was feeling increased pressure from NBC Burbank. Several middle-management executives took umbrage at his hostility toward standard network policies and procedures that all NBC series were asked to accept. He decided the best way to deflate the uprising and "lighten up" NBC was with humor—his kind of "humor."

A rough draft of the tongue-in-cheek but poorly received telegram Roddenberry sent to NBC V.P. Grant Tinker.

GRANT TINKER ℅ MORT WERNER
NBC
30 ROCKEFELLER PLAZA
NEW YORK 20 NEW YORK

IN CASE THERE ARE STILL HOLES IN ~~THE~~ NBC SCHEDULE, AM WORKING ON SOME ALTERNATES ~~PROGRAMMING~~. THE FIRST IS MARVEL MOTHER, A SWEET LITTLE OLD LADY WHO, WHEN DANGER THREATENS, CAN STEP INTO A PHONE BOOTH AND ~~KAZAAM~~ KAZAAM! SHE BECOMES A SWINGING BUXOM BLONDE. ~~THE SECOND ALTERNATE,~~ ANOTHER, IN COLLABORATION WITH HERB SOLOW, IS ~~TENTATIVELY TITLED~~ WONDER RABBI, WHO ~~CAN~~ ~~KAZAM~~ KAZAAMS INTO AN EPISCOPAL MINISTER WHOSE REVERSED WHITE COLLAR IS ACTUALLY A ~~DEADLY~~ STEEL BOOMERANG WHICH HE THROWS WITH DEADLY ACCURACY. ~~JUST A SAMPLE. LET ME KNOW IF~~ AND WE HAVE MORE! SHOULD WE ~~SHOULD~~ KEEP THINKING?

Gene Roddenberry

HERB: Unbeknownst to me, Gene sent what he thought was a humorous telegram to NBC Vice President Grant Tinker:

I asked Lydia to get Grant Tinker on the phone after receiving a copy of the telegram and talking briefly with Gene. While Lydia was dialing, Grant called.

"This is the creative force behind our most expensive new series? What's with Roddenberry?"

"I was just calling you on the other line to explain. Grant, I knew nothing about the telegram. Roddenberry thought it was cute."

"All we need is for Mort [Werner] and Don Durgin [NBC Sales Vice President] to come across amateur-night stuff like this. I sure hope you're backing Roddenberry up with good creative people."

I assured Grant we were and called Gene. We reestablished our original arrangement. Others on the series would deal with NBC on routine matters; I'd deal with NBC on policy matters and problems. Gene promised to stay away from NBC.

But he never learned one of the most important maxims of Publilius Syrus, "Never promise more than you can perform." Gene's next involvement with NBC management haunted *Star Trek* for all three years of its production.

With Roddenberry concentrating on stories and scripts, Bob Justman, though credited as Associate Producer, took over most of the producer functions: budgeting and costs, show scheduling, casting, set and costume design, film editing, music and sound effects, hiring of directors, composers, and crew members—the list was endless. Now he could staff the show with the people he wanted.

Foremost among the key people was Walter "Matt" Jefferies, who had the title of Set Designer on both pilots. (Later, Justman took on the Art Directors Union and eventually succeeded in getting Matt a "Production Designer" credit.) With the visual style of *Star Trek* often due as much to lack of money as to creativity, Matt's ingenuity and discipline would be invaluable in the series.

Since Justman could now offer a full season of employment, he was able to entice Fred Phillips to return to handle makeup. They'd need his talents to help create unusual alien beings, not to mention an endless supply of pointed ears for Spock, described by Justman as "use 'em once and throw 'em away."

BOB: And Bill Theiss would continue to create the new exotic costumes required for each episode. He'd also rework the crew uniforms to make them more attractive—or peculiar, depending upon your point of view. Gene didn't want his heroes to wear holsters for their "phaser" pistols or communicators, so Theiss came up with the solution: A piece of black Velcro was sewn onto the black uniform pants legs, and a corresponding piece was glued onto the props. The idea worked great. However, every time a communicator was unlimbered or a pistol was drawn, a loud ripping noise sounded when the two pieces of Velcro were separated. At

Courtesy Martin Nuetzel

Actress Leslie Parrish, wearing one of Bill Theiss's exotic creations.

first, it was disconcerting as everyone on the set stopped work to see whose trousers had torn.

On the financial side of things, Desilu cost estimator Bernie Widin became so helpful in the budgeting and cost-control process that Justman obtained a screen credit for him as Production Supervisor.

BOB: Once more, we were faced with the problem of finding the right cameraman to film our show. As usual, the really good ones were already working on established series. The few who were available commanded too high a salary for cash-poor Desilu, or else they were on the downhill leg of a less than illustrious career. I put the word out that I was looking for someone young, energetic, and daring. Soon after, famed feature film cameraman Harry Stradling, Sr., stopped in, accompanied by Jerry Finnerman, one of his camera operators, who, I learned twenty-seven years later, was also his godchild.

Harry wanted me to give his protégé a break. "He'll make a great cameraman, Bob."

The candidate stood there, mute, sweating, trembling. When spoken to, he became so frightened that I saw a lot of white of eye. I asked Jerry why he thought we should hire him: "I'd be taking one helluva chance. I believe you're a good camera operator. You know how to follow the action and frame each shot properly at the same time; otherwise, Harry wouldn't have you. But I don't know if you can be a leader on the set, whether you can run not only your camera crew but all the grips and electricians too, whether you can light any scene quickly and well, whether you can create the sort of dramatic mood lighting that a show like *Star Trek* demands. What would happen if you fall on your face? Are you sure you can cut it?"

It took him a while to respond. His throat was dry and he had trouble speaking. In a choked voice, he said, "I can cut it. Just tell me what you want to see and I'll give it to you. Anything you want."

"Bob, you know I wouldn't bring Jerry to you if I didn't think he was ready," said Stradling.

It was apparent to me that Finnerman was desperate to do the show. All things being equal, I felt it was worth taking a chance. Fact is, I thought it would be only a small chance. With the legendary Stradling as his teacher, he had to be good. Always believing in giving young talent a break, I would rather have someone who made a few mistakes but was really cranked up to excel rather than some tired and blasé veteran. I told Jerry I'd let him know, soon.

It didn't take long for me to check my sources. Director Jim Goldstone gave me a thumbs-up. "His dad was a special-effects cameraman. Jerry and I played on the same high school football team. He was the kicker and I "held" for him. Once, he missed the ball and almost broke my wrist, instead. But otherwise he's on the ball. I've done some shows with him, and he's a great camera operator. I think he's ready to move up."

After that, I walked across the hall to see Roddenberry. "Gene, I've found a guy who's still a camera operator. I believe he's got the stuff and I want to bump him up to be our First Cameraman."

"What do you want me say, Bob?"

"Say 'yes,' Gene."

Without hesitation, Gene replied, "Yes. Bob, if you want him, I want him."

That day, Gerald Perry Finnerman was given a new job and a new life as *Star Trek*'s Director of Photography. He was humble for a while, but later he would gain ego along with self-confidence.

To make sure Finnerman would give the show the kind of look I envisioned—dramatic lighting and camera angles that were creatively unique—I encouraged Jerry to free himself from the tired techniques of the past. "We're all in outer space, Jerry, and we're in color. NBC claims to be the first full-color network, so let's prove it for them. When you light the sets, throw wild colors in—magenta, red, green, any color you can find—especially behind the actors when they're in a close shot. Be dramatic. In fact, go overboard. Backlight the women and make them more beautiful. Take some chances. Nobody can tell you that's not the way the future will look. How can they? They ain't been there yet."

Jerry did just what was asked of him. Any doubts about hiring him disappeared when I saw the results of his work on the second series episode he photographed, "Mudd's Women." Guest stars Karen Steele, Maggie Thrett, and Susan Denberg, good-looking in real life, looked even more radiantly lovely and ravishing as they worked their magic upon Captain Kirk and crew—after Jerry worked his magic upon the three actresses.

Argyle Nelson wanted the show to be made on the home lot in Hollywood so he could "keep a close eye on the production." Justman agreed, wholeheartedly. The facilities and equipment were better at the Hollywood plant, and besides that, the *Star Trek* team would pretty much operate on its own, no matter where the show was shot.

BOB: But first, we had to accomplish the move. All the so-called permanent starship sets had to be removed from Culver City and transported to their new home in Hollywood. Unfortunately, we had discovered during filming that these "permanent" sets were much too permanent. Ideally, motion picture sets are designed to be flexible. In order to accommodate whatever camera angles are needed, walls are usually designed to be removable or "wild," so that there will be enough room for the cameras, floor lights, grip equipment, and shooting crew.

The *Enterprise* Bridge set used in the pilots looked great on film, but it was awkward to work in. Not enough of it was wild, and this lack of flexibility slowed our progress to a crawl. If we were going to make our shows in six days each, I knew we had to make some big changes.

After the sets were trucked over, I asked Matt to make every section of the *Enterprise* Bridge really wild. Matt and Roy Long, his construction supervisor, went to work.

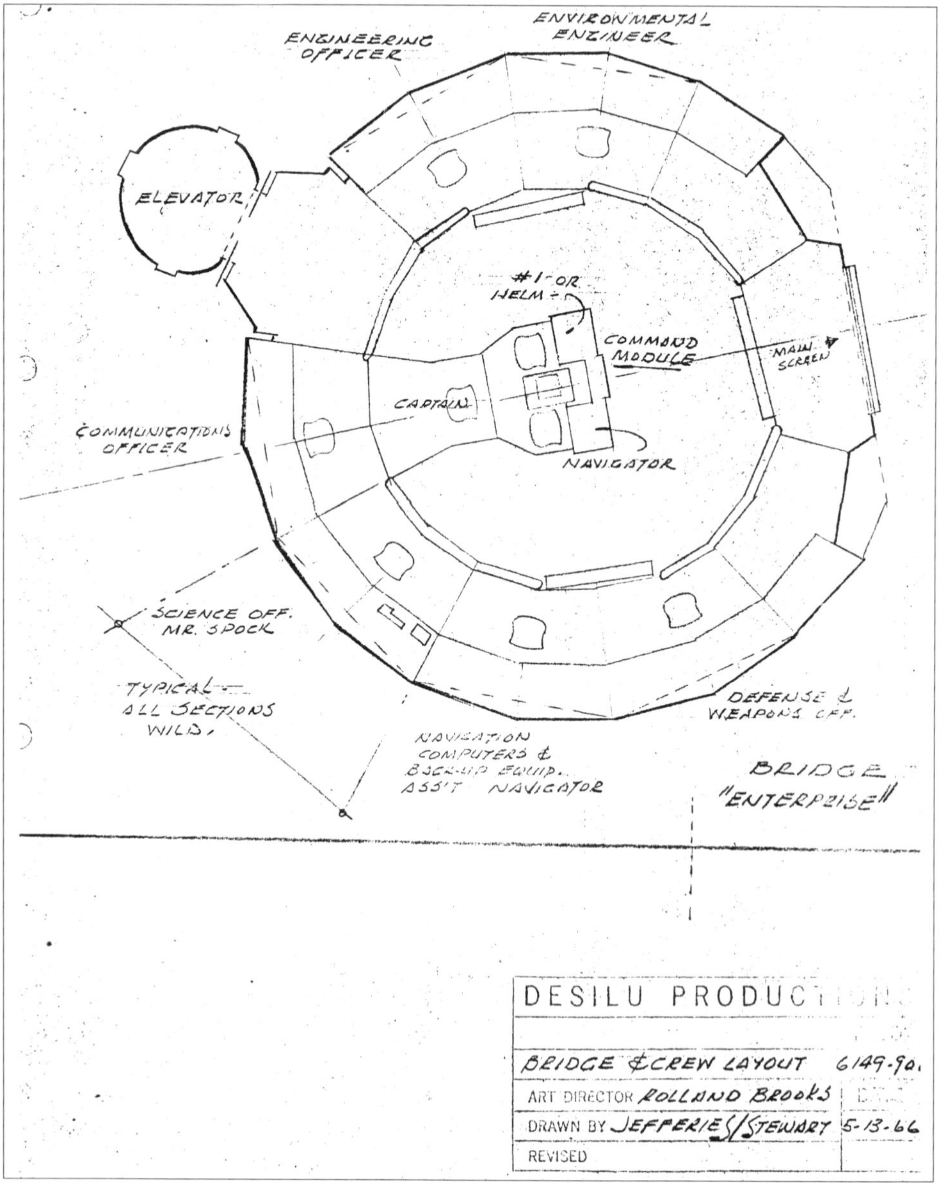

Original plan of the *U.S.S. Enterprise* Bridge set. Dated 5/13/66.

Courtesy Paramount Pictures

Three different views on the Planet set, which also used forced perspective.

Since the *Enterprise* Bridge set was essentially a complete circle with the large viewing screen in front and consoles around the rear circumference, it had made sense to divide the set into a number of pie-shaped sections. Each section was then further divided into three pieces stacked one atop the other.

The bottom piece contained the console section where the actors sat; it had wheels below to facilitate being moved. The middle piece contained the various readout screens above the console, and the top piece contained large static visuals and built-in overhead lighting "cans." The middle pieces could be pulled out without disturbing the upper sections, which were anchored to the lighting scaffold directly above and surrounding the set. Jim Rugg, the inventive new special-effects supervisor who had been hired for the series on director James Goldstone's recommendation, rewired each of the three sections separately so that no matter which piece or section of the bridge was moved, the remaining complicated and delicate electronic readouts could function undisturbed.

Courtesy Paramount Pictures

The "forced perspective" Engineering set.

To construct all the pieces of the new set, Roy Long built one complete three-piece section that was then used to make a mold from which all the other sections were cast, using a new, lightweight foam plastic. *Lightweight* was purely a relative term; the support framework was still made of wood. Compared to the wooden sections, the pieces were in fact lighter. Matt Jefferies and Roy Long had come up with an ingenious solution to a difficult problem.

The moving of the sets from the Culver City lot to Desilu's Stage 9 in Hollywood was the easy part. Making those sets shootable and positioning them all on one stage was another matter. Before the move, Jefferies and Justman labored for well over a week, spotting tracings of the various permanent sets on a scale layout of the stage floor before they agreed upon a final arrangement. Making use of every available square foot of space was of prime importance. And when necessary, some sets could be "folded" to make filming of others easier.

Their planning worked out successfully, and the layout remained the same for all three years of the series.

Justman and Jefferies squeezed enough money from the budget to pay for one major new permanent set, the engine room of the *Starship Enterprise.* Knowing that a large set was required and hurting for lack of stage space, Justman turned to forced perspective once more. Jefferies designed the set with a heavy screen separating the foreground work area from the ship's massive engines in the background. Behind the screen, the engine conduits were large closest to camera and tapered radically to a much smaller size in the rear. The film crew used pulsating reddish lighting in the background, which "emanated" from the energy generated by what appeared to be an enormous power plant—just so long as it was photographed from the proper angle.

Matt Jefferies' last big task was to satisfy Justman's request for a Planet set on Stage 10, next door, that could be used to simulate alien planet exteriors. Jefferies built a planet surface consisting of tons of sand, dozens of bogus rocks that could be moved easily (depending on who moved them and who was watching), and another forced perspective, a range of mini–mountains that encircled the set on three sides. Examples of the technique can be found in such episodes as "Man Trap," "The Deadly Years," "Amok Time," and "Metamorphosis."

As long as the camera was kept low, the mountains behind the actors looked realistic. Justman cautioned all directors to keep the camera lens well below eye height, but sometimes a director either forgot, or elected to ignore, this stricture, and the actors appeared taller than the mountains behind them, throwing the viewers' "suspension of disbelief" into total disarray.

Remembering his unsatisfactory experience with the green-painted sky on the first pilot, Justman proposed a method to color the sky of the Planet set

One of Matt Jefferies' oddly shaped doorways.

Courtesy Stephen Edward Poe

without the need to paint a new sky each time. A neutral white backing, hung high from the rafters, surrounded the Planet set and was illumined by permanently placed lamps. The lighting passed through colored "gels" and created planet skies of various hues that were selected for each episode.

BOB: No painters, no paint, no problem. Well, one problem; the colored gels either faded or burned up after a short while in front of a hot light. Even so, painting with light was still a lot cheaper than painting with paint. And the odor of the burning gels sure helped clear the sinuses.

Matt Jefferies' ingenuity paid off in uniquely creative ways. To give the impression that Captain Kirk and crew were really beaming down to "strange new worlds" and "alien planets," doorways were never rectangular; they were always triangular or trapezoidal or somehow weirdly shaped. Doors never swung open; instead, they slid up or sideways. They didn't slide down because that would entail excavating a hole in the stage floor, and financially that was out of the question.

Due to Roddenberry's continued prodding, Jefferies designed the ship's sickbay to include fully monitored hospital beds that automatically kept track of the afflicted patient's condition and displayed the readouts such as heartbeat, blood pressure, temperature, and respiration, much as modern-day intensive-care modules do today.

Two early publicity photos. Note the "not quite there" costumes.

From the collection of Robert H. Justman

BOB: One of the ideas for *Star Trek* that didn't pan out was the "great phaser caper." During preparation for the second pilot, a toy manufacturer had designed and built some phaser weapons "on spec." In return, if the series sold, the manufacturer wanted to merchandise toy replicas of these props. I was thrilled: something for nothing! But Gene finally nixed the design, and the deal fell through. Unfortunately, during the intervening period, NBC Publicity, unaware we had no rights to use the spec phasers, shot a photo session with Bill Shatner, Leonard Nimoy, and Grace Lee Whitney holding the "illegal" weapons. NBC used the photos in its "Sales Brochure." The weapons were never used in the series; the toy manufacturer never found out. Or if he did, we never heard from him.

We knew it was a total waste of time to go to a prop rental house or a store to buy our props; such things just didn't exist. As with everything else on *Star Trek,* we had to build whatever we needed, including props, wardrobe, sets, and set dressing (furniture). We were faced with having to design the much-needed and nonexistent phaser pistols. Time was short. Once more, Matt Jefferies came to the rescue. Soon, with input from Gene, he came up with a design for a small phaser weapon that could snap into a larger phaser pistol when added range and power were required. Part one of the problem was solved. (We thought it was the easiest part, but were we ever wrong!)

Then I called Wah Chang and Gene Warren at Project Unlimited, the prop design and manufacturing house that had supplied *The Outer Limits* with many of its special props and creatures. They had designed and constructed the Talosians' heads in the first pilot and would later create the Balok effigy for "The Corbomite Maneuver," the salt-sucking monster for "Man Trap," and the reptilian Gorn adversary fought by Kirk in "Arena." In *Star Trek*'s second season, their most beloved creatures were the prolific, but cute, furry little critters in "The Trouble with Tribbles."

One of Wah Chang's communicators.

Courtesy Bob Burns

Gene and Wah had a good working arrangement. Gene handled the business end of things, and Wah, an extremely talented sculptor, designed and fabricated whatever wild creatures or props were needed.

Wah Chang also designed and built the famous flip-open communicators used by Kirk and company when they beamed down from the ship to the planet below, and the medical tricorder used by Doctor McCoy. So part two of the problem was solved. (Or so we thought. Wrong again!)

In order to give work to as many studio departments as possible, the phaser pistol designs were handed over to the Desilu "prop shop," where special items were fabricated. This attempt to "keep it in the family" caused problems. The shop was able to deliver one barely acceptable "hero" working model phaser (suitable for close-up photography), but it took much too long and cost much too much. And none of the people working there could produce accurate working copies. They could cast a clumsy "dummy" copy, but they couldn't fabricate anything even remotely complicated.

Roddenberry looked at the results and said, "These are . . . uh . . . uh . . . totally . . . uh . . . unacceptable."

I was brief. I said, "Junk 'em!"

Gene turned to me. "What'll we do, Bob?"

"I'll take care of it, Gene. Just write some scripts fast. We're going to need them."

I called a meeting with Wah Chang and Gene Warren. I struck a deal and gave them Matt's detailed working drawings, and they departed, with Wah already planning how he would execute Matt's phaser pistol design, in addition to building the two other props. He finished everything perfectly and made several beautiful hero models of all three props, and all the dummy mockups that I knew the show would require. And that's when the phasers really hit the fan.

The studio's propmakers complained to their union, and their union complained to the studio that the new props couldn't be used; Wah Chang was not a union member. They insisted that we use only props built by union members at the studio. Ernest Scanlon, Desilu's Labor Relations Director, relayed the news to me. "But they're no f.....g good!" I yelled. "We already spent $7,000 on those abortions, and they can't even be photographed!" (In the sixties, $7,000 for one item was a huge sum for a TV show's prop budget.)

I was really pissed. So Ernie tried to help. He suggested that Wah Chang join the union and become an ex post facto employee of the studio. Then everything

Wah Chang's design sketch for the tricorder.

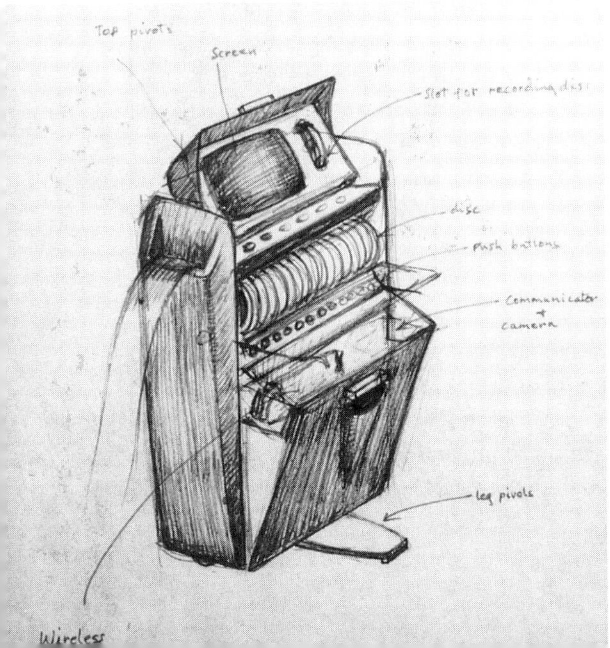

A Desilu receipt for two of Wah Chang's "ready-made" props.

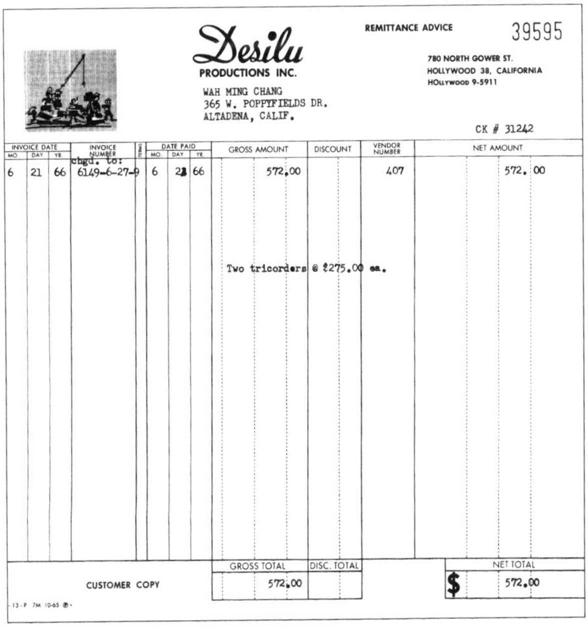
Desilu
PRODUCTIONS INC.
REMITTANCE ADVICE 39595
780 NORTH GOWER ST.
HOLLYWOOD 38, CALIFORNIA
HOllywood 9-5911
WAH MING CHANG
365 W. POPPYFIELDS DR.
ALTADENA, CALIF.
CK # 31242

INVOICE DATE MO.	DAY	YR.	INVOICE NUMBER	TERMS	DATE PAID MO.	DAY	YR.	GROSS AMOUNT	DISCOUNT	VENDOR NUMBER	NET AMOUNT
6	21	66	chgd. to: 6149-6-27-9		6	22	66	572.00		407	572.00

Two tricorders @ $275.00 ea.

CUSTOMER COPY

GROSS TOTAL	DISC. TOTAL	NET TOTAL
572.00		$ 572.00

13-P 7M 10-65

Courtesy Wah Chang

Courtesy Wah Chang

One of Wah Chang's tricorders.

would be legal—after the fact, but legal. And he could design and build anything we wanted in the future. Right?

Wrong! The union wouldn't let Wah Chang join. Talk about catch-22. If Wah could join, the union would be satisfied. But afraid that this talented artist might take work away from some of their members, they wouldn't let him join—which made the union even more satisfied.

The union had played hardball, so I decided to play hardball, too. "We didn't hire Wah. He designed and built these things himself, independently of us." (It was only a little fib. He had designed and built the "tricorder" and communicator props. But definitely not independently.) I continued, "And when we happened to see them, we liked them so much that we bought them outright, on the spot."

We were legal. Problem solved. Or so I thought. A year later, prior to our second season, the same union problem erupted all over again. So we continued to buy "ready-made" props from non-union member Wah Chang.

When you think of *Star Trek* props, you have to think of Irving Feinberg, the show's beloved property master, a special crew member who actually came from Desilu. Necessity was the mother of invention on *Star Trek.* Someone would yell, "Props, we need that new 'Feinberg' for the next scene," and Irving (usually dressed in his trademark baggy shorts that displayed his knobby knees) or his assistant, Al Jacoby, would come running with it. Since no one could ever remember the names of the various gadgets Irving put together, they were all called "Feinbergs."

When a new prop was needed, Irving had to create it. Doctor McCoy's "scalpel" was one of a pair of slim triangular Swedish-modern salt and pepper shakers that Irving bought in the May Company basement. After "operating" on his patient, McCoy would use the same device to seamlessly suture the incision.

McCoy's medical scanner was a tiny aluminum cylinder in which special effects man Jim Rugg installed a small motor that rotated a goofus little dial. The good doctor would pass the device over the body of a prostrate cast member while the gizmo's battery-powered motor ground away, courtesy of the sound-effects editors. I always claimed that McCoy could diagnose anything with the thing: heart rate, blood pressure, and even pregnancy or ingrown toenails.

HERB: Of course, if the prostrate actor wore a red tunic, he'd be declared dead. Since we couldn't kill off our cast regulars, new crewmen in red tunics portrayed by bit actors or stuntmen had to be the ones to die. Although three "red shirts" got clobbered in "The Apple," the show that holds the all-time record was "Obsession." Four of them bit the dust in that one, and two others were seriously injured. Killing red shirts became so much of a tradition that fans could always

Courtesy Paramount Pictures

Some unfortunate "red shirt" casualties from the episode "Obsession."

anticipate who was the next to go: "Uh-oh, there's a guy in a red tunic beaming down with Kirk, Spock, and McCoy. Guess who's going to get it?"

Sure enough, the guy in the red shirt would get clobbered, usually sooner rather than later, often at the end of the opening "teaser" so people would stay tuned in during the intervening commercial. "Bones" would unlimber the cylindrical gizmo, scan the victim's supine body while squinting at the readout from his medical tricorder, and then gravely announce his professional diagnosis. "He's dead, Jim."

Courtesy Greg Jein

10

And Then I Wrote

"Writers, we need writers, we need lots and lots of writers. . . ."

Not surprisingly, almost none of the following responded:

Writers who were unfamiliar with science fiction and fantasy: "What's a 'warp'?"

Writers not wanting to gamble on a new series that was more likely to be cancelled after sixteen episodes than not: "Where's my future?"

Writers who had little expectancy that the series would last long enough so their scripts could become summer repeats: "Where's the rerun money?"

Writers who understood that the "*Wagon Train* to the stars" concept for *Star Trek* scripts would be two or three times more time-consuming than actually writing *Wagon Train*: "Time is money. Include me out."

BOB: It was early March, 1966. NBC gave us a go-ahead at the same time they "picked up" all their other fall series. Unfortunately, due to *Star Trek*'s particular and peculiar writing demands, the day we were picked up we instantly fell three months behind schedule. We had no scripts, much less stories, but the September airdate to premiere our new series was immovable. Without scripts, we were nowhere. So not only did we need writers, we needed them yesterday.

And yesterday was already gone.

As is the practice with new television series seeking to hire writers, all major talent agencies, independent writers' agents, and Roddenberry's writer friends were notified that the successful second pilot was being screened. Roddenberry's explanation of the overall show would follow. Those writers who did show up expectantly filed into a Desilu projection room to see what all the fuss was about, to view the pilot for the series that was heralded as "television's ground-breaking series that will lead NBC into the new age of full-color broadcasting."

HERB: The *Star Trek* pilot screening was interrupted as the projection room door opened and closed repeatedly, sending shafts of light into the darkened room. "Boy, writers sure go to the bathroom a lot," muttered Roddenberry.

When the Desilu end credit flashed off the screen, and the lights came up, half the audience was gone. "You're right, Gene," I responded, "but the bathrooms are at their homes or offices."

Even after Roddenberry's explanation of the show and the following question and answer session, the *Star Trek* pilot wasn't a big hit with most writers. Though they were encouraged to submit story ideas, unfamiliarity with the form turned away most of them, even several of television's best dramatists who "had always wanted to take a crack at science fiction."

Roddenberry soon realized most of the writers who liked the show could not write it unless they were primed. Facing the problem head-on, he wrote a number of basic story premises—"springboards"—which he furnished to the people with whom he wanted to work. Though leading to later recriminations and Writers Guild arbitrations as to "who first had the idea and who did what to whom," Roddenberry's springboards put a number of writers to work.

HERB: All the rules about *Star Trek*'s future world existed mainly in Gene's mind. Unless he solved the familiarization problem, the number of acceptable scripts could have comfortably fit in a politician's heart. The reason was simple: Most journeyman television writers had absolutely no concept of what the series was and no idea what rules Roddenberry was talking about. And without these rules, believability would go right out the window—or, as the writers were soon to learn, out the view port.

Star Trek

Created by:
GENE RODDENBERRY

FIRST DRAFT
March 11, 1964

STAR TREK is...

A one-hour dramatic television series.

Action - Adventure - Science Fiction.

The first such concept with strong central lead characters plus other continuing regulars.

And while maintaining a familiar central location and regular cast, explores an anthology-like range of exciting human experience. For example, as varied as ...

THE NEXT CAGE. The desperation of our series lead, caged and on exhibition like an animal, then offered a mate.

THE DAY CHARLIE BECAME GOD. The accidental occurrence of infinite power to do all things, in the hands of a very finite man.

PRESIDENT CAPONE. A parallel world, Chicago ten years after Al Capone won and imposed gangland statutes upon the nation.

TO SKIN A TYRANNOSAURUS. A modern man reduced to a sling and a club in a world 1,000,000 B.C.

THE WOMEN. Duplicating a page from the "Old West"; hanky-panky aboard with a cargo of women destined for a far-off colony.

THE COMING. Alien people in an alien society, but something disturbingly familiar about the quiet dignity of one who is being condemned to crucifixion.

(See later pages for more)

Courtesy UCLA Theater Art-Special Collections Library

The first page of Gene Roddenberry's very first series proposal for *Star Trek*.

Thus was born "The *Star Trek* Writers' Guide." It was derived from Roddenberry's original series proposal, written while he was still at MGM and dated March 11, 1964, later rewritten by Roddenberry and, again, by Dorothy Fontana. In addition to containing complete descriptions of every important character in the show, the guide delineated everything a writer or director needed to know about this future universe: how far mankind had progressed, both scientifically and sociologically; how the "United Federation of Planets" was organized;

and how Starfleet, its combination space-exploration and military arm, functioned. (Photocopies of the original guide are still sold at science-fiction conventions.)

In the guide, the concepts of space travel and "warp speed," the transmutation of molecular components (the transporter effect), alien life, artificial gravity, the creation of thinking humanoids, and other ideas were presented.

As far back as the writing of the original first pilot script, Roddenberry sought advice from the scientific community. He was often in contact with Harvey P. Lynn, Jr., a scientist at the famous Rand Corporation "think tank" research facility.

On September 14, 1964, in a letter to Roddenberry, Lynn wrote: "Thanks for sending me a copy of 'The Cage'. [*sic*] It is highly exciting and hard to put down when you start to read it. I see right now that my association with you is going to cost me $400. For, when the series is shown, I'll just have to buy a color TV set." (His son, Harvey Lynn III, confirms that, indeed, a new color set was purchased.)

Lynn sent five pages of comments re: various items of scientific interest he found in the script. He also brought up a dramatic point:

> I have one final comment, which is also out of my bailiwick. Supposedly, anyone can operate the Transporter at will, even though he may be on a planet. . . . Do you really want to give him [the Captain] this capability? My reason for asking is this. Let's say that, in a future story, APRIL [later renamed Pike] is in some kind of real, not illusionary, danger. In this script, you are setting the precedent for him to just thumb his nose at the danger and high-tail it back to the *Enterprise*. What kind of fun is that? Where is the suspense? Or have I missed the point entirely?

Of course, he hadn't missed the point, and two days later Roddenberry responded, "Have your comments on 'The Cage' and find them very thoughtful and helpful. Am already making script changes which reflect them."

Later that same month, after proffering suggestions on Roddenberry's newly revised pilot script, Lynn sagely concluded his letter with a bit of tongue-in-cheek humor:

> To repeat a Cleopatra pun, "I am not prone to argue" about these points of mind which you did not choose to accept, for three good reasons. First, you are in the entertainment business and you are not making a pilot to show off scientific knowledge. If you have to bend science a little to make the story understandable and exciting, then by all means bend it. Second, my Air Force career conditioned me to give as good advice as possible to a superior officer. But if he chose another course of action or if he chose to use only part of my advice, that was his privilege. And thirdly, I'm quite satisfied with the batting average I have, as far as suggestions to you are concerned.
>
> What else can I do for you? How is the set coming along?

Roddenberry lost no time in taking him up on the offer. Lynn did a lot more for Roddenberry, who continued to contact his friend for technical advice during the production of both *Star Trek* pilots as well as the series, especially during the early part of its first season on the air.

(Desirous of rewarding Lynn for his contributions, Roddenberry wrote a memo to Herb Solow requesting a $50 "token" payment for the scientist. Solow responded: "Dear Eugene: I am in full accord with your memo and feel you should go ahead and hire your cousin Harvey Lynn as technical adviser . . . at $50 per show.")

Lynn was hired, for the first season only, and his $50 per-episode compensation was a small price to pay for suggestions that greatly benefited the development of the series concept.

But later, Lynn was advised by Roddenberry, "there will be little, if any, requirement for technical advice in *Star Trek*." Lynn wrote to Roddenberry: "Needless to say, I am disappointed, if this is true, as I enjoy the association very much, even if it has been nonproductive from your point of view."

But Lynn's contributions were very productive. In fact, they were pivotal as he described in that same letter:

> ITEM—It is now possible to telephone a computer and get a verbal answer to questions originating at more than 100 remote points. . . .
>
> Witness the "talking" computer aboard the starship *Enterprise*.
>
> ITEM—There has been developed an instrumented chair that monitors the vital functions of the body—pulse rate, respirations, heart sounds, and impulses—with no sensors attached to the person. The upholstery of the chair contains a series of electrical pickups which serve the same purpose as strapped-on electrodes. It takes the place of the stethoscope, electrocardiogram, and other clinical instruments. . . .

Jefferies's Sickbay set, which foretold scientific advances to come.

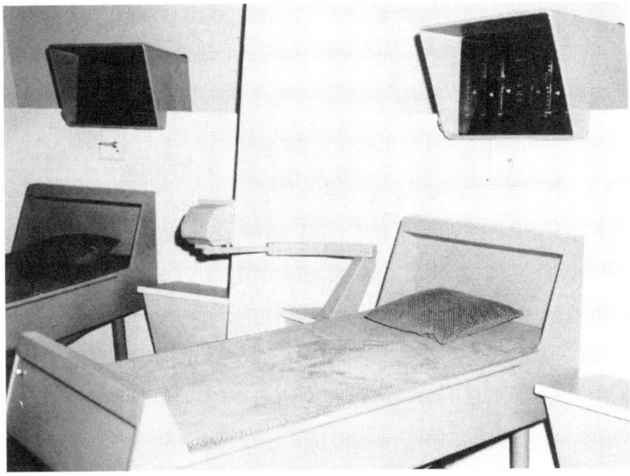

Courtesy Stephen Edward Poe

Witness the automated "medical readout" beds in sickbay aboard the *Starship Enterprise*.

Scientific fact notwithstanding, it was Roddenberry's intent to employ the world's most famous science-fiction writers and convert their futuristic ideas into the visual medium of dramatic television. The "future" belonged to them, to the science-fiction magazine writers and novelists, and to the sprinkling of science-fiction screenwriters, and Gene wanted to share their excitement.

Richard Matheson was the most experienced film writer and, as such, found *Star Trek* less of a challenge than did the others.

Several, like A. E. van Vogt, failed in their efforts to understand this plot- and budget-constrained medium. Van Vogt submitted a number of story premises that contained unusual ideas and characters. But his premises lacked story ideas and plot twists and contained elements that were unshootable.

Some of them—Robert Bloch, Ted Sturgeon, Richard Matheson, Jerry Sohl, Jerome Bixby, Norman Spinrad, George Clayton Johnson, and science fiction's incredibly angry young man, Harlan Ellison—actually wrote episodes for the show.

But to his dismay, Roddenberry soon discovered that some of the science-fiction writers had great difficulty with the transition. While their inventiveness ran amok with wild and exciting concepts, they were often incapable of developing them into believable dramas and do–able scripts. Unfortunately, they were both marvelous storytellers and lousy dramatists.

And unfortunately, Roddenberry had given himself yet another problem. Most of the science-fiction writer scripts had to be heavily rewritten—and he had to do it.

HERB: Ted Sturgeon was not only a brilliant science-fiction writer, he was a brilliant writer—period. And an evening with Ted and his wife at their Echo Park home in Los Angeles was always memorable. His vision of society was free of earthly constraints, ranging from the clothing-optional concept for his kids to "Let's go out to the cages and select the rabbit we'll cook for dinner."

This freedom from earthly constraints came into very sharp focus when Sturgeon turned his attention to writing for film. Several years after *Star Trek,* I'd optioned his famous novella *Killdozer* and made a deal with Universal to produce it as an ABC Movie of the Week. Part of the arrangement was that Ted would write the script. I gave Sturgeon an admonition: "Remember, Teddy, we have only a limited amount of production money from ABC, so focus on the character conflicts, okay?"

Sturgeon agreed and went to work converting his book into a screenplay. Some months later, he proudly handed me his adaptation. I was numbed reading the opening sequence: "a large flight of pterodactyls land on a lake." This sequence alone would cost the entire budget of the film.

"Teddy, listen. You were going to concentrate on character conflicts. What happened?"

"Nothing."

I quickly realized Ted's world did not permit him to accept that flying pterodactyls were out of the realm of character conflict. Needless to say, much judicious rewriting was needed before the film was made.

Several years later, after I left Desilu and set up shop at MGM, my fond memories of the science-fiction exotics got the better of me. I hired them. Actually, I hired four of them. Together. Teddy Sturgeon, Jerry Sohl, George Clayton Johnson, and Dick Matheson formed a creative writing company called The Green Hand. They had convinced me they would work together and create and write major science-fiction shows for MGM Television. It was one of the oddest collection of superior "nutcases ever housed in one room," as Fred Haughton, MGM TV's Head of Business Affairs defined them. Since The Green Hand was one company, they were entitled to only one office. And there they worked, day in and day out.

Word soon filtered throughout the studio regarding "them" and their work habits up in their second-floor office in the building next to the MGM East Gate. Executives strolled past my office making "crazy" signs and laughing. Eager to protect "them" from any further mockery, I invited several of the doubting executives to join me on a visit to The Green Hand. We walked up the old wooden stairs and entered. It was a sight to behold.

Dick Matheson sat at the desk; Jerry Sohl lay across the overstuffed chair; George Clayton Johnson lay on the floor staring at the ceiling; and Teddy Sturgeon stood on his head, his back leaning against the wall. And no one said anything. Nary a word. I said, "Hi." Nary a reaction. I repeated, "Hi." They continued doing their thing. I looked at the astonished visitors. "They're thinking," I explained.

Suddenly, Harlan Ellison, not a member of the team and an uninvited visitor, burst in and began haranguing The Green Hand.

"This one's *not* thinking," I explained and ushered the visitors back down the old wooden staircase.

There were two major results of the venture. First, The Green Hand miraculously created and wrote a marvelous treatment for a series. *Gestalt Team* was a most unusual giant step into the world of psychological fantasy wrapped around a commercial series format. Unfortunately, it was well ahead of its time "production-wise" and "cost-wise" as well as "thought-wise."

The second major result was their presentation to me of a plaster casting of a green hand. George Clayton Johnson still has *Gestalt Team,* and I still have the green hand.

Roddenberry eventually became friendly with a few more of America's most famous science-fiction writers: Isaac Asimov, Ray Bradbury, and Poul Anderson. But with their own schedules, wants, and goals, they never worked for him.

Near the end of the show's first season, however, Isaac Asimov became very influential in *Star Trek*'s future, and many years later, Ray Bradbury delivered an affectionate eulogy at Roddenberry's memorial service.

HERB: From the outset, believability was as major a concern as affordability. It didn't take Bob Justman long to realize that Captain Kirk and company could eas-

ily beam down to an unknown planet, breathe its noxious air—and die. Therefore, unless we clothed our galactic explorers in expensive, bulky spacesuits, the series would have a very short run!

And if they beamed down to a planet with less than normal gravity, Jim Rugg's effects crew would have to "fly" the actors around on wires, another very expensive and time-consuming procedure.

There had to be a rationale that retained the show's believability while allowing for its production on a television budget.

So Justman strongly recommended that the *Enterprise* voyage only to planets with Earthlike environments where chances were best that life forms similar to humans could have evolved. This idea mirrored the "Class M" concept that Roddenberry had previously described, but hadn't fully covered, in his March 11, 1964, sales proposal. Supposedly quoting "orders to Captain Robert M. April," he wrote: " . . . you will confine your landings and contacts to planets approximating earth-Mars [*sic*] conditions, life, and social orders."

In an April 12, 1966, memo, Justman expanded upon Roddenberry's original concept:

> As per my discussion with you and John D. F. Black this afternoon, following is a . . . direction our series should take.
>
> The *U.S.S. Enterprise* . . . has as its primary function the investigation of other worlds and civilizations, which are likely to be similar to our own. Our earth [*sic*] scientists at the time of our stories have plotted out certain areas within the galaxies which they say are likely to have . . . a chance of supporting life, as we know it. . . .
>
> Therefore, rather than having the *Enterprise* and its crew happen upon civilizations which we can relate to purely as a matter of chance, we have a situation where that is their primary function. I think that this idea will give our format a definite direction, which will be extremely useful to us in arriving at new stories.

BOB: Gene's "welcome" to the newest member of his *Star Trek* team is a much-retold story, but in later years I came to regret my participation, feeling that Gene had devised a prank that had more than a touch of sadistic humor. John D. F. Black was our first Associate Producer–Story Consultant.

Gene loved to throw office parties—usually to celebrate someone's birthday, but any excuse would do. The important thing was to take a break and party, party, party. Someone would buy a pineapple upside-down cake, we'd lay in some chips and dip and crack a bottle of bubbly, and everyone would have fun. An hour later, we'd go back to work. It never occurred to us to go home; we had a show to make.

While he liked Black, Gene felt he needed to relax a bit more. This was Black's first time ever "on staff," and he was nervous about his new position. Very nervous. When Gene spoke to him, a worried expression would cross his face, he'd squeak an answer, retreat into his office, and close the door. He wouldn't come out for hours. It was apparent to Gene that John D. F. Black needed to have "his two middle initials removed so he could relax and become a just plain John." So in late April, 1966, Gene decided to "initiate" him into our closely knit little family. And we were still a "little" family then. Production on the series was still weeks away. Only some key people were on staff, most of the crew still hadn't been hired, and Bill Shatner and the other actors had yet to report for work.

Gene called our fresh-faced and innocent Associate Producer into his office. "There's this unknown young actress named Majel Barrett I . . . ahhh . . . agreed to interview but now I can't because I have an unexpected meeting at NBC, so John, you . . . ahhh . . . interview her for me and be nice to her because she's just . . . ahhh . . . starting out in show biz and probably hasn't got any . . . ahhh . . . talent and, no, I don't know the girl at all, never met her, but her agent's a nice guy and he's a friend of a friend, so . . . ahh . . . just go through the motions, know what I mean?"

John, who had never yet conducted an actor interview, allowed as how he'd be happy to help out his boss.

Gene's plan was that, during the interview, Majel would "come on" to John and begin to disrobe, and then everyone would rush in and catch him "in the act." So after Gene "left" the studio, Majel was ushered in to be interviewed by John D. F. Black. I became suspicious that something was going on when Gene came to hide out in my office.

After the "interview" began, Gene gathered everyone outside the closed door to wait for the proper time to strike. There was only one hitch. Gene's ever-practical secretary, Dorothy Fontana, had detected a slight flaw in his plan. "How will we know when it's time?" she asked.

"I don't know," Gene whispered. He had his ear pressed against the door. "Bob, can you hear what they're doing?"

"No," I whispered back. I moved closer. I could hear Majel, but I couldn't make out what she was saying.

Majel was telling Black about her aspirations to become an actress. But when, in her best bedroom voice, she added that she would do anything, absolutely anything, to further her passionate desire, John D. F. Black began to worry. He awkwardly assured her that, while he couldn't promise her anything, he would talk things over with "the powers that be."

To show her gratitude, Majel casually eased onto her surprised host's lap, entwined her arms about his neck, and pulled him close. Gazing meaningfully into his startled eyes, she purred her eagerness to reward him, sort of "tit for tat," if he got her meaning. John certainly did. He was terrified.

Majel was doing a very realistic job of acting, but events were catching up with her. She, too, realized that she had no way to let Gene know when to spring the trap. Later, Majel told me she had never taken so much time undoing buttons. She was getting desperate because she had no idea how long it would take Gene to make his entrance and she was running out of buttons.

As she slowly and sensually began to remove her blouse, John D. F. Black tried to stand, a difficult task with Majel still sitting on his lap. He could only emit a loud, high-pitched giggle.

"I think Majel's laughing," I said.

"Are you sure it's her and not him?" asked my secretary, Sylvia T. Smith.

"Yes," said Gene, "are you sure?" He seemed worried.

I heard another high-pitched giggle. "Sounds more like a 'her' than a 'him,' " I replied.

"Maybe it's time," said Dorothy.

"I think it's time," said I.

"It's definitely time," said Gene.

He knocked on the door. Silence. I knocked. Silence. We both pounded on the door.

"Just a minute!" bleated John D. F. Black, in a very loud, very high-pitched voice. Next came scuffling noises and the sound of running feet.

We flung open the door and rushed in. Majel was seated far across the room, blushing and buttoning up. John D. F. Black was hunkered behind the desk, cowering. His face was ashen. He tried, in a frightened falsetto, to explain his innocence, that he hadn't touched her, and that she alone was to blame and he was pure as the driven snow. But the more he protested, the worse it got.

Majel, now fully buttoned, complained to me, "What took you guys so long? I thought you'd never come."

Suddenly, John noticed the room was filled with celebrants and corks were popping. He realized he'd been had, figuratively speaking of course.

"You bastards!" he yelled, having regained his normal voice. "I'll never be the same again!"

Next morning, John came to work without a tie. He was a lot looser thereafter and always ready to party with us—but he wouldn't do any more interviews. I can't say I blamed him.

Prior to her job as secretary to Roddenberry, Dorothy C. Fontana worked as a secretary for writer-producer Sam Peeples on the series *Frontier Circus.* Before that, she had sold a spec story entitled "A Bounty for Billy" to Peeples for the *Tall Man* series. But Dorothy's goal was to work as a professional filmwriter, and as yet she had never actually been hired to write a script.

Justman was impressed by the intelligence and orderly thought processes she revealed in her story analyses. He convinced Roddenberry to give her a trial assignment to write the script of "Charlie X." Roddenberry had written the story, then "junked" it, feeling the story didn't contain enough "action" and, therefore,

Courtesy NBC/Globe

Robert Walker, Jr., guest star of the episode "Charlie X."

wouldn't be acceptable to the network. But Fontana's script contained another kind of action, dramatic action that came from well-drawn characters. The script was excellent and so impressed actor Robert Walker, Jr., who had avoided taking television roles, that he agreed to guest star in the title role. And Dorothy Fontana's success led to her new career. As D. C. Fontana, she became one of the most valuable and dependable writers to ever work on *Star Trek*. When she left her job as Roddenberry's secretary in September, 1966, she wrote an eight-page single-spaced "Procedures" directive for the new secretary, Penny Unger, who succeeded her. It took a full page to detail her comments about Gene Roddenberry's desk: "Usually looks like a tornado hit it. . . . It's worth your life to open the middle drawer."

HERB: On April 12, 1966, during the early phases of script development, Bob Justman wrote a memo to Gene in which he laid out an unusual time-travel story idea.

Desilu Productions Inc.

Inter-Department Communication

TO GENE RODDENBERRY
FROM BOB JUSTMAN

DATE APRIL 12, 1966
SUBJECT STORY IDEA by BOB JUSTMAN

Dear Gene:

The Enterprise is returning to earth where refitting, rotation of crew, taking on of supplies, etc., is planned. On approaching earth there is malfunction of the ship's machinery with regard to its time warp capabilities. The Enterprise, due to this malfunction, does arrive back at a familiar planet which, of course, does turn out to be earth. But this is the earth of 1966 and not of their time.

There follows a situation with which we are becoming familiar. Every spring, about this time, there are sighting reports of UFOs. The Enterprise's shadow craft is sighted and is identified as a UFO. Kirk and Spock and the others realize upon contact with the denizens of the earth where they are in time. Thereupon, our story develops and Kirk begins to see that by breaking through time, he is starting off a whole new and different sequence of events, which will effect the history and civilization of our planet in future years. Who knows where this will lead? Perhaps it will turn out that he and Spock and the Enterprise and its crew will therefore never really exist in the future. He will also see that the whole future course of events will be changed so radically, as to cause irreparable damage to any future earth civilization. Thereupon, the problem arises as to how they are to go back and change what they have already set in motion.

Finally, after much experimentation with the ship's machinery, they do in fact go back to the moment when they arrive back at the earth in 1966. UFO reports go out again, but Kirk and the Enterprise disappear before any contact can be made with our 1966 world denizens. There only remains on earth the usual mass of spring UFO sighting reports, which is checked out by various governmental agencies and found to be without foundation.

Regards,

BOB JUSTMAN

RHJ:sts
cc: John D.F. Black

The genesis of the episode "Tomorrow Is Yesterday," for which Justman received no credit.

Gene gave no indication that he had ever read the story idea so, eight months later on December 12, 1966, in a memo entitled "WHAT'S FAIR IS FAIR," Bob again wrote to Gene.

Desilu Productions Inc.

Inter-Department Communication

TO Gene Roddenberry DATE December 1, 1966

FROM Bob Justman SUBJECT WHAT'S FAIR IS FAIR

Gene:

Attached you will find a copy of a story idea memo I wrote last April 12th. I would appreciate your perusing the memo and letting me know whether you like the idea.

If you like the idea, I would appreciate your okaying my submitting a request to be paid for an original story. I would entitle the screenplay something like "ALL OUR YESTERDAYS", or "TOMORROW THE WORLD", or "TOMORROW IS YESTERDAY".

Please let me hear from you at your earliest convenience, as otherwise I feel I shall be forced to sell this story idea to "TIME TUNNEL".

Regards,

RHJ

R. HARRIS JUSTMAN

RHJ:sts

A reminder from Justman to Roddenberry regarding his "time travel" story.

Bob's reminder produced results because the show was still suffering a dearth of intriguing and affordable scripts. Roddenberry assigned Bob's story to Dorothy Fontana, who had just gone on staff as Story Editor. Again, she wrote an excellent teleplay. The episode, "Tomorrow Is Yesterday," posed some fascinating ideas about time travel and its effects upon both the history of the past and the history of the future.

Unfortunately, Gene had a blind spot about recognizing the contribution of original material from others. On several occasions I talked with Gene about his attitude that the public must perceive him as the originator of everything that was *Star Trek*—even given the fact that most of the "original" *Star Trek* doctrines, ideas, and concepts were not original to *Star Trek* at all but, rather, were derived from current science and magazines, books, and films that predated his "*Wagon Train* to the stars." Unfortunately, Gene brushed aside any such discussions; he apparently never saw this flaw. Sometimes, Gene would joke about his colleagues' contributions by insisting that, for example, Gene Coon's creation of the Klingons and the Klingon culture, Bob Justman's many story ideas and production concepts, and my contribution of the captain's log–stardate concept all came from his "cousin in Ohio."

It was the beginning of what years later could be referred to as the "*Star Trek* myth," a legend of ideas and accomplishments that became the lightning rod for the millions of fans whose fervor and support thrust *Star Trek* into the rarefied atmosphere of near-galactic success.

So, accordingly, Gene gave Bob neither credit nor payment for the story; in fact, he never even thanked him.

BOB: At the time, I was disappointed by the fact that Gene never responded to my request to be paid for the story. I knew that he had come up with a number of story ideas for the show, "springboards" as we called them. He claimed that he wouldn't get paid for them; they were part of his duties as the creator of the show. But since I was part of the management team, I rationalized that, if Gene could do it gratis, then so could I. The important thing was to help the show in every way possible. At the time, I had no idea that Gene would receive extra money from the studio for this "extra work." Many years later when I had the facts, I came to realize that the "feet of clay" syndrome was kicking in—but at the time, I didn't want to accept that fact.

HERB: Gene's refusal to acknowledge Bob Justman's story contribution was a particularly cruel treatment of his Associate Producer and friend, especially when considering his own money demands for anything he wrote or rewrote. Part of the salary and royalty paid to series "Creator–Executive Producers" covered some rewriting of stories and scripts. After I left the studio and moved to MGM, Gene's agents submitted bills directly to the Paramount Business Affairs Department for almost every story or rewrite he did. The payments ranged from $750 to over $3,000, at times even more than what the writer of a particular script was paid. It was like putting the fox in charge of the henhouse; it was Gene, himself, deciding what stories and scripts needed rewriting. And the more stories and scripts he rewrote, the more extra money he was paid. It's no wonder that almost all the *Star Trek* writers, at one time of another, were angered over his treatment of their scripts. At the time, even Bob Justman didn't know about Gene's additional

"perks." These extraordinary payments were not reflected in the studio's weekly cost reports.

By the time I heard about Roddenberry's refusal to give RJ credit, money, or even a personal acknowledgment for his story, it was twenty-seven years later and there was nothing I could do to correct the situation.

BOB: Gene had mentioned several times that, when he was first submitting scripts to producers, he found one invaluable tool that helped guide his writing: Lajos Egri's *The Art of Dramatic Writing.*

He kept the volume at his desk and said, "I use it all the time, Bob. If a writer follows its principles, he'll never go wrong. I think you really should have a copy."

From the tone of his voice, I assumed he would spring for another copy or at least loan me his. I waited a week, but no such luck! So I went out and purchased one myself. Egri's writing style was dull, but I appreciated the principles he laid out, and I gained a better understanding of the elements of drama.

Ironically, I later used Egri's principles to review Gene's own script, "The Omega Glory." I wrote a memo in which my comments were devastating. However, not wanting to hurt his feelings, I tore up the memo and made a few suggestions orally. He took the advice, but as anyone who has seen the episode knows, it didn't do much good.

Gene Roddenberry wanted to encourage aspiring writers: To one, he felt constrained to write, in part:

> Isaac Asimov forwarded your unsolicited script to us with his personal request that we read it and comment directly to you. Needless to say, we are Asimov fans also and a simple request from him takes on something of a "command" as far as we are concerned. . . . Although we find it interesting and indicative of a talent for story . . . it does not meet *Star Trek* needs and requirements sufficiently. This is a hard thing to say to a budding writer (God knows we spent those same years budding ourselves), and, thus, we do want to make certain that none of this discourages you. . . . We cannot afford to purchase any unsolicited script that is anything short of startling in quality and immediately shootable in terms of budget, schedules, and format. . . . I do wish we had more time, since we are quite sincere in our interest in new writers.

BOB: Ordinarily, Gene had little time to read unsolicited manuscripts, and he turned that thankless task over to others: John D. F. Black, Dorothy Fontana, and me. Later, after Black left the show and Dorothy was busy writing originals and

rewriting others, more of the task fell upon my shoulders. During the show's first season, unsolicited manuscripts weren't much of a problem because *Star Trek* had yet to attract much attention from either professional screenwriters or wanna-be writers. The deluge didn't begin until some time later, near the end of the second season, when the amount of submissions approached flood proportions. Part of the deluge was due to Gene's outside appearances, where he encouraged nonprofessionals to try their hands at writing for *Star Trek.*

Now there were really two kinds of unsolicited material: unsolicited manuscripts submitted by reputable literary agents, which the studio allowed us to read, and the other kind—"unsolicited" unsolicited manuscripts submitted out of the blue, which the studio legal department ordered us to return "unread." The legal beagles didn't want us to lay the studio open to any claims of plagiarism.

These unsolicited manuscripts were returned unopened, with a note suggesting that the author get an agent to submit it "legally." And later, now legally submitted, I'd read it avidly because if an agent liked the property enough to represent the author, I wanted to see what divine inspiration motivated him to do so. It usually turned out that the divine inspiration was the prospect of a sale for cash money. There were very few, if any, literary gems.

Soon enough, Justman became so overburdened with his daily production duties that he had to analyze both solicited and unsolicited stories and scripts at home.

Roddenberry had recently discovered dictating machines and was now using them to draft memos and script scenes. He soon turned his Associate Producer on to the practice. Now, Justman could dictate his voluminous memos to a machine at home. He set some kind of a record for writing twenty-page single-spaced memos about ten-page double-spaced stories.

BOB: Every morning, I gave a new tape to my secretary, the formidable Sylvia T. Smith, to transcribe. Sylvia never complained. She came in early and left late. I often wondered why her husband put up with all the madness. Earphones on and working the machine's foot pedal, Sylvia typed the memos, her fingers flying over the keyboard at warp speed while she answered phone calls, kept a weather eye cocked at everything and everyone else, and drove the other secretaries crazy.

HERB: Bob often waited impatiently for script pages from John D. F. Black, who, with his secretary, the estimable and highly likable Mary Stilwell, worked behind closed doors. DO NOT DISTURB! When they emerged hours later, Justman complained about the paltry number of script pages that were forthcoming. Like Oliver Twist, he wanted more.

And what were they doing in there all that time? "Writing, Bob" was Black's standard reply. When the pages were really good, Justman, a glint in his eye, would confront Black. "Hey, John, this is terrific. Did Mary do all the writing again?"

Years later, after John's first marriage ended, Mary Stilwell wrote, but then as Mrs. John D. F. Black.

BOB: With John busy writing "The Naked Time," his own first original script for the series, his Story Consultant responsibilities suffered accordingly and his rewriting output became less than prodigious. Soon, Producer Roddenberry realized it was up to Writer Roddenberry to rework most of the early scripts. No *Star Trek* writer's work was immune from the process, regardless of experience, talent, or position.

John had put in a great deal of time and hard work in writing his first draft, and he was proud of every single word he had written. After turning in his script, he expected kudos from his boss.

A week later, John rushed into my office, frantically waving a mimeographed copy of Gene's rewrite of "The Naked Time."

"He can't do this to me!" trumpeted the aggrieved writer, breathing hard, his nostrils flaring with rage.

Gene had read the script, rewrote it without telling John, and sent it out to be mimeographed. Now John knew how it felt to be rewritten by the Great Bird of the Galaxy. (Several years later, the Writers Guild ruled that scriptwriters must be given the opportunity to do their own first rewrite and, if they chose not to do so, specifically forbade producers from rewriting a script without first consulting the writer.)

John had anticipated praise from his boss; instead he got his ego trampled. "He can take the damn script and shove it!" he yelled.

It took me an hour to talk him out of quitting. I knew we couldn't afford to lose him. He was a talented man, and we couldn't survive with only Roddenberry to do all the rewrites. But after Gene's heavy-handed dealing with John Black's script, the party was over and it was time to call it a day. John never again had the same positive disposition toward *Star Trek.* He came to the office every day, closed his door, and went to work. The door stayed closed most of the time. He kept precise hours, never staying late, never leaving early.

On the day his contract expired, he and Mary Stilwell opened a bottle of champagne in his office and, toasting the occasion, celebrated the fact that he no longer worked for Gene Roddenberry.

But there were two first-year *Star Trek* writers whose efforts were appreciated—even years later. Carey Wilbur and Gene Coon (using his pen name, Lee Cronin) wrote the episode "Space Seed" and created the character of Khan Noonian Singh, a role that was played by Ricardo Montalban. Little did Wilbur and Coon realize that their efforts would be used later as the basis for the second *Star Trek* motion picture, *Star Trek: The Wrath of Khan,* with Ricardo Montalban recreating his original role.

All story and script memos were addressed to Roddenberry. But memos from the show's staff weren't the only ones he received. Every version of every story and teleplay generated memos to him from two separate NBC departments.

HERB: The great majority of television series are network damage-proof: a Western is a Western; a cop show is a cop show; a three-camera situation comedy, with the mandatory living room and kitchen sets, is a three-camera situation comedy with the mandatory living room and kitchen sets. They're basic, almost standard, television forms that are popped out of familiar molds. They can withstand the usual network tinkering.

The character-driven science-fiction–fantasy concept and fragile nature of *Star Trek* made it very much the exception. As such, the series needed, almost required, an NBC program manager with experience, good taste, an appreciation for the written word, lack of ego, and absence of involvement in the very private lives of its personnel. In an ideal world, the role of a network program manager is to represent the interests of the sponsor and the network regarding series and story content and timely delivery of the product.

Former NBC President Grant Tinker, in his recent autobiography *Tinker in Television,* wrote:

> Over the years, network executives in general have become infamous for confusing their role with that of the producer. As buyers, they unquestionably have the right to the final say. Unfortunately, all too often they exercise it. This self-defeating sin is usually committed by the younger, more arrogant networkers. Veteran practitioners often have learned to be helpful, not dictatorial; that's how they survived to become veterans.
>
> For the people who make the shows, the producer–program executive relationship is a slippery slope. Someone whose hands are full simply meeting the relentless demands of supplying programs to a network schedule has very little time left over for fending off—or accommodating—supervision from the network. If the phenomenon weren't so distracting and time-consuming, it would be funny. The young network overseers come fully equipped with all the jargon and none of the skills and smarts born of real experience.

In other words—with apologies to Grant, who never once abused his prerogatives—no "tinkering." Sadly, other, lower-echelon network execs chose not to follow his example.

Unfortunately, the Program Manager assigned to *Star Trek* did not provide everything the show needed. It was another of Roddenberry's attempts to placate NBC that brought NBC Program Manager Stanley Robertson to *Star Trek.* It was an approval Gene always wished he had never given. Robertson's involvement with the show, at times, became nothing but a bad dream.

Stan Robertson, who started his career as a page, worked in the NBC Music Clearance Department in Burbank, but always kept his eyes open for the next move up. With an increase in filmed television series, Los Angeles television studios were reaping the benefits of New York's production decline. Local network departments and production companies were hiring. NBC was compelled to expand its program department, particularly in the Current Program Manager area, the representatives and overseers of series bought by the network.

Robertson, aware of the openings, lobbied both Grant Tinker and Jerry Stanley for one of the new Program Manager positions. He had been writing a column for *The L.A. Sentinel*, the leading African American newspaper in Los Angeles. He gave copies of his columns to Tinker and Stanley to establish his credentials: his writing ability and creative bent.

In the mid-1960s, NBC was desirous of promoting racial equality, not only on its television shows, but within its own management structure. Stanley Robertson, one of the few African American executives already employed by NBC, couldn't have come along at a better time. He was hired for one of the new positions.

Program Managers were assigned to series on a random basis, the only mitigating circumstance being the workload of a particular manager. Robertson drew *Star Trek* as one of his series. The only step left to make it official was to get Gene Roddenberry's approval.

HERB: Gene interviewed, questioned, interrogated everyone who had, or would have, an effect on his life, career, and *Star Trek.* Saying Gene was protective was like saying the rain is wet, the sky is blue, and the night is for love. So Roddenberry, assuming his fatherly "what do you want to be when you grow up?" posture, interviewed Robertson. He liked what he saw, liked what he heard, and enthusiastically approved NBC's new Program Manager. (Years later, former NBC Vice President Jerry Stanley reacted: "Hey, don't complain to us, Herb. Roddenberry wanted him.")

As stories and first-draft scripts were received, they were automatically sent to new Program Manager Robertson for NBC's approval. While settling into the new job, he was congenial and cooperative. But as actual production came closer, Roddenberry and Justman became concerned about Robertson's—at times—seeming lack of understanding of story outlines—and of Roddenberry himself.

The future of *Star Trek* would be fought, not in outer space, but here on Earth in a flurry of objections and accusations between two supposed allies, Roddenberry and Robertson.

Enter another NBC department: Broadcast Standards, the censors. It was a network department that operated outside Programming's jurisdiction.

BOB: Representing the network's policies relating to morals, values, and the "American way," NBC Broadcast Standards' Jean Messerschmidt found herself bearing the brunt of arguments and complaints from *Star Trek.* Her only concern was specific content, first in script and subsequently on film. Although she often bumped heads with us, Jeannie performed her job and performed it well. She was both firm and reasonable. If only she could have been *Star Trek*'s Program Manager. But there were no women executives in the Programming Department. Unfortunately, the age of feminism was years away.

HERB: Many things in life go hand in hand: Gilbert and Sullivan, Rogers and Hammerstein, Laurel and Hardy. At Desilu, a new set of bookends was added, *Star Trek* and Kellam DeForest.

A thin, rumpled Yale University scholar, Kellam operated an amazing and invaluable information research facility. Over the years, Kellam had collected, bought, begged, and borrowed books, magazines, newspapers, and whatever else he could find to enable him, and his capable and responsible assistant, Joan Pearce, to give writers and producers the real scoop. If you were writing an episode of Tarzan and had the apeman swimming, in a river, a mile wide, against the current, past three waterfalls that emptied into the southern section of Lake Victoria, but only during the rainy season when crocodiles were mating, and you wanted the name of that river, Kellam would either supply the name or bluntly advise that such a river didn't exist. He'd then offer a list of African river names meeting the criteria that the writer should consider.

As you can gather, Kellam had a field day with *Star Trek.* Because Kellam believed everything—*everything*—must be accurate!

It began with Gene Roddenberry and progressed to the writers who made up names of characters, planets, stars, nebulae, solar systems. And they made up "stardates," the numbered dates quoted by Kirk in his captain's logs. This particularly annoyed Kellam as, from script to script, he recognized that the dates were out of sequence and galactically "incorrect."

While the following is not an actual quote, Kellam might typically complain, "Based on script two, even with the *Enterprise* travelling at a near-maximum speed of warp nine, it would be impossible for the vessel to arrive at Talos IV in order to confront the Romulan space cruiser, as, in script seven, that very same Romulan ship, having been damaged in a photon-torpedo engagement in script three, could not have maneuvered into this quadrant of the universe in time. This anomaly begs explanation."

When I read the above to Kellam recently, his reaction to what I had written was enthusiastic. "I love it! That's exactly what I would have said."

Whenever Kellam became particularly exercised over writers' liberties, his comment was brief and to the point: "This begs explanation!" Kellam's phrase should be added to the list of famous *Star Trek* bumper stickers.

BOB: A number of fans noticed discrepancies in our stardates and wrote to us, joining in the madness. A stereotypical letter might say:

> In act three of last week's show, Captain Kirk's narration indicated a stardate of 4891.4 but he'd already mentioned star date 4323.7 in act one. This means he made love to Phobos 7's four-breasted alien maiden princess before he arrived and "beamed down." How can this be?
>
> Live long and prosper,
>
> (Signed) Anne Avid Fann, aged 16.56.
>
> P.S. Please send me autographed photos of everyone in the cast. Thanks.
>
> P.P.S. *Star Trek* is great. Me and my best friend watch it every week. He's a big fan, too. He's 6 feet 3.2. Ha, ha, ha.
>
> P.P.P.S. My dad and mom hate your show.

To solve the stardate problem, Gene came up with the perfect answer: "There are no constants or absolutes in deep outer space. Depending upon what quadrant of the galaxy you're in, and at what speed you're travelling, or in all three dimensions in what direction you're headed, time increases or decreases accordingly relative to time on planet Earth—or anywhere else in the universe."

His explanation seemed to satisfy even the most demanding fan. But it certainly confused me.

Although Gene Roddenberry was brilliant in creating unusual concepts and story ideas, he practiced every imaginable technique to avoid one of his primary responsibilities, that of rewriting scripts. His days were filled with story and script conferences, and he was always immediately available to approve costume designs, prop designs, hair designs, and whatever network and production matters "desperately" required his attention. At the eleventh hour, however, he'd finally begin rewriting, which almost always meant Roddenberry was still at his desk when the morning sun rose over Hollywood.

Star Trek's famous opening narration came about under the pressure of an approaching crucial deadline.

BOB: On August 1, 1966, with the season premiere set for September 8, only weeks away, I prodded Gene to write the show's opening narration. But as usual, he continued to procrastinate. With only a few days left to ship the premiere episode to NBC for broadcast, it was now or never. The episode was complete except for this necessary and long-promised element.

Finally goaded into action, Gene took a stab at writing it, incorporating Sam Peeples's pilot title, "Where No Man Has Gone Before." He sent his first version to John Black and me. Gene asked for our comments and contributions. After an exchange of memos, he incorporated some of the suggestions into what became Captain Kirk's famous opening narration:

Desilu Productions Inc.

Inter-Department Communication

TO GENE RODDENBERRY

DATE AUGUST 1, 1966

FROM BOB JUSTMAN

SUBJECT STANDARD OPENING NARRATION

Dear Gene:

It is important that you compose, without delay, our Standard Opening Narration for Bill Shatner to record. It should run about 15 seconds in length, as we discussed earlier.

Regards,

BOB

RHJ:sts
cc: John D.F. Black

Justman's memo asking Roddenberry to write the narration.

ROUGH DRAFT 8/2/66
OPENING NARRATION - STAR TRE

This is the story of the United Space Ship Enterprise. Assigned a five year patrol of our galaxy, the giant starship visits Earth colonies, regulates commerce, and explores strange new worlds and civilizations. These are its voyages... and its adventures.

Roddenberry's first rough draft.

/2/66
STAR TREK
Opening narration

This is the adventure of the United Space Ship Enterprise. Assigned a five year galaxy patrol, the bold crew of the giant starship explores the excitement of strange new worlds, uncharted civilizations and exotic people. These are its voyages and its adventures . . .

Roddenberry's revised draft.

Desilu Productions Inc.

Inter-Department Communication

TO GENE RODDENBERRY

FROM JOHN D. F. BLACK

DATE August 2, 1966

SUBJECT STAR TREK
Opening Narration

Gene....

Think the narration needs more drama.

Follows an example of what I mean... at about 15 to 17 seconds ———

KIRK'S VOICE

Space...the final frontier...endless...
silent...waiting. This is the story of
the United Space Ship Enterprise...its
mission...a five year patrol of the
galaxy...to seek out and contact all
alien life...to explore...to travel the
vast galaxy where no man has gone before
...a STAR TREK.

JDFB
John D. F.

cc: R. Justman

JDFB/ms

Black's suggested version.

GR......

Or... at about 11½ second length...

Would you believe:

KIRK'S VOICE

The U.S.S. Enterprise...star ship...
its mission...a five year patrol to
seek out and contact alien life...
to explore the infinite frontier of
space...where no man has gone before
...a STAR TREK.

JDFB

JDFB

Black's shorter version.

Desilu Productions Inc.

Inter-Department Communication

TO GENE RODDENBERRY

FROM BOB JUSTMAN

DATE AUGUST 2, 1966

SUBJECT STAR TREK
OPENING NARRATION

Dear Gene:

Here are the words you should use for our Standard TEASER Narration:

"This is the story of the Starship Enterprise. It's mission: to advance knowledge, contact alien life and enforce intergalactic law ... to explore the strange new worlds where no man has gone before".

Regards,

B

BOB

RHJ:sts
cc: John D.F. Black

Where no man has gone before. Space, ... strange ... exotic planets ... civilizations ... Alien ... This is the story of the U.S.S. Enterprise ... its adventures ... its voyages ...

STARSHIP

Justman's suggested version, with Roddenberry's handwritten annotations.

Desilu Productions Inc.

Inter-Department Communication

TO GENE RODDENBERRY

DATE AUGUST 10, 1966

FROM BOB JUSTMAN

SUBJECT STANDARD OPENING NARRATION

Dear Gene:

As per our converation last night on the phone, it is absolutely imperative that we record with William Shatner the Standard Opening Narration for the STAR TREK Main Title as soon as possible.

Need I say more? ?

Love and kisses,

X XXXX

BOB

Justman's demand that Roddenberry deliver his final draft.

On the afternoon of August 10, 1966, literally minutes after Gene finished his final version, I phoned Bill Shatner on stage, where he was working on"Dagger of the Mind," our ninth episode to be filmed. I told him to "drop everything," and then I ran across the street to the dubbing stage. Bill raced to meet me and arrived a minute later, slightly out of breath. We rehearsed the dialogue several times and made a take. Due to Bill's classical training, his delivery was excellent—but the narration sounded too contemporary. There was something lacking; it didn't seem to "ring out."

I asked the sound mixer to add reverberation to Shatner's voice. We made another take and the results were perfect. Bill had become Captain Kirk, the adventurous commander of a spacecraft of the future, when he declared:

> Space . . . the final frontier. These are the voyages of the *Starship Enterprise,* its five-year mission:
>
> . . . to explore strange new worlds . . .
>
> . . . to seek out new life and new civilizations . . .
>
> . . . to boldly go where no man has gone before.

Courtesy Greg Jein

11

New Faces of 1966: The Actors

HERB: In April, 1964, almost two months prior to the start of production, one of the lead stories in the Hollywood casting news was headlined: *STAR TREK* RECASTS . . . AGAIN!

Famous actors' agent John Gaines called and cattily whispered, "One would think you could get it right the first time, Herb . . . or even the second time." Gaines was on target. With *Star Trek* now a network series, the third time had better be right; there'd be no fourth time.

If the *Enterprise* had an interstellar space cruiser newsletter, its headlines would have read:

SHIP'S DOCTOR PAUL FIX FOLLOWS SHIP'S DOCTOR JOHN HOYT OUT OF SICKBAY AND INTO EARLY RETIREMENT!

STARFLEET OFFICER PAUL CARR DOES HIS BEST IN NOTHING ROLE AND IS LOST IN SPACE!

CREWMAN LLOYD HAYNES BEAMED BACK DOWN TO EARTH AFTER ROLE FIZZLES!

SEXY YEOMAN ANDREA DROMM FAILS TO SIZZLE! SLIPS INTO SUSPENDED ANIMATION!

Though Gene asked Casting Director Joe D'Agosta and my assistant, Morris Chapnick, to bring in candidates for the new roles, they could have saved their time, energy, and phone calls. Gene should have shared his reality: "It's a sure thing." "In the bag." He should have told them, "Don't waste your time, guys. The fix is in."

Courtesy Greg Jein

DeForest Kelley as *Star Trek*'s third ship's doctor, Leonard "Bones" McCoy.

The first indication that kismet had arrived in the *Star Trek* galaxy was when NBC decided to drop Roddenberry's *Police Story* from further contention as a fall series or possible midseason replacement. So DeForest Kelley, one of the stars of that pilot, was available.

If the *Police Story* pilot was nothing else, it was a great piece of film for Kelley. Usually typecast as a cattle rustler, renegade, outlaw, horse thief, or gambler, he was finally seen in an entirely fresh light, that of a crusty but likable police criminologist, an honest-to-goodness good guy. Gene Roddenberry made no bones (pun intended) about wanting Kelley to play the new doctor of the *Enterprise*. All agreed. De Kelley would bring a much-needed humanity to the role of Doctor McCoy. However, there remained some question as to his "wearability" over twenty-six episodes. In fact, he would not receive costar billing and was guaranteed only the actors' union minimum for series regulars, "seven out of thirteen" shows, including the pilot. No one at the studio or the network had any idea how important Doctor McCoy would become in the *Star Trek* saga to follow.

A part of the *Star Trek* legend, advanced by Gene Roddenberry and quoted numerous times by De Kelley, is that NBC turned him down for both pilot films and finally relented after seeing him in the *Police Story* pilot. Since it was I who requested and secured all network pilot and series cast approvals, let me correct the record and assure De that at no time did NBC reject him for the role of ship's doctor, because his name was never submitted for either of the pilots. It was just another case of Gene Roddenberry's not taking responsibility for his own decisions and finding scapegoats to avoid confrontation.

There was *almost* another new face aboard the *Enterprise*. If it had not been for his very aggressive agent, Jimmy Doohan, one of *Star Trek*'s most beloved actors, would not have made the cut. Shortly after NBC ordered the series, Doohan received a letter from Gene Roddenberry informing him, "We don't think we need an engineer in the series." Doohan was confused by Roddenberry's direct communication and informed his agent, Paul Wilkins, that apparently he'd been fired. Wilkins became irate and met with Roddenberry, and by the close of business that same day, Doohan was returned to the *Enterprise* engine room. Millions of fans should be thankful to Paul Wilkins for getting Doohan back on board. NBC was unaware of Roddenberry's attempt to fire Doohan.

NBC Programs head Mort Werner had sent out a directive to the producers of all the network's series concerning NBC's policy to hire more actors from diverse racial backgrounds. Desilu studio management had already taken such steps on both *Star Trek* and *Mission: Impossible*, and the following year they would do the same on *Mannix*.

Even in light of Werner's memo and Solow's desire for a racial mix on all series, Roddenberry surprisingly decided to drop Lloyd Haynes, the only African American actor in the second pilot. Solow recognized that the problem was not with Haynes as an actor, but with the dullness of the character he had to play. If a new character wasn't written for him, there would be no African American in the series's cast. Roddenberry suddenly became strangely silent on the subject.

Courtesy Greg Jein

James Doohan as Scotty, a character that Gene Roddenberry almost cut before series production began.

HERB: In May, 1965, after the series' first stories were being fleshed out into shooting scripts, there was no mention of a new character—a sexy female communications officer. Soon, however, Gene talked of inserting this new role into several scripts. He wanted to call her Lieutenant Sulu, intending to rename George Takei's character.

Even before the first shooting scripts were completed, Gene had asked D'Agosta to prepare a list of actress suggestions for this new role. Then, one day, a casting idea suddenly "engulfed" Gene: "Herb, I just remembered this actress who worked for me on *The Lieutenant*. I'm gonna bring her in. You'll like her."

The following day, Gene escorted Nichelle Nichols to my office for introductions. She was pretty, sexy, vital, and African American and would fulfill our desire to have a racially mixed cast. She was, as I later discovered, not just a sudden afterthought.

BOB: And I, as usual, was oblivious to what Herb eventually learned. I just thought Gene was pursuing the liberal bent I knew he possessed. I liked the idea that we once again had an African American in our cast, and I particularly liked the fact that the new role was for a female. And I liked Nichelle as an actress. It

took years for me to realize that Nichelle and Gene had more than just a platonic friendship. But then, I was naive at the time. According to Herb, I still am.

Solow had reservations about the new character's name. "Sulu" sounded too much like "Zulu," and the plan for racial diversity in the show might have been misread and misunderstood. So Roddenberry agreed and retained George Takei's original character name. But what to name the new communications officer? When Nichelle Nichols first came in for her interview, she was carrying a book about Africa entitled *Uhuru.* Justman explained to Roddenberry that the word *uhuru* meant "freedom" in Swahili. Roddenberry took the word, changed it to "Uhura," and gave it to his "discovery." The new character had a new name. It was almost as if he had planned everything.

BOB: Now that he once again had Nichelle, Gene inserted the new character into an already network-approved script. In "The Corbomite Maneuver," Communications Officer Dave Bailey suddenly became Navigator Dave Bailey, and some of his original dialogue was given to Nichelle, our new communications officer, Lt. Uhura. Thus, Dave Bailey had been demoted without benefit of court-martial.

Nichelle was hired as a "day player"; she wasn't a "regular" member of the cast. Nevertheless, Gene kept on writing her in: "We have to have a communications officer, Bob. Someone that the audience sees every week; someone who's part of the *Star Trek* family. Nichelle's great, and she's not that expensive. Someone else would cost a whole lot more."

As usual, our series episode budget was tight; the cast budget was even tighter. On "The Corbomite Maneuver," Nichelle was guaranteed two days' work on a "$700 for five days" rate, $140 per day. Not much today, and, come to think of it, not much then, either. But even that small amount of extra money was hard to come by.

Gene wanted her to be in the show often, so I attempted to get Nichelle into more episodes without breaking our cast budget. Even a minimum "seven out of thirteen shows" series deal like we had with DeForest Kelley, George Takei, and Grace Lee Whitney was not in the cards.

Courtesy NBC/Globe

Gene Roddenberry's "last-minute" find, actress Nichelle Nichols as Lieutenant Uhura.

I asked Joe D'Agosta to make an oral agreement with Nichelle's agent in which we "promised to keep her working as often as we could." (Gene saw to that part of the arrangement.) Her salary was prenegotiated. If she worked one day, she got a higher rate. For two days, less per day. For three days, even more so. We made up for short money by giving her a "featured player" credit. Her salary was a "no quote," meaning that we helped maintain the fiction that she was making a lot more than she actually earned. Her ego was salved and our budget was saved.

HERB: Nichelle later claimed that, at the time, she had a firm agreement with Gene Roddenberry for $1,000 per week with a guarantee of appearing in ten out of each group of thirteen episodes and costar billing, and that the studio reneged on her deal. In actuality, those were the terms her agent attempted to negotiate for her services on the *second* season of *Star Trek.* Nichelle had told her agent what Gene had promised.

But Gene, knowing full well the studio's financial conditions at the time, knew that I could not—and would not—approve anything other than the actual final terms and conditions of her employment.

To quote a March 17, 1967, memo from Business Affairs attorney Ed Perlstein to Gene Roddenberry, subject, "NICHELLE NICHOLS—*Star Trek*":

"Since Nichelle Nichols' agent, Harry Lipton of the Mitchell-Gertz Agency, requested a minimum deal of $1,000 per show for ten out of each 13, I turned down the deal as per your advice and since our budget could not withstand this extreme price. . . ."

Copies of Perlstein's memo were sent to "H. Solow; G. Coon; B. Justman; J. D'Agosta."

Gene had obviously told Nichelle what she wanted to hear and, later, told the studio to turn down the "deal."

BOB: Many years later, I encountered a young actor at a party. He introduced himself as Kyle, Nichelle's son, and reminded me that he and our oldest son, Bill, had been fast friends. They raced slot cars together several afternoons a week during the time his mother and I worked together. Bill used to call his friend "Mouse," so I never realized that the boy was Nichelle's son. While I liked Nichelle, we saw each other only at work; I didn't have much time for socializing. And at the time, the kids never thought to mention their relationship to either of us. They were just kids; adults weren't all that important.

HERB: Grace Lee Whitney was another refugee from Gene's unsold *Police Story*

Actress Grace Lee Whitney, in her role as Yeoman Janice Rand.

Courtesy NBC/Globe

Courtesy Greg Jein

Actress Majel Barrett, in her role as Nurse Christine Chapel.

pilot. She had played the part of Police Lieutenant Lilly Monroe, and, as in the case of DeForest Kelley, Grace Lee was available.

Gene liked Grace Lee. Unlike the two prior "model-type and cute" Yeoman actresses, she appeared to him as what she was—pretty, sexy, and vulnerable. Yeoman Janice Rand was piped aboard the *U.S.S. Enterprise.*

She was dressed in her William Ware Theiss–designed outfit, a short skirt that emphasized her legs and a tunic that emphasized her bosom. Grace Lee and Gene both welcomed the attention she received.

BOB: Although he was our Costume Designer, Bill Theiss was assigned by Gene the task of designing Grace Lee's hair styles. He'd bring in a sketch and, soon, with considerable input from Gene, the design would be "finalized"—almost. Then Virginia Darcy, our hairstylist, would go to work and build it on the actress.

Every time Grace Lee was brought back for inspection, Gene spent an inordinate amount of time fussing with the bouffant hair creation. Gene explained that it was necessary to invent unusual hairstyles so viewers would feel they were really witnessing the future. Well, he fussed and poked and pushed and prodded until Grace Lee finally ended up with an enormous beehive hairdo. It must have been damned uncomfortable to cart around, but she never complained. It looked so heavy and was so thickly lacquered, I joked, "You could hit it with a sledgehammer and never make a dent."

HERB: No discussion of the "new" faces who came aboard the *Enterprise* for the series would be complete without the mention of Majel Barrett, the defrocked Number One from the first pilot. Noticing her NBC-requested absence from the second pilot, I waited for Gene to plot and execute a "sneak Majel into the series" move.

Majel wasn't coy about insisting Gene make her a regular in the series. "I'm suffering from pillow talk, Herb," he'd confide in me, "severe pillow talk."

So Gene began the campaign. First he told Majel, and then subsequently hinted to several journalists "off the record," that NBC rejected Majel for the second pilot because the network executives were sexists, not wanting a series star to be a strong woman. His move embarrassed the network; later he denied ever making the statement. He conveniently forgot that the NBC execs, for both financial and moral reasons, had always favored a strong woman as a series star. They just didn't want Majel, and they resented having her forced upon them for the first pilot.

Soon, Majel deserted her apartment near MGM. Roddenberry moved her into a very convenient place around the corner from Desilu. Majel's new apartment became Gene's second home, and Desilu Studios became Majel's second home, where she became a fixture in the *Star Trek* offices. But several more moves were still needed to make Majel a fixture in the *Star Trek* series.

But for this first 1966 season, three new faces—Kelley, Nichols, and Whitney—boarded the *U.S.S. Enterprise* to join Shatner, Nimoy, Doohan, and Takei.

Courtesy Greg Jein

12

These Are the Voyages: The First Season

BOB: The real magic time was here. We had to shoot at least sixteen consecutive one-hour episodes, and the adventure into the unknown was to begin at 8:00 the following morning. I felt a bit nauseated.

The series had been prepared as well as time, and not enough money, would allow. Argyle Nelson finally agreed that we should begin filming a new series on a Tuesday, rather than a Monday, so that any last-minute needs could be taken care of on a "working day," rather than over a weekend when all our outside suppliers were closed.

I'd even been able to finagle a rehearsal day on Monday for the director and cast, something seldom done in filmed series television. Bob Aldrich had taught me the value of rehearsal time when I worked with him. It enabled the cast to begin establishing the character relationships that would persist well into the future. The rehearsal also enabled the crew to rough in lighting for the first shot the following day.

The actors had been given their makeup calls for the next morning, the first day of series production. The "call sheet" gave the crew their reporting times. All the equipment was prepared, checked out, and ready for use. So I had it checked out again, just in case. The "crab" dolly and the cameras worked fine, as did the sound-recording system, and there was more than enough 35 mm Eastman color negative film and sound recording tape on hand to last for weeks.

There were new "carbons" for the studio's ancient arc lights. The best of the studio's ancient lighting equipment had been reserved for our use, but even so, some of the big arc lights would "sing" when in use. Inside each arc, two carbon rods were mounted at ninety degrees to each other with their tips nearly touching. When turned on, the powerful 220-volt DC electricity passing between the rod tips caused them to glow white hot and emit copious quantities of bright light. From time to time, the arcs sang, emitting squeals and sputters that the electrician assigned to each arc was supposed to prevent by carefully "trimming" (adjusting) the space between the rod tips as the current burned away the carbon. If the lamp operator wasn't on the ball, unwanted noises would erupt, usually resulting in a ruined take, and the shot would have to be redone.

The big 10-K incandescent lamps were supposedly in working order, although some of them emitted sounds when turned on—or off. When the incandescent 10-K "globes" (like big light bulbs) were turned on, the heat they emitted caused the lamp's metal structure to expand, resulting in loud "pops" and assorted pinging noises. And they'd sometimes sing as well, emitting their characteristic thin high-pitched note. We'd have to watch the 10-Ks. Their noises drove everyone crazy, the sound mixer, the actors, the director—and especially me, because they ruined takes. Retakes meant more time, and more time meant—well, you know the rest.

All the actors had been fitted in their costumes. We had our daily supply of rubber ears waiting to be glued onto Leonard Nimoy. Even the first script was ready, though it contained very few original "white pages." Different colors indicated script changes, and the rest of the pages were a wild assortment of pink, yellow, blue, green, buff—name the color, we had it. But there hadn't been any script changes made in at least several hours. It looked like we were ready.

We were ready, but our new head cameraman, Jerry Finnerman, wasn't. He slowly walked into my office, as nervous as he'd been when Harry Stradling first brought him to me. His eyes seemed to bulge and his throat was so dry he could hardly speak.

"What is it, Jerry? What's the matter?"

"I . . . can't . . . do it." He sounded strangled.

"What? Can't do what?"

"Can't . . . shoot the show."

"Why not? What's wrong?"

"I think you should get . . . somebody else . . . somebody more experienced."

"What are you talking about? We start shooting tomorrow morning."

"I just can't . . . do it."

"Calm down and tell me why. Are you sick?"

Then it all came out in a rush. "I'm afraid I'll screw up and you won't like my work and you'll fire me and I'll be out of work for the next six months." (One of the rules of the cameramen's union was that, when a member moved up to a higher category, he had to stay at that level for a minimum of six months before dropping back down, even if he ended up out of work.)

That was not what I wanted to hear. "Let's look at the facts, Jerry. I've gone out on a very long limb for you and you're damn well going to be our cameraman or you'll be out of work for a helluva lot longer than six months. How does being out of work for the rest of your life sound?"

Jerry was shocked, but I was surprised—surprised at myself. I had employed a tone of voice and a kind of vitriol that was rare, even for me.

Poor Jerry couldn't even respond; he was that frightened. I calmed down. "Jerry, your resignation is not accepted. You're going to be our cameraman and you're going to be a great one. So forget all this nonsense. Go home and get some . . . I mean, try to get some sleep. Then come back tomorrow and knock 'em dead. I believe in you. I know you can do it—even if you don't."

Luckily, Jerry was more afraid of me than of his private demons. He honored his commitment. However, during the first season of the series, after viewing the "rushes" with me every day and listening to my critiques and suggestions, Jerry sometimes proceeded to the nearest men's room to throw up. But he was our cameraman, and as I had hoped, he was a great one.

That night, in Gene's office, I joined Gene, Herb, and Joe Sargent—the director of our first episode, "The Corbomite Maneuver"—for a "successful launch of the good ship *Enterprise* in the morning" drink. After what had happened earlier, I needed one. A stiff one. No one stayed very long. We wished each other luck and soon we were all on our way home. I knew I'd be spending a sleepless night, just like Jerry Finnerman.

I ate my dinner quickly, afterward going over all my notes. But I didn't go to sleep then; I went to bed. There's a distinction between the two terms. Herb was an optimist at heart. I knew that his main thought that night would be: "We can do it." And he'd go to sleep. As I tossed and turned in bed, my main thought was: "How can we do it?"

The answer didn't fully come on that night or any succeeding night. We had to do it; so we did—by being inventive. After all, we couldn't throw money at our problems; we didn't have the money. All we had were the problems. And problems do have solutions—solutions that might not be ideal but are, nevertheless, solutions.

The following morning, Tuesday, May 24, 1966, at 8:22 A.M., the cameras rolled on the first shot of "The Corbomite Maneuver," the first episode produced

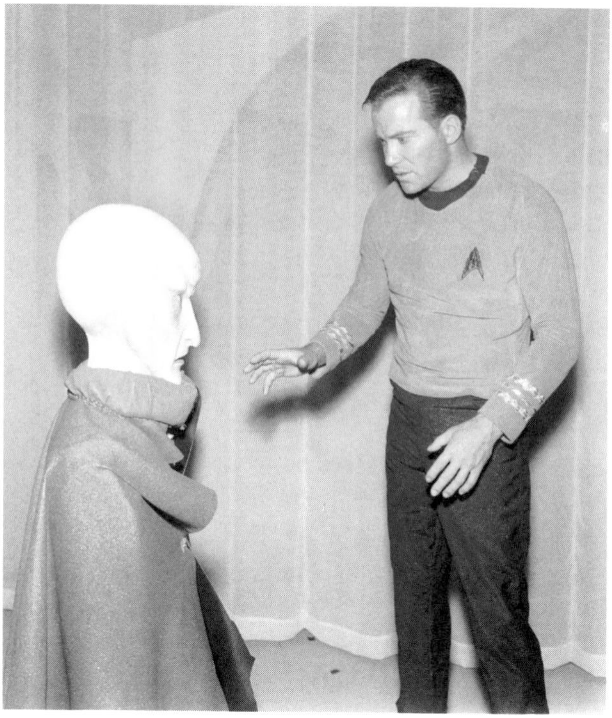

Courtesy NBC/Globe

Kirk faces the alien Balok in a publicity still. Note background, which gives away the fact that this set is a re-dress of the briefing room.

of the father of them all, the original *Star Trek* series. (Trivia buffs take note.)

Serendipity came to the fore on that first day of filming. Spock's speech patterns had been formalized during the second pilot. Herb Solow had recommended that, because English was a second language to Spock, he should speak it precisely, perfectly, and in measured cadence. But his attitudes hadn't yet been formalized.

During an extremely tense scene, Kirk and company had to face what appeared to be an incredibly powerful and frightening adversary who appeared on the ship's main viewing screen. Everyone was transfixed and fearful, even the intrepid Captain Kirk. But not Mister Spock. Director Joseph Sargent gave Leonard the key to his character by suggesting that, contrary to what was called for in the script, Spock remain aloof and deliver his one-word reaction introspectively, expressing curiosity rather than fear: "Fascinating." The Spockian attitude was defined for the future.

"The Corbomite Maneuver" contained one of Roddenberry's novel ideas. He cast a little boy to portray a bald, all-powerful adversary who used an awesome-looking dummy monster to frighten away interplanetary interlopers. Later, Gene had the boy's dialogue replaced by the deep voice of a mature actor. Gene's idea was good, but getting the bewildered child to act and enunciate at the same time gave director Joe Sargent fits. The poor kid, who was actor-director Ron Howard's brother, Clint, could hardly pronounce the complicated dialogue. But he sure did look weird in his Fred Phillips–created polished head. Sargent had to resort to making "pick-up" shots, filming one line at a time until the "all-powerful adversary" got it somewhat right. Because it was a "ship" show rather than a "planet" show, "The Corbomite Maneuver" was the tenth episode broadcast and was first seen on November 10, 1966.

HERB: In August, before the series debuted, a screening for NBC was held at Desilu, at which time the premiere episode was to be selected from the small group of episodes that could be ready in time for the first airdate, Thursday night, September 8, 1966, at 8:30 P.M. EST. (Are you still with us, trivia fans?)

NBC's and Desilu's desire was to deliver what the opening main title promised: "strange new worlds." There were really only two serious candidates: "Man Trap" and "The Naked Time." The second pilot, "Where No Man Has Gone Before," was held back because it was too expository in terms of the series con-

Child actor Clint Howard, as he appeared in "The Corbomite Maneuver."

cept and characters, a problem with most pilots telecast as series episodes. "Where No Man" was necessary for selling, not necessarily for televising. "Mudd's Women" was out of the running because the opening-night critics would have had a field day with the story of "space hookers in the galaxy." "Charlie X" was too gentle a tale, dealing with the problems of a teenager. "The Enemy Within" was another shipboard show that lacked the scope of *Star Trek*'s premise. Despite a fine performance by William Shatner, it was held back for later telecast.

BOB: I felt that "The Naked Time" made it easy for viewers to understand the main characters of our show and their relationships to each other. But the story took place mainly aboard ship. I suspected the NBC people wanted "Man Trap," because it was scarier and more exploitable than the others. I made a speech in the projection room pushing for "The Naked Time," but Gene was strangely silent and so was Herb. I suspected Herb had decided to give the network what it wanted and had cautioned Gene about making waves—but he hadn't cautioned me. I should have saved my breath. I had forgotten the "golden rule": "Those who have the gold, rule."

My recommendation was ignored, and NBC made the decision. Roddenberry and Solow agreed with them. The first show broadcast would be "Man Trap," the fourth episode filmed. It not only took place on a distant planet, but also featured a character, Nancy Crater, who had been replaced by a loathsome salt-sucking creature. I later realized NBC was right. With "Where No Man Has Gone Before" out of contention, "Man Trap" was the only viable "new worlds" premiere episode available. Later, prior to the premiere broadcast, NBC research-tested "Man Trap" at Preview House. The results confirmed NBC's and Desilu's decision to lead off with the loathsome salt-sucker.

"Man Trap" was written by George Clayton Johnson. George was an offbeat and, perhaps, almost strange person. He wore a shirt made from an American flag and would play guitar for us after delivering his latest rewrite. Watching him play, I was fascinated by his hands, with their long spatulate fingers. I'd never seen fingers with tips that splayed out so broadly. They seemed almost alien. Was it possible that . . . ? But no, I was just imagining things.

A section of *Enterprise* corridor. Note the stage on the left and one of the Styrofoam wall decorations on the right.

HERB: Offbeat and strange, however, are definitely in the eye of the beholder. George Clayton Johnson distinctly recalls meeting me for the very first time:

Courtesy Stephen Edward Poe

"I was visiting with Harlan Ellison in this little, tiny first-floor office with one window. Bob Justman had put him in there and wouldn't let him out until Harlan finished his 'City on the Edge of Forever' script.

"Suddenly, a guy dressed in old clothes and carrying a handful of papers crawled through the open window. He casually said 'hello' to Harlan and offered me his hand. 'Hi, I'm Herb Solow. I'm sneaking up on Roddenberry.' With that, the stranger walked out the door and down the hall. Harlan told me the intruder was head of production at the studio. I said to Harlan, 'Now, that's really an off-beat and strange human being!' "

Innovative storytelling wasn't enough to firmly establish, in the viewers' minds, a society several hundred years in the future. The interiors of the *Enterprise* would have to convince them they were actually "aboard" an ultramodern spaceship. Art Director Matt Jefferies continued to be faced with that design responsibility. And since he also continued to be limited in what he could afford to build, Jefferies always kept his eyes peeled for "things," in particular oddly shaped Styrofoam packaging pieces.

The search became a game. Whenever Jefferies and Justman—of "Jefferies and Justman Interiors," as Solow referred to them—walked together through the studio streets, they vied with each other to find serendipitous items. A successful walk meant finding Styrofoam packing pieces in refuse bins. Someone's garbage was someone else's treasure. The Styrofoam pieces were painted in primary colors and glued to the ship's interiors, making them look oddly modern. And the actors were cautioned, "Don't touch that piece on the aft bulkhead; it'll crumble in your hand!" Even Herb Solow was always on the lookout for more "neat things and gizmos."

HERB: Superior hand-eye coordination was necessary for brain surgeons, prestidigitators, and the guy responsible for opening the various doors on the set. He accomplished it by standing out of sight of the camera and running the "mechanisms." The mechanisms consisted of wires attached to the sides of the doors and threaded through a series of pulleys. The assistant director, standing behind camera and watching the scene, would trigger a red light that cued the offstage guy that the moment had arrived for him to open the doors. He would yank on the main wire. This activated the wires running through the pulleys and opened the doors just in time for Kirk or Spock to enter or exit.

The mechanisms always worked; the people responsible weren't as dependable. Sometimes the cue would be given too early, and the doors would open long before the actors reached them. This "magic door" syndrome usually brought an enthusiastic laugh from everyone except, perhaps, the director, who was usually behind schedule. To him, it wasn't funny.

Sometimes the cue would be given too late and the actors, trusting souls that they sometimes were, bounced off the unopened doors. This almost always brought an enthusiastic laugh, especially from the director. De Kelley was overheard to remark, "You can get killed walking to the coffee shop aboard this ultramodern space cruiser."

Later, when a builder in Santa Barbara, California, wrote to us asking for ideas on how to build sliding doors that work as quickly as those aboard the *Enterprise,* my recommendation to Bob was to tell the builder to get a different assistant director and a faster offstage guy.

There were certain limitations on the design and construction of sets. Feasibility and practicality dictated what could and could not be done. Visitors to the set, not to mention eagle-eyed viewers, were always amused that no matter how rocky and bumpy the walls of underground or cave sets on foreign planets might be, the floors were always flat and smooth. The practicality was that cameras couldn't "dolly" over bumpy floors. And when stuntmen staged fights, they had to be careful not to hit the "rocky" cave walls and crash right through. As a matter of fact, those wishing to leave the underground world in the "Devil in the Dark" episode could have punched their way out.

The 1960s saw an explosion of research in many industrial fields. Advances in aerospace and construction materials were of particular interest to Roy Long, *Star Trek*'s resourceful and innovative construction foreman.

For forty years of picture making, rocks, mountains, cave interiors, and large cut-stone walls had generally been cast in plaster. It was a very time-consuming and costly method, not to mention the weight, which created problems in moving the units. There were new advances, using plastic resin and Fiberglas, but costs, construction time, and weight problems remained.

In 1965, Roy Long experimented with and tested a "spray foam" machine that used several powerful solvents to fabricate both rigid and flexible foam forms. His continuing experiments led to a process that produced set pieces and sets that were lightweight, rugged, quickly constructed, and cost-effective. Long's success did not come without pain, however. While applying spray foam to a large planet surface set, he was overcome by a dangerous mixture of solvents in the air and was rushed to a local hospital. It was months before Long was able to return to the studio and *Star Trek*. In October 1966, he presented a paper, "Spray Foam—Application for Set Construction," to the 100th Technical Conference of the Society of Motion Picture and Television Engineers.

Star Trek could not have been produced on a television budget without Roy Long's contribution.

BOB: There was an urgent, garbled message from the set: We had to shut down. Some kind of emergency, something to do with the heat. "What heat?" I demanded, when I phoned back the stage. "This is May. You want 'hot'? Wait until August or September!"

"They just get too hot," responded the second assistant director, "and they won't work. Every time we—"

"Wait there, I'll be right down," I growled and hung up. Rushing up the studio street to Stage 9, I got even angrier. It wasn't that hot. What was with those actors? Sure, burning all those lamps made it hotter on stage, but this was ridiculous.

I stormed into the stage and spotted Bill and Leonard. "What's the matter, guys? Do you have a problem?"

"No, Bob. You have the problem," replied Leonard.

"Yeah, Bob, it's your problem. We've been ready for twenty minutes," added Bill.

"You're not hot?"

"We're not hot," said Leonard, "but your equipment is."

"My equipment?"

"If you'll pardon the expression," said Bill, grinning.

It was the equipment, specifically that which powered all the console readouts and light displays in the Bridge set. This was 1966. There were no computer chips or integrated circuits yet. Left on for any length of time, all the old-fashioned vacuum tubes, flickering lights, and wiring built up heat inside the cramped consoles until the overheated circuits blew out.

We shut down the displays during rehearsal, but that didn't solve the overheating problem. Heat built up continuously, and by afternoon the circuits overloaded within minutes of being activated. Our only solution was to rent portable air-conditioning units. Large flexible ducts snaked across the stage floor and pumped cold air onto special effects boss Jim Rugg's complicated electronics—and those people standing nearby who also needed relief from the heat.

Except during a take, the air conditioning ran constantly. Another problem solved but another problem raised: money. We couldn't use our own IATSE (International Association of Theatrical and Stage Employees) electricians because the air-conditioning guys were from a different electricians' union, IBEW (International Brotherhood of Electrical Workers). The A/C rental costs were nothing compared to the added salaries of the "cooler" electricians. And we also had to absorb the salary of a union plumber whose only duty was to hook up the water hoses. (The formula: different jurisdictions ÷ different locals = same electricity and a lot more money.) "But," as showbiz columnist Jimmy Fidler used to write, "don't get me wrong. I love Hollywood."

The money had to come from somewhere, so our set construction budget got trimmed again. Poor Matt Jefferies!

HERB: Necessity made Matt Jefferies the absolute mother of *Star Trek* invention. As Engineering Officer Scott gained importance, there came the need for a compact set where Scotty could feverishly work to effect emergency repairs on the ship's internal circuitry, when the preservation of a peaceful galaxy and the future of the *Enterprise* was in doubt. With short notice and little money, Matt designed a tall cylinder that later became known as the "Jefferies Tube." The camera could shoot straight down at Engineer Scott as he clung to the inside of the cramped set with lights flickering all around him. An assortment of bells, whistles, gongs and beeps was laid in afterward by the sound editors.

BOB: Although this was not an actual filmed scene, the action would typically go as follows:

"Bridge to Engineering. How's it going, Scotty?" Kirk looked and sounded anxious.

"Engineer-r Scott her-r-re. I'm inter-r-lacing the star-r-boar-r-d power-r-r module with the por-r-t photon tor-r-pedo tubes, Captain," said Doohan from his perch high inside the Jefferies Tube.

"We don't. . . ahhh . . . have much time left, Scotty . . . . ahhh . . . How much longer will it take?" asked Kirk. Shatner always seemed to hesitate dramatically when events overtook the captain. Actually, I always thought the dramatic pauses were a device he used while he tried to remember his lines.

"Thr-r-ee or-r four-r-r mor-r-e minutes, Captain, and I'll have war-r-p power-r-r restor-r-red," answered the intrepid ship's engineer as he probed the complicated circuitry with an instrument that resembled a futuristic combination of a soldering iron and a cuticle trimmer.

"We only have one minute left. Hurry, Scotty!"

"All r-right, Captain. I'll patch the r-rest of the reactor-r r-right into the r-r-adiation r-r-regulator-r. But don't blame me if it doesn't wor-r-k."

"Just do it, Scotty!"

"Aye, sir-r-r. Her-re goes. . . ." And after racing the clock, Scotty would bring power back at the very last moment and thereby save the good ship *Enterprise.*

Whenever shooting scripts called for the Jefferies Tube, Matt added more dojiggers and thingamajigs to it. Since there was no space available on Stage 9 to keep the contraption set up all the time, Jefferies put his tube on wheels so it could be easily moved in when it became necessary for Scotty to restore "war-rp" power and save the galaxy. Again.

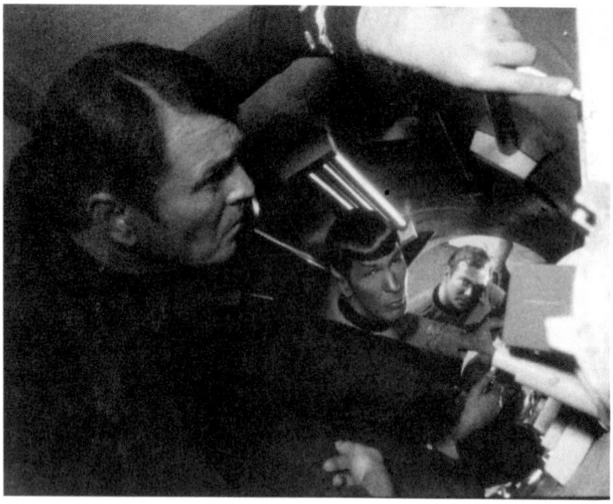

Courtesy Paramount Pictures

Scotty at work in the Jefferies Tube.

Flexibility of sets was of prime importance, with limited stage space and new sets needed for every episode. As a result of a memo from Roddenberry urging greater creativity in the use and reuse of sets, Jefferies designed the *Enterprise*'s Briefing Room so that it could be "re-dressed" and used as a recreation room or a cargo space. Similarly, Scotty's Engineering space became a shuttlecraft bay when needed.

And other sets were designed for quick conversion. Kirk's cabin became Spock's cabin became an alien passenger's cabin became Kirk's cabin all over again. Pull out a wall and stick in a different one; pull out the wall on one end and stick it back in on the other end and, with a change of furniture and fabrics, voilà!—another set!

Before alien planet interiors were designed and built, Justman, Jefferies, and Long met and discussed upcoming episodes with an eye toward revamps that would provide sets for a series of future episodes. Jefferies would change the colors of the walls and replace octagonal doorways with triangular doorways, but only infrequently would he move window walls. Having a new window was a luxury. Being able to see through to the planet exterior meant constructing a portion of planet exterior and lighting it, and that was more costly. But the same overall set dimensions were kept so that the lighting scaffolds could remain in position, fully rigged. Jefferies met every script requirement despite insufficient time and money. He was one of the most important contributors to *Star Trek*.

BOB: Matt Jefferies was the most decent and devoted human being on the production team. He never lost his cool, never lost his temper. His eyes got watery and he would find it difficult to speak when an over-budget show forced me to take away half his construction money. And I'd demand the impossible, that he still provide us with believable sets for less money than it should cost. He'd gulp a bit and finally say, in a very throaty voice, "Well . . . let me see what I can do. I'll give it a try."

So Matt would try harder, and he always came through for us. And I always felt guilty, so I sent him a memo of thanks and prodded Gene to do the same. By union contract, Matt wasn't entitled to a raise until after his first six months as a full-fledged Art Director. I talked Gene into discussing the problem with Solow. He did, and Herb "bumped him up" immediately.

Courtesy Matt Jefferies

Matt Jefferies with another of his creations, the Klingon battle cruiser.

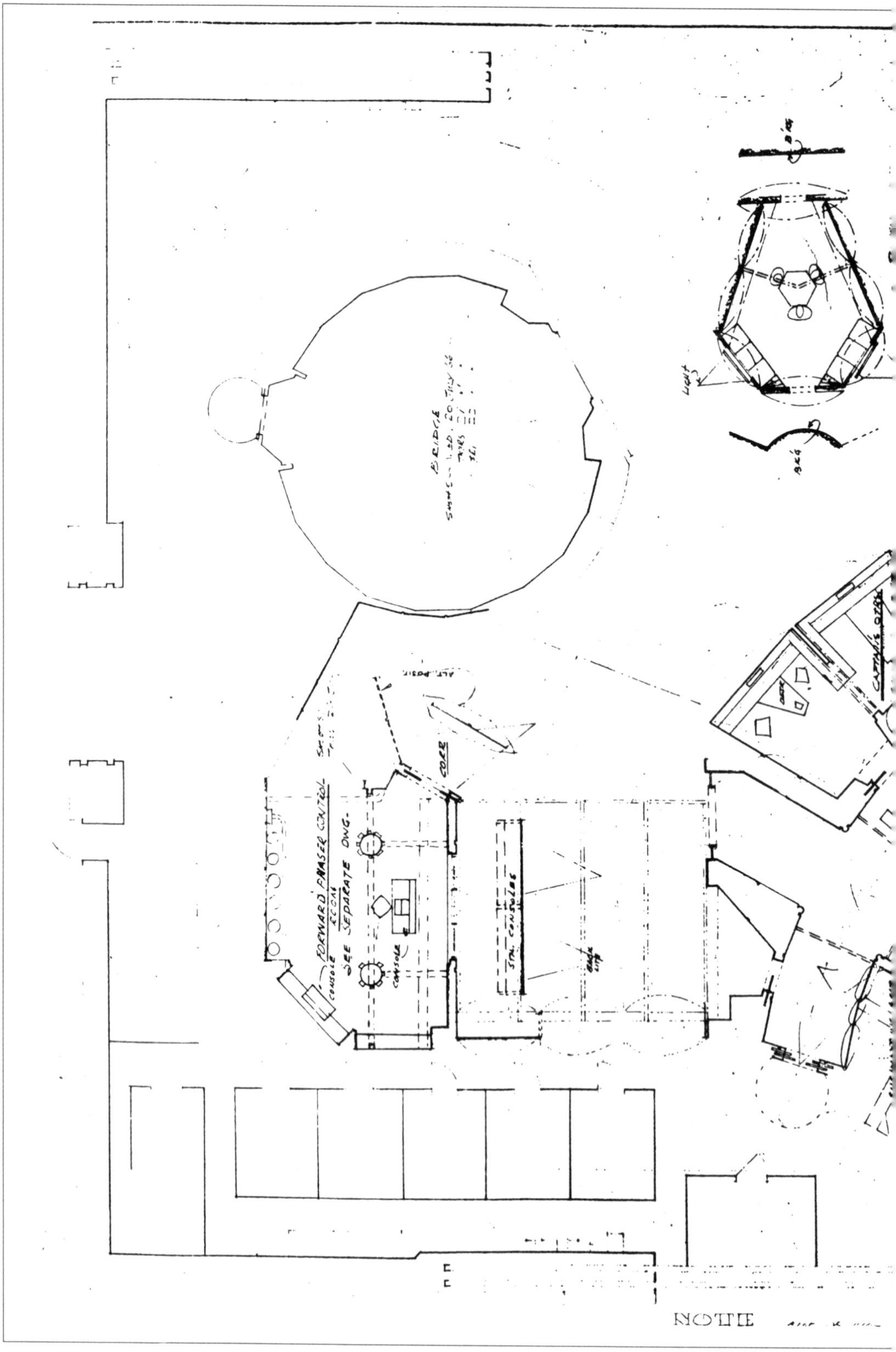
BRIDGE
FORWARD PHASER CONTROL ROOM
SEE SEPARATE DWG.
CONSOLE
CONSOLE
CORE
STA. CONSOLES
CAPTAIN'S QTRS
LIGHT
NOTE

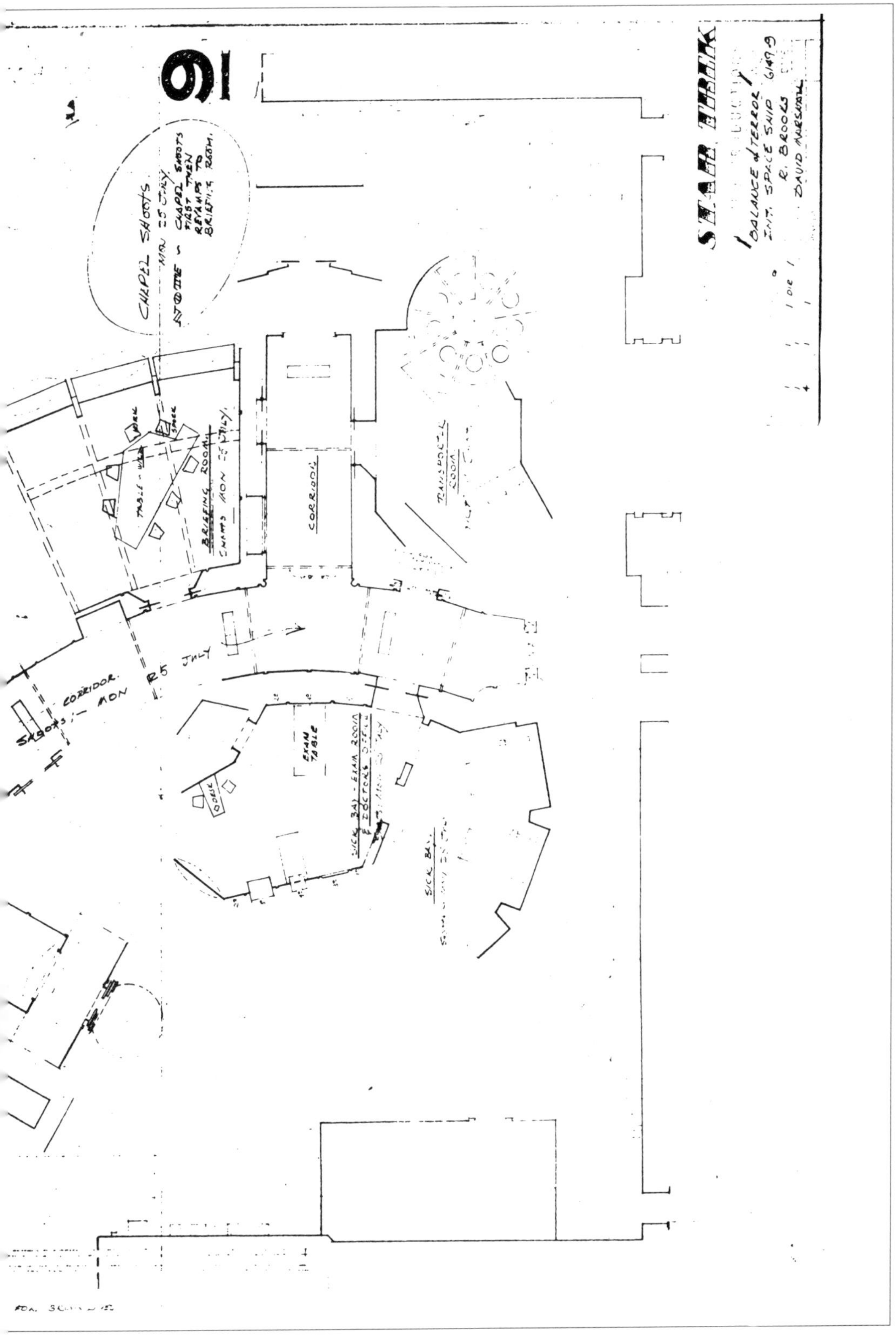

Courtesy James Cawley

Blueprints for the Enterprise sets for "Balance of Terror." Note the reuse of sets: the Briefing Room is marked to be re-dressed as the "Chapel."

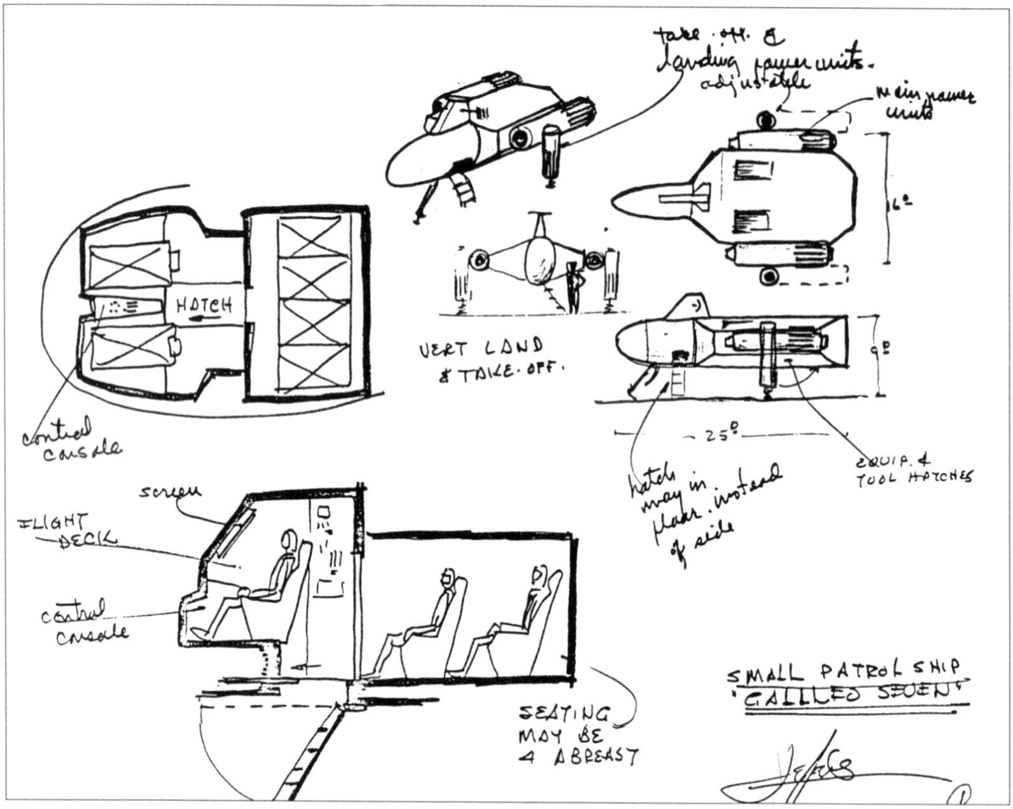

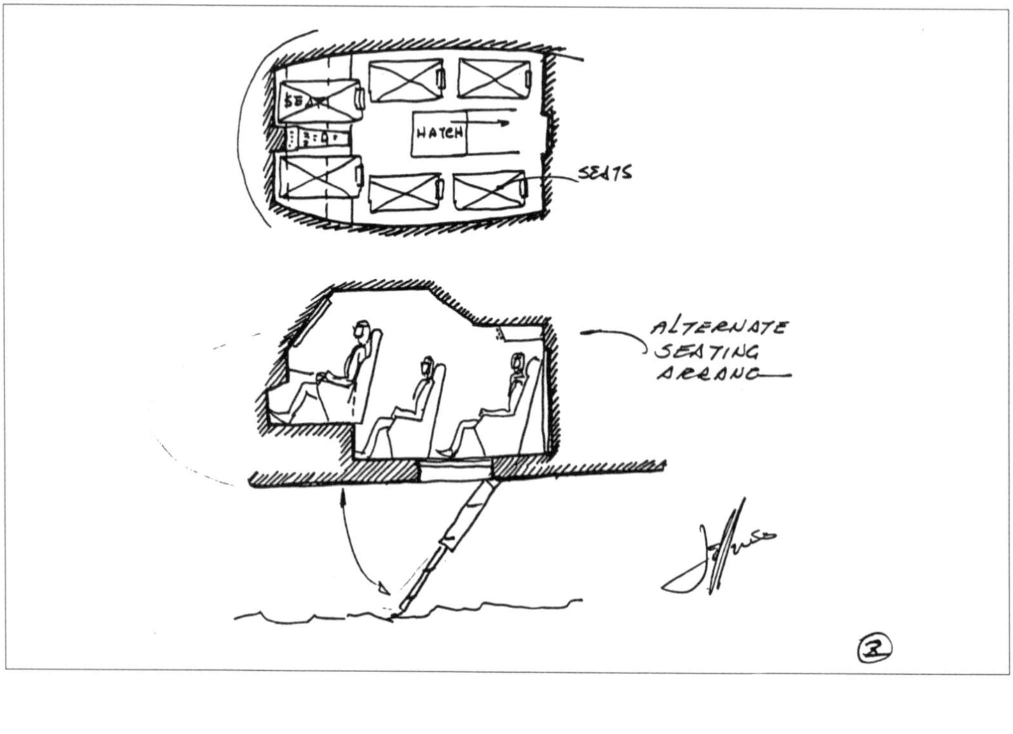

Matt Jefferies' sketches for the *Galileo 7* shuttlecraft.

Courtesy Matt Jefferies

But Matt Jefferies' own Art Directors Union scuttled Justman's attempt to wangle a better screen credit for him. By Jefferies' request, Justman had given him the highly desired credit of Production Designer on the first two series episodes produced.

It wasn't long before Jefferies' union wrote to Roddenberry, ". . . the words 'Production Designer'. . . shall not be used except upon written approval of the Union. . . . We must insist that you stop using this credit immediately and, except for the first two shows, the credits be corrected to comply with the contract." So much for fraternal relations.

Jefferies's contribution to *Star Trek* extended further than mere set design. He worked closely with Stephen Whitfield (later Stephen Poe) of the AMT Corporation, an official merchandising "licensee." Jefferies designed the plastic model of the series' *U.S.S. Enterprise* kit, which first went on the market in January 1967. Jefferies helped again by designing and consulting on the development of Klingon spaceship model kits. And later, after Jefferies designed the "shuttlecraft" *Galileo 7*, it became the basis for yet another model kit. By the time *Star Trek* was cancelled, Paramount Pictures, which had purchased Desilu, was already deriving significant merchandising revenues from sales of the model kits. But Jefferies never shared in those revenues. The man whose creativity brought millions of dollars in revenues to Paramount never saw a penny for himself.

The availability of the *Enterprise* plastic model kits not only made money for Paramount, it enabled a good deal of money to be saved on the manufacture and shooting of miniatures. AMT sent assembled models that soon became other "star cruisers" used in outer-space forced-perspective matte shots. The small *Enterprise* kit models were kept in the background while the larger *Enterprise* model cruised in the foreground. Viewers never realized they were seeing the same dinky kit models that they could buy in their neighborhood toy store. At least Justman hoped they didn't realize it. Happily, no one ever wrote in to complain.

Three uses of the commercially available *U.S.S. Enterprise* model kit on the series.

Courtesy Paramount Pictures

One of Bob Justman's "stock" reaction shots, as used in "The Corbomite Maneuver."

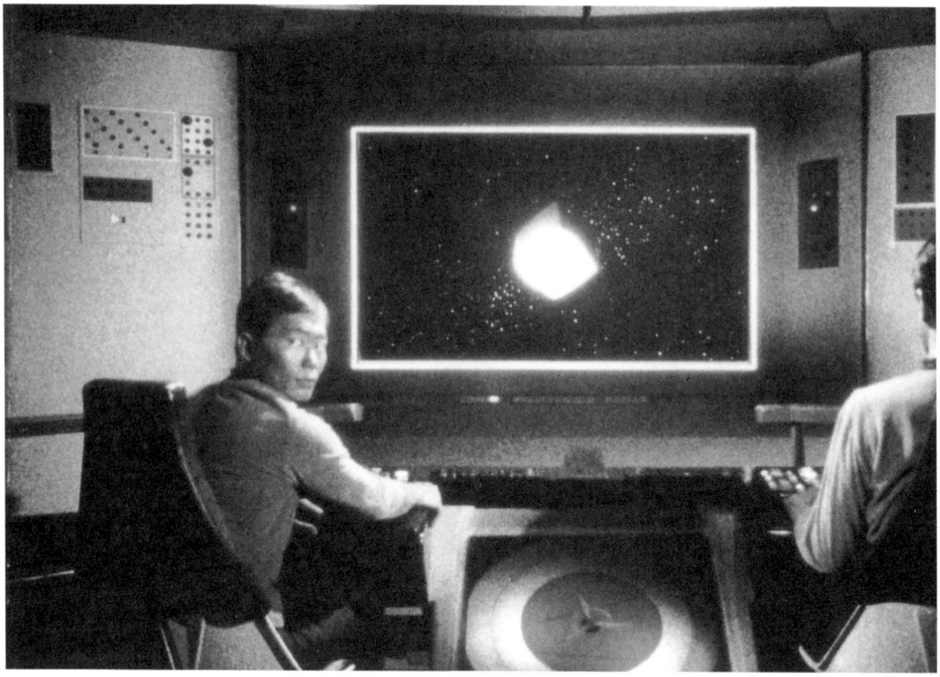

Courtesy Paramount Pictures

BOB: First-unit filming of special elements on stage with the actors for photographic matte shots is time-consuming and, therefore, expensive. We couldn't afford to stop production for an hour or more every time we needed a shot of the main "bridge viewing screen" with any of our cast in the foreground. A way had to be found to get around this sticky problem. As the well-known sign reads, we had to be able to "PLAN AHEAD."

So during the filming of the first few episodes, I took some time away from the shooting company to make tie-down "stock shots" on the ship's bridge. All optical matte work for the viewing screen would be accomplished without an accompanying loss of first-unit shooting time. There would be no further need to reshoot those angles for individual episodes.

A number of silent camera angles were set up in the rear of the set at various distances from the screen. The camera rolled, and I talked the foreground actors through their business. The shots were framed featuring George Takei in the left foreground and an extra's shoulder on the right.

"Glance back over your shoulder at where Bill Shatner's supposed to be, George, and look worried. No, I don't know what you're worried about, but we'll figure something out later."

We ran through a whole range of actions and reactions. The following season, when Walter Koenig joined the bridge crew, he was placed on the right side and we made enough shots with both him and George to satisfy any and all

requirements for the duration of the series. "Look at the screen, George, and act worried. Look at the screen, Walter, and act worried. Now look at each other, and act worried. And look at me, guys, if you need to learn how to act worried."

Star Trek continued to generate problems for Solow. Both NBC and Desilu management wanted the same thing—a successful series. But Desilu wanted more. It wanted a successful series that cost less money. That wasn't easy. *Star Trek*'s special requirements made for expenditures far above those of standard television fare.

Although individual episodes sometimes exceeded the series' budget of approximately $193,000 per episode (a high cost for a one-hour series in those days), Justman managed to place controls on all aspects of preproduction, production, and postproduction. This resulted in the series' staying slightly under budget, on average. Understanding the competitiveness between Desilu's two new one-hour series, however, the budget-conscious *Star Trek* management took umbrage at the fact that *Mission: Impossible* always exceeded its approved budget figure. This occurred because Bruce Geller paid only token attention to his budget. But then, not only was CBS paying more for *Mission* than NBC was paying for *Star Trek*, CBS Business Affairs would look more kindly on a request for additional money if that request came from Lucille Ball.

BOB: The studio's old guard continually put pressure on Herb. He tried not to put pressure on me, but Herb, regardless of his understanding of our problem, had a responsibility to his employers.

"Bob, there has to be something done to reduce our costs. We're spending ourselves right into a hole."

"Jesus Christ, Herb, we don't have enough to make the shows as it is. I keep cutting important things out of the scripts just so we can keep costs down. And Gene's getting really pissed off about it. We promised you that we'd stay on budget after Gene accepted the figures I'd worked out with you and the studio. We've kept our promise, but it isn't easy, especially when Gene sees how much Bruce Geller is going over budget on *Mission.* We shoot six days a show. Bruce shoots at least seven or eight, not to mention the so-called second-unit days he tacks on afterward. We say "yes" and mean it; Bruce says "yes" and doesn't give a damn. Ask *him* to save money, not us."

"I have, RJ. We're talking apples and oranges. You're the apples. But the oranges have more money to spend. That's the way it is, and unfortunately that's the way it's going to be."

But I was still burned. "Why don't you go back to that cheapskate network of ours and get us more money?"

"You're kidding. With Business Affairs holding the purse strings at NBC, we can consider ourselves lucky to get what we're getting now. Just give it a try, okay? That's all I'm asking."

So I tried harder; we all tried harder. And somehow, by the end of the first season's production, *Star Trek* managed to finish barely under budget overall while shooting an average of 6⅓ days per show. Unfortunately, our reward for this accomplishment, after the show was picked up for a second year, was a significantly reduced series budget. Even though NBC paid an increased license fee for the second year, the studio decided to recoup part of its first-year loss.

To make matters worse, second-year cast salaries were increased, per contract, for all the show's performers. Actually, the cast salaries were increased even higher than the contracts specified, due to an unforeseen demand by one of the show's stars. But more on that later.

Although Roddenberry and company were dealing with science fiction, it didn't mean that they could ignore the basic rules of drama. People of the future had to be as comfortable with their world as we are with ours. It was important that no one on board the *Enterprise* appear overwhelmed by "the wonder of it all." Their technology had to be as familiar and ordinary to them as our technology is to us. So Bill Shatner's flying a space cruiser in the future had to be as ordinary a process as Bill Shatner's driving an automobile today.

To achieve this goal, the staff, crew, and cast had to continually be made aware of this dramatic necessity. Accordingly, Roddenberry kept up a constant flow of memos to "ALL CONCERNED" regarding how viewers were affected by on-screen believability.

One stated:

> . . . we are not seeing the "trained group efficiency" that should characterize even a 20th Century Bridge much less one of the *U.S.S. Enterprise* in our Century. . . . *Why is this important to us?* Believability again! Our audiences simply won't believe this is the Bridge of a starship unless the characters on it seem at least as coordinated and efficient as the blinking lights and instrumentation around them. And were [*sic*] not going to believe our characters either unless there is a constant reminder they are indeed the trained kind of individuals who would have these posts of responsibility. . . . Admittedly it is first a script/dialogue problem and we will certainly try to keep an eye on it there. But we will miss and need the creative assistance of our directors in giving us movement and pace which helps keep the Bridge and routines efficient and believable.

Another Roddenberry memo suggested keeping things simple re: ship's course and speed:

> . . . much simpler to the audience and more to the point to say something like "Increase speed, lets [*sic*] overtake that vessel," or of course, something like "Give us an interception course, Navigator." In some such cases the

more precise numeral or decimal terminology can be useful as sort of a "throwaway dialogue," coming faintly from background [*sic*] as "filler" in keeping the scene alive, believable, suggesting that precise things are being measured and done without cluttering up our foreground story line.

Of all the problems, not the least was the complicated postproduction process. And as everyone agreed, it was "a bitch."

Initially, three teams of film editors were hired. Bob Swanson, who cut "The Corbomite Maneuver," headed up the first team. He worked quickly and confidently. Bruce Schoengarth cut the second episode filmed: "Mudd's Women." He was a quiet and accomplished editor. The third editor was brought to the production by Roddenberry.

BOB: Fabien Tordjmann was an excitable Frenchman, a rabid film buff who believed that cutting film was both a public art and a private discipline calculated to advance "film theory." He was enthusiastic and always ready to experiment. His initial assignment was the third episode filmed: "The Enemy Within." Fabien decided to enhance the story, utilizing an esoteric approach. However, the story had Shatner playing both Kirk and Kirk's evil alter-ego; it was already esoteric enough for the television screen. Using experimental editing techniques was, to put it mildly, counterproductive.

I urged Fabien to stay with the basics. "Just cut film the old-fashioned way, and when in doubt, 'Stay with the money.' "

"What is this stay with the money, Bob?"

"The money is the star, Fabien. The money is always the star. Just stay with Bill Shatner; he'll keep things clear so the audience won't have to work so hard to understand what's going on."

"Okay, Bob. If you insist. But there won't be any style to the editing."

"I think we'll survive that loss, Fabien. See you later." No sooner had I left his cutting room then I heard:

"Merde!"

Fabien was unaware of my return, so involved was he in untangling his feet from the hundreds of feet of film that covered the cutting room floor. As Fabien stomped about, trying to free himself from "The Enemy Within," his Moviola continued to spew out more film onto the floor.

William Shatner turned in a fine performance as Captain Kirk's evil alter ego in "The Enemy Within."

Courtesy NBC/Globe

"Merde! Merde! Merde!"

It seemed as if Fabien always had Moviola mishaps. We'd hear *"Merde! Merde, merde, merde!"* and we knew he was stepping on the film again. In dailies, we could always tell which films had been cut by Tordjmann: "They're the ones with the footprints on them."

The fourth team of editors was finally hired to remedy the expected production and postproduction slippage. With the production of "What Are Little Girls Made Of?" came Frank Keller, an amiable man and a fine editor. *Star Trek*'s picture-cutting staff was complete.

Don Rode was Assistant Film Editor. After viewing a sequence that the young editor cut, Justman gave him a chance to do the show "trailers," the one-minute "promos" that closed each episode and hyped, "Next on *Star Trek* . . ."

Justman and Rode played a game: How many individual pieces of film could be contained in a trailer without confusing the viewers? Rode set a record with a total of sixty-nine cuts—count 'em, sixty-nine cuts—in ninety feet (one minute's worth of film). Actually, there was only eighty-eight feet of film to work with; the other two feet comprised the trailer's one-foot fade-in and one-foot fade-out.

Fabien Tordjmann wasn't the only one who had theories. Justman had the "orgasm" theory for the show's trailers. Any sequence involving Captain Kirk romantically involved with a female guest star was assembled with successively shorter cuts that ended in an on-screen explosion. "Maybe nobody else will get it," exclaimed Justman, "but we will."

Rode was also assigned to assemble the famous "gag" reel for the *Star Trek* Christmas party. When dailies were run, Rode kept two lists, and Justman indicated which shots were to be used in the trailers and which flubs and mistakes to save for the gag reel.

Star Trek's music gave viewers a human point of reference for the unusual characters and events in the stories.

Alexander Courage's hauntingly melodic main title theme had served both pilots well; it would now serve the series. The charismatic four-note "ping ping ping ping" was a mysterious but welcoming beacon to viewers every week. And every time an episode would be run and rerun, Courage would receive 100 percent of the BMI music royalties—or so he thought. Roddenberry, who had never written a music lyric, chose to write one for the *Star Trek* theme, a lyric that would never be sung or used in any manner other than being printed on the published orchestral and band arrangements. Its purpose was not an expression of creativity; it was purely financial. Roddenberry, the lyricist, would now receive fifty percent of all music royalties; and Courage, the composer, would receive the remaining fifty percent.

THEME FROM STAR TREK
LYRICS BY
GENE RODDENBERRY
MUSIC BY
ALEXANDER COURAGE (BMI)
♩=152
BE- YOND
THE RIM OF THE STAR- LIGHT
MY LOVE IS WAN-D'RING IN STAR- FLIGHT
© 1966 BRUIN MUSIC CO.
110
HO. 5-3124 1527½ Vine St Hollywood, Calif.

Courage's famous theme music and Roddenberry's seldom-heard lyrics.

2.
I KNOW HE'LL FIND IN STAR CLUS-TERED
REACH- ES
LOVE STRANGE,
LOVE A STAR WO-MAN TEACH- ES
I KNOW HIS JOURN-EY ENDS NEV- ER
Hollywood, Calif
110

HIS STAR TREK WILL GO ON FOR-
EV- ER BUT TELL HIM
WHILE HE WAN-DERS HIS STAR- RY SEA RE-
MEM- BER RE-MEM-BER ME

110

4.

FROM THE LOG OF THE STAR SHIP ENTERPRIZE

October 3, 1967

Mr. Alexander Courage
12317 16th Helena Drive
Los Angeles, California 90049

Dear Sandy:

After the telephone conversation with you, I sat down and spent some time going over old notes and jogging my memory regarding our conversations so long ago regarding STAR TREK music. Perhaps this will help refresh your memory -- in my old office, the small bungalow across the lot, you and I sat down one afternoon and discussed sharing the credits on the music. I recall very distinctly that you shook your head and stated you would naturally prefer not to split the money on the theme but, on the other hand, since this was the way it was and since we were working so closely together on the concept you would go along with it. You may recall that shortly afterwards I assigned you to do the theme on POLICE STORY, unfortunately not sold, and did not ask for a similar arrangement since I had no strong notions about that music and did not expect to work as closely with you on it.

I think you know it has never been my way or policy to be unfair. On the other hand, I have always considered handshake agreements not only to be as binding as written agreements but also more important. I am certain you feel the same way and intend no effort to violate such agreement.

I am sending the enclosed to you in all hopes that a reference to your old notes on the subject will recall to your mind that conversation.

Sincerely yours,

Gene Roddenberry

Desilu STUDIOS · 780 NORTH GOWER STREET, HOLLYWOOD, CALIFORNIA 90038 · PHONE (213) HO 9-5911

Letter from Roddenberry to Courage regarding their sharing of credit and payment for *Star Trek*'s theme music.

Ed Perlstein

December 19, 1966

Gene Roddenberry

Dot Records-Nimoy Record

cc: H. Solow
L. Maizlish
P. Singer

Dear Ed:

Reference promotional copies of the STAR TREK theme record, this office could use five dozen of them for "thank you" give-aways to science fiction "greats" who are currently helping us out on a mail campaign, and other similar places.

In the matter of a Leonard Nimoy album, since it will undoubtedly contain something of the STAR TREK theme, I would expect to receive a lyric royalty. And, since "Mr. Spock" is a creation of mine (maintained against some odds) I would like to have some voice in the nature and direction of this album, nor do I feel that a special arrangement with myself and Norway Corporation on profits from that album would be at all out of order.

Reference both items in the preceding paragraph, would very much appreciate an answering memo on them at your earliest convenience.

Respectfully,

Gene Roddenberry

GR/p

Memo from Roddenberry to Desilu attorney Ed Perlstein regarding Roddenberry's "participation" role in Leonard Nimoy's record deal.

HERB: When Sandy Courage was given his contract to write the *Star Trek* music, he was unaware of a two-sentence clause toward the end of the agreement. Thinking it was more of the usual boilerplate, Sandy signed the agreement without reading it fully. The clause, inserted by Gene's attorney, Leonard Maizlish, gave Gene the right to write a lyric to Courage's theme.

Almost two years later, after NBC put *Star Trek* on its schedule, Sandy received a call from Leonard Maizlish: "Listen, from now on we will be collecting one-half of your royalties." Sandy, confused as to how this could happen, spoke to Desilu Music Department head Wilbur Hatch and Desilu attorney Ed Perlstein. "They told me there was nothing that could be done, legally," said Sandy, and when he questioned Roddenberry, Gene explained, "Hey, I have to get some money somewhere. I'm sure not going to get it out of the profits of *Star Trek.*"

Sandy felt that if the reason for the lyrics was to get singers to record the theme, to add value to the property, then that would have been acceptable. In fact, Courage would have worked with Gene to assure the musicality of the lyrics. But it was simply Gene Roddenberry taking performance royalty monies from Alexander Courage.

And as Courage points out, "Roddenberry's lyrics totally lacked musical practicality. He [Roddenberry] made two very serious errors in writing the lyrics. One, he changed the shape of the melody by adding extra beats, and two, he used a closed vowel with a z-z-z-z-z sound on the highest notes, something that gives great problems to singers."

With Gene taking half of Sandy's sole credit and royalty, I again marveled at his seemingly unending drive to fashion himself the single master, the absolute proprietor of *Star Trek.* At the time we were producing the series, I never realized the ultimate result of his actions; I'm not sure Gene ever realized the ultimate result of his actions. Simply stated, it was that the followers of *Star Trek* would look upon Gene Roddenberry as the unfettered, all-encompassing, see-all, hear-all, know-all Master of the *Star Trek* universe. And this allegiance to the Master would ensure the future success of anything related to *Star Trek.*

BOB: Owing to his involvement at Fox arranging the music for the film *Doctor Dolittle,* Sandy could do only two of the first season's episodes. Nevertheless, owing to the "royalty" issue, it's no wonder Sandy Courage lost all enthusiasm for the series and liking for Gene Roddenberry. Despite my efforts to convince him to score second-season episodes, Sandy never returned to *Star Trek.*

Roddenberry's taste for music royalties didn't stop with Courage. During the second season, after Leonard Nimoy "spoke" a record album, Gene demanded royalties and a piece of Nimoy's profits.

While Roddenberry and Nimoy argued over profit participation, Solow was interested in pushing any album that promoted the series. On December 14, 1966, he wrote a memo to Desilu Business Affairs attorney Ed Perlstein.

Desilu Productions Inc.

Inter-Department Communication

TO: ED PERLSTEIN

DATE: December 14, 1966

FROM: Herb Solow

SUBJECT: "STAR TREK" - DOT RECORDS DEAL

Thanks for the memo and the copy of the letter from Charles Grean of Dot Records. I feel very strongly that we should enter into such a record deal. I think we should push any record company that wants to do an outer space or Vulcan or any other single record or album, be it straight dramatic music, weird music, Nichelle Nichols singing, Bill Shatner doing bird calls or even the sound of Gene Roddenberry polishing a semi-precious stone on his grinder. Hopefully we and Gene will make some money out of the exploitation of the music, but, more importantly at this time, will be the amount of consumer publicity we will be receiving. The more times we can get the name STAR TREK in front of the buying public, the better it is for all of us.

Regarding any deal with Leonard Nimoy, I imagine we have our standard deal with him and can convey it to Dot records. If not, I would hope that we would have some pressure on Alex Brewis not to dampen any interest in our deal by trying to price his client out of the Dot Record business.

H.F.S.

hfs:ls

cc: Bernie Weitzman
Gene Roddenberry ✓
Howard McClay

Memo from Solow to Ed Perlstein regarding Leonard Nimoy's record deal.

Courtesy Pictorial Press Limited

Leonard Nimoy in his office, with the record album that became a sticking point between him and Gene Roddenberry.

BOB: I knew we would get dramatic and lyrical scores from our composers. The thought-provoking content of *Star Trek* caused their creative juices to flow, influencing not only their musical themes but the orchestrations as well. Although Gene felt that "electronic space music" was not the way to go, I never hesitated when a composer wanted to work an electronic instrument into the score, adding a splash of futuristic color to the proceedings. And at times, we threw away the old rules and used stand-alone music "stings" (dah-dahhhhh . . .) or unaccompanied tympany hits for dramatic emphasis. Both seemed to belong in future worlds.

With Sandy Courage unavailable, it was necessary to find composers whose talents would suit our individual and very distinctive episodes.

George Duning, famous for his award-winning score for the movie *Picnic,* was chosen for his ability to write sensitive love themes and highly emotional scores; Gerald Fried, for his use of instrumental voices to depict strange alien world cultures; Jerry Fielding, for his upbeat approach to both drama and comedy. Other composers were also important: Sol Kaplan for his intellectualism, and Sandy Matlofsky for his inventiveness.

But Fred Steiner was the brightest star in our symphonic universe. His music seemed to spring full-blown from deep within him to support and reinforce the on-screen drama. It's no wonder that Fred wrote and conducted more scores, by far, than any other *Star Trek* composer. Totally reliable and immensely talented, he wrote symphonic themes so generic that they were often reused later in the season when, for budgetary reasons, we had to "track" certain shows with previously recorded *Star Trek* music composed by him.

But there were two problems to solve with Fred Steiner. They came not from this wonderful man's music, but from the age-old conductor problem of "stomp and grunt." In addition to "miking" each of the various instrumental groups (strings, brass, reeds, percussion, etc.), Fred demanded an "overall" microphone, facing the orchestra and hanging directly above the conductor's podium, to capture the full orchestral sound.

Fred was a very energetic conductor. And when the spirit moved him during a take, he would stomp on the wooden platform. The overall microphone would pick up the noise, and the sound mixer would tear off his head set and groan: "He's stomping again!"

Great minds gathered. By the close of the next ten-minute rest period, a double thickness of wool pile carpeting covered the platform. Stomping wasn't solved, but the sound was—unless he stomped really, really hard.

Grunting was different. And at times, the grunting was, to say the least, explosive. Great minds weren't about to shove a double thickness of wool pile carpeting down Fred Steiner's throat.

We made Fred aware of the problem. He apologized profusely and honestly tried to control himself. But soon after the cue began, he'd lose himself in the music and grunt on the more intense downbeats.

We always scored a "double" (two three-hour sessions in a row). All the musicians would play during the first three hours when we recorded the "big" cues. The "grunt problem" was not as acute then, since its sound was covered up by the full orchestra. However, during the second three-hour session, as musicians no longer needed were dismissed to save overtime, the orchestra continually decreased in size, and Fred's grunts became more and more noticeable. What to do? Herb Solow suggested reorchestrating the cues and including the grunts as an integral part of the score. He was quickly invited to leave the scoring stage.

Once, on a particularly important cue, the music recording mixer devised a twofold approach to solving our problem. First, he had gradually reduced the volume on the overall mike as the various players left the stage during the second session. Then, realizing Fred's major grunts always occurred on a major downbeat, he dipped the overall mike's volume and raised it up again immediately thereafter. He compensated by slightly raising the volume on all the other microphones. Later, during the hourly ten-minute break when Fred played back the recorded cue, the composer felt "something" was amiss. He just couldn't put his finger on it. "Did you hear that, Bob?"

"Hear what, Fred?"

"I don't know. Maybe I'm imagining things. Did it sound okay to you?"

"It sounded great, Fred. Couldn't be better."

"Oh. Thanks."

"Really good. We'd better get a move on. We don't want to run over."

"Guess I'm imagining things. Okay, let's do the next cue. We don't want to run over."

Fred cared about everything, even our budget.

Music could be composed, but the sounds of the future had to be invented. Roddenberry didn't want *Star Trek* to use the sort of spaceship and galaxy sounds that had been standard in the film industry for years. This breakthrough series would have its own. Sound effects editors Joe Sorokin and Doug Grindstaff became the inventors of new noises for the multitude of devices seen in the series. Using experience gained during production of the pilots, they worked with Justman and mixed together a multitude of sound tracks, some of which were created on the spot in the dubbing stage. Some are familiar, even famous: the shimmering transporter effect that follows Captain Kirk's now-famous command to his chief engineer, "Beam me up, Scotty," the twittering noises emitted whenever he unlimbered his communicator, and the phaser pistol's characteristic warble whenever it was "set on stun" and fired at an enemy.

Defying the dictates of science, the phaser warble sound reached a crescendo when the *Enterprise* fired a broadside. Science has proved there can be no sound in the vacuum of space. But without sound effects, much of the drama and excitement of the visuals would be lost. So when the ship fired its weapons, the sound track was filled with noise and the resultant explosions were horrific. When the ship warped past camera, the noise of its passage was magnificent. Not only that, when the *Enterprise* changed course, it banked like an airplane. Without exciting visuals and exciting noises to back them up, much of the drama of the show's space miniatures would be lost. "Dramatic license" was the reason, not the excuse, why Roddenberry and his team purposefully ignored the dictates of science.

BOB: Gene was intense about using sound creatively. His interest in the effect that sound had on viewers led him to give me a special assignment. "Bob, I want you to come up with a different sound for each part of the ship."

"*Each* part, Gene?"

"Well, not *each* part, just the ones we see on screen—the individual sets. After all, I don't want to overburden you and the sound-effects people." After that attempt at humor, he waltzed off and left me moaning and groaning with a full dance card and only one possible partner, Doug Grindstaff.

Doug moaned and groaned when I told him. "Every set, Bob? Every set?"

"No, not every set. Just the ones we see."

Doug groaned again. "Not funny, Bob. Unfunny, Bob."

"Look at it this way," I said. "Once we've got the tracks laid down, they're set forever."

It took hours and hours of work by Doug and his crew. We then worked on

the dubbing stage, mixing and blending the various tracks into an individual track for each section of the *Enterprise.* They were composed of not only machine noise and the pinging of the ship's sensors, but a number of voice tracks of crew members, which supposedly emanated from communications channels.

Prior to dubbing the second pilot, Gene had sent out a "confidential" memo to "come on down" to the dubbing stage. Everyone from our offices joined in, including Gene himself, plus some people from *Mission* and even Herb Solow. We laid down separate "normal" and "red alert" dialogue tracks for the bridge so that, when an emergency arose aboard the *Enterprise,* we could inject a feeling of urgency into the scene. The effort paid off throughout all three seasons of the show.

Desilu Productions Inc.

Inter-Department Communication

CONFIDENTIAL — CONFIDENTIAL

TO Bob Justman — cc: M. Chapnick, G. Peters

DATE August 26, 1965

FROM Gene Roddenberry

dcf

SUBJECT STAR TREK - B.G. WILD LINES REQUIRED DURING FRIDAY SHOOTING

All of our people involved in editing and sound on STAR TREK have requested us to pick up some offstage, background voices for use in STAR TREK scenes 48 through 63, i.e. when the U.S.S. Enterprise is being shaken around and damaged by the force field barrier. Am sure we can get Steve and Gary to cooperate in this, just as our STAR TREK group would help them wherever necessary. As for additional voices, I leave this problem to you.

Dorothy is typing up copies of this dialogue and should have it available for you sometime Thursday.

Gene

GENE RODDENBERRY

A "confidential" memo from Roddenberry asking everyone to help record "wild" lines of dialogue.

After we finished all the generic *Enterprise* tracks, whenever a scene took place on the bridge or sickbay or the corridors, a particular sound loop was utilized to paint an audio picture of that set. The sounds weren't obtrusive but they were always there, in the background, and they helped give a feeling of reality to what was happening.

Of course, there were times when specific shows required specific dialogue "wild tracks." For *Star Trek*'s first-season "Charlie X" episode, Gene Roddenberry volunteered to record a message from a cook in the *Enterprise* galley (kitchen) when the ship's routine was turned topsy-turvy by Charlie, a disgruntled teenager with unusual powers. Gene's voice can be heard on the bridge intercom complaining, "I put meat loaf in the oven. Now, there's turkeys—real, live turkeys!"

By building all those generic sound tracks, we did save substantial time later, when dubbing individual episodes. But as with all *Star Trek*'s best-laid plans, not everything worked as envisioned.

Whenever the main bridge viewing screen was featured, a series of red lights pulsated from left to right beneath it. And every camera angle of the earlier filmed bridge view screen stock shots featured those pulsating red lights. However, the lights did not sequence in a set pattern. Unfortunately, there was no way we could have afforded to automate the sequencing. We had done it the old-fashioned way. A special-effects man, using a nail attached to an electric lead, made contact with a row of other nails attached to the individual lights and closed the circuits. He ran the nail manually across the others as a kid might run a stick along a picket fence. We hadn't realized it at the time, but when he completed a pass, his timing and speed varied. So later, the familiar "ping . . . ping . . . ping . . ." sound had to be individually hand-synchronized with each light every time we saw the pulsating red lights. It drove the sound-effects cutters so crazy, they were getting severe "ping-itis." I finally told them to sync only one ping, either the beginning or the end ping. We acted as though we'd planned it that way.

Later, while dubbing various episodes, we took reality one step beyond. We rented a special machine that was used to change the pitch of people's voices without affecting the speed of the sound track, thereby keeping the dialogue "in sync" with the picture. Although the device was large, clumsy to handle, and expensive, it helped make alien humanoids sound as alien as they looked.

In addition, sometimes we slightly overlapped a character's voice with itself at a different frequency or overlapped and staggered it a few frames out of sync so that the two sound tracks were slightly out of phase with each other. This resulted in dialogue that had an eerie, echoing, and mushy sound.

Dubbing *Star Trek* was an intricate process. Dialogue, sound effects, and music were combined by dubbing mixers who recorded everything onto clear celluloid 35 mm film carrying three separate magnetic stripes. Each of the three mixers controlled many individual tracks, each mounted on a separate thousand-foot reel, and each in sync with the picture. An episode's picture footage was divided over six reels of film, with as many as twenty or more separate reels of sound for each reel of picture, all running simultaneously.

The dubbing process for *Star Trek* took a day and a half for each episode. The producers had to work with the antiquated equipment that the Glen Glenn Sound Company staffed and maintained for Desilu. Not only was the process too time-consuming, and thus expensive, it forced producers to accept results that never fully satisfied them.

BOB: Dubbing at Desilu was a frustrating chore. We'd test-run each reel and take notes. When mistakes were found, and they always were, all the reels had to be taken down and the faulty ones corrected before they could be run again. In the meantime, we went on to the next reel so we wouldn't be sitting around for hours with nothing to do. We'd usually have to take that reel down, too.

The antiquated technology added to the problem. If a mistake was made near the end of a reel, we couldn't just back up a few feet and pick up where we'd left off. All the reels had to be taken down, rewound, remounted, and recued. Then we began dubbing that reel all over again, from its beginning. It was the way films were dubbed back in the thirties.

But we found ways to break the tension on the dubbing stage. One of our composers had gifted me with a conductor's baton. I always brought it to the dubbing stage and "conducted" the music mixer. Unknowing visitors figured this was the way films were scored.

Harry Eccles, the sound recordist (and half owner of the equipment, which he had built), stayed in the "machine room" and, in addition to listening to the sound tracks over his earphones, loved to listen to our comments. He watched us, and the action on the projection screen, through a large glass window. Harry always wanted to join in, but he couldn't leave his post. I decided to play a joke on him.

Late that night, a propman installed a large window shade on our side of the glass window. The following day, I started speaking quietly to the mixers and threw surreptitious glances at Harry. Harry pressed his earphones close to his head. I began to whisper, but he couldn't make out what I was saying. Actually, no one could; I wasn't really saying anything.

I called the mixers over to me and we all whispered. Harry came right up to the window, like a moth drawn to a flame. He was trying to read our lips. So without looking up, I reached out and pulled the window shade down. Harry was now physically out of the loop. And we had a great laugh.

But when I raised the shade to have Harry join us in the laughter, he was gone. He'd hung up his earphones and not only walked out, but quit. And we still had most of an episode to dub. I caught up to him at the studio gate. "Harry, please, it was only a joke. We didn't mean to hurt your feelings. Please come back; I'll never do anything bad to you again. I promise. Please, Harry? Please?"

Harry finally relented and agreed to return to work. So he had the last laugh.

Or did he? Harry, like Herb Solow, was an orchid hobbyist. One day, to show he bore no hard feelings, he gave me a rare and beautiful orchid that he had grown. It had an exquisite perfume. I took it home and wrote him a letter of thanks:

"Dear Harry, Jackie and I wish to thank you for your gift of that exquisitely beautiful orchid. It was delicious, but half an hour later, we were hungry again."

I guess Harry and I ended up in a draw.

Gordon Day, the sound-effects mixer, gave me my own special buttons that controlled two sound loop tracks. One track contained the sound of a woman screaming in terror. Just one horrific scream was enough to curdle the blood. The other track contained the sound of a man laughing hysterically. Only the mixers and I knew they weren't hooked into the recorder.

I noodled around with the buttons, so I could perfectly control the volume of the tracks. And then I waited for visitors. But after successfully tricking a few Desilu executives and sending them scurrying away, I still wasn't satisfied. I wanted bigger game. I waited for the biggest fish of all—Gene Roddenberry.

Gene would come by in response to our request to check out a particularly complicated dub and perhaps make suggestions. Many times we had to wait for him; I was getting upset. How busy could he be that he couldn't walk fifty feet to the dubbing stage when I phoned? We couldn't take the reel down to work on another one because it meant losing even more time. I decided to end Gene's tardiness.

We finished a reel and I called him. We waited until he showed up, late as usual. He apologized. "Sorry, guys. I got here as soon as I could."

"No problem, Gene," I said.

Gene cocked an eyebrow at me. I'd never before failed to express my annoyance at him for keeping us waiting. Was this a new Bob Justman?

I said, "Roll 'em, Eldon, please." [Eldon Ruberg was the dialogue–head sound mixer.]

Gene settled back, ready to speak out if he saw or heard any creative or technical improprieties. After a few hundred feet rolled by, I surreptitiously eased in my laugh track loop, inserting it into a shot in an alien planet corridor. It sounded like someone having a really great time, out of sight, just around the corner.

Gene began to speak, but first looked around to see who else had heard the inappropriate laughter. No one looked up. We all continued watching the show, seemingly fascinated. Gene looked puzzled. Maybe he was imagining things. He kept mum.

The action continued. Captain Kirk was preparing to make love to a beauteous alien maiden with lots of cleavage. As Kirk moved close to kiss her, he partially obscured her face. This was the moment to mini-strike! It was just a minor scream; nothing spectacular. Gene started to say something, then stopped. He looked around again. Had no one noticed anything? The expression on his face was memorable. Were we crazy? Worse yet, was *he* crazy?

Courtesy Paramount Pictures

Solow's screen credit superimposed over the Balok monster's face.

Captain Kirk was now fully into his kiss. I couldn't resist. What a scream! It practically blew everyone out of the room. Gene jumped to his feet. "Did you hear that?"

"What, Gene, what?"

"Don't tell me you didn't! I know you did! What are you doing, trying to drive me . . ." He stopped.

I was laughing so hard, I almost fell off my chair. The dubbing crew, though trying to be respectful, burst into uncontrolled laughter. Even Harry, behind the glass partition, was chuckling.

It took a while for us to calm down, especially now that Gene was laughing, too. Gene gave us very few corrections that day. And shortly after, he decided I had learned enough to be trusted and he wouldn't have to check each completed reel anymore.

One of Justman's tasks was choosing the "freeze frame" backgrounds for all the end credits. He liked using shots that were visually arresting, altering and revising the list for every episode.

BOB: My favorite was the one I finally chose for Herb, the last credit prior to the closing Desilu logo. This was the only standard credit I never changed as long as Herb ran the Desilu operation. I used a close-up of Balok, the monster from "The Corbomite Maneuver," lit, enchantingly, with color washes of angry red and bilious green, and positioned his credit, "Executive in Charge of Production," so that it

appeared just below the creature's wildly glaring eyes. I thought it a fitting tribute, as did Herb, who thanked me profusely, thereby depriving me of some heavy-duty gloating. I still have the original credit and display it in my office at home, suitably framed in the cheapest, junkiest black frame I could find.

At the beginning of this first season, Roddenberry, with his eager Associate Producer constantly at his side, closely supervised all postproduction tasks, particularly picture cutting, sound effects, and dubbing. But after the completion of the first five or six shows, Roddenberry was obliged to concentrate on the series' major problem, story and script development, so he relinquished the postproduction workload to Justman. Roddenberry continued to screen "first cuts" (director's cuts) of each episode and gave Justman and the editors detailed notes about the changes he wanted made. He also always screened "final cuts" before approving them, but his hands-on proclivities diminished. Simply stated, there would be no new episodes to complete if there were no new scripts to shoot. So it was back to the typewriter and the dictating machine for Roddenberry as he supervised the rewrite process. And with *Star Trek,* a most difficult series to write for, the rewrite process was monumental.

Scripts for theatrical films are usually guided by the director. It's the director's presumed "vision" that ultimately gets on the screen. By contrast, television series are usually supervised by the creator(s) of the series, the singular individual or group of individuals who protect their vision over the life of that series.

Justman always claimed that Roddenberry was a terrific rewriter—so good, it was almost as if rewriting were something he was born to do. In fact, many agreed he was better at rewriting scripts than at writing his own originals.

But rewriting *Star Trek* was difficult at best and often psychically painful. Despite all the writers' best efforts, almost every script required extensive changes.

Until writer-producer Gene Coon joined the creative team, it was substantially Roddenberry's responsibility, and for him a painful one. He tired easily. He never had much physical endurance, and the process wore him out. So it was no wonder that he delayed facing the problem. But avoidance became a trap for Roddenberry. After shepherding scriptwriters to their "final" draft, he delayed working on the always "must have, indispensable, absolutely necessary" rewrite until the very . . . last . . . possible . . . moment.

BOB: As usual, Gene was late with a rewrite. The company was shooting the last sequence before they would run out of material and have to shut down. I couldn't wait any longer; I walked into Gene's office to hurry the process. My past prodding hadn't accomplished anything. He was still hunched over his desk, writing. He didn't look up when I entered; he just kept working, scribbling on the mimeographed script pages with a soft-lead pencil. But he knew I was there. I waited a few minutes, then asked, "How much longer, Gene?" He didn't respond. I waited

some more. He kept on scribbling. When he looked up momentarily, pondering, he continued to ignore me. He shouldn't have done that.

I climbed up onto his desk and stood there, looking down at him. "That'll teach him to ignore me," I thought. I waited a few minutes. He scribbled even faster, made some corrections, tore several pages from the script, and handed them up to me without speaking a word and without looking up. I took them, without speaking a word, jumped down, and left to go to the set with our next scene.

Eventually, it became a standard routine: When the shooting company needed pages, I'd walk into his office without announcing myself, climb up onto his desk, and just stand there, looking down at him while he wrote. For a while, he'd try to ignore me; he'd pretend that I really wasn't there. But I was there and he knew it. And I knew that he knew it. And he knew that I knew that he knew it.

Gene never said anything to me about my barging into his office without knocking. But one day, his office door didn't open. I turned the knob and pushed harder. Nothing. I soon realized an electric latch had been installed on the door, a latch controlled by a secret buzzer that was hidden from view. All this just to keep me out.

Only his secretary, Penny Unger, knew the buzzer's location, and she had been sworn to secrecy—never, never to reveal it to me. I was frustrated—but not for long. One day when they were at lunch, I doggedly searched everywhere, behind the potted plant and file cabinets, under her desk top, and then, eureka! There it was, hidden beneath the carpet where she could press it with her foot.

I bided my time, waited until later, and casually strolled into Gene's outer office. When Penny left her desk to file some papers, I quickly pressed the buzzer, opened the door, and walked into Gene's office. The office was long and narrow and he sat in the middle. A back door was at the far end of the room. Gene was busy writing and I walked right past in silence, pretending not to see him. I headed for the back door. Gene kept his head down, writing, while *he* pretended not to see *me.* I exited his office without ever speaking a word. And he never acknowledged I'd been there and never spoke a word about it to me. It was like two enemy spaceships passing in the "neutral zone"—an outer-space standoff. We never discussed it, not even in later years. It was our own private joke and it helped cement an already close friendship.

NBC's newly appointed executive, Stanley Robertson, the network's program "rep," never had to wait for the buzzer. At first, he was welcomed by *Star Trek* personnel. During his after-hours visits, Robertson seemed to enjoy the camaraderie engendered by the informal atmosphere at the impromptu staff parties. He was affable and friendly.

"Almost too friendly," a staff member said and grinned. "I guess he forgot he's supposed to be the enemy." Someone else ascribed Robertson's behavior to the quality of the two-dollar so-called champagne provided to him: "I guess it went to his head."

Robertson's behavior was different when it came to the work environment; he was all business. He sometimes objected to both premise and content of stories and scripts, as well as the "rough cut" of each episode—but the reality was that he was NBC's representative, and that was his job. The story phase was usually the major problem, and it made for some fancy footwork on Roddenberry's part.

Story outlines weren't supposed to display a fine writing style; they merely established the premise of the episode and outlined the steps in the plot. Well-defined characters and dialogue didn't usually appear until later in the various versions of the script. It was Robertson's lack of experience and dogged determination to establish his position that caused difficulties. Without approved stories, there could be no scripts. Roddenberry complained that he had to walk Robertson through the thicket, so to speak, in order to get approval for stories that he felt the NBC exec had difficulty visualizing in their final stage, the script.

"Imagine how confused he'd be if he had to read the original stories before we rewrote them," said Justman.

An early example of Robertson's intransigence was his rejection of "Portrait in Black and White," a first-season story outline written by Gene Coon that was one of Roddenberry's favorite story concepts. On August 26, 1966, Robertson wrote: "Per our conversations of today and yesterday, this is to confirm that, in its present form, the above story outline is unacceptable. We believe that this story does not fit into the *Star Trek* concept. . . ."

Roddenberry was angered by the rejection, which helped to sour his ensuing relationship with the NBC program executive. (During the third production year, this same story was revised, finally approved by Robertson, and filmed as "Let That Be Your Last Battlefield.")

There was yet another reason to resent Robertson's so-called intrusion into Roddenberry's domain of creativity. One of the three original scripts considered for the second pilot was "The Omega Glory," written personally by the *Star Trek* creator. In December 1967, when revised and proposed to Robertson as an episode by second-season writer-producer John Meredyth Lucas, it generated a harsh "Dear John" letter:

> On March 25, 1966, prior to the production of the first season of *Star Trek* films, agreement was reached in writing with Gene Roddenberry that the above titled script would be placed in "inventory" and at his discretion reworked and again submitted to us at a future date for our re-evaluation. Except for a few minor changes, we cannot distinguish enough difference in the 1966 script and the script received last Wednesday, November 28, to warrant an approval. Our basic objections, as discussed at great length with Mr. Roddenberry in 1966 are still, we feel, valid.
>
> . . . We will, however, on the basis of my telephone conversation with

Captain Kirk encountering alien life forms.

Courtesy Paramount Pictures

> Gene Roddenberry on Monday morning in which he promised to "personally re-write Omega Glory to our satisfaction" prior to it's [*sic*] being produced, grant you an approval based on those conditions.
>
> I must remind you again, John, that we, in the future, *will take an arbitrary position*, regardless of production schedules, that no story for *Star Trek* will be approved unless you and your staff adhere to the clearly spelled out contractual requirements.

Neither Roddenberry nor Lucas appreciated the arbitrary tone of their chastisement. The fact that a copy of the embarrassing memo went to NBC Vice President Herbert Schlosser and Desilu Head of Production Herb Solow was not lost upon a seething Gene Roddenberry.

On the other hand, to do justice to the young NBC program executive, once Robertson understood and approved a story, his comments about the resultant scripts, and the series itself, were often valid and, in fact, helpful.

Writing aside, there was another reason why friction arose. Robertson pushed hard for the "strange new worlds" concept voiced in the show's opening narration. If he had his way, every episode would seek out "new life and new civilizations"—in other words, NBC wanted planet shows. In a July 6, 1966, memo to Roddenberry on the first-draft script of "Charlie X," he voiced his opinion:

> Without becoming involved in a rehash of all of the dialogue which has passed between us on this point, we are very aware, as you are, that The *Enterprise*, with all its lavishness, depth and grandeur, plus the imagination it took to construct it, is a definite *plus* as far as *Star Trek* is concerned. However, we, like you, are very aware of the dangers inherent in restricting any series of plots to the confines of only "four walls", regardless of how magnificent they are. . . .
>
> A recommendation would be that in the case of "Charlie X" and other stories not yet in production, you give some serious thought to measures by

which parts or all of our dramas might be told by action away from the *Enterprise,* possibly on planets or scientific stations, etc.

Roddenberry did give "serious thought" to Robertson's recommendation. As did Justman, who voiced his opinion that "We could do just what Stan wants. But I don't want to be around when Herb Solow tells us that Desilu has gone bankrupt."

BOB: There was another NBC department to cope with as well, and at times this department's reactions differed completely from Programming's. Programming wanted "action" and lots of it, just so long as the action wasn't unnecessarily violent or "gratuitous." (*Gratuitous* was a word that was somehow surgically implanted in every NBC executive.) However, the word *gratuitous* was open to interpretation and a certain amount of give and take. After all, if we removed all "gratuitous" violence, the average hour episode would run approximately seventeen minutes.

Broadcast Standards was the title of our other formidable opponent. It was supposedly a completely independent entity within the NBC hierarchy, and its people were referred to by one and all as the "censors." If they said "no," it was "NO!" and they always knew exactly what *gratuitous* meant. There was no recourse to any of their edicts. And since it seemed that Captain Kirk spent a large proportion of his waking hours kissing various beauteous females, script after script resulted in Broadcast Standards memo after memo cautioning us to "avoid the open-mouth kiss."

We tried—but Bill Shatner didn't.

HERB: The 1950s saw the beginning of the anti–violence, anti–smut, anti-sexual-connotation movements. Owing to the pressures of religious groups, for example, it was forbidden to say "pregnant" on television. Lucy was never pregnant with Desi, Jr.; Lucy was "with child." Strange, she sure looked pregnant. There were also the rigged game show scandals and the under-the-table payments by manufacturers to producers and crew members to feature cars, cigarettes, cameras, watches, soft drinks, kitchen appliances, and like products on their shows; it was cheap and glamorous advertising. So Broadcast Standards had been set up to keep both the network and its many suppliers squeaky clean. Who wants protest letters? Who wants government subcommittees? Not the network and definitely not its advertisers.

BOB: On every new series, the first thing any producer or upper-level staff person received from the network was a heavy packet containing the various Broadcast Standards rules by which we would, in the future, lead our production lives. We all had to sign the agreement and attest that we would abide by these strictures, or else. No "payola," no acceptance of free products for filming, no acceptance of free merchandise to be consumed at home, no nothing from no one—nohow! Actually, not a bad set of rules for one to live a life by. Too bad politicians aren't required to do the same when they take office.

Broadcast Standards' other policies were similarly both strict and rigid: not only no open-mouth kissing, no nudity—not even exposure of an inner thigh now and then, and definitely no nipples. Genitalia did not, do not, and would not ever exist.

Regarding open-mouth kissing, John D. F. Black wrote to Gene after meeting with NBC Broadcast Standards' Jeannie Messerschmidt, "to quote her . . . 'The men should not look like they were going to devour the women when they get within six inches of them . . . and open-mouthed kisses . . .' She continued on [*sic*], but I am sure you understand the nature of her comment."

Gene sent a memo to our two first assistant directors, Gregg Peters and Mike Glick, on the subject of "NBC CONTINUITY": "We have requested that you and the director on each show be put on NBC's mailing list for continuity comments, i.e. 'please see that there is no open-mouth kissing', and that sort of stuff we get from them [*sic*]."

When it came to dialogue, there were no "goddamns," even when spelled with a small "g" instead of a large "G," and a simple "go to hell" had to be negotiated.

Also, if one thought about it, there were no lavatories aboard the *Enterprise*. Characters on *Star Trek,* or on any other network television shows, did not, do not, and would not ever go to the bathroom—except possibly during the commercials when the audience did much the same.

Every story outline, every teleplay, every completed episode resulted in a memorandum from Broadcast Standards detailing items that had to be either changed or removed. Some of their admonitions were amusing, if not mind-boggling. While it occasionally steamed us, the fact was that *Star Trek* suffered no more than any other network show. All programming was subject to the same restrictions. People sometimes forget that NBC was our customer and invested millions of dollars in our show. While we objected to some of their strictures, "they were entitled."

Luckily, Jeannie Messerschmidt possessed a temperament that could subdue the wrath of an angry producer, and unlike Stan Robertson, she never demanded that we obey orders; she always said "please." And since we knew she didn't set the policy but merely carried it out, we never took her strictures personally. After all, why kill the messenger? Besides, she was a nice person, and if we lost her, we might get someone else who could really make our lives miserable.

HERB: *Star Trek* was a major employer of creative talent: writers, composers, directors, and of course those brave souls who exposed their hearts and souls to the camera, the actors. Those *Star Trek* actors were marvelous. Granted, some arrived at the stage door with more than just their acting talent. Occasional guest stars carried with them their egos, petty demands, and attitudes. But they arrived. Rather, all of them arrived, save one, the scion of America's most famous acting family, the Barrymores.

Director Gerd Oswald was preparing his second episode, "The Alternative Factor." After Gerd interviewed John Drew Barrymore for a guest-star role, after Desilu Casting negotiated and confirmed a deal with Barrymore's agents, after Barrymore spent hours in wardrobe being fitted with a specially tailored and costly costume—after all that, the morning he was scheduled to begin work, November 16, 1966, John Drew Barrymore disappeared, ignoring his role, his moral obligation, and his contract. Calls to his home, his agents, his publicist brought us no insight or explanation. They didn't have a clue. The son of the famous John Barrymore had skipped out on *Star Trek.*

Actor Robert Brown, in the role intended for missing guest star John Drew Barrymore.

Courtesy NBC/Globe

Gerd hustled and Casting hustled and the role was re-cast on a moment's notice. A special costume had to be rebuilt for replacement actor Robert Brown. The episode not only went a day over schedule, the crew and cast had to be "carried" over a holiday, which amounted to a lot of money.

With all our more serious problems, common sense should have dictated, "Forget Barrymore, hope to make up the time on future episodes, and concentrate on something more important like meeting airdates." But I was livid at Barrymore's screwing us. I held a meeting with Bernie Weitzman, Desilu's Business Affairs Vice President.

"Can you just imagine what would happen if an actor showed up for his guest-star role and we told him to leave, that we'd changed our mind and are breaching our contract? There'd be hearings, press conferences, lawsuits. Hell, Ronnie Reagan is an actor. He's running for governor this year and he's a former President of the Screen Actors Guild. He'd probably have us drummed out of Hollywood!"

"So what do you want to do, Herb?"

"I want to lodge a protest with his guild."

Bernie pointed out that if we filed a complaint and failed to follow through, we'd be doing a great injustice to the Screen Actors Guild and to Desilu. And we'd be like so many other producers and studios who initiate grievance actions and then drop them. "And we'll certainly never recoup our lost money from John Drew Barrymore."

Bernie read the anger on my face. He filed a complaint with the Screen Actors Guild.

The Screen Actors Guild Board of Directors authorized the filing of a charge of conduct unbecoming a member against John Drew Barrymore, based on our complaint. Formal charges were prepared and filed and, after giving the Barrymore scion time to respond, a Trial Board was convened.

On the evening of January 4, 1967, we showed up—all of us, Weitzman, Justman, Widen, D'Agosta—in the Screen Actors Guild boardroom, as promised. John Drew Barrymore was present. SAG President Karl Malden headed the Trial Board, which included Jeanette Nolan and Charlton Heston, among others.

Barrymore gave a very unconvincing explanation of forgetfulness; we made a very convincing presentation of our hiring practices and what creative and monetary damages Barrymore's actions had caused.

We could not have been more impressed with the SAG board's interest, sensitivity, and propriety. They could not have been more impressed that two Desilu vice presidents and *Star Trek*'s Associate Producer, head of casting, and production accountant appeared to support the complaint.

The Trial Board suspended John Drew Barrymore's membership for a period of six months, thus preventing him from working as an actor during that period of time.

Star Trek still lost the production costs, but suffice it to say, no other actor ever failed to honor his contract to appear in *Star Trek*. Of course, that didn't help director Gerd Oswald, whose episode didn't turn out to be the triumph he had planned.

Star Trek directors, like directors of most one-hour series, were itinerant workers. Granted, they had an important responsibility, controlling every aspect of the live filming process on stage, but they were, nonetheless, itinerants. Directors reported to the studio for six days of preparation work and then shot their episode—it was hoped—in another six days. Then they'd move on to pre-

Advance Information on 1966-67 Programming

Star Trek

NBC TELEVISION NETWORK

pare an episode for another series elsewhere, only occasionally returning to the *Star Trek* cutting rooms to see if everything fit together. It was the producers' responsibility to shepherd the episode to its ultimate completion and airing.

Fortunately, the director of the first *Star Trek* episode was one of the most experienced talents working in filmed television. With everyone understandably anxious, Joe Sargent's work on "The Corbomite Maneuver" was outstanding. Although he finished half a day over schedule, Roddenberry, Solow, and Justman were ecstatic. First-show jitters could have made "Corbomite" both a creative and a financial debacle. Sargent had an open invitation to direct more episodes, but he quickly moved on to "long-form" television and theatrical films.

Canadian director Harvey Hart was inventive and worked well with actors, but his camera setups were far too intricate and time-consuming for a six-day episode. The second episode, "Mudd's Women," was beautifully directed, but it went a full day over schedule. And by "camera cutting" the show at times, he made some of his footage difficult to edit. Editing choices are nonexistent when you have only a "master shot" and a dearth of other angles. Hart wasn't invited back.

Leo Penn, father of actors Sean and Christopher Penn, was highly regarded and very much in demand. But the third episode, "The Enemy Within," went three-quarters of a day over schedule despite the fact that all the action took place aboard ship.

Suddenly, anxiety and concern entered the picture. Argie Nelson and Ed Holly issued daily reports on the three over-schedule and over-budget episodes. Solow refused to return their phone calls. Roddenberry's door stayed closed to them. *Star Trek* was playing right into the hands of the old guard!

BOB: Could any quality director complete an episode on schedule? Or had Solow and his crazies sold an impossible bill of goods to Lucy?

Enter our savior.

Marc Daniels was set to direct show number four, "Man Trap." He was known as a jack-of-all-trades: theatre, movies, and television—film and live, episodic and long form, single- and multicamera. He had directed comedy—ironically Marc was an award-winning director of *I Love Lucy.* He had directed countless dramas; he had directed commercials. And in 1961, he had even directed Sir Laurence Olivier and George C. Scott in *The Power and the Glory,* a two-hour CBS television special.

"Sounds like a man who can't hold a job," I joked.

During a drought, you pray for rain. During the first year of *Star Trek,* we prayed for Marc Daniels. He finished "Man Trap" on schedule, in six days. His film work was outstanding, crisp, and energetic. Marc, his earpiece wired to the hearing aid in his shirt pocket, was a demanding general and ran the set with a firm hand.

But that success wasn't the only reason to pray for Marc. While he was directing "Man Trap," the next scheduled director was hired to direct a feature

and became suddenly unavailable. It was too late to find a replacement. We'd have to shut down.

So what could I lose? I went to Daniels, "Would you? Could you? Do both?"

Marc hunched his shoulders. "Why not?"

So while filming "Man Trap," Daniels prepared the next episode, "The Naked Time," and shot both shows back to back. "The Naked Time" finished shooting a quarter of a day under schedule. He was my hero, and I was a guy who had few heroes.

Marc was hired for multiple assignments that season. He again shot two shows back to back, "Court Martial" and Roddenberry's two-part "Envelope" script "The Menagerie," incorporating the first *Star Trek* pilot. Marc directed more episodes of *Star Trek* than anyone else. He was a marvelous talent and a wonderful man. And what a find for *Star Trek*!

It was Daniels who initiated the "cast table" rehearsals that soon became an integral part of the *Star Trek* methodology. A long table was set up in an unused portion of whichever stage was in use that day. After blocking out the action for the next camera setup, the cast members didn't return to their dressing rooms to await the call to the set for filming, as was the custom in the industry at that time. Instead, they sat with the episode director and script clerk George Rutter, at the table where they rehearsed the upcoming scenes. As a result, valuable production time was saved and performances were honed.

Among the other directors, Vincent McEveety's work on "Balance of Terror" stood out for both its style and its great energy. He also directed two back-to-back episodes, "Dagger of the Mind" and "Miri."

Although James Goldstone, director of the second pilot, was well on his way to a motion-picture career, he returned to direct "What Are Little Girls Made Of?" Not only was the episode intricate and difficult, but the script was in such bad shape that it had to be rewritten as it was filmed. Everyone on the set had to wait until fresh pages arrived from Roddenberry. "Little Girls" went two days over schedule.

Joseph Pevney was an ex-actor turned director. Some former actors become good directors; some former actors become dictatorial hacks. Pevney was the former. but more than just "good." He directed "Arena," producer-writer Gene Coon's first script for *Star Trek*.

By August 1966, with the first airdate still weeks away, Roddenberry, whose long suit had never been stamina, was running out of gas. The series desperately needed fresh and inventive story ideas. It needed a writing "machine." Roddenberry asked his agent and his writer friends for help. It came in the person of writer-producer Gene L. Coon.

Courtesy Richard Arnold

Star Trek Producer Gene L. Coon.

World War II veteran, Korean War combat radio correspondent, novelist, and screenwriter, Coon had been cranking out quality scripts in machinelike fashion for a successful CBS series, *The Wild, Wild West*, without ever missing a deadline. He'd been a fertile source of ideas for that show's other writers. Soon Gene Coon, fresh and strong and oblivious to pressure, became *Star Trek*'s savior and Justman's new "hero."

BOB: Although his title was "Producer," Coon knew he was hired to write, and write he did. He was an ever-fertile source of story ideas and "the fastest type-writer in the West." Coon churned out page after page of shootable and exciting scripts while chain-smoking his way through pack after pack of Sherman cigarillos.

And exciting scripts weren't his only contribution to *Star Trek.* In one of his rare acknowledgments of others who contributed to the series, Gene Roddenberry wrote in a February 19, 1968, letter to columnist John Stanley: "Gene [Coon] did bring many new ideas and concepts to the show, not the least was [*sic*] the arch villains, the 'Klingons' and their subculture."

Coon's appearance was deceiving. At first, to me, he looked like the stereo-typical "B-picture" banker who delighted in foreclosing on impoverished old ladies. But from his writing and his person, I soon realized Gene Coon was a romantic. He was a romantic with an obvious sense of humor, as evidenced by an accept-ing smile every time the secretary I hired for him, Andee Richardson, the first African-American woman at Desilu to become a producer's secretary, answered the phone by announcing in the heaviest, most Southern cornpone accent she could muster, "Coon's office! Coon's coon speaking." Andee was much loved by all who came in contact with her, reputedly including her onetime boyfriends Wilt Chamberlain and Godfrey Cambridge.

Andee wasn't Gene Coon's only surprise. Oddly enough, "Arena," Coon's first script for *Star Trek,* almost never happened.

HERB: Plain and simply, we were running out of scripts. Several writers hadn't delivered as promised, and suddenly, there were only two choices of action avail-able to us: either shut down the shooting company or somehow find another script. Gene Roddenberry was away and Gene Coon was busy rewriting other writers' scripts, but none of those would be ready in time. So Coon decided to take some direct action. He asked Bob if he could leave the studio a little earlier that Friday afternoon to go home, lock himself in a room, and not emerge until Monday morning with a new script. RJ was thrilled. "If you can do that, go home early every weekend."

So just before 6:00 Friday, Coon drove his Toyota Land Cruiser off the lot and did not return until midmorning Monday—with a new script in hand. Now, I was thrilled. The script was quickly put into mimeo and copies were rushed to NBC for network approval and Kellam DeForest's office for factual research and legal approvals.

But suddenly, the thrill was gone. Coon, an ardent reader of science fiction since he was a child, in his haste to create a story, had inadvertently based part of his script on a short story that had been written by Fredric Brown. Kellam's assistant Joan Pearce, who reviewed, analyzed, and wrote the research reports on all *Star Trek* scripts, recognized the story. She remembers that when she advised Coon of the problem, his reaction was a horrified "Oh my God!" Joan has

Leonard Nimoy as Spock, with guest star Jill Ireland in "This Side of Paradise."

absolutely no doubt he was unaware he had "lifted" the material. But Coon had transgressed, and there was no way we could shoot the script without buying a plagiarism lawsuit.

Gene Coon and I met with Bernie Weitzman and Ed Perlstein and formulated a plan. Business Affairs would call Brown, tell him *Star Trek* would like to buy his story, and offer a fair price. Brown was thrilled to have one of his stories on *Star Trek* and accepted the deal. We never did tell him that the script had already been written.

"Arena" was a difficult action show and was filmed mostly on location. Pevney, who was brought to *Star Trek* by Gene Coon, was possessed of both unfailing optimism and good nature and worked exceptionally well with the cast—and he brought the episode in on time. He was signed for multiple shows and ended up directing five episodes that season. Two of those episodes became famous: "The Devil in the Dark," written by Gene Coon, and "The City on the Edge of Forever," which later won a Writers Guild award for Harlan Ellison.

BOB: While Joe was directing "The Devil in the Dark," Bill Shatner got word that his father died. It was a crushing blow to him, and we immediately decided to shut down so he could fly to the funeral in Florida. With his plane not scheduled to leave until that evening, however, Bill wouldn't hear of stopping. He insisted upon finishing the day's work before leaving for the airport.

We shot around Shatner for the next few days, but when we ran out of non-Kirk material, we were forced to shut down for a day, Friday, January 20, 1967. Owing to Bill's absence, we also had to shoot an extra day. But his demeanor was impressive during this difficult time for him.

The strength of Ralph Senensky's episode, "This Side of Paradise," was that it gave Leonard Nimoy the opportunity to display the human side of his Vulcan character. "Spock laughs! Spock cries! Spock . . . what?!!"

Guest star Jill Ireland fell ill with the flu during the filming, and although wanting to continue, she finally had to take a day off under doctor's orders. Senensky handled the sensitive story and the revised schedule very well and returned to direct other emotionally sensitive stories during the show's second and third seasons.

Michael O'Herlihy, brother of actor Dan O'Herlihy, directed "Tomorrow Is Yesterday." O'Herlihy worked hard and worked fast. His film crackled with energy and he could always be depended on to finish, not merely on time, but early. The sun was always barely over the yardarm when Michael would announce, in his Irish brogue, "It's time for a drink."

BOB: O'Herlihy liked a little nip or two as well as anyone, but during the working day he was all business. I had to see Michael about something and caught up with him during a "stage move." He was hurrying to the next stage.

"Have you got a minute?" I asked, trying to keep pace with the fast-moving Irishman.

"No!" he snapped, without slowing down.

O'Herlihy's abrupt response stopped me dead in my tracks. Then I ad-libbed after him, lamely, "Thanks, Michael. You sure know how to hurt a guy."

O'Herlihy paid no attention and disappeared into the next stage. When I later reminded him of the incident, he grinned but didn't apologize. Why should he? Who was I to interfere with his schedule? Now, after the wrap, he had time for me. Eyes twinkling, he asked, "Anything important you need to discuss, Bob?"

"Nothing I can think of."

"Good," he said, grinning. "Let's have a drink, then." And he uncorked a bottle. We clinked glasses and laughed.

On this, or any other show, Michael O'Herlihy's episodes never went over schedule!

Robert Sparr directed "Shore Leave," a wildly imaginative story by Theodore Sturgeon, at that time "the most anthologized" science-fiction writer of his generation. The script, which was originally titled "Finagle's Planet," was so filled with difficult transitions and special effects that Gene Roddenberry had to go out to the location and rewrite as it was being shot. Needless to say, "Shore Leave" went importantly over schedule. But it wasn't the fault of Robert Sparr.

BOB: That episode had everything: Japanese Samurai warriors leaping in from out of nowhere; Alice in Wonderland and a human-sized rabbit; a "tame" wild tiger; a diving, strafing World War II fighter aircraft; an evil knight in armor mounted on a huge horse; and a knock-down, drag-out fistfight between Captain Kirk and a laughing ex-Academy classmate played to the hilt by actor Bruce Mars.

Sparr was terrific. He handled every revision that Gene threw at him. But certain cast regulars didn't like working with him because the immense amount of work he had to complete kept him from giving them individual attention. They prevailed upon Gene Roddenberry not to rehire him.

On June 9, 1967, I again saw the episode on the air when it was rerun and wrote a memo to both Genes:

> . . . although I realize that a great deal of effort went into the cutting of this film, I am of the opinion that Robert Sparr did a superlative job in directing this show. I realize that I am probably alone in my opinion, but I think that the conception of his shots and the motion and energy he created in his depiction of the exterior scenes was a truly creative achievement. Notwithstanding the fact that Bill Shatner and some of the other actors found much fault with Bob Sparr's abilities as a director of actors, his overall filmic judgement has definitely come through on this show. Perhaps he did not give lip service to the egos of our series regulars, but his filmic sense cannot be faulted. Bob Sparr really cared about what he was doing and I, for one, am sorry that circumstances made it impossible for us to bring him back again.

Some years later, while in Colorado producing *Then Came Bronson,* I learned that Bob Sparr and Jerry Finnerman (then Sparr's cameraman) were scouting film locations not far away. I made arrangements to visit them, but before I could, word came that their plane had gone down in the mountains. Jerry survived, but with major injuries. Bob Sparr died in the crash.

A sampling of Bill Theiss' *Star Trek* creations.

Photo by Casey Brown. Courtesy Butterfield & Butterfield

13

Haute Couture

HERB: This was Raymond Chandler's city. A city of shadows, a city that lived at night and died at dawn. Hollywood, California, U.S.A. The morning sun had not yet begun to spread its warmth over the horizon; the stillness of the night was giving way to the sounds of thousands of early rising commuters heading for work. And the dimly lit streets glistened from a brief summer shower as an elderly man walked his elderly dog.

Suddenly, two shadowy figures, clutching large plastic bags, walked quickly along the east side of Gower Street, hugging the still-dark walls of an aging office building. They stopped near the street-level window of a darkened room, and—first checking for unwanted observers, witnesses who could later testify—one figure quietly rapped on the window. Once, twice, three times. Several slats of window blind parted quickly, and a pair of steely eyes studied the shadowy figures. The

figure rapped one more time. The window opened, and the figures pushed their cargo through the open window and hastily walked back up Gower. The window closed. Were burglars at work? Was this industrial spying? Were kidnappers returning their victim?

Actually, the new costumes for this day's *Star Trek* filming had just been delivered.

Bill Theiss had monumental wardrobe problems. There were no "plain pipe racks" on which to find strange, exotic, and unearthly costumes. So on those episodes dealing with alien planets and the future, Theiss had to:

1. Design every costume and trust that late script changes didn't change the look of the characters.

2. Hope and pray actors weren't cast at the last minute, so he could fit them properly and finish the costume in time for filming.

3. Find the time and money to locate and purchase interesting materials and fabrics that were either discounted or on sale.

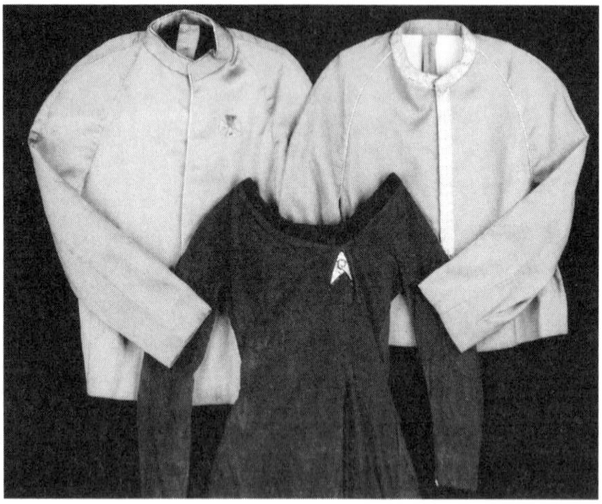

Photo by Casey Brown. Courtesy Butterfield & Butterfield

Three of Bill Theiss' uniforms.

4. Find seamstresses who had never heard the words *union* or *overtime* in a very strong union town.

5. Keep smiling! (Theiss never smiled.)

In order to accomplish his miracle, Theiss rented a small apartment one block from the studio, and the "*Star Trek* Sweatshop" was born. With shades tightly drawn to keep out inquiring eyes, seamstresses worked throughout the night. And after the completed costumes were smuggled through the street-side window of the *Star Trek* mimeograph room, they were innocently carried to the stage just in time for the actors to be dressed for the morning's work.

Except for a select few, no one, the unions in particular, ever knew of the existence of the "*Star Trek* Sweatshop."

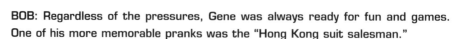

BOB: Regardless of the pressures, Gene was always ready for fun and games. One of his more memorable pranks was the "Hong Kong suit salesman."

Character actor Ted Cassidy, preparing to play the giant android Ruk in "What Are Little Girls Made Of?" had been sent to Gene's office for final makeup and wardrobe approval while Shatner and the other actors in that episode were hard at work on stage. Gene, Bill Theiss, Fred Phillips, and I were there to check out Ted's makeup.

The built-up Cassidy stood seven feet tall. As Ruk, he was totally bald and had a huge, cadaverous, bony skull with prominent cheekbones, ghostly dark deep-sunken eye sockets, and a ghastly battleship-gray complexion. His costume was a voluminous sort-of medieval monk's habit.

"No, no, he doesn't look frightening enough."

"What do you mean? He looks just right."

"Believe me, guys, he looks much too frightening!"

With such diverse opinions, Gene needed a totally objective eye—to find out for sure.

There happened to be an eager young salesman patiently waiting in the outer office to see Gene, hoping to sell some really top-quality "at-giveaway-prices" Hong Kong–made suits. Roddenberry turned to Cassidy. "Ted, this is a chance of a lifetime. How would you like to sit behind my desk and be me?"

Courtesy Paramount Pictures

Actor Ted Cassidy as "Ruk" from "What Are Little Girls Made Of?"

"Great, Gene. I wouldn't mind being you." The gentle giant smiled as he assumed the position.

Gene buzzed. "Send him in."

As the dynamic young salesman entered, carrying his sample case, the absolutely weird and unearthly-looking imposter rose to his full height and offered his hand. "How do you do?" he bellowed in his deepest, most stentorian tones. Instinctively, the entrepreneur offered his comparatively minuscule hand, only to have it totally engulfed in Ruk's enormous paw.

Ted grinned. "I'm Gene Roddenberry," he said, his eyeballs bulging ominously as he indicated the rest of us, "and these are my trusted associates." The salesman smiled uneasily as Ruk invited him to sit down. "So tell us all about your exquisite male fashion products."

The suit salesman had come across a lot of strange customers in the film business, but as he stared transfixed at Ruk, it was unmistakably clear he had never, never come across anyone remotely like "*Star Trek* creator Gene Roddenberry." He paused to collect his thoughts.

"Ah . . . well, Gene, if I can call you Gene, I represent the most outstanding tailors in Hong Kong, the finest and fastest fabric artists in the world." He nervously fiddled with the clasp of his case, finally opened it, and unfortunately spilled all the fabric samples on the floor.

"Just notice how quickly the wrinkles disappear."

Ted leaned across the desk and indicated his choice. "Can you make them 'extra large' using my favorite colors—fuchsia, mauve, and lavender?"

The salesman swallowed nervously. "Why, s-s-sure, Gene. We're the best and fastest fabric artists in the world—"

"Good," interrupted "Gene." "I'll take a dozen."

". . . but it may cost extra, what with all the extra fabric and the unusual amount of cutting and stitching." He whipped out his order pad. "I'll take your measurements now."

The charade couldn't continue. Everyone broke into laughter. Gene finally took pity on the salesman, explained the joke, and introduced him to Ted Cassidy. The salesman said he loved the experience.

Based on what we'd just witnessed, it was decided that Ted's makeup was just perfect—frightening, but not too frightening. After giving his autograph to our now-friendly entrepreneur, Ted hurried to the stage where Jimmy Goldstone was directing a scene featuring Bill Shatner. Ted was scheduled to be in the very next scene, and Jimmy was anxiously awaiting his arrival.

Incidentally, Gene did order three suits. They arrived in twelve weeks and didn't fit. Gene never noticed.

Costume Designer Bill Theiss didn't "do monsters." When creatures were required, outside specialists were consulted. Wah Chang designed and built the Gorns for "Arena." They were green and resembled some aquatic creatures he had created for *The Outer Limits.* The full-body suits were made of a rubberlike compound, but owing to their weight and limited flexibility, even stuntmen needed great endurance to wear them.

Famous stuntman and acrobat Janos Prohaska had inhabited a Wah Chang "creature" in the first pilot. He was eager to demonstrate what else he could do and came to the studio expressly to show off his wares. Janos often designed and built his own costumes and constantly experimented to create new creatures. Although small in stature, he was muscular and possessed incredible strength. When not working, Janos was a sweet man, mild, modest, and unassuming. But once inside a costume, he "became" the creature and showed a much darker side of his nature.

BOB: Janos came by our office, on spec, and donned his chimp outfit. He scuttled around the room, suddenly sprang up onto a desk, studied his surroundings and leaped to the top of a filing cabinet. He squatted, chattering and scratching himself like Cheetah, Tarzan's pet ape. His performance was impressive. But when one of the secretaries walked in, Janos leaped onto her and, in hominid fashion, attempted to take uncalled-for sexual liberties. After we pried him off her, which wasn't easy, he apologized for "the chimp's" actions.

We made a "spec" deal with Janos. If he came up with a really great creature for a script Gene Coon was writing, we'd rent it and hire him to play the part.

Janos was back within a week's time with his custom-designed creature. It was a large pancake-shaped glob of gook with a thickened raised center and fringe around its circumference. It sure didn't look like much.

As Janos took the glob out of sight to put it on, Gene Coon raised an objection. "Bob, why are we wasting time with this?"

Suddenly, the blob skittered around the corner, making straight for us. Then it stopped, curiously, backed away, and rotated in place. The blob gathered itself up, quivered, made a whimsical up-and-down movement, grunted, and skittered away again—leaving behind a large, round white "egg." Coon was dumbfounded. He had watched the creature giving birth. And when the creature suddenly turned and scurried back to nuzzle its "child," Gene was sold.

"Great!" he exclaimed, "It's perfect! Just what we need." Then he excitedly hastened back to his office to finish writing the script.

Gene Coon's "The Devil in the Dark" became one of *Star Trek*'s most famous episodes. And Janos Prohaska played his own creation, one of *Star Trek*'s most famous creatures, the highly imaginative and custom-designed mother Horta.

HERB: Somehow, Bob Justman's office became the unofficial repository for *Star Trek* creatures. First to arrive was the female salt sucker from the series opener, "Man Trap." Next came the rented female mannequin used in "The Naked Time." She had been used to portray a frozen person coated with ice, but unfortunately, when the "ice "was removed, her torso was permanently damaged. *Star Trek* became her new owner: "You break it—you bought it."

"What do we do with her?" asked propman Irving Feinberg. "She's damaged. Who would ever want a damaged naked mannequin?"

There was an immediate consensus: "Bob Justman. Give her to Bob Justman. He'll take anything."

Bob had been the *Star Trek* interior decorator when the production team moved into E building. He chose the furniture and the color scheme for the walls and carpets. His own office soon became famous for its "tasteful" combination of red carpet, white walls, and blue ceiling. "Kind of patriotic, don't you think?" he would ask. I always told Gene that the overall decor of the *Star Trek* offices beautifully complemented the *Star Trek* creator's "taste" in clothes.

To complete Bob's patriotic theme, he located several World War I recruiting posters and had them framed and hung on his walls. Featured was the famous James

Bob Justman welcomes two of the more "normal" visitors to his office.

Courtesy Karla Schneider

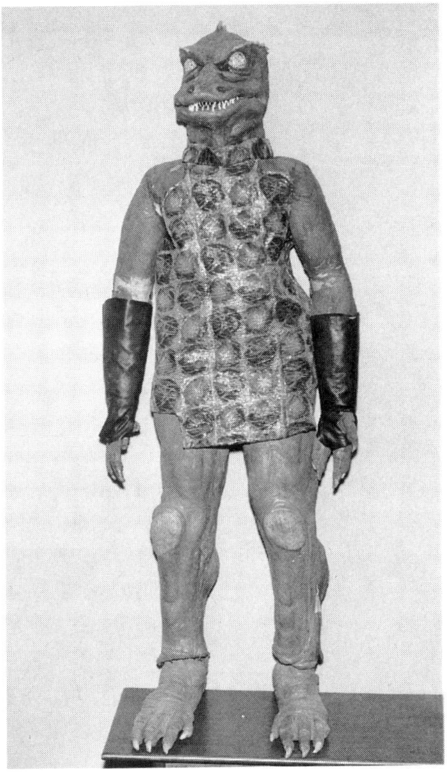

From the collection of Robert H. Justman

Montgomery Flagg poster of Uncle Sam saying "I Want You"; another was a "vicious Hun" bayoneting innocent Belgian victims. But his favorite poster depicted the seated female figure of "Columbia, goddess of liberty and the gem of the ocean," cradling a wounded Yankee doughboy in her lap. Behind her was an American flag, and above the tableau, a banner proclaimed, "The Mother of Us All."

So, yes, Justman's office was absolutely the right place. But the female mannequin was nude, and since Bob occasionally had visitors, he asked Bill Theiss to dress her in a frilly French maid's apron to "preserve decorum." Leaning against his office wall and wearing a worn-out wig, her presence contributed to engaging discussions when conversation lagged.

Then the Gorn showed up. Actually there were two of the reptilian creatures, and they stood atop a coffee table. One sported a miniskirt, so that, as Bob insisted, "My visitors will know which one is the girl."

Gene Roddenberry claimed to be progressive when it came to sexual politics, but his actual practices belied it. He wanted the actresses in the show to be visual sex objects. Even uniformed female crew members were not exempt. They were chosen on the basis of their looks, and their costumes were designed to emphasize feminine physical qualities: short skirts and high-heeled boots to show off their legs, nipped-in waists and well-filled tunics to emphasize their female figures.

Designer Bill Theiss always had to modify the crew women's costumes as Gene prodded him to make "improvements." The results? Equal opportunity for women: short skirts and lots of cleavage. And female guest stars, invariably exotic, were gowned in filmy, see-through outfits that exposed their bodies and accentuated their breasts.

BOB: No matter what he was doing, Gene always dropped everything when Theiss came to the office to display actresses in their costumes for his approval. Gene took great pleasure in making "hands-on adjustments," but sometimes the adjustments went a bit too far.

Case in point: Actress Maggie Thrett was one of the three space hookers who boarded the *Enterprise* in the first-season episode, "Mudd's Women." Gene had spent a goodly amount of time "making their costumes better." But as we filmed Maggie writhing about and attempting to entice our heroes, one of her breasts popped out from behind what little bodice was left of her costume. She quickly stuffed it back in, smiling ruefully. It didn't stay put, however, much to the crew's amusement and her embarrassment. The moment was preserved for posterity in the first of the famous *Star Trek* Christmas gag reels.

Another case in point: Sherry Jackson, former child star on *The Danny Thomas Show,* had grown up to become an exquisitely beautiful young woman. Bill Theiss brought her to the projection room where we were viewing dailies. She was scheduled to begin work shortly after lunch in "What Are Little Girls Made Of?"

and her costume had to be approved. Gene stopped the projector.

Sherry was petite, but her body was perfect. The tunic that Theiss designed for her was open on both sides, and there was no way that she could wear a bra without it being seen—as if she had any need for one. The top of her costume concealed very little. Gene felt the garment could be "improved" by making some "hands-on" adjustments.

"Maybe if we tacked the sides back a little more," I suggested and moved forward.

"I'll do it," growled Gene, shouldering me aside. He didn't need any help from me at that particular time.

Bill Shatner was in the projection room with us and tried to get into the act. "I think Bob's right. Maybe if you . . ." he volunteered and moved to help. But Gene shouldered him aside, too.

In reality, there wasn't much more that could be done to the costume without provoking an uproar from the NBC censors. So after he removed another square inch or two of fabric, Gene reluctantly approved her garment.

Courtesy NBC/Globe

Actress Sherry Jackson in one of Bill Theiss' more alluring creations.

Bill Shatner always got an odd cross-eyed look when he was acting in a big close-up and couldn't quite remember all his lines. Suddenly, the look happened, and, as a slight film of perspiration formed on his upper lip, he said, breathing heavily, "Ahhh . . . Sherry. What say you have lunch with me and I'll help you with your scenes?"

"Oh, would you?" She smiled seductively. "You're so kind. I don't know how to thank you."

"I'll bet Bill knows how," I thought.

Sherry asked for a bathrobe to cover herself. The prospect of displaying her body to a crowded studio commissary had apparently aroused her nascent modesty. As they left, Bill took her arm. She smiled a secret smile.

When they arrived at the neighboring Paramount studio commissary and saw how crowded it was, Sherry quickly removed her bathrobe and made an entrance that became legendary.

HERB: I was eating there when Sherry "did lunch." Food-laden forks were arrested midway in their journey from plate to mouth. Agents, producers, extras, technicians, and studio executives reacted as one to this vision of feminine pulchritude. Conversation in the room hushed as she paraded proudly past and, with Bill in tow, took the longest route possible to reach her table. And she smiled demurely through it all.

Gene Roddenberry on the *Enterprise* bridge.

Courtesy Stephen Edward Poe

14

Gene's Genes

There was no one else on staff to handle the production work load; the immense demands of writing and producing *Star Trek* put enormous pressure upon both Gene Roddenberry and Bob Justman, a pressure that knitted them together in an enduring relationship.

BOB: Gene always delivered his last-minute rewrites at the *very* last minute. The revised pages, with lots of penciled Roddenberry scribbling out in the margins, were immediately sent to a "mimeo house" down the street on Melrose Avenue. Stencils were typed, the script was mimeographed overnight, and it was delivered to us first thing the following morning.

On July 27, 1966, I sent a letter of appreciation to Ed Leavitt, owner of the mimeo service. I closed the letter by writing, "May the Great Bird of the Galaxy deposit stardust in your rapidly thinning locks." Copies of my letter went to Gene Roddenberry and Herb Solow.

Later that first season, I felt that a lackadaisical feeling had begun to pervade the production. It needed correction, since we still had the mountain to climb and couldn't afford to slow down, either physically or mentally. I didn't want to come down hard on any particular person or department, so I jokingly threatened that the Great Bird of the Galaxy, Gene Roddenberry, would fly over and deposit cosmic doo-doo on them if they didn't shape up.

After that, Gene was "The Bird." It became my personal nickname for him, an affectionate way to address him: "Bird, we need your rewrite now." Or, "Feeling okay, Bird? You look a smidgen tired. Why don't you take ten minutes off and rest up a bit?"

Gene liked his new name and used it in a second season memo that he sent to Gene Coon:

> Dear Encino Fats:
>
> Reference your comment the other day I should give you a memo on Bob Bloch's script "Wolf In The Fold." I gave you a memo on it! In fact, a splendid memo, one which I would not have thought would be so easily forgotten by one who professes to admire incisive writing and clear thought.
>
> Yours very truly,
> THE BIRD!

The name stuck to him for the rest of his life.

HERB: It's a well-known fact that birds eat constantly, consuming many times their own weight in a single day. But apparently, this Bird performed other tasks constantly.

Morris Chapnick, who also took to referring to Gene as Bird, later told of a closed-door meeting in Roddenberry's office. Gene was quite worried. "Morris, is there something wrong with me?

"What do you mean, Bird?"

"I can't make love more than three times a day."

Morris was impressed, if not awed. "Seems okay to me, Bird. Tell me, where does an alien go to register?"

Gene was a multidimensional person. After I got to know him better, I realized that two of those dimensions were his interest in women and sex. It was tough to ignore his constantly straying eye whenever a woman was near. If it wore a skirt, or looked like it should be wearing a skirt, Roddenberry's radar locked on instantly. You had to feel he'd accepted the earthly role of Adam, playing to hundreds, maybe thousands of Eves. Young, old, large, small, beautiful, homely, it made no difference—as long as the Miss or Mrs. or Madame conceivably might be available.

My secretary, Lydia, a refined, pleasant, and efficient woman, was at least twenty years Gene's senior. Whenever Gene walked into my office for a *Star Trek* meeting or merely to say "hello" or meet for lunch, Gene's eyes strayed and his radar antenna went into high-intensity mode. He would smile at Lydia as if she were a strawberry sundae just waiting to be devoured. But he never partook; he knew better.

My "temp" secretary, Anita Yagel, also fascinated him. She later married, and subsequently divorced, *Star Trek* actor James Doohan, aka Scotty. "I'll bet Anita's 'all woman,'" Gene speculated to me over a Cobb salad at the Hollywood Brown Derby. I had no idea how he'd come to this opinion, but I didn't want to spend time trying to figure it out. There just weren't that many hours in a day.

But after a while, I became more and more convinced that when sex was invented, the real Creator definitely had this tall, soft-spoken Texan in mind. The fact that he was already married, with two children, seemed more of a challenge to Gene than a deterrent.

BOB: I sensed that Gene was having serious family problems. There was a terrible imbalance between his time spent at work and his time spent with Eileen—and it was growing almost daily. Sure, my time with Jackie wasn't too extensive either, but we cared for each other and very much treasured our time together.

Though inwardly critical of Gene's extracurricular activities, I tried to ignore them because I liked him so much I rationalized that all idols have feet of clay. Unfortunately, when his peccadillos intruded upon my home life, I could ignore them no longer.

One evening at eight, while preparing to leave work early for once, Gene ambled into my office, something he seldom did. He was carrying a drink. "Going home, Bob?"

"Yeah. I want to see what my kids look like, now that they're almost all grown up. You leaving, too?" Everyone else on staff had already gone home.

"Ahhh . . . no . . . ahhh . . . I'm gonna stick around. Got some . . . ahhh . . . business to take care of. But I'll . . . ahhh . . . walk you to your car."

I thought, "Why would he want to walk me to my car?"

As we headed down the hall, I glanced back to his private office. The inner door was just closing, as if by magic. Gene saw what I saw.

"Bob, I'd . . . ahhh . . . like to ask a favor."

"Sure, Gene. Name it."

"I'd . . . ahhh . . . appreciate it if Eileen happens to call your house tonight, you and I . . . ahhh . . . we're . . . ahhh . . . working late together."

"But, Gene . . ."

"That's what I . . . ahhh . . . already told her."

"Oh."

"Just . . . ahhh . . . don't answer the phone if it rings. Let Jackie do it."

"Jeezus, Gene!"

But Gene was already headed back to his office. As I drove out, I wondered who was in there. Then I remembered. Majel had come by earlier. I had assumed she had gone home like everyone else.

It was bad enough he'd involved me—but Jackie, too? I was both annoyed and worried. Dinner wasn't too enjoyable; I kept waiting for the phone to ring. Luckily, Eileen never called. The following day, I cornered Gene and told him to find another patsy. I'd do most anything to help him and the show, but I drew the line at this.

It was during this time that the "wife plan" was created, and the creator was Gene Roddenberry. He called Penny Unger into his office. "Just thought I'd tell you I'm putting through a fifty-dollar raise for you."

Penny was thrilled. "Oh, thank you, Gene."

"We need to have an understanding, an ahhh . . . important understanding so the show can run more . . . ahh . . . smoothly."

Penny nodded and waited for the pitch.

"Whenever my . . . ahhh . . . wife calls and I'm with . . . ahh. . . . Majel, tell Eileen I'm . . . ahhh . . . not here, that I'm at a meeting at NBC or . . . ahhh . . . at a screening or . . . ahhh . . . at a business lunch off the lot or something. I know you're very good with people and she'll . . . ahhh . . . believe you."

Now, Penny understood. "Why sure, Gene. You're the boss."

Roddenberry's plan worked—for a while. But to paraphrase the poet Robert Burns, "The best-planned lays of mice and men gang aft agley."

Penny Unger remembers another meeting with her boss. It was 9:00 at night.

"Gene and I had a drink together in his office. I can't remember which script it was, but we had just finished a rewrite when he made a pass at me. I was really flattered and, feeling the drink, I thought, 'What the hell.'

"So we were necking on the couch when I heard Majel coming in through the back door, and at the same time, the front-door buzzer rang. Gene exclaimed, 'Oh my God, it's Eileen!'

"Majel hadn't seen us yet; she was still unlocking the back door. So I quickly put myself together and, when Majel walked in, all she saw was Gene and me sitting together having an end-of-work drink.

"Gene whispered urgently to Majel, 'Eileen's at the front door,' and Majel turned and left in one hell of a hurry. Gene quickly sat at his desk and 'buzzed' Eileen into the office. 'Just . . . ahhh . . . finishing up, dear.' He turned to me and very businesslike, said, 'Thanks, Penny. Type that up and . . . ahhh . . . distribute it in the morning.' "

HERB: Striving for success and the pressures accompanying that rocky ride awaken different emotions in different people. I worked and worried myself into the beginnings of an ulcer, not to fully develop until years later at MGM. But never having taken up weekend sports, I could make time available for my three daughters.

Bob, accepting enormous amounts of responsibility, became even more caught up on the *Star Trek* roller coaster and worked harder and with longer hours. His home became a pit stop on the fast track he was running.

Gene's womanizing side grew to new heights and proportions. He did nothing to hide, excuse, or defend his need. In fact, Gene loved the excitement so much he flaunted it. So the Roddenberry legend grew, and since Gene never cared to stop it, no one else cared to try. It was fueled by each new story and each new event.

Having heard it was Roddenberry's birthday, writer Ken Kolb entered Gene's office to congratulate him. Roddenberry wasn't there; the office appeared empty. However, Kolb noticed "a totally nude Nichelle Nichols hiding in the legwell of the desk, obviously waiting for that certain someone to show up. After all, it was Gene's birthday, and apparently Nichelle was to be the gift." Kolb said nothing to the out-of-uniform communications officer and quickly walked out of the office. The Desilu grapevine soon reported that, later, at the birthday party, Nichelle raised a few eyebrows by parading into the office from the back room wearing only a tennis sweater—and a smile.

Noted science-fiction writer Harlan Ellison still tells the tale of the various times he and John D. F. Black observed Gene, through the office window with the Venetian blinds angled so that any passerby could witness, engaged in extracurricular activities on his couch. "I couldn't believe it!" marveled Harlan. "Anybody could look in and see them."

And Gene himself bragged often about the "friendly" actresses who began showing up for late-evening casting meetings.

However, it was Lucy who unknowingly pushed the legend into big-league status. In her after-Desi years, Lucy became prudish. One of her executives remarked, recalling her lifestyle as a Goldwyn showgirl in the late thirties and early forties, "She's sure turned the corner on fun."

It was another night at Desilu and another birthday party in Gene's office and another nearly nude dancer jumping onto Gene's lap. The following morning, a Desilu loyalist told Lucy about the goings-on at *her* studio. She was outraged; this was not the kind of image she wanted for Desilu. There had been more than enough of that when she was married to Desi.

But true to form, Lucy wasn't about to confront me in person about the Roddenberry "problem." Rather, she dispatched her personal publicist, Howard McClay, to voice her displeasure. Howard was one of the few "Lucy-ites" who understood why we had to work outside of the old-school Desilu system. He also knew Roddenberry; that helped a great deal. Howard was honest and direct. He presented the concern. "Lucy has different values, ethics, and standards now, Herb. She feels that whatever goes on at the studio reflects directly upon her own public image."

Understanding Lucy's anxiety, I met with Gene and explained the problem. Gene smiled innocently and indicated that he "understood." He seemed delighted at his sudden notoriety.

Lucy never mentioned the subject again. Neither did Gene, but saying he understood meant very little. The parties, the extracurricular fun and games, all continued. However, Nichelle Nichols no longer paraded into Gene's office wearing only a tennis sweater. Instead, during the third season, as *Star Trek* post-production executive Ed Milkis met with Gene Roddenberry, Nichelle strolled into Gene's office from the back room—this time wearing only a letterman sweater. Eddie, familiar with Gene's pranks, refused to be rattled. He glanced at her, said, "Hi, Nichelle," and continued his discussion without skipping a beat.

So Lucille Ball continued being Lucy, Gene Roddenberry continued being Gene, and the legend continued to build.

BOB: I was a very good listener. Gene knew that and, several times, complained to me about the pressures of his relationships with women, which strained even his monumental patience. I had just walked into his office as he slammed the telephone receiver down. He was really upset. "Women are . . . !"

Surprised, I asked, "What's wrong, Bird?"

"Women! Eileen's unhappy; she's giving me problems. And not only that, Majel's still after me to write in a role for her as a regular, and I don't know how to do it."

Gene had tried to keep Majel happy by giving her a job as the "Computer Voice" aboard the *Enterprise.* She worked hard to perfect a mechanically dispassionate voice that still had a recognizable personality. She was successful at it and, in fact, continued to provide that disembodied voice in all the later *Star Trek* series. But first and foremost, she was an actress. She wanted to be on camera and act. She wanted to be a real member of the *Enterprise* crew.

HERB: Gene finally found a solution to the problem. He adapted the Nichelle Nichols "non-recurring" role manifestation and created Nurse Christine Chapel. As Executive Producer, Gene would see to it that this "necessary" character, Nurse Chapel, would definitely recur. And since NBC hadn't liked the dark-haired Majel in the first pilot, the "series Majel" would be a blonde—as if no one at NBC would notice. But they did.

"Well, well—look who's back," yodeled Jerry Stanley.

BOB: After seeing the first dailies in which she appeared, I cornered Gene in his office. "Gene, I didn't like the scene with Majel."

Gene just smiled, as he always did when I told him something he didn't particularly want to hear.

"The scene didn't work. She seemed awkward."

"I thought she was fine," he responded. "Maybe a little nervous this time, but she'll work out great. It's a new character for her, and she'll get even better as she goes along. I like her a lot in this role."

Pushing him further wouldn't work. But I continued to needle him about it

from time to time. His response was always the same: a smile, a short remonstration that she was "fine" in the role, and then a change of subject.

I stopped needling him after finally becoming aware of their relationship.

Years later, I realized it wasn't the actress I disliked, it was the role. Nurse Chapel was a wimpy, badly written, and ill-conceived character. In "The Naked Time," all she did was stand around and pine for Mister Spock, much the same as Yeoman Rand did for Captain Kirk. And in "Little Girls," Nurse Chapel pined for her fiancé, mad scientist Dr. Korby. The close-up shots of her eyes misting over and lower lip quivering were beautifully photographed by cameraman Jerry Finnerman, who used special lighting and diffusion lenses. But this only served to emphasize the lack of character written into the character.

In 1987, in "Haven," a first-season episode of *Star Trek: The Next Generation* that I produced, Majel created the role of the Betazoid character, Lwaxana Troi, a bold and lusty, irreverent and energetic female alien, and she played the part to the hilt. This new character became popular with viewers—and with me, too. I took pains to tell her of my changed opinion.

Despite Roddenberry's marital and extramarital relationships, his attachment to Nichelle Nichols continued throughout the run of the series.

Nichelle was in San Francisco, appearing on *The Gypsy Rose Lee Show* to introduce her new Epic record album, when she wrote the following letter to Roddenberry:

> Dear Gene "Big Daddy" Roddenberry. I adore you! Isn't it wonderful? Everything! Everything! How does it feel to be so damn big, beautiful, brilliant & successful Capitalist Executive Creator of big out of this world magnificent T. V. series? Thy Talent cup runneth over!!!!
>
> . . . My record company wants to start on the album tying in the idea of outer space. . . . So listen Big Beautiful Daddy you put your genius to work on it? After all its *all* your fault. It you hadn't believed in me Epic [recording company] would never have heard me sing . . . my life is yours Baby I love you Busy man Keep the faith Baby Hailing Frequencies Open sir, love, Nichelle

Roddenberry made suggestions to Nichols regarding her new "outer space" album. He did not, however, seek a royalty or piece of the profits.

BOB: Majel was always "just dropping in." Even when we first started production, she hung around the offices, making herself useful even though she wasn't yet acting in the series. If there was an office birthday party, and there were always office birthday parties, she'd be one of the organizers and the hostess to Gene's host.

I was the last to realize that Gene and Majel had something going. We were working late, as usual, when Gene issued a blanket invitation: "Come on over to Majel's new place for some drinks, guys."

"New place? Where's that, Gene?"

"Just around the corner. Leave your car. You can walk there faster."

So we went, and for the first time, I realized not only was Gene living a double life, he was probably paying the rent on the apartment, his "home away from home."

Majel was the perfect hostess. She was warm and outgoing as she showed off her new apartment. Gene was affectionate with her and played the part of the lord of the manor. And there were enough people enjoying themselves that night to spread the word about Gene's "place" all over the greater Los Angeles basin.

The party was still going strong when I left for home, looking forward to perhaps a full three hours' sleep before getting back to the studio.

The following morning, I took Gene aside and cautioned him. "Gene, you're skating on thin ice. You can't be that out in the open about Majel. People will find out that you're keeping her. And so will Eileen." I felt that his behavior was destructive to his wife; Eileen didn't deserve that kind of treatment.

Gene smiled; he wasn't at all perturbed. He seemed proud and, in fact, delighted in flaunting his arrangement. It gave him yet another kind of high, in addition to the one I would later become aware of during the show's second season.

The discussion of Gene Roddenberry's sexual attitudes and adventures may seem out of place when analyzing the development of *Star Trek*—but it's actually a very important component of Roddenberry's vision of the future. If he had not been the one exercising creative authority, the overall face of the show would have been vastly different. Nowhere was this more evident than with his treatment of the women of *Star Trek*.

HERB: Gene continually tended to "his" women: regulars, guest stars, and extras. Obsessively involved with their costumes, their hairstyles, their makeup—and even their footwear—he created a look best described as "available sexuality." Their costumes were as scant as possible, designed for the maximum display of breasts and legs. Yes, actresses were chosen for their acting talent, but voluptuous lips and seductive eyes were very important to him. And in most instances, the characters they portrayed were emotionally subordinate to the men of *Star Trek*. Women were, essentially, sex objects always ready for action. And they were the antithesis of the actresses starring in the other dramatic television series of that era: Barbara Bain (*Mission: Impossible*), Amanda Blake (*Gunsmoke*), Barbara Anderson (*Ironsides*), Stephanie Powers (*The Girl From U.N.C.L.E.*), and of course Barbara Stanwyck (*Big Valley*), all playing characters of substantial independence and distinction.

Everyone had a role in Gene's future world. And for Gene, a woman's role was primarily as a decorative tool in a man's workshop.

It was "different strokes for different folks" at Desilu in 1965. As Roddenberry concentrated on *Star Trek* and his after-hours avocation, Lucille Ball, very much not a *Star Trek* woman, concentrated on *The Lucy Show* and a very different interest.

HERB: The absolute rage of the country was stamps. Not postage stamps, not food stamps, not rubber stamps. The rage was S&H Green and Blue Chip merchandise stamps. Whatever you bought, wherever you bought it, retailers gave you merchandise stamps. The more you bought, the more stamps you received. And they gave you stamp books. The books consisted of blank pages; and when you managed to cover the blank pages with stamps, you hustled off to the stamp redemption centers and received, free of charge, appliances, cameras, clothing, jewelry—everything and anything. The more stamp books, the more valuable the gift.

Green Stamps and Blue Chip Stamps became so important in people's lives that, during the disastrous Bel Air, California, fire, some victims fled from their million-dollar homes clutching their Green or Blue Chip Stamp books and leaving behind their stocks, bonds, irreplaceable family photographs, valuable paintings—even their pets.

Studio cars and trucks were used by every department. Not only did they move the cast and crew to and from locations, by union regulation they were necessary to pick up and/or deliver scripts, props, cameras, wardrobe, hair goods, film, lumber—absolutely everything necessary to make films. So the studio cars and trucks were very busy, and they used an awful lot of gasoline and oil.

The Desilu Transportation Department had an arrangement with the Shell gasoline station at the corner of Melrose Avenue and Cahuenga Boulevard, several blocks from the studio. Whenever the studio vehicles needed gasoline and oil, they merely drove to the Shell station, filled up, said "Desilu charge," and drove off.

It was another Board of Directors meeting and another discussion of the usual topic, money. Ed Holly distributed his secret analysis of the seriousness of the problem, and Argie Nelson pointed out the totality of Roddenberry's, Geller's, and my own indifference to his production ideas and proposals. Except for Mickey Rudin, Art Manella, and Bernie Weitzman, it was "let's screw Solow to the wall" day. And surprisingly, Lucy joined in.

"Herb?"

"Lucy?"

"Herb, I'm concerned."

"I am also, Lucy, but I think we're moving in the right direction."

"Not that Herb. The stamps."

"The *what,* Lucy?"

"The stamps, Herb, the stamps! Who's getting all the stamps?"

"What stamps?"

"The Green Stamps, Herb! Who's getting all the goddamn *Star Trek* and *Mission: Impossible* Green Stamps from the Shell station?"

I could see that the hundreds of thousands of dollars the studio was losing wasn't such a big deal to Lucy, but the Green Stamps—now that was something else.

"Lucy, how the hell should I know who's getting all the goddamn Green Stamps? Go speak to Aaron Dorn [the head of Desilu Transportation] and ask him who's getting all the goddamn Green Stamps!"

Lucy quickly turned to her husband, Gary Morton, and snapped, "Did you ask Aaron?" Gary dropped his head and didn't answer. I quickly understood who had primed Lucy for the Green Stamp attack.

I was never told who got the goddamn Green Stamps. Sometime later, though, Gary did get a large Bentley sedan as an almost-matching bookend to Lucy's Rolls-Royce; they were parked together just below my office window. Who knows?

Courtesy Greg Jein

15

Who's on First? The Pecking Order

The Bible says:

> The Great dragon was cast out,
> that old Serpent, called the
> Devil, and Satan . . .
>
> Revelation 12:9

HERB: But in 1965, the NBC Sales Department was concerned. It was as if they believed that, after Satan had been cast out of the Garden of Eden, he was reincarnated as actor Leonard Nimoy and cast into *Star Trek* as Science Officer Spock, a pointed-eared, arched-eyebrowed "satanic" Vulcan alien.

Though it was well before the rise of the 1970s Christian fundamentalism, NBC feared its advertisers and local stations would be targets of a religious backlash protesting this "devil incarnate."

So shortly after NBC ordered the second pilot, NBC VP Herb Schlosser called. "The Sales Department wants Spock to have regular ears and eyebrows."

"NBC Sales is mad. Tell them to kindly butt out! The whole concept of having a space alien aboard the *Enterprise* would be destroyed. No deal."

"Then we might not go ahead with the second pilot. They're really serious. You'd better talk with Roddenberry."

I met with Gene and called Herb back. "Schloss, listen. Sales is living in fear while we're trying to make a successful television show."

"What did Roddenberry say?"

Courtesy NBC/Globe

Mister Spock's "satanic" guise again became a major NBC concern.

"He agrees with me. No ears, no pilot."

Several days later, Schlosser advised me NBC would approve Spock's ears for the pilot film only if "you agree to keep an open mind if *Star Trek* goes on the air as a series." I agreed. We'd fight it out later.

On the basis of the second pilot film, *Star Trek* was ordered as a weekly series by NBC and the "anti-ear, anti-Spock campaign" heated up again. Schloss continued in his role as NBC point man. "Sales says they're having serious problems selling the show to local stations in the Bible Belt. You gotta help me."

"Sales is paranoid. When they change the name of the Duke University Blue Devils, I'll consider doing something with Spock's ears."

Schloss understood, but he had NBC Sales on his back. "Will you hold off shows that really feature Spock until after the first thirteen weeks?"

I reluctantly agreed and met with Gene Roddenberry and Bob Justman. "Listen, we have a balancing act. We have to protect the show, and we have to protect Schloss. We know the Spock character will help *Star Trek* succeed, but NBC Sales has serious doubts. Can we hold back the heavy Spock shows until later?"

Bob complained, "We're already scrambling for shootable scripts. We can't hold anything back. And the optical effects just make it more difficult."

We agreed to tell NBC what they wanted to hear, but we also agreed we'd do what we had to do.

It took several weeks for us to learn the extent to which NBC Sales had gone to disguise Spock's "satanic" pointed ears. NBC had sent a very attractive *Star Trek* sales brochure to its station affiliates and advertisers. Close scrutiny showed, however, that an artist working for the NBC Sales Department had airbrushed Spock's pointy ears round in all the photographs. NBC Sales was selling a lie to the Bible Belt. Look at this book's color insert, (and facing page). You can see what that airbrushed image looked like.

Well before the series was on the air, I screened a rough cut of "The Naked Time" episode for Schlosser and other key network executives at NBC Burbank. Schloss watched with quiet intensity, but when Nurse Chapel appeared, he spoke up. "Herb, who's that?"

Wanting any explanation to be just between Schloss and me, I quickly nudged him. "I'll tell you later."

When the lights came up and everyone else left, Schloss leaned over. "Nice show, Herb."

"Thanks, Schloss. The guys do a good job."

"Now can you answer my question?"

"What question?"

"You know, about that actress who plays Nurse Chapel, the one with the blond wig?"

"Sure, Schloss. That's Majel Barrett."

"Isn't she the one Mort Werner didn't want in the series?" he recalled. "Couldn't you guys find another actress to play this part?"

This was one of those times when the truth would be painful for all concerned. I answered quickly, "Putting together a cast is like forming an orchestra. Individual actors are unimportant; it's an ensemble thing."

Courtesy James Goldstone

The airbrushed photo of Spock that appeared in the NBC sales brochure.

As I feared, my explanation didn't fly with Schloss. "Hey, Herb, I know what goes on out here in Hollywood. Tell me, who's keeping her?"

I quickly changed the subject to the really big story I'd heard about Milton Berle that was making the rounds in Hollywood and said I hoped it was all true about NBC's "King of Comedy."

But after *Star Trek* was on the air awhile, I finally confessed to Schloss and acknowledged Majel's relationship with Gene.

Schloss grinned and nudged me. "So I was right all along!"

BOB: To me, Bill Shatner was good-natured, likable, and industrious—and perfect for the role of Captain Kirk. He threw himself into the role with enthusiasm; but in his single-mindedness of purpose, he had a tendency to ride roughshod over the "lesser" performers who, to this day, complain that he had been insensitive to them and their needs. Nevertheless, he always came in well prepared, did his work, and went home. Gene was well satisfied with him. At least, he was during that first season.

Even before the show went on the air, Leonard Nimoy displayed his humanity and concern for others. One day, he asked if he could sit in on one of our casting sessions. "I'll read with all the people trying out. It'll help them a lot if they have another actor to play the scene with them."

Courtesy Greg Jein

William Shatner in a 1967 publicity pose.

Leonard had great empathy for struggling actors; he'd been one himself, recently. But after successive readings with a bunch of actors all trying out for the same role, he confessed, "Bob, I can't do it. If it's all right with you, I'd like to leave." He held his stomach, in pain. He couldn't be part of the process knowing that all those unemployed actors needed the work but only one would get the job. The rest would have to endure yet another rejection in a whole lifetime of rejections.

During the summer of 1966, before the series premiered, NBC wasn't the only entity concerned with Leonard Nimoy's ears. The other concerned party was the actor himself.

HERB: Most actor complaints were channeled to the studio via their representatives. The theory, of course, was to prevent emotional concerns from becoming confrontations. Leonard Nimoy, however, preferred dealing directly with Gene, RJ, and on occasion, me. (After I was long gone from Desilu and *Star Trek* had been cancelled, Leonard came to my home to discuss the advisability of him replacing Marty Landau in *Mission: Impossible.* Still years later, Leonard asked my advice on whether he should appear in the first *Star Trek* movie.)

But on this particular occasion, the discussion dealt with Spock's ears, and we walked the studio streets together.

"Herb, I'm a quality actor; I don't want to perceived as an alien freak."

"We want what you want, Leonard. But there's a problem. You know that we've battled NBC on more than one occasion on the subject of ears. We threatened and they threatened and we threatened again. Finally, they went along with us; the ears would stay. And we agreed not to push Spock episodes. There's no way I can change things until we're on the air and see the public's reaction."

"But I'll still be perceived as a freak."

"Leonard, let's give the viewers a chance; let's see what happens when the series is on the air."

"Well, I don't know."

"Okay, I'll make a deal with you. If the audience doesn't react as we hope they will, I'll have Roddenberry put in a scene where Doctor McCoy operates and gives you an 'ear job.' Your new ones will be round just like your . . . I mean, Spock's Earth mother's."

Leonard thought over the proposal. "Okay."

We shook on the deal.

From the collection of Herbert F. Solow

Herb Solow (l.) and Leonard Nimoy (r.).

The first four episodes to air featured Mister Spock in varying degrees. But by the time the fifth show was ready to air, "Spockmania" had erupted, and NBC's anti-Spock campaign came to a grinding halt. Desilu's mailroom was bulging with huge sacks of fan mail, most of which was addressed to Mister Spock.

HERB: NBC New York and NBC Burbank had been deluged with fan mail for Spock. An ecstatic Schlosser phoned. "New York wants all major Mister Spock episodes to air as soon as possible." So much for the Bible Belt.

Well, we'd won the battle and had a "new star" in the galaxy. But unbeknownst to all of us, we were well on the road to losing the war.

It started with William Shatner. Hired as the star of the show, paid as the star of the show ($5,000 per episode plus a secret percentage of the profits),

and billed as star of the show, he somehow thought he was the star of the show. But every morning in the special makeup room we'd built on Stage 9, Bill had to watch his costar, Leonard Nimoy ($1,250 per episode), receive sacks of mail and gifts from the fans. Bill was dismayed.

The details of the "secret" profit participation for Shatner remain clouded, even today. An analysis of in-house Desilu Business Affairs memos indicates that, as part of Shatner's basic deal, he was given five percent of *Star Trek*'s net profits of the initial television series. (By the time the series was cancelled, however, it was evident that five percent of nothing was nothing.)

A former Paramount attorney confirms that Shatner later received additional equity as part of his new *Star Trek* movie and merchandising deal. Shatner himself refuses to confirm the story. And supposedly, Shatner lost half of his total equity to his first wife as part of the divorce settlement.

Fellow *Star Trek* actors were unaware of the alleged profit participation. Surely, their dismay would be reason enough to guarantee secrecy. Recently, when this information was given to Nichelle Nichols, she exclaimed in surprise, "That explains everything!"

It would seem likely that, later, Nimoy also negotiated a *Star Trek* movie and merchandising equity position similar to that of Shatner. A former Paramount attorney will neither confirm nor deny that a Nimoy equity position exists.

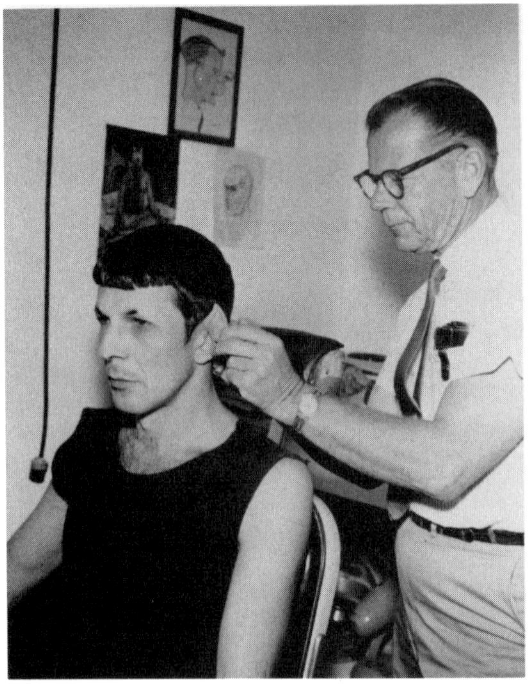

Makeup artist Fred Phillips affixing "ears" to Leonard Nimoy, part of the *Life* magazine photo shoot that caused a stir in the *Star Trek* makeup department.

Courtesy Stephen Edward Poe

HERB: The first skirmish in the war to see "who's on first" culminated one morning when a photographer from *Life* magazine set up his camera and lights around Leonard Nimoy's makeup chair and photographically recorded, for posterity, each step of Mister Spock's pointed ear application. I was there to witness the event.

Bill Shatner became annoyed. He was being totally ignored. Jimmy Doohan was there too. He recalls that "Bill's hairpiece was being applied. The top of his head was a lot of skin and a few little odd tufts of hair. The mirrors on the makeup room walls were arranged so that we could all see the laying on of his rug."

Bill's ego couldn't take it any longer. I watched as he sprang from his makeup chair and announced in true "Captain of the *U.S.S. Enterprise*" fashion, "From now on, *my* makeup will be done in my trailer." With that, Captain Kirk switched into warp drive and stormed from the room. I understood his frustration.

The second skirmish followed shortly. Leonard Nimoy was now the underbilled, underpaid, and underinvolved de facto star of *Star Trek.* Unhappy with the way the Spock character was written, and unhappy with the size of his role, Leonard complained often to Gene Roddenberry.

Scrambling to get future scripts ready, and not wanting to bow to actor complaints, Gene paid lip service to Leonard, but in effect ignored his new star. Tension between the hard-nosed producer and the equally hard-nosed actor quickly escalated. It began to affect the staff and the rest of the cast.

BOB: There was a mutiny brewing aboard the good ship *Enterprise.* Leonard grabbed me on stage one afternoon. "Bob, this script is worse than the last one. All Spock does is stand around saying 'It's illogical' or 'Ah yes, you humans do have trouble controlling your emotions.' It's bullshit, Bob! Spock should make things happen. He should motivate the action." Leonard was having much more trouble controlling his emotions than Mister Spock.

Courtesy Richard Arnold

Leonard Nimoy and Gene Roddenberry on the set of "The Cage," before serious tensions built up between the two men.

I'd heard this before from him. The problem was, he was right—but Gene wouldn't listen to him. He was so busy trying to keep shootable scripts coming that any interruption of the always-close-to-crisis writing process caused problems. Also, he had picked up the Hollywood mentality that actors should be seen and heard—but not listened to. However, I knew Gene would listen to me.

"Gene, I've been talking to Leonard."

"Tell him the answer is 'no.' "

"I won't! What he wants is good for the show and good for us. You know I wouldn't come to you otherwise."

Gene grumbled but he always made the changes. However, he made them grudgingly. And he made sure that Leonard knew he felt coerced. Their relationship deteriorated and became almost adversarial—eventually, at the end of the second season, resulting in an exchange of angry personal letters. Their uneasiness with and distrust of each other lasted until Gene's death.

Leonard confessed to me that he always regretted the deterioration of their friendship, a friendship that began well before *Star Trek.* He told me this twenty-five years later while we waited outside the chapel with the other mourners for the aerial flyover on the day of Gene's funeral.

HERB: The third and most decisive skirmish came after the end of the first season. Leonard wanted to renegotiate his contract, but as both NBC and Desilu

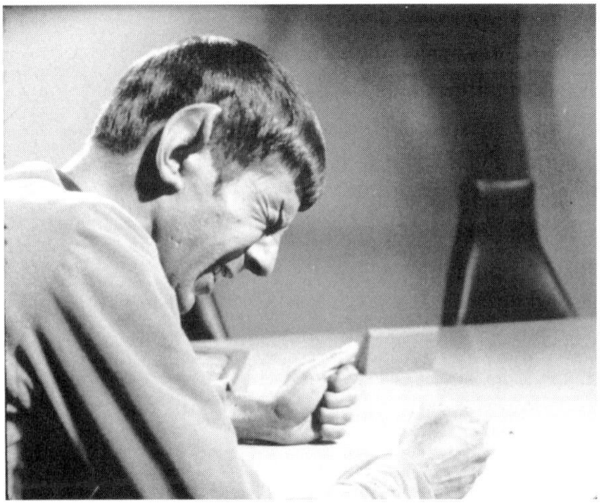

Courtesy Paramount Pictures

Mister Spock in "The Naked Time."

were losing money on the show, I told his agent to forget it. It was forgotten, but only until the show was renewed for a second year. Bill Shatner was still on "first." Leonard Nimoy was still on "second." And DeForest Kelley was still waiting in the "on-deck" circle.

By September 29, 1966, with the telecasting of the fourth episode, "The Naked Time," Mister Spock and his pointed ears had become the talk of America. Never again would Leonard mention his concern about ears to me.

NBC suddenly had a bonus—an unmitigated, unbelievable, and unexpected bonus. An instant new star had been discovered aboard the *Starship Enterprise:* a character, an actor, who stirred the imagination of millions of college students and young adults. And of course, NBC Sales was thrilled with "their" decision to keep both Mister Spock and those marvelous pointed ears.

Actors are arguably among the most competitive people in the world. More often than not, their success is measured in terms of the publicity and promotion that feeds the public's insatiable appetite for fantasy. Leonard Nimoy was a publicist's dream; William Shatner, the star, was just plain Bill.

NBC's pleasure was Roddenberry's affliction. A problem erupted when Shatner took exception to fan-mail figures being leaked to the entertainment and consumer press. Roddenberry sent out a personalized letter to Shatner's, Kelley's, and of course Nimoy's press representatives. Nimoy's publicist was Joe Sutton, a top Hollywood professional. Roddenberry did not mince words:

> . . . I'm not saying Leonard has been [one] of those . . . but we're all riding . . . in the same starship, and comparisons in any area, true or not, damage morale as nothing else can. . . . We simply won't have it and would cease to cooperate in publicity with any actor who gave out such information. *They must boost each other!*

Sutton replied, ". . .the only reference we ever made to fan mail was the positive effect Leonard's mail had in bringing forth his Dot Records contract. Never, and this pertains to the future also, was or will any comparisons be made with any other member of *Star Trek*."

To appear evenhanded, Roddenberry wrote exactly the same letter to Bob Arnold, who represented DeForest Kelley. Arnold wrote back promising "our full cooperation."

Evidently, Roddenberry struck out with his letter to Frank Liberman,

Shatner's public relations representative. Liberman's reply didn't mince words either:

> Thank you for the confidential letter in re the *Star Trek* stars.
>
> I'm sure that you're aware of the fact that Bill Shatner has always said *only* complimentary things about Leonard Nimoy and his fellow cast members. Needless to say, he will continue this policy—not only for his own good but for that of the series.
>
> Nevertheless, there has been some innuendo around town. As you may know, I called you immediately when Rona Barrett told me she was using an item in her Channel 7 Hollywood gossip to the effect that Bill was going to be replaced on the show. You weren't in, but I reached Gene Coon who immediately scotched it.
>
> The innuendo I referred to . . . comes from various gossip columnists and fan magazine editors who are looking for angles and are sometimes creating trouble on their own. This sort of thing went on with Robert Vaughn and David McCallum and I guess it will always happen when two men are involved in a series.

Courtesy Greg Jein

The usually unflappable Mister Spock.

Roddenberry also wrote to columnist Marion Dern at *TV Week* magazine:

> . . . Without taking away from my dear friend, Leonard Nimoy, any credit for a splendid job, it is Shatner's extraordinary dramatic ability and talent which often sets up the scene and gives Leonard a solid foundation and contrast which makes Mr. Spock come alive. Bill was trained in the old Canadian Shakespeare school with all its discipline and both his work and professional attitudes reflect this rich background.

Roddenberry continued to pressure the "Fourth Estate." Two years later, he wrote Charles Witbeck of the *Los Angeles Herald-Examiner*:

> . . . Mr. Spock did not "save *Star Trek* from oblivion." We agree that Leonard Nimoy has done an excellent job in protraying [*sic*] the character, but in all fairness, [I] must point out that Mr. Spock was conceived at the same time as the rest of the format and is being played today almost exactly as conceived over five years ago. We believed Spock would "catch on" and are delighted to have this belief and plan proved right.

Again, we in the *Star Trek* office are all fans of Leonard Nimoy also. He is an excellent and hard-working actor and his talents have brought many interesting dimensions to the role. His ability helped us stay on the air but to credit him with a "save" overlooks the contributions that Bill Shatner and the other extraordinarily talented actors on the show, the fine writers we had [?], the excellent directors, the whole *Star Trek* production "family". [*sic*]

But no amount of letters, meetings, or phone calls could stop the Nimoy publicity campaign. Shatner still had a better contract—more money and better billing. All Nimoy had were the ears and a lot of patience.

Courtesy Greg Jein

DeForest Kelley received a starring credit in the second-season main titles.

BOB: DeForest Kelley, who usually portrayed a professional bad guy in movie Westerns, finally became a nice guy in *Star Trek* as ship's doctor "Bones" McCoy, a pivotal role as the foil for both Kirk and Spock. He was the only one to whom the captain could unburden himself and the only one who was aware of the inner conflict waged between the Vulcan and human sides of Mister Spock.

McCoy was a brilliant man of science whose "country doctor" instincts led him to complain about not trusting his own personal molecules to the unknown dangers of transporting down to a planet's surface. Yet, despite his crusty behavior, everyone knew he was the conscience of the *Starship Enterprise.*

But Kelley, playing a brilliant man of science, could not pronounce the word *nuclear.* Yes, he knew the word was pronounced "new-clee-er" but, somehow, when the camera rolled, it always came out "nookeler."

Although Kelley's original contract called for mere "featuring" credit, Justman felt that he deserved better and always placed his name in "first position" in the end credits. On April 6, 1967, Justman wrote, in a memo to Roddenberry:

. . . I have had our contractual obligations researched by the Legal Department and can discover no objection to giving DeForest Kelley [starring] credit on our new Main Title. In addition, I have checked with Stan Robertson and he assures me that NBC welcomes the idea, as they think very highly of DeForest Kelley and the character he has helped create. Therefore, we can carry out our intention to give DeForest Kelley [starring] credit on our new Main Title for next season.

So in the second season, Kelley became an official star in the show's main title.

Roddenberry responded favorably to a request from NBC's *Today* show for a Barbara Walters interview of Shatner and Nimoy to be taped on July 10, 1967, and broadcast during the "NBC Premiere Week" of September 10. (*Star Trek*'s second-season opener, "Amok Time," was telecast on September 15, 1967.) But the *Today* show request made no mention of Kelley. Justman queried Roddenberry as to the chances for Kelley to appear as well: "De's one of our stars. He should be there with Bill and Leonard."

On the back of the letter he received from NBC Promotion Manager Terry Keegan, Roddenberry penciled four notes:

1. What will they do . . . what is format
2. Do it at 7:30 PM—OK
3. Pay for [Fred] Phillips Golden time ["golden" is 2 1/2 times the hourly salary]
4. What about deForest [*sic*] Kelley?

Although Roddenberry tried several times, he was unsuccessful in pushing for Kelley to appear together with Shatner and Nimoy. On June 12, 1967, he wrote to Justman, "Per your question about DeForest Kelley, they inform me that the TODAY SHOW has the final word on what part of the cast is to be used and wanted only Shatner and Nimoy." So the answer was "no," and as Justman had anticipated, Kelley felt slighted; his feelings were hurt.

BOB: Like good guy DeForest Kelley, George Takei also had often played bad guys. I used to kid him that, in World War II movies, he was the Japanese officer who yelled, "Yankee dogs, you die!" just before leading the inevitable banzai death charge, samurai sword in hand.

George Takei, playing Lieutenant Sulu, became one of the first Asian actors to portray a good guy on television. He was the antithesis of the so-called expressionless-unemotional-inscrutable Asian. He was so expressive in his role that I often kidded him about being "too scrutable," a description that always moved him to laughter. But then, George was so good-natured, he would laugh at most anything I said.

George never carried a samurai sword on *Star Trek,* but in "The Naked Time," he made the most of a bravura role. Infected by an insid-

Lieutenant Sulu, from "The Naked Time."

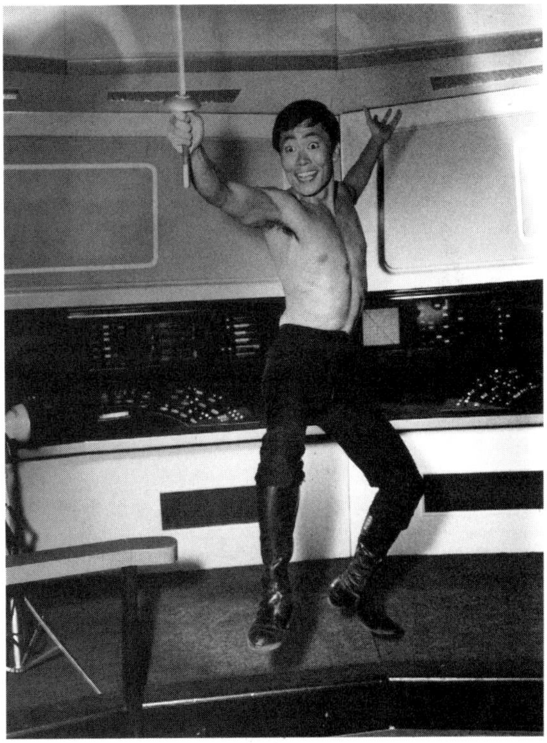

Courtesy Paramount Pictures

ious virus, Lt. Sulu went crazy. Stripped to the waist, his body glistening with perspiration, George leaped about the *Enterprise,* sword in hand, parrying and thrusting like a berserk D'Artagnan. Nichelle Nichols froze, afraid to move lest his slashing sword slice her up. She wasn't acting; she thought George had lost control, and she prayed for director Marc Daniels to yell "Cut!" She hoped George wouldn't take the command literally.

It may have been James Doohan's dramatic training in his native Canada, but during the production of the series, Chief Engineer Montgomery Scott never raised a ripple in the treacherous waters of actor relationships. Doohan reported to work on time, knew his lines, and performed them well. He never failed to deliver the goods, no matter how convoluted his scripted dialogue became.

In real life, James Doohan engineered something else. He wooed and married Herb Solow's part-time secretary, Anita Yagel. "We became very close friends with Gene and Majel. Anita became his secretary during the third production year, although Gene only showed up at the studio several times each month." The close-knit after-hours Doohan-Roddenberry relationship continued after the series went off the air.

"Gene just had to win at everything," recalls Doohan. "While we were playing pool at his house one evening and he thought I wasn't looking, Gene quickly changed the position of a ball so his shot would be easier. 'What are you doing, Gene?' I asked.

" 'Oh, nothing, Jimmy. I accidentally nudged the ball when I walked past it. Let's go. Whose shot is it?' "

And there were poker games at Doohan's house. The usual participants were Majel Barrett and Gene Roddenberry, Jackie and Gene Coon, actor Bill Campbell, and Anita and James Doohan. On one such occasion, "Gene was losing heavily but wouldn't quit. He kept doubling his bets until the friendly nickel-and-dime poker game reached a level where he owed each of us between $2,000 and $3,000. Gene was getting nasty. I wanted to stop the game and forget the money, but he wouldn't hear of it. He wanted to keep on playing until he won. I got so angry at his persistence, I took him aside and read the riot act to him. 'Listen, Gene, this is my house and when I say we stop, we stop. And that's what I say now. We forget the debts. I'll have it no other way.' Gene finally gave in and the evening was over."

Writer Don Ingalls, who at one time was a fellow Los Angeles police officer, also encountered Roddenberry's great need to win. "After Gene had become a producer, he fancied himself a chess player and kept after me to play him. He'd become a little too 'godlike' for me and I preferred not to challenge his 'superior talent.' But since I was his house guest on a particular weekend, I finally relented. And I proceeded to beat him in sixteen moves with a queen-bishop combination. For years, Gene demanded a rematch and I always refused. It drove my 'need to be in control' friend crazy."

Writer Harlan Ellison was also caught up in Roddenberry's need to win, in an incident that also involved chess. After numerous challenges, Ellison finally acceded to a game. Like Don Ingalls, Ellison beat Roddenberry in short order, and Roddenberry demanded and continued to demand a rematch. And as with Don Ingalls, Ellison continued to refuse to be a party to Roddenberry's "must win" syndrome. Ellison never played chess with him again and thereby succeeded in frustrating Roddenberry's ego.

The *Star Trek* women seemed to be mirror images of Roddenberry's sexual desires. But when the images blurred, due to internal or external problems, the mirror and a career could both be shattered. Such was the story of Grace Lee Whitney.

Everyone liked Grace Lee. Handpicked by Roddenberry to play the ship's third and final yeoman, Janice Rand, she gave the series a likable, sensual beauty and an on-board unrequited love interest for Captain Kirk. But the pressures of controlling her weight and her strained personal relationships were destructive to her career; she succumbed to the worst of emotional supports and became both alcoholic and addicted to diet pills. In the process, she lost her role. She was dropped from the series after only seven shows.

The "official" reason for Whitney's sudden departure was that the role of the yeoman limited the possibility of other romantic involvements for the energetic Captain Kirk. With an exotic new planet and an exotic new female every week, he would be free to experiment in interplanetary romances.

Grace Lee Whitney in happier days.

Courtesy Martin Nuetzel

In discussions in early September, 1966, Roddenberry, Solow, and Weitzman agreed there was no artistic or financial justification to continue her very limited role in light of the show's serious budgetary problems. Strangely, Roddenberry evinced no interest in retaining his handpicked yeoman, while Justman, opposed to "losing her," held out hope that she would return to guest star in future episodes. Roddenberry never contacted Whitney to give her the bad news. Her agent was formally advised by Desilu Business Affairs that her services were no longer required.

(Years later, there was talk of a sudden personal rift between Roddenberry and

Whitney that occurred just prior to her departure from the show. The rift supposedly guaranteed that she would never return to *Star Trek*. But she did return—in some of the *Star Trek* movies. And there was no appearance then of any ill will between them.)

Whenever Roddenberry had actress problems, be they professional or personal, he looked to his favorite scapegoat, the National Broadcasting Company. Having been successful in smuggling Majel Barrett back aboard the *Enterprise*, he turned his attention to Nichelle Nichols.

Nichols was unhappy with her small, underpaid role; Uhura did and said the same things each and every episode. The actress wanted more!

Roddenberry again pointed his finger at NBC. Word came back to Solow that NBC wanted Nichelle Nichols fired because she was an African American woman and that Roddenberry had single-handedly fought the good fight to keep her aboard the *Enterprise*. The studio rumor mill hinted that Nichelle Nichols should be thankful to him for protecting her job.

HERB: In the portion of her autobiography, *Beyond Uhura,* dealing with encountering racism at Desilu and NBC, Nichelle chose not to name those individuals who treated her with hostility and malice because of her color.

Unfortunately, by not naming names or indicating their status, she indicted all those at both companies who had anything to do with *Star Trek.* I felt a clarification was in order and subsequently discussed the issue with her.

The number of people at Desilu and NBC who, directly and indirectly, were involved in production and broadcast aspects of *Star Trek* could be conservatively put at three hundred. In my discussion with Nichelle, she averred that one middle-management executive at NBC attempted to force himself on her and one lower-level production executive at Desilu used racial epithets and made derogatory remarks. Additionally, she said that a clerk in the Desilu mailroom and a clerk in the NBC photo gallery did not treat her as they treated other performers of Nichelle's status and importance.

I told Nichelle that if I had been made aware of this totally unacceptable behavior, there was no way in Hell those deplorable actions would have been tolerated. I would have fired the Desilu executive on the spot. And the NBC executive (who, I later learned, forced himself upon other women in the industry) would have been banned from Desilu with a phone call to the President of NBC.

Nichelle further explained to me that, during the last *Star Trek* production year, the Desilu executive tearfully renounced his shameful behavior and asked her forgiveness. Nichelle, being the decent person she is, forgave him.

It must be understood that NBC executives Mort Werner, Grant Tinker, Herb Schlosser, and Jerry Stanley were unanimous in their desire to feature and protect all minorities, including women, in the product that they broadcast to the American audience. To set the record straight, once and for all, no one at NBC ever commented negatively to me about Nichelle because of her race, or

approached me or any other Desilu executive to hint, instruct, or demand that Nichelle Nichols be fired.

BOB: But there were times when the idea almost appealed to people in the projection room. Nichelle always played scenes well when they had content for her character, Uhura. But there was one constant complaint: We were seldom able to print take one of her close-ups in the Bridge set, although she usually had the same line of dialogue: "Hailing frequencies open, Captain." Sometimes it varied and it would be: "Hailing frequencies open, sir."

She'd be okay in the master shot, but when it came time to focus that big glass close-up lens on her, she'd begin to speak and it would come out sounding like "Hailing fleecrensees . . . hailing fleeklensees . . . Oh-h-h, s..t!"

We had a running bet in the projection room. I always bet against her, and sure enough, while she might get it right in the master shot, she'd seldom fail to screw up in her close-up. The camera would roll; the director would say "Action!" She'd feel that big close-up lens boring deep into her heart and soul—and she'd "go up." Thanks to her, I seldom had to buy my own lunch.

Courtesy NBC/Globe

16

Flirting with Disaster

HERB: You learn early in the one-hour series television business that your show will eventually have trouble meeting airdates. When episodes are broadcast once a week and take six or seven days to shoot, you constantly live on the broadcast-date bubble. But adding days lost owing to weekends, holidays, the usually long Christmas–New Year hiatus, and the specific optical-effects madness, the amount of time for *Star Trek* postproduction decreased almost exponentially during the last half of the production year. Eventually, the network release schedule called for *Star Trek* episodes to be broadcast almost before they were even filmed.

BOB: "You'll be sorry!" That's what the older "boots" yelled at us when our busload of recruits pulled into "boot camp," the San Diego Naval Training Center, way back in World War II. Nobody ever told us it would be easy.

And nobody ever yelled, "You'll be sorry!" when we began making *Star Trek,* but they might just as well have. Complications begat complications!

Initially, NBC screened our rough cuts at their Burbank studios and returned them the following day. But even the few precious hours the film was away from our editors contributed to the airdate problem, so after a while, we asked NBC to come to our side of the hill. All future screenings took place at Desilu.

An ordinary "rough cut" was a completed film that still needed some editorial refinements and had not yet been scored or dubbed. But on *Star Trek,* we had rOuGh CuTs! Each one was loaded with "scene missing" slugs of black "leader" film in place of the still-to-be-delivered optically composited scenes.

Stan Robertson and Jean Messerschmidt became accustomed to me narrating during the "scene missings" so they could know what was happening during the many, many times the screen went dark. If I may say so myself, I got to be a pretty good storyteller, and my description of the missing footage was often better than the finished product.

But in addition, music had to be written for those missing scenes. A composer like Fred Steiner had to depend on inspiration in order to write music for scenes he would never see until the episode was actually broadcast.

"Okay, Fred. This next cue runs from its start on the bridge back at 597 into this cut, which runs fifteen feet, from 620 to 635, and it shows the *Enterprise* shooting phasers, two blasts, with the first beginning six feet in, with three feet in between them, and each blast lasting three feet. Got that?"

A long pause. And then, "Uhh . . . yes, I think so." Fred looked at Jim Henrikson, our very talented music editor, who nodded. Fred toughed it out and asked, "Do you want the cue to tail off or do you want to 'button off' [end the cue on a crescendo] on the end?"

"I don't know. Tail it off and write a separate button. That way, we can try both."

Fred said he would do just that and went off to write the score.

Members of the beleaguered *Star Trek* postproduction team occasionally developed a sort of subjective intransigence. Film editor Bob Swanson was the series' fastest cutter, and his instincts enabled him to produce quality first cuts. But that was "all she wrote," so far as he was concerned. His attitude was, "This one's done. Let's get on to the next episode." Swanson didn't resist the minor polishing any film undergoes, but he strongly resisted any major editing changes that Roddenberry wanted to make.

Swanson felt that a show must be edited based upon what the director shot, not what the writer wrote. Roddenberry, however, often wanted to use whatever film was available to remake the episode into what he had originally envisioned in the script. Confident that his cutting couldn't be improved on, Swanson made his opinions crystal clear to Roddenberry. It all came to a head during the editing of the first segment of the two-parter "The Menagerie," made with elements from the original pilot. The two very stubborn men clashed time and time again over "inventing footage that hadn't been shot." Professional as he was, Swanson completed cutting that episode and quit, a great loss to the series. He was replaced by editor Jim Ballas, who finished the rest of the first season and most of the second before he also left—but under quite different, and what turned out to be somewhat bizarre, circumstances.

Star Trek's production and postproduction duties swamped Justman. There just weren't enough hours in a day—or night. And helping out Geller and Solow by dubbing an occasional *Mission* episode made things even worse. He requested permission from Roddenberry and Solow to find someone to help shoulder the load. He began to beat the bushes, but no one he interviewed seemed to fill the bill.

Justman, unsuccessful in his search, was so concerned about making the schedule that he wrote to Roddenberry, stating, "We are liable to end up having to play one-hour organ music concerts week after week after week. . . ."

BOB: The figures and dates were incontrovertible: We'd be unable to deliver the last third of our shows in time. I finally came to a decision—the right thing to do was to tell NBC about our problem. It wouldn't be fair to keep them in the dark. I went to see Herb Solow, not realizing I was really a "babe in the woods."

"We've got to tell the network we can't deliver the last eight shows in time."

"What did you say?!!"

"We should tell the network we can't meet their dates."

Herb stared at me, strangely. "RJ, have you lost your mind?"

"But . . ."

"We don't tell them anything!"

"But . . ."

"What they don't know won't hurt them."

"But . . ."

"There's no use worrying anybody. Just forget we had this conversation. We'll tell them when and if it ever comes to that. . . ."

"It will. Trust me."

"I trust you, RJ. So trust me: I know what I'm doing. Later, if we have to, we'll ask NBC to repeat a show . . . or two." Herb added, "In the meantime, pray for preempts."

"Preempts?"

"Yeah. There's always at least one during the holidays. When's Thanksgiving

this year?" He leafed through his desk calendar. He grinned. "There it is. November twenty-fourth, a *Star Trek* night. Guess what? Thanksgiving's on a Thursday this year. Betcha we get preempted for a special. It'll give you another week's time to play catch-up. That'll help, won't it?"

I nodded. "Do chickens have lips?"

"Remember, so far as NBC is concerned, we're in great shape."

Herb was right. NBC preempted us on Thanksgiving night for a Jack Benny special. It helped for a week or two, but eventually, Herb told NBC we wanted to schedule a repeat during Christmas week. This was one of the Nielsen nonrating weeks, or "black weeks," so advertisers wouldn't see any negative numbers that usually accompanied same-season repeats. Stan Robertson kicked and screamed, but he finally relented, and eight weeks after its initial telecast, we reran "What Are Little Girls Made Of?"

Luckily, we didn't have to ask for another repeat, much as we needed it, because in March the network preempted us again for a Ringling Brothers Circus Special.

All us clowns at *Star Trek* continued to have our own circus going, trying to meet airdates.

HERB: Happily, Gene and Bob continued driving the shows to their timely completion. Contractually, for each episode, we were obligated to deliver two 35 mm prints (and one earlier 16 mm print for Canada) to New York and one 35 mm print and one 16 mm print to Burbank for separate East-West broadcasts. At times, some of the prints weren't delivered until the day of the broadcast. The 16 mm print was run as a backup. Unfortunately, it took an extra day to manufacture.

We told NBC, "Don't worry about it. We'll get it to you." But sometimes it got there late. Luckily, it had just arrived on the only night the "film chain" chewed up the 35 mm broadcast print and NBC had to switch to the 16 mm print.

Networks ordered all their new series at the same time. Good for cop shows and Westerns—bad for *Star Trek* with its convoluted writing needs. During the show's first season, there was always a dearth of production-ready scripts. Only the first one was actually "ready" by the start of filming. And by the time the first eleven episodes had been filmed, *Star Trek* faced the prospect of an unplanned production hiatus, which not only would increase the series' already high costs, but guaranteed that the tenuous delivery schedule would become total fantasy. Not one new script was ready to shoot.

Justman asked, "Isn't there any way we can use the first pilot to tide us over until we get more scripts?"

When NBC ordered the second pilot, the strategy was to broadcast the very expensive first pilot as a Movie of the Week. However, with *Star Trek* now a weekly series, how to use "The Cage" became a serious topic of discussion. It was absurd that seventy-eight minutes of already-paid-for, expensive *Star Trek* footage was collecting dust in a Desilu film vault. (Seventy-eight minutes was the actual program length of a ninety-minute show. The remainder of the time was devoted to commercials, station breaks, etc.) Roddenberry, Solow, and Justman examined what they had, or—as they soon realized—what they didn't have.

A year earlier, Jeffrey Hunter had rebuffed Roddenberry's request to shoot added scenes to lengthen the pilot and attempt to get a theatrical release for it. There was no way Hunter would cooperate to redo it for a television episode.

With the singular exception of Leonard Nimoy, actors in the pilot crew and the series crew were different: There were two medical officers, two yeomen, two communications officers, two helmsmen, and Majel Barrett playing both Number One, the second in command, and Nurse Chapel.

Even the production itself was different. The sets, set dressings, props, and wardrobe were more refined in the series. Even Spock's ears were more realistic.

The decision was to break up the pilot story and piece it into a new story, yet to be written, that involved an "unrecognizable" Jeffrey Hunter and both the pilot and series casts. The process was similar to taking apart two somewhat related and complicated picture puzzles, moving the little irregular pieces around, and ending up with one great-looking, totally merged picture puzzle that was divisible into two parts for broadcasting back to back.

Roddenberry referred to the yet-to-be-written current series portion as the "Envelope." "The Cage" portion was the pilot that was wrapped in the Envelope, and the combined piece was referred to the "two-parter." One would think the *Star Trek* brain trust—Roddenberry, Solow, and Justman—could come up with more creative descriptions!

The two-parter touched Desilu's imagination; it had a life of its own. Solow told NBC, "Just wait until you see the two-parter." He excited the Desilu Board and the studio's agents with updates on it. Roddenberry planned a "two-parter party" when it was finished. Everyone was excited, but not John D. F. Black. He was writing the Envelope, and it wasn't easy.

Justman pressured Roddenberry to get him the pages as soon as possible. When Black finally delivered, Roddenberry took the script, disappeared into his own office, and days later emerged with a totally different version. (Black, insulted again, filed a Writers Guild grievance over payment and screen credit. Black's claims were denied.)

When Roddenberry turned over the Envelope script to Justman, he used his triumph as another reason to take another "well-deserved" vacation. Happy with what he had wrought, he sent a memo to Justman re: "THE ENVELOPE."

Desilu Productions Inc.

Inter-Department Communication

TO Bob Justman

DATE October 7, 1966

FROM Gene Roddenberry
dcf

SUBJECT THE ENVELOPE

As indication of my vast and sincere regard for you, I leave behind while I am on vacation in the High Desert, some fifty or sixty pages of sheer genius. Read and weep as did Alexander when he beheld the glories of Egypt.

Humbly,

GENE RODDENBERRY

P.S. I also leave behind Barry Trivers' "Portrait in Black and White" which you may have equally strong feelings about.

Roddenberry's memo to Justman regarding his vacation after writing the "Envelope" portion of "The Menagerie."

Now it was Justman's time to disappear into his office; he began to prepare the convoluted material.

The two-parter was named "The Menagerie," which, incidentally, was the first pilot's original title before it was changed to "The Cage." It became one of the most famous two-parters in television history. It wasn't too erotic, and it certainly wasn't too cerebral for the audience.

BOB: Stan Robertson complained whenever stories were submitted that didn't take place at least partially on an alien planet. Part of NBC's continued demand for planet shows week after week was the basic series concept of exploring "strange new worlds." Unfortunately, we couldn't afford to visit a different planet week after week.

So we consciously alternated planet shows with ship shows. Most other series called them "bottle shows," but regardless of what they were called, their purpose was the same: to save money by "bottling up" the action. There were few new sets, no expensive locations and equipment to rent, no additional union drivers to pay—and, other than the regular cast, no more than a few outside actors, which guaranteed that the episode would be a "cheapie." Our ship shows took place entirely on board the *Enterprise* and cost much less to produce.

When Marc Daniels filmed Norman Spinrad's teleplay "The Doomsday Machine" in only five days, it enabled us to average out the expensive episodes and complete the second season slightly under budget.

Curiously enough, many *Star Trek* bottle shows were enormously compelling, as indicated by both fan reaction and the ratings.

Proper preparation was the key to filming not only bottle shows but all shows. *Star Trek* required an unusual amount of preparation time. Owing to its particular needs, Justman held preproduction meetings with his key people, especially in the areas of set construction, wardrobe, special effects, and props. Even working from the first draft of the script didn't allow sufficient lead time. Unlike other series, the story outline was distributed to key personnel while the teleplay was being written. Potential problems were unearthed and remedied before it became too late. Many scripts were altered and bettered as a result of this unorthodox approach.

HERB: In the network television business, they don't hand out praise and medals for bravery, heroism, and the truth; they hand out cancellation notices. The A. C. Nielsen Company had told me our ratings were bad, NBC sales had told me our show wasn't "sold out"—that portions of the show still lacked sponsorship—and RJ kept telling me we were running a very serious risk of missing airdates. This was not the time to be seen or heard in the halls of NBC Burbank. Hiding out was the better part of valor.

Dodging network phone calls was easy, at first. Schloss or Jerry or Stanley

Robertson would call, and Lydia always said I was "off the lot." But total avoidance was a worse mistake. So I returned all network phone calls smack-dab in the middle of lunch time, knowing full well the guys were off somewhere enjoying their midday repast.

The day after an episode just made it on the air, however, Schloss left an angry message: "What the hell is going on? New York is very worried." No way could I tell the network we were having serious optical-effects delivery problems. If I did, the New York Sales's "experts" would stand tall and announce, "Well, we told you so!" and damage our credibility with NBC management. We had to devise a unique, yet easily reparable, reason for cutting it so close.

Remembering that Schloss was a very intelligent graduate of Princeton and the Yale Law School who understood things analytical, and knowing he wasn't well versed in the making of films, I returned his anxious phone call after lunch, for once.

"It's the sprocket-holer, Schloss. That's what's causing the delays."

"The what?"

"The episodes are complete. But before we can ship them, they have to go through the sprocket-holer machine so the sprocket holes can be put into the film. Without sprocket holes, you know you can't run films."

"The what?"

"But not to worry. It's being repaired as we speak. The technical people tell me the sprocket-holer will be as good as new by the end of the week."

"So I can tell New York there'll be no more problems?"

"Absolutely, Schloss. And thanks."

I don't know if Schloss ever found out I had changed motion-picture technology. (But now he will.) Regardless, the network was off our back for a while. All thanks to the "sprocket-holer."

As the demands grew for shootable scripts, lower-budget shows, cheaper effects, and deliverable episodes, the last thing Solow needed was the old guard clandestinely shooting *Star Trek* in the back. But nosy Bob Justman uncovered the ignoble plot.

HERB: Consolidated Film Industries (CFI) was one of the largest and best film labs in town. Years earlier, while with the NBC Film Division, I'd met Sid Solow, the man who ran the lab, and we traced our families as far back as the 1800s in Byelorussia. We definitely had "roots." Not only was Sid a marvelous human being, he was a marvelously honest human being. So while developing and printing both *Star Trek* and *Mission* film footage at the lab, we knew that billing-wise, CFI could be trusted. And we were right; CFI could be trusted. It was the old guard at Desilu we couldn't trust.

Bob blew into my office. "Did you know that the studio gets rebates from CFI?"

"Specifically, no; but it's something that's expected."

"Do you know what happens to the rebates?"

"I expect the lab deducts the amount from our bill."

"No! The lab bills us the standard rates, we authorize the studio to make payment, and then afterwards, the lab sends back a rebate. Do you know who gets the rebates?"

"I expect it comes back and reduces your lab costs."

"No, it doesn't! The rebates go directly to Desilu. We don't see a penny! They keep the money themselves and continue to bitch about our lab costs being too high!"

"Who told you about the rebates?"

"The lab rep."

"Why'd he tell you?"

"Simple. I asked."

I thanked Bob for the information, called Ed Holly, and expressed my anger at the studio's cover-up. He objected at first to changing the "standard studio bookkeeping" arrangement. However, after I indicated I'd be compelled to mention the facts to Bruce Geller, who would have had his attorney in Ed's office within twenty minutes, Holly retroactively applied all the rebates to both series. After all, they'd been caught with both hands stuck tightly in *Star Trek*'s pocket.

On normal series the completed film, after it's been scored and dubbed, is sent to the lab for negative cutting, color corrections, and printing. The result is called the "first trial" or "answer" print.

For the abnormal *Star Trek* series, however, the first trial prints were sometimes silent, the sound processes not yet completed. When a "picture only" print was color-corrected, a whole day was saved by not having to wait for the sound dubbing to be completed.

BOB: I ran the first of many answer prints with Roger, the Consolidated Film Labs timer, who was responsible for the film's color and density balance. He had to color-match each cut to the preceding and following cuts. Unfortunately, Roger hadn't "timed" (color-balanced) either of the pilots, so *Star Trek* was brand-new to him.

The process was tedious. It was important that the color balance be more toward the "cold" (blue) side of the spectrum rather than the "warm" (red) side, and that the dramatic lighting Jerry Finnerman had worked so hard to achieve not be compromised by a print that was too light in density. When the run was over, Roger knew he had a lot of corrections to make. "I'll work all night, Bob. We know you want it right, and it will be."

By that night, dubbing had been completed, so the following morning, Roger was able to screen the "final" answer print for me. As the first reel unfolded,

everything looked great: good balance, nice density, excellent contrast—and yet, something bothered me.

"Something's wrong, Roger."

"It looks fine to me, Bob. It's darker than I like, but that's what you wanted." Roger sounded upset. "I've never worked so hard on a print as I have on this one. You tell me what's wrong with it!"

"I don't know. But something doesn't look kosher." And as soon as I said the word *kosher*, I knew. It was Spock. He didn't look kosher.

"It's Spock. He doesn't look right."

"Spock?"

"The guy with the ears. He's the wrong color."

"Oh, him! I had a real bitch of a time with the guy. For some reason, he kept on coming out yellow. I had to crank in a lot of correction trying to make him look white again."

"He's not supposed to look white, Roger. He's supposed to look yellow."

"He is? How yellow?"

"Well, if you were Jewish, like your grandmother's chicken soup."

"That yellow?"

"That yellow."

And the problem was solved. After that, Roger made Spock look like Grandma's chicken soup.

There was one other company that desperately wanted NBC to succeed as the "full-color network." The Radio Corporation of America (RCA) not only owned NBC, it made a great deal of money selling television sets—their "government-approved RCA color-system" television sets. It followed that both companies were resolute; only the very best of color broadcasting would be seen on NBC.

HERB: The day after the series premiered to mediocre reviews from around the country, NBC decided it wasn't totally happy with *Star Trek*. But at least the CFI-Spock color problem had been solved—I thought. And RJ thought the color problem had been solved. And Roger, the film timer at Consolidated Film Industries, thought the color problem had been solved. However . . .

On the morning after the premiere, the senior color technician at NBC Master Control phoned my office with an apology and a complaint. "We sure tried last night, Mr. Solow. It just got away from us," he confessed.

"What got away?"

"But, sir, you can be a great help by getting on those guys at your lab!" He sounded aggrieved.

"Excuse me, sir, but why would I do that?"

"Well, didn't you see it?"

"Didn't I see what?

"The yellow guy! That weird-looking guy with the ears came out yellow. Yellow is tough, you know. Blue and red are easier to correct." Then he added, sadly, "We just couldn't get all the yellow out."

I thanked Master Control and advised him that Mister Spock was part Vulcan and even part-Vulcans were yellow. He allowed as how he didn't know even "part-Vulcans" were yellow and promised, in the future, to "leave him be."

Courtesy Stephen Edward Poe

17

Running on Empty

With his producing and writing responsibilities becoming even more demanding, and his unhappy family life getting more tense, the prospect of a nervous breakdown rested heavily on Gene Roddenberry.

After Roddenberry assumed the title and function of Executive Producer, Producer Coon and Asssociate Producer Justman were on the front line together and became both personal and professional friends. Soon, Coon recognized that another "writer body" was needed. During production of "Miri," in the last week of August 1966, writer Steve Carabatsos came to work as Story Consultant, and finally the writing problems seemed to be solved. But trouble loomed on an entirely different horizon.

Evidently Roddenberry had a premonition because much earlier, on April 7, 1966, he sent a memo to Justman (copies to Solow, Jefferies, Bill Heath, and the

Anderson Company) in which he wrote: ". . . we are very concerned that even Anderson's present estimated time of four weeks to completion may put us in serious trouble in getting our first two or three shows finished in time to do the audience tests which NBC insists on."

In earlier visits to the Anderson Company's Fairfax Avenue stage, Justman had been amazed to see how long it took to set up and film just one shot of the over twelve-foot model of the *Enterprise.* Using an old Fearless camera dolly and metal Durel tracks, Darrell Anderson filmed the ship by dollying toward or away from it or, for flybys, dollying past it sideways. The Anderson crew never knew whether the shots would be any good—they had to wait to see dailies. And even then, the slightest bump or wiggle, though not apparent when first screened, would show up disastrously when the shot was finally combined with the "moving-stars" background.

A moving-stars background was a combination of three star "plates," one stationary, one in which the stars moved slowly, and one in which the stars moved quickly. The final visual became complicated when all three backgrounds were composited with the footage of the *Enterprise.* If the ship's movement wasn't totally smooth, the *Enterprise* would appear to jiggle against the steady movement of the star background and the ship would look like the Model-T Ford of outer space.

As time passed, Gene Roddenberry became more anxious. "I don't want to wait to see the completed shots, Bob. I want to monitor their progress so we can avoid any problems later."

On July 14, 1966, he was worried enough to follow up with a cautionary memo to Darrell Anderson:

> . . . The purpose of this note is a friendly reminder that you and I have . . . agreed that every basic stage and component of optical work will be shown to us for comment and approval. . . .
>
> . . . This should *not* be considered as indicating any lack of faith in yours or Anderson Company's talent or creativity. Further, it simply means that *Star Trek* opticals, like stories or costumes or sets, must have a unity of one person's taste and viewpoints, good or bad.
>
> . . . I consider the above as an important part of our working agreement and arrangement. As such, if we should turn down a fully composited optical on which I have not had the opportunity to see the component parts, I would regretfully be placed in the position of having to refuse payment for the cost of making it.

For obvious reasons, Roddenberry sent copies of the memo to Solow, Justman, and Desilu Postproduction chief Bill Heath. The Anderson Company never responded, but Heath did, assuring Justman that all was well. "Don't worry, Bob. You'll have your opticals in plenty of time."

BOB: By August, Gene was pushing hard to see the composited shots of the *Enterprise* in space. Months earlier, I had drawn up a list of twenty "must-have" angles that would work in our main title and as reusable stock shots whenever we needed to show the ship orbiting a planet or zooming somewhere or other.

Remembering my visit to the Anderson Company's Fairfax Avenue special-effects stage, I became very worried. But when I checked with Bill Heath, he reassured me that things were going well with the miniature work. "Darrell doesn't want you guys to see anything until it's perfect. Like I said before, you'll have your footage in plenty of time. Tell Gene to stop worrying."

I did but it didn't take. It probably was the cop in Gene, but he had never trusted Heath. In fact, after the experience of making both pilots, Gene hated the man with a passion. I had been holding Gene off from going down to Heath's office and "cleaning his clock." Finally, the first airdate was only a month away and Roddenberry was ready to kill. "I want to see my main title and all the shots of the *Enterprise* and I want to see them *now!*"

I'd never seen gentle Gene angry before. It was a sobering sight. So I phoned Heath. "I don't care whether it's all ready or not. Show us what you've got now or I won't answer for what Gene will do."

So Darrell Anderson screened the results of his many months of work. The three of us sat in the projection room. Bill Heath wasn't there; discretion was the better part of valor.

The lights went out. The projector whirred into life. Two minutes later, the lights came back on.

We had seen maybe six good shots and some others that were partially usable. We had expected many more angles, some of which were badly needed for our series main title.

"Where's all the other shots, Darrell?"

Darrell began to shake. He jumped to his feet, screaming, "You'll never make your first airdate." Bursting into tears, he ran out of the room, still screaming, "You'll never make your first airdate! You'll never make your first airdate!"

Gene sat there in shock. I raced after Darrell and caught him outside. He was weeping. And no wonder. We later found out he had been working both day and night for months, trying to satisfy our needs. That afternoon, Darrell went to Palm Springs for a rest cure.

When I returned to the projection room, Gene was waiting for me. His expression was grim. "Come with me, Bob," he said and led me by the hand to the cutting rooms. And there, in one afternoon, piecing together scraps of film left over from both pilots, we created the now famous *Star Trek* main title. Gene actually "wrote" the sequence on a Moviola.

I wanted "the ship to zoom straight into the lens and deposit the starring credits in its wake like 'hot glowing turds' in the firmament." Gene rather liked the idea and loved the simile.

Despite Darrell's prediction, we made our first airdate. It was some kind of miracle.

The postproduction near-debacle reenergized Justman's search for "the right guy" to handle all the postproduction chores. Luckily, Roddenberry remembered Ed Milkis, a film editor who had worked for him on *The Lieutenant* at MGM.

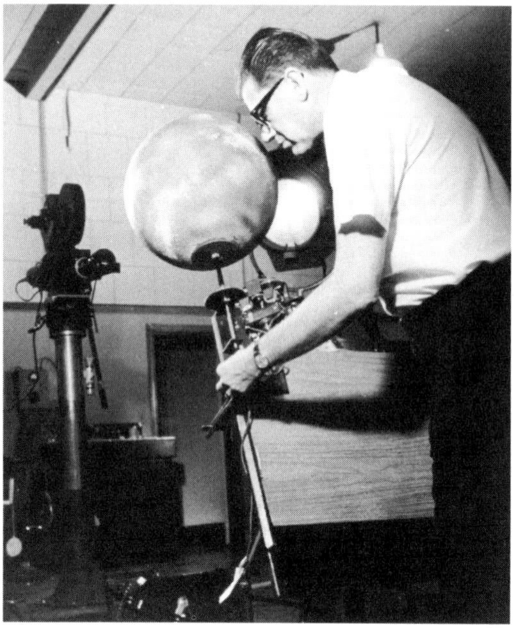

Courtesy Stephen Edward Poe

Joseph Westheimer of the Westheimer Company prepares to shoot one of *Star Trek*'s planets.

Milkis had left the film industry and gone into real estate. But when Roddenberry called, he agreed to help out "for a while." Milkis was hired as Assistant to the Producer and went to work on Wednesday, August 31, 1966.

The new executive was cool, calm, and totally unflappable. He made such an enormous difference, Justman still claims that Milkis "saved our bacon." He took over all the postproduction work and soon was running a very efficient department.

Although the series's main-title problem had been solved, the overall optical situation was a disaster waiting to happen. Bob Justman and Ed Milkis both realized that *Star Trek* needed more than one optical house. Each episode had as many effects shots as a full-length science-fiction movie. What took many months to accomplish on a major feature film literally had to be accomplished in weeks for each *Star Trek* episode. Neither the Anderson Company nor any other single company could deliver all the special effects opticals for the whole series.

Soon, Milkis had five separate optical houses supplying material for the series: the Anderson Company, the Westheimer Company, Cinema Research, Frank Vanderveer, and Film Effects of Hollywood. Although the process was substantially improved, there would always be difficulties with delivery of optical-effects shots, a problem that, in fact, persisted throughout the three-year run of the entire series.

Film Effects of Hollywood was to have replaced the Anderson Company as the show's primary supplier. While this new firm supplied some material, it couldn't supply enough, and its costs were too high for a television budget. So Justman and Milkis had to parcel out their needs to each opticals supplier on a show-by-show basis.

On the Labor Day weekend just prior to that first airdate, Roddenberry flew to Cleveland, Ohio, intent on personally introducing *Star Trek* to the country's leading science-fiction writers and fans, who had gathered at the annual World Science Fiction Convention, called "Tricon" that year. He carried a print of "Where No Man Has Gone Before" and three *Star Trek* crew uniforms, one female and one male, plus Sherry Jackson's skimpy costume from "Little Girls." Gene had made prior arrangements for a young woman to display Bill Theiss's creation, and in a rare extroverted display, very unlike Roddenberry, he hoped to fit himself into the other uniform.

Science-fiction writer Jerry Sohl remembered the uniform in a letter to Roddenberry:

> . . . I had to laugh. I remembered Gene Roddenberry who went all the way to Cleveland to prove his point at the world science fiction convention, that *Star Trek* was the greatest science fiction show ever to hit TV; and I remembered a Gene Roddenberry who sweated bullets getting into his costume and wearing it at the ball. . . .

The Sherry Jackson costume evoked a different comment. It was worn by a very attractive and well-endowed young model whose talents immediately caught the attention of famed science-fiction writer and bachelor Harlan Ellison. To quote Bjo Trimble, "We got a big kick out of watching Harlan. He was on her like a pack of fleas on a hound dog." But Harlan struck out. The woman knew how to handle the pitch, even when it came from such a creative pitchman.

Gene Roddenberry's experience in Cleveland, rubbing elbows with the most prominent members of the Science Fiction Writers of America, provided him with an idea he would exploit months later when he enlisted their aid to help save *Star Trek* from cancellation.

HERB: But that weekend, Gene's efforts paid off. "Where No Man," unlike the other television and theatrical films screened, was well received. The science-fiction aficionados at the convention were entranced by the new show. But in four days, the series would premiere on television to a national audience that thought science fiction was comic books of busty women being dragged away by alligator people, or a giant purple blob intent on dissolving Tokyo.

Earlier in the summer, NBC had devised a strategy to give its new series a head start on their ABC and CBS competition. They called it "Sneak Preview Week." It was very simple: Rather than introduce the series during the week that historically always began the fall television season, NBC—and ABC, as it later turned out—scheduled their premieres during the prior week.

A newspaper advertising blitz in the major television markets accompanied the switch and directed viewers, hungry for new programs after the long, hot summer of repeats, to sample the exciting new NBC color lineup.

The *Star Trek* newspaper ads, run on September 8, 1966, displayed an artist's

8:30 PM
in color
Welcome aboard the United Space
Ship Enterprise. Where it goes,
no program has ever gone before...
Sneak Preview!
Star Trek
starring
WILLIAM SHATNER
as Capt. James T. Kirk
(Earthman). Co-starring
LEONARD NIMOY
as Science Officer Spock

The *Star Trek* ad that ran in *The Los Angeles Times* on September 8, 1966.

sketch of Bill Shatner and Leonard Nimoy. The sketch avoided showing Nimoy's pointed ears. There were several unrecognizable characters in the background—and the *Enterprise* circling a planet, spelling out in its wake *Star Trek*. The copy read: "8:30 P.M. in color. Welcome aboard the *United Space Ship Enterprise*. [*sic*] Where it goes, no program has ever gone before."

The actors were billed: "starring WILLIAM SHATNER as Capt. James T. Kirk (Earthman). Costarring LEONARD NIMOY as Science Officer Spock (from the planet Vulcan)."

NBC also ran a full-page ad in *TV Guide*. *Star Trek* shared the space with other new NBC shows: the 7:30 premiere of *Tarzan* and the 9:30 premiere of *The Hero*. The page was headlined "SNEAKAPEEK AT NBC WEEK!" But owing to the necessary lead time of six weeks, neither the premiere episode of the new *Star Trek* series, "Man Trap," nor any of the other sneaked previews were given the very desirable half-page "*TV Guide* Close-Up."

And since CBS was still broadcasting repeats of their prior year's programs, the national ratings issued for that week failed to give an accurate picture of viewer preference over the long haul. NBC's Sneak Preview Week was a solid idea but did not bring the audience size the network expected. According to Nielsen Media Research, the *Star Trek* premiere attracted "only" 11,360,000 viewers. Its average rating for the one-hour time period was a low 20.7.

Star Trek's premiere competition on CBS was a repeat episode of *My Three Sons*, which earned a rating of 14.2, and the first half-hour of a 1961 Jerry Lewis movie, *The Ladies' Man*, which was rated 13.4. ABC aired the premiere of a new series, *The Tammy Grimes Show*, which had a rating of 13.2, and the season premiere of a popular old stand-by comedy series, *Bewitched*, which received a 18.5 rating.

Nevertheless, Lucille Ball sent a well-meaning note: "Dear Gene and the rest of you hardworking people . . . Just heard the good news, and want you to know how proud and happy I am. Looks like you really have a hit on your hands, and we all appreciate your efforts. Love, Lucy."

Her note was a lot more optimistic than the critical response would indicate.

The two most important reviews for *Star Trek* and NBC were in different editions of the entertainment industry trade paper, *Variety*. *Weekly Variety*, published in New York City, was considered the bible of the motion-picture distribution business and all those involved at the money end of radio, television, advertising, and sponsorship. On the other hand, *Daily Variety*, published in Hollywood, catered primarily to the creative side of the motion picture, radio, and television community. So for different and obvious reasons, both reviews were important.

The *Weekly Variety* review began, "*Star Trek* obviously solicits all-out suspension of disbelief, but it won't work." The *Weekly Variety* review concluded, "The biggest guessing game is figuring how this lowercase fantasia broke into the sked." The review also called Shatner and Nimoy "wooden" and referred to Mister Spock as ". . . socalled [*sic*] chief science officer whose bizarre hairdo (etc.) is a dilly." The reviewer did notice that "a quota of decorative females, most of them in vague roles, are involved in the out-of-this-world shenanigans."

And there was even more that NBC Sales and any of the participating prime-time *Star Trek* sponsors certainly did not want to read:

Star Trek's ad in the *TV Guide* fall preview edition, September 1966.

"By a generous stretch of the imagination, it [*Star Trek*] could lure a small coterie of the smallfry, though not happily time slotted in that direction. It's better suited to the Saturday morning kidvid bloc."

Legendary *Daily Variety* columnist Jack Hellman in his review of "Man Trap":

> And away we go to another planet for the sci-fi buffs to lick the dish clean. But there better be a hefty cargo of them or the Nielsen samplers may come up short. It's not for the common herd who prefer less cerebral exercises.
>
> . . . Not conducive to its popularity is the lack of meaningful cast leads. They move around with directorial precision with only violence to provide the excitement and very little of that over the hour spread.
>
> . . . The whistling sounds of the planetary devices added only to the confusion of the fleeting figures up and down the corridors.

It's understandable that all members of the Hollywood creative community enjoy being on a winning team. *Daily Variety* had just advised *Star Trek* writers, directors, actors, composers, et al. not to quit their day jobs.

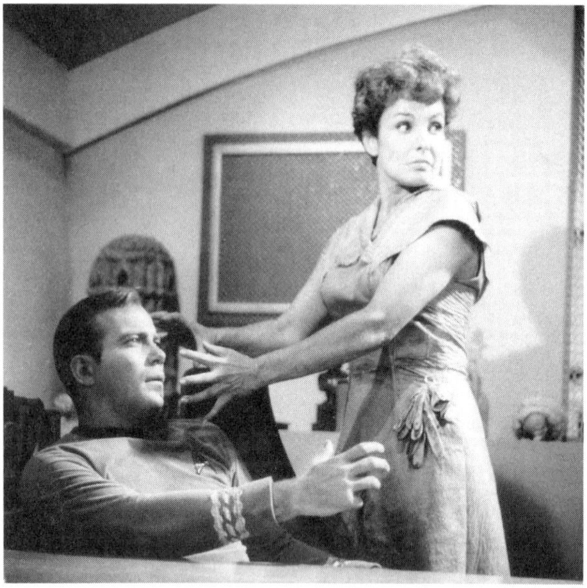

Courtesy NBC/Globe

A scene from the first *Star Trek* episode aired, "The Man Trap."

HERB: In hindsight, I shouldn't have asked Bob, in addition to his fourteen to sixteen hours a day of *Star Trek* chores, to help me out with *Mission.* But I had no other choice.

Executive Producer Bruce Geller loved to involve himself in postproduction; the cutting, scoring, and dubbing of *Mission: Impossible* fascinated him. But he was overly demanding and unforgiving when faced with what he wanted for his show. As he started taking more and more time to dub episodes—at least two full days with a lot of heavy overtime—I became very concerned. But when sound effects editor Gordon Day mentioned that Bruce had taken six hours of the entire dubbing crew's time in an attempt to get the right sound effect for a prescription pill crunch, it was definitely time to act.

Bruce acknowledged my concerns. "You get me someone I can trust and I'll pull out of dubbing."

"But you don't trust anyone," I reminded him.

"Oh, no, Herb. I trust Bob Justman. I worked with him on the pilot; he knows the show; he already dubbed some episodes. Get me Justman—and no more pill crunches!"

I apologized to Bob for asking; but he, as always, was more than happy to help out.

"You look tired, RJ. Be honest with me. Do you feel as tired as you look?"

"Actually, I feel pretty good. Maybe just a teensy bit tired, but pretty good." RJ continued, with a sardonic smile. "Anyway, while I'm dubbing *Mission,* I can use the breaks between reels to check up on the *Star Trek* sets, effects, budgets, editing, casting—and write a few dozen script memos."

So RJ accepted the additional assignment. But as the weeks passed, his smile faded, his gait slowed, his patience vanished. He thought it was just *Star Trek* that was in trouble; he never realized how much trouble *he* was in. By the time we'd begun filming our twelfth episode, "The Galileo Seven," RJ was averaging barely four hours of sleep each night and running on empty.

Overwrought and exhausted, Bob arrived home very late one night, slowly ate dinner, and totally collapsed. Jackie Justman, after tending to her husband, called Gene at home and laid down the law. "I'm taking Bob away for a rest and you'd better not interfere!"

But as could be expected, Bob refused to go away. Next morning, like those proverbial locusts, he returned to Desilu and his responsibilities. Gene told me RJ was back on the lot. First stopping at the business office, I went to see Bob and handed him two airline tickets.

"What's this?" he asked.

"Two tickets to Hawaii, made out to Robert and Jackie Justman. I found them on the street. They have to be used tomorrow."

Bob studied the tickets and handed them back to me. "Thanks, Herb. That's very thoughtful, but I'm just fine."

I dropped them on his desk. "Well, you have a choice, RJ. You and Jackie fly to Hawaii tomorrow—or you're fired!"

I left the office, and, "tomorrow," the Justmans flew to Hawaii.

BOB: One full night's sleep had already worked wonders. Concerned at first that my breakdown was psychological, I realized, however, it was merely a matter of physical exhaustion. With a bit of rest, I was confident of coming back to work fully energized. Before I left the studio, I had extracted a promise from Gene that he wouldn't do anything to Bill Heath while I was gone. No use taking a chance on things coming apart in my absence.

As Jackie and I walked through the airport terminal on the way to the plane, I caught a glimpse of Bob Hellstrom, Gene's personal assistant and "gofer," lurking nearby. He looked guilty when I walked over.

"Bob Hellstrom. What are you doing here?"

"Oh, nothing," he stammered, "just seeing a friend off. Well, so long. I hope you have a nice trip, too." He repeated, "Well, so long," and left quickly.

I was suspicious—and spotted Gene Roddenberry's fine hand at work. As we went through the boarding gate, I looked back. Hellstrom was hiding behind a column. He ducked back out of sight.

"Something's up, honey," I said. "Gene's up to something."

We boarded the plane. Jackie's seat was at the window; mine was on the aisle. Someone was already sitting in the middle. On closer inspection, we realized that Balok, the creature from "The Corbomite Maneuver," was flying to Hawaii with us. Small world, isn't it?

"Don't say anything, Jackie. Just ignore it." But she was way ahead of me and stepped past the monster, sat down, buckled up, and casually read her *New Yorker* magazine. I sat down in my seat, totally ignoring our fellow traveler.

However, a tourist seated behind us was very taken with Balok. It goes without saying, he was also very drunk.

"Hey, cutie," he yelled, "I think I'm in love." The tourist continued his one-sided conversation with Balok until the pilot marched up the aisle and angrily planted himself directly in front of me.

"Do you know this . . . thing?"

"No, sir! I never saw it before in my life."

"I'm not moving this aircraft until *it* gets off!" He paraded to the rear of the plane and left.

Shortly, a chastened Bob Hellstrom walked down the aisle. "Sorry, Bob. Gene thought . . . well, you know." Hellstrom picked up Balok and carried him off the plane.

The pilot returned and the plane taxied toward its takeoff position. We were finally off to Hawaii. But the drunk was disappointed. "Damn, I was gonna take her to a luau on the beach."

"She's a him," I said.

"Oh. In that case, aloha—and never mind!"

Once the plane was airborne, one of the two stewardesses begrudgingly announced, "a Mr. Rodderberry sent you a bottle of champagne," while the other stewardess poured a glass for us. They could have done without Balok, and they certainly could have done without the special champagne, which amounted to extra work. Every time we requested a refill, the stewardesses glared at us.

Off we soared to the land of surf, sunsets, and Sweet Leilani. We arrived at Hanalei Bay on the tropical island of Kauai, the idyllic spot where the beach scenes for the movie *South Pacific* were filmed. Remembering the monster on the plane, I sent a wire to Gene joking, "ALL US CREATURES FLY UNITED."

I shouldn't have done that.

The next morning, Saturday, October 1, 1966, I was standing in the surf. It was raining, but I didn't care. Any thought of *Star Trek* was slowly receding with the tide.

Jackie waded out into the shore break with a cablegram. I smiled. I knew it would be from Gene and it would say something nice and cute like "Hope you're having a wonderful time. Wish I was there." But what I received was something completely different.

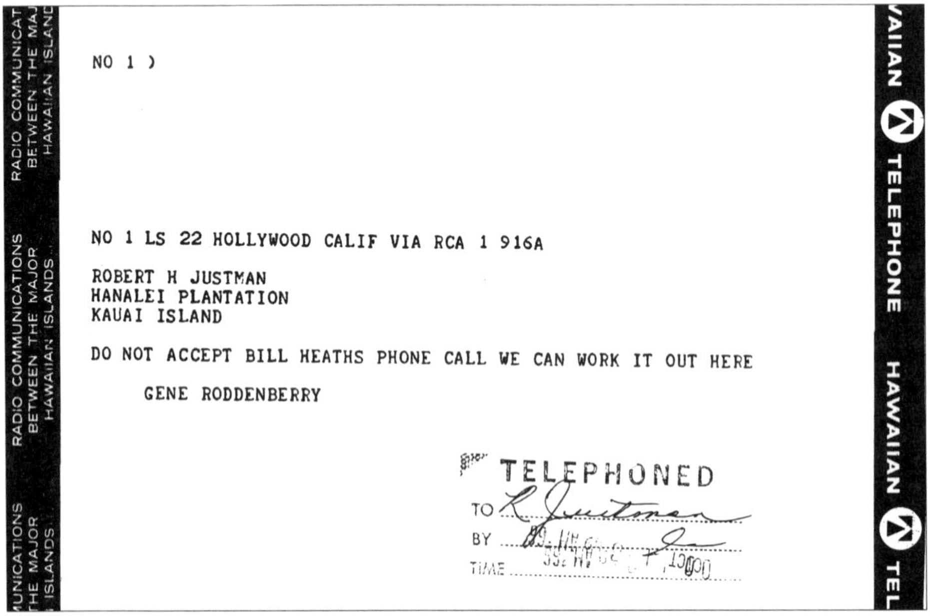
RADIO COMMUNICATIONS BETWEEN THE MAJOR HAWAIIAN ISLANDS

NO 1)

NO 1 LS 22 HOLLYWOOD CALIF VIA RCA 1 916A

ROBERT H JUSTMAN
HANALEI PLANTATION
KAUAI ISLAND

DO NOT ACCEPT BILL HEATHS PHONE CALL WE CAN WORK IT OUT HERE

GENE RODDENBERRY

TELEPHONED
TO R. Justman
BY
TIME

HAWAIIAN TELEPHONE

I went into shock; my worst fears had come true. There had been some misunderstanding, perhaps even a fight. I ran out of the water and barreled, barefoot, up the pebble-strewn path to the cliff top, and into the hotel lobby, the only place at the resort where there was a phone. Another cable awaited.

RCA COMMUNICATIONS, INC.
A SERVICE OF RADIO CORPORATION OF AMERICA
223 S. KING STREET, HONOLULU TEL. 52521

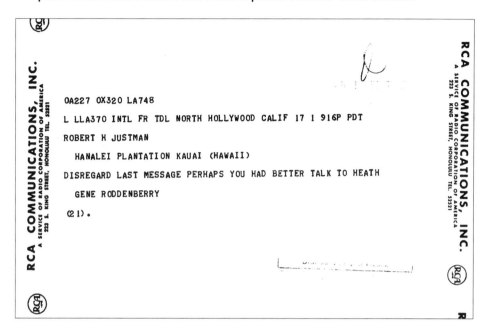

OA227 OX320 LA748
L LLA370 INTL FR TDL NORTH HOLLYWOOD CALIF 17 1 916P PDT
ROBERT H JUSTMAN
HANALEI PLANTATION KAUAI (HAWAII)
DISREGARD LAST MESSAGE PERHAPS YOU HAD BETTER TALK TO HEATH
GENE RODDENBERRY
(21).

I placed a call to the office at Desilu, but everyone had already gone. And I didn't have Bill Heath's home number. I decided to do nothing—until the following afternoon when another cablegram arrived.

RADIO COMMUNICATIONS BETWEEN THE MAJOR HAWAIIAN ISLANDS
HAWAIIAN TELEPHONE

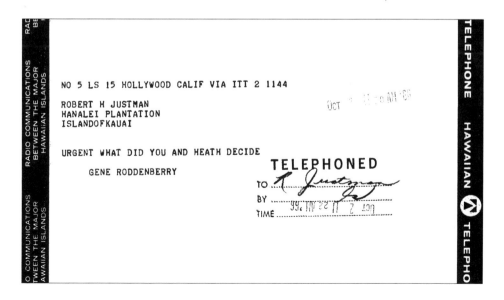

NO 5 LS 15 HOLLYWOOD CALIF VIA ITT 2 1144

ROBERT H JUSTMAN
HANALEI PLANTATION
ISLANDOFKAUAI

URGENT WHAT DID YOU AND HEATH DECIDE
GENE RODDENBERRY

TELEPHONED
TO R. Justman
BY
TIME

I spent the rest of the afternoon calling Los Angeles. Strangely, Gene was out of the office. "He hasn't gone to see Bill Heath, has he?" I asked.

"No, he left work early," answered Dorothy Fontana. "How's Hawaii? You must be having a great time. Tell me about it."

"It's hard to describe."

Gene wasn't at home either; he was out for the evening. There were no cables the next day. "Maybe they kissed and made up," I hoped. But that didn't sound likely. I was beginning to get suspicious. But I put *Star Trek* out of my mind, and we flew to the "big island," Hawaii, where Gene surfaced again.

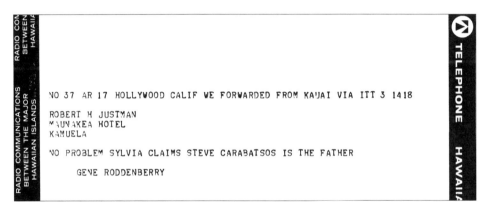

NO 37 AR 17 HOLLYWOOD CALIF WE FORWARDED FROM KAUAI VIA ITT 3 1418

ROBERT H JUSTMAN
MAUNAKEA HOTEL
KAMUELA

NO PROBLEM SYLVIA CLAIMS STEVE CARABATSOS IS THE FATHER

GENE RODDENBERRY

His cable about Sylvia seemed odd. My secretary, Sylvia, was a very married, married woman. What would her husband say? And who would tell him? Not me. For sure. He was a big guy.

And the thought of her fooling around with mild-mannered Steve Carabatsos was . . . for once, words failed me.

My burgeoning suspicions were aroused further with the arrival of the next cablegram, from sound effects editor Joe Sorokin and dubbing mixers Gordon Day and Eldon Ruberg.

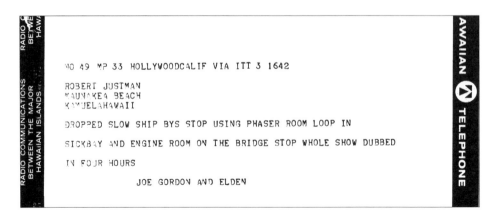

NO 49 MP 33 HOLLYWOODCALIF VIA ITT 3 1642

ROBERT JUSTMAN
MAUNAKEA BEACH
KAMUELAHAWAII

DROPPED SLOW SHIP BYS STOP USING PHASER ROOM LOOP IN
SICKBAY AND ENGINE ROOM ON THE BRIDGE STOP WHOLE SHOW DUBBED
IN FOUR HOURS

JOE GORDON AND ELDEN

I made another phone call. But again Gene was out. Sylvia was also out and nobody knew when she'd be back. I really began to smell a rat. Sylvia would never leave the office during working hours.

On Friday, September 30, 1966, when we left Los Angeles, "Galileo Seven" was finishing its last day of shooting, both on schedule and under budget. And then, another cable arrived.

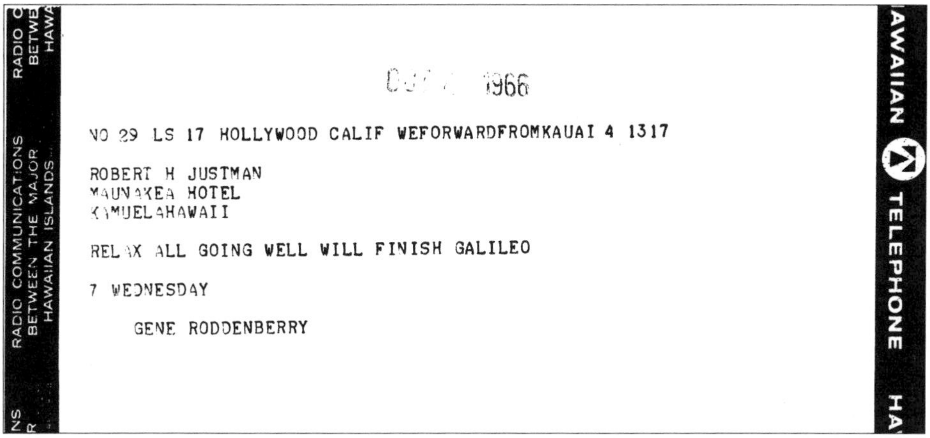

RADIO COMMUNICATIONS BETWEEN THE MAJOR HAWAIIAN ISLANDS

1966

NO 29 LS 17 HOLLYWOOD CALIF WEFORWARDFROMKAUAI 4 1317

ROBERT H JUSTMAN
MAUNAKEA HOTEL
KAMUELAHAWAII

RELAX ALL GOING WELL WILL FINISH GALILEO

7 WEDNESDAY

GENE RODDENBERRY

HAWAIIAN TELEPHONE

Everything fell into place. For an episode to suddenly go so far over schedule and budget was unheard of in the annals of television. Gene, with his warped sense of humor, was playing tricks with my mind. My suspicions were finally confirmed after another cablegram arrived.

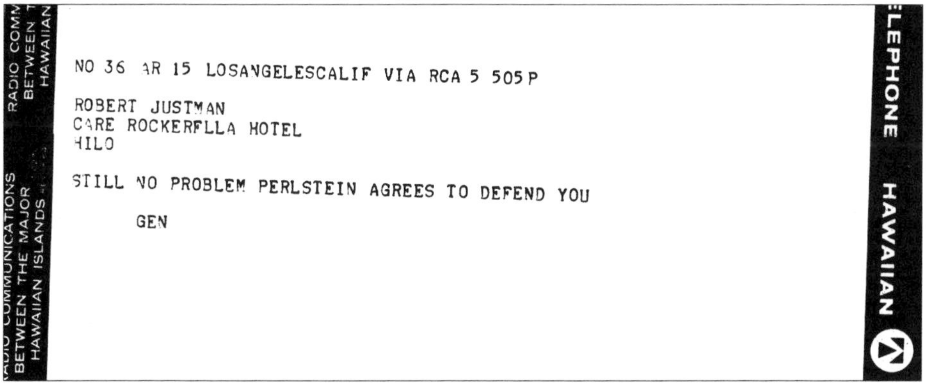

RADIO COMMUNICATIONS BETWEEN THE MAJOR HAWAIIAN ISLANDS

NO 36 AR 15 LOSANGELESCALIF VIA RCA 5 505P

ROBERT JUSTMAN
CARE ROCKERFLLA HOTEL
HILO

STILL NO PROBLEM PERLSTEIN AGREES TO DEFEND YOU

GEN

HAWAIIAN TELEPHONE

Ed Perlstein was the Desilu studio attorney. He was a great guy, but he just wrote contracts; he didn't do paternity suits.

I no longer went for the bait. Instead of worrying about the show, I waded back out into the water. It rained some more. I didn't care.

But the madness wasn't over. The day before we left for home, Jackie fell and

sprained her ankle. The following morning we rolled her out to the plane in a wheelchair. Her foot was in a cast, and she had to be carried aboard. When we finally got Jackie into a seat where she could stretch out her leg, she needed a pillow for support. I rang for the stewardess. Adding insult to injury, there were the same two stewardesses who disliked us on the flight to Hawaii. Now they disliked us even more. We couldn't wait to get home.

Justman, now well rested, was soon back in the thick of things, energized and working with renewed enthusiasm. Since he always kept the door open, he quickly discovered that his oddly decorated, creature-repository office had become the focal point of visitors to *Star Trek* headquarters. They often wandered in, just to "take a look." It never occurred to them that they were imposing upon his privacy, but the two Gorns were a real attraction.

BOB: One day months later, a father, mother, and children popped their heads in the doorway. "The kids want to see the Gorns. We'll just be a minute. You don't mind, do you?"

"Not at all," I lied, not wanting to disappoint the kids. After examining the Gorns, however, the interlopers continued to hang around and watch me try to work. Perhaps they viewed me as an exhibit, just one more weird *Star Trek* creature to tell their friends about.

Time passed. One of the kids, totally bored, lifted the "maid's" apron and screamed, "Look, Mommy, look!"

That's when I discovered that, while I was in Hawaii, the mannequin had been rendered more "lifelike" by makeup man extraordinaire Fred Phillips, egged on by Gene Roddenberry and Ed Milkis. Her nether region was anatomically correct down to the last little detail, and rather impressive, I must say. It was clearly evident that Freddy had thoroughly researched his subject.

Obviously, the visit was over, as the parents hustled the children out of the room and disappeared down the hall.

"I told you Hollywood people are dirt, pure dirt, but no, you had to bring us here, and with the kids, no less. . . ." The mother's voice faded as the interlopers left the building.

The mannequin was banished to the shower in my private bathroom to wait for more victims. When invited visitors inquired about the men's room, I was overjoyed. "Use my bathroom, instead," I insisted. "It's right in there."

Visitors would enter, unzip, and go about their business. Sooner or later, my guest felt a "presence" and glanced over his shoulder. There, lurking behind the semitransparent glass of the shower enclosure, stood a nude female figure, a towel appropriately draped over one arm. The sudden shock of seeing her never failed to invoke a start from the guest—so much so that, eventually, a "spatter shield" had to be installed around the commode.

HERB: After Bob told Gene how much he and Jackie had enjoyed the islands, *Star Trek*'s creator decided he was running out of steam himself. He turned everything over to Justman and Coon and left to try those "cool tropical drinks and those warm tropical nights." And after Gene returned from *his* Hawaiian vacation, he was gleeful as he related his successful plot to me.

Gene had told his wife, Eileen, how important it was that he get away from the pressures of *Star Trek,* the studio, the network—just everything—to be alone, by himself, on one of the out-of-the-way Hawaiian Islands, walking the beach, hiking in the hills, diving in the cool, clear water—"renewing his soul."

"She completely understood my needs," said Gene, smiling. Reservations were made, and the day he left, Eileen drove Gene to the airport.

"When we get there, she said, 'I'll just drop you off, honey.'"

"I won't hear of it, darling," he responded. "Please walk me to the boarding gate. I'm going to miss you."

Hand in hand, Gene and Eileen walked to the gate, where they kissed. Eileen waved to her husband as he walked up the ramp to board the aircraft that would carry him to the solitude he needed to renew his soul.

The stewardess directed him to First Class, third row, seat A. Gene walked down the aisle and took his assigned seat. He turned to the party in First Class, third row, seat B and said, "Hello!"

Majel Barrett looked up and smiled. "Oh, hi! Are you going to Hawaii, too?"

"Yes. Small world, isn't it?"

William Shatner and Joan Collins, as they appeared in "The City on the Edge of Forever."

Courtesy NBC/Globe

18

On the Edge of Forever: Waiting for Harlan

Waiting for Harlan Ellison wasn't exactly like waiting for Godot. Godot never showed up. Harlan did—but it took a while. The writing of Ellison's award-winning teleplay "City on the Edge of Forever" was an adventure almost as intriguing as the script itself. And it led to a curious relationship between Ellison and Bob Justman and a unique collection of memoranda between Justman and his associates.

BOB: By the time series production began, we were already hurting for scripts and wanted to get a teleplay from Harlan as soon as possible. But despite a lot of badgering, Harlan was behind schedule right from the start, taking two months to write his final revised story outline. The usual time allocation for a story was more like two or three weeks.

Although his story outline contained inherent production problems, I loved it and, in a memo to John D. F. Black, wrote: ". . . don't ever tell Harlan . . . but this outline is beautifully written. The fact that it may become rather difficult to achieve the effects that he has written into his story is another matter."

I mentioned a few problem areas: "The time vortex is described as a shimmering pillar of light set between the gray-silver rocks. It would be nice if we could find a cheaper time vortex."

And:

> On page 10, the Earthmen reel back in astonishment as the behemoth bulk of a giant wooly mammoth bursts out of the foliage within the time vortex device. At the same moment, Bob Justman reels back in agony, as he does not believe that there is any color stock film available on mastodons bursting out of foliage. Or even giant wooly mammoths.

In summation, my analysis was:

> Plenty sets, plenty speaking parts, plenty extras, plenty locations, plenty shooting time, plenty money, plenty night-for-night shooting, plenty screams from management accompanied by dire threats and reflections upon our immediate ancestry.

Fearful that the millennium would arrive before Harlan's next effort, Gene Roddenberry prevailed upon him to write his first-draft teleplay at the studio. Harlan arrived with his own typewriter, his own portable radio, and his own original approach to creativity.

Every now and then, visitors to our office building were surprised at the sight of Harlan cartwheeling down the long narrow corridor, unwinding while he took a break from the typewriter. The cubbyhole office we had assigned to Harlan was too confining. It was also the show's wardrobe storage room, so Harlan had to endure lots of interruptions. Luckily, he liked to work at night.

And there were times when Harlan, seeking to get a breath of air, would escape. He'd lock his office door from the inside, put on some loud music, and climb through the office window onto the studio street to go visit the shooting company onstage. Occasionally, he would stand in the "park" between Lucy's bungalow and the Desilu administration building and yell up to Herb Solow's second-floor office, "Herbie, can you come out and play now?" Herb worried that Lucy would overhear and misunderstand Harlan's sense of humor.

After a few weeks, however, Harlan complained we were forcing him "to work under inhuman and inhumane conditions." Since we desperately needed his final-draft teleplay, I arranged for Harlan to work and sleep inside my office until he finished the script. It was really a jail sentence. "I'm locking you in every night, Harlan, so the sooner you finish, the sooner you can go free."

Harlan would never have accepted this "imprisonment," as he termed it, if he didn't trust me. While working on *The Outer Limits,* I had prevented one of his scripts from being junked; the budget on his "Demon with a Glass Hand" was so high we couldn't afford to produce the episode. He had written his original as a "chase," and it called for many short scenes to be filmed all over Los Angeles County. It would have taken several days out of our tight shooting schedule just to account for the many "moves" for the crew and equipment, thereby leaving insufficient time to actually shoot the show. But I had an idea of how to solve the seemingly unsolvable problem.

I explained the situation to Ellison and apprised him, "We can't afford to make this episode, Harlan. The front office wants to junk the show, but I convinced them to hold off because I've got an idea about how you can salvage it."

Harlan was desperate. "Tell me how, Bob! I'll do anything to save my script!"

We were soon in my car, on the way to downtown Los Angeles and the architecturally famous Bradbury Building. I led Harlan directly into the building's basement. "We start here," said I, "and we work your way, vertically, up to the roof." Then I took him on a tour of the beautiful landmark building, pointing out where each scene could play. As we progressed upstairs from floor to floor, and finally outside onto the roof, Harlan became more and more excited by the visual and dramatic possibilities inherent in this unusual location.

"What do you think?" I asked. But I already knew the answer. Harlan was almost salivating. "It's great! I love it! And I know exactly what to do! Let's go home."

Harlan completed a warp-speed rewrite and we filmed the episode, which starred Robert Culp and was directed by Byron Haskin. "Demon with a Glass Hand" was a terrific show, and it garnered Harlan the Writers Guild Award for Most Outstanding Teleplay of the 1964–65 season.

But this was 1966, and Harlan had to finish "City on the Edge"—or else. My appreciation of his talent had begun when I first read "Demon with a Glass Hand." He would achieve much, while at times angering others who didn't appreciate his flamboyance. I, for one, appreciated both his creativity and his passion for life. We had enjoyed a good relationship during *The Outer Limits,* and now we were working together again.

This last part (supposedly the last) of the scriptwriting process took three days and nights. I had invited Harlan to sack out on my couch whenever he needed sleep, but he preferred to sleep on the carpeted floor, claiming that he found it "much more comfortable." My office was an odd place, what with the red, white, and blue color scheme and the various monsters standing around. I think Harlan found it "homey." He was there, sleeping on the floor one afternoon, when an important meeting was scheduled to begin.

The people who arrived merely stepped over Harlan, and we carried on with our business. Harlan slept through the whole thing—or so I thought. After everyone left, he opened one eye and said, "Good meeting, Bob. Now, get the hell out of here so I can get some sleep or I'll never finish the goddam script."

I did, and he did. Next morning, his teleplay was completed. His revenge upon me for locking him in my office took an odd turn. The mercurial writer ate one of the leaves from the plant on Sylvia T. Smith's desk. When I remonstrated with him, he replied, "I ate only one lousy leaf, Bob. It'll grow back. I didn't touch the stem."

Surprisingly, Harlan had finished his first-draft teleplay in three weeks. He departed for even greener pastures while we attempted to deal with what he had wrought. It was a doozy.

And it occasioned me to write another memo to John D. F. Black, saying:

"Without a doubt, this is the best and most beautifully written screenplay we have gotten to date and possibly we'll ever get this season. If you tell this to Harlan, I'll kill you."

Then came the usual litany:

> We cannot afford to make this show as it presently stands. Set construction costs, location shooting, crowds of extras, crowds of stunts, special effects onstage, special photographic effects, wardrobe costs, period props and set dressing rentals, and other costs too numerous to mention at this time. What we have to do is find a way to retain all the basic qualities contained within this screenplay and then, at the same time, make it economically feasible for us to photograph it. This is an eight-day show to my way of thinking. I would like to try for seven. [*Star Trek* episodes were budgeted for six days.]

Referring to Harlan as "Cordwainer Bird," the pen name the author occasionally threatened to use when he was rewritten, the memo finished with:

> Cordwainer has made the oft-repeated statement that this show will cost 98 cents to shoot. Please keep him out of my office. I know that he will try to convince me that this show will cost 98 cents to shoot. I can't afford to take the time to explain to him why it will cost more than 98 cents to shoot. I have been down this road before with Cordwainer. He did a segment of *The Outer Limits* entitled "The Glass Hand" [*sic*] which you may be aware of. Prior to the shooting of "The Glass Hand," Cordwainer was complaining that we were emasculating his handiwork. Emasculated or not, this show went on to win a Writers Guild Award and was also one of the best "Outer Limits" that we shot in two seasons. Tell Cordwainer that if he insists upon arguing budget with me, in the future I shall have to restrict him from my couch. He will no longer be allowed to sleep on my couch or to come in and stand on my desk. I will have him taken away by the "Civil People." He will also be denied the right to eat any leaves off my secretary's plant. He shall have to find emotional nourishment elsewhere.

Courtesy NBC/Globe

Joan Collins as Edith Keeler.

Despite their hopes, it was evident to Roddenberry and Justman that the first draft of "City" was far from being shootable. There were more than budgetary problems with this first Ellison script. Both men were concerned that some of the "guest" Starship officers, as written by Ellison for this episode, didn't behave in the upright manner Roddenberry expected from proper Starfleet personnel.

When, more than two months later and after much telephonic prodding, Ellison's "Revised Final Draft" teleplay (dated August 12 and delivered August 15, 1966) was finally read, the same concerns remained. By this time John D. F. Black was already gone and Justman wrote in his August 16th memo to the newly arrived Gene Coon:

> I have just finished reading the last draft on "City on the Edge of Forever" as written by Harlan Ellison. As you may know, this property was first

> assigned March 16, 1966. We received this draft yesterday and today is August 16, 1966. Simple arithmetic gives us the information that it has been five months since the property was first assigned. As it presently stands, this latest draft is no more inexpensive to shoot, in my opinion, than the previous version.

And Justman had other concerns:

"Although Harlan's writing is beautiful, it is not *Star Trek* that he has written. It is a lovely story for an anthology television series or a feature."

Three pages of single-spaced comments followed, including one observation that many others later also made:

". . . Spock's succeeding speech about the women that Kirk has known grates a little bit. It makes Kirk sound like a horny sailor, instead of a noble Captain."

The memo concluded with:

> I have been as frank as I possibly can be with regard to my comments on this version of the screenplay. I have not intended to be brutal in any way. It has been my experience in the past that somehow Cordwainer has gotten hold of my memos prior to my discussing them with him. At these times I have felt constrained, therefore, to read my memos to him, to save any possible embarrassment between the two of us. I would greatly appreciate it if Cordwainer could no longer obtain any of my memos with regard to his work in the future.

Having read Justman's memos about some of the problems inherent in his script, Ellison was aware that, if the script was to be made, it would have to undergo revisions. His fear that someone else, no matter how well intentioned, might not do justice to his work became a reality. After reading Story Editor Steve Carabatsos's fix, Ellison volunteered to revise his own teleplay again in "self-defense."

It took almost four months for him to deliver his *final* final draft. Although part of the delay can be attributed to his involvement in the Science Fiction Writers of America campaign to "save" *Star Trek* and part can be attributed to scripts he was writing for other television shows, it would seem that his late delivery could be attributed to the fact that he was psychologically opposed to rewriting what he had originally wrought.

In a December 20, 1966, memo to Gene Roddenberry, Justman wrote:

> I have just completed reading the "Second Revised Final Draft" of Harlan Ellison's script, which he has dated 12-1-66, even though it was delivered a hell of a lot later than that. I hear tell that there's a possibility that you, Mr. Roddenberry, will rewrite this draft to make it feasible for us to be able to photograph the story for this season's television viewers. Therefore, I address this memo to you in the hopes that it may prove of inestimable value.

Justman proceeded to list, chronologically, the various problems he found to be inherent in this latest script. In addition to the over-budget costs he anticipated, he found yet another problem—that the show might end up short:

> I am hinting that this is a 45-minute show. I will also hint, as I continue, that this show will still take about 8 or 9 days to shoot. I don't believe that much money has been saved in this version as compared with the previous versions. One does not write directions in a script about "a very small crowd of 7 or 8 people" and then give scene descriptions indicating a need for about 200 or 300 people. . . . Why don't you look at the beginning of Scene 62 and all the description contained therein and estimate to yourself how many extras you would have to hire to take care of the business indicated in the scene? Figure out how many people you would have to hire and how many people you would have to wardrobe and how many people would have to have their wardrobe altered to fit and how many cars and how many silent bits [much higher pay rate for extras who portray characters without dialogue] and how many special businesses [higher pay rate for extras who are given specific action to perform] and how many musicians and uniforms and car drivers and period [antique] cars and period trucks and set dressing in various windows and lunches and suppers and overtime and night penalty [ten to twenty percent premium on hourly rates] and golden time [2 1/2 times the hourly rate after twelve hours of "studio" work or fourteen hours of "nearby location" work] and so on and on and on and you would find your pocketbook and your brains absolutely boggled by the enormity of it all.

Of course, Justman's concerns didn't lessen his arcane sense of humor:

> Page 14A caused me to become exceedingly cruel to my wife and children the other night. And it is only one-eighth of a page. . . .
>
> . . . Scene 45 hurts me no end.

Justman finished his memo:

> Gene, I have written many, many long memos to you on the subject of this story. As always, I still feel that this is a fine story and [it] was created by an extremely talented writer. But we are in the sad position of being unfortunate enough not to be able to afford to make this story, even though it is of high quality. I feel that we have gone as far as we can go with Cordwainer and it must now devolve upon either you or Gene Coon to take this story in hand and make it shootable for us. If you don't, I fear that we must junk it. It would be immensely cheaper for us to throw away a complete screenplay of this sort, than to attempt to film it. A very dear friend of mine used to have

an expression which he used in times of stress and monetary troubles, "Your first loss is your best loss. Take your licking now and get out. It's cheaper in the long run.

The strategy paid off; Gene Coon was the next one to work on the script. Ellison had already made one very important change in the original story line: Two drug-crazed and deranged characters, Le Becque and Beckwith, had been the ones who precipitated the problems for Kirk and company. Bob Justman suggested that not only could they save money by "losing" both characters, it would also give DeForest Kelley a larger and much more important role to play in the story. So in Ellison's latest script, both characters were replaced by Dr. McCoy, and it was he, maddened by an accidental drug overdose, who motivated the action.

Most of Gene Coon's rewrite was accomplished over the Christmas and New Year's holidays, and it was delivered on January 9, 1967. On January 10, Justman wrote to Coon:

> This is pretty close to a shooting script finally. There are certain areas within it, however, which I feel need some work before we can say that we can come anywhere close to budget on the show. Among those areas are Set Construction, Night Shooting, Extras, Set Dressing, Wardrobe, etc.

There followed four single-spaced pages of specific notes and a final admonition:

> Just so that there is no misunderstanding, I want us to do this show. However, even if all my suggestions . . . are taken up by you . . . we will still be over our Series Budget. There is no doubt of it and we should not kid ourselves that we are going to get even close to a Series Budget on this particular segment.

It was time for another set of hands. Dorothy Fontana had recently become the show's new Story Editor, and the next version of Ellison's story was to be her unwanted assignment. Fontana not only was one of Ellison's most devoted admirers, she was also his friend. As such, she was aware of his already fabled explosive temperament. So with trepidation, she went to work.

Later, Justman, still concerned about costs, was more dismayed at what had happened to the beauty of Ellison's original script during the long, drawn-out revision process and wrote to Roddenberry:

> Although this latest version of Harlan's story comes closer to being producible than anything we have received to date, I would like to state that I feel there is hardly anything left of the beauty and mystery that was inherent

in this Screenplay as Harlan originally wrote it. It is very good *Star Trek* material now, but it certainly bears only structural resemblance at times to what Harlan originally delivered to us. It has none of his special magic any longer. Perhaps that is all for the best, but I, for one, feel bad about it. I'm sure you'll be able to convince me that all of the things I liked best about Harlan's writing were unsuitable for good dramatic television entertainment. Perhaps I really know it deep inside, and am trying to keep myself from realizing that knowledge. But I still feel bad. I can't help it.

During the ensuing five single-spaced pages of notes, Justman dealt with the script's specific requirements and his suggestions for accomplishing them. One of these was how to create the vortex into which Dr. McCoy, Kirk, and Spock would disappear on their way back through time. He wrote:

> . . . the "vortex" would entail an octagonal structure . . . as compared with the ruins in the immediate area. This structure would have an open entrance. Within the structure there would be some sort of a dully reflective wall, which would seem to bar any further entrance once you go inside the portal. For our purposes, this reflective wall would be removable and behind it we would have black velvet. By means of clever compositing, we could run our people into it and they would appear to disappear right through the dully reflective wall. I am sure that Ed Milkis knows what I am talking about with regard to this effect. It is somewhat similar to the old "ghost walking through a solid stone wall of the castle" effect that we used to see many, many years ago in thriller-type movies.

Although the portal eventually used was not octagonal, the methodology he suggested was employed to create the required effect.

Justman referred to Ellison again near the end of his memo:

> In closing, I would like to say that had this version of the script been turned in by some [other] writer, I am sure that we would all have been thrilled with it. My problem is that I read Harlan's original version and his [*sic*] various so-called re-workings of that version.

The memo concluded:

> Because of the amount of Sets and moves and stages . . . I don't see how this show can be shot in anything approximating a normal schedule or . . . a normal budget. In its present form, my guess is still at least 7 days and very probably 8 . . . . Please count to ten after reading this memo.

The memo was signed "MARAT-SADE."

Courtesy NBC/Globe

Mister. Spock, as he appeared in "The City on the Edge of Forever."

BOB: After several all-night sessions, Gene churned out his own revised final draft teleplay. His version is the one we began filming on the morning of February 3. And even as filming continued, revised pages kept showing up on stage. All in all, in addition to Harlan, four other writers dabbled with his script: Steve Carabatsos, Dorothy Fontana, and the two Genes—Coon and Roddenberry.

Harlan didn't take too kindly to being rewritten. In fact, he was outraged. On February 3, 1967, the day that "City on the Edge of Forever" began filming, I received a letter from his agent, which said:

Mr. Ellison would like his credit on *Star Trek* episode "City on the Edge of Forever" Production #6149-28 to read "Cordwainer Bird." I would appreciate it if this information were passed on to the appropriate people in as much as I understand the show starts shooting this week.

For Harlan to have removed his name from the episode would have been tantamount to announcing to the science-fiction community that *Star Trek* was like all the other so-called science-fiction shows: "They promise a lot; they deliver little."

Gene couldn't afford to let such a thing happen.

After a lot of fussing and hemming and hawing and, finally, according to Harlan, an "absolute threat" from Gene to keep him from ever working in Hollywood again, Cordwainer Bird was convinced to revert to being Harlan Ellison again, and his screen credit reflected that fact. Nevertheless, the uneasy truce that ensued between Harlan and Gene was never again anything even remotely approaching comfortable.

In fact, some months later, Roddenberry felt compelled to issue a not-so-veiled threat. On June 20, 1967, he sent a letter to Ellison. After apprising the writer of the extraordinarily high cost of making "City" and the resulting criticism he endured from studio management, he wrote:

. . . I would not have done it any differently. I felt under an obligation to you to produce as good a show as possible within the limits of the re-write we thought necessary. Although we have a disagreement over that re-write, every evidence is that the show was highly successful both from the mass audience aspect necessary to maintaining a show on the air, and from the critical audience as well. I note that every fanzine received has commented warmly on that Harlan Ellison episode. And our mail, including letters from S.F. writers and fans, say [*sic*] the same.

Next, never outside this office and particularly nowhere in S.F. or television circles have I ever mentioned that the script was anything but entirely yours. [The authors aver that the staff rewrites were a matter of common knowledge within the creative community.] As you know, I have recommended you to fellow producers a number of times.

Which brings me to the point of this letter. Whether true or not, I have heard from a number of sources that you have been less than faithful to your side of this arrangement. I am told you do not hesitate to accept full praise and responsibility for the show but on the other hand go out of your way to say or suggest that I treated you badly, was dishonest in my dealings with you, and showed a lack of efficiency in my tasks which only your superior writing overcame. I further understand that you have stated you intend to say or intimate something of the same at Westercon 20 and possibly at the World Science Fiction Convention in New York.

I hope this isn't true. While you are entitled to any honest opinion of me personally or professionally, you must understand that I will not permit any lies or misinformation to be circulated. At the risk of turning our currently honest disagreement into something more serious, I will fight such a thing with every weapon at my disposal. I never like to hurt a man but no man should feel he can back me into a corner where my reputation, and therefore my livelihood and therefore my family is imperiled.

I trust this letter isn't necessary. As a matter of fact, I was thinking warmly of you just the other day while in Morro Bay with Eileen and discussed you at some length. My thought at that time was attempting to find a resolution involving a problem with someone I wanted to respect. This is the course I would like to take. I sincerely hope it is yours.

Despite Ellison's anger at being rewritten, the episode, which featured a fine guest-star performance from a young Joan Collins, was *Star Trek*'s most popular episode and found great favor with the show's science-fiction audience.

"City on the Edge of Forever" had defied *Star Trek*'s rule of thumb, that the story and scriptwriting process should take no more than three months. Although the exact moment when Harlan Ellison conceived the story premise remains unknown, the episode's chronology paints a fascinating, yet atypical, picture of *Star Trek*'s creative process:

The story assignment, based on Harlan Ellison's oral presentation, was made on March 16, 1966. His first story outline was dated March 21, 1966, and was signed, in jest, "Cordwainer Bird." Perhaps he was prescient. A second revision followed, dated May 1, 1966. After his final story outline, dated May 13, 1966, was received, he was finally given the go-ahead to write the script.

His first-draft teleplay, dated June 3, 1966, was received on June 7. And a revised final-draft teleplay, dated August 12, 1966, was received on August 15. Story Editor Steve Carabatsos's rewrite of Ellison's revised final-draft teleplay, which never "went to mimeo" (not acceptable for filming and therefore neither mimeographed nor distributed) so angered Ellison that he volunteered to re-revise his revised final-draft teleplay without further compensation. This second revised final-draft teleplay, dated December 1, 1966, was received on December 19. Gene Coon further revised Ellison's last revision in a version dated January 9, 1967. Two more revised revisions followed, the first by Dorothy C. Fontana, dated January 23, 1967, and the last by Gene Roddenberry. Roddenberry's revision, dated February 1, 1967, was the one that was finally filmed. Shooting began on February 3, 1967, and finished on February 14, 1967. After six weeks of post-production work, the episode was delivered to NBC on March 27, 1967. It was telecast on April 6, 1967—well over a year after Ellison's story idea had first been approved.

"The City on the Edge of Forever" turned out to be both time-consuming and expensive to film. Instead of a normal six-day schedule, it required seven and a half days to film, and it was the most costly single episode of all three seasons.

Courtesy Paramount Pictures

The crew prepares to beam back to the ship.

Later, the studio's "Weekly Cost Summary" for the period ending May 6, 1967, revealed an estimated final cost of $245,316 for "City," well over its already-too-high episode budget of $190,635. Still later, when all the figures were in, the actual final costs came to $250,396.71, in those days a huge amount of money for a first-year television show anywhere in the industry—and a staggering amount to the near-panicked old-guard Desilu executives.

"That's a bit more than ninety-eight cents," Justman grumbled. "But you know, it was worth every penny."

HERB: A new and startling perception of Harlan dramatically appeared to me several years later, well after I convinced myself that the *Star Trek* madness was firmly in the past. In the middle of a sleepless night, a dreamlike fantasy swept into my consciousness: Harlan Ellison was more than a mere human being; he was actually the reincarnation of an incurably literate medieval alchemist, aka Wizard. The fantasy went further, revealing that centuries ago, the Wizard—the one later reincarnated as Harlan—had transmuted all his fellow sorcerers into handsome Princes, so that each of them would spend the rest of his life kissing thousands of slimy frogs, hoping beyond hope that one of the frogs would turn out to be the beauteous Princess. What the Princes didn't know was that the Wizard had her in his private quarters all along. Obviously, the Wizard wasn't playing on an even-sorcerer field.

The next morning, I realized my fantasy must have had some basis in fact. Because the "Ellison Reincarnated Wizard Theory" was as good a way as any to explain Harlan's actions at the 1967 Writers Guild of America Awards Dinner.

The dinner was held at L'Escoffier, the elegant rooftop restaurant at the Beverly Hilton Hotel in Beverly Hills, where on this night, black-tied men and beautifully gowned women gathered to celebrate and honor the best of the best. Among those writers nominated for the outstanding script in a television dramatic series was Harlan Ellison for "City on the Edge of Forever."

Desilu had "bought" a table for the big event. Sitting happily around it were the two Genes, RJ, my friend and well-known screenwriter Howard Rodman, myself, and our wives. We were all excited; there was a chance that a *Star Trek* script would be singled out for excellence and win the award. We hoped that *Star Trek* would receive some peer recognition and we all would bathe in the limelight.

The time had come; the announcement was made. "The award for the most outstanding script for a dramatic television series is—'City on the Edge of Forever'—story and teleplay by Harlan Ellison."

We were thrilled. We applauded our hero, Harlan, as he rose from his chair at another table and strode to the podium to receive his award and say a few words. Well, perhaps more than a few words; after all, the winner was Harlan.

But after Harlan finished saying all the usual nice things about his writer peers and his Guild, failing to mention *Star Trek* or even recognizing the two Genes and RJ, he quickly turned his attention to artistic integrity. And as quickly, our joy evaporated. Harlan berated the studio executive "suits," and the Executive Producers and Producers of television series, for "interfering with the writing process." I was surprised that Harlan, while he was at it, didn't berate the waiters for clearing tables while a writer was speaking.

But the ultimate insult was yet to come. Building to a passionate finale, Harlan suddenly brandished his original script high above his head, shook it in the manner of Napoleon Bonaparte preparing his armies for battle, and declared, "Remember, never let THEM rewrite you!"

The writer-dominated audience rose to their feet, en masse, and hailed this living hero who had the guts to publicly speak out against THEM! And as Harlan walked from the podium, he looked over to our table and defiantly shook his script at US.

Surprisingly, Gene Roddenberry seemed amused. He turned to us, shrugged, and smiled. "So what else is new?"

I must say I, too, was relatively calm as I picked up the two knives lying before me on the table—the dinner knife and the butter knife—and stared at them. "Which one should I use to kill Harlan?" I wondered. I decided on the butter knife; it was sort of dull and would cause more pain.

Howard Rodman, a marvelous and utterly principled writer, happened to spy writer-director Frank Pierson sitting several tables away. Some months earlier, Howard had decided to hate Frank Pierson (an Academy Award-winning writer

and former President of the Writers Guild) because Frank rewrote Howard's friend Carol Sobieski's screenplay, "Neon Ceiling," a drama that Howard felt needed no changes whatsoever. Obviously agitated by Harlan's remarks, Howard, a powerfully built man, announced he was going to tackle Frank and shove him through the huge plateglass window to plunge eight floors to the street below. We managed to restrain him. It was that kind of evening!

The Writers Guild rule for award consideration was that the writer, not the producing company, submitted the script and could submit whatever version he or she chose, be it the writer's first draft or the final shooting script, which usually had undergone many revisions and rewrites by others. Two different panels of judges then made the individual award decisions.

Some years after receiving the Writers Guild award, Ellison was in a bar when he ran into writer Don Ingalls. "Fandango," a script Ingalls wrote for *Gunsmoke*, was one of the four other contenders that lost out to Ellison's script. Ingalls had also written for *Star Trek*, and they discussed not only the series but Ellison's award-winning script. After a few drinks Harlan boasted that, before submitting his own final draft for consideration, he had "polished it up a little bit to make it even better." To this day, Ingalls remains amused by his friend Ellison's award-winning stratagem.

HERB: So when I finally realized that Harlan was a sorcerer's reincarnation, it answered that burning question: "Why did he do what he did at the Awards dinner?"

Easy. The Wizard made him do it.

Harlan takes umbrage with Ingalls' story of what occurred 28 years ago. Harlan states emphatically that he has never been in a bar, has never had a drink and that he barely knows Don Ingalls. Further, Harlan states emphatically that he submitted his actual version of the script for Award consideration and has the cover letter and Writers Guild receipt for inspection by any interested parties.

In a further interview, Don Ingalls does define the terms of his recollection. The discussion took place, not in a bar, but in the lounge at the Beverly Hilton Hotel where both alcoholic and non-alcoholic drinks were served. However, Don reiterates that, while he had no way of knowing what version Ellison did, in fact, submit to the Guild, he does know what Harlan told him at their chance meeting. Don Ingalls further volunteered that Ellison is a brilliant writer and he has only the highest respect for his talent and ability.

In his recent book "City On the Edge of Forever," Harlan refers to me as a dummy. Over one of the bi-monthly dinners that my wife, Yvonne, and I have with Harlan and his wife, Susan, I pointed out that "dummy" is a very contemptuous word. Harlan took umbrage at my statement, explaining that the word was used as a term of endearment since he did not capitalize it. If it had been capitalized—well, then it could be considered contemptuous.

Now you know why I love Harlan Ellison.

An illustration NBC produced to promote *Star Trek*'s second season.

Courtesy NBC/Globe

ACT THREE

Death and Transfiguration: The Second and Third Seasons

Courtesy Greg Jein

19

Saved by the Bell

With the February 22, 1967, completion of principal photography on "Operation Annihilate," the initial season's last episode, feelings of both enormous relief and enormous anxiety pervaded the studio. Roddenberry, Coon, Justman, and Solow shook their heads in near disbelief. Twenty-six new episodes had been filmed; adding "The Menagerie" two-parter Envelope and the second pilot made a grand total of twenty-nine first-season episodes. They truly had climbed Mount Everest. But with their mountain high also came the anxiety and the almost hourly renewal vigil. Would NBC give *Star Trek* a second year, or would NBC acknowledge the fulfillment of Desilu's impossible dream with a cancellation notice?

However, the studio had to believe there would be a second year and had to protect several key people, not only until NBC announced its 1967 fall schedule, but until the second-year shows started to prepare for shooting. Milkis was still busy with postproduction and would bridge the gap; Justman, however, had finished most of his production responsibilities, and once again there was no *Star Trek* budget to pay his salary.

Solow didn't want to lose his favorite workaholic, so he approached Bruce Geller and "suggested" that Justman be transferred to the *Mission: Impossible* postproduction budget. He had another reason for his suggestion. *Mission*'s executive producer had returned to personally dubbing the series and was taking upwards of two days to complete each episode. Justman always dubbed *Mission* in substantially less time. Geller, also busy cutting and scoring the *Mannix* pilot, bought the idea, and once again, Bob Justman began dubbing *Mission.*

The chicken-and-egg game began with NBC. What would come first, the renewal for a second season or early monies to begin the extensive story and script process should the renewal be in the offing? Waiting for renewal meant losing valuable writing time for *Star Trek*. However, if there was to be no second year, any early story money would be a total loss for NBC. The studio had requested early story money from NBC for *Star Trek*, and CBS for *Mission,* and awaited their response.

Fearing a reccurrence of the first year's script problems, Justman pushed Roddenberry hard to put pressure on NBC. Reacting in knee-jerk fashion, Gene sent a "night letter" to executives Herb Rosenthal and Mort Werner at NBC New York and Herb Schlosser at NBC Burbank. In it he threatened to shut the show down if story money wasn't immediately forthcoming.

A draft of the cable Roddenberry sent to NBC executive Herb Rosenthal regarding the need for story development money.

NBC

NIGHT LETTER TO:
MR. HERB ROSENTHAL
NATIONAL BROADCASTING COMPANY
NEW YORK, NEW YORK

CARBON COPIES TO MR. MORT WERNER
NBC
NEW YORK

MR. HERB SCHLOSSER
NATIONAL BROADCASTING COMPANY
3000 W. ALAMEDA BLVD.
BURBANK, CALIFORNIA

DEAR HERB,

RE YOUR TELEGRAM SUGGESTING FULLER DISCUSSION. MEMBERS OF MY STAFF THREATENING TO QUIT RATHER THAN UNDERGO NIGHT & DAY SCHEDULES MADE NECESSARY BY FURTHER POSTPONEMENT of INITIAL WORK. WRITERS WE HAVE TRAINED AND NURTURED ~~INFORM US THAT~~ state THEY CAN WAIT FOR US NO LONGER. I LOVE YOU ALL BUT IF STAR TREK IS GOING ANOTHER SEASON I MUST BEGIN PUTTING AT LEAST STORIES INTO WORK IMMEDIATELY. HERB, THIS IS NOT SOMETHING TO NEGOTIATE. TAKE MY WORD AS A PRO IN MY FIELD THAT THIS IS A COLD FACT COMING OUT OF TIME REQUIRED TO PLAN, DESIGN AND EXECUTE STAR TREK WITH THE QUALITY YOU WANT AND WHICH I" DEMAND. I AM WILLING TO INVEST MY TIME AND ENERGIES IN GETTING THESE NEW STORIES UNDERWAY. DESILU ALREADY DEFICIT FINANCING BUT IS WILLING TO INVEST FURTHER IN STAFF SALARIES AND FACILITIES. WHAT IS OUR PARTNER NBC INVESTING?

IF IT APPEARS LIKELY WE MAY NOT OR WILL NOT GO ANOTHER SEASON MY HARD WORK FOR THIS PARTNERSHIP DEMANDS YOU TELL ME NOW SO THAT I MAY BEGIN DEVOTING MY ENERGIES ELSEWHERE.

GENE RODDENBERRY

Threatening to shut down any series isn't an intelligent way to endear oneself to a network. But threatening in writing, for the record, to shut down a low-rated, money-losing series on the edge of extinction was not only not intelligent, it was intensely disliked by NBC's Program Department. They were only part of the renewal process. Roddenberry's continuing pressure tactics merely added their resentment to the problem of *Star Trek*'s already low ratings.

Several weeks later, without tipping its renewal hand, NBC agreed to finance the writing of six stories. Whether Roddenberry's "methods" helped secure the story money was never mentioned by NBC. However, Tinker and Schlosser, referring to the orchestrated letter and phone campaign and the "spontaneous" demonstrations at KRON-TV, the NBC-owned station in Oakland, California, and other cities, did question Gene Roddenberry's thought processes. And they wondered whether he had any interest at all in maintaining a positive working relationship with them.

Finally, with stories being written and postproduction winding down, some of the pressures were off. It was time to unwind.

BOB: "Let's all go to the Springs, Bob," suggested Gene Roddenberry. "We'll have lots of fun. And Eileen and Jackie . . . ahhh . . . can get to know each other better."

The invitation surprised me, but I was pleased because I thought perhaps Gene and Eileen had effected some kind of truce. It must have been Eileen who pushed for getting back together; Gene was still busy with his extracurricular activities. But he went on to tell me about the great times he and Eileen had shared in Palm Springs.

"Of course I'll go," said Jackie when I broached the subject, "but as far as having fun goes . . ." She didn't have to finish the sentence. So we packed for a weekend and drove down to the Spa Hotel in Palm Springs.

We met in the lobby. "Check in fast, guys," said Gene. "Then we'll all go take their famous steam and massage. Me and Bob and . . . ahhh . . . you and Jackie, honey." Eileen smiled; she seemed much friendlier.

Half an hour later, we were in the men's side, on adjoining massage tables, getting pounded senseless by two serious masseurs. After they beat on us for a while, they began kneading our flesh as if we were dough being prepared for baking. (More on that shortly.) When the ordeal was over, my whole body hurt.

Gene was still raring to go. "Well, Bob? Wasn't that great? Next, a steam! It'll do . . . ahhh . . . wonders for you, get rid of all the . . . ahhh . . . poisons."

Entering what could best be described as "Dante's Inferno," we sat on a bench of scorching hot tiles. My rear end was burning. Gene, eyes closed, sat there, smiling and looking cool. Half an hour later, I was well-done. When we left the sauna, however, Gene was still blood-rare.

"Ahhh . . . Bob, wasn't that . . . ahhh . . . great? You . . . ahhh . . . don't want a cold shower, do you?"

"You go ahead. I'll wait out here."

"I'll skip it, too. Actually, I like the next part best. We get to take a nap. When it's over, you'll feel totally refreshed."

We were led to two marble slabs. "Oh, great, here's where we nap," Gene exclaimed gleefully.

An attendant dressed in white trousers, white T-shirt, and white sneakers arrived, quickly removed our sweat-soaked sheets, and wrapped fresh sheets around us that had been soaked in ice water. I lost my breath and went into shock. The attendant directed me to climb onto my marble slab and stretch out. Every point of bodily contact with the slab hurt. Whatever position I tried, I felt pain.

Gene, however, enthusiastically climbed up onto his marble slab and went right to sleep.

Half an hour later, Gene awakened, yawned, and stretched. "I feel a great difference, Bob. Don't you?"

"I sure do."

"Hasn't this been a real experience?"

"Right, Gene—a real experience. I'll never forget it."

Jackie met me back in our hotel room.

"How was it for you?" we both asked.

"Don't ask," we both answered.

Next afternoon, when it came time to leave, Gene was, once again, enthusiastic. "Let's do it again, Bob. I hope you enjoyed it as much as I did."

"So do I, Gene."

It was clear to me that Gene needed to have others along to help lessen tension between himself and Eileen. While hoping his marriage would hold up, I wasn't optimistic considering the double life he was leading.

NBC always insisted that the A. C. Nielsen ratings were but one of the many tools used to determine the popularity and audience for series. True, it was only one of the tools, but it was the most accurate as well as the only publicly disseminated information indicating the competitive nature of the networks and their shows. It was easy to see who was winning and who was losing. There was no doubt about it; the ratings were the most heavily weighted of all the network research tools. They were the basis of the price structures NBC charged advertising agencies; the basis on which companies spent their hard-earned advertising dollars; the basis on which NBC Sales, Programming, and Research management would determine *Star Trek*'s future.

Star Trek's ratings were both positive and negative signs of whether the series would be renewed for a second season. Although the "numbers were low," they were steadily low—no dramatic fluctuations week after week.

Courtesy Herb Schlosser

NBC Vice President of Programs, West Coast, Herb Schlosser, who later became network president.

That was the positive, indicating an intensely loyal audience. These forerunners of "Trekkers" watched *Star Trek* because they liked the series, not tuning in or out because of a prior week's episode or the *TV Guide* advance description of the upcoming week's episode.

The negative was a serious one. *Star Trek*, due to its audience "age and gender" appeal, would be most successful in an early-evening time period. But the programming and sales structure of network television necessitated a building-block effect. Shows on a given night were expected to move their audience on to the following shows, building to the late evening prime-time shows, more adult in nature, that would capture the time period and all those big advertiser dollars. However, the building-block effect did not work if the early-evening show had no appreciable audience. Compared to today's practices, the approach to ratings in the mid-sixties was basic and unsophisticated. At that time, NBC and CBS research executives put major emphasis on raw audience figures, rather than indicating a particular series's demographics—the raw or total audience broken down by age, sex, buying power, etc. Staunch loyalty didn't count; numbers of bodies counted. That was the 1966 reality, and *Star Trek* had failed to deliver.

Herb Schlosser remains convinced that if one of today's NBC series delivered the demographics that *Star Trek* delivered thirty years ago, that series would definitely be renewed, year in and year out.

Vibrations from NBC suggested that the *Enterprise* was nearing its last voyage!

BOB: Everyone worried about the ratings—the NBC execs, the studio execs, the staff, the crew, the cast, the guard at the gate—and Leonard Nimoy. They all had the same questions: "Will we get picked up?" And "When will we hear?"

In addition to salary, Leonard had two major concerns: first, that the show wouldn't be picked up, and second, that if we were picked up, he'd have another agonizing year of putting on and taking off his—by then—world-famous ears.

This concern led, inexorably, to the second "ear-job" story. When Leonard first complained to Herb about his ears, he worried about being perceived as a freak. That was no longer a concern. The ears had made him famous. Now he wanted to have his cake and eat it, too.

Leonard approached me on the studio street. "How're the network wars going, Bob? Any news about a pickup?"

"Nothing yet, Lenny. But if your fans have anything to say about it, we'll be back on the air next season."

"I've been hoping, Bob, that if we do go again, you can do something about my makeup. Shatner scoots in for a quick makeup job, gets dressed, and fifteen minutes later he's ready to shoot. Forgetting wardrobe time, I have to come in at least an hour and a half early—just for makeup. And then, it's another half hour every night just to take off the damn ears. And it hurts. The skin on my ears is always raw. I'd certainly appreciate whatever you can do about this."

Leonard was much too serious for me to let the opportunity pass. "Funny you should ask, Lenny. I was going to mention something to you if we get picked up. You see, I've got this plastic surgeon friend in Beverly Hills . . ."

I looked at him. So far, he was buying it; he must have been really desperate. I continued, "If we get picked up, the doc says he can do a simple procedure, right in his office. In and out the same day. He can make your own ears permanently pointy, just like Spock's."

Leonard was thrilled. "Great!" Then a thought struck him, "But what happens afterward, if we get cancelled?"

"He just does another operation and puts 'em back, the way they were before."

"Great, just great!" But as he thought about it, his smile began to fade.

It was time to leave. "I have to dub an episode. So long, Lenny." I hurried away.

"You son of a bitch!" he yelled. "You almost had me going."

"Almost?" I yelled back.

"You son of a bitch!" he repeated. But this time Leonard was laughing.

Late one night in November of 1966, Roddenberry looked up from the script he'd been rewriting, stared at the wall of his office, and saw the handwriting. If the hoped-for ratings increase failed to develop, three years of hard work might all have been for naught. *Star Trek* would end its life as merely a noble experiment in trying to bring an intelligent science-fiction series to television. And with no new projects in development, not only would *Star Trek* be gone, Gene would be out of work.

Harlan Ellison was still in the midst of his last "City on the Edge of Forever" rewrite when Roddenberry proposed a "Save *Star Trek*" campaign, utilizing the help of the Science Fiction Writers of America. He and Ellison were still on good terms; their falling-out had yet to occur. Ellison liked the idea and volunteered to help organize "The Committee," an advisory group of famous science-fiction writers. In a December 1, 1966, letter sent, on behalf of The Committee, to all members of the SFWA, Ellison initiated a write-in campaign to "save" *Star Trek*:

> It's finally happened. You've been in the know for a long time, you've known the worth of mature science fiction, and you've squirmed at the adolescent manner with which it has generally been presented on television. Now, finally, we've lucked-out, we've gotten a show on prime time that is attempting to do the missionary job for the field of speculative fiction. The show is *Star Trek*, of course, and its aims have been lofty. *Star Trek* has been carrying the good word out to the boondocks. Those who have seen the show know it is frequently written by authentic science fiction writers, it is made with enormous difficulty and with considerable pride. If you were at the World Science Fiction Convention in Cleveland you know it received standing ovations and was awarded a special citation by the Convention. *Star Trek* has finally showed the mass audience that science fiction need not be situation comedy in space suits. The reason for this letter—and frankly, the appeal for help—is that we've learned this show, despite its healthy growth, could face trouble soon. The Nielsen Roulette game is being played. They say, "If mature science fiction is so hot, howzacome that kiddie space show on the other network is doing so much better?" There's no sense explaining it's the second year for the competition and the first year for *Star Trek*; all they understand are the decimal places. And the sound of voices raised. Which is where you come in.
>
> *Star Trek*'s cancellation or a change to a less adult format would be tragic, seeming to demonstrate that real science fiction cannot attract a mass audience. We need letters! Yours and ours, plus every science fiction fan and TV viewer we can reach through our publications and personal contacts.

Important: Not form letters, not using our phrases here; they should be the fan's own words and honest attitudes. They should go to: (a) local television stations which carry *Star Trek*; (b) to sponsors who advertise on *Star Trek*; (c) local and syndicated television columnists; and (d) *TV Guide* and other television magazines.

The situation is critical; it has to happen *now* or it will be too late. We're giving it all our efforts; we hope we can count on yours.

Sincerely, Harlan Ellison for The Committee

Then began the wait. The science-fiction community at large had been challenged. How would they respond?

In his *TV Guide* review of the series, Isaac Asimov had made some negative comments about *Star Trek*'s lack of scientific accuracy. Roddenberry responded in a gentle and flattering November 29, 1966, letter:

> . . . A person should get facts straight when writing anything. So, as much as I enjoyed your article, I am haunted by this need to write you with the suggestion that some of your facts were not straight. And just as a writer writing about science should know what a galaxy is, a writer writing about television has an obligation to acquaint himself with the pertinent aspects of that field. In all friendliness, and with sincere thanks for the hundreds of wonderful hours of reading you have given me, it does seem to me that your article overlooked entirely the practical, factual and scientific problems involved in getting a television show on the air and keeping it there. Television deserves much criticism, not just SF alone but all of it, but that criticism should be aimed, not shot-gunned. For example, *Star Trek* almost did not get on the air because it refused to do juvenile science fiction, because it refused to put a "Lassie" aboard the space ship, and because it insisted on hiring Dick Matheson, Harlan Ellison, A.E. Van Vogt, [*sic*] Phil Farmer, and so on. (Not all of these came through since TV scripting is a highly difficult specialty, but many of them did.) . . .

HERB: To my knowledge, Gene was never ordered or even asked by either NBC or Desilu to do juvenile science fiction—or put a "Lassie" aboard the *Enterprise*—or not hire the leading science-fiction writers he mentioned. This was Gene's way of allying himself with Asimov.

Roddenberry's letter continued:

> . . . We do spend several hundred dollars a week to guarantee scientific accuracy. And several hundred more dollars a week to guarantee other forms of accuracy, logical progressions, etc. Before going into production we made up a "Writer's Guide" covering many of these things and we send out

new pages, amendments, lists of terminology, excerpts of science articles, etc., to our writers continually. . . .

. . . Despite all this we do make mistakes and will probably continue to make them. The reason—Thursday has an annoying way of coming up once a week, and five working days an episode is a crushing burden, an impossible one. The wonder of it is not that we make mistakes, but that we are able to turn out once a week science fiction which [is] . . . the first true SF series ever made on television. We like to think this is what we are doing. Certainly, that is what we are trying to do, and trying with considerable pride. And I suppose with considerable touchiness when we believe we are criticized unfairly or as in the case of your article, damned with faint praise. Quoting Ted Sturgeon who made his first script attempt with us (and now seems firmly established as a contributor to good television), getting *Star Trek* on the air was impossible, putting out a program like this on a TV budget is impossible, reaching the necessary mass audience without alienating the SF audience is impossible, not succumbing to network pressure to "juvenilize" the show is impossible, keeping it on the air is impossible. We've done all of these things. Perhaps someone else could have done it better, but no one else did.

Again, if we are to believe our letters (now mounting into the thousands), we are reaching vast numbers of people who never before understood SF or enjoyed it. We are, in fact, making fans—making future purchasers of SF magazines and novels, making future box office receipts for SF films. We are, I sincerely hope, making new purchasers of "The Foundation" novels . . . "I, Robot", "The Rest Of The Robots", and other of your excellent work. . . .

. . . If mention was to be made of SF in television, we deserved much better. And as much as I admire you in your work, I felt an obligation to reply.

And, I believe, the public deserves a more definitive article on all this. Perhaps *TV Guide* is not the marketplace for it, but if you ever care to throw the Asimov mind and wit toward a definitive TV piece, please count on us for facts, figures, sample budgets and practical production examples, and samples of scripts from rough story to the usual multitude of drafts, samples of mass media "pressure", and whatever else we can give you. . . .

. . . Eileen asked me to send her best regards along to Mrs. Asimov whose kindness she remembers well from the Cleveland convention.

Asimov wrote back immediately to make amends for his negative comments:

. . . I completely neglected to say that I liked *Star Trek* very much. . . .

. . . Some friends, who are fans of *Star Trek* (I have extremely intelligent friends) have pointed out my failing in extremely forceful language and on re-reading my article I feel very ashamed at having lost a chance to support good science fiction before a large audience merely because I was so intent on being funny. . . .

. . . Is there anything I can do that would usefully express my appreciation of the sterling efforts you are making to produce an adult science fiction show of high quality?

Asimov followed up several days later with yet another "mea culpa" and stated, ". . . I would love to be able to boost *Star Trek* anywhere, and if you think

Courtesy Richard Arnold

Isaac Asimov (l.) with his good friend Gene Roddenberry (r.) at a *Star Trek* convention in the 1970s.

you would like it, I would ask *TV Guide* if they would like me to do an article on *Star Trek* for them . . . . I will give *Star Trek* favorable mentions every chance I get and do whatever I can to help it."

It is written that a soft answer turneth away wrath. As a result of Roddenberry's first letter, Asimov turned from being a detractor into one of the most influential and enthusiastic supporters of the series. And he and Roddenberry became friends, exchanging letters regularly.

Soon, the renewal campaign began to bear fruit. Science-fiction fans across the nation protested the perceived cancellation and wrote to complain. NBC received so many letters that it realized, belatedly, that it had something of a bull by the tail.

The identities of those families who participated in the Nielsen rating sample were top secret. The last thing the A. C. Nielsen Company wanted was an interested party attempting to manipulate ratings. The "Nielsen families" totaled 1,200, and these 1,200 homes were the ratings base for all network television series. Therefore, as a component representing the viewing habits for over sixty million American families, a single family's likes or dislikes could, at times, alter the destiny of those television series with tenuous renewal potential.

After the "Cordwainer Bird" credit flare-up between Roddenberry and Harlan Ellison, the aggrieved writer had done a bit of complaining within the science-fiction community. The news traveled fast because, in the February 24, 1967, issue of a science-fiction "fanzine" entitled *DEGLER!*—directly beneath the news of world-famous science-fiction author Charles Beaumont's death—the following item appeared:

> *HARLAN ELLISON TO QUIT HOLLYWOOD:* Harlan Ellison, who has been active in Hollywood writing screenplays and scripts for Television, has apparently decided to break completely with the Hollywood scene. The details available indicate that Ellison submitted a script to *Star Trek* which was altered considerably by Gene Roddenberry, executive producer of the show. When Ellison found out about the changes, he fired off a sharp letter to Roddenberry. This resulted in a letter from Roddenberry to Ellison culminating in the announced break in relations between the two. Ellison has, however, announced that he is sick of the Hollywood grind and intends to pull out entirely. It is the opinion of this editor that either Harlan has over-reacted tremendously, or he became burdened with a surplus of book contracts and decided to pull out of one area, Hollywood, in order to devote his entire time to writing for publication, and do so in a manner which would suggest a sudden impulse. With Harlan Ellison, it's difficult to decide which is more plausible.

Embarrassed over the article, on March 6, 1967, a contrite Ellison sent a letter to Roddenberry, enclosing a copy of the *DEGLER!* article.

HARLAN ELLISON

6 March 67

Gene:

I received this fan "newszine" in the mail today. I was appalled and infuriated by the "news item" on page one. I called the editor of the sheet and chewed him out, insisting on a retraction. I have sent him a letter for publication, additionally, the sum of which is: it is nobody's fucking business. I send you this note, and the newsheet, so you will know from me that I had nothing to do with it, nor care to see this sort of item bandied about, nor indeed feel any less rankled by it than I would think you might be. I have done what I can do to rectify the situation, such as it might be.

To keep the books balanced, considering this a debt on my side, I have contacted the Nielsen Family in this area, for this week (whose identity is supposed to be secret, but who are friends of mine), and I have asked them as a special favor to kindly watch STAR TREK this week, and so log it in on their Nielsen record. Out of 52,000 "families" in the country, it is a small repayment, I grant you, but it was the maximum available to me.

If the books remain unbalanced, I'm sure you'll let me know.

Again, I'm sorry this happened.

Harlan

Ellison's letter to Roddenberry.

Either Ellison's reference to "52,000 families" was off by 50,800 families, or else he was confused and meant to point out that each Nielsen family was worth a total of 52,000 families in the ratings.

Ellison's letter was quite an interesting if unorthodox gift, but did not influence NBC. Prior to release of that week's Nielsen ratings, which covered the March 9, 1967, broadcast of "Devil in the Dark," NBC had already advised the studio that *Star Trek* would live another year to continue its exploration of distant galaxies and other new airdates.

On March 9, 1967, an NBC announcer, broadcasting live over the closing credits of "Devil in the Dark," informed the audience, "*Star Trek* will be back in the fall. And please, don't write any more letters." It was the first time in television history that a network directly informed viewers that their favorite series had been renewed. Refusing to heed NBC's request and wanting to express their joy, however, hordes of loyal fans wrote thank-you letters to the network.

HERB: While everyone at Desilu was pleased with the good news, something didn't quite make sense. I scratched my head; what was behind NBC's renewal of *Star Trek*?

Sold-out sponsorship?

"Far from it."

Passable ratings?

"Barely."

More intelligent viewers?

"Probably, but meaningless."

Hard-core younger audience?

"Sure, but still meaningless."

Viewers with great buying power?

"Not really."

No better series to schedule?

"There were lots of candidates."

Protest calls?

"Yes, but organized, not spontaneous."

Protest letters?

"Yes, but organized, not spontaneous."

Demonstrations?

"Yes, but they were personally embarrassing to NBC executives."

If the campaign to "Save *Star Trek*" was the major reason for the series being brought back for a second year, was there possibly some other factor in the mix?

Networks make unexpected and seemingly illogical decisions for corporate reasons, not viewer reasons. I never bought the campaign to "Save *Star Trek*" as the only reason the series was brought back for a second year. Perhaps something else, something more related to money and profit, helped change NBC's mind.

In 1950, the Federal Communications Commission formed the National Television System Committee (NTSC) to coordinate the proposed new color television service. The new service would have to be compatible with the existing black-and-white service, so that color television could be received by the twenty-five million black-and-white sets then in use.

RCA (NBC) and CBS Laboratories (CBS) developed competing systems. But the CBS single–color-gun system, though initially approved by the NTSC, was incompatible, and after limited use in 1951, it was abandoned. RCA's three–color-

When you're first in Color TV, there's got to be a reason.
See "Star Trek" on RCA Victor Color TV. Shown above, The Hathaway
• Like Automatic Fine Tuning that gives you a perfectly fine-tuned picture every time.
• A new RCA tube with 38% brighter highlights.
• Advanced circuitry that won't go haywire.
• And over 25 years of color experience.
• You get all this and more from RCA VICTOR.
RCA
The Most Trusted Name in Electronics

An October 1967 *TV Guide* ad run by RCA, citing *Star Trek* as a reason to buy a color television.

Courtesy Doug Drexler

gun system was compatible with black-and-white sets; and in 1954, the FCC authorized NBC, using the RCA system, then known as the NTSC Compatible System, to begin broadcasting color television programs. But viewers had no immediate interest in color television, most likely due to the high cost of the new color television sets. It would take until 1965 before color receivers using the

RCA system were purchased in any substantial numbers. It went without saying that RCA had an enormous financial interest in popularizing color television. Their color-television development costs alone were estimated at $130 million, a substantial amount of money at that time.

In 1966, NBC, at the behest of RCA, commissioned the A. C. Nielsen Company to do a study on the popularity of color television series as opposed to all television series. The results were expected—and very unexpected.

Favorite series were popular whether or not they were viewed in color. For example, NBC's *Bonanza* series was a top-rated series on the overall national ratings list as well as on the color ratings list.

However, in December 1966, with *Star Trek* having been on the air only three months, an NBC executive called with some news. The Nielsen research indicated that *Star Trek* was the highest-rated color series on television. I distributed the information to the *Star Trek* staff. We thought it was all very interesting, nothing to write home about, and went back to work. We were wrong; we failed to see the importance of the research.

Perhaps those initial and subsequent Nielsen color series ratings contributed to giving *Star Trek* a second year of life. Putting aside low national ratings and lack of sponsors, perhaps a reason for renewing *Star Trek,* other than all the phone calls, letters, and demonstrations at NBC, was its position as the top-rated color series on the "full-color network." NBC's parent company was RCA. *Star Trek* sold color television sets and made money for RCA.

When I recently presented this theory to Tom Sarnoff, former Vice President of NBC and son of RCA founder and communications pioneer David Sarnoff, he found it very interesting. "I don't know, Herb, but you make a very good point. I really wouldn't be surprised if that's what happened. It's a good theory. As you said on *Star Trek,* it's not illogical."

Herb Schlosser, however, wasn't sure about the theory. "*Star Trek* was renewed because it was good and it was different. And we were proud to have it on NBC."

But the former NBC President did recall, "Even though the color program value from a rating point of view was projected as only one-half a rating point, NBC did, in fact, make every effort to convince suppliers to produce their series in color by paying an additional $7,500 per hour episode."

Regardless, there was a kicker to the theory. While RCA made money selling color television sets, both NBC and Desilu would continue to lose money on the unsuccessful yet full-color *Star Trek.*

After the NBC renewal, Roddenberry sent a personalized telegram of thanks to each of the science-fiction writers on The Committee of SFWA who were so instrumental in the "Save *Star Trek*" campaign: Poul Anderson, Isaac Asimov, Robert Bloch, Lester del Rey, Harlan Ellison, Philip José Farmer, Frank Herbert, Richard Matheson, Theodore Sturgeon, and A. E. van Vogt. The telegram read the same for each addressee.

DOMESTIC SERVICE
Check the class of service desired; otherwise this message will be sent as a fast telegram
TELEGRAM
DAY LETTER
NIGHT LETTER

WESTERN UNION TELEGRAM

W. P. MARSHALL, CHAIRMAN OF THE BOARD
R. W. McFALL, PRESIDENT

INTERNATIONAL SERVICE
Check the class of service desired; otherwise the message will be sent at the full rate
FULL RATE
LETTER TELEGRAM
SHORE-SHIP

NO. WDS.-CL. OF SVC.	PD. OR COLL.	CASH NO.	CHARGE TO THE ACCOUNT OF	TIME FILED

Send the following message, subject to the terms on back hereof, which are hereby agreed to

NZ/LH 19 PD TDL HOLLYWOOD CALIF FEB 27 300P PST

SINCERE GRATITUDE DEAR ____________ FOR ALL YOU'VE DONE TO HELP.
WILL TRY TO LIVE UP TO YOUR FAITH IN US.

GENE RODDENBERRY
STARTREK

BD
DESILU STUDIOS
780 NORTH GOWER
HOLLYWOOD CALIF
HOL 9-5911

Roddenberry's "thank you" telegram to the science-fiction writers.

It was the least he could do. Especially since, unbeknownst to all the faithful, Desilu had paid the full cost of Roddenberry's campaign.

In addition to his work on The Committee, Isaac Asimov helped out in other ways. The popularity of Mister Spock still rankled William Shatner, who claimed that he "was carrying the load" as captain of the *Enterprise* while Leonard Nimoy was getting the lion's share of the attention. On June 19, 1967, photography was completed on "Amok Time," the fifth episode filmed that season. That same day, Roddenberry wrote to Asimov and voiced his concerns:

> . . . Wish you were out here. I would dearly love to discuss with [you] a problem about the show and the format. It concerns Captain James Kirk and

Courtesy NBC/Globe

A publicity still from "Amok Time."

of the actor who plays that role, William Shatner. Bill is . . . generally rated as fine an actor as we have in this country. But we're not getting the use of him that we should and it is not his fault. It's easy to give good situations and good lines to Spock. And to a lesser extent the same is true of the irascible Dr. McCoy. . . .

. . . And yet *Star Trek* needs a strong lead, an Earth lead. Without diminishing the importance of the secondary continuing characters. But the problem we generally find is this—if we play Kirk as a true ship commander, strong and hard, devoted to career and service, it too often makes him seem unlikable. On the other hand, if we play him too warm-hearted, friendly and so on, the attitude often is "how did a guy like that get to be a ship commander?" Sort of damned if he does and damned if he doesn't situation. Actually, although it is missed by the general audience, it is Kirk's fine handling of a most difficult role that permits Spock and the others to come off as well as they do. But Kirk does deserve more and so does the actor who plays him. I am in something of a quandry [*sic*] about it. Got any ideas?

Asimov did have a number of ideas. On June 22, 1967, he wrote a follow–up letter to Roddenberry:

. . . In some ways, this is the example of the general problem of first banana/second banana. The star has to be a well-rounded individual but the supporting player can be a "humorous" man in the Elizabethan sense. He can specialize. Since his role is smaller and less important, he can be made highly seasoned, and his peculiarities and humors can easily win a wide following simply because they are so marked and even predictable. . . .

Undoubtedly, it is hard on the top banana (who like all actors has a healthy streak of insecurity and needs vocal and constant reassurance from the audience) to feel drowned out. Everybody in the show knows exactly how important and how good Mr. Shatner is, and so do all the actors, including even Mr. Shatner. Still when the fan letters go to Mr. Nimoy, and articles like mine concentrate on him, one can't help feeling unappreciated.

What to do? Let me think about it and write another letter in a few days. I don't know that I'll have any magic solutions, but you know, some vagrant thought of mine might spark some thought in you and who knows—

On July 10, 1967, Asimov wrote again.

ISAAC ASIMOV
45 GREENOUGH STREET
WEST NEWTON
MASSACHUSETTS 02165

10 July 1967

Mr. Gene Roddenberry
STAR TREK
Desilu Studios
780 North Gower Street
Hollywood, California, 90038

Dear Gene,

I appeared in TIME last week (July 7th issue, pp. 55-56) and in the course of the two columns on me, a favorable mention of STAR TREK managed to be included. How about that?

But anyway, I promised to get back to you with my thoughts on the question of Mr. Shatner and the dilemma of playing lead against such a fad-character as "Mr. Spock."

The more I think about it, the more I think the problem is psychological. That is, STAR TREK is successful, and I think it will prove easier to get a renewal for the third year than was the case for the second. The chief practical reason for its success is Mr. Spock. The excellence of the stories and the acting brings in the intelligent audience (who aren't enough in numbers, xx alas, to affect the ratings appreciably) but Mr. Spock brings in the "teen-age vote" which does send the ratings over the top. Therefore, nothing can or should be done about that. (Besides, Mr. Spock is a wonderful character and I would be <u>most</u> reluctant to change him in any way.)

The problem, then, is how to convince the world, and Mr. Shatner, that Mr. Shatner is the lead.

It seems to me that the only thing one can do is lead from strength. Mr. Shatner is a versatile and talented actor and perhaps this should be made plain by giving him a chance at a variety of roles. In other words, an effort should be made to work up story plots in which Mr. Shatner has an opportunity to put on disguises or take over roles of unusual nature. A bravura display of his versatility would be impressive indeed and would probably make the whole deal a great deal more fun for Mr. Shatner. (He might also consider that a display of virtuosity would stand him in great stead when the time---the <u>sad</u> time---came that STAR TREK had finished its run and he must look elsewhere.)

Then, too, it might be well to unify the team of Kirk and Spock a bit, by having them actively meet various menaces together with one saving the life of the other on occasion. The idea of this would be to get people to think of Kirk when they think of Spock.

And, finally, the most important suggestion of all---ignore this letter, unless it happens to make sense to you.

Isaac Asimov

Isaac Asimov's response to Roddenberry's request for advice.

Roddenberry wrote his thanks to Asimov:

> . . . Your comments on Shatner and Spock were most interesting and I have passed them on to Gene Coon and the others. We've followed one idea immediately, that of having Spock save his Captain's life in an up-coming show. I will follow your advice about having them much more a team, standing more closely together. As for having Shatner play more varied roles, we have been looking in that direction and will continue to do so. But I think the most important comment is that of keeping them a close team. Shatner will come off ahead by showing he is fond of the teenage idol [Mister Spock]; Spock will do well by displaying great loyalty to his Captain. In a way it will give us *one* lead, the team.

And Spock did, indeed, save his captain's life in "Obsession," then being scripted by writer Art Wallace under Coon's supervision. In fact, Spock rose to the occasion again in "Spectre of the Gun," which was written well before its third-season production by Coon under his pseudonym "Lee Cronin."

But reality was reality. Team concept or no, Mister Spock continued to be the "star" in *Star Trek*.

No series had more impact on television history than *Star Trek*. Yet no one ever figured out what there was, or wasn't, about the show that never impressed members of the National Academy of Television Arts and Sciences (NATAS). The Academy's membership nominated and subsequently voted the "Emmy" awards.

In the spring of 1967, Desilu was again in the news, big time. *Mission: Impossible* and *The Lucy Show* received nominations for the best of almost everything: best show, best acting, best writing, best directing, best music, best photography, best film editing, best sound. You name it, they got it. *Star Trek* was nominated for best one-hour dramatic series, one acting award (Leonard Nimoy as best supporting actor in a dramatic series), and three technical awards: sound and film editing, photographic special effects, and mechanical special effects. The three series shared a total of fourteen nominations. Everything from the reawakened Desilu was best, best, best—or so it seemed.

But on June 4, 1967, as the nineteenth annual Emmy Award ceremony came to its close, after Lucy had swept up her Emmy and Bruce Geller and *Mission* had swept up theirs, the *Star Trek* contingent, decked out in their rented tuxedos and seated at their assigned tables, had politely accepted the fact that their names had not been called; their contributions had not been honored. There was no reason for any anxiety; they had lost. *Star Trek* had been shut out.

HERB: Our table was just to the right of center, very close to the bandstand. Bruce Geller, Barbara Bain, and *Mission* Producer Joe Gantman had already

Courtesy Greg Jein

At Isaac Asimov's suggestion, Roddenberry made Kirk and Spock more of a team.

removed their dessert plates and proudly positioned their glistening gold Emmys before them. Roddenberry, Coon, and Justman, having little choice, continued trying to enjoy their desserts.

It was exciting; the studio was taking home a total of eleven Emmy awards. The word had already been passed—a celebration party at my house when it was all over. But looking at my "running score" slip of paper, I wondered who would come. Lucy and Gary wouldn't join the group. And no one would blame the two Genes and Bob for "being tired and wanting to get home."

It was time for a commercial during the live telecast; we waited impatiently for the one award remaining before the evening ended: music. Composer Lalo Schifrin's *Mission: Impossible* theme music was among the five nominees for Best Musical Score. But coming out of the commercial, the Master of Ceremonies told a couple of lame jokes, thanked everyone for their attendance, and waved good night. The 1967 Emmy Awards show was over!

What happened to the Best Musical Score? I was concerned and upset and rushed to the stage to corner Thomas Freebairn-Smith, the man in charge of the Emmy awards for the Academy.

"You forgot the music award!"

"No, no, Herb; there isn't any music award."

"What are you talking about?"

"The music committee didn't feel any of the nominated scores were up to the standards of television."

"'The standards of television?' Are you guys crazy? Every week *Mission: Impossible* and *Star Trek* are pushing the standards of television to new heights."

"There's nothing to discuss, Herb."

"*Star Trek,* recipient of *no* awards tonight, is the most innovative series in television history, breaking every boundary there is—and you're telling me about the 'standards of television'?"

Freebairn-Smith, having more important matters to attend to, turned abruptly and walked away. Case closed.

The celebration at the house was, as expected, a *Mission: Impossible* affair. A good time was had by all—but not the ignored Lalo Schifrin. And definitely not the people from *Star Trek.* They were already at home, asleep.

The 1967 Emmy Awards ceremony was the beginning of an unenviable record for *Star Trek*. It was never to receive an Emmy in any major category and became the bridesmaid of one-hour series, while *Mission: Impossible*, receiving multiple Emmys year after year, became the bride. Interestingly enough, to this day, no actor in any of the *Star Trek* spin-off series has ever won an Emmy.

In fact, *Star Trek* received very few awards, and when it did, in most instances they were expected. It was no surprise that the only true science-fiction series on television that employed true science-fiction writers would receive the "Hugo" award from the attendees at the World Science Fiction Convention. Similarly, the Science Fiction Writers of America gave it the "Nebula" award. Acknowledging episodes that occasionally ventured into fantasy and horror, an award was received from "Sci-Fi Guy" Forrest J Ackerman's Count Dracula Society.

The only mainstream popularity award ever bestowed on *Star Trek* was the Gold Medal as top television show of the year in *Photoplay* magazine's 1967 Annual Poll.

Courtesy Stephen Edward Poe

20

Money, Money, Money

BOB: Johnny Carson, who starred in NBC's *Tonight Show* for so many years, used to perform a routine in which, after the answer was announced, he would open an envelope and read the question to which it pertained.

For me, with a new season staring us in the face, "rock and roll" was the answer.

The question was, "Why are we spending so much time and money dubbing our shows when we can do it cheaper and better?"

When he heard that, Herb Solow got really interested. Both *Star Trek* and *Mission* had been picked up for a second season, and with the addition of *Mannix*, the studio had three series that cost more than it could afford.

I continued, "It takes a day and a half to dub *Star Trek* and two days to dub *Mission*. *Mannix* will take at least a day and a half. Herb, we can save half a day on each dub if the studio puts in rock and roll."

An early publicity still of Mister Spock.

(Rock and roll was an automated process that enabled a dubbing crew to merely roll a reel back to a specified footage to correct a mistake rather than take down all the reels and start all over again.)

"RJ, you mean we hire Little Richard to score the shows?"

"Wrong! Bill Haley and the Comets—right! And not only does rock and roll save overtime on the dubbing crew and sound-effects editors, it frees up half a day's time for each series producer and cuts at least a half day off our delivery schedules." That was the capper. Herb bought the sales pitch. Next season, we'd really "rock and roll."

Not content with getting the rock-and-roll dubbing equipment, Justman turned his attention to Desilu's aged stage-lighting equipment. He proposed that the studio purchase a number of the new lightweight and compact "quartz lights" to permanently rig *Star Trek*'s main sets.

Solow bought the idea, because it would save substantial lighting time. To Justman's surprise and pleasure, Ed Holly bought the idea too, because not only would the quartz lights be fully amortized in one production year, they would free up a number of heavier, older lamps that Desilu could lease to rental customers.

HERB: At first, I approved a second-season *Star Trek* episodic budget of almost $192,000. Soon, because I perceived it to be the proper thing to do, I cut the budget down to $187,500—not because I wanted the studio to make more money, but rather because I wanted it to lose less money.

By this time, Leonard's popularity had convinced him of what we already knew: He had the most important role and was the most important actor in the series.

Leonard's agent, Alex Brewis, was a likable, energetic man, highly experienced in overcoming the daily obstacles of getting acting jobs for his clients, but not accustomed to confronting studios with demands to renegotiate a series star's contract. As Leonard recalls, Alex held a series of meetings with him, his most important client, and discussed the proper approach to convince the studio to bring his client up to "star level." Their main discussion focused on Leonard's salary. Signed contract be damned; the decision was to demand $3,000 per episode and settle for $2,500, thus doubling his contractual salary, but still giving him only fifty percent of what Shatner was originally being paid.

The studio would have been amenable to the $2,500 request. But that wasn't to be. As Alex approached my office, he overheard a phone conversation I was having with Marty Landau's agent. The deal with Landau, one of the *Mission: Impossible* stars, was no deal. The studio had no options on his services per his choice and ours, so every year I renegotiated a new deal directly with Landau and then, afterwards, phoned his agent to run through the figures. Brewis thought he heard me confirming a combined per-episode salary for Landau and his wife, *Mission* star Barbara Bain, of $11,000. He had heard incorrectly. (In a million years, I wouldn't pay that much!) He became incensed. "If they're worth $11,000, then my client, Leonard Nimoy, is worth at least $9,000."

So Alex Brewis made his demands—and a threat: "$9,000 per episode, star billing, star perks, a larger percentage of merchandising money and greater script input, or else Mr. Nimoy will not report for shooting." (Years later, Leonard laughed, remembering that when he heard how Brewis had "improved" his demands from $2,500 to $9,000, he "almost had a heart attack.")

Nimoy, who not only enjoyed but found it necessary to be involved in all negotiations, stated his position quite clearly and succinctly in a April 6, 1967, letter he sent to Desilu attorney and contract negotiator Edwin Perlstein.

April 6,1967

Mr. Edwin Perlstein
Desilu Productions, Inc.
780 N. Gower Street
Hollywood, California 90038

Dear Mr. Perlstein:

I am in receipt of your option pick-up letter and feel I must inform you, that under the terms and conditions as stated in the contract and as subsequently amended in your verbal offer, I do not feel I can perform the services you call for.

I believe my reasons for this position were clearly stated in our telephone conversation of Thursday March 30.

I believe I have made my ideas quite clear, but my representatives will be happy to discuss any further ideas Desilu may have towards a happier resolution of this situation.

Since the studio has chosen to take a "freeze" attitude, I am prepared to deal with whatever "consequences" may arise from my action, if in fact there should be any.

I feel in all fairness that you are entitled to as much advance notice of my intentions as possible.

Sincerely,

Leonard Nimoy

LN:mw

CC: Herb Solow
Bernard Weitzman
Gene Roddenberry

Certified mail
Return receipt requested

Nimoy's letter informing Desilu attorney Ed Perlstein of his refusal to come back to work.

Although Nimoy's letter was addressed to Perlstein, the Business Affairs attorney had no authority to make a decision and functioned only as the studio's point man. Herb Solow, Bernard Weitzman, and Gene Roddenberry, who were "copied" on this and all other related correspondence, were the people who would actually make the final decision.

BOB: We had to face the possibility that a new actor might have to be hired to play Mister Spock. Gene had already sent a "CONFIDENTIAL" memo to Gene Coon, Dorothy Fontana, and me regarding the "LEONARD NIMOY CONTRACT NEGOTIATION." Gene complained about Leonard's "totally impossible demands" and advised us, "We have no choice but to suspend him and take legal action."

Roddenberry's memo to Gene Coon regarding Nimoy's contract dispute.

CONFIDENTIAL

Gene Coon cc: Bob Justman
D.C. Fontana

April 1, 1967

Gene Roddenberry

LEONARD NIMOY
CONTRACT NEGOTIATION

Dear Gene:

Sorry to have to greet you back with this news, but our contract negotiations with Leonard Nimoy and his representatives seem stalemated. There is a possibility that we might have to start our second year of STAR TREK or even continue the show without Leonard Nimoy as "Mister Spock". Naturally, we hope we can avoid this, but despite our efforts to offer Nimoy a contract well above the original contract, an offer which I believe was eminently fair, his agents have placed totally impossible demands upon the Studio and upon Norway Corporation. They include such things as the absolute right to direct three episodes of STAR TREK during the coming year, Guest Star demands on other shows, a right the exclusively negotiate for himself records and merchandising on the Spock character, plus money demands that we could not meet this year and scaled up demands over future years that we could not meet then either.

We have a contract with Nimoy, once signed by both sides in good faith at the beginning of STAR TREK. Since we find it impossible to bargain with him, since they refuse to accept our best offers, or even discuss them reasonably, we've lhad no option but to inform Nimoy and his agents that he is picked up on the original contract and ordered to report for work per our schedule. He counters that he will refuse to report -- at which time we have no choice but to suspend him and take legal action.

Accordingly, I've been working with Joe D'Agosta on re-creating the part and creating a new Vulcan Science Officer, who can go to work on our first show.

Frankly, Nimoy and his representatives are very near trying to blackjack us into submission, by holding "Mister Spock" as hostage. In their enthusiasm over a first-year success, over considerable mail volume and public adulation, they are kidding themselves into believing a very successful and much-wanted actor named Nimoy joined us and did it all. And that our posture should be totally that of humble gratitude. I won't play that game, nor will Desilu.

I'm sorry about this. Naturally, I hope sweet reason will prevail. But if it does not, we must be prepared to continued STAR TREK with the same excitement and quality it has always had.

GENE RODDENBERRY

GR:sts

Casting Director Joe D'Agosta was asked to prepare an "off-the-record" list of "VULCAN POSSIBILITIES." But the three-page list had a hidden purpose. It was a ploy, a bit of psychological warfare designed to induce Leonard to capitulate. Once agents were contacted regarding a possible Spock replacement, Gene knew it wouldn't be long before the news got back to Leonard and he felt the pressure of look-alike actors' being considered for "his" role.

We already had potential replacements who had actually appeared on the show in roles that called for them to wear pointed ears. Early in the first season, Gene had decided that the Romulan enemies, as well as the Vulcan good guys, should have pointed ears, and he cast Mark Lenard as a Romulan commander. Gene reran the episode. He liked what saw; Mark could definitely replace Leonard. However, Mark Lenard's strong physical presence lacked the depth and sensitivity that had endeared Nimoy to his fans.

The next choice was Larry Montaigne. Not only was he a good actor, but of all those on the list, he came closest to Nimoy's looks and physicality. When Larry Montaigne was hired to play Spock's rival for the hand of T'Pring (played by Arlene Martel) in "Amok Time," the studio took an open option on his services for the series—just in case. Regardless of the many names on the list, only Mark Lenard and Larry Montaigne were seriously considered as replacements for Leonard. But as we say on planet Vulcan, "when push comes to shove," everyone wants Leonard Nimoy.

Courtesy Paramount Pictures

Mark Lenard, one of the proposed replacements for Leonard Nimoy.

March 30, 1967

TO: GENE RODDENBERRY
cc: Herb Solow

FROM: JOE D'AGOSTA

RE: VULCAN POSSIBILITIES

"A" LIST

MARK LENNARD

WILLIAM SMITHERS

LIAM SULLIVAN

LLOYD BOCHNER

JOE MAROSS

DONALD HARRON

EDWARD MULHARE

JAMES MITCHELL

MICHAEL RENNIE

MARK RICHMAN

CHARLES ROBINSON

CHRIS ROBINSON

STEWART MOSS

DAVID CANARY

JOHN ANDERSON

DAVID CARRADINE

A list of possible replacements for Nimoy.

VULCAN POSSIBILITIES Page 2

"B" LIST

ANTHONY JAMES

PERRY LOPEZ

GEORGE BACHMAN

ALAN BERGMANN

LEE KINSOLVING

BLAISDELL MAKEE

BILL FLETCHER

HENRY DARROW

ANTHONY GEORGE

CURT LOWENS

JACQUES DENBEAUX

MAXWELL REED

VULCAN POSSIBILITIES Page 3

"C" LIST

LAWRENCE MONTAIGNE

RON HAYES

PATRICK HORGAN

PAUL MANTEE

BRUCE WATSON

ROBERT YURO

RICHARD EVANS

JOE RUSKIN

TED MARKLAND

LEE BERGERE

JOHN RAYNER

HERB: The ramifications were huge. The extra money demanded by Nimoy was bad enough. The problem was that if he got an increase, all the other contract actors would be standing in line for theirs.

NBC, suffering financial losses on *Star Trek* due to lack of sponsorship, refused to pay any additional monies. Desilu had no money allocated for additional cast salary increases. Even though I felt Leonard deserved more money and recognition for his contributions to the show, the studio surely wouldn't pay the increase. It continued to lose money on the series, which pleased several gloating members of the Board of Directors and angered Lucille Ball.

So the empty threats and the mind games began. I met with Alex Brewis and explained the NBC-Desilu money problems—and *I* made threats. "If your client doesn't report to work under his current contract, the studio will consider him to be in breach of that contract, terminate him, sue him, and find some other actor to wear the pointed ears. Remember, it's not important who plays the role; any good actor can do that. It's the pointed ears that count; they're the star."

The studio position was reported to Leonard. He was upset at my reference to "any good actor" being able to play the Spock role. But he had his job to do. And I had mine.

The final skirmish came a week later. NBC, the original campaigner against the Spock character and the pointed ears, hearing through Leonard's agent that he might walk off the show, was also furious. "What are we hearing, Herb? You're thinking of replacing Nimoy? Are you out of your mind? Our management would go ballistic. Research tells us he's the most popular part of the whole damn show!"

The war was lost. Nimoy got more money: $2,500 per show plus $100 for expenses, better billing, a more lucrative merchandising deal, and more script input. The other actors received additional increases. DeForest Kelley had already gotten costar billing. As I expected, NBC contributed nothing. Desilu now continued to lose even more money on *Star Trek*.

Leonard Nimoy was definitely on "first." Bill Shatner was on "second." And DeForest Kelley was now on "third."

Many of the stories surrounding Roddenberry are based on his inability to deny good things said about him. Some years ago a journalist, confused with his facts, asked him how long he produced *Have Gun Will Travel*. Roddenberry was actually one of the contributing writers to the series. But rather than deny any producership, he talked about the several years he wrote scripts for *Have Gun*. The journalist subsequently, and mistakenly, confirmed that Roddenberry produced the series, and that "fact" was added to the Roddenberry myth. Needless to say, Sam Rolfe, the cocreator and Producer of *Have Gun*, wasn't too thrilled.

A publicity photo promoting *Star Trek*'s new, second-season time slot: Friday at 8:30.

Courtesy Greg Jein

HERB: Gene Roddenberry rarely denied anything good. If a visitor to Hollywood approached him on the street and asked, "Pardon me, sir, but aren't you Clark Gable?" Gene wouldn't say "yes," and he wouldn't say "no." Rather, he'd expound on "the unpredictable weather we're having" or "the idiots who run network television." The stranger would leave, still not quite sure if he really had encountered Clark Gable.

With the actors having received more money because of "*L'affaire* Leonard," and Gene having received more money because that's what was called for in his contract, Bob Justman opened his pay envelope to find he, too, had been given a raise. RJ was thrilled.

The next day, walking with Gene, he said, "Bird, thanks for the 'bump.' With the kids in private school, we can use the extra money."

Gene kept on walking.

Bob persisted. "It's great. I really appreciate your generosity. Thanks again."

"Ahhh . . . sure, Bob."

Several days later, I saw RJ on the dubbing stage. He told me of his good fortune.

"I told Gene how much I appreciated the raise, but I really feel guilty taking it. The show is running over budget, and, well, you know how I feel."

"Hey, Bob, do me a favor and stop it. Even with the extra money you're still underpaid. Enough said. Go dub a show or something."

Twenty-five years later, RJ mentioned that 1967 raise to me. He was still feeling guilty over accepting it and recalled Gene's awkward reaction when he thanked him.

"It was as if he didn't know anything about it," added Bob.

"I thought you knew, RJ. Gene didn't know anything about it."

"Then who gave me the raise?"

"Me! And the least you can do is say 'Thank you.' "

Bob was chagrined. He twirled his mustache. "Thank you," he said.

"You're welcome, Bob. Now, go dub a show or something."

Star Trek's renewal came with a caveat: a new time period. The *Enterprise* would no longer explore those strange new worlds every Thursday night. Beginning in September 1967, armchair explorers would have to wait until Friday nights at 8:30. At least those would who weren't at the movies, a fraternity party, the bowling alley, or out on dates. But there was a rationale. Although some of the series's audience—high school and college students—would be lost, it was hoped that *Star Trek* could be the recipient of good ratings passed on from a more successful lead-in, *Tarzan.* It's interesting to note that when *Star Trek* first premiered in 1966, *Tarzan* was its lead-in for the premiere night only. The following week *Tarzan* was moved to Friday at 7:30. Perhaps, after a year, NBC knew much more about their audience flow. Perhaps.

A publicity still from "Amok Time," the first episode of the second season.

Courtesy NBC/Globe

21

A Shoe Drops: The Second Season

BOB: A shoe had dropped; in fact, a whole lot of shoes had dropped. Knowing they'd continue to lose money on each episode produced, cash-poor Desilu cut our budget.

When I brought Matt Jefferies in for yet another budget meeting, the Art Director's eyes began to water up again. "Bob, you're going to say, 'Less money for sets.' I know the tune so well I could dance to it."

"Matt, it's not my favorite song, either. But can you do it?"

"I'll try." And he set about to make it happen.

But the set-construction budget wasn't the only victim. All the other cash items took a beating: guest stars, supporting cast, extras, and set dressing and property purchases and rentals. Things got so bad that Gregg Peters, the show's new Unit Manager, was later accused of watering down the morning coffee on the set and cutting the doughnuts in half to save money.

Courtesy Stephen Edward Poe

One of Matt Jefferies' inexpensive sets, from the episode "Bread and Circuses."

NBC's order for the second season was the first shoe that dropped. The network chose to hedge its bet. Yes, the renewal order was twenty-six episodes, but it contained a "cut-back" provision: Only sixteen episodes were firm; the remaining ten episodes would become firm when and if NBC exercised an option. If the series didn't meet NBC's ratings expectations, the sixteenth show would be our last show—ever.

But we had to budget on the basis of a full twenty-six–episode order. A budget based on only sixteen shows would have blown our amortized per-episode fixed costs all to hell. And it always remained very much in our minds that the old guard was still out there just waiting for over-budget tab runs to further bolster their position. You don't have to be paranoid to have enemies. But it sure helps.

We also had to plan for a full twenty-six–episode season when it came to

scripts. In no way could we be caught short on scripts should NBC exercise its option. Stories might never have "gone to script" and scripts might never have been filmed, so writing commitments had to be made.

And setting directors was chancy as well. Locking in freelance directors for a full season was tantamount to guaranteeing them employment. If there was no episode to shoot, shaking the director's hand and saying, "Sorry!" wouldn't quite make it. What would suffice was full payment of a fee for not directing.

I decided to mainly use only two directors for the second season. It would be more efficient to have successful *Star Trek* veterans alternating episodes, rather than run the risk of breaking in directors new to the show. The main second-season directors would be Marc Daniels and Joe Pevney.

It was a good deal for Marc and Joe. Not only were they guaranteed employment, they could get an early look at stories and scripts. So as soon as we received the order for the sixteen shows, I made firm commitments with them for the early part of the season. We also had a handshake agreement for later; Marc and Joe gave us first refusal rights on their services. They would touch base with me before taking assignments elsewhere.

The alternating-director concept was also creatively and monetarily advantageous to us. Marc and Joe understood the series' concept, worked well with the cast, and would deliver quality work. And lest we forget, they were living proof that quality episodes could be brought in, not only on time but on budget as well.

The story money advanced by NBC paid dividends. While the writing staff didn't complete quite as many scripts as hoped for prior to the start of production, the scripts were in substantially better shape, both quantitatively and qualitatively, compared to those available in the rocky beginning of the previous season.

Of course, certain minor headaches continued to crop up. Stories still underwent a rough going-over from Stan Robertson. On May 15, 1967, he grudgingly approved the outline for "Return to Tomorrow" and stipulated that "the highly 'cerebral' portions of the story would be eliminated and the complex nature of the plot would be materially simplified."

Coon was particularly displeased with Robertson's stipulation. "I don't understand that man, Bob."

"What's so hard to understand, Gene?" asked Justman. "What's cerebral for the goose is sauce for the gander. Stan's like the guy in Hamlet who said, 'The play . . . pleased not the million; 'twas caviare to the general.' "

Gene Coon grinned. "Are you quoting Shakespeare again? Please, don't quote Shakespeare, Bob. Me and Stan don't understand it."

BOB: Gene Coon loved to dabble in casting. His dabbling days were over, however, after he met the twins we later referred to as the "Mudd Sisters."

"I, Mudd" needed a number of sets of female twins. Finding them was going slowly, and time was getting short. We needed them to make "split-screen shots"

Courtesy Paramount Pictures

Harry Mudd and three sets of android twins.

that would optically manufacture quartets or octets of beauteous females. Harry Mudd's armies of pretty androids would start out as real, honest-to-goodness, in-the-flesh, female twins.

Joe D'Agosta rushed into my office. "Good news! I found a couple of girls hanging around the corner of Hollywood and Vine."

"Joe, aren't you taking our 'space hooker' analogy a little too seriously?"

"Hey, Bob. They're twins!" announced Joe, proudly.

Now that made sense, so Joe brought them in and we escorted the twins into Gene Coon's office.

They had recently arrived from Minnesota to make money in Hollywood, had never acted before, and were willing to try anything. Identical, but certainly not really very pretty, the twins wore wedgies and the shortest of skirts. One of them brought along her pet, a young wildcat named Marlon.

Coon stared at the animal, considering, then reconsidering, whether he should pet it.

"Oh, don't worry about Marlon, silly! He's a tame wildcat."

Gene reached out gingerly and touched the tame wildcat. Marlon squinted his eyes and scrunched up his nose.

"See, Marlon likes you."

"Okay, now, ladies," interrupted Joe, "why don't you both stand over here, take these pages, and read for us?" He handed several pages of dialogue to the twins.

"But what do I do with Marlon?" asked the pet owner.

"That animal *does* like me," observed Coon. "Here, I'll hold him."

So Gene, happily holding the "tame" wildcat in his lap, turned his attention to the twins as they began to read. Unfortunately, the twins' comprehension, pronunciation, and delivery left too much to be desired. In the meantime, Marlon began squirming and snarling and struggling to get free, while simultaneously shredding Gene's shirt and pants and skin with its razor-sharp talons.

The twins stopped reading, and we all stared curiously at Marlon slicing up Coon, and Coon stubbornly refusing to let loose of the enraged animal.

"What a cute little . . . oh . . . ow . . . ouch . . . pretty little . . . ouch . . . pet you have. Did it take long to . . . ouch . . . ow . . . train Marlon?" Gene's shirt and pants were in bloody ribbons when he finally accepted defeat and released the tame wildcat.

The twins were a bust as actresses, but we hired them anyhow, as extras—with the proviso that they leave their pet at home. Joe left to try to find twins who could act; Gene Coon left to get his wounds treated and a new shirt and pants.

After his experience with Marlon, Coon took time out only to cast guest stars and other important roles. And then, only with those actors who arrived at the studio without pets.

Star Trek became inundated with pets of a different order when Dorothy Fontana found an untried young writer: David Gerrold. Gerrold had written an unsolicited script, which he called "A Fuzzy Thing Happened."

While Fontana found much right with the script, Bob Justman found much wrong.

BOB: Although the concept was amusing, the story was just too cute. I feared that, with the script calling for Shatner and company to milk everything for laughs, it would lead to a loss of believability. Kirk, Spock, and the others were real people, and real people just did not behave that way; our finely drawn characters should never parody themselves.

Even after Gerrold made some staff-demanded revisions, the script was still found lacking, so it underwent an extensive rewrite by Gene Coon. It was retitled and filmed as "The Trouble with Tribbles," and it became one of the most popular of all the *Star Trek* episodes. So popular was it that Gerrold made a secondary career as a result of this one script, writing the books *The World of Star Trek* and *Star Trek's Trouble with Tribbles*, and guesting at *Star Trek* and science-fiction conventions. Despite its popularity, Justman, admittedly a minority of one, felt that the episode, while well made, was too farcical to be believable.

The actual source of the idea for "Tribbles" has been laid at the feet of famed science-fiction writer Robert Heinlein. Belatedly recognizing the similarity between it and the "Martian Flat Cats" story in Heinlein's *The Rolling Stones*,

Roddenberry had a problem: A lot of money had been invested in an episode with a clouded provenance; broadcasting it could result in a lawsuit. On the other hand, not broadcasting it would result in Desilu "eating" $187,500. A phone call to a very understanding Robert Heinlein cleared up the problem. Heinlein reasoned that, since the episode had not yet been broadcast, a simple "mea culpa" from Roddenberry was sufficient to remedy the problem.

BOB: David came back to work with Gene and me during the first season of *Star Trek: The Next Generation* and helped contribute to the new show's development. He also wrote a script titled "Fire and Ice," which Gene junked due to its "homosexual content." That troubled me. Although I had never liked David's original "Tribbles" script for the first series, I liked this one a lot and believed that it ought to be produced. But I fought a losing battle to change Gene's mind. Later, David departed from the series in unhappy circumstances, along with D. C. Fontana.

So with the writing seemingly under control, it appeared that the only major problem was completing the postproduction work in time for each episode to meet its projected airdate.

"Stan Robertson's really feeling his oats this season," complained Justman at a lunch meeting with Solow. "All that power's gone to his head. Even more than before."

Solow could not care less. "Maybe so, RJ, but we promised we'd deliver. And on time. We're going to do it."

"Mr. Briggs, neither snow nor sleet nor rain nor lack of talent will stay us from our duly appointed mission," Justman joked. But he was worried. Murphy's Law was still operative. There was no way of knowing where and when it would strike next.

BOB: Everything was ready. We had scripts to shoot; we had Gene Coon, the incredible writing machine; and we still had Gene Roddenberry to do emergency rewrites. With Unit Manager Gregg Peters handling production and Assistant to the Producer Ed Milkis handling postproduction, all our needs were well in hand. I made sure that Eddie, Gregg, and I kept each other apprised of everything we were doing, so that no matter what happened to one of us, the other two could handle the load. And with Marc Daniels and Joe Pevney alternating director chores, the series would be in capable hands.

Murphy's Law was revoked; it could not strike. Curfew would not ring tonight.

Ed, Gregg, and I had a few drinks together that Friday night before our last relatively peaceful weekend. We would start shooting on Monday morning, May 2, 1967.

"Bob, you're limping. What happened?" asked Eddie.

"I don't know. Must've pulled a muscle; it hurts like hell." I felt lots of pain in my upper right thigh.

"Have another Scotch," suggested Gregg. "It'll still hurt, but you won't care."

Courtesy NBC/Globe

One of Gene Coon's fine episodes, "Metamorphosis," which introduced the character Zephram Cochrane, the inventor of warp drive, played by Glenn Corbett.

"Don't mind if I do." I had another, hoping the alcohol would help. It didn't. We finished our drinks, wished each other luck next Monday, and headed home.

The following morning I was on my way to the hospital in an ambulance.

Ten days later, when Ed, Gregg, and Joe Pevney came to see me, I was still flat on my back recovering from one lulu of an infection in my right hip joint. My right leg was up in the air, in traction. A week later, I was home on crutches and raring to go back to work.

During my hospital stay, an odd thing occurred—a surprise visit from Gene Roddenberry to my hospital room one night. He sneaked in long after the official visiting hours were over. Even though I was semidrugged, it was evident he was drunk as a skunk. Awkwardly, he mumbled some maudlin words about our friendship and how important I was to him and *Star Trek,* and he entreated me to "get well real soon." Then he stumbled out. I fell asleep worrying whether he would get home safely.

HERB: RJ may have felt that everything was in good hands when he took ill, but his absence was important enough to me to advise Lucille Ball in a May 8, 1967, activity report:

> . . . on the negative side, the associate producer of *Star Trek,* who has been greatly responsible for the economic production of the series, has been

hospitalized for the past week and a half and is not expected to return to us for approximately another two weeks. This has somewhat slowed us down in getting our budgets and productions in order. . . .

BOB: It was a great day when I returned, because Eddie and Gregg had arranged a special welcome. I entered my office to find both Gorns stretched out together on my couch, the "girl" atop the "guy," in a position expressly prohibited by the California State Penal Code. I was touched.

But more importantly, good planning had paid off; the show had functioned well without me. In an odd and painful way, we had triumphed over Murphy's Law.

Ed Milkis continued his unflappable ways, handling the myriad postproduction tasks. Gregg Peters had been promoted to Unit Manager and was now responsible for all production and budget matters. He celebrated by purchasing a brand-new automobile.

BOB: Gregg was very happy with his new "wheels," a Thunderbird "hard top," and showed it off to one and all. As he got into his new car one evening, Sylvia T. Smith and Eddie Milkis passed by. "Nice car, Gregg!" Gregg nodded and grinned proudly; then he cranked it up. SCREECH! SCREEECH! SCREEEECH! Terrible sounds emanated from the engine compartment.

Startled, Sylvia jumped back. "What's wrong with your car, Gregg?"

"I don't know," answered Gregg. "It was fine this morning." He turned the engine off, then turned it back on again. SCREECH! SCREEECH! SCREEEECH! The noise was so horrendous he turned the engine off again.

"Something's wrong with the engine," volunteered Milkis.

"I can tell that, Eddie. Believe me. But what is it?" Gregg tried again. SCREECH! SQUEALLL! SCREEEECHHHH!

"Sounds like the fan belt's slipping," said Milkis.

Gregg turned off the ignition. "You think so?" He turned the ignition back on. SCREECH! SCREEECH, SCREECHHH! He nodded agreement. "That's it, the fan belt's slipping."

Gregg left the engine running and got out of the car. By now, the noise had attracted a small crowd. Eddie, Sylvia, and the others watched as Gregg went to the front of the car and opened the hood. SCREECH! YOWWWL!! Tufts of fur flew everywhere as a badly frightened and rather damaged studio cat leaped out of the engine compartment and sped away, complaining mightily.

"Your car sounds fine, Gregg, but I think your cat needs work," said Eddie Milkis.

In 1987, almost twenty years later, while preparing to film the opening two-hour episode of *Star Trek: The Next Generation*, Ed Milkis and Bob Justman planned to refurbish the *Enterprise* sets that had been built for the *Star Trek* movies and use them on the new series. And once again, they encountered a studio cat problem.

BOB: When the studio guard unlocked the stage, we were assailed with an unbelievably intense odor. Cats had been defecating on the floors of the sets for months on end. Cats lead a good life at motion-picture studios: lots of food to scavenge and lots of rodents to hunt. And sound stages make a great cat house in which to live and bring up a family.

No matter where we walked, there were piles of excrement. It was an obstacle course just to go twenty feet. We finally gave up. The studio would have to send in a cleaning crew. Just before we left the stage, one particularly mangy-looking cat crossed our path. Holding my nose, I turned to Eddie and quipped, "Isn't that the cat from Gregg's car?"

"Yeah," said Eddie, holding his nose, "it took twenty years, but it finally got even with us."

A different car, a 1966 pearl-gray Pontiac Bonneville Brougham, also had a role in the production of *Star Trek*. James Doohan noticed the sleek beauty parked on the lot and fell in love with the automobile. He had to have it. Checking around, Doohan found it was owned by Steve Whitfield [later, Steve Poe], then writing *The Making of Star Trek*.

Doohan went to see him. "Steve, I just love your car. Would you want to sell her?"

"Actually, Jimmy, I would. But you don't want that car. It's haunted."

"Sure it is. Now, how much do you want for her?"

"Okay, Jimmy, I lied. It's actually cursed. Forget about it."

"No, Steve, if you'd like to sell her, then I'd like to buy her—'haunted' or not."

"Let me explain. Since I've had it, other cars have hit it four separate times. That's four times, and there was never anyone inside; it was always parked at the curb. It has to be the most accident-prone automobile ever built."

"Steve, I'm a grown man standing here and begging you. Sell me your car, man!"

Doohan continued to bug Whitfield until he finally relented. Doohan bought the "haunted" 1966 pearl-gray Pontiac Bonneville Brougham.

Several months later, Whitfield saw Doohan on the lot. "Hi, Jimmy. What's new?"

"Nothing, Steve, nothing," mumbled Doohan. "Listen, I have to get to the set."

"Sure. By the way, how's the car?"

"The car? Oh, the car," replied an embarrassed Doohan. "To be honest with you, the car was parked in front of the house, and an old man hit her, and it took forty-nine days before she was properly repaired and repainted. And six months later, while I was wheeling her around town, her entire right front end fell off, right there in the middle of the street. I couldn't believe she was so accident-prone. You know, lad, I think she was cursed, even haunted! I sold the damn thing!"

Star Trek had a continuing need for special props. In early August 1967, Justman invited Milkis and Peters to a meeting in which Project Unlimited would again arrange to sell some new props to the show, props they conveniently "already owned"—although the props had not yet been designed and manufactured. This time, it would be the furry little tribbles. Although they had never met Project Unlimited's Wah Chang and Gene Warren, Milkis and Peters were impressed with the firm's previous work for *Star Trek*. They particularly admired Wah Chang's creativity and were eager to meet him in person.

BOB: But they weren't ready for what they saw. I hadn't told them that Wah Chang was crippled from the effects of polio. So Ed and Gregg could only watch and react in stunned sympathetic silence as Wah Chang made a stiff-legged torturous entry, both of his legs encased in jointed metal braces that had to be unlocked at the knees before he could sit. After introductions were made, Gene Warren unlocked Wah Chang and we all sat down.

Other than saying, "Glad to meet you," Gene Warren was silent throughout the whole meeting. But I knew he'd be making mental notes about delivery dates, costs, and billing procedures. Wah Chang and I did all the talking. We discussed design, cost, and delivery date while Eddie and Gregg just sat there, listening.

When the meeting was over, Wah Chang straightened out the braces and locked them into place, a process that resulted in lots of metallic clicking noises. With Wah Chang's legs now rigidly extended out in front of him, he needed help to rise. Gene Warren, in a well-practiced move, helped lift him to his feet. Wah Chang departed, the way he entered, clicking and clanking as he slowly strode, stiff-legged, toward the door. Braces locked at the knees, Wah Chang had to swing each leg from the hip. Throughout it all, Gene Warren stayed close, for support, but still said nothing other than "good-bye."

After our two guests were gone, there was a long moment when no one spoke. Eddie and Gregg exchanged glances. Then Eddie said, "I'm impressed, Bob."

"Me, too," said Gregg, "really, really impressed."

Eddie continued. "But I've got a problem. I know what Wah Chang does." He hesitated. "But tell me, just what does Gene Warren do?"

I took my time, looked at them very seriously, and then replied, "He oils Wah Chang every morning."

After a few seconds of stunned silence, the laughter erupted. Tears ran down Eddie's cheeks, and Gregg laughed so hard that he fell out of his chair onto the floor.

Sound technician Frank Oakden was a familiar presence on the set. But both cast and crew soon realized that Oakden was a talented caricaturist. From his close-to-camera vantage point, Frank captured the human side of those people who made *Star Trek*.

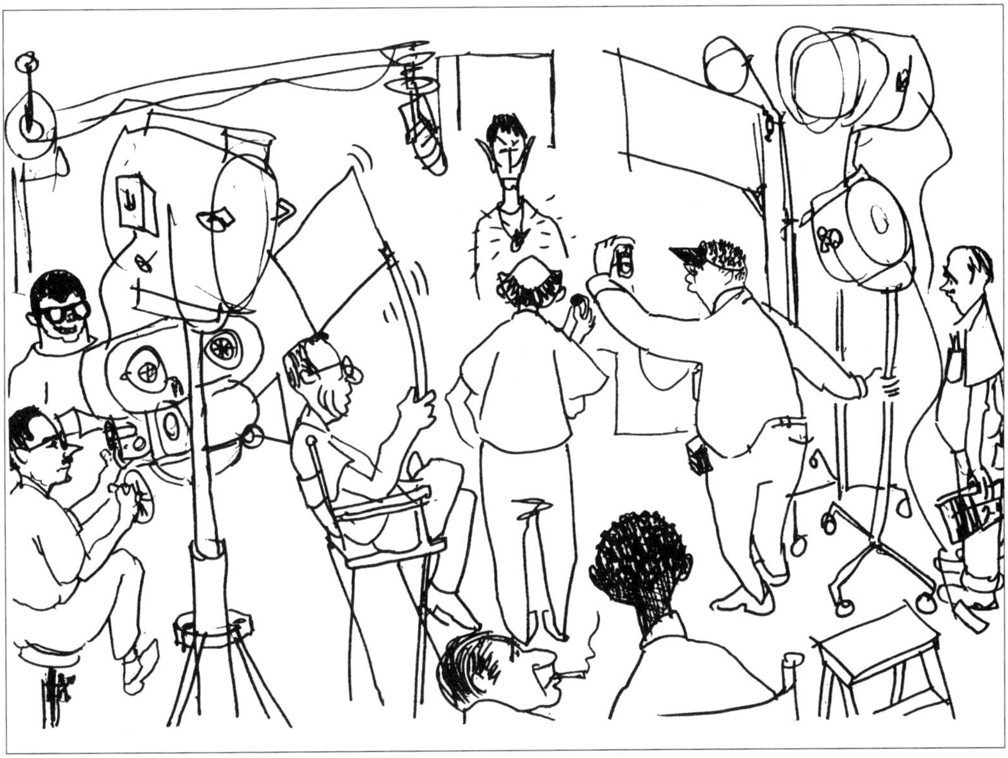

It takes a heap of people to light Mister Spock's close-up.

Courtesy Frank Oakden

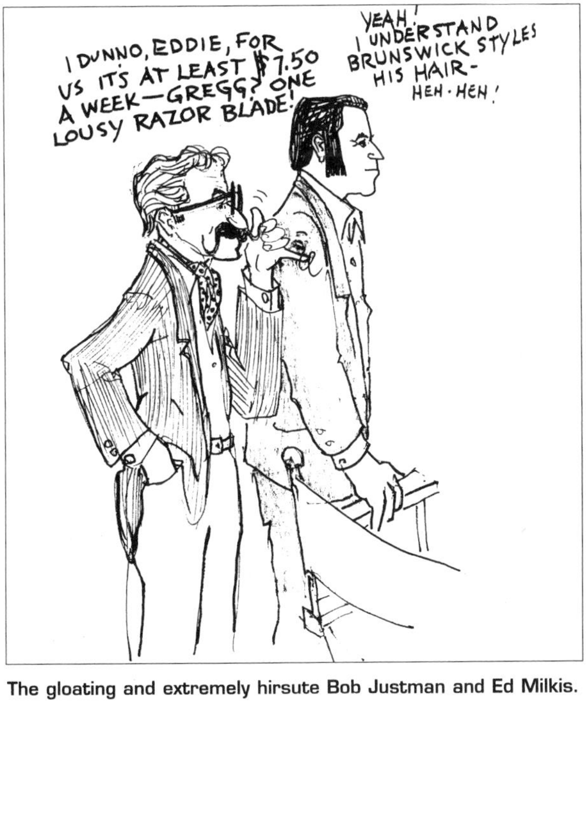

The gloating and extremely hirsute Bob Justman and Ed Milkis.

The bald but exceedingly thrifty Gregg Peters.

Caricatures of the cast and crew by Sound Technician Frank Oakden. Courtesy of Frank Oakden.

The ever-efficient Lieutenant Uhura never fails to put on a brave front.

The heroic Captain Kirk battles the elements.

The resourceful and scientific Engineer Scott can solve *any* problem.

The usually good-natured Shatner didn't like the way he was caricatured. But there was also something else bothering him.

BOB: Bill Shatner stopped me in the middle of the studio street. This was the first time he'd ever complained to me about anything and he was furious. "Look at this goddamn uniform, Bob!" The bottom of his velour tunic was headed north and barely concealed his stomach. He tugged to pull the fabric down over the top of his uniform trousers, which were headed south.

"The goddamn material shrinks more every time it's cleaned. The women are the ones who are supposed to have the bare midriffs on this show, not me!"

I already knew about the problem from watching dailies. All costumes, by Screen Actors Guild contract, had to be cleaned after each use. So every night the uniforms went to the cleaners, and every morning they came back to the studio a smidgen smaller and a shade less colorful.

"You're right, Bill. I'll take care of it."

I knew that shrinkage was only one part of the problem. The other part was Bill himself. As a professional, he worked out strenuously and went on a diet before he began this new TV season. He looked terrific when he reported for the first show, slimmed down to photogenic proportions. But as the season progressed and time passed, he gained weight, mainly in his midsection. So the top of his pants and the bottom of his tunic moved inexorably away from each other as they got smaller and he got larger.

Also, Bill wore lifts to help him attain his advertised height of 5'11", and the high heels threw his posture awry, pushing out his stomach and making him look slightly swaybacked. The eternally slim Leonard Nimoy and DeForest Kelley were much easier to outfit.

"Your f.....g studio is a cheap f.....g studio!"

"Not mine, Bill—ours. It's our studio and we love it. By the way, has anyone ever told you that you're beautiful when you're angry?"

His inborn good nature took hold. He laughed. "Do something, will you?" He was mollified, for now.

"I will. I promise." After all, I thought, we do want our brave, dashing captain to look the part.

My gaze shifted to his hairline. Examining balding actors' hairlines was a habit I'd picked up over the years. The "lace" that anchored the front of his toupee glistened. I made a mental note to tell the makeup man about it before we filmed Shatner again.

I was tempted to ask Bill if he had ever found the so-called missing hairpiece. But no, discretion was the better part of valor.

We had begun the first season with two new toupees for Bill because his own "personal" ones were too ratty-looking. He would wear one toupee while the other piece was being cleaned in the makeup department. But somehow, one of them disappeared during the hiatus between seasons. Each hairpiece cost $200, a princely sum in those days. So we expected to get our money's worth from them.

We had always planned to have two Shatner pieces at the start of each season, and we expected to have the same two when the season ended. Somehow, there was only one left when Fred Phillips, our makeup man, took inventory after the last episode was filmed.

The hairpieces were made for Bill; he was the only one they fit. The missing toupee had been left in the makeup room. It didn't just get up and walk out by itself. I was sure the cleaning lady wasn't guilty; she already had a wig. Who could have taken it? And why?

I couldn't resist: "Ever find that missing 'toup,' Bill?"

"Who, me? Nope. It was in the makeup room when I left that night. I told you, ask Fred. Surely, you don't think that I . . . ?" He was the very soul of innocence. But I had made my point. He knew that I knew.

So we had to have a new hairpiece built for him. And later, by the time *Star Trek* was cancelled after three seasons, Bill ended up with an expanded personal collection of toupees.

Courtesy Greg Jein

Nichelle Nichols, wearing the wig that remains missing to this day.

Actually, this didn't surprise me. Actors historically tended to treat wardrobe and other items created for them as their own, taking things home with them at the end of their employment. And since no one else could use the goods, producers usually looked the other way. Bill couldn't very well wear his *Star Trek* uniforms outside the studio. Actors are weird, but not that weird. But hairpieces were another thing; they were expensive.

Bill wasn't the only one whose hair ended up on the lost-in-action list. During the second season, I sent a memo to Gene complaining:

> Majel Barrett's wig has disappeared. Nobody, including Majel, knows what has happened to it [and] Nichelle Nichols' wig has disappeared. She borrowed it when she finished working and claims that she returned it, but neither Freddie [Phillips] nor Pat Westmore [hair stylist] know [*sic*] anything about it being returned. That takes us up to here on missing hair goods.

Gene didn't respond to my memo, so I cornered him in his office. "Did you find out about Majel?" I asked.

"What do you mean?" he replied, suddenly anxious. "Find out what?"

"About her missing wig."

"Oh." He seemed curiously relieved. "Well, I asked her and she says she has no idea where it is."

"Yeah, I'll bet. What about Nichelle's wig?"

He didn't respond.

"Did you ask her?" I persisted.

He just looked at me and smiled sheepishly. "Come on, Bob. What do you want me to do? Go search her apartment?"

"Yeah. She probably keeps it with all those tennis sweaters."

Hair figured prominently in the case of another *Enterprise* crew member. Soon after the series debuted, Roddenberry was on the prowl to add yet another character to his show's already large cast. He wanted someone who would appeal to younger television viewers. In a September 22, 1966, memo to casting director Joe D'Agosta, he wrote:

> Keeping our teenage audience in mind, also keeping aware of current trends, let's watch for a young, irreverent, English-accent "Beatle" type to try on the show, possibly with an eye to him reoccurring. Like the smallish fellow who looks to be a hit on *The Monkees*. Personally I find this type spirited and refreshing and I think our episode could use that kind of "lift." Let's discuss.

In the spring of 1967, with a second season of *Star Trek* now a *fait accompli*, Roddenberry set out in earnest to find his new "Monkee." But while the hairstyle would remain, the nationality would change. No more "English-accent Beatle type" for him; Roddenberry intended to go where only one other TV show had gone before. Like *The Man from U.N.C.L.E.*, *Star Trek* would have a Russian as one of the good guys.

And of all places, the recommendation came directly from the Kremlin! *Pravda*, the official newspaper of the Communist Party, had criticized *Star Trek* as being "typically capitalistic" and questioned why there was no Russian crewman aboard the *Enterprise*. After all, the Soviets were doing quite well in the race for outer space.

Roddenberry liked the idea. By having someone from behind the Iron Curtain on "our side," he intended to show that people with opposing philosophies not only could learn to get along, but could in fact set aside their differences and cooperate to bring about a better future for humankind.

On the recommendation of director Joseph Pevney, actor Walter Koenig was interviewed for the part of Lieutenant Chekov, the series' new Russian crew member. Pevney recalls that "Walter had the worst Russian accent you ever heard." But Roddenberry was taken with the actor and selected him to play the role after first making certain that a Beatle-type hairstyle would work on the new recruit.

Koenig brought both sensitivity and dedication to his role, qualities that mirrored his own personality.

On October 10, 1967, after *Pravda* criticized his show as being "typically capitalistic," Roddenberry wrote to that newspaper's editor.

October 10, 1967

Mr. Mikhail V. Zimyanin
Editor
PRAVDA
Central Committee of Communist Party
of the Soviet Union
Moscow, Russia

Dear Mr. Zimyanin:

About ten months ago one of the stars of our television show, STAR TREK informed us he had heard that the youth edition of your newspaper had published an article regarding STAR TREK to the effect that the only nationality we were missing aboard our USS Enterprise was a Russian. We were certainly most flattered to even have mention from so far away and wondered if perhaps you could confirm that there was such an article and if so could we possibly presume upon you for a copy of it.

Incidentally, as soon as we heard of this article we added that Russian character. His name is Chekov, and he is, we feel, a great addition to our show.

Very sincerely yours,

Gene Roddenberry
Executive Producer
STAR TREK

GR/p

Letter from Roddenberry to the editor of the Soviet newspaper *Pravda*.

HERB: Because Gene tended to carry on about his new relationship with the USSR, Bob Justman decided to take his boss down a peg. The next day, when Gene returned from lunch, RJ feigned excitement. "Gene! While you were out, we got an angry phone call from Moscow. Some guy at *Pravda* kept on saying 'Nyet, nyet,' and don't write him any more 'typically capitalistic letters.' "

Gene was taken aback. "Really?"

"Yeah. And then, he complained you spelled 'Chekov' wrong; it's 'Check Off'—C-H-E-C-K O-F-F!"

Gene was struck dumb.

"And not only that, he said to tell you, 'Loosen up. Spend the two dollars and give Comrade Koenig a decent haircut.' "

"He has a great haircut!" sputtered Gene. "Those guys don't . . ." Then, realizing he'd been had, he stopped, reached into his pocket, pulled out some money and said, "Here's two bucks, Bob. Take care of it. And while you're at it, get one for yourself."

Courtesy Greg Jein

Actor Walter Koenig, photographed here wearing a Russian-looking tunic.

Star Trek came to the attention of other publications as well. A written inquiry was received from *Mad* magazine. *Star Trek* had finally "arrived." The magazine wanted to do a parody and requested both "approbation" and some photographs of the cast for the artist who would illustrate the piece. (In later years, the show was "honored" several more times.) Gene Roddenberry replied, "For once we are ahead of *Mad*, although it may be the last time. We are already setting up photos which we think you will like.

"Thank you for the letter. Incidentally, what is 'approbation'? Anything around here with more than two syllables we use on the show."

BOB: Penny Unger was on the phone to me in the dubbing stage. "Bob, Gene wants to see you in his office."

"I'll come over as soon as we've finished the dub."

Five minutes later, Penny called again. "Gene wants to know how much longer."

"Tell him I've got another full reel to dub and we have to finish it tonight."

Five minutes later, another call. "Bob, Gene says he has to see you now."

"Tell him to wait, or we won't make our airdate."

Penny covered the mouthpiece, relayed my message, and replied, "He said, 'now'!"

Courtesy Richard Arnold

Star Trek "arrives" in *Mad* magazine.

"I said,'no!' N-o spells no. And stop bothering me." I hung up and went back to work. Two minutes later, Eddie Milkis and Gregg Peters showed up. I glanced at them, waved, and turned my attention back to the screen. Next thing I knew, Eddie and Gregg picked me up by my arms and hastily carried me out of the dubbing stage, across the studio street, and into Building E.

"What's going on?"

They didn't respond. They just went faster.

"Have you guys gone crazy?"

We entered Gene's office on the run.

"Surprise! Surprise! Happy birthday to you, happy birthday to you, happy birthday, dear Boh-ob, happy birthday to you."

Gene was grinning. He had a glass in his hand, and it was evident he'd started without us. Eddie and Gregg were laughing—and breathing hard. People were crowded into the office. And Majel was slicing a pineapple upside-down cake. Someone uncorked another bottle of André "champagne" and poured a glass of two-dollar sparkling wine for me.

"Happy birthday, Bob," said Gene, his eyes twinkling. "You . . . ahhh . . . did know it was your birthday, didn't you?"

"No. I guess I forgot."

"Well, we didn't. Cheers!"

"Thanks, Bird. It was a real surprise."

That pleased him. We clinked glasses and drank. I drained mine, quickly. As soon as the party got into full swing, I snuck out and returned to the dubbing stage. We finished the show that night and made the delivery date.

I knew all along it was my birthday, but I didn't want to disappoint Gene because he so enjoyed surprising people.

But there was more to working on *Star Trek* than mere fun and games. Long-lasting relationships are often born on movies and television series. *Star Trek* was no exception, with a veritable round-robin of duos: Solow-Justman to Justman-Roddenberry to Roddenberry-Coon to Coon-Solow and back again to Solow-Justman. And there were others.

One member of the *Star Trek* family at Justman's surprise party was the show's first "apprentice" assistant director, Charles Washburn. Not only was he one of the first African Americans to enter the Directors Guild of America's apprentice training program, he was the first African American crew member to work on the *Star Trek* series. Washburn arrived for the beginning of the show's second season.

Washburn stayed with *Star Trek* and became a full-fledged second assistant director for the show's third and final year. Justman became a surrogate father to "Charlie" in a relationship that has endured over the years.

In *Star Trek*'s second season, there was another relationship, and it was clearly destined for trouble. Its emotional and financial ramifications were still being experienced many years later.

BOB: The last time Jackie and I ever socialized with the Roddenberrys, Eileen seemed almost hostile. Actually, I couldn't blame her. I knew it wasn't that she didn't like anyone with whom Gene was friendly; it went much deeper than that. Gene was leading a new life, a separate life from which she was excluded, a life that centered more and more on Majel. Eileen's marriage was nearing an end. She was just plain unhappy.

This time, Gene invited us to dinner. From our previous outings with them, Jackie and I knew that they liked to collect and polish semiprecious jewels and set them into homemade jewelry. Jackie had about ten very small rubies, the remnants of some jewelry that her mother had given her. While small, they were quite pretty, though probably worth no more than two or three hundred dollars. We decided to give them to Eileen as a present, something she could use for her hobby.

When we gave them to her, she didn't say "Thanks" or "Oh, you shouldn't have." Fact is, she didn't say much of anything else that night. Gene looked embarrassed, but, afterwards never said anything to me about it.

When we got home that night, Jackie simply said, "Well, another fun evening with the Roddenberrys."

I took her comment as a hint. Once burned, their fault; twice burned, our fault. While we continued to socialize with Gene and Eileen at a party or other group gathering, as couples we didn't get together after that. The tension had made things too uncomfortable.

One of those gatherings was a Sunday-afternoon party the Roddenberrys hosted at their large Holmby Hills home on Beverly Glen. Howard Rodman, Chris Knopf, E. Jack Neuman, Richard Simmons, Gene Coon, and other writer friends were among the guests. Intelligent people spoke quietly to each other. It was a beautiful sunny afternoon, and it seemed as if time were passing slowly.

Gene Coon and I had become good friends. My wife, Jackie, and I had socialized with him and his wife, Joy. Joy was an artist and had a penchant for wearing eyeglasses with outrageously colored harlequin frames. She was quirky, but both intelligent and genuine. Jackie and I enjoyed being with her.

Gene Coon and I stood together in the living room, sipping our drinks and looking out through the leaded-glass windows. Joy, Jackie, and some other women stood together in the sunlit, flower-filled garden. Joy was laughing, talking animatedly. It was an idyllic scene, one I'll never forget.

I turned to Gene. "Joy looks happy."

He nodded and watched for a while. He took another sip and turned to me. "She doesn't know it, but I'm leaving her tomorrow. She'll get the divorce papers in the morning."

I couldn't take it in, at first. What he was saying was monstrous, and yet he'd said it so matter-of-factly.

He continued, "I haven't told anyone yet. Only you."

I couldn't respond.

"I've found my first love, again—the girl I thought I'd lost forever. And we're still in love, just like before. We're going to get married." He raised his glass and drank again. His hand trembled. He was overcome with guilt. He had to unburden himself to someone.

I watched Joy laughing in the garden. She was happy, but after tomorrow that would all change. At this moment, I knew more about what would happen to her life than she did. And I knew Gene was suffering terrible guilt. I found Jackie and made some excuse, and we left the party.

I hardly slept that night. Tomorrow, Joy's life would be shattered. And there was nothing I could do about it.

Years later, Gene's friend, actor Bill Campbell, told me that Joy had, in fact, sensed something for several days prior to that fateful Sunday. Her husband had seemed preoccupied and strangely aloof. But when she queried Gene, "Is anything wrong? Is there something you're not telling me?" he assured her that everything was fine, that she was imagining things. So Joy supposed that he'd let the pressures of making *Star Trek* affect him too much.

Despite his feelings of guilt, Gene Coon was happy with his new love. As if it wasn't confusing enough dealing with the two Genes, we now had another Jackie to go along with my wife, Jackie.

Gene Coon and Jackie Mitchell had met at a radio school in Los Angeles. He was in his early twenties; she was only eighteen. They cherished their time together, but both were shy people, so their love for each other went unexpressed. Joy, Gene's future wife, also attended the training school, and they were all friends—so much so that after graduation, Gene, Joy, and Jackie all ended up working for the same eleven dollars a week at the same radio station in Virginia. But they soon went their separate ways, Jackie pursuing her modeling career and Gene and Joy eventually marrying.

What followed, over the years, was both pleasure and pain—all the trappings of a soap opera. Jackie Mitchell, then a successful model, saw Gene Coon, then a successful Hollywood producer and writer, being interviewed on television. She wrote to him, to say hello and recall the past, but purposefully put no return address on the envelope. The letter evoked such a loving memory of her that Gene hired a private detective and enlisted the aid of his secretary,

Andee Richardson, to try to find Jackie. Two years later the search finally bore fruit.

Jackie Mitchell, now working as an actress at Universal Studios in Hollywood, received a message from her agent to call *Star Trek* producer Gene Coon. Thinking it was for a job interview, she went to see him. After so many, many years apart, they met once again. They were inseparable after that meeting. Within the week, Gene decided to divorce Joy and marry his first love.

Jackie Coon was both charming and beautiful and, in her career as a model, had been the "legs" in the Hanes hosiery ads. We had dinner with them a few times. Gene seemed happier than I'd ever seen him before.

Now saddled with the costs of an expensive divorce and having to provide for both Joy and Jackie, Coon found that his *Star Trek* income wasn't enough to meet his obligations. So while continuing to produce and write *Star Trek*, he began to moonlight for other shows as a writer. Coon worked under at least one pseudonym: Lee Cronin.

Working an almost eighteen-hour day, Coon faced the impossible task of meeting the deadlines imposed by both *Star Trek* and his outside work. He was flirting with both physical and mental disaster.

At a story meeting with a longtime friend, Coon mistakenly showed the writer a scathing critique of the friend's story that had been prepared by Bob Justman. The writer, his sensitivities shattered, verbally attacked Coon, angrily telling him what he could do with Justman's memo, the story, and the assignment. Soon after, Justman went in and found Coon sitting at his desk with his head cradled in his arms. He was sobbing.

BOB: I wrote my last memo to Gene Coon on September 5, 1967, one day after the Labor Day holiday. He left the show that week, exhausted; he had come close to a complete nervous breakdown. Another shoe had dropped.

Coon's departure was a big blow to Roddenberry, who announced, "We'll have to find someone else to take his place. But no one will ever be able to fill his shoes."

What Gene meant was he would have to buckle down and work harder now—at least until he found a replacement.

HERB: With *Star Trek* now well into its second season, Gene Roddenberry had already achieved a semblance of the cult status he would later enjoy. Working hard and late in his office, as usual, Gene took a breather when I dropped by one night. He looked spent; the strain on him was obvious, but I thought it was all due to the pressures of producing a show like *Star Trek*. It turned out that there were other pressures, as well.

"I don't have enough time for everything in a single day, Herb." He took a drag on his cigarette. "And there are . . . aaah . . . all those . . . ahhh . . . women."

"Women?"

"Yes. They keep after me . . . ahhh . . . all the time. They all want me to . . . ahhh . . . father their children."

As Bob Justman later said, "Gene Roddenberry, the creator, had become Gene Roddenberry, the Creator."

With the renewals of *Star Trek* and *Mission: Impossible*, and with CBS ordering the *Mannix* series in addition, Desilu now faced a production year that would guarantee the studio would lose even more money. Saving dollars, therefore, became the order of the day.

Gary Morton yearned to be involved in the operation of the studio; he wanted something to do. As part of the "Save the Money" campaign, Gary proposed building an exterior "European Street" on the Gower lot. The street would feature a quaint cobblestone road bordered by European-style false storefronts. The theory was the three series, especially *Mission*, would "location" on the lot, thus saving substantial money.

HERB: Bud Brooks, head of the Desilu Art Department, carried a handful of plans and sketches into my office. "I'd like to go over the plans for the European Street, Herb."

"What European Street?"

"Gary's European Street. You knew about it."

"I thought it was a joke, Bud. There's no room on the lot to build a European or any other kind of street."

"It's no joke. Lucy's approved it and wants your input." Bud rolled out the plans.

It was another one of those old-guard games. They really didn't care about my input. What they cared about was my acceptance of the idea, tantamount to guaranteeing that all three series would use the "location."

"Something looks odd, Bud."

"Well, the scale is a little different."

"How different?"

Bud was somewhat uncomfortable. "Well, in order to fit on that little park area across from the commissary, all the buildings will be in three-quarter scale."

"Give me an example of three-quarter scale."

Bud became very uncomfortable. "Well, for example, Disneyland is built in three-quarter scale."

"Hold it, Bud. Gary is spending hundreds of thousands of dollars to build a Mickey Mouse European Street?"

"Lucy and Gary want *Mission: Impossible, Mannix,* and *Star Trek* to use it," added the talented but embarrassed art director.

"Please take a message to Lucy, Gary, Argie, Ed, and all others on the 'building committee': Peter Graves, Martin Landau, Greg Morris, and Peter Lupus are all well over six feet tall. Barbara Bain is nearly five foot nine. Mike Connors is six foot four, and Leonard Nimoy is over six feet. They would all look stupid and ridiculous in a three-quarter-scale set. Now Shatner could work on the European Street without wearing his lifts; that would make him closer to Mickey Mouse size. But he would never do that, and I would never ask him. So, folks, there is no way in Hell that any of the three series will ever work in Gary's folly."

"No input, Herb?"

"No input! But to protect yourself, Bud, leave the plans and I'll have Bob Justman and Barry Crane [*Mission: Impossible*'s Associate Producer and Production Manager] study them and express their own opinions."

After RJ looked over the plans, he had but one word to describe the European street: "Toonerville!" After Barry Crane looked over the plans, he had several words: "Herb, they're all very, very sick people."

During my time at the studio, the three Desilu one-hour series, and almost all the rental shows, never "locationed" on the European Street. Recently, a former Desilu auditor confirmed that the studio lost several hundred thousand dollars on Gary's pet project.

However, while Solow laughed at "Toonerville," there were few tears of joy in his eyes. With a zealousness to save money, he had made several budget decisions he would later have preferred not having made. Although they affected very little and weren't at all obvious to viewers, one of them, the modification in Sandy Courage's main title theme, was the most emotionally significant casualty of the budget wars.

Everyone on the show loved the soprano voice that soared high over Sandy's orchestral sounds. Although the audience wasn't aware of its presence within the music, its effect was palpable. The voice had a humanity that enriched the score. It was used in both pilots and all the first-season shows. But when Solow was presented with certain facts and figures, his love affair with the voice began to wane.

HERB: With the possibility of a full twenty-six episodes for *Star Trek* in its second year, the likelihood of postnetwork syndication became more of a reality. There would now be fifty-five one-hour shows to sell to local stations. And if the series was lucky enough to go into a third or fourth year, the possibility of financially breaking even became a small light, yet a light nonetheless, at the end of the tunnel.

Business Affairs had prepared a rerun cost schedule indicating who must be paid additional money every time an episode was repeated. It was pointed out that while no musicians would receive rerun fees under the agreement with the American Federation of Musicians, the soprano singer, Loulie Jean Norman, having been hired under a Screen Actors Guild agreement, had to be treated as an actress. She would receive rerun fees.

The money was small, but the issue was huge. If money could be saved for the rest of *Star Trek*'s life by replacing a human sound with an electronic sound, why shouldn't a reasonable and responsible management make the change? It was a good argument.

I called RJ and told him not to hire the soprano again for the new season. He wasn't happy, but the change was made. Since Sandy Courage never watched the series after the first season, he was totally unaware of the change until we informed him twenty-seven years later.

If I were faced with doing it over again, the soprano would have stayed. But we still wouldn't have "locationed" in "Toonerville."

BOB: As the search for cost-saving ideas continued, Herb Solow came up with one based solely on human greed. It was called the "Proposed Series Incentive Plan" and offered a bonus to directors who could bring their shows in for less (much less) money than budgeted.

"Good idea, Herb," I enthused. I knew it was a good idea but couldn't resist a dig. "What are you smoking? I want to change brands."

"It is a good idea, RJ. You're just jealous."

Herb's idea was creative, but practically speaking, it didn't help. With six-day schedules and seven-day scripts, directors Marc Daniels and Joe Pevney didn't have a prayer of ever earning an incentive bonus. Try as they might, it was all they could do just to finish on time.

"Nice try, Herb," I said later.

"You've missed the point," he explained. "Not only haven't we paid out any incentive bonuses, the shows did finish on time."

"Just like they always did?"

"Okay. Then how about directors paying us when they go over?"

In addition to the manifold scriptwriting and postproduction problems, Roddenberry began to have problems with Shatner. While Nimoy continued to press for improvements in his role, Shatner had very few complaints. He was the hero: He carried the storyline, handled most of the physical action, and got to make love, not war, when it came to the fair sex.

HERB: Bill Shatner's problem was rather more prosaic. It stemmed from complaints by directors and their assistants that no one could use the phone on stage because Bill was "always on the damn thing," and it was slowing things down. Inaccessibility to telephones is and has been the actors' lament since the days of Alexander Graham Bell. They had to speak to their agents—and girlfriends, stock brokers, fitness trainers, bookies . . .

To remedy the problem, I had another stage phone put in—now we had one for incoming and one for outgoing calls. Soon, both phones were in constant use, but at least company business could be handled in case of an emergency. But it

Courtesy Paramount Pictures

Dr. McCoy faces a gladiator in the episode "Bread and Circuses."

was still hard to pry Bill away from the phone when he was needed on camera. He continued to be a problem. Directors still complained they were losing time.

BOB: It wasn't all Bill's fault; he was in practically every scene. Since it was the only way he could transact his other business during working hours, he had to use either the phone on the stage or one in the *Star Trek* offices.

Tired of hearing daily complaints from the stage, Gene Roddenberry laid down the law: no more personal phone calls on stage. Bill, smarting from the reprimand, angrily countered, "Then put a private phone in my dressing room, and I won't have to tie up the goddamn stage phone."

Gene tried, but Herb Solow said, "No! If Bill Shatner gets a phone, then Leonard wants a phone, De wants a phone, Nichelle wants a phone, Jimmy wants a phone, George wants a phone, Walter wants a phone, and Majel probably wants a phone. And think about *Mission.* Peter Graves wants a phone, Marty Landau wants a phone, Barbara Bain wants a phone, Greg Morris wants a phone, and Peter Lupus probably wants a phone. And don't forget *Mannix.* Mike Connors will definitely want a phone. Even though they say they're all willing to pay for it, that isn't the problem. If you think you have a circus now, just wait until the assistant

directors try to get *all* the actors off their phones. The only Desilu actor on the lot who ever had a dressing room phone is Lucille Ball. And she owns the place."

Gene, caught in the middle, had to say "no" to Bill again. So Bill, his ego bruised, stopped speaking to Gene. And he continued to monopolize the stage phones—both incoming and outgoing.

HERB: Bill also failed to recognize that his single-minded approach to his role tended to alienate his fellow performers. They became victims of his need to dominate all the action. Only Leonard and DeForest were relatively safe. The others, especially Jimmy, George, and Walter, sometimes found themselves either shunted to the sidelines or deprived of the chance to deliver meaningful dialogue—or both.

On the recommendation of the departing Gene Coon, talented writer-director John Meredyth Lucas, while in the midst of a multiple writing and directing assignment on *Mannix*, was hired as *Star Trek*'s new producer.

The thirteenth episode of the season, "The Trouble with Tribbles," had finished filming just before Labor Day, and the next show, "Bread and Circuses," would begin on Tuesday, September 12. Even prior to his Monday, September 11th arrival, Lucas was already receiving stories and scripts from *Star Trek*. By the next day, he had become the new primary addressee of all the voluminous Justman story and script memos.

Lucas was no neophyte in the film business. His mother had written, among other screenplays, the original *Ben-Hur*. His stepfather was Michael Curtiz, the Academy Award–winning director of *Casablanca*. And having recently produced the very successful and star-driven television series *Ben Casey*, Lucas thought he had seen it all. However, his welcome on his first day of *Star Trek* was an eye-opener—even for him:

> Nobody was speaking to anyone else. Gene wanted me to meet the cast and crew, so he took me out to Bronson Canyon where the company was shooting on location. Shatner came around a corner, and when he saw Gene, he turned around and went the other way. And the cast was fighting too. All the actors complained to me about all the other actors.

Lucas settled easily into the difficult routine of writing—and rewriting—for *Star Trek*. But there was yet another surprise to come for the show's new writer-producer. On November 2, 1967, Lucas received a belated welcome in the form of a "Dear John" letter from Stan Robertson, which, compared to the complaint he later wrote to Lucas regarding "The Omega Glory," sounded even more ominous:

> This will confirm our telephone conversation of this afternoon in which I advised you that the ["A Private Little War"] rough cut was, in the form in which screened, unacceptable. Although we realize that certain cuts in the film have been made since our viewing, we have chosen to re-screen the film

and view the results of these changes tomorrow afternoon at which time we will decide on the acceptability of the episode.

We realize, John, that the episode in question was not produced by you but, as a guideline for the future, we must reiterate our position that the costuming, the implied sex, and the forms of violence as we discussed, are totally unacceptable to NBC for airing over our facilities.

We strongly urge that you pass our feelings along to your creative staff so that in the future we can avoid such a situation as we currently have facing us.

Unfortunately, John Lucas was unaware of the continuing skirmishes with Programs and Broadcast Standards. Bob Justman, however, was right in the thick of things.

BOB: Pains were taken to purposefully leave extra expletives in the scripts, so that Broadcast Standards could remove them. The expletives were bargaining chips to use when needed. There were times, however, when we used the actual film as the ultimate bargaining chip.

In "A Private Little War," Marc Daniels had directed a scene in which a shapely primitive maiden—played by actress Nancy Kovack (later to wed symphony conductor Zubin Mehta)—bathed beneath a small waterfall. We intercut that shot with one of a nearby Captain Kirk, staring at the maiden—and visibly salivating. Since Nancy was, indeed, nude to the waist, Marc made sure that she was carefully turned away from camera. Nonetheless, if the viewer strained very hard, an occasional small portion of Nancy's breast could be seen. Ed Milkis viewed the episode with me before we submitted it to Broadcast Standards for approval.

Ed Milkis was aghast. "Bob, how the hell are you gonna get away with that shot? Broadcast Standards will have a heart attack. They'll cut it down to nothing."

"How long does the shot run, Eddie?"

"Oh, about fifteen feet [ten seconds]."

"We've got more, right?"

"Sure, lots more. But we'll be lucky to keep half of what we've got in there now."

"Tack on another fifteen feet and send it over."

"You dirty dog." Eddie grinned. The extra footage was added, and the show was dispatched to Burbank.

Bear (or bare) in mind that when the "A Private Little War" script was first submitted for approval, Broadcast Standards had advised:

"Please make certain that Nona's behavior . . . is kept within the bounds of television propriety; caution also on her costuming. Caution on the embraces between Nona and Tyree and, later, between Nona and Kirk; avoid the open-mouth kiss."

When the restored episode was screened by Broadcast Standards, their reaction was predictable. "You can't show this sort of thing on television. Why, you can actually see part of her . . . her . . ."

"Tit?"

"Breast, Bob, breast. You'll have to lose the shot."

"This is a major story point. We can't take it out!"

There followed lengthy haranguing by both sides. Finally, like reasonable people, we reached an acceptable compromise. "If you cut the shot down by half, Bob, we'll approve the episode."

"Great! Thanks. . . ."

"After you send it back with the trim already made."

"Don't you trust me?"

"Of course we do, but send it back just in case."

We removed the added footage, and they approved the show exactly the way it was originally cut. They got what they wanted—and so did we.

But the real surprise came when NBC's Program Department screened the show. Not even Stan Robertson liked it, even though there was lots of action, lots of hairy primitive aliens clad in furry animal skins running around and shooting each other with bows and arrows, lots of mumbo-jumbo incantations and healing with mysterious jungle herbs—and lots of jeopardy for Captain Kirk and company.

"A Private Little War" was eventually approved by one and all and was first broadcast on February 2, 1968. Surprisingly, Stan Robertson never seemed to realize that the story was supposed to be an allegory about the growing "police action" in Vietnam. In fact, no one at NBC made the connection and took us to task. But the audience did; we got letters. Lots of them.

HERB: It was generally understood that low-rated shows always did better in the summer, as viewers watched those they chose to avoid during the fall, winter, and spring. And during the summer months, the ratings did in fact increase. But as the summer reruns ended and *Star Trek* premiered with a new day and time, its ratings again began to slide.

Gene Roddenberry always felt that if the show had retained its original time, ratings would have continued to build as it attracted new converts. However, Gene was thinking with his heart, not with his head. Networks existed only by delivering entertainment to a mass audience. With a projected sixteen million *Star Trek* viewers, even adding an additional million during the 1967–68 television season wouldn't enable NBC to attract enough advertiser dollars to pay all the bills.

The building-block theory, that the lead-in series would deliver additional audience to *Star Trek*'s new Friday night time, unfortunately remained a theory. There was a major financial problem. If the share of audience wasn't high enough to convince NBC to pick up the additional ten episodes, *Star Trek*'s episodic costs would be horrendous.

While *Star Trek*'s status remained tenuous, it was quickly becoming the darling of popularity polls. In *TV Week*'s Second Annual Poll, which listed "Favorites by Age Group," *Star Trek* was chosen favorite by the two most important age groups: twenty-to-thirty and thirty-to-forty. (*Mission: Impossible* took second spot in both age groups as well as in the "under twenty" category.) *Tarzan*, *Star Trek*'s lead-in, was well down in the *TV Week* standings at number thirty-one out of thirty-three series. *Tarzan* was most definitely a very poor building block.

But the *TV Week* poll and other newspaper polls around the country were unscientific contests. Series with ardent fans tended to win unscientific contests.

An oddball approach to measure *Star Trek*'s popularity dealt with the sales of *Enterprise* model kits. Until then, the most successful plastic model was the Munster model car kit, of which a million copies were sold in a period of two years. More than a million *Enterprise* model kits were sold in *Star Trek*'s first year of production. Obviously, *Star Trek* had tremendous appeal to younger viewers, a prime requirement for a successful television series then—as it is today.

But in the real world, the networks subscribed to the A. C. Nielsen Company; if you wanted to win, you won with *their* ratings and *their* share of audience.

Desilu, its agents, and Roddenberry—all entities with a financial stake in the series—continued to pressure NBC into ordering the last ten shows. There was seemingly no understandable reason for the network to do so.

BOB: "We're not going to help you out with preempts like we did last season," threatened Stanley Robertson, sitting in my office, a month before we went on the air. "You have to deliver on time, and that means ten days prior to airdate. This year, there'll be no excuses."

"We'll deliver on time, Stan—a week early for sure. We're scheduled to deliver at least ten days early, but based on past experiences, it would be damn foolish for us to guarantee it."

That wasn't good enough for him. Stan was on a tear; his tone hardened. "*Star Trek* is not a hit—definitely not a hit. I feel you should know, Bob, that if you have trouble meeting airdates again this year, your show's position with us . . ."

His voice trailed off; however, I knew a threat when I heard one. But Robertson was a messenger; he wasn't in any position to threaten us. I resented the way he spoke—as if we were naughty children who needed a good scolding.

And there was a complicating factor, caused by the renegotiated second-year order of only sixteen episodes with an option for an additional ten. The option exercise date was October 16.

I cautioned, "Stan, you ought to know that we'll finish our sixteenth show on October fifth."

He didn't understand the significance of that date.

"It means we'll have to shut down that night and then wait until October sixteenth for NBC to make up its mind. That's almost two weeks we're going to lose for postproduction on shows seventeen through twenty-six, and it's bound to affect our deliveries. Of course, if NBC doesn't order the last ten shows, then this discussion is all academic."

Stan's face was a study.

"We'll probably lose part of our crew because we can't afford to carry them while we're waiting for a pickup. That's really going to hurt. Also, because the earliest we could start up again would be October seventeenth, we had to make directorial commitments on that basis. So if we're picked up early and continue to work without laying off, we might have to pay off a director or two for shows they'll never shoot—but that's still better than shutting down."

Stan left my office shortly thereafter. I hoped he would carry the message regarding the need for an early pickup back to headquarters.

A month later, Herb Solow pressured NBC into making a commitment for two additional "interim" episodes, making a total of eighteen shows and thereby avoiding a production hiatus. NBC finally ordered the remaining eight shows, nineteen through twenty-six—but not until October 18.

And sure enough, owing to the resultant late change in directorial assignments, we had to pay off a scheduled commitment to director Vincent McEveety. True to form, NBC Business Affairs reneged on the agreement to reimburse us for the additional costs. I got pissed all over again and complained to Herb Solow.

Herb's response? "RJ, this is the television business. We're paid to put up with lunacy." Then he grinned. "But look at the results. We got the last ten shows."

It was official. On October 18, 1967, Herb Solow sent a memo to "ALL CONCERNED."

Solow's memo informing "All Concerned" that NBC had ordered a full twenty-six second-season episodes.

FORM 40

PARAMOUNT TELEVISION PRODUCTIONS, INC.
INTER-OFFICE COMMUNICATION

Date October 18, 1967

To ALL CONCERNED

From Herbert F. Solow

Subject STAR TREK

Please be advised that NBC has picked up its option to guarantee a minimum commitment for this season of 26 episodes.

H.F.S.

Courtesy NASA JPL

Scientists from the Jet Propulsion Laboratory wearing Spock ears while monitoring the *Mariner V* on its October, 1967, fly-by of Venus.

It seemed that things were looking up for *Star Trek*. With a total of fifty-five episodes guaranteed, the odds for a third season, if not more, seemed to improve.

Although Roddenberry later claimed that NBC executives didn't understand *Star Trek*, many of them not only understood it, but actively supported it. During the second season, Stanley Frank wrote an article for *TV Guide* entitled "Who Said TV Had to Make Sense?" He quoted "'Dave' Klein, VP, Audience Measurement, NBC":

> Take *Star Trek*. The scripts have no scientific validity. The producer and the writers haven't the foggiest notion about the operation of a space ship or conditions on other planets. I am not putting you on. They don't know what the hell they are doing. But every week we get hundreds of letters with long analyses of what's happening. Viewers develop the stories through their fantasies.

Herb Schlosser sent a copy of Klein's response to "Coon, Roddenberry, Solow." Klein, whose first name is actually Paul, wrote to *TV Guide*:

> Statements attributed to me concerning the program *Star Trek* in Stanley Frank's article on McLuhanism are incorrect.
>
> Contrary to being without "scientific validity" (a phrase I have never used in my life), *Star Trek* is the only scientific fiction show on television *with* a scientific basis. It is fiction, though, and it is television and it does allow the viewer to participate. In fact it allows the viewer to go beyond even the scope of the writer.
>
> I was instrumental in recommending *Star Trek* for the NBC schedule last year and have been one of its staunchest supporters during the agony of renewal time.
>
> Messrs. Roddenberry and Coon and the whole *Star Trek* staff have deserved the public's approval, NBC's faith in them, and as topping to the cake, were just honored by the National Space Club in Washington for their *scientific validity*.

A new corporate player had recently arrived on the scene. Charles G. Bluhdorn, Board Chairman and founder of Gulf & Western Industries, Inc., had come west to Tinsel Town to mix it up with the Hollywood types. Bluhdorn, who had started his multimillion-dollar business by making automobile bumpers, was now going to make movies. In October, 1966, he bought Paramount Pictures, Desilu's immediate studio neighbor to the east. The word was that Bluhdorn wanted also to move heavily into the television production business. The word was accurate. Shortly thereafter, former CBS Network Vice President John Reynolds was announced as the new President of Paramount Television.

HERB: Corporate, bright, and personable, John was one of the more highly respected television executives in town. I knew him from my CBS days, so it was no surprise when, several weeks later, John called and suggested we have lunch. It was the very best of good-neighbor policies.

By the time we ordered our desserts, however, John made a proposal. Paramount needed someone to take care of television development and production. Would I be that someone? His overture was very unexpected; it required thought well beyond dessert. The reemerging Desilu had been a success story, so why abandon it now? On the other hand, each Desilu day was a battle with "the forces of yesterday," and it didn't seem to be getting much better. Why continue to put up with the madness? I asked John to give me some time to think it over.

Several weeks later, after a particularly upsetting occurrence involving Ed Holly and his numbers game, I called John. But before I could accept his propos-

DAILY VARIETY DAILY

Vol. 135 No. 45 Hollywood, California - 90028, Friday, May 5, 1967 13 Ten Cents

SOLOW IN NEW JOB AT OLD DESK

NEWSMEN MAKE WEIGHT FELT WITHIN AFTRA

Network newsmen now have a place on the national board of American Federation of TV and Radio Artists, as well as guaranteed delegate status at the upcoming annual AFTRA convention.

AFTRA national board has adopted a rule which will add eight newsmen members to the board: three each in L.A. and N.Y., and one each in Chi and Washington. Three-year terms apply for all.

A dozen special newsmen convention delegates also are now assured, four to come from here and N.Y. and two each from Chi and Washington. The L.A. convention group, now at 126 in number, thus will be increased to 130. One rep each from the local ABC, NBC and CBS News staffs will be assured, the fourth to be determined from the next highest votes received.

This new representation of newsmen, on paper and in reality,

(Continued on Page 16)

Stan Bergerman Gives 20-Bed Wing To M.P. Hospital

Stanley Bergerman, former Universal producer and now a real estate broker and developer, has gifted the Motion Picture Relief Fund with an undisclosed amount to finance a 20-bed hospital wing, now under construction at the agency's Country

(Continued on Page 4)

Pat Boone, NBC Agree To Terminate Program

Pat Boone and NBC have mutually agreed to the termination of his contract as star of a daytime stripper, effective after his 184th taped show July 1.

Actor-singer asked out so he can accept flock of bookings in clubs,

(Continued on Page 16)

Jack Warner Tells Court TV Spots Didn't Hurt Stevens 'Sun'

Jack L. Warner yesterday testified that George Stevens' "A Place In The Sun" was, and is, an "excellent" pic — so good that in the last year he screened it for Warner Bros. producers and directors, because he explained he cannot get directors to use dissolves such as employed by Stevens in "Sun."

Praise notwithstanding, Warner, who appeared as one of Paramount's defense witnesses, said that the March, 1966, NBC-TV airing of "Sun" did not harm the pic. Blurbs, he added, were well-placed. As a professional, Warner said, he follows the story.

In routine documentation of

(Continued on Page 17)

Skelton's CBS Summer Sub His Own 'Spotlight'

CBS-TV has made a firm 26-week commitment for a new series, "Spotlight," to be produced by Red Skelton's Van Bernard Productions in England, by ATV.

Series, consisting of 26 music and comedy hours, will begin airing in June in the slot now occupied by the Skelton show, will be seen for 10 weeks, during the summer hiatus. Thereafter the "Spotlight" shows will be aired as spex during the regular season.

It's an unusual deal, one with a hands-across-the-ocean concept, utilizing British and U.S. talent.

Seymour Berns, producer of Skelton's series, will be exec producer of the series, and Howard Leeds and Bernie Rothman are writers.

Each show will have two co-hosts, at least one an American,

(Continued on Page 16)

Par To Finance 'Brotherhood'

Paramount will finance and release "The Brotherhood," an original script about U.S. underworld by Lewis John Carlino which Kirk Douglas and Martin Ritt will produce under their joint Bryna-Ritt banner. Package, previously reported, stars Douglas under Ritt's direction. Film rolls Sept. 15, with shooting in Sicily and N.Y.

Prior to "Brotherhood," Douglas will star in "The Pineapple Print" for Universal, and after it, Ritt remains at Par for "The Molly Maguires."

Phyllis Diller Seeks Vegas TV Station License

Washington, May 4. — Phyllis Diller may not fit the image of a television executive, but she has applied at Federal Communications Commission for Channel 13 in Las Vegas, off the air since the FCC took away the license of KSHO-TV. Miss Diller owns 80% of Diller Broadcasting Corp., one of a number of applicants for the channel. The cut-off date for applications is now past, and all will be thrown together in a comparative hearing.

Among the other applications are filings by Meyer "Mike" Gold, who runs KLUC, AM-FM, Vegas, on behalf of Clark County Communications Inc., and Lotus Television of Las Vegas. The latter is a joint venture by Lotus Theatre Corp. and Leonard Hornsby and has ties to KENO, Vegas AM.

LEAVES DESILU TO HEAD PAR'S TV PRODUCTION

By Dave Kaufman

Herbert F. Solow has resigned as production veepee of Desilu Productions to become production chief of Paramount TV Productions, but won't even change offices in the process.

Unusual situation derives from the fact that Gulf & Western, which owns Paramount, has reached an agreement to buy Desilu, and that deal is now being finalized. Consequently, although Solow has exited his Desilu position, he retains his office, and will continue to supervise its series.

Solow's official title with PTV, of which John T. Reynolds is prexy, is v.p. in charge of programming. Reynolds had been in negotiations with Solow for some time anent his taking over the PTV post, even before Gulf-Western had reached agreement with Desilu on the buyout.

Just how the two operations—Desilu and Paramount—will mesh

(Continued on Page 16)

3-Ply Univ. Pact For Dick Simmons

Universal has signed Richard Alan Simmons to an exclusive producer-writer-creator contract for motion pictures and tv.

Simmons worked for U as a screenwriter in the 1950's. He last produced a Filmways tv pilot, which did not sell, was creator-producer of "The Trials Of O'Brien" last year.

Bout With The Boss? Take To The Air

New York, May 4. — WNBC manager George Skinner, who received critical praise for his stand-in work as a news commentator during the AFTRA strike, is reportedly joining KNBC-TV as a news air talent.

Skinner took over WNBC a couple of years ago and launched the New York flagship's talk-news format. Format has never really taken off, and Skinner in recent months has been hassling with Stephen Labunski, ever since the latter became president of the NBC Radio Division (he had been prez of the radio network, but recently took over as chief also of the radio o&o's).

The front page of *Daily Variety*, which announces Solow's new position as V. P. of Paramount TV Productions.

From the collection of Herbert F. Solow

(l. to r.) Joseph Gantman (*Mission: Impossible* producer), Bruce Geller (*Mission: Impossible* creator), Herb Solow and his daughters (Bonnie, Jamie, and Jody), Gene Roddenberry, and Wilton Schiller (*Mannix* producer) at good-bye birthday party on stage for Herb Solow, who was "leaving" Desilu to join Paramount.

al, John removed all choice by advising that Gulf & Western was preparing to buy Desilu. The bottom line was, whether I rejected his offer or accepted his offer, I'd still end up running television production for Paramount.

In February of 1967, Gulf & Western announced their intention to acquire Desilu, for which they would pay $17 million. Since Gulf & Western had already acquired Paramount Pictures, it proceeded to merge the two neighboring studios. In early May, Herb Solow officially resigned his position at Desilu and was appointed "Vice President, Programs, Paramount Television."

HERB: The Desilu mimeograph machine worked overtime as Lucy prepared her "sincere" thanks to her employees. After four years of rebuilding a dying studio, I received the "To all employees" mimeographed memo advising:

". . . I have sold the studio. Thanks for everything. Love, Lucy."

And there was that little heart logo from *I Love Lucy* at the end.

I probably should have been thankful for the mimeographed memo. It was better than a letter bomb.

Though the actual legal and official closing date of Gulf & Western's acquisition of Desilu was July 27, 1967, Lucy returned to the studio one day earlier, to participate in a ribbon-cutting ceremony. Sharing a pair of scissors, Lucy and Charlie made the cut, and the flimsy metal fence that had separated the two studios for generations came down. Whether Lucy expected her Desilu Productions to continue as a Paramount Television production arm was, and is, subject to debate. But the bottom line was that *Star Trek*, *Mission: Impossible*, and *Mannix* now belonged to Gulf & Western and Paramount Pictures. History would show that Gulf & Western's purchase of *Star Trek* alone, the low-rated, money-losing second-year series on NBC, would become one of the most spectacular business moves in entertainment history.

Courtesy Greg Jein

22

If They Give You Any Trouble, Screw Them!

HERB: In the later summer of 1967, my secretary, Lydia, received a call from John Reynolds's secretary. The Gulf & Western financial people had looked over the Desilu production figures and were concerned. Charlie Bluhdorn wanted to visit the *Star Trek* set to see, for himself, exactly what was going on.

Since I still kept my old office, I walked across the lot to the Paramount side and met Bluhdorn. As we walked toward the *Star Trek* stages, I could see the great verve and drive that had made him so successful. I could also see that Charlie hadn't the slightest idea how films were made.

No one on the set recognized Bluhdorn, and my being there was no big deal. So it was business as usual. Director Marc Daniels made several takes in order to get the correct look on Shatner's face. Nimoy's head turn took a couple of takes and Nichelle Nichols's "hailing frequencies open . . ." went on for at least five takes.

Bluhdorn continued to stare in utter disbelief until he signaled me to join him outside the stage.

"Listen, Herb, it's obvious why that 'Star show' is costing so much money. Why do you let the director shoot the same scene over and over again? It's just not cost-effective. I want it to stop."

Charlie walked back to the Paramount side of the studio muttering something about Hollywood "crazies." And I quickly realized I'd jumped out of the frying pan and into corporate America. But there was more of corporate America yet to come.

BOB: Soon, another shoe was about to drop. And this shoe was a heavy one. When it hit the deck, it sent out a shockwave that registered high on the studio's Richter scale. And mine too.

HERB: An ideological disease had spread throughout the East Coast business community. Unfortunately, it had been carried to the television production business by the corporate thinkers at Gulf & Western. The disease was called MBA, and it supposedly had originated at the Harvard Business School. Being an Ivy League graduate myself, I foolishly thought perhaps I'd be immune to the cancerous ideology. That was not to be the case.

Soon after Desilu's absorption, it was time to forecast the future of Gulf & Western Industries. Each division was called upon to prepare its own five-year plan that would be presented to the Gulf & Western Board of Directors. A select Senior Executive Committee was established to oversee the preparation of this event. One of the committee members contacted me and explained the coming exercise. Actually, he had first contacted Paramount Television President John Reynolds, and John referred him to me. I appreciated that because production was the principal activity at my division, Paramount Television. A guideline memo would be sent to me, after which an informal meeting would be held to finalize our approach to the formal presentation.

Several days later, a twenty-six-page outline arrived at my office. I read the guidelines and called my committee guy—with questions.

"Could you please tell me what is meant by my 'product line'?"

"Your product is your product line."

"You mean, like *Star Trek*?"

"Correct. *Star Trek* is a component of your product line."

"Okay. Now, there's a term, ROI. What does the French word for 'king' have to do with television?"

My committee guy was getting upset. "No, no! ROI refers to your 'return on investment'!"

"Ah-h-h. Now, one of the questions refers to how I propose 'enlarging our market potential.' Could you explain that to me?"

My guy was getting downright nasty. "How to increase the number of your buyers, of course!"

"You mean how do I make more networks? Is that it?"

"Well, I guess so," affirmed my committee guy. "Anything else?"

"No. Nothing else." That was quite enough.

BOB: Herb came by and showed me the "plan" he was supposed to implement. "What do you think, RJ?"

I read it, unbelievingly. "We don't manufacture widgets here, Herb. Don't they know this is show business? This whole thing is f.....g gobbledegook!"

"I thought it might amuse you."

"It's Loony Tunes time. What are you going to do?"

"I'll think of something."

HERB: The select committee arrived and, after first meeting with the Paramount Motion Picture Division, they showed up in my conference room. The eight-man committee was very serious and very formal. They all wore ties. I was a little uncomfortable and somewhat embarrassed, as my L.L. Bean pullover shirt was wrinkled and faded.

The head man explained that he had previously been the Director of Advertising for the American Safety Razor Company and therefore was well versed in television production, "so you'll have no problem discussing creative matters with me."

John Reynolds sat by my side hoping for the best as I rose to address the select committee. Considering the aftermath of the meeting, I could not have hoped for a more pleasant and understanding ally.

"Gentlemen, I have given very serious thought regarding Paramount Television's presentation to the Gulf & Western Board of Directors. As we are possibly the most visual component of all Gulf & Western divisions, the expectation would seem to be that Paramount Television would make its presentation utilizing the most advanced visual concepts."

They nodded.

"Therefore, Paramount Television, in order to accrue maximum potential, will not do the expected, but rather will employ one of the most important and highly revered educators in the United States to judiciously and succinctly present our new five-year plan."

They nodded and smiled. The American Safety Razor guy added, "Good thinking. I like the educational angle."

"Paramount Television will be employing as its spokesman that leading educator, Professor Irwin Corey!"

(Professor Irwin Corey was a crazed, outlandish, and pontificating comic who wore a filthy, wrinkled formal dinner suit, disheveled hair, and dirty sneakers. This undomesticated human being was hysterically funny and famous with TV audiences for running through the studio set of NBC's *The Tonight Show* and physically attacking the cameras.)

The select committee momentarily absorbed my proposal. Finally, each member of the committee responded with how much he loved the educator approach and applauded my choice of the famous educator, Professor Irwin Corey. They were very, very serious. John Reynolds, trying hard to control himself, led the select committee from my office.

Gulf & Western's "show-business acumen" convinced me it was time to move on. The following day I thanked John Reynolds for his many kindnesses and resigned my position. John later issued a press release attributing my resignation to "a difference over management policies."

Solow Resigns as V.P. Of Paramount TV

NEW YORK — Herbert F. Solow, vice president of Paramount Television Productions, a division of Paramount Pictures Corp., has resigned from that post, it was announced on Friday. John T. Reynolds, president of Paramount Television, attributed the resignation to "a difference over management policies."

Solow formerly held the same position with Desilu Productions, which company earlier this year was acquired by Gulf & Western Industries, parent company of Paramount Pictures.

(Above) From the *Motion Picture Daily* front page. "A difference over management policies . . ."

Before leaving the lot that day, I spoke to Roddenberry. "Eugene, there's something you can do for me. I hope *Star Trek* will get a third year. And I sense you might not invite John Meredyth Lucas back—which I think would be unfortunate. But, Bob Justman has been the de facto producer and backbone of the series from the very beginning. I know it and you know it. But whether John Lucas, or someone else, handles the writer–producer chores, I really want to see Bob finally named Producer. It would be unconscionable if you didn't reward him for all he's done to make the show a success."

"I've felt that way all along, Herb. I'll take care of it."

"Great, Eugene. I'll call you in a couple of weeks; you can buy me lunch."

Two things never resulted from that conversation. One, Gene never bought me lunch. Two, he moved Bob up—but to Co-Producer. He hired someone else as Producer.

(During our book interview with him, John Lucas divulged that, near the end of that second season, Gene had confided to him, "Justman is not your friend." The truth is that Bob was very much John's friend and supporter, and he was horrified to hear this falsehood. Actually, Bob had always wondered why Lucas was not invited back for the third season of the show. We both still don't know. And neither does John Meredyth Lucas.)

My first call after resigning was to Herb Schlosser at NBC. "Schloss, tell me if you hear of anything around town. I just quit."

Two weeks later I was developing new television shows as Vice President of Television Production for MGM. At least MGM President Robert O'Brien had heard of Professor Irwin Corey.

I hated to walk away from *Star Trek*, *Mission: Impossible,* and *Mannix,* but the following year I had three new series on the air—*Medical Center* on CBS, *The Courtship of Eddie's Father* on ABC, and *Then Came Bronson* on NBC—upon which I would again be working with Bob Justman. And not long after that, Gene Roddenberry, Bruce Geller, and I would be working together on movies.

So much for MBAs in the television production business.

BOB: We were all sad when Herb left. He was the architect of Desilu's success, bringing to prime-time television three new one-hour shows: *Star Trek*, *Mission: Impossible,* and *Mannix.* During his tenure, he carefully selected the best creative talents he could assemble, browbeat the networks into buying what those talents had created, and protected us and the shows when threatened by network and/or studio executives. Without him, *Star Trek* would never have happened in the first place. And without him, *Star Trek*'s struggle to remain on the air would only become more desperate.

Even after Solow left Paramount, he continued to support *Star Trek*. On January 30, 1968, he wrote to Ronald P. Jensh at Jefferson Medical College Hospital:

> Your letter is most appreciated, and I am very happy to see that a carbon copy was sent to Gene Roddenberry. Gene Roddenberry is the creator and executive producer of *Star Trek* and is, in fact, the guiding creative mind behind the brilliant and inventive thinking that has made *Star Trek* probably the most fascinating show on the air. It is true that the series is on the verge of being canceled. It is also true that many important professional men have rushed to its aid, and for this the people who produce *Star Trek* and I are most grateful. Though my official relationship with the *Star Trek* series is ended, I have now become a television viewer and for that alone have great hopes that *Star Trek* can continue on the air.
>
> With your permission I will send your letter on to NBC. Thank you most kindly for taking the time from your busy schedule for jotting down your kind words.

BOB: With Herb gone, our new overseers didn't waste time getting down to the business of cutting the budget. They had an interesting approach, pitting science-fiction series against science-fiction series: *Voyage to the Bottom of the Sea,* a 7:30 CBS series primarily for children and the ultimate in "shipboard" series, versus *Star Trek*'s adult exploration of distant planets. It was the old apples and oranges ploy. Paramount Television President John Reynolds pointed out that *Voyage*'s budget was lower than *Star Trek*'s budget and leaned heavily on us to cut our show down to child-size.

I prepared a four-page memo for Gene to sign that listed twenty-six major areas where *Star Trek*'s costs had to be higher or where Fox didn't charge its show for elements that we had to pay to Paramount. Reynolds knew the difference. Perhaps now, I thought, we could get back to work without further interference.

But was I ever wrong! The old guard may have been gone, but the "new guard" were digging in their heels.

Paramount's Production Department dictated that *Star Trek*'s budgets be revamped to fit their budget forms and accounting charge numbers. Justman, Milkis, and Peters oversaw the conversion and, not surprisingly, the total per-episode revised budget came out a bit less, i.e., $185,000, as compared to a previous $187,500. However, after perusing a copy of the "Studio Facilities Agreement," they found much to be discouraged about. Items that previously had been included as part of "facilities and services" were now to be paid for—in cash.

Justman informed Roddenberry, "We are now considered to be paying guests instead of members of the wedding." So while the final budget figure was less than before, the final costs would be noticeably higher.

Justman complained, wryly, "I guess they don't appreciate us. We don't even get an 'attaboy' from them for saving money by continuing to use up all the old Desilu memo forms instead of ordering new ones from Paramount."

With Herb Solow no longer available to offer protection to *Star Trek*, Gulf & Western had made an end run. It would be the first of many.

Douglas Cramer, former Vice President of ABC, was hired to replace Solow. Recognizing the politics of coming into an ongoing operation, he didn't interfere with *Star Trek*; he was hired to develop new programs for Paramount, not play nursemaid to someone else's apparently unsuccessful series.

BOB: But those directly involved with *Star Trek* were concerned, and by the time the Christmas holidays rolled around, everyone was already asking, "When do we hear about next season?" They were aware that the changed time period hadn't resulted in better ratings. No one was really sanguine about our prospects.

Don Rode and I had made additions to the gag reel, which we showed to the cast and crew at *Star Trek*'s second annual Christmas party. Everyone enjoyed what they saw, but underneath there was a feeling of tension, especially amongst the cast members. They were working hard, and with dedication, for the past two seasons, but their egos hadn't survived intact. Those who had to play second fiddle did harbor some resentments.

So it was no wonder that they laughed even harder than anyone else at the gag reel shot where stuntman Jack Perkins had difficulty pronouncing the word *skewer*. As he waved his sword at Kirk and Spock, Jack was supposed to order his henchmen, "If they give you any trouble, skewer them!" Unfortunately, what he said was, "If they give you any trouble, screw them!" which is the way certain people came to feel that second season.

The film clip was taken from "Bread and Circuses," which Gene Roddenberry had rewritten as it was being filmed. After viewing the dailies, Gene wrote a memo to director Ralph Senensky in which he suggested that all dialogue should be "carefully enunciated in future."

Consensus had it that William Shatner was a "professional" actor in every sense of the word. And until that second annual *Star Trek* Christmas party on

Stage 9, there was never a clue that Captain Kirk couldn't handle criticism well.

During the course of the festivities, Shatner led a toast and made a short extemporaneous speech to the cast and crew. It was a pep talk in which he lauded everyone's work and predicted that *Star Trek* was finally going to be a big winner in the network ratings war.

Who knows? Perhaps he envisioned winning an Emmy for "leading actor in a one-hour drama series." If hard work had been a deciding factor, he could have won, hands down. As Shatner finished his remarks, predicting the series would grace the airwaves for many years to come, he basked in the resulting applause and headed for the bar.

"Fill her up," he said. While he waited for a refill, film editor Jim Ballas walked up to the bar for his refill.

"Nice speech, Bill," complimented Ballas.

"Thanks. Well, bottoms up."

"I'll drink to that," said Ballas, volunteering, "I've been cutting 'The Omega Glory.' It's a real turkey."

"Is that so?"

"You know, Bill, everyone says you're a real good actor . . ."

"Thanks. *I* like to think so."

". . . but you always telegraph your reactions. And in this episode, it's more of a problem than ever. It doesn't make my job any easier . . ."

"What???!!!"

". . . because they're so darned hard to cut around. The camera doesn't lie, you know. Why don't you . . . ?"

Shatner exploded. Nasty words were exchanged. People gathered around. Shatner yelled at Ballas; hard-nosed Ballas yelled back. Neither one gave ground. Fearing they would come to blows, several partygoers separated them. Later, Shatner went to Roddenberry and expressed his outrage. Jim Ballas, working on his last episode for that season, never finished cutting it. He was replaced by editor Bill Brame. Ballas didn't return for the third season.

And Shatner never won a "Best Actor" Emmy.

The last episode of the second season wrapped on January 10, 1968. It was called "Assignment: Earth" and had been planned by Roddenberry and written by Art Wallace as a spin-off pilot, an episode within the series that was intended to find its own life as a separate new series on the next NBC fall schedule. Roddenberry recognized that if *Star Trek* was cancelled, an *Assignment: Earth* series would keep him on the air—and employed.

Spin-off pilots always have the problem of trying to serve two masters and serve them well, as both a good episode and a great pilot. Recognizing that dif-

Courtesy NBC/Globe

Teri Garr and Robert Lansing from the episode "Assignment: Earth." Note Teri Garr's shortened skirt.

ficulty, Roddenberry not only spent more than his usual amount of time revising the Art Wallace script, he reinserted himself into all phases of the episode's production.

BOB: Gene got into everything: sets, props, special effects, casting of actors, casting of black pussycat, and costumes—especially costumes.

The clothes worn by guest star and potential new series lead Robert Lansing were not a problem. He wore what any self-respecting alien visitor would wear: a Brooks Brothers suit and sincere tie. But owing to Gene's odd taste in ladies' ready-to-wear, Lansing's costar, Teri Garr, made a fashion statement that set back haute couture at least several hundred light-years. I watched resignedly as Gene, up to his old tricks, kept costume designer Bill Theiss busy, taking a tuck here and a trim there, attempting to improve what was essentially a patterned woolen skirt that could have started life as my maiden aunt's throw rug.

Teri understood the machinations of show business, having come from a performing family, so she didn't object when, just before her first scene on stage, Gene went to work on her costume again. He kneeled down, gathered up her already scant skirt, and told Bill Theiss, "It's too long, Bill." Teri rolled her eyes.

Theiss objected. "But, Gene, her costume is cut on the bias. It'll look . . . silly."

Gene persisted. "No, it'll look great. Take three inches off." Bill rolled his eyes. Gene compromised. "Okay, two inches."

Theiss sighed, took Teri by the hand, and led her back to her dressing room. A seamstress followed them, also rolling her eyes. Five minutes later, they were back. Teri's skirt was appreciably higher.

"There," said Gene, "now it looks great."

Teri looked embarrassed as she was called to the set for her first shot. But Gene was pleased as punch. "Just great. That's something else again. Right, Bill?"

"Whatever you say, Gene."

"No, Bill, you just don't understand. We want the audience to notice her. She should look different—out of the ordinary."

"She does, Gene. Believe me."

Bill's sarcasm didn't escape Gene. He shook his head, smiling. "You're prejudiced, Bill."

"Call it biased, Gene," he said, "like her skirt."

Courtesy Stephen Edward Poe

(l. to r.) William Shatner, Unit Production Manager Gregg Peters, First Assistant Director Rusty Meek, and Bill Theiss dressed for the second-season wrap party on the last day of filming.

Despite Roddenberry's efforts, "Assignment: Earth" was neither a good episode nor a great pilot. It wasn't even a good pilot. In fact, it was well below average and was immediately discounted as a potential series by the network. So the second production season ended, not with a whimper—but not with a bang, either.

Owing to an earlier start on scripts, a more efficient and experienced staff and crew, and the existence of permanent sets that had already been paid for, the twenty-six second-season shows were brought in at the Paramount-mandated $185,000 per episode versus a cost of $193,000 for the first season. This meant a savings to the studio of $208,000—and it was accomplished despite new studio charges, contractual cast cost escalations, and Nimoy's renegotiated second-year salary.

BOB: By the end of the second season, Gene was spending more and more time away from work, having fun with Majel. He bought a motorcycle and dressed in black leather. Majel had a matching outfit. It made for quite a sight as Gene, astride a small Honda, motored away from the office and out the studio auto gate with Majel hanging on behind.

HERB: Very few images remain etched in our minds over a lifetime, but one of mine took place at the corner of Wilshire Boulevard and Barrington Avenue in West Los Angeles. It was a chilly February evening as my daughters and I sat in the car waiting for the traffic light to change. I glanced to my left to see what car was making all the racket, revving its engine for a drag strip blastoff, and looked squarely at a Honda with two of the most "with it" bikers I'd ever seen. They wore the finest of matching black leathers, boots, and black helmets; even the bike was shiny black. "It's surprising what crazy teenagers can afford nowadays," I marveled.

As I rolled down the window to get a better look at society gone wrong, the "teenagers" turned to check out their "let's burn rubber" competition. And I was looking into the faces of Gene Roddenberry and Majel Barrett. The shock was mutual. No one spoke. Finally, the light changed and they zoomed away.

One of my daughters inquired, "Daddy, was that Gene Roddenberry?"

"Gee, honey," I said, "I certainly hope not."

One Sunday afternoon, Bob and Jackie Justman walked into the very prestigious Biltmore Hotel in Santa Barbara for lunch. As they passed, they couldn't help noticing Roddenberry and Majel Barrett, dressed in full leather gear, enjoying a drink at the bar. The Justmans decided to lunch elsewhere, but worried whether the bikers would get back to Los Angeles in one piece.

But Justman became even more concerned when he discovered Roddenberry had stepped up his use of "harmless" substances. Roddenberry had graduated from taking pills to keep him awake while finishing rewrites to the use of other mood-altering substances.

BOB: Gene began to roll his own "cigarettes." He knew I disapproved and tried to convince me that "There's . . . ahhh . . . nothing wrong with 'grass,' Bob. You ought to try some. It has no . . . ahhh . . . bad side effects like booze and tobacco. It ought to be . . . ahhh . . . legalized, but there's too many . . . ahhh . . .

powerful groups opposed to it, like the . . . ahhh . . . liquor lobby and the tobacco companies."

I couldn't come to terms with what I had heard. I thought, "What are you talking about? You're an ex-cop. How long have you been smoking that stuff?" But I couldn't say it. I kept silent. After all, it was his life. But I was disappointed in him.

Gene saw me shake my head and he smiled. We never discussed the subject again.

Later, after Gene Roddenberry and Majel Barrett married, he pursued interests that had little to do with the television business. Life in the fast lane seemed to have its attractions for both of them, but especially for him.

Many years later, Roddenberry acknowledged to author Yvonne Fern, in her book, *Gene Roddenberry: The Last Conversation*, that he lived his sexual life by his own unique set of rules:

> I practice what I preach. There may be times when I feel like "dipping my wick" and I do so. When it's right. When it feels good. People may say "Oh, that Gene Roddenberry. He's no good. He's an unfaithful husband." I say unfaithful to what?
>
> . . . They may condemn me for breaking a vow they think I made. Whereas in fact, I didn't make it. I could never adhere to an agreement that deprived me of myself. Majel and I have our own agreement.

Perhaps, but agreement or not, speculation has it that she suffered as a result of her unqualified love for him.

BOB: There was another aspect of Gene Roddenberry's character—something that perplexed me even more—that we did discuss.

Gentle as he seemed, Gene sometimes displayed a sadistic side to his nature when, at parties and in Majel's presence, he hinted at affairs with other women. Her reaction seemed to please him. She looked stricken. I felt tremendous empathy for her.

Alone later, I called him on it. "That's kind of cruel, Gene. You hurt her when you say those things."

Strangely, Gene even took a perverse kind of pleasure from that. He smiled. "You're . . . ahhh . . . mistaken, Bob. You don't . . . ahhh . . . know her like I do. Besides, it . . . ahhh . . . adds a little . . . ahhh . . . spice to the mix."

A publicity still from the third-season episode "Spock's Brain." Courtesy NBC/Globe

23

First, the Good News: The Final Season

In November 1967, *TV Guide* carried a letter from a viewer complaining that the second season's episodes bore small resemblance to the promise contained in the first season's shows.

The viewer's concerns were discussed at great length by Justman and Roddenberry. Justman was particularly concerned with the direction the series had taken under the pressures of time, money, and NBC's desire to attract more viewers by moving the series away from science fiction–fantasy and more toward action-adventure.

BOB: Gene promised to pay more attention to the scripts still in the works for that season. "And next season, Bob, we'll concentrate more on mind-bending 'sci-

fi' concepts. And I'll write some originals, too. I've got some ideas that'll blow you away. That is, if there is a next season."

I smiled, knowing he had already begun masterminding his second "Save *Star Trek*" campaign.

The ratings hadn't improved at all since the move to Friday nights. Prospects for another season now looked bleak. But a new force had arrived. Trekkies! (At least, that's what they were called then. Today, they're "Trekkers.") Even before the annual Christmas-week layoff, Roddenberry was busy orchestrating his "Save *Star Trek* Campaign, #2."

At the September, 1966, World Science Fiction Convention, in Cleveland, Ohio, Roddenberry had met a determined science-fiction fan, "Bjo" Trimble, and her husband, John. He had charmed her into allowing his *Star Trek* costumes to be displayed during the fan-made costume competition. It didn't take him long to realize that Bjo Trimble was a force in the science-fiction fan cosmology. She had both the energy and the contacts to help him further *Star Trek*'s popularity and, therefore, his own career.

BOB: I had noticed a stranger lurking about our offices. She seemed to be friendly with Gene and was often in his office. When I came in, she usually left.

One day, I asked, "Gene, who the hell is that?"

"Oh, that's Bjo."

"Bee-joe?"

"Yes. She's got a lot of pull with our fans. I've hired her to help out on our letter-writing campaign."

***"Our* letter-writing campaign? *What* letter-writing campaign?"**

Whereupon Gene explained his renewal strategy. "I've hired Bjo to run our letter-writing campaign." The studio would reimburse him for her expenses on this massive nationwide effort. (Years later, I learned that Bjo was never "hired" and had volunteered to work without pay.)

Gene gloated, "We'll bury NBC up to their eyeballs in protest letters, Bob. They'll never know what hit them." Then he swore me to secrecy. If NBC were to find out that he was masterminding the effort, it would be all over for *Star Trek*—and him.

"If it ever comes out, we'll deny everything," said Gene. "It would be our ass."

"If it ever comes out, denials won't help," I said. "And it will be your ass, not ours."

After that, whenever Bjo and I passed in the hall, we'd say "Hi." But that's about as far as it went with us. She was busy doing her thing; I was busy doing mine.

Soon, Bjo's letter-writing campaign began to bear fruit. U.S. Postal Service workers began to complain about the poundage of mail they had to deliver to NBC. It seemed to be increasing exponentially.

HERB: It didn't take long for Herb Schlosser to call me at MGM. For the second year in a row, NBC was receiving thousands of letters protesting "the cancellation of *Star Trek.*" Schloss assured me that no such decision had been made; in fact, many programming executives favored a *Star Trek* renewal. NBC had begun to smell a rat, spelled R-O-D-D-E-N-B-E-R-R-Y. But in no way could they prove his involvement. And as the volume of mail increased and its often strident content was magnified, Roddenberry's campaign didn't endear the "Trekkies" to the harassed executives who had to cope with the man-made phenomenon.

As the volume of mail increased, Roddenberry crowed about it in a February 19, 1968, letter to newspaper columnist John Stanley:

> Thank you for the copy of the article you wrote on *Star Trek* for the *Miami Herald Sunday Magazine*. Splendid! All of us here in the production staff really appreciate it, as we do your genuine enthusiasm for the show and all the other help you have given us. As of last week we received ten thousand dollars advance story money for our third season and although no NBC schedule has been published, things look fairly secure for us. However, knowing networks, I won't believe it until I do see the published schedule and have the re-order firm in hand.
>
> On that score, we heard from a New York source that letters to the Network (probably counting too [*sic*] names on the many petitions received) passed the *one million* mark! It's hard to believe that figure and I'm trying to check up on it, but whatever the final tally, we do know the letters to NBC began to pique [*sic*] a couple of months ago and at one time I heard they received over two thousand a day. Whatever the final tally, it's obvious now it was the all-time-high fan response to any show, including the "greats" like PLAYHOUSE 90, ROBERT MONTGOMERY and others. As a matter of fact, some think it has shaken the Network's faith in the Neilsons [*sic*] and, indeed, I received some indication of that when I was back there a couple of months ago and talked to the Network's statistical and audience survey experts. We were off the schedule, wiped out, finished, about six to eight weeks ago. But the letters kept coming, increasing in volume rather than leveling off, upset them enough that a committee was formed of six Network Vice Presidents to investigate the matter. Shortly afterward, we began to reappear on the schedule again.

In his book *I Am Not Spock*, Leonard Nimoy maintained that the actual NBC count was 114,667 pieces of mail received between December 1, 1967, and March 1, 1968, of which 52,151 pieces of mail were received in the month of February. Roddenberry's estimate that "one million pieces" were received certainly differs greatly. Herb Schlosser states categorically that it would have been inconceivable that the network received a million pieces of mail. However, according to Alan Baker, who was Director of Program Publicity for NBC during those years, *all* reports of the *Star Trek* mail "counts" were greatly inflated. Baker was responsible for seeing that each and every letter received a reply. "During those days, NBC was very meticulous about responding to our viewers," states Baker. "I'm sure the other networks were also, but at NBC it was a very strong point."

The number of pieces of mail received by NBC when an average series was near cancellation, or had already been cancelled, typically fell between 2,500 and 4,000. A huge mail response protesting the cancellation of a series with intensely dedicated fans might go as high as 5,000 to 6,000 letters.

Prior to the campaign to save *Star Trek*, the high-water mark for letters received by NBC for any show concerned the announced televising of Ulu Grosbard's Broadway play, *The Investigation*. The drama dealt with Nazi war crimes and, through an error in executive sensitivity, was scheduled to air, without commercials, just prior to Passover and Easter. The mail response was overwhelming, causing NBC to reschedule the broadcast. Even the wife of RCA and NBC founder and television pioneer General David Sarnoff wrote in to protest the announced airing. According to Baker, the total number of letters objecting to the insensitive scheduling of *The Investigation* was 10,000 pieces.

"During the months of January and February, 1968, NBC's *Star Trek* mail count totaled 12,000 pieces," Baker states. "This was such an enormous amount for the NBC mailroom to handle, we had to hire two temporary employees to deal with the volume. The two worked a full week along with the regular staff just replying to the *Star Trek* mail. If we had received the amount of mail the *Star Trek* people said we received, believe me, I would have known about it."

Despite Roddenberry's contention that *Star Trek* was already locked into NBC's schedule, the network's Program Department maintained an ever-fluid, ever-evolving "possible" lineup for the coming season. Since no new pilots were yet completed, and important ratings of current series were yet to be received, there was no guarantee the possible schedule would come to pass. So whether Roddenberry's claims about being "off the schedule" and then "on the schedule again" were factual, or even meaningful, the flood of letters arriving certainly caught the attention of NBC.

HERB: In the mid-sixties students at the University of California at Berkeley had taught young people all over America that demonstrations were good and demonstrations worked. Find a cause; have a demonstration.

A college student at Cal State Northridge was also an intern on the staff of the NBC Press Department in Burbank. He worked under Press and Publicity Vice President Hank Rieger, one of the most highly respected professionals in that field.

It was just another business day in early January at NBC when two pieces of intelligence shattered Rieger's calm. The first came from Rieger's college-student

intern, who had insider news: "The Save *Star Trek* Committee is going to picket NBC."

"The what?" asked Rieger.

"I'm on this committee at the college. We don't want to see *Star Trek* cancelled. It's part of a big national movement."

"Well, we've been picketed before. You know, a dozen or so people with signs."

"This may be different, Mr. Rieger. I think there'll be more than a dozen. A lot more."

The second piece of intelligence came shortly thereafter; a representative of the Burbank Police Department tipped Hank off. A group of college students from Cal Tech had applied for and had been granted a permit to parade in front of NBC Studios. The informant warned, "Our department is going to mobilize. They're talking thousands!"

Now concerned, Hank Rieger went to see Herb Schlosser. "Herb, in all my years in this business, I've never heard of anything like this happening."

Schloss did not take the information lightly and arranged an immediate executive meeting to discuss NBC's response. In addition to Schloss and Hank Rieger, Program Vice President Jerry Stanley, Facilities Vice President Dick Welsh, and Legal Vice President Richard Harper Graham attended the meeting.

After each man made his point relative to NBC's legal responsibilities and community relations, the discussions boiled down to just who would represent NBC and meet with the "maddening" (purposeful pun) throng. Dick Welch and Dick Graham were ruled out, as they had very little to do with *Star Trek*.

"Don't look at me," suggested a worried Jerry Stanley. "You're head of the West Coast, Herb. You go speak to them."

"But, Jerry, you're responsible for programs out here and *Star Trek* is one of your programs. Besides, you're much taller and heavier than me. You could take a blow better."

"Then you come with me, Herb. I'll protect you with my taller and heavier body."

"No, I don't think so. Better still, we need someone who understands publicity and promotion—you know, relating to our audiences. Hank will go with you."

Hank was thunderstruck. "I will?"

Several evenings later, hordes of chanting, torch-carrying student demonstrators from Cal Tech, Cal State, Pasadena City College, and even USC, many of them holding placards and banners, paraded down Alameda Street and congregated on the lawn in front of NBC Broadcast Stages 2 and 4. And as Schloss and several other NBC executives watched from their windows above, Jerry Stanley and Hank Rieger walked out of the executive building to deal with the demonstrators.

The protest leaders very politely and succinctly spelled out their desire to have the series remain on NBC and presented a written declaration to that effect. Jerry and Hank made their very polite corporate statements: "NBC appreciates your interest in *Star Trek.* We, here on the West Coast, support a renewal. Your views will definitely be considered by our management in New York."

The meeting was never confrontational. If anything, it was more a love-in because the NBC Burbank Program and Press Departments did, in fact, support a renewal and had been urging top management in New York to give *Star Trek* another chance. Herb Schlosser and Grant Tinker had an expression to describe those series they wanted renewed, "p and p"—popular and proud. They both felt *Star Trek* was "p and p."

To this day, Hank Rieger feels the Burbank demonstration was one of the main reasons *Star Trek* was renewed.

And no one, absolutely no one, knew that during the demonstration, the real organizer sat on his motorcycle, wearing his helmet and watching, unrecognizable. Gene Roddenberry was smiling like a cat who just swallowed a renewal.

The phenomenon was also visited upon NBC New York, where in front of 30 Rockefeller Plaza, a sizable contingent from MIT, not to mention other prestigious Eastern seaboard colleges and universities, held their own "Save *Star Trek*" demonstration.

The protesters outside the NBC Burbank offices.

Courtesy Stephen Edward Poe

On January 9, after the march on NBC, Roddenberry wrote a gleeful letter to Asimov:

Dear Isaac,

Thought you would be pleased and amused by the following. On Saturday night about 300 students from [the] California Institute of Technology, supported by students from other local colleges, marched on NBC West Coast headquarters in Burbank.

Although we knew it was going to happen, it was the students [*sic*] idea to do it and we very carefully stayed out of the picture. I did ride my motorcycle up, disguised by the hard hat and plastic face shield, watched from a distance. I was pretty safe since I looked rather like a member of "Hells Angels" and this is hardly the image NBC executives have of its executive producers. Almost froze to death during it since the march happened at 8:00 P.M. and it was getting down to freezing in Burbank at that time.

Rather exciting. They marched from a nearby park and they could be heard coming several blocks away as they chanted various slogans. It was a torchlight parade, extremely well ordered and mannerly. They had a parade permit from the Burbank Police Department who stopped traffic at the intersections for the kids. In fact the Police were very complimentary. The students, were, as one would expect from Cal-Tech, very clever in their signs, music, and proclamation which was handed over to NBC Program Executives in a nice little ceremony. Placards read things like "We know [?] doesn't have

Courtesy Stephen Edward Poe

Note the "Mr. Spock for President" bumper sticker.

> a heart—but don't you General Sarnoff?", *"Star Trek* . . . si! Neilson [*sic*] . . . no!", and "Mr. Spock for President"! We all felt rather complimented in that we've never heard of another television show that has had its own student march and demonstration.
>
> The "Asimov telegrams" went out on schedule. About 250 of them. As with the student march and other things, naturally we have to stay out of the picture and plead total ignorance if confronted by our enemy the network. If they know we have any part in any of this, then the whole value of it is immediately lost. For some strange reason I don't feel at all immoral about such protestations of innocence on our part since the networks invented this silly game and made up the rules for it. . . .

On February 14, 1968, a month after "the march on Burbank," Roddenberry wrote a valentine to Chief Rex Andrews of the Burbank Police Department:

> This is a long overdue "thank you" for a splendid attitude and intelligent police work displayed by officers of the Burbank Police Department during the Cal-Tech "*Star Trek* March on NBC" last month. I have rarely heard so many compliments toward a police department. And it was particularly interesting that much of this comment came from high school and college age young people who too often display an "anti-police" bias. As a former officer myself (LAPD) I know that some such bias is merited but that much of it is not and as a citizen and ex-police officer I am very pleased that departments like yours are doing such an excellent job of not only eliminating reasons for such bias but also doing positive things to bring the police and young people closer together. You have the friendship of all here at *Star Trek*.

During this "Save *Star Trek*" campaign, NBC Vice President Herb Schlosser's private telephone number was disseminated. The obvious culprit was Gene Roddenberry, and he hinted as much to Herb Solow. But Roddenberry wasn't talking for the record, and the leaking of Schlosser's phone number resulted in a very annoyed executive and a very busy phone line. Schlosser could be heard saying:

"Hello. Who? How did you get this number? How dare you call me on my private line? What show? *Star Trek*? No, I can't promise you that! I said, I can't . . . . Yes, I know it's a good show. Okay, a great show. Okay, a very great show. Thanks for calling—but please, don't call me anymore. Are you threatening me? Who is this? I never heard of you. And tell your friends to stop calling me. I'll be sorry? Stop calling or *you'll* be sorry! I'm going to . . . I'm going . . . I'm going to hang up. I'm hanging up now! Good-bye. Good-bye!!!"

He slammed the receiver down. The phone rang immediately. "Hello? Who? Herb Schlosser? No, no one here by that name. You have the wrong number. Sorry!"

While Roddenberry's reach was not yet global, much less interplanetary, it definitely was transcontinental. A fan, Wanda Kendall, was flown by Roddenberry to New York from Los Angeles, where another devoted fan, Joan Winston, had helped stir things up outside NBC New York on behalf of a series renewal. NBC had been outflanked.

Neither NBC nor participants in the "Save *Star Trek*" campaign ever realized that Roddenberry was recompensed for a December, 1967, expense listed as "Round Trip Air Fare—Miss Wanda Kendall LA-NY-LA (SAVE *Star Trek* Campaign) plus cash for expenses. $350.00."

Roddenberry's memo regarding the "expenses" he incurred in his secret campaign to save the show.

Desilu Productions Inc.

Inter-Department Communication

TO EMMET LAVERY JR.

FROM GENE RODDENBERRY

DATE March 12, 1968

SUBJECT Expenses

Dear Emmet:

Per our discussions, here is a list of expenses which I personally incurred in regard to the SAVE STAR TREK Campaign.

1/68	Copy Master- 5,000 Bumper Stickers-(Less $100.00 donated by M.S.E.I.) Mr. Spock For President $303.52
11/67	A.A.A. Glass Co.- 54 Sets STAR TREK Glasses- for publicity, fans, public relations,press (Gifts) $263.00
12/67	Round Trip Air Fare- Miss Wanda Kendall LA-NY-LA (SAVE STAR TREK Campaign plus cash for expenses. $350.00
11/67	Pacific Athletic Company-STAR TREK Tee Shirts. for promotion purposes. $60.60.

TOTAL: $977.12

But phone calls, letters, and mass picketing weren't the only harassing tactics. One evening, as NBC executives in New York left for home, they were annoyed to discover "Mr. Spock For President" bumper stickers affixed to their automobiles parked inside a secure area. Wanda Kendall's mission had paid off. But no one associated with the campaign came forward to claim credit for the unusual political statement.

However, on March 12, 1968, Roddenberry wrote a memo to Paramount Studio's Emmet Lavery, Jr., in which he requested repayment for "expenses which I personally incurred in regard to the SAVE *Star Trek* Campaign."

The first item, dated "1/68" was for "Copy Master—5,000 Bumper Stickers —(Less $100.00 donated by M.S.E.I.) Mr. Spock For President $303.52."

Luckily for Roddenberry, the NBC executives never discovered the source of those very same bumper stickers. (M.S.E.I. was the public relations firm, McFadden, Strauss, Eddy, and Irwin. Among their clients were Desilu Studios and Gene Roddenberry. It was in their definite interests that *Star Trek* be renewed.)

NBC executives reacted angrily to all the manipulation, but for the second year in a row, in an on-the-air live announcement, *Star Trek* fans were informed at the close of the March 1 episode, "The Omega Glory," that *Star Trek* had been renewed for a third season.

Roddenberry had already heard the news and, after the announcement, sent a telegram to the cast confirming that they'd have a third season together. Leonard Nimoy, ever on the alert to "protect his character" of Mister Spock, buttonholed Justman to complain about the way his role had been written during the recently completed second year of the show.

BOB: Much of what Leonard said made sense to me. As he was the de facto star in *Star Trek,* the better we made use of his talents, the better the series would become. As our resident Vulcan himself would put it, "It's only logical that Spock's importance be realized by all the writers and taken into account from the very beginning of the scriptwriting process."

So I suggested he put his beefs down on paper (yes, in a logical way) and present them in memo form rather than going to see Gene in person and running the risk of a possible confrontation. It wouldn't do Leonard any good to put Gene's back up against a wall. Better to let Gene digest the letter in private and think about its possibly useful ramifications before responding. My theory was, "You get further using a carrot than a stick."

Leonard wrote the memo on February 21, 1968, and sent me a "CONFIDENTIAL" copy of it along with a note of thanks. He began the memo by writing:

Dear Gene:

It gives me great pleasure to know that it is you sitting behind the Producers [*sic*] desk talking the stories with the writers for the new season. Deep inside me, I feel that your talent, your taste, and your efforts, will again

make *Star Trek* and "Mr. Spock" a fulfilling experience, in spite of the amazingly complex pressures which exist in this project. In short, I do believe that our goals are the same, and I would like to take this opportunity to express a few thoughts pertaining to *Mr. Spock.*

Leonard thereupon expounded at length about how ". . . in a brief time there were built in this character far more dimensions than one finds in a group of characters put together on television."

Leonard added:

> Public response indicated that we had done a *groovy* thing. The Scientists [*sic*] admired his logical precise and scientific mind. The Hippies [*sic*] dug his cool and his mysticism. The kids revelled in his strength and his sharp dry wit, to say nothing of his fascinating ears.

Leonard then summed up his complaints about the Spock character in the *"Second Season":*

> I shall try and be fair. There were some very gratifying moments. But, looking back from this vantage point, Spock seems to have added up to:
>
> 1) a raised eye-brow
>
> 2) "Fascinating" . . . "Logical" . . . "Illogical". . .
>
> 3) The "Spock" pinch
>
> 4) "I am sorry Captain, but at the present time, and with the present information, I am unable to give you anything more specific than that. . . ."
>
> 5) "The planet is Class M, Captain not unlike your Earth, and capable of supporting human life. . . ."
>
> 6) Some comedy sketch dialogue between Spock and McCoy, often petty in nature, and usually kept [*sic*] with "Gentlemen, will you please stop the bickering amongst yourselves, I need answers not arguements [*sic*]." (Captain Kirk)

Leonard next complained about being in scenes where he had nothing to do:

> Gene, I can't tell you how many times scenes were introduced with: Kirk and Spock enter, followed by several pages of dialogue during which we cut to Spock for a raised eye-brow, and finally Kirk and Spock leave, [*sic*] There were times when the writer had so completely forgotten that he had introduced Mr. Spock into the scene that he forgot to have Spock make the exit with Kirk, and tag the scene simply with *Kirk Leaves.*

After more examples of how badly his part was written, Leonard concluded with a passionate plea:

Please Gene, let Captain Kirk be a giant among men, let him be the best damned Captain in the fleet, let him be the best combat officer in the fleet, let him be the greatest lover in the fleet, let him be capable of imerging [*sic*] unscathed from a brawl with five men twice his size, but above all let him be a LEADER, which to me means letting your subordinates keep their balls.

Despite the "aggravation" he claimed he endured from Nimoy, Roddenberry—urged on by Justman—said he would "make things better" for Nimoy in the upcoming third season. He was elated with the pickup and the possibility of a favorable new time. When NBC President Don Durgin announced *Star Trek*'s renewal, he indicated a new time of Monday at 7:30 for the show. In subsequent conversations with network executives, Tuesday night was mentioned as an alternative. But Monday night appealed most to Roddenberry. Although no promises were made by NBC, he rejoiced to Justman, "Monday night looks firm, Bob. Looks like it'll be seven-thirty."

BOB: Gene seemed really reenergized. Finally, after what he had called a "disastrous move" to Friday night, it seemed as if we'd have a chance to become successful. He looked forward to higher ratings, and he promised to become fully involved with the show again. And he intended to satisfy Leonard Nimoy's complaints. With Gene back at the helm, *Star Trek* was now going to be better than ever.

It all sounded hunky-dory to me. With both Gene Coon and John Lucas gone, only the Great Bird of the Galaxy could work magic with our scripts. And he was enthusiastic about getting back to work. We had already received story money in advance of the renewal, and we put it to good use: Writers were already hard at work. The future seemed bright. It was just too good to be true.

Then another shoe dropped. NBC had been busy, juggling its lineup of shows in its attempts to solidify a successful schedule. We got a new time all right, but it wasn't Monday night at 7:30. We didn't even get to keep Friday night at 8:30. It would be Friday night at 10:00, a time that Gene knew would guarantee failure. Our audience was bound to shrink; high school and college students didn't stay home on Friday nights and, at 10:00, our younger fans were in bed and fast asleep.

Gene's enthusiasm disappeared. With the certainty that the third season would be the show's last season, he pulled back and began to investigate other, greener pastures. Just a little while before, he had promised NBC that he would devote all his energies to personally producing *Star Trek* as he had during the first half of the first season. Now, he just seemed to give up. And I wasn't the only one to notice.

Word of his attitude began to spread. I prevailed upon Gene, for the sake of morale, to effect some damage repair.

He sent a letter to everyone working on the show.

Star Trek

A DESILU PRODUCTION IN ASSOCIATION WITH NORWAY PRODUCTIONS

FROM THE LOG OF THE STARSHIP ENTERPRISE

March 28, 1968

Assume the Paramount production people have gotten in touch with you by now or will shortly do so. I am looking forward to working again with you on a third year of STAR TREK.

You may have heard we were somewhat disappointed with our Friday 10:00 P.M. time slot but we have been disappointed before and have confounded the experts by coming out on top. With your help we intend to do this again.

We will have practically the whole team back with us as far as we know now. My post on the show will be Executive Producer. Contrary to anything you may have heard, I intend to stay very much with the show and will give it close guidance and loving care. This will also give me some time to write some of next season's scripts myself -- as well as develop new properties on which you and I someday may be involved.

This marks the third year of STAR TREK and I have every hope that you and I will be together to celebrate its Bar Mitzvah.

Warmest regards,

Gene R

GeneRoddenberry

BCC: Mort Werner Herb Schlosser, John Reynolds Emmet Lavery
Leonard Maizlish, Alden Schwimmer

Will Love

APR 1 1968

HERBERT S. SCHLOS

Desilu STUDIOS · 780 NORTH GOWER STREET, HOLLYWOOD, CALIFORNIA 90038 · PHONE (213) HO 9-5911

Roddenberry's memo reassuring everyone that he would remain involved in the show in its third season.

Courtesy Greg Jein

From the episode "And the Children Shall Lead."

Gene made sure that NBC top brass were sent a copy of his message to the troops. Herb Schlosser scribbled a "Well done" on his copy and sent it back to Gene. It later proved to be a sad prophecy: Schlosser's office received his copy and date-stamped it April 1, 1968—April Fool's Day.

Everyone at *Star Trek* was reassured and buoyed up by the "good news" from Gene. George Merhof, the "thinking man's gaffer," sent a handwritten reply to Roddenberry:

> You must know that I am looking forward to another interesting and, I am sure, productive season with the *Star Trek* family.
>
> It is a comfortable feeling to know that you are going to be more closely involved this season. Although I have never had the feeling you had cast us adrift, I missed seeing you on the set at frequently as you were the first season. I shall be happy to be aboard.

Merhof's "comfortable feeling" didn't last long, as Roddenberry had no intention of fulfilling his promise. He didn't even go through the motions. It is a myth that Roddenberry was forced to "quit" the show because NBC had gone back on its word to schedule the show on Monday night at 7:30. He merely no longer saw a future for *Star Trek*.

With Roddenberry losing heart, Justman was the only one on staff who could keep everything together. He and Roddenberry had already discussed his moving up to full producer for the series' third year. Justman had already proved he could handle all the duties of a "line" producer and was confident he could ride herd on stories and scripts too.

In fact, on March 13, 1968, in a story memo on "And the Children Shall Lead" by writer Edward J. Lakso, Justman reminded Roddenberry:

> You will note that several ideas that I expressed to Ed Lakso have been utilized well by him in this story. . . . I mention these things to strengthen the point I made with you recently that I contributed heavily in a creative way to most of the properties we filmed [during] the preceding two seasons.

In addition to his usual responsibilities, Bob Justman was now acting as the de facto story editor, reading, analyzing, and writing reports to Roddenberry on all the unsolicited stories and teleplays arriving in the *Star Trek* offices every day. But Roddenberry had become so diffident that he seldom bothered to read Justman's comments.

There was really no one to handle all the rewriting chores. John Meredyth Lucas would write and direct a few episodes, but he was no longer on staff to rewrite other scripts. And Dorothy Fontana, busy on her own originals, couldn't devote much time to rewrites.

Justman had earlier discussed the problem with Roddenberry and, in a March 11, 1968, memo, had strongly suggested the immediate need to hire a skilled Story Consultant who could function as a rewrite man under his supervision. Roddenberry's response was, "Who would you recommend, Bob?"

BOB: It kind of boggled me that the Executive Producer couldn't find a Story Editor for his own series. The word was out in the somewhat incestuous writers' world that there wasn't much of a future writing for Roddenberry and *Star Trek*—and obviously Gene no longer cared enough to make even the slightest effort to find someone himself.

Although there were a number of fine writers whose work I respected, they preferred to freelance while trying to develop shows of their own. Story editing on a series was a thankless task; it took guts and gumption to rewrite someone else's words in the high-pressure world of television deadlines. And it helped, of course, to have talent. I winnowed my long list down to two contenders. One was available; one wasn't.

But before any Story Editor was hired, Gene had a surprise for me. "Good news, Bob," Gene said, smiling. "I'm going to keep my Executive Producer title after all. *Star Trek*'s going to have a new producer this year."

"Great, Gene." This was what I had waited for. I would finally get the title to go along with what I actually did. And there'd be monetary recognition as well.

"Fred Freiberger's coming in as our new producer next Monday. He'll be a big help to me riding herd on stories and scripts."

I'm sure the smile froze on my face. "Gene, I thought I was going to produce. That was the understanding."

"Oh, you will, Bob. Fred'll be Producer, and you'll be Co-Producer."

It was like a good news–bad news joke. Only this one was on me.

It took a while, but later, the reality dawned on me that neither NBC nor the new Paramount TV management team would have agreed to my becoming the show's sole Producer. To them, I was a "nuts and bolts" kind of guy, not someone with enough creativity to run a complicated series like *Star Trek.* But if Herb Solow had still been at the studio, things would have turned out differently.

HERB: Fred Freiberger was an experienced television writer-producer who also had the good fortune to be represented by Roddenberry's agent, Alden

Courtesy Paramount Pictures

Robert H. Justman's "Co-Producer" credit.

Schwimmer. Schwimmer had instant access to Roddenberry. In fact, Gene had interviewed Freddie prior to the first production year, but owing to a planned trip to Europe, Freiberger bowed out of any consideration. Gene Coon was hired later that year. With John Meredyth Lucas not returning for the third season's production, Roddenberry again turned to Schwimmer—and Alden again turned to Fred Freiberger. A meeting was held to discuss what producing *Star Trek* would entail.

Since Freddie had never written a *Star Trek* script—or story—Gene felt it important for him to write one before being considered for the job. Freiberger, not interested in auditioning, told Gene to buy him based on his past experience or hire someone else. Roddenberry, at Schwimmer's urging, made the commitment.

Gene was then confronted with a choice. He could step up and fight for the equally shared credit for Bob Justman, or he could take the path of least resistance and not fight for his friend and associate. Gene took the path of least resis-

tance. Fred was named Producer. Bob, who for two years had in actuality been the line producer handling every aspect of the show, was treated like an also-ran.

Gene was a stand-up guy for himself, but not, unfortunately, for others. Paramount Television and NBC preferred that a writer follow in the steps of Roddenberry, Coon, and Lucas as the producer of *Star Trek.* Television historically separated the producer function into creative and production, or "above-the-line" and "below-the-line," even though the two tended to overlap. In most instances, especially on difficult production series, the producership was equally divided. If the responsibilities had been divided on *Star Trek,* the Producer credits should have listed both Fred Freiberger and Bob Justman.

BOB: My anger had nothing to do with Fred personally. I liked him a lot. Understanding the difficulty of the situation, I helped indoctrinate him into the unusual world of *Star Trek.* I thought it significant, however, that Fred reported for work on April 1, 1968—April Fool's Day. He couldn't have known what he was getting into. Even so, the joke was on me.

Gene, Fred, Bill Shatner, and I met a week prior to production to discuss the *Star Trek* creative process. And a Friday night "getting acquainted" party was held on stage for both cast and crew. But the upbeat mood of the office staff and the shooting company had already begun to fade. Soon, *Star Trek* would no longer be a fun place to work.

Over the years, Freiberger had employed writer Arthur H. Singer in various capacities. Recognizing the immediate need for writing support, he saw to it that Singer was hired as *Star Trek*'s new Story Consultant, with his employment commencing on April 15, 1968. (Since Singer's salary was to be $1,000 per week, appreciably more than what Justman received, Justman's salary was increased accordingly.) Freiberger was unaware that Arthur Singer was one of the two writers whom Bob Justman had recommended to Roddenberry and whom Justman himself had intended to employ.

Singer turned out to be both bright and hardworking. But as the production season progressed, he sometimes became frazzled under the unrelenting pressures of the job, and the scripts suffered. The problem wasn't him—the problem was that Roddenberry stayed on his Olympian perch as Executive Producer and no longer did any of the rewriting. The "Roddenberry touch" was no longer present in the scripts.

But strangely enough, despite his failure to recognize Justman's important creative contributions to the series as well as his de facto Producer role, Roddenberry continued to depend on him to solve Roddenberry's problems.

On May 14, 1968, Roddenberry wrote a "*PERSONAL*" memo to Co-Producer Justman entitled "Actors & Scripts."

Desilu Productions Inc.

Inter-Department Communication

TO ROBERT JUSTMAN DATE May 14, 1968

FROM GENE RODDENBERRY SUBJECT Actors & Scripts

PERSONAL

Dear Bob:

Forgot to mention that I got a telephone call the other day from Bill Shatner who mentioned having read a yellow cover script of "The Last Gunfight". He was a little shakey about it but I quickly and I think thoroughly assured him that Fred Freiberger was aware of all the story problems and would clear them up.

The point of this, however, is to question whether or not we want to send our yellow cover versions to our actors as we have done in the past? Naturally, they are all very nervous as they have always been in the past over any change in producing staff. Until we get squared away and they see demonstrated in final versions and on stage that Freiberger is a highly capable "pro", maybe we should hold off sending them first draft versions.

I've directed this to you since you are more acquainted with the actors and past experience. Leave it to your judgement whether you want to talk to Freiberger about this, assuming you agree.

GENE RODDENBERRY

Roddenberry's memo to Justman regarding the actors' concerns about the quality of new Producer Fred Freiberger's first-draft scripts.

[The Last Gunfight" script referred to by Roddenberry was filmed one week later but retitled "Spectre of the Gun."]

Justman did talk to Freiberger, who agreed that not sending the "yellow cover" scripts would exacerbate the problem. "When actors have problems with a script, it's better to make them partners in the solution," Bob reasoned, "and sometimes, they come up with great ideas."

And although Roddenberry continued as an absentee landlord, there were some touchy problems that Justman presented directly to him in memo form with a recommendation for action. One problem concerned William Shatner:

> . . . it also might be a good way to get a fairly close look at Bill [Shatner] and see what sort of physical shape he is in at the present time. Come to think of it, perhaps it would be a good idea to have this get-together before the end of this week, so that if Bill is on the pudgy side, it can be suggested that he start slimming down right away.

Roddenberry did pursue the problem of Shatner's weight. In a "*CONFIDENTIAL*" memo addressed to Ed Milkis, with copies to Freiberger and Justman, he wrote:

> Please coordinate this with Fred and Bob, but I think we *must* bring Shatner's weight problem and the result of it on film to Shatner's attention. You will remember we once talked about finding some unflattering film clips where belly, face, etc., made the angle unusable [*sic*] or almost unusable. We discussed having an inexpensive print made of three or four such angles, sending it to him from the producer or myself with a friendly note, even at the risk of shaking him up a bit.
>
> Many who saw the Emmy Awards commented that he appeared very heavy. Even though he has taken off a little poundage since the end of last season, if he follows his usual pattern of putting it on again we are likely to have him heavier than ever before long.
>
> If Bob and Fred like the idea of proceeding in this direction, we'd better get it done fast.

BOB: It got done fast. But Bill didn't have to be goaded with unflattering photos. Gene's memo went out on the first shooting day; we invited Bill to the dailies the following day. He saw himself on screen and that was all he needed. Bill immediately went on a crash diet.

So Fred Freiberger had become *Star Trek*'s new "main man." This was evident not only by his title, but by the fact that Roddenberry went so far as to turn over his spacious office to Freiberger. Roddenberry moved away from the *Star Trek* office building and into a small single room at the other end of the lot, turning his back on the series although he continued to draw his Executive Producer salary. Freiberger later described his *Star Trek* ordeal. "I thought I could never have a more unpleasant experience in my life than when I, a Jewish kid from the Bronx, parachuted out of a burning B-17 over Germany to land in the midst of eighty million Nazis. But that was before my association with *Star Trek*. My ordeal in a German prison camp only lasted two years. My travail with *Star Trek* has spanned twenty-five years and still counting."

HERB: It wasn't too difficult to understand Freddie's pain. Not only was he thrown into a nest of feuding actors at a recalcitrant studio; but when the show's captain, Roddenberry himself, deserted ship and turned over his command, Freiberger was suddenly alone at the top.

There were times, though, when all wasn't painful. It was just plain weird.

"While I was moving my personal stuff into Gene's office," recalled Fred, "I noticed there was a peephole in the door. I was curious and asked Bobby Justman what that was all about. When Bobby told me Gene used to check on whether his wife, Eileen, was in the outer office, I sensed I was suddenly in a strange new world."

That was driven home even more for Freddie when Paramount Business Affairs confronted him with "a major expense-account scam."

Fred still laughs. "Bill Shatner had turned in an expense account that listed a breakfast charge of $15. The studio was concerned; $15 was a lot of money for breakfast. Since I was the producer of the series, they instructed me to discuss the matter with my star. I didn't want to make waves with Paramount, so I pointed out the disparity to Shatner."

"Well, let's see, Freddie," explained Bill, "I had bacon and two eggs and some toast, coffee . . . and oh yes, a glass of orange juice. It was good and actually was worth $7.50."

"Yes Bill, but that's the studio's point. Breakfast is $7.50; you charged them $15."

"Right, $7.50 for me and $7.50 for my dog."

"Your dog?"

"Sure, my dog and I always breakfast together and we usually order the same things."

Freiberger reported back to Paramount Business Affairs that Shatner's breakfast charge was legitimate.

But the continuing Shatner-Nimoy strife was no laughing matter. Nimoy's constant demand for scripts with a more involved Spock—and a Spock who maintained his original character values—and Shatner's insistence that *he* was still the star of the series put unusual pressures on Freiberger. In his desire to solve the problem, *Star Trek*'s new producer, frustrated and fed up with the bickering, arranged a meeting with the players: Shatner, Nimoy, and Roddenberry.

Freiberger held the meeting in Roddenberry's old office, where he explained the complex nature of the situation, something that Roddenberry had been well aware of for at least two years. Freiberger then proceeded to confess that those pressures were preventing him from properly performing his role as the series's producer. Shatner and Nimoy hung on his every word.

"Gee, I'm sorry to hear that, Fred," said Roddenberry. "I hope you get it straightened out real soon." Roddenberry stood. "Well, I have to go now." As Roddenberry started to leave his old office, Freiberger stopped him and asked

Courtesy Greg Jein

A third-season publicity photo of Kirk and Spock.

the million-dollar question: "Gene, please tell me. Who's the star of the series? Is it Bill—or is it Leonard?" Both actors leaned forward, eagerly.

Roddenberry became quiet. He grabbed a cigarette, lit it quickly, inhaled deeply, and stared wide-eyed into the space above him. "Ahh . . . I see," he mused. He looked out the window, shook his head in Buddha-like fashion, but said nothing else. He looked at neither Bill nor Leonard. Perhaps he was hoping they would jump into the conversation and solve the matter, actor to actor. They did not.

It was up to *Star Trek*'s creator. "You're really putting me on the spot, Fred," said Roddenberry.

"Sorry, Gene, but I have to know," responded Freiberger. "Is it Bill—or is it Leonard?"

Roddenberry walked toward the door to leave, but turned and stared, angrily, at Freiberger. Roddenberry was sweating. "It's Bill. Bill is the star of the series."

Roddenberry left immediately, and a smiling Shatner and a sullen Nimoy returned to the set. Freiberger, though he got his answer, had unfortunately failed to realize how deep-seated the animosities were in Roddenberry's "happy" *Star Trek* family. Putting Roddenberry on the spot with Shatner and Nimoy present had permanently damaged his relationships with both Nimoy and Roddenberry.

To this day, Freiberger continues to fend off the negative comments advanced by Roddenberry, Nimoy, and other series regulars relative to Fred's creative guidance of *Star Trek*'s final year.

The Charles Bluhdorn philosophy of corporate management had taken hold at Paramount well before production commenced on *Star Trek*'s third season. The studio turf was divided up into three separate and competing entities: Facilities, Motion Pictures, and Television. Each had to struggle for success by competing with the others. But Facilities seemed to hold all the cards. It maintained the physical plant, the stages, and all the equipment, which it rented to the other two divisions.

> **BOB: It reminded me of the games in ancient Rome. Motion Pictures and Facilities would enter the arena as gladiators, fully armed with sword and shield, and fight to a draw. Then Television would enter, unarmed, to face both of them. Guess who would win?**

But again to Justman's surprise and pleasure, Ed Holly, now the head of Paramount's Facilities Division, was agreeable to suggestions regarding the purchase of much-needed equipment—reasoning that, if better tools would benefit *Star Trek*, they also would benefit the whole studio.

Prompted by Justman, Roddenberry sent a memo to everyone on the series regarding the new "working relationships between the Facilities Division . . . and us" and assured everyone that Facilities "will do everything in its power to cooperate—and in return asks only that our attitude be honest and sincere. . . . We do not just intend to pay lip service to this agreement."

Roddenberry made sure that a "blind copy" of the memo, which praised Holly, was sent to both Ed Holly and Ted Leonard, Paramount Television's

Production Manager. It wouldn't hurt to be on their good side. His show was going to need all the help it could get.

BOB: Mixing metaphors, while Facilities had turned out to be a pussycat, the new corporate management at Paramount Television was a real kettle of fish.

NBC would be paying more for the series for its third year. But even as we were preparing our new series budget, the new guys in the front office rejected it out of hand. The new figure would have to be $178,500—$9,000 less than the Desilu budget—no ifs, ands, or buts. And we had to meet this mandated series budget despite the contractual increases in cast salaries.

The reasons were simple. The broadcast license fees from NBC (including the additional monies from repeats) were still insufficient to allow Paramount to break even. Projected foreign sales were minuscule. And management was sure this would be *Star Trek*'s last season, so there wouldn't be enough episodes to "strip" the show in syndication. All management wanted was to cut its losses and get out.

The buck, or the lack of bucks, stopped at my desk. Gene was no help; he was out to lunch, literally and figuratively. Every third-season episode would suffer; there were no exceptions.

As usual, Matt Jefferies's set construction budget took another, nearly fatal, hit—less money for sets and fewer sets per episode. I also sliced money from the Guest Star, Supporting Players, and Extras accounts.

We couldn't afford to shoot on location because Transportation, Location Rentals, and Catering allocations were eliminated. To save overtime, directors would have to finish their episodes in fewer hours per day, which meant reduced coverage for editing. Scripts underwent simplification to make them less expensive to produce. Not surprisingly, it also made them very dull.

"We're writing radio shows," I protested. "All the actors can do now is stand around and talk to each other."

It seemed that Paramount management, in its need to save money on a dying series, was doing its very best to kill both the goose and the gold-plated egg. No longer would stories and scripts be junked. "A Portrait in Black and White" was one of the original stories by Gene Coon, written under his pen name of Lee Cronin, that were carried forward into the third production year. It wouldn't do to waste the investment, so good money was thrown after bad. Oliver Crawford was hired to write the teleplay, which, although it had an intriguing premise, suffered from the same fault as the original story—a lack of physical action. The script was now entitled "Let That Be Your Last Battlefield," and a talented director, Jud Taylor, was hired to shepherd the episode.

In a meeting held a week prior to filming, Taylor, Freiberger, Justman, and Singer agreed that not only were they about to embark on the production of a dull, drab, and totally pedestrian episode, they also didn't have a clue as to the "look" of the aliens. The discussion centered on what to do about it, if anything. Toward the end of the meeting, Jud Taylor made an offhand suggestion, "What would happen if we made the two opposing characters half-black and half-white? You know, one color from the waist up and another color from the waist down . . . but each one opposite?" Taylor's suggestion was enthusiastically adopted; it solved their problems. Refinements were discussed and soon all were in agreement; the two characters would be half-black and half-white—but with the colors separated vertically rather than horizontally.

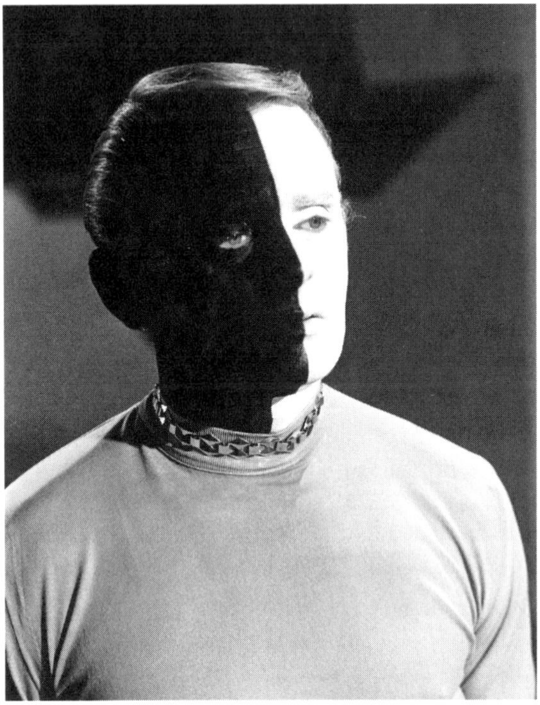

Courtesy Greg Jein

Actor Frank Gorshin, as he appeared in the episode "Let That Be Your Last Battlefield."

The completed film, with its half-black–half-white concept, was roundly criticized by some for being a heavy-handed attempt to preach. Nevertheless, the film made a valid point with viewers. And it was infinitely better with bicolored people than without.

Jud Taylor wasn't the only "new" director for *Star Trek* in its last season. Marc Daniels and Joseph Pevney no longer alternated assignments. Seeking a fresh approach, Bob Justman added other directors to the roster. Some of them, who had previously done excellent work on *Star Trek*, were Ralph Senensky, Vincent McEveety, and John Meredyth Lucas. Others, like the talented Marvin Chomsky and John Erman, were new to the show.

During the second "Save *Star Trek*" campaign, Bjo and John Trimble also helped organize Lincoln Enterprises, a *Star Trek* memorabilia merchandising company that Roddenberry set up, as he later told Solow, "to give Majel something to do."

The normal print run for *Star Trek* scripts was more than was needed for every person on the series, every department at the studio, and a handful of departments at NBC. After the formation of Lincoln Enterprises, however, the script run was increased. Paramount later discovered that the extra scripts, owned by the studio, had somehow found their way to Lincoln Enterprises and were being sold via mail order and at *Star Trek* and science-fiction conventions—an apparent violation of the studio's basic bargaining agreement with the Writers Guild of America.

Shortly after production commenced on the third-season shows, film editor Don Rode needed a short shot of the *Enterprise* warping through space. He recalled seeing it in one of the first-season episodes and figured the rest of it must be among the "trims" and "outtakes" (unused pieces of printed footage) in the fireproof and security-locked *Star Trek* film vault. So he arranged for a studio guard to unlock the large walk-in vault. Rode was surprised to find it was empty. All the trims of scenes, all the unused scenes—everything was gone.

He questioned the guard. "What happened to all the film that was here?"

"Oh," responded the guard, "they took it away."

"What do you mean, 'they' took it away?"

"Well, Mr. Roddenberry and his friend, that girl from *Star Trek*, Mabel something, backed a truck up to the vault and took it. Mr. Roddenberry said it was no longer being used and the studio was going to throw it away. Why? Is there something wrong?"

Rode found a different shot of the *Enterprise* to use. The "missing" film had already been reported to the studio. Shortly thereafter, in addition to scripts, individual frames of film from *Star Trek* were being sold by Lincoln Enterprises. It was a sensitive matter for the Paramount executives, as the film was owned by the studio and not Gene Roddenberry. The upshot was that everyone pretended not to know what had happened. So it continued to happen.

The final fate of some of the missing *Star Trek* film: three of the filmclips sold by Lincoln Enterprises.

The first recorded history of *Star Trek* came from a very unexpected source. In 1966, Stephen E. Whitfield (later known as Stephen Poe), who was working as National Advertising and Promotion Director of the AMT Corporation, a manufacturer of toy model kits, attended an affiliates meeting at which film clips of NBC's new fall series were screened. After this first exposure to *Star Trek,* Whitfield became doubly hooked. First and foremost, he wanted to acquire the *Enterprise* model rights for AMT. Second, he wanted to write the contemporaneous history of the exciting new series.

Working with Matt Jefferies and Desilu, Whitfield negotiated the contract for AMT to acquire the marketing rights to the model of the *Enterprise.* Permission to write a book about the making of *Star Trek* would have to come from Gene Roddenberry.

Whitfield says, "Although I was not the first person to approach Roddenberry with the idea, he finally made a deal in August 1966, several weeks before the series premiered." The terms of the agreement gave Whitfield carte blanche access, night or day, to all the files, the set, actors, technicians, et al.

The "surreal" set for "Spectre of the Gun."

Roddenberry also agreed to edit the manuscript as it progressed. Whitfield, however, had to give Roddenberry fifty percent of the book's royalties, or there was no deal. Roddenberry's explanation to Whitfield was, "I had to get some money somewhere. I'm sure not going to get it from the profits of *Star Trek*." He had used the same phrase before with composer Alexander Courage.

During the time it took to write *The Making of Star Trek*, Whitfield continually requested that Roddenberry edit the newly written material. But Roddenberry procrastinated and finally read the book after it was typeset, and in galleys, and spent "one long night" with Whitfield "making changes." Owing to the book's printing deadline, very few changes were incorporated, and the book was published much as Whitfield had written it. However, at the suggestion of the publisher, Roddenberry's name appeared on the book's cover along with author Whitfield's name. Ballantine Books considered it a "marketing ploy."

The Making of Star Trek was Whitfield's first book. He never regretted the fifty-fifty deal he made with Roddenberry. It was a substantial portion to give away, but otherwise he never would have had the opportunity to become the first chronicler of television's most successful unsuccessful series.

BOB: Gene Coon was gone, but his influence continued to be felt. As a condition of being let out of his contract, he had promised to complete work on a number of his story premises if *Star Trek* was renewed for a third season.

"The Last Gunfight" was one of the stories that he was developing at the time he left *Star Trek*. But now, Coon was working elsewhere on an exclusive contract, and legally he could write only for Universal Television, his new employer. Intending to honor that contract, Coon explained that he would not be able to write the teleplay for "Gunfight." Being a man of his word, however, Gene Coon arranged for "Lee Cronin" to complete the assignment. It was filmed and retitled "Spectre of the Gun."

"Lee Cronin" also contributed two third-season stories, "Wink of an Eye" and "Let That Be Your Last Battlefield," as well as writing the story and teleplay for "Spock's Brain," an episode in which, as a result of a suggestion from me, Spock's purloined brain, after being rescued, takes over during surgery and instructs Dr. McCoy exactly how to go about reinserting it back where it came from—inside Spock's skull. Many fans consider that one show to be a worthy candidate for the worst *Star Trek* episode of all time.

Gene Coon had come full circle. While he officially worked on *Star Trek*, "Lee Cronin" had written for other shows. With Coon now working on another series, "Lee Cronin" became an important contributor to *Star Trek*.

His "Spectre of the Gun" was an excellent script with two major drawbacks. First, as expected, Stan Robertson objected to the story, feeling it did not fit his view of science fiction because "It's just an excuse to do a Western and nobody wants to see our guys in Western garb." His comment was ignored.

Second, and more important, it required new sets, locations, and wardrobe. That meant more money—and more money just wasn't in the cards. So rather than junk the script, Justman approached director Vincent McEveety with the cost-saving concept of using a stylized Western street consisting of buildings with false fronts and no sides. An angry-red-sky backing would complete the strange setting for the relentless story line that led to an inevitable fate during the final "shootout" at the O. K. Corral.

"Spectre of the Gun" was a triumph for McEveety and Justman—and "Lee Cronin." It also provided Walter Koenig his first important role on the series.

BOB: While cutting this episode, film editor Fabien Tordjmann confided that his wife, Josette, was enduring excruciating headaches, and yet medical tests were inconclusive. He didn't know where to turn next.

My wife and Josette had become friendly. One day Jackie came home, worried. Josette hadn't shown up for a lunch they had planned together.

Next morning, Fabien, distraught, told me the problem had been diagnosed. His wife had a brain tumor. She would have to be operated upon. During surgery, the doctors discovered that owing to its invasion of the brain stem, the tumor was already inoperable.

We gave Fabien time off so he could be with her. Nothing could be done to relieve Josette's suffering. She lingered for three months and finally, mercifully, she died. Fabien wept; his was a tragic loss. Nothing we did could comfort him, but fortunately, he agreed to come back to work. At least we could keep him occupied during this trying time.

Things were different on set this third time around. While Cameraman Jerry Finnerman's previous lack of self-confidence had disappeared, his ego had grown. He had begun carrying a swagger stick on stage with which he goosed unsuspecting crew members. Later in the season, Finnerman received an offer to photograph a motion picture starring Sidney Poitier. Justman, hoping the daunting experience of doing a feature film might help bring the now-confident cinematographer back down to earth, released him from his obligation and then made camera operator Al Francis the show's new Director of Photography. Finnerman never returned to the good ship *Enterprise*—and, years later in an interview for *American Cinematographer* magazine, he gave sole credit to Gene Roddenberry for giving him his break, forgetting all about Bob Justman. Justman remarked, wryly, "No good deed goes unpunished." In later years, Finnerman photographed several TV series: *The Bold Ones*, *Night Gallery*, and the highly successful *Moonlighting*. While he never returned to the *Enterprise*, he did, in fact, return many years later to function as a sometime second-unit Director of Photography for *Star Trek: Deep Space Nine*.

BOB: A quarter-century later, I met Al Francis again at a Thanksgiving party at Bill Shatner's house in Malibu. He was still working in the business. When he saw me, he became emotional and hugged and kissed me for giving him his break. He should have hugged and kissed Jerry Finnerman.

Other new careers began during this third and last season. Interestingly enough, three talented writers all broke in as a result of unsolicited submissions that Justman read and recommended to Roddenberry—and they were all women: Jean Lisette Aroeste ("Is There in Truth No Beauty?" and "All Our Yesterdays"), Judy Burns ("The Tholian Web"), and Joyce Muskat ("The Empath"). But finding new writing talent provided only temporary satisfaction.

BOB: Stan Robertson continued to give us a hard time over stories and scripts. He wanted more planet stories and fewer shipboard stories. At my urging, Roddenberry, in an April 3, 1968, letter to Stan, wrote:

> **. . . despite fears to the contrary, our shipboard tales have consistently turned out to be among our most exciting and colorful action-adventure episodes. If what you mean is that you want the exotic, the strange and unusual, the unexpected and the fearsome, there is no rule which says these items cannot and have not been introduced just as successfully as on a bizarre landscape. Yes, we want the bizarre landscapes too; we want both. NBC should keep in mind that our ship, after all, is our "familiar home base" and is as important to the fabric of our show as "BONANZA's" [*sic*] house and ranch which has been the locale of a great number of their most exciting episodes. [*Bonanza* was a very successful NBC-owned and produced in-house show.] In that regard, to help counteract any "sameness" about the ship, we are presently planning this season the addition of new and interesting ship areas, including a "simulated outdoor recreation area" complete with foliage, turf, running water, and etc. [Actually not accomplished until the 1987 premiere episode of *Star Trek: The Next Generation.*]**
>
> **When you say you want to be fresh and different this year and then, on the other hand, say you believe it a major mistake to have Kirk "marry" a lovely native girl—I think there is a potential contradiction.**
>
> **As NBC discovered with the case of Mr. Spock's ears, in an alien heritage, anything different you do involves a risk and thus becomes suddenly frightening to people. If there was ever a rule of entertaining and exciting action-adventure drama, it is that to get in Stan Robertson's words, "a fresh-**

er and a newer look" requires doing things that to some may appear "risky". *Taste* in execution of the idea is what takes the risk out of it, while keeping the freshness. If we make every decision on our show, Stan, on the basis of pandering to "contemporary people with contemporary views on morals, manners, etc.", you just ain't going to get what you're asking for.

Two weeks passed, and nothing changed. Stan evidently hadn't taken Gene's advice to heart. The show was foundering and maybe, as sharks do, he smelled blood in the water. We had enough to handle without being sniped at from a supposedly friendly quarter. Fred Freiberger and I met with Gene, and I laid out the ineffectiveness of his last letter. Gene got really steamed and sent off another missive to Robertson:

> This refers to the last group of letters received from you on *Star Trek* story outlines sent NBC.
>
> First, all future correspondence should be directed to Fred Freiberger, line producer of *Star Trek,* and Robert Justman, co-producer. A copy also to Arthur Singer, our new story consultant.
>
> To be perfectly honest, Stan, your last letters had me sorely tempted to include here a request that you omit sending me copies of your future story comments. Your statement, "we *must* and *will* insist upon more novel material than we have accepted in the past" is misleading and totally unacceptable. You have gotten in the past and will continue to get some of the most imaginative and novel concepts in television writing today. If we are going to refer to the records, let's do so fully—including the fact that many of our most varied and most successful episodes were sent to script over your own strong objections.
>
> This is not to say you have not been an excellent program manager. We have appreciated your help, talent, and friendship. But let's establish again at the beginning of this third season that on a show as complex and difficult as *Star Trek* the *producer* must produce the show. We recognize NBC's several contractual rights regarding content but we have no intention of permitting others to take over our contractual functions. You'll find that Fred Freiberger feels no less the way I do. We welcome comment but no one here is going to sit quietly when we receive letters which seem to suggest that on the slender basis of a story outline you can guess all our plans and conversations about the story and can make the final omniscient decision that it will or will not translate into a good or varied script.
>
> Your letters had all the earmarks of some form of "ultimatum" and if this does in fact reflect NBC thinking I suggest you have Herb Schlosser contact me immediately.
>
> Yes, you will continue to receive shipboard stories and probably several in a row. I am surprised you are not aware by now that this is always followed

DAILY VARIETY DAILY

Vol. 139 No. 65 Hollywood, California - 90028, Wednesday, June 5, 1968 13 Ten Cents

SOLOW REVITALIZING MGM-TV

MAKES 4 WEB DEVELOPMENT DEALS, 1 PILOT

By Dave Kaufman

Determined to restore MGM-TV to a front-running position, tv production chief Herbert F. Solow has initiated a great deal of activity at the Culver City lot, gearing projects for the 1969-70 season.

As part of the broad program he has also hypoed activity in the vidfilmery's animation division and documentary department.

Solow, who became tv production veepee last January when the studio's vidfilm fortunes were at their

(Continued on Page 12)

STRIKE-RACKED FRANCE LOSES PIX TO ITALY

By Hank Werba

Rome, June 4—Film producers are moving out of strikebound France and readjusting film-making plans on the Italian side of the border.

Caught by the strike in Nice, Commonwealth producer Henry Weinstein is reassembling the cast of "Madwoman of Chaillot" to shoot remaining five weeks of the schedule here.

Weinstein, according to cast member Richard Chamberlain, received support from striking French film technicians to resume activity today for four days, or long enough for director Bryan Forbes to finish off his big street location set before moving here.

Chamberlain was doubtful even

(Continued on Page 13)

Valenti Reports Progress On Classification Plan

New York, June 4—"Steady progress in reaching agreement on a voluntary industrywide plan to rate motion pictures according to audiences and with self-enforcement" was reported today by Jack J. Valenti, prexy of Motion Picture Assn. of America, after a meeting between MPAA officials and a special committee of the National Assn. of Theatre Owners.

Valenti said NATO prexy Julian Rifkin joined in the sentiments expressed in his statement. "Obviously there are a good many bases yet to be touched," Valenti continued, "but the harmony of this meeting and the dispatch with which a number of problems were resolved encourages Mr. Rifkin and me to believe that within a very short time an effective plan can be constructed and accepted by all segments of the industry."

Ahmanson Off MCA Board By New Law; Stock Split 3-2

Chicago, June 4—At the annual meeting of MCA stockholders here today, directors were reduced from seven to six. Howard F. Ahmanson, board chairman of Home Savings and Loan Association, complied with a recent National Housing Act amendment that prohibits a director of one savings-and-loan holding company from serving as director of another (MCA's Columbia Savings and Loan Association) without prior approval of the Federal Savings and Loan Insurance Corp.

Approval was denied, and Ahmanson withdrew as a nominee.

During a brisk, 18-minute meeting, Jules C. Stein, Milton R. Rackmil, Lew R. Wasserman, Charles B. Thornton, Walter M. Heymann and Charles Miller were reelected to the board without opposition.

An amendment increasing authorized common shares without par value to 9,750,000, effecting a 3-for-2 split, was adopted, effective at 5 p.m. EDT tomorrow.

The conversion ratio on MCA convertible preferred stock also

(Continued on Page 13)

Baldwin-Montrose, Chris-Craft Pitch W7 On Merger

New York, June 4 — Baldwin-Montrose and Chris-Craft topper Herbert Siegel is understood to have gone to the coast last week to discuss merger with Warner Bros.-7 Arts. (Chairman-chief exec Eliot Hyman, financial veep Alan Hirschfield and other top W7 execs were then in Hollywood for studio confabs.)

The angle is that Chris-Craft, owner of several television stations and the largest U.S. maker of pleasure boats, would be part of a large "leisure-time" complex, including, of course, W7's existing pic and tele production. It is understood that discussions are in an elementary stage, however. No comment was obtainable today.

Chris-Craft recently merged with Baldwin-Montrose, the chemical maker (and one-time owner of General Artists Corp.), which Siegel headed. Siegel is the vet of the Paramount proxy wars.

Stockholders OK Loew's Bid To Take Over CCC

New York, June 4—Stockholders of Loew's Theatres at a special meeting here today overwhelmingly approved company's bid to acquire Commercial Credit Co. of Baltimore.

Approved was an exchange involving Loew's $45 principal amount, 5½% convertible subordinated debentures, to be offered for each share of Commercial. Also okayed was increase in authorized shares from 10,000,000 to 15,000,000.

Commercial has disapproved of Loew's bid and warned its shareowners not to accept it. Last Friday Sen. Tydings of Maryland claimed in a speech that the exchange offer had been leaked to Wall Street sources a few days before it was publicly disclosed on April 25.

Discussion in the meeting at

(Continued on Page 13)

Presnell In 'Wagon'

Harve Presnell has been signed by Alan Jay Lerner for a costarring role in "Paint Your Wagon" for Paramount.

The picture, also starring Lee Marvin, Clint Eastwood and Jean Seberg, will roll in Baker, Ore., June 24, Joshua Logan directing.

Roddenberry Starts Feature Filming In 2-Pic NGC Deal

Producer Gene Roddenberry has made a two-picture deal with National General Corp. This will be the theatrical-film debut of Roddenberry, exec producer of Paramount TV's "Star Trek" series on NBC-TV.

He will be producer-writer on both films. One property has been decided and he will pick the second. Roddenberry soon will go to Mexico to eye film facilities there and decide whether the first picture will be shot there, in Hollywood, or elsewhere.

Roddenberry will continue his functions with "Trek," having been given ample time to turn out the pix.

Chamberlin To Rein All MGM Postprod'n

MGM has promoted Merle Chamberlin to new post of exec post-production supervisor of worldwide film activities. He will remain headquartered here, but will work more closely with studio's foreign film-makers, particularly in London.

Chamberlin, who has been editorial administrator past 15 years, joined MGM in 1930.

Solow strikes again! Note the announcement of the Roddenberry feature film deal—the films were never made.

up by a similar number of planet stories. It happens that way because that is the way stories sometimes come in. If you will refer to your schedule of the last two seasons you will see they were not shot nor did they air in that order.

Further, I suggest you keep in mind that story outlines are at best rough blueprints of a script—they are a small part of the constant flow of communication between producer and writer, a working tool among story telling professionals. If you want story outlines so finely rewritten and polished that every point is touched, every problem is solved, every dramatic value totally realized, and every possible doubt erased, then someone had better start petitioning NBC to run *Star Trek*'s [*sic*] in 1969-70. [An error. Roddenberry meant 1968-69.]

I was as pleased to read Gene's letter as I imagined Stan wasn't. Not only did it help reduce some of the pressures being placed on us, it was a succinct and marvelously clear expression of a producer's rights and his freedom to bring ideas to life. My respect for Gene's ability to turn a phrase increased yet again.

Low ratings weren't the only thing that was taking a toll upon morale. By mid-September 1968, the start of the broadcast season, Justman already knew that *Star Trek* would soon begin losing its audience. This season wouldn't measure up to the previous two. All the negative factors he had encountered were taking their toll, a toll that could be assuaged by only one thing: the end of his association with *Star Trek*.

BOB: If Herb had still been there, at least I would have been rewarded with full producer status. Former Paramount Television President John Reynolds later told Herb Solow, "Justman was the guy who made everything run." But evidently, others at the studio didn't appreciate my contributions to the show. That bothered me—a lot.

And to cap it all off, I was tired from three seasons of exhausting work. The thrill was gone.

Gene had distanced himself from the daily chores of supervising the series. Without Gene's insights about the series, Fred Freiberger and Arthur Singer had to labor to understand *Star Trek.* I was all alone struggling against insuperable odds.

I despaired about the show's loss of quality. By the time episodes were filmed, whatever excitement existed in the original stories and scripts had been diluted by a rewriting process that was no longer overseen by Gene Roddenberry; it was now strictly budget-driven. There were no highs and no lows—just a boring inbetween. My never-ending battle to cut costs without compromising quality had failed. The *Star Trek* I knew, and was proud to be a part of, was no more.

By the midpoint of the production season, I dreaded coming to work every day. It felt like being in prison—and I wanted out.

I expressed my concerns to new Paramount Television Vice President Doug Cramer, who was sympathetic. But he asked me to stay with *Star Trek* and

From the collection of Herbert F. Solow

(L. to r.) Herb Solow, Bob Justman, and director William Graham on the set of the "Then Came Bronson" pilot.

promised I could have my pick of the new pilots he was preparing for the following spring.

"I'd love to do a pilot for you, Doug. Just let me out of my contract now and I promise to be available in the spring. I won't take another job in the meantime."

Doug said he'd get back to me. His answer was eventually relayed by Business Affairs Vice President Emmet Lavery, Jr. The answer was "No. But we'll give you more money." They didn't understand; they thought my request was a ploy. But I was just plain burnt out. I needed to leave *Star Trek.*

No one is indispensable. We were shooting our fourteenth episode, and there were only ten left to finish out the season. And with Eddie Milkis and Gregg Peters now functioning as Associate Producers, *Star Trek*'s production and postproduction would be in capable hands.

Emmet informed me that the studio couldn't keep me from leaving "if you really wanted to." His meaning was implicit: If I left, I'd regret it.

While angered over Paramount's none-too-veiled threat, I still tried to put everything in proper perspective when a new player entered the decision-making process. Herb Solow, the man who had originally involved me with *Star Trek* and who had left Paramount to become head of MGM Television, called. "Hey, RJ, what's doing? Are you having any fun?"

I described the situation. In retrospect, I realized Herb, who always had his ear to the ground, had gotten wind of what was going on.

"Listen, RJ, I can't tell you what to do, but if you're interested, I have a new project, a two-hour pilot for NBC called *Then Came Bronson.* It needs a producer—a full producer. Why don't you come on over here and have some fun again?"

I was still torn until Herb added, "Nobody's ever attempted to do a show like this before. They say it can't be done, so I thought you might like to try it with me."

The following morning I went in to the studio and quit. And for the next eighteen years, I was persona non grata at Paramount.

HERB: When Bob came over to MGM, he carried with him a fond memento of his *Star Trek* days, the mannequin from his bathroom. She was immediately installed in his new bathroom shower and continued to startle visitors after they were counseled not to use the men's room down the hall, but the one behind his office.

When Bob eventually left MGM, he presented the mannequin to me, and she was moved into my office in the Thalberg Building. Several weeks prior to the famous MGM auction, I flew to Cannes for the annual film festival. When I returned to the studio, after the auction, the mannequin was nowhere to be found. I truly believe she was sold along with Brando's fedora from *Guys and Dolls,* Gable's vest from *Gone with the Wind,* and Judy Garland's famous ruby slippers from *The Wizard of Oz.* The mannequin from *Star Trek* was in good company.

The close of *Star Trek*'s third production year was markedly different from years one and two. Other than the show's most devoted fans, no one seemed to care whether it would be renewed. There were no marches, no massive letter writing and phone campaigns, no leading science-fiction writers leading the charge—nothing. Neither Roddenberry nor Paramount nor Ashley-Famous lifted a finger to promote the dying series.

In NBC's New York offices, top management executives discussed the ramifications of finally cancelling *Star Trek.* Program Publicity Director Alan Baker, who oversaw the NBC replies to all the "Save *Star Trek*" protests, warned Mort Werner, "If you cancel it, I'll bet we're gonna take a lot of heat." Mort replied, "Bet we don't."

Mort Werner won the bet.

HERB: There's a saying that echoes far out in space: "It ain't over until the fat Talosian sings." And after seventy-nine episodes of joy and sorrow, birthday parties and bad marriages, lifelong friendships and short-lived hostilities, broken dreams and pride of performance, *Star Trek* was cancelled at the end of its third year. The fat Talosian had finally sung.

The first prime-time, adult science-fiction, color television series would always be looked on as a gallant and expensive effort—that failed. *Star Trek* was consigned to perpetual oblivion in the most distant quadrant of the most distant galaxy—to a place where all unsuccessful series go to die. It would never be heard from again.

A photo of a September, 1976, *Star Trek* convention.

Courtesy NBC/Globe

ACT FOUR

Rebirth: Star Trek Lives!

Courtesy Greg Jein

24

Reborn in Reruns

The countdown to oblivion began with the shooting of the last episode, "Turnabout Intruder." Seven dull and uneventful days later, on January 9, 1969, it was over. Adding insult to injury, the seventy-ninthth episode had run one day over schedule and $6,000 over budget. Freiberger remembers, "The last shot was made at 11:30 that night and there wasn't even a wrap party on the set." Several members of the cast and crew got together afterward to remember the past years and made empty promises to meet again.

"The series just wound down; it didn't wind up," recalls Ed Milkis.

Captain Kirk and the crew of the *Enterprise* had finally landed, and the dismantling of *Star Trek* began.

close
up

STAR TREK (C)
7:30 (10) (4) **TURNABOUT INTRUDER**

Return: "Star Trek" enters a new time slot with its final first-run episode.

William Shatner's talents are showcased as he acts out the personalities of a male and a female: Captain Kirk and Dr. Janice Lester, a paranoiac scientist who has transferred her mind into Kirk's body—and his mind into hers.

Only subtle changes (certain mannerisms, a marked emotionalism) indicate that the Captain's body is possessed by Dr. Lester. Driven by an ambition to command, she seeks also to satisfy her personal hatred for Kirk, who once spurned her.

Dr. Lester: Sandra Smith. Spock: Leonard Nimoy. Dr. McCoy: DeForest Kelley. Dr. Coleman: Harry Landers. Scott: James Doohan. Sulu: George Takei. Chekov: Walter Koenig. (60 min.)

A *TV Guide* "Close Up" for *Star Trek's* final episode, "Turnabout Intruder."

Three of the series' original and most important players were already gone. Coon, Solow, and Justman did not have to be part of what would have been an agonizing time for them.

Gene Roddenberry, having accepted defeat many months earlier, had all but deserted the series. He packed up his few remaining personal belongings and moved off the lot to National General Studios, where he was busy working on a new *Tarzan* movie script.

Fred Freiberger stayed on for another four weeks to oversee the editing of the remaining episodes.

Ed Milkis remained after everyone else had left to manage postproduction of the last handful of episodes and their delivery to NBC. Since he was the sole survivor on staff, Milkis also became the recipient of all *Star Trek* correspondence and phone calls, mostly from inquisitive and irate fans. "I was the fall guy," he wryly notes.

Bill Shatner fielded offers to star in various new television series.

Leonard Nimoy accepted Bruce Geller's offer to replace Martin Landau on *Mission: Impossible.*

The other actors, looking for work, called their agents.

The office staff and the stage crew either left the studio for greener pastures or were absorbed into the Paramount operation.

The major elements of the *Enterprise* bridge were donated to the Theater Arts Department at UCLA. The set was eventually trashed. Other sets, specific to

Star Trek, were "folded" and put into storage while all the "flats" (lightweight walls) were either revamped for use by other productions or junked.

(10) (4) STAR TREK—Adventure (C)
Return: The series enters a new time slot with "Turnabout Intruder." See the Close-up on opposite page for details. (60 min.)
[Postponed from an earlier date.]

***TV Guide*'s listing for *Star Trek*'s final episode, "Turnabout Intruder."**

Props and set dressings were stored in the old RKO construction mill on the "Desilu side" of Paramount. Months later, unknown individuals broke into the "mill" and illegally removed many of the props, including hundreds of furry tribbles, as well as set dressings. The mill door was left open and people came from all over the studio to scavenge what remained.

Most of the costumes were stored in the studio's wardrobe department, but Bill Theiss kept some items for his personal collection. In later years some of the costumes also disappeared after persons unknown broke into the wardrobe department at night.

Shatner's, Barrett's, and Nichols's "missing" hairpieces were never recovered.

The last new episode of *Star Trek* to be broadcast on NBC was "Turnabout Intruder." It aired on Tuesday, June 3, 1969, at 7:30 P.M., and its Nielsen rating was indicative of NBC's displeasure and its audience's defection over the three-year network life span. The episode, which was aired on a new night and time, received a rating of only 8.8. Its competition on CBS was *Lancer,* which rated 14.7, and ironically, the Harve Bennett–produced *Mod Squad* on ABC, which rated 15.2. From the premiere of "Man Trap" to the finale "Turnabout Intruder," despite all the letter-writing campaigns, marches on and harassment of the network, after all the petitions and phone calls and everything else, *Star Trek*'s Nielsen ratings had dropped by well over fifty percent from birth to death.

If shareholders of Gulf & Western had been privy to the financial records of Desilu Studios and Desilu Productions, they would have surely questioned the $17-million purchase. The only asset that would appear to have any recognizable value was the land. And even if it was overvalued, Desilu Gower shared a common border with Paramount Pictures, and it was the only expansion possibility for the major studio. It made sense for the future.

Desilu's three television series, however, were quite another matter. The good news was that their ownership gave the newly reorganized Paramount Television Division three ongoing network series, which amounted to a marvelous base of operations. The bad news was that all three series were running in the red. Every time a new episode was broadcast, the studio lost money. But management could make a case for *Mission: Impossible* and *Mannix.* Both series had good ratings, and with an expectation of yearly renewals, sufficient episodes would be available for a syndication package. There could be some value there. (Each series did, in fact, remain on the air for seven years.)

Star Trek, however, was a far different matter. It was costly to produce and low-rated. And the Nielsen ratings never indicated any major audience growth. So, with an expected early cancellation, before a sufficient number of episodes could be produced to at least make a syndication package, *Star Trek* had the honor of having been the most financially negative aspect of the Desilu purchase. Paramount considered it to be a total loss.

Under the terms of the original deal between Desilu and Norway Productions (Roddenberry's company), the studio retained overall control of the property. However, net profits (if there would ever be any) were to be shared among Desilu, Norway Productions, NBC, and Bill Shatner.

While NBC's share of the eventual profits came only from the original series episodes and related merchandising receipts, the network has, in fact, profited handsomely over the years. (The practice of networks receiving profit participation in series licensed for broadcast was later prohibited by the FCC's Financial Interest Regulation that also outlawed their participation in syndication rights. It did not, however, prohibit NBC from its previously negotiated continuing interest in the series.)

Incidentally, Roddenberry's and Shatner's percentages were later reduced by their subsequent divorces.

HERB: At the time of the series's cancellation, any Paramount executive, or for that matter, any entertainment industry figure who predicted there could ever be *Star Trek* profits would have been immediately incarcerated in the nearest asylum for the severely insane. It was that bad.

However, a year after the series was cancelled, Roddenberry approached Paramount with a simple proposal: Would Paramount give him control of the *Star Trek* rights, so he could attempt to do something with the property? After analyzing *Star Trek*'s domestic syndication sales potential, foreign television sales potential, the talent rerun costs, foreign dubbing costs, print, insurance, shipping, and sales costs, Paramount saw little future potential in the property, and on an upper-management level there was even some talk of a counteroffer to Roddenberry. Theoretically, Paramount would sell all its *Star Trek* rights, title, and equity position to Roddenberry. The price discussed was reputed to be $150,000. For the first time, a value had been placed on the much-maligned property; money had been discussed.

At that time, Roddenberry's major income came from his appearances on the college lecture circuit and the sale of "memorabilia." He was supporting his ex-wife and two daughters and a new wife, while trying to maintain some image of success in the highly competitive Hollywood community. He simply did not have $150,000.

Roddenberry's financial condition at the time was such that he even needed to sell his sailboat. But he couldn't; there were no buyers. James Doohan, however, felt that Roddenberry wasn't going about the sales process correctly and volunteered to sell the boat, as his friend's agent, in return for a sales commission of ten percent. Roddenberry jumped at the offer. Doohan ran ads in several papers and soon found a buyer for $19,000. Roddenberry was elated, took the deal, and, when reminded of the ten percent sales commission, wrote out a check to Doohan for $1,900.

But Roddenberry cautioned, "Listen, Jimmy. Hold onto the check for a while. Okay?" That was okay to Doohan.

However, five days later, more than "a while" in Doohan's vocabulary, the check was used to make a down payment on a house he and his wife, Anita, were buying. When he mentioned that to Gene and Majel Roddenberry, they seemed both shocked and offended, as if Doohan was spending money they had counted on for other uses.

"This was really strange to me," said Doohan. "Gene had a great house in the hills, a condo at La Costa that cost at least $1,000 a month, nice cars—you know. How could he be upset over $1,900?"

But now that Paramount had placed a value on the *Star Trek* rights, Roddenberry supposedly countered by offering to sell, for cash, a portion of his own future profits. The discussions never went any further. Equity in *Star Trek* did not change hands; no money changed hands. If the talks had come to fruition, it would have been questionable who, at the time, would have gotten the better deal.

BOB: So *Star Trek* was dead. Or was it?

The accepted story is that the series began to develop its syndication afterlife in 1972, well after its network cancellation. Actually, that wasn't exactly true.

The year was 1967, shortly after the Gulf & Western purchase of Desilu and its absorption into Paramount. The place was the Hotel Warwick in New York City, and the occasion was a Saturday-morning breakfast meeting between Dick Block, President of Kaiser Broadcasting, and Bob Newgard, head of Paramount Domestic Syndication. Kaiser Broadcasting owned five major-market UHF stations—Philadelphia, Boston, Cleveland, Detroit, and San Francisco—and Block was always on the lookout for an inexpensive program buy. Years earlier he had wanted to buy the CBS network reruns of one of his favorite series, Rod Serling's *The Twilight Zone*. But heeding well-intentioned advice from his fellow executives, Block dropped the idea and the purchase. *The Twilight Zone* went on to become one of the most successful syndication packages ever to come off the networks. Another of Block's favorite series was *Star Trek,* and he wasn't about to be talked out of that one.

Unfortunately for him, however, *Star Trek* was still running on NBC, and the series' future was the reason for the Kaiser-Paramount breakfast meeting. Block proposed buying the syndication rights to *Star Trek before* it was cancelled, something relatively unheard of at the time. He would pay less than the going rate; after all, he was guaranteeing the sale and the money. No contract was to be prepared or signed until after *Star Trek*'s network cancellation. The two men shook on the deal, and a year and a half before *Star Trek* was cancelled by NBC, Kaiser Broadcasting bought what turned out to be seventy-nine episodes of *Star Trek* for their local stations.

In the early seventies, Kaiser's UHF stations had neither the range nor audience of the VHF stations in their markets and had to augment their programs by mounting them differently, promoting them differently, and marketing them differently. Kaiser's research indicated the prime viewers of *Star Trek* were young males. Gambling that young males were not heavy viewers of television news programs, Block and Barry Thurston, who worked for Block in Oakland, California, decided to schedule the *Star Trek* reruns at 6:00 P.M., directly opposite their competitor stations' newscasts. As if that wasn't enough, they decided to run the original, uncut network films, regardless of the fact that the shows allowed for more program content and less commercial time. Block further decided to run the episodes in the order they had run on NBC and, as a matter of fact, had an announcement made, on each one of the episodes, of the exact time and date of the initial NBC telecast. And after running them daily for sixteen weeks, the station started over and ran them daily for another sixteen weeks, and another and another. The audience reaction was terrific. All the Kaiser Broadcasting stations saw startling increases in audience for their 6:00 P.M. time period, with WKBS, Channel 48, in Philadelphia amassing the highest *Star Trek* ratings of all.

There is very good reason to believe that Block's and Thurston's programming approach to *Star Trek* was of major importance to the unparalleled syndication success of the cancelled series. Incidentally, the Kaiser stations eventually followed the *Star Trek* reruns with reruns of *Mission: Impossible. Mission* performed very badly in its time period. Thus, after years of losing battles with *Mission: Impossible*, *Star Trek* had finally come out on top where it counts: in the ratings—and in the money.

Star Trek on the Kaiser Broadcasting stations was a major programming achievement, and word of the rating success soon spread to independent stations in other cities. The original seventy-nine episodes were scheduled in late afternoon and early evening time periods and run, rerun, and rerun again all over the country—and, eventually, all over the world.

BOB: The show began to spawn generation after generation of Trekkers. Both fans and nonfans delighted in its arcane phraseology: "Beam me up, Scotty," and "He's dead, Jim."

"I grok Spock" stickers began to appear on automobile bumpers everywhere. From *Saturday Night Live* and *Mad* magazine to NASA's space shuttle *Enterprise*, the show had become a cultural phenomenon. Thousands of *Star Trek* conven-

tions were launched everywhere and probably saved the hospitality business in the seventies: A zillion "Trekkies" (or "Trekkers") wearing pointy ears and decked out in "Federation" uniforms converged on a million Hilton Hotels to cohabit with each other—strictly in a cultural sense, so far as I know.

Gulf & Western had bought Desilu for an estimated $17 million and merged it into Paramount Pictures. In 1986, well before his death, Roddenberry confided to Bob Justman his estimate that Paramount had "made over $1 billion" from its ownership of the *Star Trek* merchandising rights, reruns of the original series, and the *Star Trek* feature films thus far produced. Since then, the total has grown considerably, with three new television series—*Star Trek: The Next Generation*, *Star Trek: Deep Space Nine*, and *Star Trek: Voyager*—as well as the additional *Star Trek* feature motion pictures, videocassettes, books, magazines, toys, clothing, souvenirs, memorabilia. The list goes on and on. By 1994, it was estimated that Paramount had grossed over $1.4 billion from its ownership and exploitation of the basic original property.

And now a spate of *Next Generation* movies has begun. How many more will follow?

HERB: With the resurgence of *Star Trek* as a viable television property, a renewed Gene Roddenberry reentered the world of network television. He made a term deal with Universal Television, and both Gene and Universal pinpointed NBC as the best network to approach for pilot-development money. The project was called *The Questor Tapes,* and a pilot was filmed at Universal. Herb Schlosser liked it very much and ordered twelve scripts to be written. Later, burned by NBC's and Universal's difficulties in dealing with Gene, Herb Schlosser called me with a plea for help—and an offer. "How about going into business with Roddenberry to produce a series we want to do with him at Universal?"

"Please don't ask me that, Schloss. Gene has changed since the early days of *Star Trek.* It's almost as if he's become one of those gods he used to write about. One film would be fine, but the thought of working together on a four- or five-year television series is too much to ask."

The series was never made. The twelve scripts are collecting dust at Universal, and *The Questor Tapes* pilot was broadcast by NBC as a Movie of the Week.

Recently, Leonard Nimoy recounted an interesting story about his own short-lived association with *The Questor Tapes.* After NBC contracted for the pilot film, Gene Roddenberry phoned Nimoy and asked whether he would be interested in the starring role in both the pilot and possible series. Nimoy read the script that Roddenberry sent to him and indicated his interest in the project. He was soon assured that his agent was negotiating a deal for his services as the star of the new show.

Subsequently, Roddenberry arranged for Nimoy to meet with him at Universal Studios to discuss the script and begin fittings for the star's wardrobe. The arrangement was for them to meet in the Universal Wardrobe Department. Nimoy arrived and waited for Roddenberry to show up, in the meantime chatting with the male costumer assigned to the pilot. He knew that Roddenberry, being a busy man, was sometimes late for his appointments.

"The costumer seemed very ill at ease," recalled Nimoy, "and he soon left the room to make a phone call."

Shortly thereafter, director Richard Colla arrived and, after the usual "hello" and "how are you?" casually asked Nimoy why he was there.

"Why, I'm here to fit my wardrobe on the pilot," responded the actor. "I understand you're directing, Dick."

"Yes, I am. . . " acknowledged Colla. He hesitated, then continued, ". . . but didn't anyone tell you?"

"Tell me what?" queried Nimoy.

Dick Colla seemed very ill at ease. "Well, to tell you the truth, we've already hired Robert Foxworth for the starring role."

Nimoy smiled all-knowingly, thanked Dick Colla for his straightforwardness, and went home. Leonard Nimoy laughed when he told this story to Solow and Justman, albeit ruefully. And *they* laughed upon hearing it, albeit just as ruefully. They knew, as he did, that Gene Roddenberry never liked to be the bearer of bad tidings.

HERB: In 1973, Gene Roddenberry approached Paramount and expressed his desire to write and produce a *Star Trek* movie. The idea was well received, but Paramount would accept him only as a writer. Based on their past dealings with him and the negative word of mouth in the industry concerning his lack of control over director Roger Vadim on the MGM movie *Pretty Maids All in a Row,* he was unacceptable to Paramount as a producer.

While I was producing at Warner Brothers in 1973, Gene called and explained "the Mexican standoff." According to him, "Paramount can't make a *Star Trek* movie without me, and I can't make a *Star Trek* movie without Paramount. They'll go along only if you're the producer. I'll write the script."

Later, I learned that Paramount could have, in fact, legally made a *Star Trek* movie without Gene, but hesitated to do so, not wanting to alienate the show's many fans.

Gene's proposed story was a one-paragraph premise entitled "The Cattlemen," which bore some resemblance to H. G. Wells's book *The Time Machine.* This premise had been included with eight others in an early rough draft

writer's guide that Gene and Dorothy Fontana prepared in 1964. The story concerned:

> . . . an Earth colony on the planet Regulus that had survived by shifting to a meat-producing economy. Dr. Boyce [ship's doctor in the first pilot] discovers the "cattle" are intelligent beings and Captain April [the original name for Captain Pike in the first pilot] tries to enforce the statutes regarding the protection of intelligent alients [*sic*] . . . Then April discovers the bitter irony—it is a necessary part of the "cattle's" life cycle that they be killed and eaten, for this plants within the eater the seeds of the animal's continued existence and gradually the "host" begins to change and becomes one of the "cattle" himself. . . .

It was obvious to me that Gene's story premise would have to be rewritten because it did not foreshadow an enjoyable night at the movies.

Despite my misgivings, I phoned Paramount President Frank Yablans to discuss the venture. Frank was enthusiastic and estimated that the film could gross a minimum of $30 million. *Star Trek* would have been a major hi-tech space movie, years before George Lucas had given any thought to *Star Wars.* But it was not to be.

While Gene and I spent time discussing how to fix the story, my agent, Robin French, negotiated a standard producer's deal for me with Paramount. Leonard Maizlish began negotiations for Gene.

A money problem arose. Maizlish and Roddenberry refused to accept the scriptwriting fee and equity proposed by Paramount. Although this was only Gene's second movie deal, he demanded more money than Paramount was willing to pay. Gene pointed out that MGM had paid him $100,000 for adapting the novel *Pretty Maids All in a Row.* He chose to forget that I was the MGM executive who had hired him and paid him the $100,000, and that it was a generous deal for a script at the time, and particularly good for Gene, considering his financial situation. But for whatever reason, he demanded more money. Having trouble even closing a deal with Gene, Paramount saw nothing but more trouble in the future and backed away from the project.

Gene never wrote the script; this "first" *Star Trek* movie was never made. *Star Trek: The Motion Picture* wasn't made until six years later. In the interim, George Lucas astonished moviegoers with *Star Wars. Star Trek,* an early-on sure winner, became an also-ran in Hollywood's race for space.

Later, two Paramount Business Affairs attorneys were discussing the senselessness of Roddenberry's negotiating himself out of writing a major movie. One of them decried Gene's reasoning: "He lost the deal arguing over nickels. Nickels!"

But some other attempts to cash in on the franchise were also less than successful.

Courtesy NBC/Globe

Two illustrations from the *Star Trek* animated series.

Guided by Lou Scheimer, president of Filmation, a Saturday-morning animated *Star Trek* series was launched on NBC in 1973. Roddenberry was contracted to be the creative force behind the cartoon series, but he delegated that chore to Dorothy Fontana, who was hired as the Associate Producer–Story Editor. The plan was to hire the original series stars to provide their character voices. However, with the budget constraints and usual practice of Saturday-morning cartoon series, Majel Barrett and James Doohan were to "double" the voices of Nichelle Nichols, George Takei, and Walter Koenig. This action was not appreciated by Leonard Nimoy, who threatened to forgo the animated series unless all the original series stars were hired to voice themselves. Roddenberry and Filmation relented, but hired only Nichols and Takei. Walter Koenig wrote an episode. The cartoon series wasn't successful and was cancelled after twenty-two episodes.

In 1977, Roddenberry and Paramount attempted to launch a new series, *Star Trek: Phase II*. Roddenberry wrote a two-hour pilot script and a revised writer's guide, and endeavored to recreate the atmosphere and beginnings of the original series. However, Leonard Nimoy, wanting new and different challenges, chose not to participate in the "rehash." Without the saturnine Vulcan, the new *Starship Enterprise* never got off the ground.

Finally, in 1978, Paramount, recognizing *Star Trek*'s big-screen potential, put aside its aversion to Gene Roddenberry (taking into account the importance of his name) and contracted for him to produce *Star Trek: The Motion Picture*. However, plagued by faulty planning, a faulty script, and faulty supervision, it was a total misadventure. The production went tens of millions of dollars over budget, making *Star Trek: The Motion Picture* the most over-budget film in the history of Paramount Pictures. Unfortunately, owing to the unexpectedly high cost of the film, it failed to be the commercial hit that Paramount anticipated, although owing to receipts from ancillary markets, the film eventually did make money. The studio felt that Roddenberry was ill-equipped as a motion picture producer and removed him from consideration as the producer of any future *Star Trek* movies.

Recognizing the continuing commercial potential of *Star Trek* movies, however, Paramount hired Harve Bennett to produce, and occasionally write, many of the subsequent features. This was the very same Harve Bennett who, years earlier as an ABC Program Manager, had been ordered thrown off the *April Savage* set by Roddenberry. Bennett's films were all produced with budgetary restraint and were successful at the box office.

However, the Roddenberry myth and the *Star Trek* legend had taken such a hold on the millions of *Star Trek* fans that Paramount, to avoid a box-office backlash, relented and hired Roddenberry for the succeeding *Star Trek* movies, but only as a highly paid "consultant." He could read the scripts and make suggestions, but the studio was under no obligation to accept or implement his input.

Courtesy Greg Jein

25

All Our Yesterdays

In 1902, the Canadian medical historian, Sir William Osler, wrote, " . . . The foolishness of yesterday has become the wisdom of tomorrow." *Star Trek*'s detractors might have called it foolishness, but they can't deny the firestorm it generated.

Without a doubt, Gene Roddenberry was the spark that ignited it all. But the embers glowed brighter and brighter as many professionals made meaningful contributions that continually fueled *Star Trek*'s growth and development—so much so that without those contributions, the glowing embers would have died.

Those contributors are forever etched in our minds, some more deeply remembered than others.

Courtesy Carole Werner Teig

The front and back of the invitation for Mort Werner's memorial service.

HERB: First, let's talk about the NBC guys—Werner, Tinker, Schlosser, and Stanley. They financed two pilots and the series, represented us well with their top management, and kept us on the air for three full seasons despite bad ratings and bad reviews.

I remember that every time Mort Werner returned to New York after visiting NBC's West Coast suppliers, he spent his airline travel time writing postcards to the producers and studio executives who supplied NBC with product, thanking them for their help. *Star Trek* actually owed its existence to Mort.

Shortly before Mort died, Grant Tinker visited him in Hawaii. A victim of Alzheimer's disease, Mort didn't recognize his close friend and associate.

And, after Mort died and *Daily Variety* carried the NBC-paid full-page announcement, Grant felt there should be something more for Mort. He arranged and paid for a commemorative dinner to honor his friend and former boss. On June 13, 1990, two months after Mort's death, several dozen of his friends packed the banquet room of Matteo's Restaurant and traded stories and remembrances about the friendly and unassuming NBC program executive who was so instrumental not only in their own lives, but in giving the post–Golden Years of television a new style and purpose.

It was an executive and producer Who's Who of television: Grant Tinker, Herb Schlosser, Lee Rich, Sylvester "Pat" Weaver, Jerry Leider, Sheldon Leonard, Jackie Cooper, Bud Grant, Roy Huggins, Frank Price, Leonard Stern, Tom McDermott, and others of equal prominence. Egos were checked at the door. After dinner, I asked former NBC President Herb Schlosser why he flew in from New York and former NBC President and legendary program innovator (the *Today* show, *The Tonight Show*) Pat Weaver why he drove down from Santa Barbara. Both men simply replied, "For Mort."

It's very easy to remember Grant Tinker. He was, and still is, the most throughly trustworthy, decent, thoughtful, and talented executive I have ever dealt with in the television industry. Long before my Desilu days, I returned to NBC for the opportunity to work with him; if he was to call me today to join him in a television venture, I'd be in his office tomorrow.

Much of the network's support of *Star Trek* came about because of Grant's understanding of the creative process. He conditioned NBC to accept the television boundaries we continually expanded and defended us from in-house criticism. Grant loved *Star Trek,* understood Gene Roddenberry, and was always available when we needed him. What more could I ask?

I remember that soon after Herb Schlosser moved to Los Angeles, he experienced his first earthquake. He called to report the "strange occurrence," announcing, "The water in my pool has whitecaps." When he mangled Spanish-rooted street and city names, I explained that La Canada is not pronounced La Can-a-da, but rather La Can-yada; La Cienega was not La See-a-negga; Sepulveda wasn't Sep-ull-veeda. When his pet keeshond had ticks, he drove his Beverly Hills dog to my house on Saturday mornings to have me, a serious German Shepherd owner, remove the little bloodsuckers. Schloss had a nice dog.

And our personal friendship was key to his support of *Star Trek.* It afforded him some firsthand knowledge of what the series was all about and afforded me a clearer insight into NBC's desire to "make the series work."

I remember Jerry Stanley, who broke into a very important meeting at MGM with confidential information—a freight car filled with "difficult to find" fresh dates had tipped over near Burbank, and ten thousand pounds of fruit were there for the taking. He knew I enjoyed dates, and I was ready to leave my meeting and drive to Burbank until I learned his freight-car story was a total fabrication. The incident had absolutely nothing to do with *Star Trek,* but reminded me that Jerry always had a strange sense of humor. How else would he have supported some of the things we did on the series?

I remember that seven years after I resigned from Paramount, one of my daughters and I were walking in the Beverly Hills shopping area when a harsh, crackling voice demanded, "Herb, where's Giorgio's [the clothing store]?" We turned and stared at an old lady with bleached red hair and deeply wrinkled skin. "Herb, where's Giorgio's?" she demanded again.

I didn't recognize her until my daughter whispered, "Daddy, it's Lucy." It was the first time Lucy had spoken to me since shortly before she sold the studio.

At the time, we'd had a very intense discussion regarding my refusal to give Gary Morton an executive role in the production of all three series. Lucy had glared at me. "Herb, you think my husband is a shit, don't you?"

"Stop acting like Lucy Ricardo, will you, please?" I had retorted. We stared at each other for a few moments, and then what would turn out to be our last employer-employee meeting was over.

Twelve years later on a crowded street, it seemed as if nothing had ever happened. I answered her question. "Sorry, Lucy, I have no idea where Giorgio's is."

We traded small talk. There was no mention of *Star Trek, Mission: Impossible, Mannix,* or the old studio. Lucy congratulated me on some of the things I'd done, then turned and slowly walked away. The Desilu part of my life finally ended. I never saw Lucy again.

I remember the actors on the series. I enjoyed working with them, but Leonard Nimoy was the most distinctive. Where most other series regulars were concerned with the size of their roles each week—"How many lines do I have?"—Leonard was more concerned with the quality of his lines and Spock's impact on the particular story. Battling for dramatic integrity did not necessarily ingratiate him with those who were constantly rewriting scripts while fighting budgets, costs, delivery schedules, and studio policies. But Leonard performed a positive service, not only for his own character, but for the relationships of all the characters. He was the unbilled guardian of dramaturgy. It's easy to understand why, in recent years, Leonard Nimoy, the actor, is also recognized for his preeminence as a film producer and director.

I remember Gene Coon. After his divorce from his wife, Joy, and subsequent marriage to Jackie, his world consisted of great heights and, tragically, even greater depths. He no longer lived a balanced life; normalcy would never touch him again.

A year after the divorce, Joy Coon was stricken with cancer. Her illness devastated her former husband. As Joy lay dying in the hospital, Gene asked to see her. He needed to express his grief—and guilt—and to say goodbye. She refused his request and died without ever seeing her ex-husband again. Gene was shattered.

The happiness of his second marriage helped Gene Coon deal with his burden of guilt. He was working steadily, and Gene and Jackie were like kids in love and spoke often of the house they were building in Cambria, near the famous Hearst Castle, a few hundred miles north of Los Angeles. However, bad times would soon return, and his second marriage was destined to be short-lived.

I saw little of Gene and Jackie Coon socially, but Gene's and my paths continued to cross professionally. We were working together on developing some projects at Warner Brothers when Gene Coon's world crashed again—this time forever.

On Monday, July 2, 1973, I waited in our office. Gene Coon was late for a meeting. Gene was rarely late for meetings, and I became concerned.

An hour later, he walked in, carrying a cylinder of oxygen and a mask.

"What the hell is that?" I asked.

Gene looked terrible and coughed as he spoke. "Sorry, Herb, the goddamn smog is getting worse. I've been really feeling it lately. It's sure not helping my bronchitis." Coon lit up one his constant companions, a Sherman cigarillo. He inhaled deeply. "So tell me, what's happening with NBC?"

We reviewed the new series presentation we were scheduled to make Thursday morning at NBC. We were very well prepared.

Coon snuffed out the cigarillo, pressed the oxygen mask close to his nose, and took a long, deep breath. "Jackie made a doctor's appointment for me tomorrow. I think I'll rest a few days and meet you at NBC Thursday. Okay?"

"No problem, Gene. Ten o'clock in Schlosser's office. Get there a little early so we can get up to speed and discuss our presentation. And take care of yourself."

Late Wednesday afternoon, Jackie Coon called. "Herb, the doctor wants to run some more tests tomorrow. Gene was wondering if you can take the NBC meeting without him."

"Absolutely, Jackie. I'll call him after the meeting with a report. How's he feeling?"

"About the same. Can you believe this smog?"

"No." But Gene was a rugged guy, a Korean War veteran who had seen a lot of military action. Strange that smog should affect him so much.

The NBC meeting went well; they ordered a pilot script, "The Adventures of Diamond Smith." When I got back to the office, I called Gene Coon. His phone didn't pick up, and the answering service didn't know where he could be reached. "Please ask him to call. I have good news."

Friday afternoon, Gene Coon called from a hospital. His voice was shallow, and he gasped for air as he spoke. "Herb, Jackie was going to call, but she's at the library getting me some books to read." He paused. "It's not too good."

I tried for more information. Gene merely repeated, "It's not too good." We agreed I'd visit him Monday and discuss our pilot script order.

At 7:00 Sunday morning, six days after he was examined by his doctor, Gene Coon died in Jackie's arms. The X-rays had shown a lump the size of a grapefruit in his lungs. The original diagnosis of smog-induced bronchitis had turned out to be inoperable cancer.

Actor Bill Campbell, Gene Coon's close friend, believes the great burden of guilt he carried over his first wife, Joy, was so painful that he truly welcomed death.

I remember Majel Barrett. Always cheerful, helpful, and professional, Majel sometimes found herself caught in the web of Gene's machinations, and I truly believe she suffered both personally and professionally because of it. Majel's acting career certainly would have grown and flourished without the limitations of her *Star Trek* role.

Further, NBC's decision to drop Majel's Number One character from the second pilot (and thus the subsequent series) opened the door for another actor to assume the role of second-in-command of the *Enterprise.* The actor was Leonard

Nimoy, and Mister Spock moved up from being third star of the first pilot to costar of the second pilot and series. Since scripted roles are written based on the "importance" of the series stars, the door was opened for Mister Spock to shine. And not only did he shine, he became the brightest of all the stars in the *Star Trek* universe.

And lastly, I remember Gene Roddenberry. He and I quickly became the best of friends after our first meeting in 1964, although we never socialized together. Our lifestyles and values were quite different.

However, over the years, as Gene continued his seemingly never-ending conflict with authority, it became difficult for me to continue working with him. Our close friendship would last only about nine years. Gene had a lot of good qualities, but his need for self-glorification stood in the way of continuing our personal and professional association.

Star Trek was Gene's only successful creation. It was a great show. But I'm convinced that his establishment of scapegoats when dealing with authority prevented him from achieving further success. However, his talent and his ego helped propel Gene Roddenberry's *Star Trek* well beyond its intended role as mere television entertainment.

I regret that Gene never publicly or privately thanked Desilu and its executives and NBC and its executives for supporting him and his series. He became a very famous and a very wealthy man because of the opportunity they afforded him. Moreover, when the going got tough, Gene failed to keep his part of the bargain and, in essence, abandoned *Star Trek* in its third, and final, year. He was already on to new ventures.

My last conversation with Gene was in 1973, during the ill-fated negotiations with Paramount for him to write and me to produce what would have been the first *Star Trek* movie. The fact that, years later, Paramount finally relented and allowed him to produce *Star Trek: The Motion Picture* convinced me that it wasn't the money that caused Gene to negate the all-but-finalized deal. Based on our very close working relationship in the trenches at Desilu, I knew that, even though Gene initiated the discussions, he could not emotionally accept the public knowledge that someone else was producing "his" movie. I would have enjoyed producing this first movie, but if it was not to be, it was far from an end-all. I was working elsewhere, doing other things and getting on with my life.

The inability to forge the first movie deal wasn't the cause of my major disappointment with Gene. My displeasure grew over the years as he reinvented the origins of *Star Trek,* further enlarging the *Star Trek* legend and the Gene Roddenberry myth. While there is no denying that Gene created the root, the core from which the series grew, there were other important contributors to its growth: Gene Coon, Bob Justman, Matt Jefferies, and me. Unfortunately, the credit for our contributions was washed away in the wake of Gene's disinclination to honor them, and by doing so, he assumed their authorship.

Star Trek went into formal development in 1964 as a commercial television series with Gene Roddenberry, Desilu, and NBC all hoping to make money from the project. It's important to understand that, first and foremost, *Star Trek* was not created or developed as a critical study of truth, life's fundamental principles, or concepts of reasoned doctrines. We just wanted a hit series.

The basic *Star Trek* philosophy was developed by its producers and writers during its production. However, a profound and metaphysical overlay was superimposed over the years as popularity begat popularity and viewers saw and defined a subjective something that validated and increased their appreciation of the show. The fact that so many fans saw, and continue to see, so much more in *Star Trek* than we ever realized was there makes me happy and proud beyond belief.

RJ and I talked with many of the people who worked on *Star Trek* from 1964 to 1969. There was one overriding emotion, one common thread present in our conversations. Even with the disappointments of impossible schedules and frazzled relationships, every one of us believed—every one of us insisted—that it was, absolutely, the best time of our lives.

BOB: I remember working at home late one night during the first season of *Star Trek,* analyzing stories and scripts and, strangely enough, not feeling tired at all. In fact, I felt exhilarated. By all rights, I should have been exhausted; yet while at dinner, I could hardly wait to finish eating and get back to work. What made me feel so excited? I pondered the question for a while.

And then it came to me: *Star Trek* wasn't just a grand adventure for Kirk and Spock and McCoy and the others; it was a lot more than that. *Star Trek* was also a grand adventure for Gene Roddenberry and Herb Solow and me—three explorers embarking upon a journey into the unknown, truly a journey where no man had ever gone before. No one else working in television had ever attempted anything so audacious, and yet there we were, charting a perilous course into the unknown.

"We're pioneers too," I thought, "facing unknown perils, yet eager to come to grips with them." It was then I realized, "We're not doing what Kirk and Spock do; rather, they're doing what we do: taking chances by facing the great unknown, blazing paths to the future."

Our task was so dangerous, I almost laughed aloud with glee. I could have worked all night and never faltered, and I couldn't wait to go back to the studio the next morning.

Herb was so right; it was, absolutely, the best time of our lives.

I remember everyone: Ed Milkis, Matt Jefferies, Lucy, the people at NBC, the studio execs, the cast, the crew, even the cop at the gate—and Herb.

Lastly, I, too, remember Gene Roddenberry, the man who used *Star Trek* as a platform to advance his view of mankind's future, a future that embraced non-human cultures. I remember him predicting: "Given the countless billions of stars in our universe, there must be millions of planets out there where intelligent life exists. Someday, people from our planet will encounter them."

Star Trek's creator employed the show's stories, allegorically, to further his optimistic premise that "there will be no Armageddon for mankind" and that "the future is bright." His ideas and the future he created for all of us convinced me that, sociologically speaking, he was the most advanced thinker I had ever met. Genius had touched him.

And I remember something else. In November, 1977, soon after Paramount announced that *Star Trek: The Motion Picture* was in the works, Gene phoned me and suggested, "Let's have lunch together. Just the two of us. We'll talk about the movie. I'll call you next week to set a time."

I was thrilled. Gene had used this approach in the past when he wanted me to work with him on his Warner Brothers pilot, *Planet Earth.* But this time I waited in vain for his phone call. After several weeks, I tried calling him but he was always "out of the office." He never returned any of my calls. I was mystified.

Finally, I asked my agent, Bill Haber, at CAA (Creative Artists Agency), to find out what was wrong. He couldn't get an answer from Gene. "He's avoiding you, Bob," advised Bill. "You might as well forget it."

It was a bitter disappointment. Later, after screening the movie, I was convinced that, had I been there, some of the mistakes made in making the film could have been avoided. Afterwards, the subject of the movie was never brought up between us—other than one time, seven years later, back at the place where it all began.

In September 1986, word went out that a new *Star Trek* series was in the works. Soon Gene phoned, this time suggesting I come by to screen various science-fiction movies with him and Ed Milkis. I swallowed my pride and did so. This time, things were different; and soon, eighteen years after leaving Paramount, I was back preparing the first season of *Star Trek: The Next Generation*—which only goes to prove the old Hollywood adage: "You'll never work in this town again—until we need you."

Although I had sworn never to produce another television series, I couldn't resist making *Star Trek* again, not only to make it better than it ever was but to prove that, unlike the first series, it could be a success.

But I had to confront Gene about not being a part of the first *Star Trek* movie. I told him, "You broke my heart, Gene." Gene didn't respond. He couldn't. But I'd made my point; I never brought the matter up again.

After that, my relationship with Gene became much closer. There were lots of hugs and kisses from him, and he even went so far as to say, "Love you, Bob!" whenever we finished a meeting.

From the collection of Robert H. Justman

Gene Roddenberry (l.) and Bob Justman (r.) in 1989 at the "wrap" party for the second season of *Star Trek: The Next Generation.*

And he meant it. It was as if he sensed the end—his end—wasn't far off, and he wanted to make amends for the disappointments he had caused in the past. In fact early in our preparation for *Star Trek: The Next Generation,* Gene went so far as to give me a $5,000 bonus check. "I want you to have it because you deserve it——even more," he declared.

In the fall of 1986, during my initial preparation of *Star Trek: The Next Generation,* it was clearly evident that Gene was in bad shape physically. He would be out of breath after walking a hundred feet, and he had to drive a golf cart to visit the stages or other parts of the lot.

It was great to be back together with Ed Milkis again. We had maintained our friendship over the years, and he had become a highly successful producer of both television and feature films. Eddie was under contract with Paramount and had agreed to "help out" on the new show. After about five months, however, he became disgusted with some of the studio television executives and even more disgusted with Gene's attorney and business manager, Leonard Maizlish. Maizlish, attempting to "protect" his friend and client, had become destructive to the series and interfered with everything Eddie and I were doing. Eddie walked—in late April, 1987, even before we began filming the first episode, "Encounter At Farpoint."

And I stayed—but only for a while. Even before the first season ended, I told Gene and Paramount that I didn't want my option picked up for a second year. I didn't tell them the real reason: that Leonard Maizlish (who had promised that I

From the collection of Herbert F. Solow

Composite photo of the "team" that produced *Star Trek*'s second pilot, the one that sold to NBC and started the phenomenon.

would get a "piece" of the show—a piece that somehow never materialized) had gotten to me as well. For the first time in my life, I began to suffer from hypertension.

Despite all the hugs and kisses and an offer to bump me up to Executive Producer, I left the show in late April, 1988, after completing my work on "The Neutral Zone," the last episode of the new series' first season. I had some good years left and wanted to enjoy them.

Gene and I remained close during the ensuing three and a half years. But every time I saw him, I was struck by how much he seemed to be deteriorating. He was a ghastly sight when I visited him at the UCLA Medical Center Hospital after he had been operated upon to relieve pressure upon his brain. His head had been shaved, and he was still weak from the surgery. It took two nurses to move his large frame from his bed to a nearby chair. He had difficulty speaking, but he smiled at me constantly.

On October 17, 1991, an ailing, wheelchair-bound Gene came to visit me at my home. Ernie Over, the devoted man who helped care for Gene, wheeled him inside. Gene had been looking forward to this visit, as had I. He wasn't in good shape, having suffered a number of strokes and the surgery to reduce pressure on his brain. But the surgery couldn't correct his condition; it only relieved the symptoms for a while.

I knew he didn't have much longer to live and that he had refused any further efforts to lengthen his life. He didn't want to prolong the agony, both for himself and for the people he loved. Gene seemed to enjoy the visit and told me, "I'd like to come back again real soon." He smiled a lot, but I did most of the talking. At times, he was lucid and responded well and then, suddenly, he'd seem to slip away.

I had to ask; it had been on my mind for years. This was my last opportunity. "Gene, remember the rubies Jackie and I gave Eileen?"

Gene smiled and nodded at me.

"Did she ever do anything with the rubies, Gene? Did she make jewelry with them?"

Gene smiled and nodded.

"She seemed angry that night, so angry I thought maybe she threw them away."

Gene smiled and nodded.

I looked at Ernie: was I getting through? He shook his head. The visit was over. Ernie wheeled Gene outside and put him into the Rolls-Royce. As Ernie crossed around to the driver's side, I leaned in close to Gene. "Gene, I want you to know something. I never f....d you. Maybe other people let you down, but not me. Not ever."

His smile faded. I looked into his eyes. Did something flicker there, or was it my imagination? I kissed him good-bye and he smiled once more. I never saw him again. He died exactly one week later.

Epilogue

Live Long and Prosper

Many of the major players in the development and production of the original *Star Trek* series are still active in the entertainment industry. Others have retired; still other have passed away. This is where they all are now:

Darrell Anderson (*Star Trek* optical-effects supervisor) retired from the optical-effects business. The Howard Anderson Company remains a leading optical-effects supplier to the entertainment industry.

Desi Arnaz (actor-producer) was never successful in show business after his divorce from Lucy. He remarried and moved to Del Mar, where he had a stable of racehorses. He died in 1986.

Ted Ashley (talent agency owner) sold his interest in International-Famous Agency (formerly Ashley-Famous) and later became the head of Warner Brothers. He is now retired.

Lucille Ball (actress; Desilu Studios owner) formed another production company, Lucille Ball Productions. After the failure of her new series, *Here's Lucy,* and the motion picture, *Mame,* Lucy performed in various TV specials. She retired after her role as a bag woman in a less than memorable television movie, *The Stone Pillow.* She died in 1989.

Majel Barrett (*Star Trek* actress: "Number One," "Nurse Chapel") married Gene Roddenberry in 1969 at a Shinto ceremony in Japan. She gave birth to a son, Rod, in 1974. In addition to running Lincoln Enterprises, a *Star Trek* merchandising firm, she has successfully continued her acting career, appearing in two *Star Trek* movies as well as playing the popular Lwaxana Troi character in the television series *Star Trek: The Next Generation* and *Star Trek: Deep Space Nine.* She is a well-loved and frequent guest star at science-fiction conventions and actively supports the continued exploration of space.

Harve Bennett (ABC Programs Manager) became an ABC Vice President. He left to produce several highly successful TV series. He later wrote and produced several of the *Star Trek* movies and is still very active in the television and motion picture industries.

John D. F. Black (*Star Trek* writer; Associate Producer) continued his writing career with numerous films and television series, some of which involved Herb Solow and Bob Justman.

Dick Block (President, Kaiser Broadcasting), who made the initial syndication purchase of *Star Trek,* presently resides in Los Angeles, California, and works as an independent television consultant.

Charles Bluhdorn (CEO, Gulf & Western) built Gulf & Western, later to be renamed Paramount Communications, into one of America's leading corporations. He died February 19, 1983.

Robert Butler (director, first *Star Trek* pilot) is a successful director and screenwriter of motion pictures. He created the popular television series *Remington Steele* and directed the pilot films of *Hill Street Blues, Moonlighting, Lois and Clark,* and *Sisters.*

Ted Cassidy (*Star Trek* actor: "Ruk" in "What Are Little Girls Made Of?") continued his acting career until his death on January 16, 1978.

Wah Chang (*Star Trek* prop and creature designer-builder) worked on many other shows, designing masks and headdresses for such major films as *The King And I* and *Can-Can*. Elizabeth Taylor wore one of his most spectacular creations in *Cleopatra*. Now retired from prop and costume making, he resides in Carmel Valley, California with his wife, Glen. He is widely recognized as an accomplished sculptor.

Morris Chapnick (executive assistant to Roddenberry and Solow) became an assistant director and unit manager for films and television. He also works as a commercial photographer.

Gene L. Coon (*Star Trek* writer-producer) continued his successful writing career. After five happy years of marriage to his second wife, Jackie, he died of cancer on July 8, 1973.

Jacqueline Coon–Fernandez (actress) remarried and now lives in Florida. She has continued her modeling career.

Alexander "Sandy" Courage (composer of *Star Trek* theme music) is still active in the music and film world. He lives in Malibu, California.

Douglas S. Cramer (Vice President, Paramount Television) is a highly successful producer of television shows and movies. He is a leading art connoisseur and has amassed an important collection of contemporary art.

Joe D'Agosta (Desilu Casting Director) joined Herb Solow at MGM as Talent Vice President. He is still active as a casting director.

Marc Daniels (*Star Trek* Director) later directed the first episode of *Man From Atlantis* for Herb Solow and Bob Justman. He died in 1989 after a long and successful career in films, television, and theatre.

Kellam DeForest (head of research for *Star Trek*) eventually sold DeForest Research, but continues to serve the film industry as a consultant. He lives in Santa Barbara, California.

James Doohan (*Star Trek* actor: "Engineer Scott") portrays "Scotty" in the *Star Trek* movies and is a popular guest star at science-fiction conventions. He is writing a book about his life.

Harlan Ellison (writer, "City on the Edge of Forever") writes films, books, articles, and film critiques and is a major participant in all areas of the science-fiction genre.

Gerald Perry Finnerman (*Star Trek* cameraman) continues to work as a cinematographer in the film industry.

Dorothy C. Fontana (*Star Trek* writer; Story Editor) scripted the opening two-hour episode of *Star Trek: The Next Generation* and held a staff position on the series during its first season. Together with writer David Gerrold, she later initiated and won a Writers Guild arbitration against both Paramount and Roddenberry. She continues her successful writing career.

Fred Freiberger (third-season *Star Trek* producer) is active in the entertainment industry as a writer and producer.

Bruce Geller (writer-producer; *Mission: Impossible* creator) wrote and produced television and motion picture films, some in conjunction with Herb Solow. He died tragically at the height of his career when his private plane crashed on a mountainside near Santa Barbara on May 21, 1978.

David Gerrold (writer, "The Trouble with Tribbles") wrote a nonfiction book entitled *The World of Star Trek*. After working on the first season of *Star Trek: The Next Generation*, Gerrold failed in his attempt to garner a remunerative "created by" credit on the new series. Gerrold writes popular science-fiction novels, writes for television, and is a frequent guest at *Star Trek* conventions.

James Goldstone (*Star Trek* second-pilot director), after a successful career as a motion picture director, teaches film at Bennington College. He remains active in films as a writer-director.

Ernest Haller (cameraman) died on October 21, 1970, five years after photographing the second *Star Trek* pilot.

Byron Haskin (Associate Producer, first *Star Trek* pilot) continued to work in films and television, lending his expertise in the area of optical special effects. Before retiring in 1968, Haskin directed *The Power*, a theatrical film for producer George Pal. He died in 1984.

Edwin Holly (Desilu Vice President) continued as an executive with Paramount Pictures and later became an executive with the William Morris Agency. He has since retired.

Jeffrey Hunter (starred as "Captain Pike" in the first *Star Trek* pilot) died as the result of a fall on May 27, 1969, one week prior to the broadcast of *Star Trek*'s final episode. He never attained stardom in films.

Walter M. "Matt" Jefferies (*Star Trek* Art Director; Production Designer) retired from the film business and now restores and flies period airplanes as a hobby. He is considered one of America's leading aviation artists.

George Clayton Johnson (writer, "Man Trap") continues to write science fiction stories, novels, and films.

Robert H. Justman (*Star Trek* Associate Producer; Co-Producer) went on to produce many other television shows, including *Man from Atlantis*, with Herb Solow, and the television pilot *Planet Earth*, with Gene Roddenberry. After producing the first season of *Star Trek: The Next Generation*, he eagerly withdrew from television production and now spends his time writing and lecturing at science-fiction conventions, and, as a reserve captain, continues his more than twenty-three-year secondary law-enforcement career in the Los Angeles County Sheriff's Reserve.

Steve Kandel (writer, "Mudd's Women" and "I, Mudd") is active as a television and motion picture writer.

Oscar Katz (President, Desilu Productions) retired from the television business after leaving Desilu and became a securities analyst and stock market investor. He died of pneumonia in Los Angeles on January 4, 1996.

Sally Kellerman (guest star, second *Star Trek* pilot) has starred in many films and television shows. She originated the role of "Hot Lips" Houlihan in the movie *M.A.S.H.*

DeForest Kelley (*Star Trek* actor: "Doctor McCoy") continued his acting career and reprises his role as Doctor McCoy in *Star Trek* movies. He makes occasional appearances at science-fiction conventions as an honored guest.

Walter Koenig (*Star Trek* actor: "Ensign Chekov") portrayed Ensign Chekov in the *Star Trek* movies and continues to act in films and the theatre. He has also become a successful author and frequently guest-stars at science-fiction conventions.

Gary Lockwood (guest star, second *Star Trek* pilot) starred in Stanley Kubrick's *2001*. Since then, he has appeared in numerous other motion pictures and television shows. When not acting, he pursues his favorite avocation, designing and building custom homes.

John Meredyth Lucas (second-season *Star Trek* writer-producer) returned to again work with Gene Roddenberry, writing the two-hour script "Katumba" for the ill-fated *Star Trek* television series resurrection, *Star Trek II.* Today, Lucas continues to be active in film and television. He remarried after the death of his first wife and now resides in Corona del Mar, California.

Harvey P. Lynn, Jr. (scientist; *Star Trek* technical advisor) continued his work at the Rand Corporation and, thereafter, at another prominent research facility. He died on New Year's Eve, December 31, 1986, one month after his eagerly looked-forward-to retirement.

Leonard Maizlish (attorney--business manager) negotiated all of Roddenberry's *Star Trek* contracts and the divorce agreement between his client and Eileen Roddenberry. Until he became physically incapacitated, he helped defend the Roddenberry estate and Majel Barrett Roddenberry against various lawsuits initiated by Eileen Roddenberry. Maizlish died on September 7, 1994.

Howard McClay (head of Desilu Publicity) continued as Lucille Ball's publicist until his death on December 9, 1980. Lucille Ball, who never attended funerals, attended his Rosary, showing her great respect for him.

Jean Messerschmidt (Director, NBC Standards and Practices) retired from NBC after many years of devoted service. She lives in Squim, Washington.

Edward K. Milkis (*Star Trek* Associate Producer) went on to become a producer of many successful television shows, including *Happy Days, Laverne and Shirley, Bosom Buddies,* and *Mork and Mindy.* He also was a producer on films like *Silver Streak* and *Foul Play.*

Ricardo Montalban (guest star: "Khan," in "Space Seed") later starred in the highly successful *Fantasy Island* television series. He is active in the film community, promoting the casting of Latino actors in theatre, movies, and television.

Gary Morton (husband of Lucille Ball) ran Lucille Ball Productions after Lucy sold Desilu. He remained married to her until she died.

Argyle Nelson (Desilu Vice President) retired after the sale of Desilu, ending a lengthy and distinguished career in film production. He died on August 14, 1970.

Nichelle Nichols (*Star Trek* actress: "Lieutenant Uhura") became a role model to many others as one of the first African American actresses to play an important role in a television series. She has starred in *Star Trek* movies, makes personal appearances at science-fiction conventions, and tours with her nightclub act. She has written her autobiography, entitled *Beyond Uhura.*

Leonard Nimoy (*Star Trek* actor: "Mister Spock") has continued his acting career, has written and directed for the theatre, and has become a successful director of such films as *Star Trek: The Search for Spock*, *Star Trek: The Voyage Home*, *The Good Mother*, and *Three Men And A Baby*. In 1994, he initiated his own new comic book line, "Primortals."

Susan Oliver (guest star, first *Star Trek* pilot) continued to act in both motion pictures and television and also gained national fame as an aviatrix. She died on May 9, 1990.

Joan Pearce (*Star Trek* researcher), who later established the firm of Joan Pearce Associates, continues to supply research services to the motion picture and television industries. She handles all *Star Trek* research matters for Paramount Pictures.

Samuel Peeples (writer, second *Star Trek* pilot) retired from actively writing for television but remains a great resource for many science-fiction writers. He lives in Santa Rosa, California.

Gregg Peters (*Star Trek* Associate Producer; Unit Manager) retired from the film industry. He lives in Pacific Palisades, California, and devotes his time to his interest in painting.

Joseph Pevney (*Star Trek* director) retired and moved to Palm Desert, California, where he pursues his passion as a ham radio operator.

Fred Phillips (*Star Trek* makeup supervisor) continued to work as a make-up artist until he was forced to retire due to encroaching blindness. He died on March 21, 1993.

Stephen E. Poe (author, aka Stephen E. Whitfield) left AMT after writing *The Making of Star Trek*. He enjoys a successful career as an author and is now writing a book about the new series *Star Trek: Voyager*. He lives in Reno, Nevada.

Janos Prohaska (stuntman, "The Devil in the Dark") remained active as a stuntman and creator of monsters in the film industry until his death on May 9, 1974.

John Reynolds (President, Paramount Television) resigned to become President of Los Angeles television station KTLA and later President of Golden West Broadcasting. He retired from show business, but remains active as a major charity fund-raiser.

Henry "Hank" Rieger (NBC Vice President) is still very active in the television industry as editor-publisher of *Emmy* magazine, the publication of the National Academy of Television Arts and Sciences.

Stanley Robertson (NBC Program Manager for *Star Trek*) unexpectedly resigned from NBC in 1976 after becoming Vice President of Motion Pictures for Television. He had been with the network for nineteen years.

Eileen Roddenberry (first wife of Gene Roddenberry) never remarried. She has been awarded substantial amounts of money from lawsuits she initiated against her former husband and his estate.

Gene Roddenberry (*Star Trek* creator) married Majel Barrett in a Shinto ceremony in Japan after divorcing his wife, Eileen. He wrote and produced other television pilots and the film *Pretty Maids All in a Row* at MGM for studio chief Herb Solow. He returned to Paramount to produce *Star Trek: The Motion Picture*, was credited as Creative Consultant on the other *Star Trek* movies, and was Executive Producer of *Star Trek: The Next Generation*, which reunited him and Justman. He died on October 24, 1991.

Don Rode (*Star Trek* Assistant Film Editor) became a full-fledged film editor and continues to work in the industry.

Milton "Mickey" Rudin (attorney for Lucille Ball and Desilu) continues his successful law career representing major figures in the entertainment industry.

Herbert Schlosser (NBC Vice President) became President of NBC and, later, Vice President of its parent company RCA. He is presently Senior Advisor in Broadcasting and Entertainment for Wertheim Schroder & Company, Inc.

Alden Schwimmer (talent agent) left the entertainment industry to become an attorney. He also works *pro bono* for the state of California, defending indigent people.

William Shatner (*Star Trek* actor: "Captain Kirk") continued his acting career, starring in several successful network TV series and the *Star Trek* movies, one of which he directed. He has written several science fiction novels and cowrote the books *Star Trek Memories* and *Star Trek Movie Memories*. His Tek War books were adapted for television as a series.

Arthur Singer (*Star Trek* third-season Story Consultant) died of pneumonia in New York City on March 19, 1978.

Jerry Sohl (writer, "The Corbomite Maneuver"), author of the famous novel *The Lemon Eaters,* remains active as a prominent science-fiction writer.

Herb Solow (Desilu Vice President; Executive in Charge of Production) became Vice President in Charge of Worldwide Theatrical and Television Production at MGM and later produced a number of theatrical and television motion pictures. He now works as a motion picture writer and producer. He is married to Yvonne Fern, author of the critically acclaimed *Gene Roddenberry: The Last Conversation.*

Robert Sparr (*Star Trek* Director, "Shore Leave") directed motion pictures and television films until his accidental death in 1969, in a plane crash while scouting location in Colorado with Jerry Finnerman.

Jerome Stanley (NBC Director of Current Programs) retired from NBC after 25 years. He now resides in Rancho Mirage, California—and golfs every day!

Fred Steiner (*Star Trek* composer) continued to write and conduct music for films and television. One of the many scores he created, the main title music for *Perry Mason,* became justly famous. Steiner eventually gained a PhD at the University of Southern California and later taught music composition there. Although he has since retired and now lives in Santa Fe, New Mexico, he continues to teach and lecture.

Leslie Stevens (writer-producer; creator of *The Outer Limits*) has continued an illustrious career, writing and producing for television, motion pictures, and the legitimate theatre.

George Takei (*Star Trek* actor: "Mister Sulu") continues to act in both film and theatre and is the editor-at-large of *Transpacific* magazine, the leading Pacific-rim periodical. He has been active in Los Angeles politics and served on the Board of Directors of the Southern California Rapid Transit District. He also guests at science-fiction conventions and has written his autobiography, *To The Stars.*

William Ware Theiss (*Star Trek* costume designer) continued to design costumes for films and television, including *Harold and Maude* and *Star Trek: The Next Generation.* He died on December 15, 1992. His personal collection of *Star Trek* costumes and designs was auctioned for the benefit of his estate in December, 1993.

Grant Tinker (NBC Vice President) founded MTM Productions with his wife, Mary Tyler Moore. He later returned to NBC to become Chairman of the Board and CEO. Afterward, he formed a partnership with Gannett Publications and purchased the former Desilu Culver studios, where both *Star Trek* pilots had been filmed. He is the author of the book, *Tinker in Television: From General Sarnoff to General Electric.*

Fabien Tordjmann (*Star Trek* film editor) continued his career editing films and television. Later remarrying, he produced several films in Canada. He now represents European moviemakers in the United States.

Bjo Trimble (volunteer organizer of the "Save *Star Trek*" campaign) and her husband John continue to be active in science-fiction fandom and make numerous personal appearances at conventions both here and abroad. She is the editor of *Bjo Trimble's Sci-Fi Spotlite*, a popular newsletter "for fans of Science Fiction, Fantasy & Horror Films, Television, & the entertainment field."

Charles Washburn (*Star Trek* second assistant director) became a Director. Bob Justman later hired him as a first assistant director on the opening season of *Star Trek: The Next Generation.*

Bernard L. Weitzman (Desilu Vice President) went on to hold major executive positions at various film studios after the sale of Desilu. He is now working with game show host Monty Hall, developing a cable television network for senior citizens.

Mort Werner (NBC Vice President of Programs) retired and moved to Hawaii, where he died of Alzheimer's disease on April 14, 1990.

Grace Lee Whitney (*Star Trek* actress: "Yeoman Rand") joined Alcoholics Anonymous and, after a hard struggle, successfully turned her life around. She frequently lectures on the problems of alcoholism and is often a guest star at *Star Trek* and other science-fiction conventions.

Acknowledgments

During the preparation of this book, many friends and former associates and employees at Desilu Studios, Paramount Television, and the National Broadcasting Company were most generous in giving us both their time and their memories.

It is often said that filmmaking is a collaborative effort. We have found that the writing of history can be collaborative as well. While honoring the requests of those who asked to remain anonymous, we would like to acknowledge the other contributors, in alphabetical order:

Those who were there:

Alan Baker; Howard Barton; Bill Blackburn; Dick Block; Robert Butler; William Campbell; Wah Chang; Morris Chapnick; Alexander Courage; Gordon Day;

Kellam DeForest; James Doohan; Harlan Ellison; Jacqueline (Coon) Fernandez; Dorothy C. Fontana; Fred Freiberger; James Goldstone; Don Ingalls; Walter "Matt" Jefferies; George Clayton Johnson; Jacqueline Justman; Gary Lockwood; Stephen Kandel; DeForest Kelley; Walter Koenig; Ken Kolb; John Meredyth Lucas; Penny Unger Marciaro; Edward K. Milkis; Nichelle Nichols; Leonard Nimoy; Frank Oakden; Joan Pearce; Sam Peeples; Joseph Pevney; Stephen E. Poe (Whitfield); John Reynolds; Henry "Hank" Rieger; Majel Barrett Roddenberry; Don Rode; Thomas Sarnoff; Herbert Schlosser; Sylvia T. Smith; Jerome Stanley; George Takei; Jud Taylor; Grant Tinker; Fabien Tordjmann; Bjo Trimble; Bernard Weitzman; Grace Lee Whitney; Bernard Widin

And those who supplied information:

Arnold Anisgarten; Richard Arnold; *Daily Variety*; the Directors Guild of America; Barbara Ditlow, Writers Guild of America, West; Joel Engel; Tom Gilbert; *The Los Angeles Times*; Harvey P. Lynn III; Nielsen Media Research; Ernie Over; *TV Guide*

And those who helped:

Yvonne Fern; Brigitte J. Kueppers, UCLA Arts-Special Collections Library; Paul Lenburg, VP, ASI Market Research; Robert McCracken, Archivist, Paramount Pictures; Leslie Mathieson; Bonnie Solow; our agent, Richard Pine—and our editor at Pocket Books, Kevin Ryan.

We thank them all for their assistance and guidance.

HERBERT F. SOLOW AND ROBERT H. JUSTMAN
Los Angeles, California
February 14, 1996

Authors' Biographies

HERBERT F. SOLOW

Herb Solow joined the mailroom of the William Morris Agency in New York City shortly after graduation from Dartmouth College in 1953. After his promotion to talent agent in 1956, Solow moved to NBC as Program Director of California National Productions and its subsidiary, the NBC Film Division, which was the network's in-house film unit. In 1960 Solow was transferred to Los Angeles, shortly before NBC, reacting to government regulations relative to network ownership of syndication companies, dissolved the NBC Film Division.

Solow then joined CBS as Director of Daytime Programs, West Coast, subsequently returning to NBC a year later as Director of Daytime Programs.

He left his NBC Daytime Programs position and joined Desilu Studios in 1964. Appointed Vice President of Production a year later, Solow personally oversaw the development, sales, and production of *Star Trek, Mission: Impossible,* and *Mannix.*

After Desilu was sold to Gulf & Western and combined with Paramount Studios, Solow joined Metro-Goldwyn-Mayer as Vice President of Television Production, overseeing the development, sale, and series production of *Medical Center, The Courtship of Eddie's Father,* and *Then Came Bronson.*

Solow was subsequently appointed Vice President of Worldwide Motion Picture and Television Production for MGM. During that period, he hired Gene Roddenberry to write and produce a theatrical film, *Pretty Maids All in a Row,* based on the novel by Francis Pollini and directed by Roger Vadim. Among the other films made under his helm at MGM were *Ryan's Daughter,* directed by David Lean; *Brewster McCloud,* directed by Robert Altman; *Shaft,* directed by Gordon Parks; *Zabriskie Point,* directed by Michelangelo Antonioni; *Kelly's Heroes,* directed by Brian Hutton; *Alex in Wonderland,* directed by Paul Mazursky; *The Strawberry Statement,* directed by Stuart Hagmann; and *The Gang That Couldn't Shoot Straight,* directed by *Star Trek* pilot director James Goldstone.

In 1973, he left MGM to become an independent filmmaker and formed Solow Productions. He cocreated and produced the television series *Man from Atlantis.* He was also involved in the production of the English movie *Brimstone and Treacle,* written by Dennis Potter and starring Sting, Joan Plowright, and Denham Elliot. His last feature film production was *Saving Grace,* starring Tom Conti, Giancarlo Giannini, and Edward James Olmos.

Solow is a member of the Writers Guild of America and the Directors Guild of America and serves on the Foreign Film, Documentary, and Special Effects Committees of the Academy of Motion Picture Arts and Sciences. He is currently an independent writer-producer and also lectures on television and film production.

Herb Solow and Yvonne Fern, having met in a vortex of impossible circumstance and celestial attraction, and having the good sense to realize that their lives had been a preparation for each other, married at the home of Bob and Jackie Justman. Mr. and Mrs. Solow are now writing a fictional account of their quixotic and bewitching romance.

ROBERT H. JUSTMAN

Bob Justman has gone from gofer to Executive Producer during a career that spans more than thirty-five feature motion pictures and five hundred television episodes, pilots, and movies.

After Navy service in World War II and college at UCLA, Justman began his film career in 1950 with $50-a-week jobs on independent films. In 1953, he became an assistant director and worked with director Robert Aldrich on the films *Apache* with Burt Lancaster, Jean Peters, and Charles Bronson; *The Big Knife* with Jack Palance, Rod Steiger, Ida Lupino, and Shelley Winters; *Attack* with Palance, Lee Marvin, and Eddy Albert; and Mickey Spillane's *Kiss Me Deadly.*

Soon afterward, he entered the fledgling television industry to freelance on such disparate fare as *The Adventures of Superman, The Thin Man, Northwest Passage, Stoney Burke, The Outer Limits,* and many, many others.

In 1964, he met Herb Solow and Gene Roddenberry and was hired as the assistant director on "The Cage," the first *Star Trek* pilot. He was soon back, but now as the Associate Producer of the second *Star Trek* pilot and the series that followed. He became Co-Producer for the show's third and final season.

In late 1968, under Solow's aegis at MGM, he produced the lyrical series *Then Came Bronson,* starring Michael Parks. He joined with Roddenberry at Warner Brothers to produce a science-fiction pilot, *Planet Earth,* and later worked again with Solow on *Man from Atlantis.* The TV series *Search, McClain's Law,* and *MacGruder & Loud* followed. Justman was also Executive in Charge of Production on *Gideon's Trumpet,* a Hallmark Hall of Fame two-hour special starring Henry Fonda, John Houseman, and José Ferrer.

In October, 1986, he teamed up again with Roddenberry to produce and help create the most successful syndicated television show of this or any other era, the Peabody Award-winning *Star Trek: The Next Generation.*

Justman has served on the Boards of Directors of both the Directors Guild of America and the Producers Guild of America and is a member of the Academy of Television Arts and Sciences. He presently divides his time between writing, lecturing, and guesting at science-fiction and *Star Trek* conventions at home and abroad. For more than twenty-three years he has pursued a secondary avocation, a voluntary career in law enforcement that included a lengthy stint "working the street" as a uniformed Reserve Deputy Sheriff. He recently retired as captain of a Reserve Company that provides consultant services to the Los Angeles County Sheriff's Department.

He has been married to his beauteous and incredibly tolerant Jackie for the past thirty-eight years.

Index